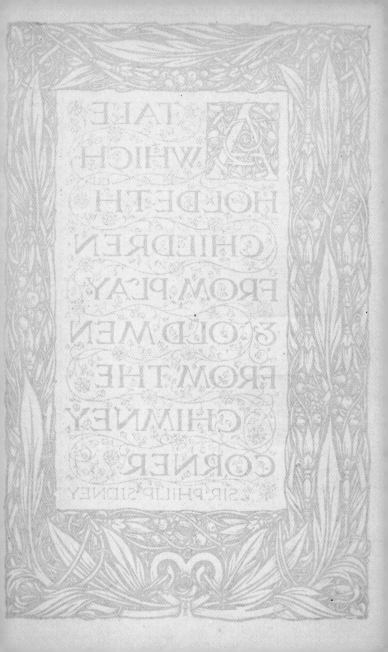

A TALE
WHICH

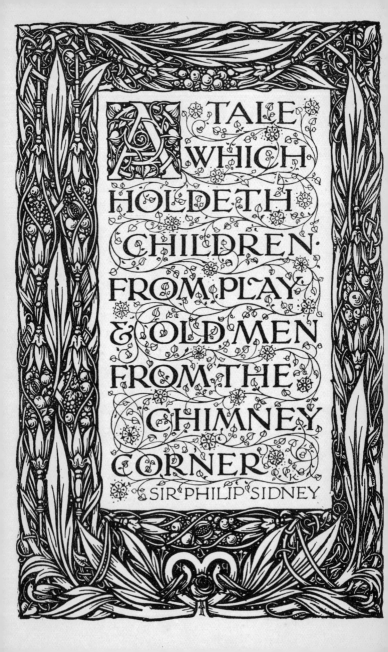

A TALE WHICH HOLDETH CHILDREN·FROM·PLAY & OLD MEN FROM·THE CHIMNEY CORNER

SIR·PHILIP·SIDNEY

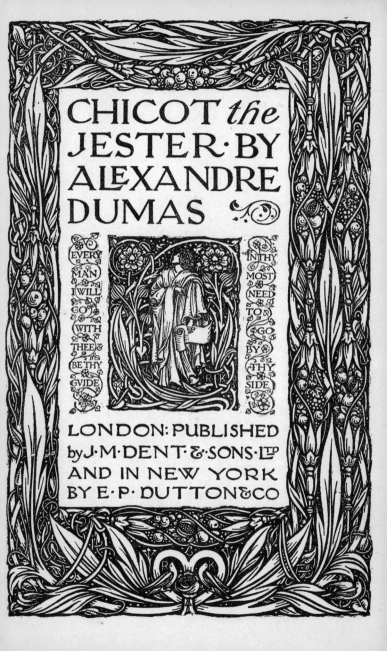

CHICOT *the* JESTER · BY ALEXANDRE DUMAS

EVERY MAN I WILL GO WITH THEE & BE THY GVIDE

IN THY MOST NEED TO GO BY THY SIDE

LONDON: PUBLISHED by J·M·DENT·&·SONS·Lᵀᴰ AND IN NEW YORK BY E·P·DUTTON&CO

CHICOT the JESTER · BY ALEXANDRE DUMAS

LONDON: PUBLISHED
by J·M·DENT & SONS LD
AND IN NEW YORK
BY E·P· DUTTON & CO

INTRODUCTION

AMONG the separate cycles into which Dumas wrought his
picked threads of history, the Valois romances form a very
brilliant group. We have already had in these "Everyman"
volumes *La Reine Margot*, re-titled in her English dress,
Marguerite de Valois. The present story, *La Dame de Monsoreau*, re-titled *Chicot the Jester*, forms another item in the
cycle, although it is in no respect a direct continuation of the
Margot book. Of Chicot himself, it is scarcely needed to say
more than that, whatever Maquet did in unearthing the
bones of the character from history, it was Dumas himself
who lent the atomy flesh and blood, and gave the last fillip
that galvanised him into reality. As for the romantic counter-
feit of Bussy d'Amboise, Dumas had already, we may remember, discovered him, and introduced him into his *Henri
Trois*. Now he resumed the saga of this most congenial
hero with a zest and an adventurous resource that he never
excelled in all his writing and fighting on paper. In the
death of Bussy, we have a unique exhibition of Dumas' art.
Mr. Andrew Lang, one of the best Dumas critics and appre-
ciators on this side the channel, has already set the episode
high, very high indeed, in the epic scale. He says there are
four great fights of one man against a multitude, which stand
apart: "The death of Gretir the Strong, the death of Gunnar
of Lithend, the death of Hereward the Wake, and the death
of Bussy d'Amboise." In the treatment alike of Chicot and
Bussy we see the signs of that high conceit of the Man-against-
Odds which gives the romance of Dumas a touch of the
transcendental, of something more than a tale-teller's use of
sensation piled up for effect. But it would be easy, following
other friendly critics of the Valois romances, to show how
much of the recorded sensation of lust and blood which he
might have taken from history (to say nothing of the scan-
dalous chronicles) Dumas forbore to use. He was not the
unscrupulous artist he has often been accused of being; but

he looked in history for the things, the characters, the culminating episodes, the predicaments of life and death, which counted to him. He liked to see strong passions and dramatic motives taking effect, whether in a prince, a prince's jester, a duke, a duke's mignon, a great lady or a demi-dame: and in Henri Trois and his circle he found (or Maquet found for him) splendid material. When he wrote *La Dame de Monsoreau* or *Chicot the Jester*, he was at the very prime of his rapid and tireless invention. It belongs to the year 1846, the year associated also with *Le Chevalier de Maison Rouge*, and follows pretty closely in the record the *Three Musketeers* and *Monte Cristo*. Dumas was born in 1802, and died in 1870.

E.R.

The following is the list of his published works:—

POETRY AND PLAYS.—Elégie sur la Mort du Général Foy, 1825; La Chasse et l'Amour (in collaboration), 1825; Canaris (Dithyramb), 1826; La Noce et l'Enterrement (in collaboration), 1826; Christine (or Stockholm, Fontainebleau et Rome), 1828; Henri III. et sa Cour, 1829; Antony, 1831; Napoléon Bonaparte, ou Trente Ans de l'Histoire de France, 1831; Charles VII. chez ses grands vassaux, 1831; Richard Darlington, 1831; Térésa, 1832; Le Mari de la Veuve (in collaboration), 1832; La Tour de Nesle, 1832; Angèle (in collaboration), 1833; Catherine Howard, 1834; Don Juan de Marana, ou la Chute d'un Ange, 1836; Kean, 1836; Piquillo, comic opera (in collaboration), 1837; Caligula, 1837; Paul Jones, 1838; Mademoiselle de Belle-Isle, 1839; l'Alchimiste, 1839; Bathilde (in collaboration), 1839; Un Mariage sous Louis XV. (in collaboration), 1841; Lorenzino (in collaboration), 1842; Halifax, 1842; Les Demoiselles de Saint-Cyr (in collaboration), 1843; Louise Bernard (in collaboration), 1843; Le Laird de Dumbicky (in collaboration), 1843; Le Garde Forestier (in collaboration), 1845; L'Oreste, 1856; Le Verron de la Reine, 1856; Le Meneur des Loups, 1857; Collective Eds., *Théâtre*, 1834-36, 6 vols., 1863-74, 15 vols. Dumas also dramatised many of his novels.

TALES AND NOVELS, TRAVELS.—Nouvelles Contemporaines, 1826; Impressions de Voyage, 1833; Souvenirs d'Antony (tales), 1835; La Salle d'Armes (tales), 1838; Le Capitaine Paul, 1838; Acté, Monseigneur Gaston de Phébus, 1839; Quinze Jours au Sinaï, 1839; Aventures de John Davy, 1840; Le Capitaine Pamphile, 1840; Maître Adam le Calabrais, 1840; Othon l'Archer, 1840; Une Année à Florence, 1840; Praxide; Don Martin de Freytas; Pierre le Cruel, 1841; Excursions sur les bords du Rhin, 1841; Nouvelles Impressions de Voyage, 1841; Le Speronare (travels), 1842; Aventures de Lyderic, 1842; Georges; Ascanio; Le Chevalier d'Harmental, 1843; Le Corricolo; La Villa Palmieri, 1843; Gabriel Lambert; Château d'Eppstein; Cécile; Sylvandire; Les Trois Mousquetaires; Amaury; Fernande, 1844; Le Comte de Monte-Cristo, 1844-5; Vingt Ans après, 1845; Les Frères Corses; Une Fille du Régent; La Reine Margot, 1845; La Guerre des Femmes, 1845-6; Le Chevalier de Maison-Rouge, 1846; La Dame de Monsoreau, 1846; Le Batard de Mauléon, 1846; Mémoires d'un Médecin, 1846-8; Les Quarante-cinq, 1848; Dix Ans plus tard, ou le Vicomte de Bragelonne, 1848-50; De Paris à Cadix, 1848; Tanger, Alger, et Tunis, 1848; Les Milles et un

Fantômes, 1849; La Tulipe Noire, 1850; La Femme au Collier de Velours, 1851; Olympe de Clèves, 1852; Un Gil Blas en Californie, 1852; Isaac Taquedem, 1852; La Comtesse de Charny, 1853-5; Ange Pitou, le Pasteur d'Ashbourn; El Satéador; Conscience l'Innocent, 1853; Catherine Blum; Ingénue, 1854; Les Mohicans de Paris, 1854-8; Salvator, 1855-9 (the two last with Paul Bocage); L'Arabie Heureuse, 1855; Les Compagnons de Jéhu, 1857; Les Louvres de Machecoul, 1859; Le Caucase, 1859; De Paris à Astrakan, 1860.

OTHER WORKS.—Souvenirs de 1830-42, 1854; Mémoires, 1852-4; Causeries, 1860; Bric-à-brac, 1861; Histoire de mes Bêtes, 1868; Memoirs of Garibaldi, Reminiscences of various writers, historical compilations, etc.; Children's Tales; Histoire d'un Casse-Noisette, La Bouillie de la Comtesse Berthe, Le Père Gigogne.

CONTENTS

PART FIRST

Contents

xiii

LIST OF CHARACTERS

PERIOD, 1578

HENRI III., King of France.

FRANÇOIS, Duc d'Anjou, his brother, formerly Duc d'Alençon.

AURILLY, a lute-player, the confidant of Duc d'Anjou.

LOUISE DE LORRAINE, wife of Henri III.

CATHERINE DE MÉDICIS, the Queen Mother.

CHICOT, the King's jester, a Gascon gentleman.

HENRI DE BOURBON, King of Navarre.

MADEMOISELLE DE MONTMORENCY, " la Fosseuse," his mistress.

M. AGRIPPA D'AUBIGNÉ, his friend.

COMTE LOUIS DE CLERMONT, called Bussy d'Amboise.

M. CHARLES BALZAC D'ANTRAGUES,
FRANÇOIS D'AUDIE, Vicomte de Ribeirac, } friends of Bussy d'Amboise.
M. DE LIVAROT,

FRANÇOIS D'ÉPINAY DE SAINT-LUC, favourite of Henri III.

JEANNE DE COSSÉ, his wife.

MARÉCHAL DE BRISSAC, her father.

M. BRYAN DE MONSOREAU, chief huntsman.

DIANE DE MÉRIDOR, his wife, " La Dame de Monsoreau," in love with Bussy d'Amboise.

BARON DE MÉRIDOR, Diane's father.

RÉMY LE HAUDOUIN, a young surgeon.

GERTRUDE, Diane's servant.

M. D'ÉPERNON,
M. DE SCHOMBERG,   } friends of the king.
M. DE MAUGIRON,
JACQUES DE LEVIS, Comte de Quélus,
M. DE CRILLON, an officer of the king.

HENRI, Duc de Guise,
CARDINAL DE LORRAINE,
DUC DE MAYENNE,
DUCHESS DE MONTPENSIER, his sister,
MAÎTRE NICOLAS DAVID, an advocate,   } Leaguers, conspiring against
M. PIERRE DE GONDY,   Henri III.
M. LE GOUVERNEUR D'AUNIS,
M. DE CASTILLON,
BARON DE LUSIGNAN,
M. CRUCÉ,
M. LECLERC,

CHANCELLOR DE MORVILLIERS.

M. DE NANCEY, Captain of the Guards.

JOSEPH FOULON, superior of the Convent of Sainte Geneviève.

CLAUDE BONHOMET, host of the " Corne d'Abondance."

M. BERNOUILLET, of the hostelry of La Croix.

MAÎTRE LA HURIÈRE, of the Belle Etoile Inn.

BROTHER GORENFLOT.

CHICOT THE JESTER

PART FIRST

CHAPTER I

THE WEDDING OF SAINT-LUC

On the evening of a Sunday in the year 1578, a splendid fête was given in the magnificent hotel just built opposite the Louvre, on the other side of the water, by the family of Montmorency, who, allied to the royalty of France, held themselves equal to princes. This fête was to celebrate the wedding of François d'Épinay de Saint-Luc, a great friend and favourite of King Henri III., with Jeanne de Cossé-Brissac, daughter of the marshal of that name.

The banquet had taken place at the Louvre; and the king, who had been with much difficulty induced to consent to the marriage, had appeared at the feast with a stern expression of countenance not at all appropriate to the occasion. His costume was in harmony with his face; he wore that suit of deep chestnut in which Clouet has presented him to us at the wedding of Joyeuse. And this royal spectre, solemn and majestic, had chilled all the spectators, but, above all, the young bride, at whom he cast many angry glances. The reason of all this was known to every one, but was one of those court secrets of which no one likes to speak.

Scarcely was the repast finished, when the king had risen abruptly, thereby forcing every one to do the same. Then Saint-Luc had given a long look to his wife, as if to draw courage from her eyes, and approaching the king had said, " Sire, will your Majesty do me the honour to accept the fête which I wish to give to you this evening at the Hôtel de Montmorency? " This was said in an imploring tone, but Henri, with a voice betraying both vexation and anger, had replied,—

" Yes, Monsieur, we will go, although you certainly do not merit this proof of friendship on our part."

Then Madame de Saint-Luc had humbly thanked the king, but he had turned his back without replying.

" Is the king angry with you? " asked the young wife of her husband.

A

" I will explain it to you later, my love, when this anger shall have passed away."

" And will it pass away? "

" It must."

Mademoiselle de Brissac was not yet sufficiently Madame de Saint-Luc to insist further; therefore she repressed her curiosity, promising herself to satisfy it at a more favourable time.

They were therefore expecting Henri III. at the Hôtel de Montmorency at the moment in which our story commences. It was already eleven o'clock, and the king had not arrived. Saint-Luc had invited all the king's friends and all his own, and the princes and their favourites, particularly those of our old acquaintance the Duc d'Alençon, who on the accession of Henri III. had become Duc d'Anjou. But the Duc d'Anjou had not been present at the banquet in the Louvre, nor did it appear that he would attend the fête at the Hôtel de Montmorency.

As to the King and Queen of Navarre, they were, as we have said in a former work, safe at Navarre; and there they made open opposition to the king, fighting at the head of the Huguenots.

The Duc d'Anjou, according to his custom, also made opposition, but an opposition hidden and treacherous, in which he took care to keep himself out of sight, pushing forward those of his friends who had not been warned by the example of La Mole and Coconnas, whose terrible death our readers probably have not forgotten. Of course, his favourites and those of the king lived in a state of antagonism, which brought on rencontres two or three times a month, in which it was rare that some one was not killed or badly wounded.

As for Catherine, she was at the height of her wishes; her favourite son was on the throne, and she reigned through him, while she pretended to care no more for the things of this world, and to be concerned only for the salvation of her soul.

Saint-Luc, very uneasy at the absence of all the royal family, tried to reassure his father-in-law, who was much distressed at this menacing absence. Convinced, like every one else, of the friendship of Henri for Saint-Luc, he had believed he was allying himself to royal favour; and now it began to look as if his daughter had, on the contrary, married something like a disgrace. Saint-Luc tried hard to inspire in him an assurance which he did not feel himself; and his friends, Maugiron, Schomberg, and Quélus, clothed in their most magnificent costumes, stiff in their splendid doublets, with enormous frills, added to his annoyance by their ironical lamentations.

" Eh, *mon Dieu!* my poor friend," said Jacques de Levis, Comte de Quélus, " I believe now that you are done for. The king is angry that you laughed at his advice, and M. d'Anjou because you laughed at his nose." [1]

" No, Quélus, the king does not come because he has made a pilgrimage to the monks of the Bois de Vincennes; and the Duc d'Anjou is absent because he is in love with some woman whom I have forgotten to invite."

" But," said Maugiron, " did you see the king's face at dinner? Was that the paternal face of a man who is about to take his staff and make a pilgrimage? And as for the duke, if he could not come, his gentlemen might. Do you see one of them here? Look, a total eclipse,—not even that swaggerer Bussy."

" Oh, gentlemen," said the Duc de Brissac, in a despairing tone, " it looks like a complete disgrace. *Mon Dieu!* how can our house, always so devoted to his Majesty, have displeased him? "

The young men received this speech with bursts of laughter, which did not tend to soothe the marquis. The young bride was also wondering how Saint-Luc could have displeased the king. All at once one of the doors opened, and the king was announced.

" Ah!" cried the marshal, " now I fear nothing; if the Duc d'Anjou would but come, my satisfaction would be complete."

" And I," murmured Saint-Luc, " I have more fear of the king present than absent, for he comes only to do me some ill turn,—just as the Duc d'Anjou stays away for the same purpose."

But, nevertheless, he ran to meet the king, who had abandoned at last his sombre costume, and advanced resplendent in satin, feathers, and jewels. But at the instant he entered, another door opened just opposite; and a second Henri III., clothed exactly like the first, appeared, so that the courtiers, who had run to meet the first, turned round at once to look at the second.

Henri III. saw the movement and exclaimed, " What is the matter, gentlemen? "

A burst of laughter was the reply. The king, not naturally patient, and less so that day than usual, frowned; but Saint-Luc approached and said, " Sire, it is Chicot, your jester, who is dressed exactly like your Majesty, and is giving his hand to the ladies to kiss."

Henri laughed. Chicot enjoyed at his court a liberty similar

[1] The small-pox had so badly served the Duc d'Anjou that he seemed to have a double nose.

to that enjoyed thirty years before by Triboulet at the court of
François I., and forty years after by Langely at the court of
Louis XIII. Chicot was not an ordinary jester. Before being
" Chicot " he had been " De Chicot." He was a Gascon gentleman, who, ill-treated by M. de Mayenne on account of a rivalry
in a love-affair, in which Chicot had been victorious, had taken
refuge at court, and paid the king for his protection by telling
him the truth.

" Eh, M. Chicot," said Henri, " two kings at a time are too
many."

" Then," replied he, " let me continue to be one, and you play
Duc d'Anjou; perhaps you will be taken for him, and learn
something of his doings."

" So," said Henri, looking round him, " Anjou is not here? "

" The more reason for you to replace him. It is settled; I
am Henri, and you are François. I will play the king, while
you dance and amuse yourself a little, poor king."

The eyes of the king rested on Saint-Luc. " You are right,
Chicot, I will dance," he said.

" Decidedly," thought Brissac, " I was wrong to think the
king angry; he is in an excellent humour." And he stepped
briskly this way and that, congratulating every one, and especially congratulating himself on having given his daughter to so
great a favourite of the king.

Meanwhile Saint-Luc had approached his wife. She was not
a beauty, but she had fine black eyes, white teeth, and a dazzling
complexion.

" Monsieur," said she to her husband, " why did they say that
the king was angry with me? He has done nothing but smile
on me ever since he came."

" You did not say so after dinner, dear Jeanne, for his look
then frightened you."

" His Majesty was doubtless out of humour then, but now—"

" Now it is far worse; he smiles with closed lips. I would
rather he showed me his teeth. Jeanne, my poor child, he is
preparing for us some disagreeable surprise. Oh, do not look
at me so tenderly, I beg; turn your back to me. Here is
Maugiron coming; converse with him, and be amiable to him."

" Do you know, Monsieur," said Jeanne, smiling, " that is a
strange request, and if I should follow it to the letter they might
think—"

" Ah ! " said Saint-Luc, with a sigh, " it would be very
fortunate if they did think so." And turning his back upon

his wife, who was greatly astonished, he went to pay his court to Chicot, who was playing his part with a most laughable majesty.

The king danced, but seemed never to lose sight of Saint-Luc. Sometimes he called him to repeat to him some pleasantry, which, whether droll or not, made Saint-Luc laugh heartily. Sometimes he offered him out of his comfit-box confectionery and candied fruits, which Saint-Luc found excellent. If he disappeared for an instant, the king sent for him, and seemed not happy if he was out of his sight. All at once a voice rose above all the tumult.

"Oh!" said Henri, "I think I hear the voice of Chicot; do you hear, Saint-Luc? The king is angry."

"Yes, Sire, it sounds as though he were quarrelling with some one."

"Go, and see what it is, and come back and tell me."

As Saint-Luc approached, he heard Chicot crying out in the nasal tones which the king sometimes employed, "I have made sumptuary laws, but if they are not enough I will make more; at least they shall be numerous, if they are not good. By the horn of Beelzebub, six pages, M. de Bussy, that is too much." And Chicot, swelling out his cheeks and putting his hand to his side, imitated the king to the life.

"What does he say about Bussy?" asked the king, frowning, when Saint-Luc returned.

Saint-Luc was about to reply when the crowd, opening, showed to him six pages, dressed in cloth of gold, covered with chains, and bearing on their breasts the arms of their master, sparkling in jewels. Behind them came a young man, handsome and proud, who walked with his head raised and a haughty look, and whose simple dress of black velvet contrasted with the splendour of his pages. This was Bussy d'Amboise. Maugiron, Schomberg, and Quélus had drawn near to the king.

"See," said Maugiron, alluding to the unexpected presence of Bussy, and the continued absence of the Duc d'Anjou, to whom Bussy belonged, "here is the servant, but where is the master? Are you in disgrace with him also, Saint-Luc?"

That "also" struck Saint-Luc to the heart.

"Why should he follow Bussy?" said Quélus. "Do you not remember that when his Majesty did M. de Bussy the honour to ask him if he wished to belong to him, he replied that being of the house of Clermont, he had no need to belong to any one, and should be content with belonging to himself, certain that he should find in himself the best prince in the world?"

The king frowned, and bit his mustache.

"Yet," said Maugiron, "whatever you say, he serves the Duc d'Anjou."

"Then," coolly replied Quélus, "it is because the duke is greater than the king."

No observation could have been more annoying to the king than this, for he detested the Duc d'Anjou; and although he did not answer, he was seen to turn pale.

"Come, come, gentlemen," ventured Saint-Luc, trembling, "a little charity for my guests, if you please; do not spoil my wedding-day."

This remark probably recalled to Henri another subject of his thoughts. "Yes," he said, "let us not spoil Saint-Luc's wedding-day, gentlemen." And as he said this, he twisted his mustache with a crafty air that did not escape the poor husband's notice.

"Oh!" said Schomberg, "is Bussy allied to the Brissacs?"

"Why that question?" said Maugiron.

"Because here is Saint-Luc defending him. What the devil! in this poor world where every one has enough to do in defending himself, we defend, it seems to me, only our relatives, our allies, and our friends."

"Gentlemen," said Saint-Luc, "M. de Bussy is neither my ally, my friend, nor my relative; he is my guest." The king gave him an angry look. "Besides," he hastened to add, terrified by that look of the king, "I do not defend him the least in the world."

Bussy approached gravely behind his pages to salute the king, when Chicot cried, "Oh, there! Bussy d'Amboise, Louis de Clermont, Comte de Bussy, do you not see the true Henri? Do you not know the true king from the false? He to whom you are going is Chicot, my jester, who makes so many jokes that sometimes I almost die with laughing at him."

Bussy continued his way, and was about to bow before the king, when he said, "Do you not hear, M. de Bussy? You are called;" and amid shouts of laughter from his favourites, he turned his back to the young captain.

Bussy reddened with anger, but he affected to take the king's remark seriously, and turning round towards Chicot, "Ah, pardon, Sire!" said he, "there are kings who resemble jesters so much that you will excuse me, I hope, for having taken a jester for a king."

" *Hein!* " murmured Henri, " what does he say? "

" Nothing, Sire," said Saint-Luc, who during all that evening seemed to have received from heaven the mission of peace-maker,—nothing, absolutely nothing."

" Nevertheless, Maître Bussy," said Chicot; " it was unpardonable."

" Sire, pardon me! I was preoccupied."

" With your pages, Monsieur? " said Chicot. " You ruin yourself in pages; and, *par la mordieu*, it is infringing our prerogatives."

" How is that? " said Bussy, who understood that by indulging the jester he should humiliate the king. " I beg your Majesty will explain; and if I have really done wrong I will confess it in all humility."

" Cloth of gold for them, while you a gentleman, a colonel, a Clermont, almost a prince, wear simple black velvet! "

" Sire," said Bussy, turning towards the king's favourites, " as we live in a time when lackeys dress like princes, I think it good taste for princes to dress like lackeys."

And he returned to the young men in their splendid apparel the impertinent smiles which they had bestowed on him a little before. They grew pale with fury, and seemed only to wait the king's permission to fall upon Bussy.

" Is it for me and mine that you say that? " asked Chicot, speaking like the king.

Three friends of Bussy's now drew near to him; these were Charles Balzac d'Antragues, François d'Audie, Vicomte de Ribeirac, and Livarot. Seeing all this, Saint-Luc conjectured that Bussy was sent by Monsieur to provoke a quarrel. He trembled more than ever,—for he found himself placed between two powerful enemies, who had chosen his house for their field of battle. He ran to Quélus, who seemed more excited than the rest, and placing his hand upon the young man's sword, " In Heaven's name, dear friend," he exclaimed, " be quiet and let us wait! "

" Eh, *parbleu!* Be quiet yourself! " he cried. " That block-head's blow reaches you as well as me. Whoever says anything against one of us speaks against all of us; and whoever insults us all touches the king."

" Quélus, Quélus," said Saint-Luc, " think of the Duc d'Anjou, who is behind Bussy,—the more watchful because he is absent,

the more to be feared because he is invisible. I presume you
will not do me the wrong to think that I am afraid of the servant;
I fear the master."

" Eh, *mordieu !* what need we fear? we belong to the king.
If we get into peril for him he will protect us."

" You, yes; but me! " said Saint-Luc piteously.

" Ah! why the devil do you marry, knowing how jealous the
king is in his friendships? "

" Good! " thought Saint-Luc, " every one thinks of himself,
—let us not, then, forget it; and since I wish to live quietly,
at least during the first fortnight of my marriage, let us try to
make a friend of M. d'Anjou." And he advanced towards
Bussy.

After his impertinent speech, Bussy had looked round the
room to see if any one would take notice of it. Seeing Saint-Luc
approach, he thought he had found what he sought.

" Monsieur," said he, " is it to what I said just now that I
owe the honour of the conversation you appear to desire? "

" Of what you have just said, I heard nothing. No, I saw
you, and wished to salute you, and thank you for the honour
you have done me by your presence here."

Bussy, who knew the courage of Saint-Luc, understood at
once that he considered the duties of a host paramount, and
answered him politely.

Henri, who had seen the movement, said, " Oh, oh! I fear
there is mischief there; I cannot have Saint-Luc killed. Go
and see, Quélus. No, you are too rash; you, Maugiron."

But Saint-Luc did not let him approach Bussy, but came to
meet him, and returned with him to the king.

" What have you been saying to that coxcomb? " asked the
king.

" I, Sire? "

" Yes, you."

" I said good-evening."

" Oh! was that all? " growled the king.

Saint-Luc saw that he had made a blunder. " I said good-
evening,—adding that I would have the honour of saying good-
morning to-morrow."

" Good! I suspected it, you wicked fellow," said Henri.

" Will your Majesty keep my secret? " said Saint-Luc, pretending to speak in a low tone.

" Oh, *pardieu !* if you could get rid of him without injury to
yourself—" The favourites exchanged a rapid glance, which

Henri III. seemed not to notice. " For," continued he, " that rascal's insolence is too great."

" Yes, yes," said Saint-Luc, " but some day he will find his master."

" Oh! " said the king, " he manages the sword well. Why does he not get bit by some mad dog? That would rid us of him quite comfortably." And he threw a spiteful glance at Bussy, who, with his three friends, walked back and forth, jostling and laughing at those who he knew were most hostile to the Duc d'Anjou, and consequently most friendly to the king.

" *Corbleu !* " cried Chicot, " do not be so rude to my friends, M. de Bussy, for I draw the sword, though I am a king, as well as if I were a jester."

" Ah, the rogue! " murmured Henri; " upon my word, he sees things as they are."

" If he continues such pleasantries, I will chastise Chicot, Sire," said Maugiron.

" No, no, Maugiron, Chicot is a gentleman. Besides, it is not he who most deserves punishment, for it is not he who is most insolent."

This time there was no mistaking; and Quélus made signs to D'O and D'Epernon, who had been in a different part of the room, and had not heard what was going on. " Gentlemen," said Quélus, leading them apart, " come to the council; you, Saint-Luc, go and finish making your peace with the king."

Saint-Luc approached the king, while the others drew back into a window.

" Well," said D'Epernon, " what do you want? I was making love to the wife of Joyeuse; and I warn you, if your recital be not interesting, I shall not forgive you."

" I wish to tell you that after the ball I set off for the chase."

" For what chase? "

" That of the wild boar."

" What possesses you to go in this cold to be killed in some thicket? "

" Never mind; I am going."

" Alone? "

" No, with Maugiron and Schomberg. We hunt for the king."

" Ah, yes, I understand," said Maugiron and Schomberg together.

" The king wishes a boar's head for breakfast to-morrow."

A 2

"With the neck dressed *à l'Italienne*," said Maugiron, alluding to the turn-down collar which Bussy wore in contrast to their ruffs.

"Ah, ah!" said D'Epernon, "I understand."

"What is it?" asked D'O; "for I do not."

"Ah! look round you."

"Well, I am looking!"

"Is there any one who laughs in our faces?"

"Bussy, I think."

"Well, that is the wild boar the king wants."

"You think the king—"

"He asks for it."

"Well, then, so be it. But how do we hunt?"

"In ambush; it is the surest."

Bussy remarked the conference, and not doubting that they were talking of him, approached, laughing, with his friends. "Look, Antragues, look, Ribeirac," said he, "how they are grouped; it is quite touching. It might be Euryalus and Nisus, Damon and Pythias, Castor and— But where is Pollux?"

"Pollux is married, so that Castor is left alone," said Antragues.

"What can they be doing?" said Bussy, looking at them insolently.

"I bet they are inventing some new starch."

"No, gentlemen," said Quélus, smiling; "we are talking of the chase."

"Really, Signor Cupid," said Bussy; "it is very cold for that. It will chap your skin."

"Monsieur," replied Maugiron, politely, "we have warm gloves, and doublets lined with fur."

"Ah! that reassures me," said Bussy. "Do you go soon?"

"To-night, perhaps," said Schomberg.

"In that case I must warn the king; what will he say to-morrow, if he finds his friends have caught cold?"

"Do not give yourself that trouble, Monsieur," said Quélus; "his Majesty knows it."

"Do you hunt larks?" asked Bussy, with an impertinent air.

"No, Monsieur, we hunt the boar; we absolutely must have the head of a boar."

"And the animal?" asked Antragues.

"Is started," said Schomberg.

"But it is necessary to know which way he is going," said Livarot.

" We will try to find out," said D'O.   " Will you hunt with us, M. de Bussy ? "

" No, really, I cannot," replied the latter, continuing the conversation in the same tone.   " To-morrow I must go to the Duc d'Anjou for the reception of M. de Monsoreau, to whom Monseigneur has just given the place of chief huntsman."

" But to-night ? " asked Quélus.

" Ah! to-night I have a rendezvous in a mysterious house of the Faubourg St. Antoine."

" Ah, ah ! " said D'Epernon, " is the Queen Margot here incognito, M. de Bussy ?—for we understand that you have inherited from La Mole."

" No, it is some time since I renounced that heritage: it is now some one else."

" And that person expects you in the Faubourg St. Antoine ? " asked D'O.

" Just so; indeed, I will ask your advice, M. de Quélus."

" Do so; although I am not a lawyer, I pride myself on giving good advice, especially to my friends."

" They say the streets of Paris are unsafe, and that is a lonely place.   Which way do you counsel me to take ? "

" Why, I advise you to take the ferry-boat at the Pré aux Clercs, get out at the corner, and follow the quay until you arrive at the great Châtelet, and then go through the Rue de la Tixer-anderie until you reach the faubourg.   Once at the corner of the Rue St. Antoine, if you pass the Hôtel des Tournelles without accident, it is probable that you will arrive safe and sound at your mysterious house."

" Thanks for your route, M. de Quélus, I shall be sure to follow it."   And saluting the five friends, he went away.

As Bussy was crossing the last salon, where Madame de Saint-Luc was, her husband made a sign to her.   She understood at once, and going to meet Bussy, stopped him.

" Oh, M. de Bussy," said she, " every one is talking of a sonnet you have made."

" Against the king, Madame ? "

" No, in honour of the queen; do repeat it to me."

" Willingly, Madame; " and offering his arm to her, he went off, repeating it.

During this time Saint-Luc drew softly near his friends, and heard Quélus say, " The animal will not be difficult to follow; so then, at the corner of the Hôtel des Tournelles, opposite the Hôtel St. Pol."

"Each with a lackey?" asked D'Epernon.

"No, no, Nogaret; let us be alone, and keep our own secret, and do our own work. I hate him; but he is too much a gentleman for a lackey to touch."

"Shall we go out all six together?" asked Maugiron.

"All five, if you please," said Saint-Luc.

"Ah! it is true; we forgot that you are married."

"In fact," said D'O, "it is right enough that poor Saint-Luc should remain with his wife the first night after his marriage."

"You are wrong, gentlemen," said Saint-Luc; "it is not my wife who keeps me,—though you will agree that she is well worth staying for,—it is the king."

"The king! how so?"

"Yes; his Majesty wishes me to return with him to the Louvre."

The young men looked at him with a smile which Saint-Luc sought in vain to understand.

"What would you have?" said Quélus. "The king is so wonderfully attached to you that he can't do without you."

"Besides, we have no need of Saint-Luc," said Schomberg; "let us leave him, then, to his king and to his wife."

They heard the king's voice calling Saint-Luc.

"Gentlemen," said he, "the king calls me. Good sport; *au revoir!*"

And he left them; but instead of going straight to the king, he ran to where Bussy stood with his wife.

"Ah, Monsieur, how hurried you seem!" said Bussy. "Are you going also to join the chase? It would be a proof of your courage, but not of your gallantry."

"Monsieur, I was seeking you."

"Really?"

"And I was afraid you had gone. Dear Jeanne, tell your father to try to stop the king, while I say a few words in private to M. de Bussy." Jeanne hastened away, understanding nothing, but perceiving that her mission was important.

"I wish to say to you, Monsieur," continued Saint-Luc, "that if you have any rendezvous to-night, you would do well to put it off, for the streets are not safe; and that if perchance your rendezvous should take you in the direction of the Bastille you would do well to avoid the Hôtel des Tournelles, where there is a place in which several men could hide. This is what I wished to say; I know you fear nothing, but reflect."

At this moment they heard Chicot's voice crying, "Saint-

Luc, Saint-Luc, do not hide yourself; I am waiting for you to return to the Louvre."

"Here I am, Sire," cried Saint-Luc, rushing forward. Near Chicot stood the king, to whom one page was giving his ermine mantle, another his gloves extending to his elbows, and a third the velvet mask lined with satin.

"Sire," said Saint-Luc, addressing the two Henris at the same time, "I will have the honour of lighting you to your litters."

"No," said Henri, "Chicot goes one way, and I another. My friends are good-for-nothings, who have run away and left me to return alone to the Louvre. I had counted on them, and they have failed me. Now, you see, I cannot go back alone in this way. You are a grave married man, and must take me back to the queen. Come, my friend, my litter is large enough for two."

Madame de Saint-Luc, who had heard this, tried to speak, to say a word to her husband, to tell her father that the king was carrying away her husband, but Saint-Luc, placing a finger on his mouth, indicated the necessity for silence and circumspection.

"*Peste!*" said he to himself; "now that I am on good terms with François d'Anjou, I mustn't quarrel with Henri de Valois. —Sire," added he, aloud, "I am ready. I am so devoted to your Majesty that at your command I would follow you to the end of the earth."

When the king took leave the others followed, and Jeanne was left alone. She entered her chamber, and knelt before the image of a saint to pray, then gave orders that she should be left alone, and that a lunch should be prepared for her husband. M. de Brissac sent six men to the Louvre to escort him on his return. But two hours later one of them returned, saying that the Louvre was closed, and that before closing, the captain of the watch had said, "It is useless to wait longer, no one will leave the Louvre to-night; his Majesty is in bed."

The marshal carried this news to his daughter, who declared that she was too anxious to go to bed, and would sit up and wait for her husband.

CHAPTER II

HOW IT IS NOT ALWAYS HE WHO OPENS THE DOOR WHO ENTERS THE HOUSE

THE Porte St. Antoine was a kind of vault in stone, similar to our present Porte St. Denis, only it was attached by its left side to buildings adjacent to the Bastille. The space at the right, between the gate and the Hôtel des Tournelles, was large and dark, little frequented by day, and quite solitary at night, for all passers-by took the side next to the fortress, so as to be in some degree under the protection of the sentinel. Of course, on winter nights the passers-by were still more timorous than on summer nights.

The night in which the events which we have recounted and are about to recount took place was cold and dark. Before the gate on the side towards the city were the walls of the church of St. Paul, and of the Hôtel des Tournelles. At the end of this hotel was the niche of which Saint-Luc had spoken to Bussy. No lamps lighted this part of Paris at that epoch. In the nights when the moon charged herself with the lighting of the earth the Bastille rose sombre and majestic against the starry blue of the skies; but on dark nights there seemed only a thickening of the shadows where it stood. On the night in question, a practised eye might have detected in the angle of the wall of the Tournelles several black shades, which moved enough to show that they belonged to poor devils with human bodies, who seemed to find it difficult to preserve their natural warmth as they stood there, apparently awaiting some event. The sentinel from the Bastille, who could not see them on account of the darkness, could not hear them either, for they talked almost in whispers. However, the conversation did not want interest.

" This Bussy was right," said one; " it is a night such as we had at Warsaw, when Henri was King of Poland, and if this continues we shall freeze."

" Come, Maugiron, you complain like a woman," replied another. " It is not warm, I confess; but draw your mantle over your eyes, and put your hands in your pockets, and you will not feel the cold."

" Really, Schomberg," said a third, " it is easy to see that you

are German. As for me, my lips bleed, and my mustaches are
stiff with ice."

"It is my hands," said a fourth; "on my honour, I would
not swear I had any."

"You should have taken your mamma's muff, poor Quélus,"
said Schomberg.

"Eh, *mon Dieu!* have patience," said a fifth voice; "you
will soon be complaining that you are hot."

"I see some one coming through the Rue St. Paul," said
Quélus.

"It cannot be he; he named another route."

"Might he not have suspected something, and changed it?"

"You do not know Bussy; where he said he should go, he
would go, if he knew that the Devil were lying in wait to bar
his passage."

"However, here are two men coming."

"Faith! yes," said two or three voices.

"Let us charge," said Schomberg.

"One moment," said D'Epernon; "do not let us kill good
bourgeois or poor women. Hold! they stop."

In fact, the two persons who had attracted the attention of
the five companions had stopped, as if in uncertainty.

"Oh, can they have seen us?"

"We can hardly see ourselves!"

"See, they turn to the left; they stop before a house; they
are searching."

"Faith! yes."

"One would say that they mean to enter," said Schomberg.
"Eh! wait. Is it possible that he is trying to escape us?"

"But it is not he, for he was going to the Faubourg St.
Antoine."

"Eh!" said Schomberg, "what assurance have you that the
cunning fellow did not give you, by accident or by intention,
a false indication?"

"In fact, that might be," said Quélus.

At this supposition they all rushed out, sword in hand,
towards the two men who had stopped before the door.

One of the men had just introduced a key into the lock;
the door had yielded and was about to open, when the noise
of their assailants made them turn.

"What is this? Can it be against us, Aurilly?" said one.

"Ah, Monseigneur," said the other, who had opened the door,
"it looks like it. Will you name yourself, or keep incognito?"

"Armed men! an ambush!"

"Some jealous lover; I said the lady was too beautiful not to be watched."

"Let us enter quickly, Aurilly; we are safer within doors."

"Yes, Monseigneur, if there are not enemies within; but how do you know—"

He had not time to finish. The young men rushed up; Quélus and Maugiron made for the door to prevent their entering, while Schomberg, D'O, and D'Epernon prepared to attack in front.

"To death! to death!" cried Quélus, always the most ardent of the five.

Suddenly he who had been called Monseigneur turned towards Quélus, who was in front, and crossing his arms proudly, said, "I think you cried 'To death!' referring to a son of France, M. de Quélus."

Quélus drew back, trembling and thunderstruck; "Monseigneur le Duc d'Anjou!" he cried.

"The Duc d'Anjou!" repeated the others.

"Well," said François, with a threatening air, "do we still say, 'To death! to death!' my gentlemen?"

"Monseigneur," stammered D'Epernon, "it was a joke; forgive us."

"Monseigneur," said D'O, "we did not dream of meeting your Highness here!"

"A joke!" said the duke, without honouring D'O with a reply; "you have an odd manner of joking, M. d'Epernon. Since it was not intended for me, whom did your jest menace?"

"Monseigneur," said Schomberg; "we saw Saint-Luc leave the Hôtel de Montmorency and come this way; it seemed strange to us, and we wished to see what took him out on his wedding-night."

The explanation was plausible, for in all probability the Duc d'Anjou would learn in the morning that Saint-Luc had not slept at the Hôtel de Montmorency, and that intelligence would agree with what Schomberg had now said.

"M. de Saint-Luc,—you took me for him, gentlemen?"

"Yes, Monseigneur," the five companions replied in chorus.

"M. de Saint-Luc is a head taller than I am."

"It is true, Monseigneur," said Quélus; "but he is just of the height of M. Aurilly."

"Besides, the night is very dark, Monseigneur," replied Maugiron.

" And seeing a man put a key in a lock, we took him for the principal," added D'O.

" Monseigneur cannot suppose that we had the shadow of an evil thought towards him, even that of disturbing his pleasures."

While listening thus to the answers more or less logical which surprise and fear permitted, François, by a skilful strategic manœuvre, had left the threshold of the door, and followed step by step by Aurilly, his lute-player and usual companion on his nocturnal rambles, had already moved so far from the door that it could not be distinguished from those near it. " My pleasures!" said he, angrily; " what makes you think I was seeking pleasure?"

" Ah, Monseigneur, in any case, and for whatever purpose you may have come, pardon us, and let us retire," said Quélus.

" It is well; adieu, gentlemen."

" Monseigneur," added D'Epernon, " your Highness can rely on our discretion."

The Duc d'Anjou, who had already started to withdraw, paused, and bending his brows, said, " Discretion, M. de Nogaret; and who, pray, asks you for discretion?"

" Monseigneur, we supposed that your Highness, alone at this hour, and followed by your confidant—"

" You are mistaken. This is what is to be believed,—what I wish you to believe."

The five gentlemen listened in the most profound and respectful silence.

" I was going to consult the Jew Manassès, who reads the future; he lives, as you know, in Rue de la Tournelle. In passing, Aurilly saw you, and took you for the watch, and we therefore tried to hide ourselves in a doorway. And now you know what to believe and say; it is needless to add that I do not wish to be followed;" and he turned away.

All bowed and took leave of the prince, who turned several times to follow them with his eye while he took some steps in the opposite direction.

" Monseigneur," said Aurilly, " I am sure these men have bad intentions. It is near midnight, and this is a lonely quarter; let us return home, I beg."

" No, no," said the prince, pausing; " let us profit by their departure."

" Your Highness is deceived; they have not gone, but have returned to their retreat. Look in the angle of the Hôtel des Tournelles."

François looked, and saw that Aurilly was right; it was evident that they waited for something, perhaps to see if the duke were really going to the Jew.

"Well, Monseigneur," continued Aurilly, "what do you decide? I will do whatever your Highness may command, but I think it not wise to remain."

"*Mordieu!* yet it is annoying to give up."

"Yes; but it can be put off. I told your Highness that the house is taken for a year; we know the lady lodges on the first story. We have gained her maid, and have a key which opens the door. With all these advantages we can wait."

"You are sure that the door yielded?"

"Yes, to the third key I tried."

"By the way, did you shut it again?"

"Yes, Monseigneur."

Aurilly did not feel so sure that he had shut the door as that he had opened it; but his assurance removed all doubt from the prince's mind.

"But," said the prince," I should not have been sorry to ascertain—"

"What they are doing there, Monseigneur? I can tell you with certainty; they are lying in wait for some one. Let us go. Your Highness has enemies; who knows what they might dare against you?"

"Well, I will go; I shall return some other time." And the duke went away, promising to pay off the gentlemen for their interruption.

They had hardly disappeared when the five companions saw approach a cavalier wrapped in a large cloak. The steps of his horse resounded on the frozen ground, and a feeble ray of moonlight, struggling through the clouds and the snow-laden atmosphere, silvered the white plume in his cap. He cautiously restrained the impatience of his horse, compelling him to move slowly.

"This time," said Quélus, "it is he."

"Impossible," said Maugiron.

"Why?"

"Because he is alone, and we left him with Livarot, Antragues, and Ribeirac, who would not have let him run such a risk."

"It is he, however; do you not recognise his insolent way of carrying his head?"

"Then," said D'O, "it is a snare."

"In any case, it is he; and so, to arms!"

It was indeed Bussy, who came carelessly down the Rue St. Antoine, and followed precisely the route given him by Quélus; he had, as we have seen, received the warning of Saint-Luc, and although naturally startled by those warning words, had parted from his friends at the door of the Hôtel de Montmorency. It was one of those bravadoes delighted in by the valiant colonel, who said of himself, " I am but a simple gentleman, but I bear in my breast the heart of an emperor; and when I read in Plutarch the exploits of the ancient Romans, I think there is not one that I could not imitate." And besides, he had thought that perhaps Saint-Luc, who was not ordinarily one of his friends, merely wished to get him laughed at for his precautions; and Bussy feared ridicule more than danger. He had, even in the eyes of his enemies, earned a reputation for courage which could only be sustained by the rashest adventures. Therefore, like one of Plutarch's men, he had dismissed his three companions,—a vigorous escort, which would have secured to him the respect of a squadron,—and alone, armed only with a sword and poniard, he advanced towards the house where awaited him, not a mistress, but simply a letter, which the Queen of Navarre sent him every month on the same day, and which he, according to his promise to his beautiful Marguerite, went for himself, alone, and at night.

When he arrived at the Rue St. Catherine, his active eye discerned in the shade the forms of his adversaries. He counted them; " Three, four, five," said he, " without counting the lackeys, who are doubtless within call. They think much of me, it seems. The devil! here is a good deal of trouble for one man! That brave Saint-Luc did not deceive me; and were his even the first sword to pierce me, I would cry, ' Thanks for your warning, friend!' " So saying, he continued to advance, only his right arm moved freely under his cloak, of which his left hand, without apparent movement, had unfastened the clasp.

It was then that Schomberg cried, " To arms! " and the cry being repeated by his four companions, they all sprang forward towards Bussy.

" Ah, gentlemen," said Bussy, " it appears that you wish to kill me. I am the wild boar you had to hunt. Well, gentlemen, the wild boar will rip up a few of you; I swear it to you, and I never break my word."

" Possibly," said Schomberg; " but it is none the less bad manners in you, M. de Bussy d'Amboise, to talk to us on horseback while we listen on foot." And as he spoke, the arm of the young man, covered with white satin, which glistened in the moonlight, came from under his cloak, and Bussy felt his horse give way under him. Schomberg had, with an address peculiar to himself, pierced the horse's leg with a kind of cutlass, of which the blade was heavier than the handle, and which had remained in the wound. The animal gave a shrill cry, and fell on his knees. Bussy, always ready, jumped at once to the ground, sword in hand.

"Ah!" cried he, "my favourite horse; you shall pay for this." And as Schomberg approached incautiously, miscalculating the reach of the sword at Bussy's side, as one might miscalculate the length of a coiled snake, Bussy's arm and sword were suddenly thrust out and wounded him in the thigh. Schomberg uttered a cry.

"Well!" said Bussy, "have I kept my word? One already. It was the wrist of Bussy, and not his horse's leg, you should have cut."

In an instant, while Schomberg bound up his thigh with his handkerchief, Bussy presented the point of his long sword to his four other assailants, disdaining to cry for help, but retreating gradually,—not to fly, but to gain a wall against which to support himself, and prevent his being attacked behind,—making all the while constant thrusts, and feeling sometimes that soft resistance of the flesh which showed that his blows had taken effect. Once he slipped and instinctively looked at the ground. That instant sufficed for Quélus to give him a wound in the side.

"Touched!" cried Quélus.

"Yes, in the doublet," said Bussy, who would not even acknowledge his hurt. And rushing on Quélus, with a vigorous effort he made his sword fly from his hand. But he could not pursue his advantage, for D'O, D'Epernon, and Maugiron attacked him with fresh fury. Schomberg had bound his wound, and Quélus picked up his sword. Bussy made a bound backwards, and reached the wall. There he stopped, strong as Achilles, and smiling at the tempest of blows which rained around him. All at once he felt a cloud pass over his eyes. He had forgotten his wound; but these symptoms of fainting recalled it to him.

"Ah, you falter!" cried Quélus, redoubling his blows.

"Judge of it!" cried Bussy. And with the hilt of his sword he struck him on the temple. Quélus fell under the blow. Then furious, wild, he rushed forward, uttering a terrible cry. D'O and

D'Epernon drew back; Maugiron was raising Quélus, and held him in his arms; Bussy broke the sword of Quélus with his foot, and wounded the right arm of D'Epernon. For a moment he was conqueror, but Quélus recovered himself, and four swords flashed again. Bussy felt himself lost. He gathered all his strength to retreat, and moved backwards step by step to regain the wall. Already the perspiration was cold on his brow; and the ringing in his ears and the cloud over his eyes warned him that his strength was giving way. He sought for the wall with his left hand; to his astonishment, it yielded. It was a door not quite closed. Then he regained hope and mustered all his strength for a last effort. For a second his blows were so rapid and violent that all those swords were drawn back or were lowered before him. Then he glided to the other side of the door, and turning, closed it with a strong push of the shoulder. The spring clicked in the lock. It was all over; Bussy was out of danger, and was victorious, inasmuch as he had escaped. He heard the furious blows of his enemies on the door, their cries of rage, and wrathful imprecations. Then the floor seemed to fail under his feet, and the walls to move. He made a few steps forward, and fell on the steps of a staircase. He knew no more, but seemed to descend into the silence and obscurity of the tomb.

CHAPTER III

HOW IT IS SOMETIMES DIFFICULT TO DISTINGUISH A DREAM FROM THE REALITY

BUSSY had had time, before falling, to pass his handkerchief under his shirt, and to buckle the belt of his sword over it, so as to make a kind of bandage to the open wound whence the blood was flowing; but he had already lost so much blood that in consequence of that loss he had fainted away, as we have seen. During his fainting-fit, this is what Bussy saw, or thought he saw: He found himself in a room with furniture of carved wood, with a tapestry of figures, and a painted ceiling. These figures, in all possible attitudes, holding flowers, carrying arms, seemed to him to be stepping from the walls. Between the two windows appeared the portrait of a woman, glowing with light; only it seemed to Bussy that the frame of that portrait was the casing of a doorway. He, fixed to his bed, lay regarding all this. All at once the woman of the portrait seemed to move; and an adorable creature, clothed in a long white robe, with fair hair falling over her shoulders, and with eyes black as jet, with long lashes, and with a skin under which he seemed to see the blood circulate, advanced towards the bed. This woman was so wonderfully beautiful that Bussy made a violent effort to rise and throw himself at her feet. But he seemed to be confined there by bonds like those which keep the dead body in the tomb, while the soul mounts to the skies. This forced him to look at the bed on which he was lying, and it seemed to him one of those magnificent beds sculptured in the reign of François I., to which were suspended hangings of white damask embroidered in gold.

At the sight of this woman the people of the wall and ceiling ceased to occupy his attention; she was all to him, and he looked to see if she had left a vacancy in the frame. But suddenly she disappeared; an opaque body interposed itself between her and Bussy, moving slowly, and stretching out its arms as though it were playing blind man's buff. Bussy felt in such a passion at this that had he been able, he would certainly have attacked this inopportune visitor; but as he made a vain effort, the new-comer spoke. " Well," said he, " have I arrived at last? "

" Yes, Monsieur," said a voice so sweet that it thrilled through Bussy; " and now you may take off your bandage."

Bussy made an effort to see if the sweet voice belonged to the woman of the portrait, but it was useless. He saw only the pleasant face of a young man, who had just taken off his bandage, and was looking curiously about him.

" To the devil with this man! " thought Bussy, and he tried to express his thought by speech or gesture, but both were impossible to him.

" Ah, I understand now," said the young man, approaching the bed; " you are wounded, are you not, my dear monsieur? Well, we will try to cure you."

" Is the wound mortal? " asked the sweet voice again, with a sad accent, which brought tears into the eyes of Bussy.

" I do not know yet; I am going to see. Meanwhile he has fainted."

This was all that Bussy could comprehend. He thought he heard the rustling of a dress, as if some one were leaving the chamber; he seemed to feel a red-hot iron in his side, and then he lost all consciousness.

Afterwards, it was impossible for Bussy to fix the duration of this insensibility. When he woke, a cold wind blew over his face, and harsh voices sounded in his ears; he opened his eyes to see if it were the persons on the tapestry quarrelling with those on the ceiling, and in the hope that the portrait was still there, turned his head in all directions. But there was neither tapestry nor ceiling visible; and the portrait had also disappeared. He saw at his right only a man with a white apron spotted with blood; at his left, a monk, who was raising his head; and before him, an old woman mumbling her prayers. His wondering eyes next rested on a mass of stone before him, in which he recognised the Temple, and above that, the cold white sky, slightly tinted by the rising sun. He was in the street.

"Ah, thank you, good people," said he, "for the trouble you have taken in bringing me here. I wanted air, but you might have given it to me by opening the window; and I should have been better on my bed of white damask and gold than on the bare ground. But never mind, there are in my pocket—unless you have already paid yourselves, which would have been prudent—some twenty golden crowns; take, my friends, take."

"But, my gentleman," said the butcher, "we did not bring you here, but found you here as we passed."

"Oh, the devil! and the young doctor, was he here?"

The bystanders looked at one another.

"It is the remains of delirium," said the monk. Then, turning to Bussy, "My son, I think you would do well to confess," said he.

Bussy looked at the monk with a bewildered air.

"There was no doctor, poor young man," said the old woman; "you were here alone, and as cold as death. See, it has snowed a little, and your place is marked in black upon the snow."

Bussy then remembered having received a sword stroke, glided his hand under his doublet, and felt his handkerchief in the same place, fixed over his wound by his sword-belt.

"It is singular," said he.

Already profiting by his permission, the lookers-on were dividing the contents of his purse with many pitiful exclamations at his condition.

"There," said he, when the distribution was finished, "that is very good, my friends; now take me to my hotel."

"Ah, certainly," said the old woman, "poor dear young man; the butcher is strong, and then he has his horse, on which you can ride."

"Yes, my gentleman, my horse and I are at your service."

" Nevertheless, my son," said the monk, " while the butcher goes for his horse I think you would do well to confess."

" What are you called? " asked Bussy.

" Brother Gorenflot."

" Well, Brother Gorenflot, I trust my hour has not yet arrived; and as I am cold, I wish to get quickly home and warm myself."

" What is your hotel called? "

" Hôtel de Bussy."

" How! " cried all, " you belong to M. de Bussy? "

" I am M. de Bussy himself."

" Bussy! " they all cried out; " the brave Bussy, the scourge of the favourites! Hurrah for Bussy! " And the young man, lifted to the shoulders of his hearers, was carried in triumph to his hotel, while the monk went away counting his share of the twenty crowns, shaking his head and murmuring, " If it was that bully, Bussy, I don't wonder he wouldn't confess! "

When he got home Bussy sent for his usual doctor, who found the wound not dangerous.

" Tell me," said Bussy, " has it not been already dressed? "

" Upon my word," said the doctor, " I am not sure."

" And was it serious enough to make me delirious? "

" Certainly."

" Ah! " thought Bussy, " was that tapestry, that frescoed ceiling, that bed, the portrait between the windows, the beautiful blond woman with black eyes, that doctor playing blind man's buff,—was this all delirium? Is nothing true but my combat? Where did I fight? Ah, yes, I remember: near the Bastille, by the Rue St. Paul, I leaned against a door, and it opened; I shut it, and then I remember no more. Have I dreamed or not? And my horse! My horse must have been found dead on the place. Doctor, pray call some one."

The doctor called a valet. Bussy inquired, and heard that the animal, bleeding and mutilated, had dragged itself to the door of the hotel, and at daybreak had been found there, neighing. Then the alarm had extended through the hotel; all the servants, who adored their master, had gone out to look for him, and the greater part of them had not returned.

" It must have been a dream," thought he again; " how should a portrait come down from the wall and talk to a doctor with a bandage on his eyes? I am a fool. And yet, as I remember it, that portrait was very charming. It had—" and he set himself to recalling the characteristics of the portrait.

As he passed in review those details, a trembling of love warmed and animated his heart. " And I dreamed all that!" he exclaimed. " *Mordieu!* it is impossible. No one has such dreams as that. Let us recapitulate." And he went over for the hundredth time the history of the previous evening. " We fought roughly. I entered a passage-way; I found myself ill, and then,—ah! there it is again; it is that *and then* that kills me. There was a fever, a delirium, a dream after that, *and then*— And then," he added with a sigh, " I found myself in the street, where a monk wished me to confess.—Doctor," said he, " shall I have to keep the house a fortnight again for this scratch, as I did for the last? "

" We shall see; can you walk? "

" I seem to have quicksilver in my legs."

" Try."

Bussy jumped out of bed, and walked quickly round his room.

" That will do," said the doctor, " provided that you do not go on horseback, or walk ten miles the first day."

" Capital! you are a doctor. However, I saw another last night. Ah, yes, I saw him plainly; I have his face engraved on my mind, and if ever I meet him, I shall know him."

" I advise you not to seek for him, Monsieur; one has always a little fever after a sword-wound. You should know that, who have had a dozen."

" Ah, *mon Dieu!* " cried Bussy, struck with a new idea, " did my dream begin outside the door instead of inside? Was there no more a staircase and a passage than there was a bed with white and gold damask, and a portrait? Perhaps those wretches, thinking me dead, carried me to the Temple, to divert suspicion, should any one have seen them hiding. Certainly, it must be so, and I have dreamed the rest. *Mon Dieu!* if they have procured for me this dream which torments me so, I swear to make an end of them all."

" My dear seigneur," said the doctor, " if you wish to get well, you must not agitate yourself thus."

" Excepting, however, that good Saint-Luc," continued Bussy, without hearing what the doctor said; " he acted as a friend, and my first visit shall be to him."

" But not before five this evening."

" If you wish it; but, I assure you, it is not going out and seeing people which will make me ill, but staying quietly at home."

" Well, it is possible; you are always a singular patient.

Act as you please, only I recommend you not to get another wound before this one is healed."

Bussy promised to do his best to avoid it, and after dressing, called for his litter to take him to the Hôtel de Montmorency.

CHAPTER IV

HOW MADAME DE SAINT-LUC HAD PASSED THE NIGHT

LOUIS DE CLERMONT, commonly called Bussy d'Amboise, was a perfect gentleman, and a very handsome man. Kings and princes had sought for his friendship; queens and princesses had lavished on him their sweetest smiles. He had succeeded La Mole in the affections of Marguerite de Navarre; and the good queen of tender heart, who after the death of the lover whose history we have written doubtless felt the need of consolation, had committed for the handsome and brave Bussy d'Amboise so many follies that even her husband, insensible so long, was moved by them. And the Duc François would never have pardoned him, had it not gained over Bussy to his interests. Here again the duke sacrificed his love to that secret and irresolute ambition which during the entire course of his existence was to bring him so many sorrows and to produce for him so little fruit.

But in the midst of all his successes of war, ambition, and intrigue, Bussy had continued to be like one who is inaccessible to every human weakness; and he who had never known fear had never known love,—at least until the period which we have now reached.

When the servants of M. de Saint-Luc saw Bussy enter, they ran to tell M. de Brissac.

" Is M. de Saint-Luc at home? " asked Bussy.

" No, Monsieur," said the *concierge*.

" Where shall I find him? "

" I do not know, Monsieur. We are all very anxious about him, for he has not returned since yesterday."

" Nonsense! " said Bussy, astonished.

" It is true, Monsieur."

" But Madame de Saint-Luc? "

" Oh, she is here."

" Tell her I shall be charmed if she will allow me to pay my respects to her."

Five minutes after, the messenger returned, saying Madame de Saint-Luc would be glad to see M. de Bussy.

When Bussy entered the room, Jeanne went to meet him. She was very pale, and her jet-black hair made her look more so; her eyes were red from her sleepless night, and there were traces of tears on her cheeks.

"You are welcome, M. de Bussy," said she, "in spite of the fears your presence awakens."

"What do you mean, Madame? How can my presence announce to you misfortune?"

"Ah! there was a meeting last night between you and M. de Saint-Luc? confess it."

"Between me and Saint-Luc!" repeated Bussy, in astonishment.

"Yes, he sent me away to speak to you; you belong to the Duc d'Anjou, he to the king; you have quarrelled. Do not hide anything from me, M. de Bussy, I beseech you! You must understand my anxiety. He went with the king, it is true— but afterwards? Confess to me the truth. What has happened to M. de Saint-Luc?"

"Madame, this is marvellous. I expected you to ask after my wound—"

"He wounded you? He did fight, then?"

"No, Madame; not with me at least. It was not he who wounded me. Indeed, he did all he could to save me. Did he not tell you so?"

"How could he tell me? I have not seen him."

"You have not seen him? Then your porter spoke the truth?"

"I have not seen him since eleven last night."

"But where can he be?"

"I ask you that question."

"Oh, *pardieu!* tell me about it, Madame," said Bussy, who suspected what had happened; "it is very droll."

The poor woman looked at him with astonishment.

"No, it is very sad, I mean. I have lost much blood, and scarcely know what I am saying. Tell me this lamentable story, Madame."

Jeanne told all she knew,—how the king had carried him off, the shutting of the doors of the Louvre, and the message of the guards.

"Ah, very well, I understand," said Bussy.

"What! you understand?"

"Yes; his Majesty took him to the Louvre, and once there he could not come out again."

"And why not?"

"Ah! that is a State secret."

"But my father went to the Louvre, and I also; and the guards said they did not know what we meant, and that M. de Saint-Luc had probably returned home."

"All the more reason that he should be in the Louvre."

"You think so?"

"I am sure of it, and if you wish to assure yourself—"

"How?"

"By seeing."

"Can I?"

"Certainly."

"But if I go there, they will send me away, as they did before."

"Would you like to enter the Louvre, I ask you?"

"For what purpose?"

"To see Saint-Luc."

"But if he is not there?"

"Eh, *mordieu!* I tell you he is there."

"It is strange!"

"No, it is royal."

"But you, then, can enter the Louvre?"

"Certainly. I am not the wife of Saint-Luc."

"You confuse me."

"Come, nevertheless."

"What do you mean? You pretend that the wife of Saint-Luc cannot enter the Louvre, and you propose to take me there with you?"

"Not at all, Madame; it is not the wife of Saint-Luc whom I propose to conduct thither,—a woman! Bless you, no!"

"You laugh at me, and it is very cruel, in my distress."

"No, dear lady, listen. You are young, you are tall, and have black eyes; you are like my youngest page, who looked so well in the cloth of gold yesterday."

"Ah, what folly, M. de Bussy!" cried Jeanne, blushing.

"I have no other method but this. If you wish to see Saint-Luc—"

"Oh, I would give all the world to see him!"

"Well, I promise that you shall without giving anything."

"Oh, but—"

"I told you how."

" Well, I will do it; shall I send for the dress? "

" No, I will send you a new one I have at home; then you must join me this evening at the Rue St. Honoré, and we will go together to the Louvre." Jeanne began to laugh, and gave her hand to Bussy.

" Pardon my suspicions," said she.

" Willingly. You will provide me an adventure which will make all Europe laugh. It is I who am obliged to you." And taking leave, he went home to prepare for the masquerade.

Bussy and Madame de Saint-Luc met at the appointed time. Jeanne looked beautiful in her disguise. At the end of the Rue St. Germain l'Auxerrois, they met a large party, in which Bussy recognised the Duc d'Anjou and his train.

" Ah," said he, " we will make a triumphal entry into the Louvre.—Eh, Monseigneur! " cried he to the duke.

The prince turned. " You, Bussy? " cried he, joyfully; " I heard you were badly wounded, and I was going to your hotel."

" Faith, Monseigneur! if I am not dead, it is thanks to no one but myself. You get me into nice situations; that ball at Saint-Luc's was a regular snare, and they have nearly drained all the blood out of my body."

" *Par la mort!* they shall pay for it, Bussy; they shall pay dearly."

" Yes, you say so," said Bussy, with his usual liberty, " and you will smile on the first you meet."

" Well! accompany me to the Louvre, and you shall see."

" What shall I see, Monseigneur? "

" You will see how I shall speak to my brother."

" Listen, Monseigneur; I will not go to the Louvre to receive a rebuff. That will do for princes of the blood and for favourites."

" Be assured; I have taken the matter to heart."

" You promise me reparation? "

" I promise you shall be content. You hesitate still, I believe? "

" Monseigneur, I know you so well."

" Come, I tell you."

" This is good for you," whispered Bussy to Jeanne. " There will be a frightful quarrel between the brothers, who hate each other, and meanwhile you can find Saint-Luc.—Well," said he to the prince, " I follow you; if I am insulted, at least I can always revenge myself."

And he took his place near the duke, while his page kept close to him.

"Revenge yourself? No, Bussy," said the prince. "I charge myself with it. I know your assassins," added he, in a low tone.

"What! your Highness has taken the trouble to inquire?"

"I saw them."

"How so?" cried Bussy, astonished.

"Oh! I had business myself at the Porte St. Antoine. They barely missed killing me in your place. Ah, I did not know it was you they were waiting for, or else—"

"Well?"

"Had you this new page with you?" asked the prince, without finishing his sentence.

"No, I was alone; and you?"

"I had Aurilly with me; and why were you alone?"

"Because I wish to preserve my name of the brave Bussy."

"And they wounded you?"

"I do not wish to give them the pleasure of knowing it, but I had a severe wound in the side."

"Ah, the wretches! Aurilly said he was sure they were bent on mischief."

"How! you saw the ambush; you were with Aurilly, who uses his sword as well as his lute; you thought they had bad intentions; you were two and they were only five,—and you did not watch to give aid?"

"Bless you! what would you have? I didn't know for whom they were in ambush."

"'Mort diable!' as King Charles IX. would say, when you saw the king's friends, you might have known that they intended harm to friends of yours. Now, as there is hardly any one but myself who has courage to be your friend, you might have guessed that it was I."

"Oh, perhaps you are right, my dear Bussy; but I did not think of all that."

When they entered, "Remember your promise," said Bussy. "I have some one to speak to."

"You leave me, Bussy?"

"Yes, I must, but if I hear a great noise I will come to you; so speak loud."

Then Bussy, followed by Jeanne, took a secret staircase,

traversed two or three corridors, and arrived at an antechamber.
"Wait here for me," said he to Jeanne.

"Ah, *mon Dieu!* you leave me alone!"

"I must, to provide for your entrance."

CHAPTER V

HOW MADAME DE SAINT-LUC ARRANGED FOR THE SECOND NIGHT OF HER MARRIAGE

BUSSY went straight to the sleeping-room of the king. There
were in it two beds of velvet and satin, pictures, relics, perfumed
sachets from the East, and a collection of beautiful swords.
Bussy knew the king was not there, as his brother had asked to
see him; but he knew that adjoining this chamber there was a
little room which was occupied in turn by all the king's favourites,
and which he now expected to find occupied by Saint-Luc, whom
the king in his great affection had carried off from his wife.
Bussy knocked at the antechamber common to the two rooms.
The captain of the guards opened.

"M. de Bussy!" cried he, in astonishment.

"Yes, myself, dear M. de Nancey; the king wishes to speak
to M. de Saint-Luc."

"Very well," replied the captain; "let some one tell M. de
Saint-Luc the king wants him."

"What is he doing?"

"He is with Chicot, waiting for the king's return from his
brother."

"Will you permit my page to wait here?"

"Willingly, Monsieur."

"Enter, Jean," said Bussy; and he pointed to the embrasure
of a window, where she went to hide herself. Saint-Luc entered,
and M. de Nancey discreetly withdrew beyond reach of their
voices.

"What does the king want now?" cried Saint-Luc, angrily.
"Ah! it is you, M. de Bussy?"

"Myself, dear Saint-Luc; and before everything, let me
thank you for the service you rendered me."

"Ah! it was quite natural; I could not bear to see a brave
gentleman like you assassinated. But I understood that you
were killed."

" I came only a little short of it; but in a case like that a little is enormous."

" How was it? "

" Yes; I got a pretty wound with a sword, which I repaid with interest, I think, to Schomberg and D'Epernon. As for Quélus, he may thank the bones of his head; they are the hardest I ever knew."

" Ah! tell me about it, it will amuse me," said Saint-Luc, yawning.

" I have no time at this moment, my dear Saint-Luc; and besides I have come for something else. You are very much bored here, it seems? "

" Royally,—that tells all."

" Well, I have come to wake you up,—what the devil! one service deserves another."

" You are right; and that which you render me is not less than mine to you. One dies of ennui as surely as by a thrust of the sword; it takes more time, but is more certain."

" Poor count! " said Bussy; " you are, then, a prisoner, as I suspected? "

" Completely. The king pretends that no one else can amuse him as I do. He is very good, for since yesterday I have made more grimaces than his ape, and have said more rude things to him than his jester."

" Well, it is my turn to render you a service; can I do it? "

" Yes, go to the Marshal de Brissac's and reassure my poor little wife, who must be very uneasy, and will think my conduct very strange."

" What shall I say to her? "

" Eh, *pardieu!* tell her what you see,—that I am a prisoner, and that the king talks to me of friendship like Cicero, who wrote on it; and of virtue like Socrates, who practised it."

" And what do you reply to him? " said Bussy, laughing.

" *Morbleu!* I reply to him that as to friendship I am an ingrate, and as to virtue I am an unbeliever. That doesn't prevent his persisting and repeating to me with sighs, ' Ah, Saint-Luc, friendship, then, is but a chimera! Ah, Saint-Luc, virtue, then, is but a name! ' Only, after saying it in French, he says it again in Latin and repeats it in Greek."

At this sally, the page, to whom Saint-Luc had not yet given the least attention, laughed aloud.

" What do you expect, dear friend? He wanted to touch your feelings. But is that all I can do for you? "

" Ah, *mon Dieu !* I fear so."

" Well, that is done."

" How so? "

" I suspected all that has happened, and have already informed your wife."

" And what did she say? "

" At first she would not believe; but I trust now," continued he, glancing towards the window, " she will yield to evidence. Ask me, then, to do something else,—something difficult, impossible even; I shall undertake it with pleasure."

" Then, bring here the griffin of Signor Astolpho; I will mount behind you, and you will take me to my wife; afterwards, if you like, you can continue your journey to the moon."

" A more simple thing would be to take the griffin to your wife and bring her here."

" Here? "

" Yes; here."

" To the Louvre? "

" Even to the Louvre. That would be still more amusing, would it not? "

" Oh, *mordieu !* I should say so."

" You would be bored no longer? "

" Upon my soul, no."

" For you are bored, you said? "

" Ask Chicot. Since this morning I have a horror of him, and proposed to fight him. The monkey was angry enough to make one burst with laughter, and yet I didn't move an eyebrow. If this thing goes on I shall kill him outright to distract my mind, or I will make him kill me."

" *Peste !* don't play that game; you know Chicot is a rough swordsman. You would be much more *ennuyé* in a coffin than you are in your prison."

" Faith! I don't know about that."

" Come," said Bussy, laughing. " would you like to have me give my page to you? "

" To me? "

" Yes, a wonderful lad."

" Thank you," said Saint-Luc; " I detest pages. The king offered to send for the one of my own who would most please me, and I declined. Offer him to the king, who is arranging the service of his house."

" Bah! " said Bussy, insisting; " try him, at least."

B

" Bussy," said Saint-Luc, annoyed, " it is not kind in you to make fun of me in this way."

" Let me leave him."

" But I say no."

" When I tell you that I know that you need him? "

" No, no, no! a hundred times no! "

" Holloa, page, come here! "

" *Mordieu !* " cried Saint-Luc.

The page left the window and came forward, blushing.

" Oh, oh! " murmured Saint-Luc, stupefied, on recognising Jeanne in Bussy's livery.

" Well! shall I send him away? "

" No, no! Ah, Bussy, Bussy, I owe you an eternal friendship! "

" Take care! you cannot be heard, but you can be seen."

" It is true," said Saint-Luc; and having taken two steps towards his wife, he took three in retreat.

Indeed, M. de Nancey was beginning to wonder what was going on, when a great noise was heard from the gallery. " Ah, *mon Dieu !* " he cried, " there is the king quarrelling with some one."

" I really think so," replied Bussy, affecting inquietude; " can it be with the Duc d'Anjou, who came with me? "

The captain of the guards went off in the direction of the gallery.

" Have I not managed well? " said Bussy to Saint-Luc.

" What is the matter, then? "

" M. d'Anjou and the king are at this moment tearing each other to pieces. It will be a superb scene, and I must hurry so as not to lose it. You can take advantage of the brawl to place in safety the handsome page I give you; is it possible? "

" Yes, *pardieu !* and if it were not, I should have to make it so; but fortunately, I am supposed to be ill, and am confined to my chamber."

" In that case, adieu, Saint-Luc. Madame, remember me in your prayers." And Bussy, rejoicing in having played the king an ill turn, went off to the gallery, where the king, red with fury, was swearing to the duke, who was pale with anger, that in the scene of the preceding night Bussy was the aggressor.

" I affirm to you, Sire," cried the duke, " that D'Epernon, Schomberg, and Quélus were waiting for him at the Hôtel des Tournelles."

" Who told you so? "

" I saw them with my own eyes."

" In that darkness? The night was pitch dark."

" I knew their voices."

" They spoke to you? "

" They did more,—they took me for Bussy and attacked me."

" You? "

" Yes, me."

" And what were you doing there? "

" What does that matter to you? "

" I wish to know; I am curious to-day."

" I was going to Manassès."

" To Manassès, a Jew? "

" You go to Ruggieri, a poisoner."

" I go where I like; I am the king."

" That is not a reply, it is arrogance."

" Besides, as I said, Bussy was the aggressor."

" Where? "

" At Saint-Luc's ball."

" Bussy provoked five men? No, no, he is brave, but he is not a fool."

" *Par la mordieu !* I tell you I heard the provocation myself. Besides, he was capable of it, in spite of what you say; he has wounded Schomberg in the thigh, D'Epernon in the arm, and half killed Quélus."

" Ah, really! he didn't tell me that; I congratulate him."

" I will make an example of this brawler."

" And I, whom your friends attack in his person and in my own, will know if I am your brother, and if—"

At this moment Bussy, dressed in pale-green satin, entered.

" Sire," said he, " receive my humble respects."

" *Pardieu !* here he is," cried Henri.

" Your Majesty, it seems, was doing me the honour of speaking of me."

" Yes, and I am glad to see that in spite of what they told me your appearance indicates good health."

" Sire, blood drawn improves the complexion, so mine ought to be good this morning."

" Well, since they have wounded you, complain, and I will do you justice."

" I complain of nothing, Sire."

Henri looked astonished. " What did you say? " said he to the duke.

" I said that Bussy had received a wound in his side."

" Is it true, Bussy? "

" Since your Majesty's brother has so stated," said Bussy,
" it must be true; a first prince of the blood would not lie."

" And yet you do not complain? "

" I shall never complain, Sire, until they cut off my right hand
to prevent my revenging myself, and then I will try to do it
with the left."

" Insolent! " murmured Henri.

" Sire," said the duke, " do justice; we ask no better.   Order
an inquiry, name judges, and let it be proved who prepared
the ambush and the intended murder."

Henri reddened.   " No," said he, " I prefer this time to be
ignorant where the wrong lies, and to pardon every one.   I
wish these enemies to make peace, and I am sorry that Schomberg and D'Epernon are kept at home by their wounds.   Come,
M. d'Anjou, which of my friends was the most violent, in your
opinion,—since you say that you saw them? "

" Sire, it was Quélus."

" Faith! yes," said Quélus; " his Highness is right."

" Then," said Henri, " let M. de Bussy and M. de Quélus
make peace in the name of all."

" Oh, oh! " said Quélus, " what does that mean, Sire? "

" It means that you are to embrace here, before me."

Quélus frowned.

" Ah, Signor," cried Bussy, turning towards Quélus, and
imitating the Italian manner of a pantaloon, " will you not do
me this favour? "

The sally was so unexpected, and Bussy had made it with
such animation that the king himself laughed aloud.   Then,
approaching Quélus, Bussy threw his arms round his neck,
saying, " The king wishes it."

" I hope it engages us to nothing," whispered Quélus.

" Be easy," answered Bussy, " we shall meet soon."

Quélus drew back in a rage, and Bussy, still imitating the
pantaloon, made a pirouette and went out of the gallery.

CHAPTER VI

LE PETIT COUCHER OF HENRI III

AFTER this scene, beginning in tragedy and ending in comedy, the king, still angry, went to his room, followed by Chicot, who asked for his supper.

" I am not hungry," said the king.

" It is possible; but I am in a rage, and I must bite something, if only a leg of mutton."

The king pretended not to hear. He unclasped his cloak, took off his cap, and advancing to the passage which led to Saint-Luc's room, separated from his own only by a wall, said to Chicot, " Wait here for me till I return."

" Oh, do not be in a hurry, my son," said Chicot. When he could no longer hear the footsteps of the king, he opened the door and called, " Holloa!"

A valet came. " The king has changed his mind," said Chicot, " he wishes a good supper here for himself and Saint-Luc; above all, plenty of wine and—despatch."

The valet went to execute the orders, which he believed to be the king's. Henri meanwhile had passed into Saint-Luc's room. He found him in bed, having prayers read to him by an old servant who had followed him to the Louvre, and shared his captivity. In a corner, on an armchair, her head buried in her hand, slept the page.

" Who is that young man? " asked the king.

" Did not your Majesty authorise me to send for a page? "

" Yes, doubtless."

" Well, I have profited by the permission, Sire."

" Oh!"

" Does your Majesty repent of having allowed me this little indulgence? "

" No, no; on the contrary, amuse yourself, my son. Well, how are you? "

" Sire, I am very feverish."

" Really, your face is red. Let me feel your pulse; you know that I am something of a doctor."

Saint-Luc held out his hand with visible ill-humour.

" Oh! " said the king, " intermittent, agitated."

" Yes, Sire, I am very ill."

" Be easy; I will have you cared for by my own physician."

" Thank you, Sire, but I hate Miron."

" I will watch you myself."

" Sire, I could not allow it."

" You shall have a bed in my room, and we will talk all night. I have a thousand things to say to you."

" Oh!" cried Saint-Luc, in despair, " you see me ill, and you want to keep me from sleeping. *Morbleu*, Doctor, you have a queer way of treating your patients! *Morbleu*, Sire, you have a strange way of loving your friends!"

" What! you wish to remain alone, suffering as you are?"

" Sire, I have my page, Jean."

" But he sleeps."

" That is what I like best; he will not, at any rate, prevent my sleeping too."

" Well, come and assist at my going to bed."

" Then I shall be free to come back to bed?"

" Perfectly."

" Well, so be it. But I shall make a bad courtier, I assure you; I am dying with sleep."

" You shall yawn at your ease."

" Sire, if your Majesty will leave me, I will be with you in five minutes."

" Well, then, five minutes, but no longer."

As soon as the door was shut, the page jumped up. " Ah, Saint-Luc," she cried, " you are going to leave me again? *Mon Dieu!* I shall die of fright here. Suppose they discover me!"

" My dear Jeanne, Gaspard here will protect you."

" Then I may as well go back," said the young woman, blushing.

" If you really wish it, Jeanne," said Saint-Luc, sadly, " you shall. But if you are as good as you are beautiful, if you have any feeling in your heart for me, you will wait here a little. I shall suffer so much from my head and nerves that the king will not long keep so sad a companion, and will send me back to bed."

Jeanne lowered her eyes. " Go, then," she said; " I will wait. But, like the king, I say, ' Come soon.' "

" My dear Jeanne, you are adorable. Trust me to return as soon as possible. Besides, I have an idea, which I will tell you when I return."

" An idea which will restore your liberty?"

" I hope so."

" Then go."

" Gaspard," said Saint-Luc, " prevent any one from entering

here, and in a quarter of an hour lock the door, and bring me
the key to the king's room. Then go home and tell them not
to be uneasy about Madame the Countess, and come back
to-morrow."

Gaspard, smiling, promised to obey the orders, and the young
woman blushed as she heard them.

Saint-Luc kissed his wife's hand, and went to the king, who
was already growing impatient. Jeanne, alone and trembling,
hid behind the curtains of the bed.

When Saint-Luc entered, he found the king with his feet
buried in flowers, of which the stalks had been cut off that they
might not irritate the delicate skin of his Majesty. Roses,
jasmines, violets, and wall-flowers, in spite of the severe weather,
formed a soft and fragrant carpet for Henri III. The chamber,
of which the roof was painted, had in it two beds, one of which
was so large as to occupy nearly a third of the room. It was
hung with gold and silk tapestry, representing mythological
figures, and the windows had curtains to match. From the
centre of the ceiling hung, suspended by a golden chain, a silver
gilt lamp, in which burned a perfumed oil. At the side of the
bed was a golden satyr, holding in his hand a candelabrum containing four rose-coloured wax candles, also perfumed.

The king, with his naked feet resting on the flowers, was
seated on a chair of ebony inlaid with gold; he had on his knees
seven or eight young spaniels, who were licking his hands. Two
servants were curling his hair, his mustaches, and beard; a third
was covering his face with a kind of cream, which had a most
delightful scent.

" Here," cried Chicot, " the grease and the combs, I will try
them too."

" Chicot," said Henri, " your skin is too dry and will absorb
too much cream, and your beard is so hard it will break my
combs.—Well, my son," said he, turning to Saint-Luc, " how
is your head?"

Saint-Luc put his hand to his head and groaned.

" Imagine!" continued Henri, " I have seen Bussy
d'Amboise."

" Bussy!" cried Saint-Luc, trembling.

" Yes, those fools! five of them attacked him, and let him
escape. If you had been there, Saint-Luc—"

" I should probably have been like the others."

" Oh, no! I wager you are as good as Bussy. We will try
to-morrow."

" Sire, I am too ill for anything."

Henri, hearing a singular noise, turned round and saw Chicot eating up all the supper that had been brought for two.

" What the devil are you doing, M. Chicot? " cried Henri.

" Taking my cream internally, since you will not allow me to do it outwardly."

" Ah, traitor! " cried the king, turning his head, so that the pasty finger of the valet filled his mouth with cream.

" Eat, my son," said Chicot, gravely. " I am not so despotic as you are. Internally or externally, I allow both."

" Monsieur, you stifle me," said Henri to the valet. " Let some one go for the captain of the guards," he cried, " this instant! "

" What for? " asked Chicot, emptying a porcelain cup of chocolate.

" To pass his sword through your body."

" Ah, let him come, we shall see! " cried Chicot, putting himself into such a comical attitude of defence that every one laughed.

" But I am hungry," cried the king; " and the wretch has eaten up all the supper."

" You are capricious, Henri; I offered you supper, and you refused. However, your *bouillon* is left; I am no longer hungry, and I am going to bed."

Meantime old Gaspard had brought the key to his master.

" And I also," said Saint-Luc, " for I can stand no longer."

" Stay, Saint-Luc," said the king, " take these," and he offered him a handful of little dogs.

" What for? "

" To sleep with you; they will take your illness from you."

" Thanks, Sire," said Saint-Luc, putting them back in their basket; " but I have no confidence in your receipt."

" I will come and visit you in the night, Saint-Luc."

" Pray do not, Sire, you will only disturb me; " and saluting the king, he went away. Chicot had already disappeared; and there remained with the king only the valets, who covered his face with a mask of fine cloth plastered with the perfumed cream, in which were holes for the eyes, nose, and mouth; a cap of silk and silver fixed it on the forehead and ears. They next covered his arms with sleeves made of wadded silk, and then presented him with kid gloves, also greased inside. These mysteries of the royal toilet finished, they presented to him his soup in a golden cup. Then Henri said a prayer, a short one that night, and went to bed.

When well settled on his pillows, Henri ordered the flowers to be carried away, which made the atmosphere of the chamber heavy with perfume. The windows were opened for a few moments to renew that atmosphere too charged with carbon. Then the valet closed the doors and curtains, and called in Narcissus, the king's favourite dog, who, jumping on the bed, settled himself at once on the king's feet. The valet next put out the wax lights, lowered the light of the lamp, and went out softly.

Already more tranquil and nonchalant than the lazy monks of his kingdom in their fat abbeys, the King of France no longer remembered that there was a France; he slept.

Every noise was hushed; and one might have heard a bat fly in the sombre corridors of the Louvre.

CHAPTER VII

HOW, WITHOUT APPARENT CAUSE, THE KING WAS CONVERTED IN THE NIGHT

THREE hours passed thus. Suddenly a terrible cry was heard, which came from the king's room. All the lights in his room were out, and no sound was to be heard except this strange call of the king's,—for it was he who had called out.

Soon was heard the noise of furniture falling, porcelain breaking, steps running about the room, and the barking of dogs mingled with new cries. Almost instantly lights burned, swords shone in the galleries, and the heavy steps of the guards were heard.

"To arms!" cried all; "the king calls!"

And the captain of the guards, the colonel of the Swiss, and some attendants, rushed into the king's room. Twenty torches illumined the scene. Near an overturned chair, broken cups, and disordered bed, stood Henri, looking terrified and grotesque in his nightdress, his hair on end, his eyes fixed. His right hand was extended, trembling like a leaf in the wind, and his left held his sword, which he had seized mechanically. He appeared dumb through terror, and all the spectators, not daring to break the silence, waited with the utmost anxiety.

Then appeared, half dressed and wrapped in a large cloak,

the young queen, Louise de Lorraine, blond and gentle, who led the life of a saint upon earth, and who had been awakened by her husband's cries.

"Sire," cried she, also trembling, "what is the matter? *Mon Dieu!* I heard your cries, and I came."

"It—it is nothing," said the king, without moving his eyes, which seemed to be looking in the air for some form invisible to all but him.

"But your Majesty cried out. Is your Majesty suffering?" asked the queen.

Terror was so visibly painted on the king's countenance that it began to gain on the others. They recoiled; they advanced; they devoured with their eyes the person of the king, to assure themselves that he had not been wounded or struck by lightning or bitten by some reptile.

"Oh, Sire!" cried the queen, "in Heaven's name do not leave us in this suspense! Will you have a doctor?"

"A doctor, no," cried Henri, in the same tone; "the body is not ill, it is the mind. No doctor; a confessor."

Every one looked round; nowhere was there to be seen any traces of what had so terrified the king. However, a confessor was sent for; Joseph Foulon, superior of the convent of Ste. Geneviève, was torn from his bed to come to the king. On the arrival of the confessor, the tumult ceased, and silence was reestablished. Every one conjectured and wondered; the king was confessing.

The next day the king rose early, and began to read prayers; then he ordered all his friends to be sent for. They sent to Saint-Luc, but he was suffering more than ever. His sleep, or rather his lethargy, had been so profound that he alone had heard nothing of the tumult in the night, although he slept so near. He begged to be left in bed. At this deplorable recital, Henri crossed himself, and sent him a doctor.

Then he ordered that all the scourges from the convent should be brought to him, and going to his friends, distributed them, ordering them to scourge one another as hard as they could.

D'Epernon said that as his right arm was in a sling, and he could not return the blows he received, he ought to be exempt; but the king replied that that would only make it the more acceptable to God.

He himself set the example. He took off his doublet, waistcoat, and shirt, and struck himself like a martyr. Chicot tried to laugh, as usual, but was warned by a terrible look that this was not the right time, and he was forced to take a scourge like the others.

All at once the king left the room, telling them to wait for him. Immediately the blows ceased as by enchantment; only Chicot continued to strike D'O, whom he hated, and D'O returned the blows as well as he could. It was a duel with whips.

The king went to the queen, gave her a pearl necklace worth twenty-five thousand crowns and kissed her, which he had not done for a year. Then he asked her to put off her royal ornaments and put on a sack. Louise, always good, consented, but asked why her husband gave her a necklace, and yet made such a request.

" For my sins," replied he.

The queen said no more, for she knew better than any one how many he had to repent of.

Henri returned, which was a signal for the flagellation to recommence. D'O and Chicot, who had not ceased, were covered with blood. The king complimented them, and called them his true and only friends. In ten minutes the queen arrived, with her sack on her shoulders. Then tapers were distributed to all the court, and bare-footed, through the snow, all the courtiers and fine ladies went to Montmartre, shivering at first, but soon warmed by the furious blows which Chicot administered to all within reach of his discipline. At five o'clock the promenade was over, the convents had received rich presents, the feet of all the court were swollen, and the backs of the courtiers sore. There had been tears, cries, prayers, incense, and psalms. Every one had suffered, without knowing why the king, who danced the night before, scourged himself to-day. As for Chicot, he had escaped at the Porte Montmartre, and with Brother Gorenflot had entered a public-house, where he ate and drank. Then he had rejoined the procession and returned to the Louvre.

In the evening the king, fatigued with his fast and his exercise, ordered himself a light supper, had his shoulders washed, and then went to visit Saint-Luc.

Since the evening before, the king was entirely changed. All his thoughts were turned towards the vanity of human affairs, towards penitence and death. " Ah," he said with the deep tone of a man weary of life, " God has done well to render life so bitter."

" Why so, Sire? "

" Because then man, instead of fearing death, longs for it."

" Speak for yourself, Sire, I do not long for it at all."

" Listen, Saint-Luc; will you follow my example? "

" If I think it a good one."

" I will leave my throne, you your wife, and we will enter a cloister. I will call myself Brother Henri—"

" Pardon, Sire, if you do not care for your crown, of which you are tired, I care very much for my wife, whom I know so little. Therefore I refuse."

" Oh, you are getting better, it seems."

" Infinitely better, Sire; I feel quite joyous, and disposed for happiness and pleasure."

" Poor Saint-Luc! " cried the king, clasping his hands.

" You should have proposed that to me yesterday, Sire. Oh! yesterday I was ill and cross; I would have thrown myself into a well for a trifle. But this evening it is quite a different thing. I have passed a good night and a charming day. *Mordieu*, hurrah for happiness! "

" You swear, Saint-Luc."

" Did I, Sire? but I think you swear sometimes."

" I have sworn, Saint-Luc, but I shall swear no more."

" I cannot say that; I will not swear more than I can help, and God is merciful."

" You think he will pardon me? "

" Oh, I speak for myself, not for you, Sire. You have sinned as a king, I as a private man; and we shall, I trust, be differently judged."

The king sighed. " Saint-Luc," said he, " will you pass the night in my room? "

" Why, what should we do? "

" We will light all the lamps, I will go to bed, and you shall read prayers to me."

" No, thank you, Sire."

" You will not? "

" On no account."

" You abandon me, Saint-Luc? "

" No, I will stay with your Majesty if you will send for music and ladies, and have a dance."

" Oh, Saint-Luc, Saint-Luc! " cried the king, in terror.

" I am wild to-night, Sire; I want to dance and drink."

" Saint-Luc," said the king, solemnly, " do you ever dream? "

" Often, Sire."

" You believe in dreams? "

" With reason."

" How so? "

" Dreams console for the reality. Last night I had a charming dream."

" What was it? "

" I dreamed that my wife—"

" You still think of your wife? "

" More than ever, Sire; well, I dreamed that she, with her charming face,—for she is pretty, Sire—"

" So was Eve, who ruined us all."

" Well, my wife had procured wings and the form of a bird, and so, braving locks and bolts, she passed over the walls of the Louvre, and came to my window, crying, ' Open, Saint-Luc; open, my husband! ' "

" And you opened? "

" I should think so! " exclaimed Saint-Luc, with enthusiasm.

" Worldly! "

" As you please, Sire."

" Then you woke? "

" No, indeed; the dream was too charming. And I hope to-night to dream again; therefore I refuse your Majesty's obliging offer. If I sit up, let me at least have something to pay me for losing my dream. If your Majesty will do as I said—"

" Enough, Saint-Luc. I trust Heaven will send you a dream to-night which will lead you to repentance."

" I doubt it, Sire; and I advise you to send away this libertine Saint-Luc, who is resolved not to amend."

" No, no; I hope before to-morrow, grace will have touched you as it has me. Good-night, I will pray for you."

CHAPTER VIII

HOW THE KING WAS AFRAID OF BEING AFRAID

WHEN the king left Saint-Luc, he found the court, according to his orders, in the great gallery. Then he gave D'O, D'Epernon, and Schomberg an order to retire into the provinces, threatened Quélus and Maugiron with punishment if they quarrelled any more with Bussy, to whom he gave his hand to kiss, and then embraced his brother François. As for the queen, he was prodigal in politeness to her,—to such a degree that those present drew from it a most favourable augury for the succession to the crown of France.

When the usual time for retiring approached, the king seemed trying to retard it. At last ten o'clock struck. "Come with me, Chicot," then said he. "Good-night, gentlemen."

"Good-night, gentlemen," said Chicot; "we are going to bed. I want my barber, my hair-dresser, my *valet de chambre*, and, above all, my cream."

"No," said the king, "I want none of them to-night; Lent is going to begin."

"I regret the cream," said Chicot.

The king and Chicot entered the room which we already know.

"Ah, Henri," said Chicot, "I am, then, the favourite to-night. Am I handsomer than that Cupid, Quélus?"

"Silence, Chicot! And you, gentlemen of the toilet, go out."

They obeyed, and the king and Chicot were left alone.

"Why do you send them away?" inquired Chicot; "they have not greased us yet. Are you going to grease me with your own royal hand? It would be an act of humility."

"Let us pray," said Henri.

"Thank you, that is not amusing. If that be what you called me here for, I prefer to return to the bad company I have left. Adieu, my son. Good-night."

"Stay," said the king.

"Oh! this is tyranny. You are a despot, a Phalaris, a Dionysius. All day you have made me tear the shoulders of my friends with cow-hide, and now we are to begin again. Do not let us do it, Henri; when there are but two, every blow tells."

"Hold your tongue, miserable chatterer, and think of repentance!"

"I repent! And of what? Of being jester to a monk? *Confiteor*, I repent; *mea culpa*, it is a great sin."

"No sacrilege, wretch!"

"Ah, I would rather be shut up in a cage with lions and apes than with a mad king. Adieu, I am going."

The king locked the door.

"Henri, you look sinister; if you do not let me go, I will cry, I will call, I will break the window, I will kick down the door."

"Chicot," said the king, in a melancholy tone, "you take advantage of my misery."

"Ah, I understand! you are afraid to be alone. Tyrants always are so. Take my long sword, and let me take the scabbard to my room."

At the word "afraid," Henri shuddered, and he looked nervously around and seemed so agitated and grew so pale that Chicot began to think him really ill, and said, "Come, my son, what is the matter? tell your troubles to your friend Chicot."

The king looked at him and said, "Yes, you are my friend, my only friend."

"There is," said Chicot, "the abbey of Valencey vacant."

"Listen, Chicot; you are discreet."

"There is also that of Pithiviers, where they make such good pies."

"In spite of your buffooneries, you are a brave man."

"Then do not give me an abbey, give me a regiment."

"And even a wise one."

"Then do not give me a regiment, make me a counsellor; but no, when I think of it, I should prefer a regiment or an abbey. I prefer not to be a counsellor, for I should be always forced to be of the king's opinion."

"Hold your tongue, Chicot, the terrible hour is approaching."

"Ah! you are beginning again."

"You will see; you will hear."

"See what? hear what?"

"Wait, and the event will show you. Chicot, you are brave?"

"I boast of it, but I do not wish to try. Call your captain of the guards, your Swiss, and let me go away from this invisible danger."

"Chicot, I command you to stay."

"On my word, a nice master. I am afraid, I tell you. Help!"

"Well, rascal, if I must, to keep you silent, I will tell you all."

"Ah!" cried Chicot, drawing his sword, "once warned, I do not care; tell, my son, tell. Is it a crocodile? My sword is sharp, for I use it every week to cut my corns. You say, then, Henri, that it is a crocodile?" And Chicot sat down in the armchair with his drawn sword between his legs.

"Last night," said Henri, "I slept—"

"And I also," said Chicot.

"Suddenly a breath swept over my face."

"It was the dog, who was hungry, and who licked your grease."

"I half awoke, and felt my beard bristle with terror under my mask."

"Ah! you make me tremble deliciously."

" Then," continued the king, in a trembling voice,—" then a voice sounded through the room with a doleful vibration."

" The voice of the crocodile! yes, I have read in Marco Polo that the crocodile has a voice like the crying of children; but be easy, my son, for if it comes, we will kill it."

" ' Listen! miserable sinner,' said the voice—"

" Oh! it spoke; then it was not a crocodile."

" ' Miserable sinner,' said the voice, ' I am the voice of your Lord God.' "

" The voice of God! "

" Ah, Chicot, it was a frightful voice."

" Was it like the sound of a trumpet, according to Scripture? "

" ' Are you there?' continued the voice. ' Do you hear, hardened sinner? Are you determined to persevere in your iniquities? ' "

" Ah, really, really, really," said Chicot; " but the voice of God says very nearly what your people are saying, it seems to me."

" Then, Chicot, followed many other reproaches, which I assure you were most painful."

" But still, continue a little, my son; repeat what the voice said, that I may know whether God was well informed."

" Impious! if you doubt I will have you chastised."

" I? I do not doubt; all that astonishes me is that God has waited so long to reproach you. He has become very patient since the Deluge. So, my son, you were dreadfully afraid? "

" Oh, yes, the marrow seemed to dry in my bones."

" As in Jeremiah; it is quite natural. On my word, I do not know what I should have done in your place. And then you called? "

" Yes."

" And they came? "

" Yes."

" And there was no one here? "

" No one."

" It is frightful."

" So frightful that I sent for my confessor."

" And he came? "

" Immediately."

" Now, be frank, my son; tell the truth for once. What did he think of your revelation? "

" He shuddered."

" I should think so! "

" He made the sign of the cross; he ordered me to repent, as God had directed."

" Very well; there can be no harm in repenting. But what did he think of the vision, or rather, of the audition? "

" That it was a miracle, and that I must think of it seriously. Therefore, this morning—"

" What have you done? "

" I gave one hundred thousand livres to the Jesuits."

" Very well."

" And scourged myself and my friends."

" Perfect! but afterwards? "

" Well, what do you think of it, Chicot? It is not to the jester I speak, but to the man of sense, to my friend."

" Ah, Sire, I think your Majesty had the nightmare."

" You think so? "

" Yes, it was a dream, which will not be renewed, unless your Majesty thinks too much about it."

" A dream? No, Chicot, I was awake; my eyes were open."

" I sleep like that."

" Yes, but then you do not see; and I saw the moon shining through my windows, and its light on the amethyst in the hilt of my sword, which lay in that chair where you are."

" And the lamp? "

" Had gone out."

" A dream, my son, only a dream."

" Why do you not believe, Chicot? It is said that God speaks to kings when he wishes to effect some great change on the earth."

" Yes, he speaks, but so low that they never hear him."

" Well, do you know why I made you stay? That you might hear as well as I."

" So that, should I repeat what I hear, it may be thought that I utter some buffoonery. Chicot is such a nobody, so insignificant, so mad, that if he should repeat it to any one he would not be believed. Not well played, my son."

" Why not rather believe, my friend," said the king, " that I confide this secret to your well-known fidelity? "

" Ah, do not lie, Henri; for if the voice comes it will reproach you with that falsehood, and you have sins enough without it. But no matter. I accept the charge; I shall not be sorry to hear the voice of the Lord. Perhaps he will have a word for me also."

" Well, what is it best to do? "

"Go to bed, my son."

"But—"

"Do you think perchance that by sitting up you will prevent the voice of God from speaking? A king surpasses other men only in the height of his crown; and when he is bareheaded, believe me, Henri, he is sometimes a little smaller than other men."

"Well, then, you remain?"

"I said so."

"Well, then, I will go to bed."

"Good."

"But you will not?"

"Certainly not; I will stay here."

"You will not go to sleep?"

"Oh, that I cannot promise; sleep is like fear, my son, a thing independent of will."

"You will try, at least?"

"Be easy; I will pinch myself. Besides, the voice would wake me."

"Do not joke about the voice."

"Well, well, go to bed."

The king sighed, looked round anxiously, and glided tremblingly into bed. Then Chicot settled himself in his chair, arranging round him the pillows and cushions.

"How do you feel, Sire?" said he.

"Pretty well; and you?"

"Very well; good-night, Henri."

"Good-night, Chicot; do not go to sleep."

"Of course not," said Chicot, yawning enough to break his jaws.

And they both closed their eyes, the king to pretend to sleep, Chicot to sleep really.

CHAPTER IX

HOW THE ANGEL MADE A MISTAKE AND SPOKE TO CHICOT, THINKING IT WAS THE KING

THE king and Chicot remained thus for some time. All at once the king jumped up in his bed. Chicot awoke at the noise.

"What is it?" asked he, in a low voice.

"The breath on my face."

As he spoke, one of the wax lights went out, then the other, and the rest followed. "Oh, oh!" said Chicot, "what a breath!" Chicot had hardly pronounced these words when the lamp also went out, and the room was lighted only by the last gleams of the fire. At the same moment they heard a hollow voice, saying, apparently from the end of the room,—

"Hardened sinner, art thou there?"

"Yes, yes, Lord," said Henri, with chattering teeth.

"Oh!" thought Chicot, "that is a very hoarse voice to come from heaven; nevertheless, it is dreadful."

"Do you hear?" asked the voice.

"Yes, Lord, and I am bowed down under thy wrath."

"Do you believe you obeyed me by all the exterior mummeries which you performed yesterday, without your heart being touched?"

"Very well said," thought Chicot. He approached the king softly.

"Do you believe now?" asked the king, with clasped hands.

"Wait."

"What for?"

"Hush! leave your bed quietly, and let me get in."

"Why?"

"That the anger of the Lord may fall first on me."

"Do you think he will spare me for that?"

"Let us try," and he pushed the king gently out and got into his place.

"Now, go to my chair, and leave all to me."

Henri obeyed; he began to understand.

"You do not reply," said the voice; "you are hardened in sin."

"Oh, pardon, pardon, Lord!" cried Chicot, imitating the king's nasal tones. Then he whispered to Henri, "It is strange, —do you notice, my son?—the good God doesn't recognise Chicot!"

"What can it mean?"

"Wait."

"Wretch!" said the voice.

"Yes, Lord, yes," said Chicot,—"yes, I am a hardened sinner, a dreadful sinner."

"Then acknowledge your crimes and repent."

"I acknowledge to have been a great traitor to my cousin Condé, whose wife I seduced; and I repent."

"Oh, hush!" said the king, "that is so long ago."

"I acknowledge," continued Chicot, "to have been a great

rogue to the Poles, who chose me for king, and whom I abandoned one night, carrying away the crown jewels; and I repent."

"Ah!" whispered Henri, "why recall that? That is all forgotten."

"I must continue to cheat him; let me alone."

"Go on," said the voice.

"I acknowledge having stolen the crown from my brother D'Alençon, to whom it belonged of right, as I had formerly renounced it on accepting the crown of Poland."

"Knave!" said the king.

"Go on," said the voice.

"I acknowledge having joined my mother, to chase from France my brother-in-law, the King of Navarre, after having destroyed all his friends, and my sister, Queen Marguerite, after having destroyed all her lovers, of which I heartily repent."

"Ah!" whispered the king, angrily.

"Sire, let us not offend God, by trying to hide what he knows as well as we do."

"Leave politics," said the voice.

"Ah!" cried Chicot, with a doleful voice, "it is my private life I am to speak of?"

"Yes."

"I acknowledge, then, that I am effeminate, idle, and hypocritical."

"It is true," said the voice, with a hollow sound.

"I have ill-treated women, my wife especially,—a worthy woman."

"One ought to love one's wife as one's self, and prefer her to all things," said the voice angrily.

"Ah!" cried Chicot, in a despairing tone, "then I have sinned deeply."

"And you have made others sin by your example."

"It is true."

"You have almost ruined that poor Saint-Luc."

"Bah!" said Chicot, "are you very sure, *mon Dieu*, that I have not ruined him altogether?"

"No, but that may easily happen to him and to you too, if you do not send him home to-morrow morning to his wife."

"Ah!" said Chicot to the king, "the voice seems to be friendly to the house of Cossé."

"And you must make him a duke and his wife a duchess, as a recompense for her days of premature widowhood."

" *Peste !* " said Chicot; " the angel is much interested for M. de Saint-Luc. Devil take me! one would think he had the good God up his sleeve! "

" Oh! " cried the king, without listening to Chicot's jesting remarks, " this voice from on high will kill me."

" Voice from the side, you mean," said Chicot.

" How, voice from the side? "

" Yes; can you not hear, my son, that the voice comes from that wall? Henri, the good God lodges in the Louvre."

" Blasphemer! "

" Why, it is honourable for you, Henri; I congratulate you. But you do not seem to receive him with much honour. What! the good God is in the Louvre, is separated from you by only a wall, and you do not go to make him a visit! Come, now, Valois, I don't recognise you in that; you are not polite."

At that moment a stick of wood in the fireplace took fire, and throwing a light into the chamber, illumined Chicot's face, which wore such an expression of amusement that the king was astonished. " What! " said he, " have you the heart to laugh? You dare—"

" Yes, and so will you in a minute. Be reasonable, and do as I tell you. Go and see if the good God be not in the next room."

" But if the voice continues? "

" Well, I am here to answer. He is vastly credulous. For the last quarter of an hour I have been talking, and he has not recognised me. It is not clever! "

Henri frowned. " I begin to believe you are right, Chicot," said he.

" Go, then."

Henri opened softly the door which led into the corridor. He had scarcely entered it when he heard the voice redoubling its reproaches, and Chicot replying.

" Yes," said the voice, " you are as inconstant as a woman; as soft as a Sybarite, as irreligious as a heathen."

" Oh! " whined Chicot, " is it my fault if I have such a soft skin, such white hands, such a changeable mind? But from to-day I will be different; I will wear coarse linen—"

Meantime Henri advanced along the corridor, and noticed with surprise that as Chicot's voice grew fainter, the other became louder, and that it seemed to come from Saint-Luc's room, in which he could see a light. He stooped down and peeped through the keyhole, and immediately grew pale with anger. "*Par la mordieu!*" he murmured, "is it possible that any one has dared to play me such a trick?"

This is what he saw through the keyhole: Saint-Luc, in a dressing-gown, was roaring through a tube the words which the king had found so terrible, and beside him, leaning on his shoulder, was a lady in white, who every now and then took the tube from him, and spoke through it, while stifled bursts of laughter accompanied each sentence of Chicot's, who continued to answer in a doleful tone.

"Jeanne de Cossé in Saint-Luc's room! A hole in the wall! Such a trick on me! Oh, they shall pay dearly for it!" And with a vigorous kick he burst open the door.

Jeanne rushed behind the curtains to hide herself, while Saint-Luc, his face full of terror, fell on his knees before the king, who was pale with rage.

"Ah!" cried Chicot, from the bed,—"ah, mercy! Holy Virgin! I am dying!"

Henri, seizing in a transport of rage the trumpet from the hands of Saint-Luc, raised it as if to strike. But Saint-Luc jumped up and cried, "Sire, I am a gentleman; you have no right to strike me!"

Henri dashed the trumpet violently on the ground. Some one picked it up; it was Chicot, who, hearing the noise, judged that his presence was necessary as a mediator. He ran to the curtain, and drawing out poor Jeanne, all trembling, "Oh!" said he, "Adam and Eve after the Fall. You send them away, Henri, do you not?"

"Yes."

"Then I will be the exterminating angel." And throwing himself between the king and Saint-Luc, and waving the trumpet as a flaming sword over the heads of the guilty couple, he said, "This is my paradise, which you have lost by your disobedience; I forbid you to return to it." Then he whispered to Saint-Luc, who had his arm round his wife, "If you have a good horse, kill it, but be twenty leagues from here before to-morrow."

CHAPTER X

HOW BUSSY WENT TO SEEK FOR THE REALITY OF HIS DREAM

When Bussy returned home again, he was still thinking of his dream. " *Morbleu!* " said he, " it is impossible that a dream should have left such a vivid impression on my mind. I see it all so clearly,—the bed, the lady, the doctor. I must seek for it; surely I can find it again." After having the bandage of his wound rearranged by a valet, he put on high boots, took his sword, wrapped himself in his cloak, and set off for the same place where he had been nearly murdered the night before, and nearly at the same hour.

He went in a litter to the Rue Roi de Sicile, then got out, and told his servants to wait for him. It was about nine in the evening; the curfew had sounded, and Paris was deserted. Bussy arrived at the Bastille; then he sought for the place where his horse had fallen, and thought he had found it. He next endeavoured to repeat his movements of the night before, retreated to the wall, and examined every door to find the corner against which he had leaned; but all the doors seemed alike.

" *Pardieu!* " said he, " if I were to knock at each of these doors, question all the lodgers, spend one thousand crowns to make valets and old women speak, I might learn what I want to know. There are fifty houses; it would take me at least five nights."

As he spoke, he perceived a small and trembling light approaching.

This light advanced slowly and irregularly, stopping occasionally, moving on again, and going first to the right, then to the left, then for a minute coming straight on, and again diverging. Bussy leaned against a door, and waited. The light continued to advance, and soon he could see a black figure, which, as it advanced, took the form of a man, holding a lantern in his left hand. He appeared to Bussy to belong to the honourable fraternity of drunkards, for nothing else seemed to explain the eccentric movements of the lantern. At last he slipped over a piece of ice and fell. Bussy was about to come forward and offer his assistance; but the man and the lantern were quickly up again, and advanced directly towards him, when he saw, to his great surprise, that the man had a bandage over his eyes.

" Well! " thought he, " it is a strange thing to play at blind man's buff with a lantern in your hand. Am I beginning to dream again? And, good heavens! he is talking to himself. If he be not drunk or mad, he is a mathematician.''

This last surmise was suggested by the words that Bussy heard.

" Four hundred and eighty-eight, four hundred and eighty-nine, four hundred and ninety,'' murmured the man; " it must be near here.'' And then he raised his bandage, and finding himself in front of a house, examined it attentively.

" No, it is not this,'' he said. Then, putting back his bandage, he resumed his walk and his calculations. " Four hundred and ninety-one, four hundred and ninety-two, four hundred and ninety-three, four hundred and ninety-four; I must be near the place.'' And he raised his bandage again, and approaching the door next to that against which Bussy was standing, he began again to examine.

" Hum! " said he, " it might be, but all these doors are so alike.''

" The same reflection I have just made,'' thought Bussy.

The mathematician replaced his bandage and continued his walk. " Four hundred and ninety-five, four hundred and ninety-six, four hundred and ninety-seven, four hundred and ninety-eight, four hundred and ninety-nine—if there is a door opposite me, it should be the one.''

In fact there was a door, and it was the one at which Bussy stood; so that when the presumed mathematician raised his bandage he found that he and Bussy were face to face.

" Well? " said Bussy.

" Oh! " cried he, stepping back.

" Hold! " cried Bussy.

" It is not possible! " cried the unknown.

" Yes; but it is extraordinary. You are the doctor? ''

" And you the gentleman? ''

" Precisely.''

" *Mon Dieu!* how strange! ''

" The doctor,'' continued Bussy, " who yesterday dressed a wound for a gentleman? ''

" Yes, in the right side.''

" Exactly so. You had a gentle, light, and skilful hand.''

" Ah, sir, I did not expect to find you here.''

" But what were you looking for? "

" The house."

" Then you do not know it? "

" How should I? They brought me here with my eyes bandaged."

" Then you really came here? "

" Either to this house or the next."

" Then I did not dream? "

" Dream? "

" I confess, my dear friend, I believed all that adventure— except the wound, of course—to have been a dream."

" Well! " said the young doctor, " you do not surprise me, Monsieur."

" Why so? "

" It has seemed to me that some mystery was hidden there."

" Yes, my friend,—a mystery which I propose to bring to light; you will help me, will you not? "

" Willingly."

" What is your name? "

" Monsieur, to such a question I ought perhaps to reply by looking fierce, and saying, ' Yours, Monsieur, if you please; ' but you have a long sword, and I only a lancet. You seem to me a gentleman, and I cannot appear so to you, for I am wet and dirty. Therefore I reply frankly: I am called Rémy le Haudouin."

" Very well, Monsieur; I thank you. I am Louis de Clermont, Comte de Bussy."

" Bussy d'Amboise! the hero Bussy! " cried the young doctor, joyfully. " What, Monsieur, you are that famous Bussy? "

" I am Bussy," replied he. " And now, wet and dirty as you are, will you satisfy my curiosity? "

" The fact is," said the young man, " that I shall be obliged, like Epaminondas the Theban, to stay three days at home, for I have but one suit of clothes. But pardon! you would do me the honour to question me, I think? "

" Yes, Monsieur, I was about to ask how you came to this house? "

" Monsieur the Count, this is how it happened: I lodge in the Rue Beautreillis, five hundred and two steps from here. I am a poor surgeon, not unskilful, I hope."

" I can answer for that."

" And I have studied much, but am without any patients. Seven or eight days ago, a man having received behind the

Arsenal a stab with a knife, I sewed up the wound and cured him. This made for me some reputation in the neighbourhood, to which I attribute the happiness of having been last night awakened by a pleasant voice."

" A woman's? "

" Yes, but, rustic as I am, I knew it to be the voice of a servant. I know them well, since I have heard those voices oftener than the voices of mistresses."

" And what did you do? "

" I rose and opened my door; but scarcely had I done so, when two little hands, not very soft, but not very hard, put a bandage over my eyes."

" Without saying anything? "

" ' Oh!' she said, ' come, do not try to see where you are going. Be discreet; here is your recompense;' and she placed in my hand a purse."

" Ah! and what did you say? "

" That I was ready to follow my charming conductress. I did not know if she were charming or not; but I thought that the epithet, even if exaggerated, could do no harm."

" And you asked no more? "

" I had often read stories of this kind in books, and I had remarked that they always turned out well for the doctor. Therefore I followed, and I counted five hundred and two steps."

" Good! then this must be the door."

" It cannot be far off, at all events, since this time I have counted up to four hundred and ninety-nine,—unless she led me by some indirect course, which I half suspect."

" But did she pronounce no name? "

" None."

" But you remarked something? "

" All that one could with one's fingers,—a door with nails, then a passage, and then a staircase—"

" On the left? "

" Yes; and I counted the steps."

" How many? "

" Twelve. Then I think we came to a corridor, for they opened three doors."

" Well? "

" Then I heard another voice, and that belonged to the mistress, I am sure; it was sweet and gentle."

" Yes, yes, it was hers."

" Good! it was hers."

" I am sure of it."

" Then they pushed me into the room where you were, and told me to take off my bandage, when I saw you—"

" Where was I? "

" On a bed."

" A bed of white and gold damask? "

" Yes."

" In a room hung with tapestry? "

" Exactly."

" And a painted ceiling? "

" Yes, and between two windows—"

" A portrait? "

" Yes."

" Representing a woman about nineteen years old? "

" Yes."

" Blond, and beautiful as an angel? "

" More beautiful."

" Bravo! what did you do then? "

" I dressed your wound."

" And upon my soul, you did it well."

" As well as I could."

" Admirably! this morning it was nearly well."

" It is owing to a salve which I have compounded, and which appears to me sovereign; for many times, not knowing on whom to try experiments, I have made wounds on myself, and they were always well in two or three days."

" My dear M. Rémy you are a charming man, and I have taken a great liking to you. Well, afterwards? "

" You fainted again. The voice asked me how you were."

" From where? "

" From a room at the side."

" So you did not see the lady? "

" No."

" And you replied? "

" That the wound was not dangerous, and in twenty-four hours would be well."

" She seemed pleased? "

" Charmed; for she cried, ' What happiness, *mon Dieu !* ' "

" She said ' What happiness!' My dear M. Rémy, I will make your fortune. Well? "

" That was all. I had no more to do; and the voice said, ' M. Rémy—' "

" She knew your name? "

" Yes. ' M. Rémy,' said she, ' be a man of honour to the last; do not compromise a poor woman carried away by an excess of humanity. Replace your bandage, and let them take you straight home.' "

" You promised? "

" I gave my word."

" And you kept it? "

" As you see, for I am seeking now."

" You are an honest man, and here is my hand," cried Bussy.

" Monsieur, it will be an eternal glory for me to have touched the hand of Bussy d'Amboise. However, I have a scruple."

" What is it? "

" There were ten pistoles in the purse."

" Well? "

" It is too much for a man who charges five sous for his visits when he does not give them gratis; and I was seeking the house—"

" To return the purse? "

" Yes."

" My dear M. Rémy, it is too much delicacy; you have earned the money well, and may surely keep it."

" You think so? " said Rémy, well-pleased.

" I assure you; only it is not the lady who should pay you, for I don't know her, and she doesn't know me."

" There, you see, still another reason."

" I meant to say only that I also owe you a debt."

" You owe me a debt? "

" Yes, and I will pay it. What are you doing in Paris? Come, give me your confidence, my dear M. de Rémy."

" What am I doing? I am doing nothing; but I would do something if I had patients."

" Good! that happens well; I will give you a patient. Will you have me? I am famous practice; for there is scarcely a day when I do not deface God's noblest work for others, or they do it for me. Will you undertake the care of all the holes I make in the skin of others, or others make in mine? "

" Ah, Monsieur the Count! I am too unworthy."

" No; you are just the man I want. You shall come and live with me; you shall have your own rooms, and your own servants. Accept, or upon my word, you will lacerate my soul."

" Monsieur the Count, I am so delighted that I know not how to express to you my joy. I will work; I shall have patients."

"But, no, I tell you that I keep you for myself and my friends. Now, do you remember anything more?"

"Nothing."

"Ah, well! help me to find out, if it be possible."

"How?"

"Let us see; you, who are a man of observation, who count steps, feel along the walls, distinguish voices,—how do you account for the fact that after being doctored by you I found myself by the Temple, close to the ditch?"

"You?"

"Yes, I. Did you help to take me there?"

"Certainly not, and I should have opposed it if they had consulted me; for the cold might have done you much harm."

"Then I am in the dark. Will you search a little more with me?"

"I wish all that you wish, Monsieur; but I fear it will be useless. All these houses are alike."

"Well, we must come again by day."

"Yes; but then we shall be seen."

"Then we must inquire."

"We will, Monseigneur."

"And we shall unravel the mystery, believe me, Rémy, now that there are two of us to work."

CHAPTER XI

M. BRYAN DE MONSOREAU

IT was more than joy, it was almost delirium which agitated Bussy when he had acquired the certainty that the lady of his dream was a reality, and had, in fact, given him that generous hospitality of which he had preserved the vague remembrance in his heart. He would not let the young doctor go, but made him, dirty as he was, get into the litter with him; he feared that if he lost sight of him, he too would vanish like a dream. He would have liked to talk all night of the unknown lady, and explain to Rémy how superior she was even to her portrait; but Rémy, beginning his functions at once, insisted that he should go to bed. Fatigue and pain gave the same counsel, and these united powers carried the point.

The next day Bussy, on awaking, found Rémy at his bedside.

The young man could hardly believe in his good fortune and wanted to see Bussy again to be sure of it.

"Well!" said he, "how are you, Monsieur the Count?"

"Quite well, my dear Æsculapius; and you, are you satisfied?"

"So satisfied, my generous protector, that I would not change places with the king. But I now must see the wound."

"Look." And Bussy turned round for the young surgeon to take off the bandage. The wound looked well; it was nearly closed. Bussy, quite happy, had slept well, and sleep and happiness had aided the doctor.

"Well," said Bussy, "what do you say?"

"I dare not tell you that you are nearly well, for fear you should send me back to the Rue Beautreillis, five hundred paces from the famous house."

"Which we will find, will we not, Rémy?"

"I should think so!"

"Well, my friend, look on yourself as one of the house; and to-day, while you move your things, let me go to the fête of the installation of the new chief huntsman."

"Ah! you want to commit follies already."

"No, I promise to be very reasonable."

"But you must ride."

"It is necessary."

"Have you a horse with an easy pace?"

"I have four to choose from."

"Well, take for to-day the one you would choose for the lady of the portrait you know."

"Ah! I think I do know it, Rémy; you have found the way to my heart for ever. I feared you would prevent my going to this chase, or rather this imitation of one, for the ladies of the court, and many from the city, will be admitted to it. Now, Rémy, this lady may be there. She certainly is not a simple *bourgeoise;* those tapestries, that bed, so much luxury as well as good taste, show a woman of quality, or at least one who is rich. If I were to meet her there!"

"All is possible," replied Rémy, philosophically.

"Except to find the house," sighed Bussy.

"Or to enter it when we have found it," added Rémy.

"Oh! I have a method."

"What is it?"

"To get another sword-wound."

"Good! that gives me the hope that you will keep me."

"Be easy, I feel as if I had known you for twenty years; and, by my faith! I could not do without you."

The handsome face of the young doctor grew radiant with joy.

"Well, then," said he, "it is decided; you go to the chase to look for the lady, and I go to look for the house."

"It will be curious if we both succeed," said Bussy; and upon that they parted, more like two friends than like master and servant.

A great chase had been appointed in the Bois de Vincennes for M. de Monsoreau to enter on his functions of chief huntsman. Most people had believed, from the scene of the day before, that the king would not attend, and much astonishment was expressed when it was announced that he had set off with his brother and all the court. The rendezvous was at the Point St. Louis. It was thus they named a cross-road where the martyr king used to sit under an oak-tree and administer justice. Every one was therefore assembled here at nine o'clock, when the new officer, object of the general curiosity, unknown as he was to almost every one, appeared on a magnificent black horse. All eyes turned towards him.

He was a man about thirty-five, tall, marked by the small-pox, and with a disagreeable expression. Dressed in a jacket of green cloth braided with silver, with a silver shoulder-belt, on which the king's arms were embroidered in gold; on his head a cap with a long plume; in his left hand a spear, and in his right the *éstortuaire!* destined for the king,—M. de Monsoreau might look like a terrible warrior, but not certainly like a handsome cavalier.

"Fie! what an ugly figure you have brought us, Monseigneur!" said Bussy to the Duc d'Anjou; "are these the gentlemen that your favour goes to seek in the provinces? Certainly, one could hardly find such in Paris, which is nevertheless well stocked with ugliness. They say that your Highness made a great point of the king's appointing this man."

"M. de Monsoreau has served me well, and I recompense him," replied the duke.

"Well said, Monseigneur,—it is rare for princes to be grateful; but if that be all, I also have served you well, and should wear the embroidered jacket more gracefully, I trust, than M. de Monsoreau. He has a red beard, I see also, which is an additional beauty."

---

[1] The *éstortuaire* was a stick which the chief huntsman presented to the king, to put aside the branches of the trees when he was going at full gallop.

"I never knew that a man must be an Apollo or Antinous to fill an office at court."

"You never heard it, Monseigneur?" said Bussy, with great coolness; "that is astonishing!"

"I consult the heart and not the face,—the services rendered, and not the services promised."

"Your Highness will say I am very curious; but I search, and uselessly, I confess, to discover what service this Monsoreau can have rendered you."

"Ah, Bussy," said the duke, sharply, "you have said it; you are very curious, even too curious."

"Just like princes," cried Bussy, with his ordinary freedom; "they ask you everything, but if you ask a question in return, you are too curious."

"Well! go and ask M. de Monsoreau himself."

"Ah! you are right. He is but a simple gentleman, and if he do not reply, I shall know what to say."

"What?"

"Tell him he is impertinent." And turning from the prince, Bussy approached M. de Monsoreau, who was in the midst of the circle.

Bussy approached, gay and smiling, with his hat in his hand. "Pardon, Monsieur," he said, "but you seem all alone. Has the favour which you enjoy already made you enemies?"

"I do not know, Monsieur, but it is probable. But may I ask to what I owe the honour that you do me in invading my solitude?"

"By my faith! to the great admiration that M. le Duc d'Anjou has inspired in me for you."

"How so?"

"By recounting to me the exploit for which you were made chief huntsman."

M. de Monsoreau grew so frightfully pale that the marks in his face looked like black spots on his yellow skin; at the same time he looked at Bussy in a manner that portended a violent storm.

Bussy saw that he had started wrong, but he was not a man to draw back; on the contrary, he was one of those who generally repair an indiscretion by an impertinence.

"You say, Monsieur," said Monsoreau, "that the duke recounted to you my last exploit?"

"Yes, Monsieur, at full length,—which, I confess, has given me a strong desire to hear the story from your own lips."

M. de Monsoreau clasped his dagger tighter in his hand, as though he longed to attack Bussy. "Upon my word, Monsieur," said he, "I was quite disposed to acknowledge your courtesy by acceding to your request; but unfortunately here is the king arriving, so we must leave it for another time."

Bussy, looking around, met the eyes of the Duc d'Anjou; the prince smiled in his most malicious manner.

"Master and servant," thought Bussy, "both make an ugly grimace when they laugh; what, then, must it be when they weep?"

The king loved handsome faces, and was therefore little pleased with that of M. de Monsoreau. However, he accepted with a good grace the *éstortuaire* which he presented to him, kneeling, according to custom. As soon as the king was armed, the chase began.

Bussy watched narrowly every one that passed, looking for the original of the portrait, but in vain; there were pretty, even beautiful and charming women, but the charming creature for whom he sought was not there. He was reduced to conversation, and the company of his ordinary friends. Antragues, always laughing and talking, was a great amusement to him in his ennui.

"We have a frightful chief huntsman," said he to Bussy; "what do you think of him?"

"I find him horrible; what a family it must be if his children are like him! Do you know his wife?"

"He is not married."

"How do you know?"

"From Madame de Veudron, who finds him very handsome, and would willingly make him her fourth husband. See how she keeps near him."

"Of what region is he lord?"

"He has numerous estates."

"Situated?"

"In the direction of Anjou."

"He is rich, then?"

"They say so; but he is nothing more. He belongs, it seems, to the inferior nobility."

"And who is mistress to this rural magnate?"

"He has no mistress. The worthy man undertakes to be unique among his fellows. But see, there is M. le Duc d'Anjou calling to you."

"Ah, faith! he must wait. I am curious about this man.

c

I find him singular. I hardly know why, but I have a presentiment that I shall have a bone to pick with him. And then that name,—Monsoreau!"

"Oh! it comes from Mons Soricis; Livarot knows all about that. Here, Livarot! this Monsoreau—"

"Well?"

"Tell us what you know about him—"

"Willingly."

"Is it long?"

"No, it is short. In three words I will tell you what I know of him, and what I think of him,—I fear him."

"Good; that is what you think. Now tell us what you know."

"Listen. I was going home one night—"

"It begins in a terrible manner."

"Pray let me finish. It was about six months ago; I was returning from my uncle D'Entragues's, through the wood of Méridor, when all at once I heard a frightful cry, and I saw pass, with an empty saddle, a white horse, rushing through the wood. I rode on, and at the end of a long avenue darkened by the approaching shades of night, I saw a man on a black horse; he seemed to fly. Then I heard again the same cry; and I distinguished before him on the saddle a woman, on whose mouth he had his hand. I had a gun in my hand; you know I aim well, and I should have killed him, but my gun missed fire."

"Well?"

"I asked a wood-cutter who this gentleman on the black horse was, and he said, 'M. de Monsoreau.'"

"Well," said Antragues, "it is not so uncommon to carry away a woman, is it, Bussy?"

"No; but at least one might let her cry out."

"And who was the woman?"

"No one could tell me that."

"Come," said Bussy, "decidedly he is a remarkable man; he interests me."

"So remarkable," said Livarot, "that he has a terribly bad reputation."

"Do you know anything else about him?"

"No; but he is much feared by his tenantry. However, he is a good hunter, and will fill his post better than Saint-Luc would have done, for whom it was first destined."

"Do you know that the Duc d'Anjou is still calling you?"

" Good! let him call. Have you heard what is said about Saint-Luc? "

" No; is he still the king's prisoner? " asked Livarot, laughing.

" He must be," said Antragues, " since he is not here."

" Not at all; he set off at one o'clock this morning to visit his country-house with his wife."

" Banished? "

" It looks like it."

" Impossible! "

" True as the gospel."

" According to Saint Luke? "

" No, according to Marshal de Brissac, who told me so this morning."

" Ah! that is interesting news. That will injure Monsoreau."

" I have it," said Bussy.

" What have you? "

" I have found it."

" Found what? "

" The service that he rendered to the duke."

" Who,—Saint-Luc? "

" No; Monsoreau."

" Really."

" Yes, you shall see; come with me." And Bussy, followed by Livarot and Antragues, galloped after the Duc d'Anjou.

" Ah, Monseigneur," said he, " what a valuable man that M. de Monsoreau is! "

" Ah, really! then you spoke to him? " said the prince, smiling.

" Certainly."

" And asked him what he had done for me? "

" Certainly; that was my only purpose in addressing him."

" And he answered you? " asked the duke, more smiling than before.

" Immediately, and with the greatest politeness."

" Come, what did he say to you, my brave Hector? "

" He confessed that he was your purveyor."

" Of game? "

" No; of women."

" What do you mean, Bussy? " cried the duke, angrily.

" I mean, Monseigneur, that he carries away women for you on his great black horse, and that as they are ignorant of the

honour reserved for them, he puts his hand on their mouths to
prevent their crying out."

The duke frowned, ground his teeth with anger, grew pale,
and galloped on so fast that Bussy and his companions were left
in the rear.

"Ah, ah! it seems that the joke is a good one," said Antragues.

"And so much the better that every one does not seem to
find it a joke," said Bussy.

A moment after, they heard the duke's voice calling Bussy.
He went, and found the duke laughing. "Oh!" said he, "it
appears that what I said was droll."

"I am not laughing at what you said."

"So much the worse; I should like the honour of having
made a prince laugh who hardly ever does so."

"I laugh, my poor Bussy, at your inventing a false story to
find out the true one."

"No, the devil take me, Monseigneur, I told you the truth!"

"Well, then, as we are alone, tell me your little history.
Where did it happen?"

"In the wood of Méridor."

The duke grew pale again, but did not speak.

"Decidedly," thought Bussy, "the duke is mixed up with
that story. Come, Monseigneur," said he, "as M. de Monsoreau
seems to have found the method of pleasing you so well, teach
it to me."

"*Pardieu!* yes, Bussy, I will tell you how. Listen: I met
by chance, at church, a charming woman; and as some features
of her face, which I saw only through a veil, recalled to me a
lady whom I had much loved, I followed her, and found out
where she lived. I have gained over her servant, and have a
key of the house."

"Well, Monseigneur, all seems to go well for you."

"But they say she is a great prude, although free, young,
and beautiful."

"Ah! you are romancing."

"Listen; you are brave, and love me?"

"I have my days."

"For being brave?"

"No, for loving you."

"Well, is this one of the days?"

"I will try and make it one if I can serve your Highness."

"Well, I want you to do for me what most people do only for
themselves."

" Make love to her, to find out if she be a prude? "

" No, find out if she has a lover.   I want you to lie in wait and discover the man who visits her."

" There is a man then? "

" I fear so."

" Lover, or husband? "

" That is what I want to know."

" And you want me to find out? "

" Yes, and if you consent to render me that service—"

" You will make me the next chief huntsman."

" Upon my word, Bussy, I should feel under the greater obligation to you since I have never done anything for you."

" Oh! you have discovered that at last."

" Well, do you consent? "

" To watch the lady? "

" Yes."

" Monseigneur, I confess I do not like the commission."

" You offered to do me a service, and you draw back already?"

" Because you want me to be a spy."

" No, I ask you to be my friend.   Besides, don't imagine that I give you a sinecure; you may have to use your sword."

" Monseigneur, this is a sort of thing that every man must do for himself, even if he be a prince."

" Then you refuse? "

" Faith! yes, Monseigneur."

The duke frowned.   " Well, I will go myself," said he; " and if I am killed or wounded, I shall say that I begged my friend Bussy to undertake the task, and that for the first time in his life he was prudent."

" Monseigneur, you said to me the other night, ' Bussy, I hate all those favourites of the king who are always laughing at and insulting us; go to this wedding of Saint-Luc's, pick a quarrel, and try to get rid of them.'   I went; they were five, and I was alone.   I defied them all; they lay in wait for me, attacked me all together, and killed my horse, yet I wounded three of them.   To-day you ask me to wrong a woman.   Pardon, Monseigneur, but that is past the service which a prince should exact from a gallant man, and I refuse."

" So be it; I will do my work myself, or with Aurilly, as I have done already."

" Oh! " said Bussy, with a sudden thought.

" What? "

" Were you engaged in this enterprise the night when you saw the ambush laid for me? "

" Yes."

" Then your beautiful unknown lives near the Bastille? "

" Opposite the Rue St. Catherine. It is a dangerous place, as you know."

" Has your Highness been there since? "

" Yesterday."

" And you saw? "

" A man spying all about, doubtless to see if any one was watching him. He probably saw me, for he stopped still before that door."

" Was he alone? "

" Yes, at first. Afterwards he was joined by another, with a lantern in his hand."

" Ah! "

" Then they began to talk together, and at last, tired of waiting, I went away. And before I venture into the house, where I might be killed—"

" You would like one of your friends to be killed there? "

" Or rather that my friend, not being prince, not having the enemies that I have, and besides, being accustomed to adventures of that kind, should ascertain the nature of the risk I may run, and report to me."

" In your place, Monseigneur, I would give up this woman."

" No, she is too beautiful."

" You said that you hardly saw her."

" I saw her enough to distinguish splendid blond hair, magnificent eyes, such a complexion as I never saw before, and a wonderful shape! "

" Ah, ah! "

" You understand that one does not easily renounce such a woman."

" No, I feel for you."

" You jest."

" No, on my word; and to prove it, if you will give me my instructions, and tell me the house, I will watch this evening."

" You retract your decision, then? "

" There is no one but the pope infallible; now tell me what I am to do."

" You will have to hide a little way off, and if a man enter, follow him to find out who he is."

" But if in entering he close the door behind him? "

" I told you I had a key."

" Ah! true; then there is only one more thing to fear, that I should follow the wrong man to the wrong door."

" You cannot mistake; this door is the door of a passage-way, and at the end of the passage-way there is a staircase; mount twelve steps, and you will be in a corridor."

" How do you know all this, if you have never been in? "

" Did I not tell you I had gained over the servant? She told me all."

" *Tudieu!* how convenient it is to be a prince! I should have had to find out all for myself, which would have taken me an enormous time, and I might have failed after all."

" Then you consent? "

" Can I refuse your Highness? But will you come with me to show me the house? "

" Useless; as we return from the chase we will make a détour, and pass through the Porte St. Antoine, and I will point it out to you."

" Very well, and what am I to do to the man if he comes? "

" Only follow him till you learn who he is. I leave to you your mode of action."

" Then your Highness authorises me to act as for myself? "

" Precisely."

" I will do so, Monseigneur."

" Not a word to any one."

" No, on my honour."

" And you will go alone? "

" Alone, I swear to you."

" Well, then, it is settled; I show you the door on our way home. Then you come with me; I give you the key, and this evening—"

" I act in your stead; it is all understood."

Bussy and the prince then rejoined the rest. The king was charmed with the manner in which M. de Monsoreau had conducted the chase, and the latter was congratulated by the king and by the Duc d'Anjou.

" Monseigneur," then said M. de Monsoreau to the duke, " I am very happy to receive these compliments, since it is to you that I owe my place."

" But you know that you must go to-night to Fontainebleau, where the king will hunt to-morrow and the day after."

" I know, Monseigneur; I am prepared to start to-night."

" Ah, M. de Monsoreau, there is no more rest for you," said

Bussy; "you wished to be chief huntsman, and you are so, and now you will have at least fifty nights' rest less than other men. Luckily, you are not married."

At this joke Monsoreau's face was covered once more with that hideous paleness which gave to him so sinister an aspect.

CHAPTER XII

HOW BUSSY FOUND BOTH THE PORTRAIT AND THE ORIGINAL

THE chase terminated about four o'clock in the evening, and at five all the court returned to Paris. As they passed by the Bastille, the duke said to Bussy, "Look to the right, at that little wooden house with a statue of the Virgin before it; count four houses from that. It is the fifth you have to go to, just fronting the Rue St. Catherine."

"I see it; and look! at the sound of the trumpets announcing the king all the windows are filled with gazers."

"Except of the house I show you, where the curtains remain closed."

"But there is a corner lifted," said Bussy, with a beating heart.

"Yes, but we can see nothing. The lady is well-guarded. However, that is the house. At the hotel I will give you the key."

When Bussy returned, he said to Rémy, "Have you discovered the house?"

"No, Monseigneur."

"Well, I believe I have been more lucky."

"How so, Monsieur? Have you been seeking?"

"No, I only passed through the street."

"And you recognised the house?"

"Providence, my dear friend, has mysterious ways."

"Then you are sure?"

"Not sure, but I hope."

"And when shall I know if you are right?"

"To-morrow morning."

"Meanwhile, do you want me?"

"No, my dear Rémy."

"Shall I not follow you?"

"Impossible."

"At any rate, be prudent, Monseigneur."

" Ah! the recommendation is useless; my prudence is well known."

Bussy dined like a man who does not know when he will sup, then, at eight o'clock, choosing the best of his swords and attaching in spite of the king's orders a pair of pistols to his belt, went in his litter to the corner of the Rue St. Paul. He easily recognised the house again, and then, wrapped in his cloak, hid at the corner of the street, determined to wait for two hours, and at the end of that time, if no one came, to act for himself. He had scarcely been there ten minutes when he saw two cavaliers coming. One of them dismounted, and gave his horse to the other, who was probably a lackey; and after seeing him return by the way they had come, after seeing him and the two horses disappear in the darkness, he advanced to the house which Bussy was watching, and after glancing round to see if he were observed, opened the door and went in. Bussy waited two or three minutes, and then followed him. He advanced slowly and softly, found the staircase, and went up. In the corridor he stopped, for two reasons: the first was that he perceived his legs becoming weak under the weight of his emotion; and the second was that he heard a voice say, " Gertrude, tell your mistress that it is I, and that I must come in."

This was said in an imperious tone, and a moment after Bussy heard a woman's voice say, " Pass into the drawing-room, Monsieur, and Madame will come to you."

Then he heard the sound of a door shutting. He made a few steps silently, and extending his hand, felt a door. He went in, found a second, in which was a key; he turned it, and entered the room trembling from head to foot. The room in which he found himself was dark, except for the light shining from another. By this he could see two windows, hung with tapestry, which sent a thrill of joy through the young man's heart. On the ceiling he could faintly see the mythological figures; he extended his hand and felt the sculptured bed. There was no more doubt; he was in the room where he had awakened on the night of his wound.

Bussy hid behind the bed-curtains to listen. He heard in the adjoining room the impatient step of the unknown; from time to time he stopped, murmuring between his teeth, " Will she come? " Presently a door opened, and the rustling of a silk dress struck on Bussy's ear. Then he heard a woman's voice, expressive at once of fear and disdain, saying, " Here I am, Monsieur, what do you want now? "

" Oh, oh! " thought Bussy, " If that man is the lover I congratulate the husband."

" Madame," replied the man, " I have the honour of telling you that, forced to set off to-morrow morning for Fontainebleau, I come to pass the night with you."

" Do you bring me news of my father? "

" Madame, listen to me—"

" Monsieur, you know what we agreed yesterday, when I consented to become your wife,—that, before all things, either my father should come to Paris or I should go to him."

" Madame, as soon as I return from Fontainebleau we will set out. I give you my word of honour; but meanwhile—"

" Oh, Monsieur! do not close that door, it is useless; I will not pass a single night under the same roof with you until I am reassured in regard to my father." And the woman who spoke so decidedly blew into a small silver whistle, which made a sharp and prolonged sound. It was the method employed for calling servants.

Immediately the door opened, and a young, vigorous-looking girl entered. As she went in she left the door open, which threw a strong light into the room where Bussy was hid, and between the two windows he saw the portrait. " Gertrude," said the lady, " you will not go to bed, and you will remain within hearing of my voice."

The young woman retired without making any reply.

Bussy now crept noiselessly along to where he could peep into the room. However carefully he moved, the floor creaked. At the noise the lady turned; she was the original of the portrait, the fairy of his dream. The man, seeing her turn, turned also; it was M. de Monsoreau.

" Ah! " thought Bussy, " the white horse, the woman carried away,—there is some terrible history."

Bussy, as we have said, could see them both. She was standing up, pale and disdainful; he, sitting, not pale, but livid, moved his foot impatiently.

" Madame," said he, at last, " do not hope to continue with me this character of a persecuted woman. You are at Paris, in my house; and still more, you are Comtesse de Monsoreau,— that is to say, my wife."

" If I am your wife, why refuse to conduct me to my father? Why continue to hide me from the eyes of the world? "

" You have forgotten the Duc d'Anjou, Madame."

" You assured me that once your wife I should have no more to fear from him."

" That is to say—"

" You promised me that."

" But still, Madame, I must take precautions."

" Well, Monsieur, when you have taken them, return to me."

" Diane," said the count, who was growing visibly angry,— " Diane, do not make a jest of this sacred tie."

" Act so, Monsieur, that I can have confidence in the husband, and I will respect the marriage."

" Oh, this is too much! " cried the count. " I am in my own house, you are my wife; and even if hell should come to help you, this very night you shall be mine."

Bussy put his hand on his sword-hilt, and made a step forward, but Diane did not give him time to appear.

" Stay," said she, drawing a poniard from her belt, " here is my answer." And rushing into the room where Bussy was, she shut the door and locked it, while Monsoreau exhausted himself in menaces and in blows on the door.

" If you break this door you will find me dead on the threshold."

" And be easy, Madame," said Bussy, enclosing Diane in his arms, " you will have an avenger."

Diane was about to utter a cry, but she comprehended that the only danger which threatened her came from her husband. She trembled, but was silent.

M. de Monsoreau struck violently with his foot, then convinced that Diane would do as she had threatened, he went out of the drawing-room, shutting the door violently behind him. Then they heard him going down the stairs.

" But you, Monsieur," said Diane, releasing herself from Bussy's arms, and taking a step backwards, " who are you, and how came you here? "

" Madame," said Bussy, opening the door and kneeling before her, " I am the man whose life you preserved. You cannot think that I come to your house with any bad designs."

As the light streamed in, Diane recognised him at once. " Ah! you here, Monsieur? " she cried, clasping her hands. " You were here; you heard all? "

" Alas! yes, Madame."

" But who are you? Your name, Monsieur? "

" Madame, I am Louis de Clermont, Comte de Bussy."

" Bussy! you are the brave Bussy! " cried Diane, naïvely,

without suspecting with what joy that exclamation filled the young man's heart. "Ah, Gertrude," she continued, turning to her servant, who, hearing her mistress talking to some one, had entered in terror,—" Gertrude, I have no more to fear, for from this time I place myself under the safeguard of the most noble and loyal gentleman in France." Then, holding out her hand to Bussy, "Rise, Monsieur," said she; "I know who you are, now you must know who I am."

CHAPTER XIII

WHO DIANE WAS

BUSSY rose, bewildered at his own happiness, and entered with Diane into the room which M. de Monsoreau had just left. He looked at Diane with astonishment and admiration; he had not dared to hope that the woman whom he had sought for would equal the woman of his dream, and now the reality surpassed all that he had taken for a caprice of his imagination. Diane was about nineteen years old; that is to say, in that period of youth and beauty which gives the purest colouring to the flower, the finest complexion to the fruit. There was no mistaking the looks of Bussy; Diane saw that she was admired, and she had no force to interrupt Bussy's ecstasy. At length she comprehended the necessity of breaking that silence which said too much.

"Monsieur," said she, "you have told me who you are, but not how you came here."

"Madame, the cause of my presence here will come naturally out of the recital you have been good enough to promise me; I am sure of it, from some words of your conversation with M. de Monsoreau."

"I will tell you all, Monsieur; your name has been sufficient to inspire me with full confidence, for I have often heard of it as that of a man of honour, loyalty, and courage."

Bussy bowed, and Diane went on.

"I am the daughter of the Baron de Méridor; that is to say, the only heiress of one of the noblest and oldest names in Anjou."

"There was," said Bussy, "a Baron de Méridor, who, although he could have saved himself, came voluntarily and gave up his sword at the battle of Pavia when he heard that the king was a prisoner, and begged to accompany François to Madrid, partook his captivity, and left him only to come to France and negotiate his ransom."

" It was my father, Monsieur; and if ever you enter the great hall of the Château de Méridor you will see, given in memory of this devotion, the portrait of François I., painted by Leonardo da Vinci."

" Ah! " said Bussy, " in those times kings knew how to recompense their followers."

" On his return from Spain my father married. His first two children, sons, died. This was a great grief to the Baron de Méridor, who lost all hope of seeing his life continued in an heir. When the king died, my father abandoned the court, and shut himself up with his wife in the Château de Méridor. It was there that I was born, ten years after the death of my brothers.

" Then all the love of the baron was concentrated on the child of his old age; his love for me was more than tenderness,—it was idolatry. Three years after my birth I lost my mother. That, certainly, was a new sorrow for the baron; but I, too, young to know what I had lost, continued to smile, and my smiles helped to console my father. As I was all to him, so was he also all to me. I attained my sixteenth year without dreaming of any other world than that of my sheep, my peacocks, my swans, and my doves, without imagining that this life would change, or wishing that it should.

" The Château de Méridor was surrounded by vast forests, belonging to the Duc d'Anjou; they were filled with deer and stags, whom no one thought of tormenting, and who had grown quite familiar with me. Some of them would even come when I called them; and one, a doe,—my favourite Daphné, my poor Daphné,—would come and eat out of my hand.

" One spring I had missed her for a month; I thought her lost, and was ready to weep for her as for a friend, when she reappeared with two little fawns. At first they were afraid of me, but seeing their mother caress me, they soon learned to do the same.

" About this time we heard that the Duc d'Anjou had sent a governor into the province, and that he was called the Comte de Monsoreau. Why did that name, when I heard it pronounced, strike me to the heart? I can account for that painful sensation only as a presentiment. A week passed, during which every one spoke of the new governor. One morning the woods resounded with the sound of the horn, and the barking of dogs. I ran to the park, and arrived just in time to see Daphné, followed by her two fawns, pass like lightning, pursued by a pack of hounds. An instant after, mounted on a black horse, M. de Monsoreau flew past me.

" I cried out and implored pity for my poor *protégée*, but he did not hear me. Then, without thinking of the anxiety which my absence would cause my father should he become aware of it, I ran in the direction of the chase; I hoped to meet either the count or some of his suite, and determined to implore them to stop that pursuit, which tore my heart. I ran for some time without knowing whither, and lost sight of both dogs and hunters.

" Soon I could not even hear them, so I sat down at the foot of a tree and began to cry. I had been there about a quarter of an hour, when I heard the chase again. The noise came nearer and nearer, and, darting forward, I saw my poor Daphné again. She had but one fawn with her now; the other had given way through fatigue, and without doubt had been torn to pieces by the dogs. She herself was growing visibly tired; and the distance between her and the hounds was less than when I saw her first.

" As before, I exerted myself in vain to make myself heard. M. de Monsoreau saw nothing but the animal he was chasing; he passed more quickly than ever, with his horn to his mouth, which he was sounding loudly. Behind him, two or three hunters animated the dogs with horn and voice. All passed me like a tempest, and disappeared in the forest. I was in despair; but I ran on once more, and followed a path which I knew led to the Château de Beaugé, belonging to the Duc d'Anjou, and which was about six miles from the Château de Méridor. It was not till I arrived there that I remembered that I was alone, and far from home.

" I confess that a vague terror seized me, and that then only I thought of the imprudence and folly of my conduct. I followed the border of the lake, intending to ask the gardener —who, when I had come there with my father, had often given me bouquets—to take me home, when all at once I heard the sound of the chase again. I remained motionless, listening, and I forgot all else. Nearly at the same moment the doe reappeared, coming out of the wood on the other side of the lake, but pursued so closely that she must be taken immediately. She was alone; her second fawn had fallen. But the sight of the water seemed to reanimate her, and she plunged in as if she would have come to me. At first she swam rapidly, and I looked at her with tears in my eyes, and almost as breathless as herself; insensibly her strength failed her, while the dogs seemed to grow more and more earnest in their pursuit. Soon some of them reached her, and stopped by their bites, she ceased to advance; at this moment, M. de Monsoreau appeared at the border of the lake and jumped off his horse. Then I collected all my strength to cry for pity, with clasped hands. It seemed to me that he saw me, and I cried again. He heard me, for he looked at me; then he ran towards a boat, entered it, and advanced rapidly towards the animal, who was fighting among the dogs. I did not doubt that, moved by my voice, he was hastening to bring her succour, when all at once I saw him draw his hunting-knife and plunge it into the neck of the poor animal. The blood flowed out, reddening the water of the lake, while the poor doe uttered a doleful cry, beat the water with her feet, reared up, and then fell back dead.

" I uttered a cry almost as doleful as hers, and fell fainting on the bank. When I came to myself again, I was in bed, in a room of the Château de Beaugé, and my father, who had been sent for, was weeping near me. As it was nothing but over-excitement, the next morning I was able to return home; but for three or four days I kept my room. Then my father told me that M. de Monsoreau, who had seen me when I was carried to the château, had come to ask after me; he had been much grieved when he heard that he had been the involuntary cause of my accident, and begged to present his excuses to me, saying that he could not be happy until he had his pardon from my own lips.

" It would have been ridiculous to refuse to see him; so in spite of my repugnance I granted his request. He came the next day; I felt that my behaviour must have seemed strange, and I excused it on the ground of my affection for Daphné. The count swore twenty times that had he known I had any interest in his victim, he would have spared her with pleasure; but his protestations did not convince me, nor remove the unfavourable impression I had formed of him. When he took leave, he asked my father's permission to come again. He had been born in Spain and educated at Madrid, and it was a pleasure to my father to talk over the place where he had been so long a prisoner. Besides, the count was of good family, deputy-governor of the province, and a favourite, it was said, of the Duc d'Anjou; my father had no motive for refusing his request, and it was granted. Alas! from this moment ceased, if not my happiness, at least my tranquillity. I soon perceived the impression I had made on the count; he began to come every day, and was full of attentions to my father, who showed the pleasure he took in his conversation, which was certainly that of a clever man.

" One morning my father entered my room with an air graver than usual, but evidently pleased. ' My child,' said he, ' you always have said that you would be happy never to leave me.' ' Oh, my father,' cried I, ' you know that it is my dearest wish.' ' Well, my Diane,' continued he, bending over me to kiss me, ' it depends now on yourself to have your wish realised.' I guessed what he was about to say, and grew so pale that he stopped before touching my forehead with his lips. ' Diane, my child, what is the matter? ' cried he. ' M. de Monsoreau, is it not? ' stammered I. ' Well? ' said he, astonished. ' Oh! never, my father, if you have any pity for your daughter, never—' ' Diane, my love,' said he, ' it is not pity I have for you, but idolatry; you know it. Take a week to reflect, and if then—' ' Oh, no, no!' cried I, ' it is useless; not a day, not a minute! No, no, no!' and I burst into tears. My father adored me, and he took me in his arms and gave me his word that he would speak to me no more of this marriage.

" Indeed, a month passed, during which I neither heard of nor saw M. de Monsoreau. One morning we received an invitation to a grand fête which M. de Monsoreau was to give to the Duc d'Anjou, who was about to visit the province whose name he bore. To this was added a personal invitation from the prince, who wrote that he remembered seeing my father at court, and would be pleased to meet him again. My first impulse was to beg my father to refuse, but he feared to offend the prince, so we went. M. de Monsoreau received us as though nothing had passed, and behaved to me exactly as he did to the other ladies.

" Not so the duke. As soon as he saw me he fixed his eyes on me and scarcely ever removed them. I felt ill at ease under these looks, and without telling my father why I wished to leave the ball, I urged him so strongly that we left early. Three days after, M. de Monsoreau came to Méridor; I saw him from the window, and shut myself up in my own room. When he was gone, my father said nothing to me, but I thought he looked gloomy.

" Four days passed thus, when, as I was returning from a

walk, the servants told me that M. de Monsoreau was with my
father, who had asked for me several times, and had desired
to be immediately informed of my return. Indeed, no sooner
had I entered my room than my father came to me.

" ' My child,' said he, ' a motive which I cannot explain to
you forces me to separate myself from you for some days.
Do not question me, but be sure that it is an urgent one, since
it determines me to be a week, a fortnight, perhaps a month,
without seeing you.' I trembled, though I could not conjecture
to what danger I was exposed; but I fancied that those two
visits of M. de Monsoreau boded me no good. ' Where am I to
go, my father? ' I asked. ' To the Château de Lude, to my
sister, where you will be hidden from all eyes. You will go by
night.' ' And do you not accompany me? ' ' No, I must stay
here, to ward off suspicion; even the servants must not know
where you are going.' ' But then who will take me there? '
' Two men whom I can trust.' ' Oh, *mon Dieu*, father! ' I cried.
The baron embraced me. ' It is necessary, my child,' said he.

" I knew my father's love for me so well that I said no more,
only I asked that Gertrude, my nurse, should accompany me.
My father left me, telling me to get ready.

" At eight o'clock (it was dark and cold, for it was the middle
of winter) my father came for me. We descended quietly,
crossed the garden, when he opened a little door leading to the
forest, and there we found a litter waiting, and two men; my
father spoke to them a long time, giving them directions about
me, it seemed. Then I got in, and Gertrude with me.

" My father embraced me once more, and we set off. I was
ignorant what danger menaced me, and forced me to leave the
Château de Méridor. I did not dare to question my conductors,
whom I did not know. We went along quietly, and the motion
of the litter at last sent me to sleep, when I was awakened by
Gertrude, who, seizing my arm, cried out, ' Oh, Mademoiselle,
what is the matter? '

" I passed my head through the curtains. We were surrounded by six masked cavaliers, and our men, who had tried
to defend me, were disarmed. He who appeared the chief of
the masked men approached me, and said, ' Reassure yourself,
Mademoiselle, no harm will be done to you, but you must follow
us.' ' Where? ' I asked. ' To a place,' he replied, ' where, far
from having anything to complain of, you will be treated like
a queen.'

" That promise seemed to me more frightful than a threat

would have been. ' Oh, my father! my father!' I cried.
' Listen, Mademoiselle,' said Gertrude; ' I know the country,
and I am strong; we may be able to escape.' That assurance
was far from quieting my fear; and yet it is so comforting to
find one's self supported that I recovered a little strength, and
said, ' You must do as you will with us, gentlemen; we are but
two poor women, and cannot defend ourselves.' One of the
men then took the place of our conductor, and changed the
direction of our litter."

Here Diane stopped a moment, as if overcome with emotion.

" Oh, continue, Madame, continue! " cried Bussy.

It was impossible for Diane not to see the interest she inspired
in the young man; it was shown in his voice, his gestures, his
looks. She smiled sadly, and continued:

" We continued our journey for about three hours, then the
litter stopped. I heard a door open; a few words were exchanged. We went on, and I fancied we were crossing a draw-
bridge. I was not wrong,—for on looking out of the litter, I
saw that we were in the courtyard of a château. What château
was it? We did not know. Often, during the route, we had
tried to discover where we were, but we seemed to be in an
endless forest.

" The door of our litter was opened, and the same man who
had spoken to us before asked us to alight. I obeyed in silence.
Two men from the château had come to meet us with torches;
they conducted us into a bedroom richly decorated, where a
collation waited for us on a table sumptuously laid out.

" ' You are at home here, Madame,' said the same man, ' and
the room for your servant is adjoining. When you wish for
anything, you have but to strike with the knocker on this door,
and some one who will be constantly in the antechamber will
wait on you.' This apparent attention showed that we were
guarded. Then the man bowed and went out, and we heard
him lock the door behind him.

" Gertrude and I were alone. She was about to speak, but
with my finger I made a sign to her to be silent, for perhaps
some one was listening. The door of the room which had been
shown us as Gertrude's was open, and we went in to examine
it. It was evidently the dressing-room to mine, and was also
locked. Both rooms apparently opened into the same antechamber. We were prisoners. Gertrude approached me and
said in a low tone, ' Did Mademoiselle remark that we mounted
only five steps after leaving the court?' ' Yes,' said I. ' There-

fore we are on the ground-floor?' 'Doubtless.' 'So that—' said she, pointing to the windows. 'Yes, if they are not barred.' 'And if Mademoiselle had courage.' 'Oh, yes! I have.'

"Gertrude then took a light, and approached the window. It opened easily, and was not barred; but we soon discovered the cause of this seeming negligence on the part of our captors. A lake lay below us, and we were guarded by ten feet of water better than we should have been by bars to the window; but in looking out I discovered where we were. We were in the Château de Beaugé, where they had brought me on the day of my poor Daphné's death. This château belonged to the Duc d'Anjou, and a sudden light was thrown upon our capture. I looked at the lake with a gloomy satisfaction; it was a last resource against violence, a supreme refuge against dishonour. We shut the window again, and I threw myself, dressed, on my bed, while Gertrude slept in a chair by my side. Twenty times during the night I woke, a prey to sudden terror; but nothing justified it, excepting the place where I found myself, for all seemed asleep in the château, and no noise but the cry of the birds interrupted the silence of the night. Day appeared, but only to confirm my conviction that flight was impossible without external aid; and how could that reach us? About nine they came to take away the supper and bring breakfast. Gertrude questioned the servants, but they did not reply.

"All was explained to me by our being at the Château de Beaugé, and by the pretended respect which surrounded us. The Duc d'Anjou had seen me at the fête given by M. de Monsoreau, and had fallen in love with me. My father had been warned and had designed to deliver me from the pursuit of which, doubtless, I was to be the object. He had sent me away from Méridor; but either by the treachery of a faithless servant or by an unhappy chance, his precaution had become fruitless, and I had fallen into the hands of the man against whom he had in vain sought to protect me. I dwelt upon that explanation,—the only one that seemed probable, and the one that, in fact, was true.

"Being entreated by Gertrude, I drank a glass of milk and ate a piece of bread.

"Our morning was consumed in forming fruitless plans for escape; and yet we could see a boat fastened to the shore, with its oars in it, only a hundred feet from us. Could we only have reached that, we might have been safe.

"They brought us our dinner in the same way, put it down, and left us. In breaking my bread I found in it a little note. I opened it eagerly, and read,—

"A friend watches over you. To-morrow you shall have news of him and of your father.

"You can imagine my joy. The rest of the day passed in waiting and hoping. The second night passed as quietly as the first; then came the hour of breakfast, waited for impatiently, for I hoped to find another note. I was not wrong. The note was as follows:—

"The person who had you carried off will arrive at the Château de Beaugé at ten o'clock this evening; but at nine the friend who watches over you will be under your windows with a letter from your father, which will command the confidence you perhaps might not otherwise give. Burn this letter.

"I read and re-read this letter, then burned it as I was desired. The writing was unknown to me, and I did not know from whom it could have come. We lost ourselves in conjectures, and a hundred times during the morning we went to the window to see if we could see any one on the shores of the lake, but all was solitary. An hour after dinner some one knocked at our door and then entered. It was the man who had spoken to us before. I recognised his voice; he presented a letter to me.

"'Whom do you come from, Monsieur?' I asked. 'Will Mademoiselle take the trouble to read, and she will see.' 'But I will not read this letter without knowing from whom it comes.' 'Mademoiselle can do as she pleases; my business is only to leave the letter,' and putting it down, he went away. 'What shall I do?' I asked Gertrude. 'If I might venture to offer advice to Mademoiselle, it would be to read that letter. Perhaps it contains warning of some danger, which, being thus warned, we may escape.' I opened and read."

Diane, at this moment, rose, opened a desk, and from a portfolio drew out a letter. Bussy glanced at the address and read, "To the beautiful Diane de Méridor." Then looking at Diane, he said, "It is the Duc d'Anjou's writing."

"Ah!" replied she, with a sigh, "then he did not deceive me." Then, as Bussy hesitated to open the letter, "Read," said she; "chance has initiated you into the most secret history of my life, and I wish to keep nothing from you."

Bussy obeyed and read:—

An unhappy prince, whom your divine beauty has struck to the heart, will come at ten o'clock to-night to apologise for his conduct towards you,— conduct which he himself feels has no other excuse than the invincible love he entertains for you.   FRANÇOIS.

" Then this letter was really from the duke? " asked Diane.

" Alas, yes! it is his writing and his seal."

Diane sighed. " Can he be less guilty than I thought? " said she.

" Who, the prince? "

" No, M. de Monsoreau."

" Continue, Madame, and we will judge the prince and the count."

" This letter, which I had then no idea of not believing genuine, rendered still more precious to me the intervention of the unknown friend who offered me aid in the name of my father; I had no hope but in him. Night arrived soon, for it was in the month of January, and we had still four or five hours to wait for the appointed time. It was a fine frosty night; the heavens were brilliant with stars, and the crescent moon lighted the country with its silver beams. We had no means of knowing the time, but we sat anxiously watching at Gertrude's window. At last we thought we saw figures moving among the trees, and then distinctly heard the neighing of a horse.

" ' It is our friends,' said Gertrude. ' Or the prince,' replied I. ' The prince would not hide himself.' This reflection reassured me. A man now advanced alone; it seemed to us that he left another group under the shade of the trees. He went straight to the boat, detached it from its fastening, and stepped into it, and the boat glided silently towards us. As it approached, my eyes made violent efforts to pierce the obscurity, and I thought I recognised first the tall figure, then the features of M. de Monsoreau. I now feared the help almost as much as the danger. I remained mute, and drew back from the window. Arrived at the wall, he secured his boat, and I saw his head at our window. I could not repress a cry.

" ' Ah, pardon,' said he, ' but I thought you expected me.' ' I expected some one, Monsieur, but I did not know it was you.' A bitter smile passed over his face. ' Who else,' said he, ' except her father, watches over the honour of Diane de Méridor? ' ' You told me, Monsieur, in your letter, that you came in my father's name.' ' Yes, Mademoiselle, and lest you should doubt it, here is a note from the baron,' and he gave

me a paper. I went from Gertrude's chamber into my own.
I knelt before the fire, and by the light of the flame I read:—

"MY DEAR DIANE,—M. de Monsoreau can alone extricate you from
your dangerous position, and this danger is great. Trust, then, to him
as to the best friend that Heaven can send to us. I will tell you later
what from the bottom of my heart I wish you to do to acquit the debt
we shall contract towards him.

"Your father, who begs you to believe him, and to have pity on him,
and on yourself, BARON DE MÉRIDOR.

"I knew nothing positive against M. de Monsoreau; my
dislike to him was rather from instinct than reason. I had to
reproach him only with the death of a doe,—a very light crime
for a hunter. I then went to him. 'Well?' said he. 'Monsieur, I have read my father's letter; it tells me you will take me
hence, but it does not tell me whither you will take me.' 'I
will conduct you to where the baron waits for you, Mademoiselle.'
'And where is that?' 'In the Château de Méridor.' 'Then I
shall see my father?' 'In two hours.' 'Ah, Monsieur, if you
speak truly—' I stopped. The count waited for the end of my
sentence. 'Count on my gratitude,' said I, in a trembling tone,
for I knew what he might expect from my gratitude. 'Then,
Mademoiselle,' said he, 'you are ready to follow me?' I looked
at Gertrude with anxiety. It was easy to see that the sinister
face of the count was not more reassuring to her than it was to
me. 'Reflect that each minute that passes is most precious,'
said he; 'I am nearly half an hour behind time now. It will
soon be ten o'clock, and then the prince will be here.' 'Alas!
yes.' 'Once he comes I can do nothing for you but risk without
hope that life which I now risk with the certainty of saving you.'
'Why did not my father come?' I asked. 'Your father is
watched. They know every step he takes.' 'But you—'
'Oh! I am different; I am the prince's friend and confidant.'
'Then if you are his friend—' 'Yes, I betray him for you. It
is true, as I told you just now, I am risking my life to save you.'
This seemed so true that although I still felt repugnance I could
not express it. 'I wait,' said the count. I looked at Gertrude,
who was as undecided as I was. 'See!' said M. de Monsoreau;
'if you still doubt, look there.' I looked, and saw on the
opposite shore a body of cavaliers advancing. 'It is the duke
and his suite,' said he. 'Mademoiselle, Mademoiselle,' said
Gertrude, 'there is no time to lose!' 'Too much time has been
lost already,' said the count. 'In Heaven's name, decide!' I
fell upon a chair, and my strength failed me. 'Oh, *mon Dieu!*
mon Dieu! what shall I do?' I murmured. 'Listen,' said the

count; ' they are knocking. In five minutes it will be too late.'
I tried to rise, but my limbs failed me. ' Help, Gertrude!' I
feebly cried,—' help!' ' Mademoiselle,' said the poor girl, ' do
you hear the door opening? Do you hear the horses in the
court?' ' Yes! yes!' I said, exerting myself to rise; ' but I
have no strength.' ' Oh! is that it?' she said; and taking me
in her arms, she raised me as if I had been an infant, and placed
me in the arms of the count.

" On feeling that man's touch I shuddered so violently that I
nearly fell into the lake; but he held me fast and placed me in
the boat. Gertrude followed without aid. Then I noticed that
my veil had come off, and was floating on the water. I thought
they would track us by it, and I cried, ' My veil! catch my veil!'
The count looked at it and said, ' No, no, better leave it.' And
seizing the oars, he rowed with all his strength. We had just
reached the bank when we saw the windows of my room lighted
up. ' Did I deceive you? Was it time?' said M. de Monsoreau.
' Oh, yes, yes!' cried I, ' you are indeed my saviour.'

" The lights seemed to be moving about from one room to the
other. We heard voices, and a man entered from whom all the
others stood apart. That man approached the open window,
looked out, saw the floating veil, and uttered a cry. ' You see
I did well to leave the veil,' said the count, ' the prince believes
that to escape him you threw yourself into the lake; and while
he searches for you we will escape.' Then indeed I trembled at
the dark depths of that mind that could in advance reckon on
such an expedient."

CHAPTER XIV

THE TREATY

THERE was a moment's silence. Diane seemed almost overcome. Bussy was already vowing eternal vengeance against
her enemies. She went on:—

" Scarcely had we touched the shore when seven or eight men
ran to us. They were the count's people, and I thought I recognised among them the two men who had escorted me when I
left Méridor. A groom held two horses,—a black one for the
count and a white one for me. The count helped me to mount,
and then jumped on his own horse. Gertrude mounted behind
one of the men, and we set off at full gallop. The count held the

bridle of my horse. I said to him that I was a sufficiently good horsewoman to dispense with this, but he replied that the horse was inclined to run away. When we had gone for about ten minutes I heard Gertrude's voice calling to me, and turning, I saw that our troop was divided; four of the men were going off with Gertrude by a lateral path which led into the forest, while the Comte de Monsoreau and the other four continued with me along the same road. 'Gertrude!' I cried; 'Monsieur, why does she not come with me?' 'It is an indispensable precaution,' said the count; 'if we are pursued we must leave two tracks; and in two directions chance lookers-on must be able to say that they have seen a woman carried away by men. There is then a chance that M. d'Anjou may take a wrong road, and go after your servant instead of you.' Although specious, this reply did not satisfy me; but what could I do? Besides, the path which the count was following was the one which led to the Château de Méridor. In a quarter of an hour, at the rate at which we were going, we should have been at the château, when all at once as we came to a cross-road which I knew well, the count, instead of following the road to the château, turned to the left and took a road which led away from it. I cried out, and in spite of our rapid pace had already my hand on the pommel, in order to jump off, when the count, who, without doubt, watched all my movements, leaned towards me, seized me round the waist, drew me off my horse, and placed me on the saddle before him. This action was so rapid that I had only time to utter a cry. M. de Monsoreau put his hand on my mouth, and said, 'Mademoiselle, I swear to you on my honour that I act only by your father's orders, as I will prove to you at the first halt we make. If this proof appears to you insufficient you shall then be free.' 'But, Monsieur,' cried I, pushing away his hand, 'you told me you were taking me to my father!' 'Yes, I told you so because I saw that you hesitated to follow me, and a moment's more hesitation would have ruined us both, as you know. Now, do you wish to kill your father? Will you march straight to your dishonour? If so, I will take you to Méridor.' 'You spoke of a proof that you acted in the name of my father.' 'Here it is,' said the count, giving me a letter, 'keep it and read it at our first stopping-place. If, when you have read it, you wish to return to Méridor, you are free; but if you have any respect for your father's wishes, you will not.' 'Then, Monsieur,' I replied, 'let us reach quickly our stopping-place, for I wish to know if you speak the truth.' 'Remember, you follow me

freely.' ' Yes, as freely as a young girl can who sees herself
placed between her father's death and her own dishonour on the
one hand, and on the other the obligation to trust herself to the
word of a man whom she hardly knows. However, I follow you
freely, Monsieur, as you shall see if you will give me my horse
again.' The count called to one of his men to dismount and give
me his horse. ' The white mare cannot be far away,' said he to
the man. ' Seek her in the forest and call her; she will come
like a dog to her name or to a whistle. You can rejoin us at
La Châtre.' I shuddered in spite of myself. La Chatre was ten
leagues from Méridor, on the road to Paris. ' Monsieur,' said I,
' I accompany you, but at La Châtre we make our conditions.'
' Mademoiselle, at La Châtre you shall give me your orders.' At
daybreak we arrived at La Châtre, but instead of entering the
village we went by a cross-road to a lonely house. I stopped.
' Where are we going?' I asked. ' Mademoiselle,' said the
count, ' I appeal to yourself. Can we, in flying from a prince
next in power to the king, stop at a common hostelry in the
middle of a village, where the first one who sees us will denounce
us? One man may be bribed, but not an entire village.'
' Well,' said I, ' go on.' We resumed our way. We were
expected, for a man had ridden on before to announce our
arrival. A good fire burned in a decent room and a bed was
prepared. ' This is your room,' said the count; ' I will await
your orders.' He went out and left me alone. My first thought
was for my letter. Here it is, M. de Bussy; read."

Bussy took the letter and read:—

MY BELOVED DIANE,—As I do not doubt that, yielding to my prayer,
you have followed the Comte de Monsoreau, he must have told you that
you had the misfortune to please M. le Duc d'Anjou, and that it was this
prince who had you forcibly carried away and taken to the Château de
Beaugé; judge by this violence of what the prince is capable, and with
what you were menaced. Your dishonour I could not survive; but there
is a means of escape,—that of marrying our noble friend. Were you
Comtesse de Monsoreau, the count would protect you as his wife. My
desire is, then, my dear child, that this marriage should take place as soon
as possible; and if you consent, I give you my paternal benediction, and
pray God to bestow upon you every treasure of happiness.

Your father, who does not order, but entreats,

BARON DE MÉRIDOR.

" Alas!" said Bussy, " if this letter be from your father, it is
but too positive."

" I do not doubt its being from him, and yet I read it three
times before deciding. At last I called the count. He entered
at once; I had the letter in my hand. ' Well, have you read it?'

said he. 'Yes,' I replied. 'Do you still doubt my devotion and respect?' 'This letter imposes belief on me, Monsieur; but in case I yield to my father's wishes, what do you propose to do?' 'To take you to Paris, Mademoiselle; that is the easiest place to hide you.' 'And my father?' 'As soon as there is no longer danger of compromising you, you know he will come to you, wherever you are.' 'Well, Monsieur, I am ready to accept your protection on the conditions you impose.' 'I impose nothing, Mademoiselle,' answered he; 'I simply offer you a method of safety.' 'Well, I will accept this safety on three conditions.' 'Speak, Mademoiselle.' 'The first is, that Gertrude shall return to me.' 'She is here.' 'The second is that we travel separately to Paris.' 'I was about to propose it to you.' 'And the third is that our marriage, unless I myself acknowledge some urgent necessity for it, shall take place only in presence of my father.' 'It is my earnest desire; I count on his benediction to draw upon us that of Heaven.'

"I was in despair. I had hoped for some opposition to my wishes. 'Now, Mademoiselle,' said he, 'allow me to give you some advice.' 'I listen, Monsieur.' 'To travel only by night.' 'Agreed.' 'To let me choose the route, and the places where you should stop. All my precautions will be taken with the sole aim of escaping the Duc d'Anjou.' 'I have no objection to make, Monsieur.' 'Lastly, at Paris, to occupy the lodging I shall prepare for you, however simple and out of the way it may be.' 'I only ask to live hidden, Monsieur; the more out of the way, the better it will suit a fugitive.' 'Then, as we are agreed on all points, Mademoiselle, it only remains for me to present to you my humble respects, and to send to you your maid.' 'On my side, Monsieur, be sure that if you keep all your promises, I will keep mine.' 'That is all I ask,' said the count, 'and that promise assures me that I shall soon be the happiest of men.'

"With these words he bowed and went out. Five minutes after, Gertrude entered. The joy of this good girl was great; she had believed herself separated from me forever. I told her all that had taken place. As I finished, we heard the sound of a horse's hoofs. I ran to the window; it was M. de Monsoreau going off at a gallop on the road by which we had come. Why did he take that direction instead of going forward? That was something I could not understand. However, he had fulfilled the first article of the agreement in restoring Gertrude to me, and the second in taking himself away. Besides, whatever direction he might take, his departure reassured me. We passed all the day in that little house, served by our hostess; in the evening the chief of our escort appeared, and asked me for my orders. As the danger seemed to me greater so long as I was near the Château de Beaugé, I answered that I was ready to go. Five minutes later he returned to say that they awaited me. At the door I found my white mare. We travelled all night and stopped at daybreak. I calculated we had gone about thirty-five miles; but my horse had a very easy pace, and when we left the house a fur cloak had been thrown over me to protect me from the cold. It took us seven days to reach Paris in this manner, and I saw nothing of the count. We entered the city at night, and the first object I saw, after passing through the gate, was an immense monastery; then we crossed the river, and in ten minutes we were in the Place de la Bastille. Then a man, who seemed to be waiting for us, advanced and said, ' It is here.' The chief of our escort jumped off his horse, and presented me his hand to dismount also. A door was open, and the staircase lighted by a lamp. ' Madame,' said the man to me, ' you are now at home. At this door the mission I received comes to an end; may I flatter myself I have fulfilled it according to your wishes, and with the respect enjoined upon us?' ' Yes, Monsieur,' said I, ' I have only thanks to give you. Offer them in my name to all your men; I would wish to reward them in a better manner, but I possess nothing.' ' Do not be uneasy about that, Madame,' said he; ' they are largely recompensed.'

"Then the little troop went away, and we went up the stairs of our house, and found ourselves in a corridor. Three doors were open; we entered the middle one, and found ourselves in the room where we now stand. It was lighted up as at this moment. On opening the door of my bedroom, to my great astonishment I found my own portrait there. It was one which had hung at Méridor, and the count had doubtless begged it of my father. I trembled at this new proof that my father regarded me already as his wife.

"Nothing was wanting in the rooms; a fire burned in the grate, and a supper was ready in the sitting-room. I saw with satisfaction that it was laid for one only. ' Well, Mademoiselle,' said Gertrude, ' you see the count keeps his promises.' ' Alas! yes,' I replied with a sigh, for I would have preferred that by breaking his word he should have given me an excuse to break mine. After supper we examined the house, but found no one in it. The next day Gertrude went out, and from her I learned that we were at the end of the Rue St. Antoine, near the Bastille. But this intelligence was nothing to me, for I had never been in Paris and knew but little about it.

" The day passed by without bringing anything new. In the evening, just as I sat down to supper, some one knocked. Gertrude and I looked at each other. There was a second knock. ' Go and see who is knocking,' I said. ' If it be the count?' asked Gertrude. ' You must open to him; he has kept his promises, and I must keep mine.' A moment later Gertrude returned. ' It is the count, Madame,' said she. ' Let him come in,' I replied. Gertrude retired and gave place to the count, who appeared upon the threshold. ' Well, Madame,' he asked me, ' have I faithfully kept my part of the agreement?' ' Yes, Monsieur,' I replied, ' and I thank you.' ' You are willing, then, to receive me?' he added, with a smile in which all his efforts could not suppress the irony. ' Enter, Monsieur.' The count approached and remained standing. I made a sign to him to be seated. ' Have you any news, Monsieur?' I asked. ' From where and of whom, Madame?' ' Of my father and of Méridor, before all!' ' I have not been to Méridor, and have not seen the baron.' ' Then of Beaugé, and the Duc d'Anjou?' ' I have been to Beaugé, and have spoken to the duke.' ' What does he say?' ' He appears to doubt.' ' Of what?' ' Of your death.' ' But you confirmed it?' ' I did all I could.' ' Where is the duke?' I then asked. ' He returned to Paris yesterday. One does not like to stay in a place where he thinks he has the death of a woman to reproach himself with.' ' Have you seen him in Paris?' ' I have just left him.' ' Did he speak of me?' ' I did not give him time; I spoke incessantly of a promise which he made to me.' ' What is it?' ' He promised me as a reward for services rendered to him, to make me chief huntsman.' ' Ah, yes,' said I, thinking of my poor Daphné, ' you are a terrible hunter, I know; and as such you have some claim to the place.' ' It is not as hunter that I shall obtain it, Madame, but as a servant of the prince; it is not because I have a claim to it that he will give it to me, but because M. le Duc d'Anjou dare not be ungrateful to me.'

" There was in all these replies, notwithstanding the respectful tone in which they were uttered, something that frightened me, —the expression of a dark and implacable will. I remained silent for a moment. ' Am I permitted to write to my father?' said I. ' Doubtless; but your letters may be intercepted.' ' Am I forbidden to go out?' ' Nothing is forbidden; but I beg to point out to you that you may be followed.' 'At least I must go on Sunday to mass?' 'It would be better not; but if you do, I advise you to go to Ste. Catherine.' 'Where is that?' 'Just opposite you.' There was a silence. Then I said, 'When shall I see you again, Monsieur?' 'When I have your permission to come.' 'Do you need it?' 'Certainly; as yet I am a stranger to you.' 'Have you not a key to this house?' 'Your husband alone has that right.' 'Monsieur,' said I, half frightened at this unnatural submission, 'you can return when you like, or when you think you think you have anything important to communicate.' 'Thanks, Madame,' said he, 'I will use your permission, but not abuse it. I know you do not love me, and I will not abuse a situation which forces you to receive me. You will, I trust, gradually become accustomed to the thought, and be willing, when the moment shall arrive, to become my wife.' 'Monsieur,' said I, 'I appreciate your delicacy and frankness. I will use the same frankness. I had a prejudice against you which I trust that time will cure.' 'Permit me,' said he, 'to partake this anticipation and live in the hope of that happy moment.' Then, bowing respectfully, he went out."

CHAPTER XV

THE MARRIAGE

" A STRANGE man," said Bussy.

" Yes, is he not, Monsieur? When he was gone I felt sadder and more frightened than ever. This icy respect, this ironical obedience, this repressed passion, which now and then showed itself in his voice, frightened me more than a will firmly expressed, and which I could have opposed, would have done. The next day was Sunday; I had never in my life missed divine service, so I took a thick veil and went to Ste. Catherine's, followed by Gertrude. No one seemed to remark us.

" The next day the count came to announce to me that the duke had fulfilled his promise, and had obtained for him the place of chief huntsman, which had been almost promised to a favourite of the king, M. de Saint-Luc. I began to hope that since the Duc d'Anjou believed me to be dead, and the danger therefore no longer existed, I should cease to be bound to the count. Seven more days passed by without bringing anything new, except two visits of the count. His manner was still cold and respectful; but I have explained to you how strange, I might almost say threatening, were that coldness and respect. The next Sunday I went again to the church. Imprudently, in the midst of my prayers, I raised my veil; besides, in the house of God I thought only of God. I was praying earnestly for my father, when Gertrude touched me on the arm. I raised my head and saw with terror M. le Duc d'Anjou leaning against a column, and looking earnestly at me. A man stood by him, who seemed to be his confidant rather than his servant."

"It was Aurilly," said Bussy, "his lute-player."

"Yes, that was the name that Gertrude told me afterwards."

"Continue, Madame," said Bussy; "I begin to see the whole plot."

"I drew my veil quickly over my face, but it was too late; he had seen me, and if he had not recognised me, at least my resemblance to her whom he believed dead had deeply interested him. Uneasy, I left the church, but found him standing at the door, and he offered the holy water to me as I passed. I feigned not to see him, and went on. We soon discovered that we were followed. Had I known anything of Paris, I should have attempted to lead them wrong; but I knew no more of it than from the church to the house, nor did I know any one of whom I could ask a quarter of an hour's hospitality,—not a friend, and only one protector, whom I feared more than an enemy."

"Oh, *mon Dieu!*" cried Bussy, "why did not Heaven, or chance, throw me sooner in your path?"

Diane thanked the young man with a look.

"But pray go on," said Bussy; "I interrupt you, and yet I am eager to hear more."

"That evening M. de Monsoreau came. I did not know whether to tell him of what had happened; but he began, 'You asked me if you could go to mass, and I told you you were free, but that it would be better not to do so. You would not believe me; you went this morning to Ste. Catherine's, and by a fatality the prince was there and saw you.' 'It is true, Monsieur; but I do not know if he recognised me.' 'Your face struck him; your resemblance to the woman he regrets appeared to him extraordinary. He followed you home, and made inquiries, but learned nothing, for no one knew anything.' 'Mon Dieu!' I cried. 'The duke is persevering,' said he. 'Oh! he will forget me, I hope.'

" ' No one forgets you who has once seen you,' said he; ' I did all I could to forget you, and I have not succeeded.' And the first passionate look that I had seen flashed from the eyes of the count. I was more terrified by it than I had been by the sight of the prince. I remained silent. ' What will you do? ' asked the count. ' Can I not change my abode,—go to the other end of Paris, or better still, return to Anjou? ' ' It will be useless; the duke is a terrible bloodhound, and now that he is on your track, he will follow you wherever you go till he finds you.' ' Oh, *mon Dieu!* you frighten me.' ' It is not my intention to do so; I tell you the simple truth.' ' Then what do you advise me to do? ' ' Alas!' said he, with a bitter irony; ' I am a man of poor imagination. I had formed a plan; but it does not suit you. I renounce it; but do not ask me to form new ones.' ' But the danger is perhaps less pressing than you imagine.' ' The future will show us, Madame,' said the count, rising. ' I can but add that the Comtesse de Monsoreau would have the less to fear from the prince, as my new post places me under the direct protection of the court.' I replied only by a sigh. What the count had said seemed sensible and reasonable. He waited a moment, as if to give me plenty of time to answer; but I had not strength enough. He remained standing ready to withdraw. A bitter smile passed over his lips; he bowed and went out. I thought I heard him swearing as he went downstairs.

" The next day, when Gertrude went out, she was accosted by a young man whom she recognised as the one who had accompanied the prince, but she remained obstinately silent to all his questions. This meeting inspired me with profound terror; I feared that M. de Monsoreau would not come, and that they would invade the house in his absence. I sent for him, and he came at once. I told him all about the young man, whom I described.

" ' It was Aurilly,' he said; ' and what did Gertrude answer? ' ' She did not answer at all.' ' She was wrong,' said he. ' Why? ' ' We must gain time.' ' Time? ' ' Yes, I am now dependent on the Duc d'Anjou; in a fortnight, in a week perhaps, he will be in my power. We must deceive him to get him to wait.' ' *Mon Dieu!* ' ' Certainly; hope will make him patient. A complete refusal will push him to extremities.' ' Monsieur, write to my father; he will throw himself at the feet of the king. The king will have pity on an old man.' ' That will be according to the king's humour, and to whether he be for the time friendly or hostile to the duke. Besides, it would take six days for a messenger to reach your father, and six days for him to come here. In twelve days if we do not stop him, the duke will have done all he can do.' 'And how to stop him?' I cried. M. de Monsoreau did not answer. I understood his thought and lowered my eyes. 'Monsieur,' said I, after a moment of silence, 'give your orders to Gertrude, and she will follow your instructions.' A smile passed over the lips of M. de Monsoreau at this first appeal to his protection. 'Madame,' said he, 'will you permit me to pass two or three hours in your room? I may be seen going out, and would rather wait till dark.'

"I signed him to sit down. We conversed; he was clever and had travelled much, and at the end of the time I understood, better than I had ever done before, the influence he had obtained over my father. When it grew dark he rose and took leave. During the evening Gertrude and I approached the window, and could distinctly see two men examining the house. They approached the door several times. All the lights had been put out, and they could not see us. The next day, Gertrude, when she went out, found the same young man in the same place. He spoke to her again, and this time she answered him. On the following day she told him that I was the widow of a counsellor, who, being poor, lived in retirement. He tried to learn more, but could extract nothing further from her. The next day, Aurilly, who seemed to doubt her story, spoke of D'Anjou, of Beaugé, and Méridor. Gertrude declared these names to be entirely unknown to her. Then he avowed that he came from the Duc d'Anjou, who had seen and fallen in love with me; then came magnificent offers for both of us,—for her, if she would introduce the prince into my house, and for me, if I would receive him.

"Every evening M. de Monsoreau came, to hear what was going on, and remained from eight o'clock to midnight, and it was evident that his anxiety was great. On Saturday evening, he arrived, pale and agitated.

"'You must promise to receive the duke on Tuesday or Wednesday,' said he. 'Promise! and why?' 'Because he has made up his mind to come in, and he is just now on the best terms with the king; we have nothing to expect from the king.' 'But before then will anything happen to help me?' 'I hope so. I expect from day to day the event which is to place the duke in my power. But to-morrow, I must leave you, and must go to Monsoreau.' 'Must you?' I cried with an emotion of joy and terror. 'Yes, I have there a rendezvous which is indispensable to bring about the event of which I speak.' 'But if you fail, what are we to do?' 'What can I do against a prince, if I have no right to protect you? We must yield to bad fortune.' 'Oh, my father! my father!' I cried.

" The count looked at me. 'What have you to reproach me with?' said he. 'Nothing; on the contrary.' 'Have I not been devoted as a friend, and respectful as a brother?' 'You have behaved throughout like a gallant man.' 'Had I not your promise?' 'Yes.' 'Have I once recalled it to you?' 'No.' 'And yet you prefer to be the mistress of the duke to being my wife?' 'I do not say so, Monsieur.' 'Then decide.' 'I have decided.' 'To be Comtesse de Monsoreau?' 'Rather than mistress of the duke.' 'The alternative is flattering.' I remained silent. 'No matter,' said the count. 'Let Gertrude gain time until Tuesday, and on Tuesday we will see.'

" The next day Gertrude went out, but did not meet Aurilly. We felt more frightened at his absence than we had done at his presence. Night came, and we were full of terror. We were alone and feeble, and for the first time I felt my injustice to the count."

" Oh, Madame! " cried Bussy, " do not be in a hurry to think so; in all his conduct there is something which we do not know, but which we will find out."

" The evening came, and with it increasing terror. I was determined not to fall living into the hands of the Duc d'Anjou. I had provided myself with a dagger, and was resolved to stab myself in the presence of the prince the moment he or any of his attendants attempted to lay hands on me. We barricaded ourselves in our chambers. By an incredible negligence the street door had no bolt on the inside. We hid the lamp and placed ourselves at the window.

" All was quiet until eleven o'clock. Then five men came out of the Rue St. Antoine, and hid themselves by the Hôtel des Tournelles. We began to tremble; were they there for us? However, they remained quiet, and a quarter of an hour passed; then we saw two other men approach. By the moonlight Gertrude recognised Aurilly. 'Alas, Mademoiselle! it is they,' murmured the poor girl. 'Yes,' I replied, trembling, 'and the five others are to help them.' 'But they must force the door,' said Gertrude, 'perhaps the neighbours will come and help us.' 'Oh, no, they do not know us, and they will not fight against

D

the duke. Alas, Gertrude, I fear we have no real defender but the count.' 'Well, then, why do you always refuse to marry him?' I sighed."

CHAPTER XVI

THE MARRIAGE (continued)

" THE two men approached the window. We gently opened it a little way, and heard one say, 'Are you sure it is here?' 'Yes, Monseigneur, quite sure,' said the other. 'It is the fifth house from the corner of the Rue St. Paul.' 'And you are sure of the key?' 'I took the pattern of the lock.' I seized Gertrude's arm in terror. 'And once inside,' he went on, 'the servant will admit us; your Highness has in your pocket a golden key as good as this one.' 'Open, then.' We heard the key turn in the lock, but all at once the ambushed men rushed forward, crying, 'To death! to death!' I could not understand this, only I saw that unexpected help had come to us, and I fell on my knees, thanking Heaven. But the prince had only to name himself when every sword went back into the scabbard, and every foot drew back."

" Yes, yes," said Bussy; " it was for me they came, not for the prince."

" However, this attack caused the prince to retire, and the five gentlemen went back to their hiding-place. It was evident that the danger was over for that night, but we were too anxious and excited to go to bed. Soon we saw a man on horseback appear, and then the five gentlemen immediately rushed on him. You know the rest, as the gentleman was yourself."

" On the contrary, Madame," said Bussy, who hoped that the young woman in her recital would betray some secret feeling of her heart, " I know only that I fought and then fainted."

" It is useless to tell you," continued Diane, with a blush, " the interest that we took in the combat, so unequal, but so valiantly sustained. Every incident in it drew from us a shudder, a cry, a prayer. We saw your horse fall, and we thought you lost, but it was not so; the brave Bussy merited his reputation. At last, surrounded, menaced on all sides, you retreated like a lion, facing your foes, and came to lean against our door; the same idea came to both of us, to go down and open to you. Gertrude looked at me. 'Yes,' I said, and we ran towards the staircase; but we had barricaded the door, and it

took us some minutes to move the furniture, and as we arrived
on the stairs we heard the door shut. We stopped, and looked
at each other, wondering who had entered. Soon we heard
steps; and a man appeared, who tottered, threw up his arms,
and fell on the first step. It was evident that he was not pursued; that he had put the door, so luckily left open by the duke,
between him and his adversaries, and, wounded dangerously,—
to death, perhaps,—had thrown himself down at the foot of the
stairs. In any case we had nothing to fear; it was he who
needed our help. Gertrude ran and brought the lamp. We
were not mistaken; you had fainted. We recognised you as the
brave gentleman who had so valiantly defended himself, and
without hesitation we resolved to help you. In a moment you
had been carried to my room and laid upon the bed. Gertrude
had heard of a wonderful cure made by a young doctor in the
Rue Beautreillis, and she offered to go for him. ' But,' said I,
' he might betray us.' ' I will take precautions,' said she.
She took money and the key, and I remained alone near you,
and—praying for you."

"Alas!" said Bussy, "I did not know all my happiness,
Madame."

"In a quarter of an hour Gertrude returned, bringing the
young doctor with his eyes bandaged. I remained in the salon
when he was brought into the chamber. There he was allowed
to take off his bandage."

"Yes, it was at that moment I recovered my senses and saw
your portrait and thought I saw you enter," said Bussy.

"I did so; my anxiety was stronger than my prudence. I
questioned the young doctor; he examined your wound and
answered for your life, and I was relieved."

"All that remained in my mind," said Bussy, "like a dream;
and yet something told me," added he, laying his hand upon his
heart, "that I had not dreamed."

"When the surgeon had dressed your wound, he drew from
his pocket a little bottle containing a red liquor, of which he put
some drops on your lips. He told me it was to counteract the
fever and produce sleep. In fact, a moment later you closed
your eyes again and fell back fainting. I was frightened, but
the doctor reassured me. All was going well, he said, and there
was nothing more to do except to let you sleep. Gertrude then
bandaged his eyes again, and took him back to the Rue Beautreillis. But she thought she perceived that he counted the
steps."

" In fact, Madame," said Bussy, " he did count them."

" This supposition frightened us. We feared he would betray us. We resolved to get rid of every trace of the hospitality we had shown you; but it was especially important for us to get rid of you. I mustered all my courage; it was two o'clock, and the streets were deserted. Gertrude was strong, and I aided her; and between us we carried you to the Temple. Luckily we met no one; but when we returned, I fainted with emotion."

" Oh, Madame! " cried Bussy, " how can I ever repay you for what you have done for me? "

There was a moment's silence, and they heard the clock of Ste. Catherine's church strike. " Two o'clock," cried Diane, " and you here! "

" Oh, Madame, do not send me away without telling me all,— without showing me in what way I may be useful to you! Suppose that God had given you a brother, and tell this brother what he can do for his sister."

" Alas! nothing now; it is too late."

" What happened the next day? " said Bussy; " what did you do on that day, when I thought constantly of you, without feeling sure, however, that you were not a delirious dream, a vision of my fever? "

" During that day, Gertrude went out, and met Aurilly. He was more pressing than ever. He said nothing of the night before, but asked for an interview for his master. Gertrude appeared to consent, but she asked until the Wednesday following—that is, to-day—to decide. Aurilly promised that his master would use no violence until then. We had, then, three days before us. That evening, M. de Monsoreau returned. We told him all, except about you.

" ' Yes,' said he, ' I heard of all this; then he has a key.' ' Can we not change the lock? ' ' He will get another key.' ' Put on bolts.' ' He will come with ten men and force the door.' ' But the event which was to give you full power over him? ' ' Is postponed indefinitely perhaps.' I stood silent, with perspiration on my brow; for I could no longer conceal from myself that the only way to escape the Duc d'Anjou was by becoming the wife of the count.' ' Monsieur,' said I, ' the duke has promised to wait till Wednesday; I ask you to wait till Tuesday.' ' Tuesday evening I will be here, Madame,' said the count; and without another word he went out.

" I followed him with my eyes, but instead of going away, he stood in the corner by the Hôtel des Tournelles, and seemed determined to watch me all night. Every proof of devotion he gave me was like a knife in my heart. The two days passed rapidly, but what I suffered it is impossible to describe. When Tuesday evening came I felt exhausted, and all emotion seemed dead within me.

" Gertrude went to the window. ' Madame,' she cried, ' four men! I see four men! They approach; they open the door; they enter!' ' Let them enter,' I said, without making a movement. ' But those four men are doubtless the duke and his followers.' For an answer, I drew my poniard and placed it near me on the table. ' See,' said I. An instant after Gertrude returned. ' It is the count,' said she. I replaced the poniard in my dress without a word. Only I turned my head towards the count. Doubtless he was startled on seeing how pale I was. ' Gertrude tells me,' said he, ' that you took me for the duke, and were ready to kill yourself.' It was the first time I had ever seen him moved. Was that emotion real, or pretended? ' Gertrude was wrong to tell you,' said I; ' since it was not the duke, all goes well.' There was a brief interval of silence. ' You know that I am not alone?' said the count. ' Gertrude saw four men.' ' You know who they are?' ' I presume one is a priest, and the others witnesses.' ' Then you are ready to become my wife?' ' It was so agreed; only I stipulated that, except in an urgent case, I would marry you only in the presence of my father.' ' I remember; but do you not think the case urgent?' ' Yes, and the priest may marry us, but until I have seen my father, I will be your wife only in name.'

" The count frowned and bit his lips. ' I do not wish to coerce you,' said he. ' You are free; but look here.' I went to the window, and saw a man wrapped in a cloak, who seemed trying to get into the house."

" Oh, *mon Dieu !*" cried Bussy; " and this was yesterday? "

" Yes, about nine o'clock. Presently another man, with a lantern, joined him. ' Who do you think those two men are?' asked M. de Monsoreau. ' I think they are the duke and his confidant,' I answered."

Bussy uttered a groan.

" ' Now,' said M. de Monsoreau, ' shall I go or stay?' I hesitated a moment; yes, in spite of my father's letter, in spite of my sworn promise, in spite of the danger present, palpable, threatening,—yes, I hesitated! and if those two men had not been there—"

" Oh, unhappy that I am!" cried Bussy; " the man in the

cloak was myself; and he who carried the lantern was Rémy le Haudouin, that young doctor you sent for."

" You? " cried Diane, stupefied.

" Yes, I,—I who, more and more convinced of the reality of my dream, sought for the house where I had been, and the woman, or rather angel, who had appeared to me. Oh, I am unfortunate! Then," continued he, after a pause, " you are his wife? "

" Since yesterday."

There was silence again, broken only by their hurried breathing.

" But," said Diane, at last, " how did you enter this house? " Bussy silently showed his key.

" A key! where did you get it? "

" Had not Gertrude promised the prince to enter to-night? He had seen M. de Monsoreau here, and also myself, and fearing a snare, sent me to find out."

" And you accepted this mission? " said Diane, in a tone of reproach.

" It was my only method of getting near you. Will you reproach me for having sought what is at once the greatest joy and the greatest grief of my life? "

" Yes, for it is better that you should see me no more, and forget me."

" No, Madame; God has brought me to you to deliver you from the toils in which your enemies have taken you. Listen: from the moment when I saw you I devoted to you my life. The mission which I imposed on myself is now beginning. You wish for news of your father? "

" Oh, yes! for, in truth, I know not what has become of him."

" Well, I charge myself with finding out; only cherish a kind remembrance of him who henceforth will live but for you."

" But this key? "

" This key I restore to you, for I will receive it only from your hands; but I pledge you my word as a gentleman that never sister could confide the key of her apartments to a brother more devoted or more respectful."

" I trust to the word of the brave Bussy. Here, Monsieur," and she gave back the key.

" Madame, in a fortnight we shall know more; " and, saluting Diane with a respect mingled with love and sadness, Bussy took leave. Diane listening to his retreating steps with tears in her eyes.

CHAPTER XVII

HOW HENRI III. TRAVELLED, AND HOW LONG IT TOOK HIM TO GET FROM PARIS TO FONTAINEBLEAU

THE sun, which shone four or five hours after the events which we have just recorded had taken place, saw, by his pale light, Henri III. set off for Fontainebleau, where a grand chase was projected. A crowd of gentlemen, mounted on good horses and wrapped in their fur cloaks, then a number of pages, after them lackeys, and then Swiss, followed the royal litter. This litter, drawn by eight mules richly caparisoned, was a large machine, about fifteen feet long and eight wide, on four wheels, furnished inside with cushions and curtains of silk brocade. In difficult places they substituted for the mules an indefinite number of oxen.

This machine contained Henri III., his doctor, his chaplain, Chicot, four of the king's favourites, a pair of large dogs, and a basket of little ones, which the king held on his knees, and which was suspended from his neck by a golden chain. From the roof hung a gilded cage containing turtle-doves, quite white, with a black ring round their necks. Sometimes the collection was completed by the presence of two or three monkeys of the *ouistiti* or *sapajou* species,—the monkey being an animal much in favour with the court of the last Valois. Thus in the numerous pamphlets and satirical verses of the period this litter was sometimes referred to as Noah's Ark.

Quélus and Maugiron employed themselves in plaiting ribbons, a favourite diversion of that time; and Chicot amused himself by making anagrams on the names of all the courtiers. Just as they passed the Place Maubert, Chicot rushed out of the litter, and went to kneel down before a house of good appearance.

" Oh! " cried the king, " if you kneel, let it be before the crucifix in the middle of the street, and not before the house. What do you mean by it? "

But Chicot, without attending, cried out in a loud voice, " Good God! just God! here is—I recognise it, I shall always recognise it—here is the house where Chicot suffered, if not for thee, my God, for one of thy creatures! I have never prayed for vengeance on M. de Mayenne, author of my martyrdom, nor on Nicolas David, his instrument. No; Chicot is patient, Chicot can wait, although it is now six years, including one leap year, that Chicot has added the interest to the little open account between him and MM. de Mayenne and Nicolas David. Now at ten per cent., which is the legal rate, since it is the rate paid by the king, the accumulated interest doubles the principal in seven years. May, then, my patience last another year, so that the fifty blows of a stirrup-leather which I received in this house by the orders of that assassin of a Lorraine prince and that bully of a Norman advocate, and which drew from Chicot a pint of blood, may amount to a hundred blows and two pints of blood for each of them; so that M. de Mayenne, fat as he is, and Nicolas David, long as he is, will no longer have blood or hide enough to pay Chicot, and will have to make a bankruptcy of fifteen or twenty per cent., expiring under the eightieth or eighty-fifth blow of the rod! In the name of the Father, and of the Son, and of the Holy Spirit, so may it be!"

" Amen!" said the king.

Chicot then returned to the litter, amid the wondering looks of the spectators.

" Why, Chicot, what does all this mean?" said the king.

" Sire, it means that Chicot is like the fox; he licks the stones where his blood fell, until against those very stones he crushes the heads of those who spilled it."

" Explain yourself."

" Sire, in that house lived a girl whom Chicot loved,—a good and charming creature, a lady. One evening when he went to see her, a certain prince, who had also fallen in love with her, had him seized and beaten, so that Chicot was forced to jump out of a window; and as it was a miracle that he was not killed, every time he passes the house he kneels down and thanks God for his escape."

" You were, then, well beaten, my poor Chicot?"

" Yes, Sire, and yet not as much as I wished."

" Why,—for your sins."

" No, for those of M. de Mayenne."

" Oh, I understand! your intention is to render to Cæsar—"

" Not to Cæsar, Sire; Cæsar is the great general, the valiant warrior, the eldest brother, who wishes to be King of France. No, you must settle with him; pay your debts, and I will pay mine."

It was three o'clock in the afternoon when they arrived at Juvisy and the great hostelry of the Cour de France.

Chicot, looking out of the litter, saw at the door of the hotel several men wrapped in cloaks. In the midst of them was a short stout person, whose large hat almost covered his face. They went in quickly on seeing the litter, but not before the appearance of this person had had time to excite Chicot's attention. Therefore he jumped out, and asking a page for his horse, he withdrew to a corner of the wall, where he was concealed in the early shades of night, and allowed the *cortége* to go on without him towards Essonnes, where the king expected to sleep. Then, when the last of the party had disappeared, when the retreating sound of the wheels on the pavement had died away in silence, he left his hiding-place, made a turn around the château, and presented himself at the door of the hotel as if he came from Fontainebleau. On passing by the window Chicot cast a rapid glance through the glass, and saw with pleasure that the men whom he had noticed were still there, and among them the short and fat man to whom he had appeared to give particular attention. He then entered the hotel, went into the opposite room, asked for a bottle of wine, and placed himself so that, although he could not be seen, no one could pass by without being seen by him.

"Ah!" said he to himself, "shall I be forced to make my payment sooner than I expected?"

Soon Chicot found that by keeping the door open he could both see into the room and hear what was said.

"Gentlemen," said the short fat man to his companions, "I think it is time to set out; the last lackey of the *cortége* is out of sight, and I believe now that the road is safe."

"Perfectly so, Monseigneur," replied a voice which made Chicot tremble, and which came from the mouth of a person as tall as the other was short, as pale as he was red, and as obsequious as he was arrogant.

"Ah! Maître Nicolas," said Chicot to himself, quietly laughing, "'tu quoque?' That is good. It will be odd if I let you slip this time!" He emptied his glass and paid the host, so that he need not be delayed, when he should wish to leave.

The precaution was well taken, for the seven persons who had attracted Chicot's attention also paid, or rather the short fat person paid for all, and they took the road to Paris. Chicot followed them at a distance. They entered by the Porte St. Antoine, and went into the Hôtel de Guise. Chicot waited outside a full hour, in spite of cold and hunger. At last the door reopened, but instead of seven cavaliers wrapped in their cloaks, seven monks came out, with their hoods over their faces, and carrying immense rosaries.

" Oh! " said Chicot, " is, then, the Hôtel de Guise so embalmed in sanctity that wolves change into lambs only by entering it? This becomes more and more interesting." And he followed the monks as he had followed the cavaliers, for he believed them to be the same.

The monks passed over the bridge of Notre-Dame, crossed the Cité and the Petit Pont, and went up the Rue Ste. Geneviève.

" Oh! " said Chicot, as he passed the house where he had kneeled in the morning, " are we returning to Fontainebleau? In that case I have made a round."

However, the monks stopped at the door of the abbey of Ste. Geneviève, in the porch of which stood another monk, who examined every one's hand.

" Why," said Chicot, " it seems that to be admitted to-night into the abbey one must have clean hands. Decidedly, something extraordinary is happening! "

Then he saw with astonishment monks appear from every street leading to the abbey,—some alone, some walking in pairs, but all coming to the abbey.

" Ah! " said Chicot, " is there a general chapter at the abbey to-night? I have never seen one, and I should like it much."

The monks entered, showing their hands, or something in them, and passed on.

" I should like to go also," thought Chicot, " but for that I want two things,—a monk's robe, for I see no layman here, and then this mysterious thing which they show to the porter, for certainly they show something. Ah, Brother Gorenflot, if you were here! "

The monks continued to arrive, till it seemed as if half Paris had taken the frock.

" There must be something extraordinary to-night," thought Chicot. " I will go and find Gorenflot at the Corne d'Abondance; he will be at supper."

CHAPTER XVIII

BROTHER GORENFLOT

To the beautiful day had succeeded a beautiful evening, only as the day had been cold, the evening was still colder. There was one of those frosts which make the lights in the windows of an hotel look doubly tempting. Chicot first entered the dining room, and looked around him, but not finding there the man he sought for, went familiarly down to the kitchen. The master of the establishment was superintending a frying-pan full of whitings. At the sound of Chicot's step he turned.

"Ah! it is you, Monsieur," said he; "good-evening, and a good appetite to you."

"Thanks for the two wishes, though one of them is made as much for your own profit as for mine. But that depends."

"That depends?"

"Yes, you know that I can't bear to eat alone."

"If necessary, Monsieur, I will sup with you."

"Thanks, my dear host, but though I know you to be an excellent companion, I seek for some one else."

"Brother Gorenflot, perhaps?"

"Precisely; has he begun supper?"

"No, not yet; but you must make haste nevertheless, for in five minutes he will have finished."

"Brother Gorenflot has not begun his supper, and in five minutes he will have finished, do you say?" And Chicot shook his head,—a sign which in all countries stands for incredulity.

"Monsieur, it is Friday, and the beginning of Lent."

"Well, and what then?" said Chicot, who did not hold a high opinion of Gorenflot's religious austerity.

Bonhomet shrugged his shoulders.

"Decidedly, something must be out of order in the sublunary machine," said Chicot. "Five minutes for Gorenflot's supper! I am destined to see wonders to-day."

Chicot then advanced towards a small private room, pushed open the door, and saw the worthy monk, who was turning negligently on his plate a small portion of spinach, which he tried to render more savoury by the introduction into it of some cheese. Brother Gorenflot was about thirty-eight years of age and five feet high. However, what he wanted in height he made up in breadth, measuring nearly three feet in diameter from shoulder to shoulder, which, as every one knows, is equal to nine feet of circumference. Between these herculean shoulders, rose a neck of which the muscles stood out like cords. Unluckily this neck partook of the same proportions; it was short and thick, which at any great emotion might render Brother Gorenflot liable to apoplexy. But knowing this perhaps, he never gave way to emotions, and was seldom so disturbed as he was when Chicot entered his room.

"Ah, my friend! what are you doing?" cried Chicot, looking

at the vegetables and at a glass filled with water just coloured with a few drops of wine.

" You see, my brother, I sup," replied Gorenflot, with a voice as resonant as the clock of his abbey.

" You call that supper, Gorenflot,—herbs and cheese? "

" We are in the beginning of Lent, Brother; we must think of our souls," replied Gorenflot, raising his eyes to heaven.

Chicot looked astounded; he had so often seen Gorenflot feast in a different manner during Lent.

" Our souls! " said he; " and what the devil have herbs and water to do with them? "

" We are forbidden to eat meat on Wednesdays and Fridays."

" But when did you breakfast? "

" I have not breakfasted, my brother," said the monk.

" Not breakfasted! Then what have you done? "

" I have composed a discourse," said Gorenflot, raising his head proudly.

" A discourse, and what for? "

" To deliver this evening at the abbey."

" Stay! " thought Chicot, " a discourse this evening; that is strange! "

" And I must be quick and go there, or perhaps my audience will grow impatient."

Chicot thought of the infinite number of monks he had seen going to the abbey, and wondered why Gorenflot, whom certainly he had never thought eloquent, had been chosen to preach before M. de Mayenne and the numerous assemblage. " When are you to preach? " said he.

" At half-past nine."

" Good; it is still a quarter to nine; you can give me a few minutes. *Ventre de biche!* we have not dined together for a week."

" It is not our fault, but I know that your duties keep you near our King Henri III., while my duties fill up my time."

" Yes, but it seems to me that is so much the more reason why we should be merry when we do meet."

" Yes, I am merry," said Gorenflot, with a piteous look; " but still I must leave you."

" At least, finish your supper."

Gorenflot looked at the spinach and sighed, then at the water, and turned away his head. Chicot saw that it was time to begin the attack. " Do you remember," said he, " the little dinner at the Porte Montmartre, where, while the king was scourging himself and others, we devoured a teal from the marshes of the Grange Batelière, with a sauce made with crabs, and we drank that nice Burgundy wine—what do you call it? Is it not a wine which you yourself discovered?"

"It is the wine of my country, La Romanée."

"Yes, yes, I remember; it was the milk you sucked as a baby, worthy son of Noah."

"It was good," said Gorenflot; "but there is better."

"So says Claude Bonhomet, who pretends that he has in his cellar fifty bottles in comparison with which that is paltry."

"It is true."

"True! and yet you drink that abominable red water, when you have only to reach out your hand to drink such wine as that? Fie!" And Chicot, taking the glass, threw the contents out of the window.

"There is a time for all, my brother," said Gorenflot, "and wine is good when one has nothing to do after drinking it except to praise the God who made it; but water is better when one has a discourse to pronounce."

"Opinions differ, for I, who have also a discourse to pronounce, am going to ask for a bottle of Romanée. What do you advise me to take with it, Gorenflot?"

"Not these herbs; they are not nice."

Chicot, seizing the plate, threw it after the water, and then cried, "Maître Claude!"

The host appeared.

"Maître Claude, bring me two bottles of your Romanée, which you call so good."

"Why two bottles," said Gorenflot, "as I do not drink it?"

"Oh! if you did I would have four or six, but when I drink alone, I drink but little, and two bottles will be enough."

"Indeed; two bottles are reasonable, and if you eat no meat with it, your confessor will have nothing to reproach you with."

"Oh, of course not; meat on a Friday in Lent!" And going to the larder, he drew out a fine capon.

"What are you doing, Brother?" said Gorenflot, following his movements with interest.

"You see I am taking this carp, for fear some one else may get hold of it. On Fridays in Lent there is a general demand for eatables of this kind."

"Carp!" cried Gorenflot, astonished.

"Yes, a carp," said Chicot, showing him the tempting bird.

"And since when has a carp had a beak?"

" A beak! do you see a beak?   I only see a nose."

" And wings? "

" Fins! "

" Feathers? "

" Scales, my dear Gorenflot; you are drunk."

" Drunk! I, who have eaten only spinach and drunk only water? "

" Well, your spinach has overloaded your stomach, and your water has mounted to your head."

" *Parbleu!* here is our host, he shall decide."

" So be it, but first let him uncork the wine."

Maître Bonhomet uncorked a bottle and gave a glass to Chicot.   Chicot swallowed and smacked his lips.   " Ah! " said he, " I am a bad taster, and my tongue has no memory; I cannot remember if it be better or worse than that at Montmartre.   Here, my brother, enlighten me," said he, giving a little to the monk, who was looking on with eager eyes.

Gorenflot took the glass, and drank slowly the liquor it contained.   " It is the same wine," said he; " but I had too little to tell whether it be better or worse."

" But I want to know," said Chicot.   " *Peste!* I don't want to make any mistake; and if you had not a sermon to preach, I would beg you to taste that wine a second time."

" If it will give you pleasure, my brother."

Chicot half filled the monk's glass.   Gorenflot drank with great gravity.

" I pronounce it better," said he.

" Bah! you have an understanding with our host."

" A good drinker ought at the first draught to recognise the wine, at the second, the quality, and at the third, the age."

" Oh, I should like to know the age of this wine."

" Give me a few drops more, and I will tell you."

Chicot filled his glass.   He drank it off, and then said, " 1561."

" Right," cried Claude Bonhomet, " that's what it is exactly."

" Brother Gorenflot," cried Chicot, " they have canonised men at Rome who were worth less than you."

" A little habit," said Gorenflot, modestly.

" And talent; for I flatter myself I have the habit, and I could not do it.   But what are you about? "

" Going to my assembly."

" Without eating a piece of my carp? "

" Ah, true; you know still less of eating than drinking. Maître Bonhomet, what is the name of this creature? "

The innkeeper looked astonished. "*Parbleu!* it is capon," said he.

"A capon!" cried Chicot, with an air of consternation.

"Yes, and a fine one."

"Well!" said Gorenflot, triumphantly.

"Well! it seems I was wrong; but as I wish to eat this capon, and yet not sin, be so kind, Brother, as to throw a few drops of water upon it, and christen it a carp."

"Ah, ah!"

"Yes, I pray you, save me from mortal sin."

"So be it," cried Gorenflot, "but there is no water."

"It is said, I don't now remember where," said Chicot, "'You will use in a case of urgency whatever is at hand.' The intention is all; baptise it with wine, my brother. The capon will be perhaps a little less Catholic, but quite as good." And Chicot refilled the monk's glass. The first bottle was finished.

"In the name of Bacchus, Momus, and Comus, trinity of the great Saint Pantagruel, I baptise thee, carp," said Gorenflot. And dipping the ends of his fingers in the wine, he let fall two or three drops upon the capon.

"Now," said Chicot, clicking his glass against that of the monk, "to the health of the newly baptised; may it be cooked to perfection, and may Maître Bonhomet add to the excellent qualities which it has received from nature."

"To his health!" cried Gorenflot, interrupting a hearty laugh to swallow his wine.

"Maître Claude," said Chicot, "put this carp at once on the spit, cover it with fresh butter with shalots in it, put some toast in the frying-pan, and serve it hot."

Gorenflot approved with a motion of his head.

"Now, Maître Bonhomet," said Chicot, when he saw his directions obeyed, "some sardines and a tunny fish, meanwhile; it is Lent, and I wish to make a dinner without meat. And let me have two more bottles of that excellent wine of 1561."

The smell of the cookery began to mount to the brain of the monk. His tongue watered, his eyes shone; but he still controlled himself and even made a movement to rise.

"Then you leave me, after all?" said Chicot.

"I must," said Gorenflot, raising his eyes to heaven.

"It is very imprudent of you to go to pronounce a discourse fasting."

"Why?"

"Because your lungs will fail you. Galen has said it: 'Pulmo hominis facile deficit' ('Man's lungs are weak, and easily fail ')."

" Alas! yes," said Gorenflot; " I have often experienced that myself. If I had had lungs I should have been a thunder of eloquence."

" You see, then? "

" Luckily," Gorenflot continued, falling back in his chair,— " luckily, I have zeal."

" Ah! but zeal is not enough; I advise you to eat some sardines, and drink a little of this nectar."

" A single sardine, then, and one glass."

Chicot gave him the sardine, and passed him the bottle. He himself took care to keep sober.

" I feel myself less feeble," said Gorenflot.

" *Ventre de biche !* " said Chicot, " when one has a discourse to pronounce it is not a question of feeling less feeble; one should be altogether strong. Were I in your place I would eat the two fins of that carp; if you eat no more, there is danger that you will feel the wine."

" Oh, the devil! " said Gorenflot, " I didn't think of that."

And as at this moment they brought in the capon, Chicot cut off a leg and thigh, which Gorenflot soon despatched.

" Body of Christ! " said Gorenflot, " what a delicious fish! "

Chicot cut off the other leg and gave it to Gorenflot, while he ate the wings. " And famous wine," said he, uncorking the third bottle.

Once started, once warmed up, once quickened in the depths of his immense stomach, Gorenflot could not stop. His appetite was enormous; he finished the bird, and then called to Bonhomet. " Maître Claude," said he, " I am hungry; did you not offer me an omelet just now? "

" Certainly."

" Well, bring it."

" In five minutes," said the host, who, upon a wink from Chicot, went out hastily to prepare what was ordered.

" Ah! " said Gorenflot, letting fall upon the table his enormous fist, armed with a fork, " this is better."

" Is it not? " said Chicot.

" And if that omelet were here, I could eat it at a mouthful, as I swallow this wine at a gulp." And he swallowed a quarter of the third bottle.

" Ah! you were ill, then? "

" I was foolish, friend; that cursed discourse weighed on my mind. I have been thinking of it for days."

" It ought to be magnificent."

" Splendid."

" Tell me some of it while we wait for the omelet."

" No, no; not a sermon at table."

" We have beautiful discourses at the court, I assure you."

" About what? "

" About virtue."

" Ah, yes! he is a very virtuous man, our King Henri III."

" I do not know if he be virtuous; but I know that I have never seen anything there to make me blush."

" *Mordieu!* I can easily believe it. It is a long time since you have blushed, you old rake! "

" Oh! " said Chicot, " I, a rake,—I, who am abstinence personified, continence in flesh and bone! I, who follow all the processions and observe all the fasts! "

At this moment Maître Bonhomet entered with the omelet and two more bottles.

" Bring it here," cried the monk, with a smile which showed his thirty-two teeth.

" But, friend, I thought you had a discourse to pronounce."

" It is here," cried Gorenflot, striking his forehead.

" At half-past nine."

" I lied; it was ten."

" Ten! I thought the abbey shut at nine."

" Let it shut," said Gorenflot, looking at the light through the ruby wine in his glass,—" let it shut; I have a key."

" A key of the abbey! "

" Here in my pocket."

" Impossible; I know the monastic rules. They would not give the key to a simple monk."

" Here it is," said Gorenflot, hilariously showing a piece of money."

" Oh, money! ah, I understand! You corrupt the porter that you may go in when you please, wretched sinner! "

Gorenflot opened his mouth to his ears with the happy and gracious smile of an intoxicated man. " Sufficit," he stammered; and he began to put back the money into his pocket.

" Wait," said Chicot; " wait a moment. That is a strange piece of money! "

" An effigy of the heretic, with a hole through his heart."

" Yes, I see it is a tester of the Béarn king's, and here is a hole."

"A blow with a dagger; death to the heretic! He who kills a heretic is sure of Paradise."

"Ah, ah!" thought Chicot, "at last the affair is taking shape; but the wretch is not yet drunk enough;" and he filled his glass again.

"To the mass!" cried Gorenflot, drinking it off.

Chicot remembered the porter looking at the hands of the monks, and said, "Then if you show this to the porter—"

"I enter."

"Without difficulty?"

"As this wine into my stomach." And the monk absorbed a new dose.

"Peste!" said Chicot, "if the comparison is just you must enter without touching the sides."

"That is to say," stammered Gorenflot, dead drunk, "for Brother Gorenflot they open both folds of the door."

"And you pronounce your discourse?"

"And I pronounce my discourse. I arrive—do you hear? The assembly is numerous and select. There are barons, counts, and dukes."

"And even princes?"

"And even princes. I enter humbly among the faithful of the Union—"

"The Union—what does that mean?"

"I enter among the faithful of the Union; they call Brother Gorenflot, and I advance—"

At these words the monk rose. "And I advance," continued he, trying to do so; but at the first step he rolled on the floor.

"Bravo!" cried Chicot, lifting him up and placing him on a chair; "you advance, you salute the audience, and you say—"

"No, it is my friends who say, 'Brother Gorenflot,'—a fine name for a Leaguer, is it not?"

"A Leaguer," thought Chicot; "what truths is this wine going to bring out?"

"Then I begin." And the monk rose, and leaned against the wall.

"You begin," said Chicot, holding him up.

"I begin, 'My brothers, it is a good day for the faith; my brothers, it is a very good day for the faith; my brothers, it is an exceedingly good day for the faith.'"

After that superlative, Chicot saw that nothing more could be gained from the monk, and let go of him. Brother Gorenflot, who had maintained his equilibrium only by Chicot's support, slipped along the wall, and in falling hit the table with his feet and knocked off several empty bottles.

" Amen! " said Chicot.

In another moment a thunderous snoring shook the windows.

" Good," said Chicot, " the capon is taking effect, and our friend is in for twelve hours' sleep. I can easily undress him."

He then untied the monk's robe and pulled it off, then rolled Gorenflot in the table-cloth and covered his head with a napkin, and hiding the monk's frock under his cloak, passed into the kitchen.

" Maître Bonhomet," said he, handing him a rose noble, " here is for our supper, and for my horse; and pray do not wake the worthy Brother Gorenflot, who sleeps like one of the elect."

" No, no; be easy, M. Chicot."

Then Chicot ran to the Rue St. Etienne, put on the monk's robe, took the tester in his hand, and at a quarter to ten presented himself, not without a beating heart, at the wicket of the Abbey Ste. Geneviève.

CHAPTER XIX

HOW CHICOT FOUND OUT THAT IT WAS EASIER TO GO IN THAN OUT OF THE ABBEY

CHICOT, in putting on the monk's frock, had taken an important precaution,—that of increasing the width of his shoulders by a skilful disposition of his cloak and other garments which the frock made superfluous. His beard was of the same colour as Gorenflot's; and he had so often amused himself with mimicking the monk's voice and manner of speaking that he could do it perfectly. Now, every one knows that the beard and the voice are the only things which are recognisable from under the depths of a monk's hood. Chicot exhibited his coin, and was admitted without difficulty, and then followed two other monks to the chapel of the convent. In this chapel, built in the eleventh century, the choir was raised nine or ten feet above the nave, and you mounted into it by two lateral staircases, while an iron door between them led from the nave to the crypt, into which you had to descend by as many steps as there were in the ascent to the choir. In the choir there was a portrait of Saint Geneviève, and on each side of the altar were statues of Clovis and Clotilda.

Three lamps only lighted the chapel, and the imperfect light gave a greater solemnity to the scene. Chicot was glad to find that he was not the last, for three monks in grey robes entered after him and placed themselves in front of the altar. Soon after, a little monk, doubtless a lad belonging to the choir, came and spoke to one of these monks, who then said aloud, "We are now one hundred and thirty-six."

Then a great noise of bolts and bars announced that the massive doors were closed. The three monks were seated in armchairs, like judges. The one who had spoken before now rose and said, " Brother Monsoreau, what news do you bring to the Union from the province of Anjou? "

Two things made Chicot start; the first was the voice of the speaker, which seemed more suited to the battle-field than to a church; the second was the name of Monsoreau, known to the court only within the last few days. A tall monk passed with a firm and bold step through a portion of the assembly, and mounted a chair.

" My brothers," said a voice which Chicot recognised at once as that of the chief huntsman, " the news from Anjou is not satisfactory,—not that we fail there in sympathy, but in representatives. The progress of the Union there had been confided to the Baron de Méridor; but he, in despair at the recent death of his daughter, has in his grief neglected the affairs of the League, and we cannot at present count on him. As for myself, I bring three new adherents to the association. The council must judge whether these three, for whom I answer, as for myself, ought to be admitted into the Union."

A murmur of approbation ran through the assembly and continued until Brother Monsoreau had returned to his place.

" Brother la Hurière! " cried the same monk, who appeared to call on the faithful according to his own caprice, " tell us what you have done in the city of Paris."

A man now took the chair and said, " My brothers, you know I am devoted to the Catholic faith, and that I have given proofs of this devotion on the great day of its triumph. Yes, my brothers, I glory in saying that I was one of the faithful servants of our great Henri de Guise, and that I followed his orders strictly. I have now noted all the heretics of the Quartier St. Germain l'Auxerrois, where I still keep the Hôtel de la Belle Etoile, at your service, my brothers. Now, although I no longer thirst for the blood of heretics as formerly, I do not delude myself as to the real object of the holy Union which we are forming. If I am not deceived, brothers, the extinction of individual heretics is not all we aim at. We wish to be sure that we never shall be governed by a heretic prince. Now, my friends, what is our situation? François II., who promised to be zealous, died without children. Charles IX., who was zealous, died without children. Henri III. will probably do the same; and there remains only the Duc d'Anjou, who not only has no children, but seems lukewarm towards the holy League."

At this point several voices interrupted the orator, and among them that of the grand huntsman.

"Why do you say lukewarm?" said the voice; "and why do you make that accusation against the prince?"

"I say lukewarm because he has not given his adhesion to the League, although the illustrious brother who has interrupted me promised it positively in his name."

"Who tells you that he has not given it,—since there are new adherents? You have no right, it seems to me, to suspect any one so long as the report is not made."

"It is true. I will wait, then; but after the Duc d'Anjou, who is mortal, and has no children, to whom will the crown fall? To the most ferocious Huguenot that can be imagined, to a renegade, a Nebuchadnezzar!" Here the acclamations were tremendous.

"To Henri de Béarn," continued he, "against whom this association is chiefly directed,—to Henri, who the people at Pau, or Tarbes, think is occupied with his love-affairs, but who is in Paris!"

"In Paris! impossible!" cried many voices.

"He was here on the night when Madame de Sauve was assassinated, and perhaps is here still."

"Death to the Béarnais!" cried several.

"Yes, doubtless, and if he comes to lodge at the Belle Etoile, I answer for him; but he will not come. One does not catch a fox twice in the same hole. He will lodge with some friend,—for he has friends, the heretic. The important thing is to know them. Our Union is holy, our League is loyal, consecrated and blessed and encouraged by our holy Father, Pope Gregoire III.; therefore I demand that it be no longer kept secret, but that we go into the houses and canvass the citizens. Those who sign will be our friends, the others our enemies; and if a second Saint Bartholomew come, which seems to the faithful to be more necessary daily,—well, we will do as we did at the first; we will spare God the trouble of separating the good from the wicked."

Thunders of acclamation followed. When quiet was restored, the grave voice of the monk who had already spoken several times was heard saying, " The proposition of Brother la Hurière, whom the Union thanks for his zeal, will be taken into consideration by the superior council."

The plaudits increased. La Hurière bowed several times in acknowledgment, and descending from the chair, returned to his place, bending under the weight of his triumph.

" Ah, ah! " thought Chicot, " I begin to see clearly into all this. The Guises are forming a nice little party, of which they will be the masters. So the great Henri, who is a general, will have the army; so the fat Mayenne will have the citizens; so the illustrious cardinal will have the Church. And some fine morning my son Henri will find that he has nothing left, and will be politely invited to enter a monastery. But what will they do with the Duc d'Anjou? "

" Brother Gorenflot! " then cried the monk.

Whether because he was preoccupied with his reflections or because he was not yet accustomed to the name, Chicot made no reply.

" Brother Gorenflot," cried the little monk, in a voice which made Chicot start; for it sounded like a woman's. However, he rose, and speaking like the monk, said,—

" Here I am; I was plunged in profound meditation." He feared to remain silent, for the members had been counted, and therefore the absence of a member would have provoked an examination. Therefore, without hesitation, he mounted the chair and began,—

" My brothers, you know that I purvey for the convent, and have the right of entering every dwelling. I use this privilege for the good of religion. My brothers," continued he, remembering Gorenflot's beginning, " this day, which unites us, is a good one for the faith. Let us speak freely, my brothers, since we are in the house of God.

" What is the kingdom of France? A body. ' Omnis civitas corpus est.' What is the first requisite of a body? Good health. How do we preserve this? By prudent bleedings at times. Now it is evident that the enemies of our religion are too strong; we must therefore once more bleed that great body we call society. This is what is constantly said to me by the faithful, who give me ham, eggs, or money for the convent."

Several murmurs of approbation interrupted Chicot, who continued, " Some may object that the Church abhors blood.

'Ecclesia abhorret a sanguine.' But mark this, my dear brethren; the theologian does not say what blood the Church abhors. In fact, 'Fons malus corruptorum sanguis, hereticorum autem pessimus!'" And I wager that it is not the blood of heretics. And then, another argument: I said, 'the Church;' but we are not the Church only. Brother Monsoreau, who spoke so well just now, has, I doubt not, his huntsman's knife in his belt. Brother la Hurière manages the spit with facility; I, myself, who speak to you,—I, Jacques Gorenflot,—have carried the musket in Champagne. It now remains to us to speak of our chiefs, of whom it seems to me, poor monk as I am, that there is something to say. Certainly, it is very well and prudent to come at night under a monk's robe to hear Brother Gorenflot preach; but it appears to me that their duties do not stop there. So much prudence may make the Huguenots laugh. Let us play a part more worthy of the brave people that we are, or rather, that we wish to appear. What do we want? The extinction of heresy. Well, that may be cried from the house-tops, it seems to me. Why not march in holy procession, displaying our good cause, and our good partisans?—not like the thieves, who keep looking round them to see if the watch is coming. Who is the man who will set the example? Well, it is I, Jacques Gorenflot; I, unworthy brother of the order of Saint Geneviève, poor and humble purveyor of the convent. It shall be I, who with a cuirass on my back, a helmet on my head, and a musket on my shoulder, will march at the head of all good Catholics who will follow me. This I would do, were it only to make those chiefs blush who, while defending the Church, hide, as if their cause was a bad one."

This speech, which corresponded with the sentiments of many there, was received with shouts of applause; and the more so, as up to this time Gorenflot had never shown any enthusiasm for the cause. However, it was not the plan of the chiefs to let this enthusiasm proceed. One of the monks spoke to the lad, who cried in his silvery voice, " My brothers, it is time to retire; the sitting is over."

The monks rose, all determined to insist on the procession at the next meeting. Many approached the chair to felicitate the author of this brilliant speech; but Chicot, fearful of being recognised, threw himself on his knees and buried his head in his hands, as if in prayer. They respected his devotions, and went towards the door. However, Chicot had missed his chief aim. What had made him leave the king was the sight of M.

de Mayenne and Nicolas David, on both of whom he had, as
we know, vowed vengeance; and although the duke was too
great a man to be attacked openly, Nicolas David was not, and
Chicot was so good a swordsman as to feel sure of success if he
could but meet him. He therefore watched the monks as they
went out, and perceived to his terror that each, on going out,
had to show some sign again. Gorenflot had told him how to
get in, but not how to get out again.

CHAPTER XX

HOW CHICOT, FORCED TO REMAIN IN THE ABBEY, SAW AND HEARD THINGS VERY DANGEROUS TO SEE AND HEAR

CHICOT hastened to get down from his chair, and to mingle with
the monks, so as to discover, if possible, what sign they used
to regain the street, and to procure that sign if there was still
time. By peeping over their shoulders, he found out that it
was a farthing, with a star cut in the middle. Our Gascon had
plenty of farthings in his pocket, but unluckily none with a
star in it. Of course, if on coming to the door he was unable
to produce the necessary signs, he would be suspected and
examined. He gained the shade of a pillar, which stood at the
corner of a confessional, and stood there wondering what he
should do. An assistant cried, " Is every one out? the doors
are about to be shut."

No one answered; Chicot peeped out and saw the chapel
empty, except that the three monks still kept their seats in
front of the choir.

" Provided they do not shut the windows, it is all I ask,"
thought Chicot.

" Let us examine," said the lad to the porter. Then the
porter lifted a taper, and, followed by the lad, began to make
the tour of the church. There was not a moment to lose.
Chicot softly opened the door of the confessional, slipped in,
and shut the door after him. They passed close by him, and
he could see them through the spaces of the sculpture.

" The devil! " said Chicot to himself, " that porter brother,
that little monk, and those three monks will not stay in the
church for ever; once they are gone, I will pile chairs upon
benches, Pelion on Ossa, and get out of the window. Ah, yes!
but when I have done that, I shall be, not in the street, but in

the court. I believe it will be better to pass the night in the confessional. Gorenflot's robe is warm; it will be a night not so heathenish as I might have made it, and I can reckon it towards my salvation."

"Extinguish the lamps," now cried the lad; and the porter, with an immense extinguisher, put out the lamps and left the church dark, except for the rays of the moon, which shone through the windows. The clock struck twelve.

"*Ventre de biche!*" said Chicot, "midnight in a church! Henri, if he were here, would be nicely frightened; but, luckily, I am less timid. Come, Chicot, my friend, good-night, and sleep well."

Then Chicot pushed the inside bolt, made himself as comfortable as he could, and shut his eyes. He was just falling asleep when he was startled by a loud stroke on a copper bell.

"Oh!" said Chicot, opening his eyes and listening; "what is the meaning of that?"

At the same time the lamp in the choir was relighted, and showed the three monks still there.

Brave as he was, Chicot was not exempt from superstitious fears. He made the sign of the cross, murmuring, "Vade retro, Satanas!" But as the lights did not go out at the holy sign, Chicot began to think that he had to deal with real monks and real lights. At this moment one of the flag-stones of the choir was slowly raised, and a monk appeared through the opening, after which the stone quietly fell into its place. At this sight Chicot's hair stood on end, and he began to fear that all the priors and abbés of Ste. Geneviève from Optaf, dead in 533, down to Pierre Boudin, predecessor of the present superior, were coming from their tombs, and were going to raise with their bony heads the stones of the choir. But this doubt did not last long.

"Brother Monsoreau," said one of the monks to him who had just made so strange an appearance, "has he arrived whom we await?"

"Yes, Monseigneur," said he.

"Open the door, that he may come to us."

Monsoreau descended to open the door between the staircases, and at the same time the monk in the middle lowered his hood, and showed the great scar,—that noble sign by which the Parisians recognised their hero.

"The great Henri de Guise himself!" thought Chicot, "whom

his very imbecile Majesty believes occupied at the siege of La
Charité. Ah! and he at the right is the Cardinal de Lorraine,
and he at the left M. de Mayenne; but where, then, in all this
business, is Maître Nicolas David? "

In fact, as if to give immediate confirmation to Chicot's suppositions, the monks on the right and left lowered their hoods
and exposed to view the large brow and piercing eye of the
famous cardinal, and the face infinitely less noble, of the Duc
de Mayenne.

"Ah! I recognise you," said Chicot,—"a trinity not very
holy, but very visible. Now let us see what you are going to
do; I am all eyes. Let us see what you are going to say; I
am all ears."

At that very moment Monsoreau had reached the iron door
of the crypt, which opened before him.

"Did you think he would come?" said La Balafré to his
brother the cardinal.

"I was so sure of it that I have under my cloak wherewith
to replace the holy vial."

And Chicot perceived, by the feeble light of a lamp, a silver
gilt box, richly chased. Then about twenty monks, with their
heads buried in immense hoods, came out of the crypt, and
stationed themselves in the nave. A single one, conducted by
M. de Monsoreau, mounted the staircase, and placed himself at
the right of M. de Guise.

Then M. de Guise spoke. "Friends," said he, "time is precious; therefore I go straight to the point. You have heard
just now, in the first assembly, the complaints of some of our
members, who tax with coldness one of the principal persons
among us,—the prince nearest to the throne. The time is
come to render justice to this prince; you will hear him, and
will judge for yourselves whether your chiefs merit the reproach
of coldness and apathy made by one of our brothers, the monk
Gorenflot, whom we have not judged it prudent to admit into
our secret."

At this name, pronounced in a tone which showed bad intentions towards the warlike monk, Chicot in his confessional could
not help laughing quietly.

"Monseigneur," said the duke, now turning towards the
mysterious personage at his right, "the will of God appears to
me manifest; for since you have consented to join us, it shows
that what we do is well done. Now, your Highness, we beg of
you to lower your hood that your faithful friends may see with

their own eyes that you keep the promise which I made in your name, and which they hardly dared to believe."

The mysterious personage now lowered his hood, and Chicot saw the head of the Duc d'Anjou appear, so pale that by the light of the lamp it looked like that of a marble statue.

"Oh, oh!" thought Chicot, "the duke is not yet tired of playing for the crown with the heads of others!"

"Long live Monseigneur le Duc d'Anjou!" cried the assembly. The duke grew paler than ever.

"Fear nothing, Monseigneur," said Henri de Guise; "our chapel is deaf, and its doors are well closed."

"My brothers," said the Comte de Monsoreau, "his Highness wishes to address a few words to the assembly."

"Yes, yes!" cried they.

"Gentlemen," began he, in a voice so trembling that at first they could hardly distinguish his words, "I believe that God, who often seems insensible and deaf to the things of this world, keeps, on the contrary, his piercing eyes constantly on us, and remains thus careless in appearance only in order to remedy, by some great blow, the disorders caused by the foolish ambitions of men. I also have kept my eyes, if not on the world, at least on France. What have I seen there? The holy religion of Christ shaken to its foundation by those who sap all belief under the pretext of drawing nearer to God; and my soul has been full of grief. In the midst of this grief I heard that several noble and pious gentlemen, friends of our old faith, were trying to strengthen the tottering altar. I threw my eyes around me and saw on one side the heretics, from whom I recoiled with horror, on the other side the elect, and I come to throw myself into their arms. My brothers, here I am."

"Amen!" said Chicot, in a low tone.

The applause and bravos resounded through the chapel. Then the cardinal, turning to the duke, said, "You are among us of your own free will?"

"Of my free will, Monsieur."

"Who instructed you in the holy mystery?"

"My friend, the Comte de Monsoreau, a man zealous for religion."

"Then," said the Duc de Guise, "as your Highness has joined us, have the goodness to tell us what you intend to do for the League."

"I intend to serve the Catholic religion in all its demands."

"*Ventre de biche!*" thought Chicot, "what fools these are to hide themselves in order to say such things as that! Why not propose this right out to the king? It would suit him excellently,—processions, macerations, extirpation of heresy, fagots, and *auto-da-fés!* Go on, worthy brother of his Majesty, noble imbecile, go on!"

And the duke, as if sensible of the encouragement, proceeded, "But the interests of religion are not the sole aim which you gentlemen propose. As for me, I see another; for when a gentleman has thought of what he owes to God, he then thinks of his country, and he asks himself if it really enjoys all the honour and prosperity which it ought to enjoy. I ask this about our France, and I see with grief that it does not. Indeed, the state is torn to pieces by different wills and tastes, one as powerful as the others. It is, I fear, to the feebleness of the head, which forgets that it ought to govern all for the good of its subjects, or only remembers this royal principle at capricious intervals, when the rare acts of energy are generally not for the good, but the ill of France, that we must attribute these evils. Whatever be the cause, the ill is a real one, although I accuse certain false friends of the king rather than the king himself. Therefore I join myself to those who by all means seek the extinction of heresy and the ruin of perfidious counsellors."

This discourse appeared profoundly to interest the audience, who, throwing back their hoods, drew near to the duke.

"Monseigneur," said the Duc de Guise, "in thanking your royal Highness for the words you have just uttered, I will add that you are surrounded by people devoted not only to the principles which you profess, but to the person of your Highness; and if you have any doubt, the conclusion of this sitting will convince you."

"Oh, oh!" murmured Chicot, "if I am not mistaken all that I have seen is but a preamble, and something is about to happen here more important than all the fiddle-faddle that has preceded."

"Monseigneur," said the cardinal, "if your Highness still experiences any fear, the names of those who now surround you will, I hope, reassure you. Here is M. le Gouverneur d'Aunis, M. d'Antragues, M. de Ribeirac, and M. de Livarot,—gentlemen whom your Highness doubtless knows to be as brave as loyal. Here are, besides, M. de Castillon, M. le Baron de Lusignan, MM. Cruce and Leclerc, all ready to march under the guidance of your Highness to the emancipation of religion and the throne. We shall, then, receive with gratitude the orders that you will give us."

The Duc d'Anjou could not repress a movement of pride. These Guises, so proud that they never could be made to bend, talked of obeying.

Then M. de Mayenne said, " You are by your birth and by your wisdom, Monseigneur, the natural chief of the holy Union; and we ought to learn from you what our conduct should be with regard to the false friends of his Majesty of whom you just now spoke."

" Nothing more simple," replied the prince, with that feverish excitement which in weak natures supplies the place of courage; " when venomous plants grow in a field, we root them up. The king is surrounded, not by friends, but by courtiers, who ruin him, and cause a perpetual scandal in France and all Christendom."

" It is true," said the Duc de Guise, in a gloomy tone.

" And," said the cardinal, " these courtiers prevent us, who are his Majesty's true friends, from approaching him, as we have the right to do by our birth and position."

" Let us, then," said M. de Mayenne, abruptly, " leave to the common Leaguers, to those of the first League, the care of serving God. In serving him they will serve those who speak of him to them. As for us, we will attend to our affairs. Certain men annoy us; they defy us, they insult us, and they continually fail in respect to the prince whom we honour, and who is our chief."

The Duc d'Anjou grew red.

" Let us destroy," continued Mayenne, " to the last man, that cursed race whom the king enriches with the fragments of our fortunes; and let each of us charge ourselves with the life of one. We are thirty here; let us count."

" I," said D'Antragues, " charge myself with Quélus."

" I with Maugiron," said Livarot.

" And I with Schomberg," said Ribeirac.

" Good! " said the duke; " and there is Bussy, my brave Bussy, who will undertake some of them."

" And we too! " cried the rest.

M. de Monsoreau now advanced. " Gentlemen," said he, " I claim an instant's silence. We are resolute men, and yet we fear to speak freely to one another; we are intelligent men, and yet we are deterred by foolish scruples. Come, gentlemen, a little courage, a little hardihood, a little frankness. It is not of the king's favourites that we think; there does not lie our difficulty. What we really complain of is the royalty which we are

under, and which is not acceptable to a French nobility,—
prayers and despotism, weakness and orgies, prodigality for
fêtes which make all Europe laugh, and parsimony for everything that relates to war and the arts. Such conduct is not
weakness or ignorance, it is madness."

A dead silence followed this speech. Every one trembled at
the words which echoed his own thoughts. M. de Monsoreau
continued, " Must we live under a king, foolish, inert, and lazy
at a time when all other nations are active? All the nations
are working gloriously towards some purpose, while we sleep!
Gentlemen, pardon me for saying before a prince, who will perhaps blame my temerity (for he has the prejudices of family),
that for four years we have been governed, not by a king, but
by a monk."

At these words the explosion so skilfully prepared and as
skilfully kept in check for the last hour, by the circumspection
of the chiefs, burst out with violence.

" Down with the Valois! " they cried, " down with Brother
Henri! Let us have for chief a gentleman prince, a chevalier
king, a tyrant if necessary, but not a monk."

" Gentlemen! " said the Duc d'Anjou, hypocritically, " let
me plead for my brother, who deceives himself, or rather, who
is deceived. Let me hope that our wise remonstrances, that
the efficacious intervention of the power of the League, will
bring him back into the right path."

" Hiss, serpent, hiss! " said Chicot.

" Monseigneur," replied the Duc de Guise, " your Highness
has heard, perhaps rather too soon, but still you have heard a
sincere expression of the meaning of the association. No! we
are not really thinking of a league against the Béarnais, nor of
a league to support the Church, which will support itself; no,
we think of raising the nobility of France from its abject condition. Too long we have been kept back by the respect we
feel for your Highness, by the love which we know you to have
for your family. Now all is revealed, Monseigneur, and your
Highness will assist at the true sitting of the League. All that
has passed is but preamble."

" What do you mean, Monsieur the Duke? " asked the prince,
his heart beating at once with alarm and ambition.

" Monseigneur, we are united here, not only to talk, but to
act. To-day we choose a chief capable of honouring and en-
riching the nobility of France; and as it was the custom of the
ancient Franks when they chose a chief to give him a present

worthy of him, we offer a present to the chief whom we have chosen."

All hearts beat, and that of the prince most of any; yet he remained mute and motionless, betraying his emotion only by his paleness.

"Gentlemen," continued the duke, taking something from behind him, "here is the present that in your name I place at the feet of the prince."

"A crown?" cried the prince, scarcely able to stand, "a crown to me, gentlemen?"

"Long live François III.!" cried all the gentlemen, drawing their swords.

"I! I!" cried the duke, trembling with joy and terror. "It is impossible! My brother still lives; he is the anointed of the Lord."

"We depose him," said the duke, "waiting for the time when God shall sanction, by his death, the election which we have made, or rather, till one of his subjects, tired of this inglorious reign, forestalls by poison or the dagger the justice of God."

"Gentlemen!" said the duke, feebly.

"Monseigneur," then said the cardinal, "to the scruple which you so nobly expressed just now, this is our answer,—Henri III. was the anointed of the Lord, but we have deposed him; it is you who are going to be so. Here is a temple as venerable as that of Rheims, for here have reposed the relics of Saint Geneviève, patroness of Paris; here has been embalmed the body of Clovis, our first Christian king. Well, Monseigneur, in this holy temple, I, one of the princes of the Church, and who may reasonably hope to become one day its head, I tell you, Monseigneur, that here, to replace the holy oil, is an oil sent by Pope Gregoire XIII. Monseigneur, name your future Archbishop of Rheims, name your constable; and in an instant, it is you who will be king, and your brother Henri, if he do not give you up the crown, will be the usurper. Child, light the altar."

Immediately, the lad, who was evidently expecting that order, came out from the vestry with a lighter in his hand, and presently fifty lights shone round the altar and choir.

Then was seen on the altar a mitre glittering with precious stones, and a large sword ornamented with *fleurs de lis*. They were the archbishop's mitre and the constable's sword. At the same moment the organ began to play the *Veni Creator*. This sudden stroke, managed by the three Lorraine princes, and which the Duc d'Anjou himself did not expect, made a profound impression on the spectators. The courageous grew bolder than ever, and the weak grew strong. The Duc d'Anjou raised his head, and with a firmer step than might have been expected, walked to the altar, took the mitre in his left hand and the sword in his right, and presented one to the cardinal and the other to the duke. Unanimous applause followed this action.

"Now, gentlemen," said the prince to the others, "give your names to M. de Mayenne, grand master of France, and the day when I ascend the throne, you shall all be chevaliers of the order."

"*Mordieu!*" thought Chicot, "what a pity I cannot give mine! I shall never have another such opportunity."

"Now to the altar, Sire," said the cardinal.

"M. de Monsoreau, my colonel, MM. de Ribeirac and d'Antragues, my captains, and M. de Livarot, my lieutenant of the guards, take your places."

Each of those named took the posts which, at a real coronation, etiquette would have assigned to them. Meanwhile, the cardinal had passed behind the altar to put on his pontifical robes; soon he reappeared with the holy vial. Then the lad brought to him a Bible and a cross. The cardinal put the cross on the book and extended them towards the Duc d'Anjou, who put his hand on them, and said, "In the presence of God, I promise to my people to maintain and honour our holy religion as a Christian king should! And may God and his saints aid me!"

Then the Duc de Guise laid the sword before the altar, and the cardinal blessed it and gave it to the prince. "Sire," said he, "take this sword, which is given to you with the blessing of God, that you may resist your enemies, and protect and defend the holy Church and the kingdom which is confided to you. Take this sword, that with it you may exercise justice, protect the widow and the orphan, and repair disorders, so that, covering yourself with glory by all the virtues, you will deserve to reign with him whom you represent upon the earth, and who with the Father and the Holy Spirit reigns throughout all ages."

Then the prince returned the sword to the Duc de Guise, and knelt down. The cardinal opened the gold box, and with the point of a golden needle drew out some holy oil; he then said two prayers, and taking the oil on his finger traced with it a cross on the head of the prince, saying, "Ungo te regem de oleo sanctificato, in nomine Patris et Filii et Spiritûs Sancti."

The lad wiped off the oil with an embroidered handkerchief. Then the cardinal took the crown, and, holding it over the head of the prince, said, "God crown thee with the crown of glory and justice!" Then, placing it, "Receive this crown in the name of the Father, the Son, and the Holy Ghost!"

All brandished their swords and cried, "Long live François III.!"

"Sire," said the cardinal, "you reign henceforth over France, for you are consecrated by Pope Gregoire XIII. himself, whom I represent."

"Gentlemen," said the prince, "I shall never forget the names of the thirty gentlemen who first judged me worthy to reign over them; and now adieu, and may God have you in his holy keeping!"

The Duc de Mayenne led away the new king, while the other two brothers exchanged an ironical smile.

CHAPTER XXI

HOW CHICOT LEARNED GENEALOGY

WHEN the Duc d'Anjou had gone, and had been followed by all the others, the three Guises entered the vestry. Chicot, thinking that of course this was the end, got up to stretch his limbs, and then, as it was nearly two o'clock, once more disposed himself to sleep.

But to his great astonishment the three Lorraine princes almost immediately came back again, only this time without their frocks, and in their usual costume. On seeing them appear, the lad burst into so hearty a fit of laughing that Chicot caught the impulse, and he too began to laugh, without knowing why.

"Do not laugh so loud, sister," said the Duc de Mayenne; "they are hardly gone out, and might hear you."

"His sister?" said Chicot, going from one surprise to another. "Is that little monk a woman?"

In fact, the seeming lad threw back his hood and displayed a head as charming and intelligent as was ever painted by Leonardo da Vinci,—black eyes full of fun, but which could assume an expression almost terrible in its seriousness, a little rosy mouth, and a round chin terminating the perfect oval of a rather pale face. It was Madame de Montpensier, a dangerous siren who had the soul of a demon with the face of an angel.

"Ah, Brother Cardinal," cried she, in a paroxysm of laughter, "how well you acted the holy man! I was really afraid for a minute that you were taking the affair seriously; and he letting

E

himself be greased and crowned! Oh, how horrid he looked with his crown on!"

" Never mind," said the duke, " we have got what we wanted, and François cannot now deny his share. Monsoreau, who doubtless had some hidden interest of his own to serve, led the thing on well, and now D'Anjou cannot abandon us, as he did La Mole and Coconnas."

Chicot saw that they had been laughing at M. d'Anjou, and as he detested him, would willingly have embraced the Guises for that hoax,—excepting Mayenne, whose share in the embrace he would rather have given to Madame de Montpensier.

" Let us return to business," said the cardinal; " is all well closed? "

" Oh, yes! " said the duchess, " but if you like I will go and see."

" Oh, no; you must be tired."

" No; it was too amusing."

" Mayenne, you say he is here? "

" Yes."

" I have not seen him."

" I believe you; he is in concealment."

" Where, then? "

" In a confessional."

These words sounded in Chicot's ears like the hundred thousand trumpets of the Apocalypse.

" Then he has heard and seen all? " asked the duke.

" Never mind, he is one of us."

" Bring him here, Mayenne."

Mayenne descended the staircase and came straight to where Chicot was hiding. He was brave, but now his teeth chattered with terror. " Ah," thought he, trying to get out his sword from under his monk's frock, " at least I will kill him first." And with the intention of putting that courageous project into execution, Chicot, having at last found the hilt of his sword, had already put his hand on the latch of the door when the duchess called out,—

" Not that one, Mayenne; the confessional to the left."

" It was time," thought Chicot, as the duke turned away, " but who the devil can the other be? "

" Come out, Maître Nicolas David," said Mayenne; " we are alone."

" Here I am, Monseigneur," said a man, coming out of the confessional.

" You have heard all ? " asked the Duc de Guise.

" I have not lost a word, Monseigneur."

" Then you can report it to the envoy of his Holiness Gregoire XIII. ? "

" Everything."

" Now, Mayenne tells me you have done wonders for us; let us see."

" I have done what I promised, Monseigneur; that is to say, I have found a way of seating you without opposition on the throne of France ! "

" They also ! " thought Chicot; " every one, then, wants to be King of France ! "

Chicot was gay again, for in the first place, he felt safe once more; and in the second place, he had discovered a conspiracy by which he hoped to ruin his two enemies.

" To gain a legitimate right is everything," continued Nicolas David, " and I have discovered that you are the true heirs, and the Valois only a usurping branch."

" It is difficult to believe," said the duke, " that our house, however illustrious it may be, comes before the Valois."

" It is nevertheless proved, Monseigneur," said David, drawing out a parchment. The duke took it.

" What is this ? " said he.

" The genealogical tree of the house of Lorraine."

" Of which the root is ? "

" Charlemagne, Monseigneur."

" Charlemagne ! " cried the three brothers, with an air of incredulous satisfaction, " impossible ! The first Duc de Lorraine was contemporary with Charlemagne, but his name was Ranier, and he was not related to that great emperor."

" Wait, Monseigneur; you may be sure I have not raised a point to which any one may give the lie. What you want is a long lawsuit, during which you can gain over, not the people,— they are yours,—but the parliament. See, then, Monseigneur, here it is: Ranier, first Duc de Lorraine, contemporary with Charlemagne; Guilbert, his son; Henri, son of Guilbert—"

" But—" said the duke.

" A little patience, Monseigneur. Bonne—"

" Yes," said the duke, " daughter of Ricin, second son of Ranier."

" Good; to whom married ? "

" Bonne ? "

" Yes."

" To Charles de Lorraine, son of Louis IV., King of France."

" Precisely. Now add, ' brother of Lothaire, despoiled of the crown of France by the usurper, Hugh Capet.' "

" Oh, oh! " said the duke and the cardinal.

" Now, Charles de Lorraine inherited from his brother Lothaire. The race of Lothaire is extinct; therefore you are the only true heirs of the throne."

" What do you say to that, Brother? " cried the cardinal.

" I say that unluckily there exists in France a law they call the Salic law, which destroys all our pretensions."

" I expected that objection, Monseigneur," said David; " but what was the first application of the Salic law? "

" The accession of Philippe de Valois, to the prejudice of Edward of England."

" What was the date of that accession? "

" 1328," said the cardinal.

" That is to say, three hundred and forty-one years after the usurpation of Hugh Capet, two hundred and forty years after the extinction of the race of Lothaire. Then, for two hundred and forty years your ancestors had already had a right to the throne before the Salic law was invented. Now, every one knows that the law cannot have any retroactive effect."

" You are a clever man, Maître Nicolas David," said the Duc de Guise, looking at the advocate with admiration not unmixed with contempt.

" It is very ingenious," said the cardinal.

" It is very fine," said Mayenne.

" It is admirable," said the duchess. " Then I am a princess royal. I will have no one less than the Emperor of Germany for a husband."

" My God," said Chicot, " thou knowest that I have never made to thee other prayer than this: Lead us not into temptation, and deliver us from lawyers! "

The Duc de Guise alone remained thoughtful in the midst of the general enthusiasm. " And to think," he murmured, " that such subterfuges are necessary to a man of my build! To think that before rendering obedience, the people give attention to parchments like that instead of reading a man's rank in the lightning of his eyes or of his sword! However," he continued, " the genealogy is good, and here are the two hundred gold crowns which my brother Mayenne has demanded for you, Maître Nicolas David."

"And here are two hundred others," said the cardinal, "for the new mission with which we are about to charge you."

"Speak, Monseigneur, I am ready."

"We cannot commission you to carry this genealogy yourself to our holy Father, Gregoire XIII."

"Alas! no; my will is good, but I am of too poor birth."

"Yes, it is a misfortune. We must therefore send Pierre de Gondy on this mission."

"Permit me to speak," said the duchess. "The Gondys are clever, no doubt, but ambitious, and not to be trusted."

"Oh, reassure yourself! Gondy shall take this, but mixed with other papers, and not knowing what he carries. The pope will approve, or disapprove, silently, and Gondy will bring us back the answer, still in ignorance of what he brings. You, Nicolas David, shall wait for him at Châlons, Lyon, or Avignon, according to your instructions. Thus you alone will know our true secret."

Then the three brothers shook hands, and embraced their sister, who had just brought to them their monk's frocks. Then, after assisting in putting them on, she drew her hood down over her eyes, and went, preceding the others, to the door, where they disappeared, followed by Nicolas David, whose crowns of gold clinked at every step. Behind them the porter drew the bolts, and then came in and extinguished the lights. Dense darkness filled the church and revived in Chicot that mysterious horror which already more than once had made his hair stand on end. Then the sound of the monk's sandals on the pavement became fainter until it ceased altogether. Five minutes—very long to Chicot—passed by without any interruption of the silence.

"Good!" said Chicot, "it seems that this time all is really finished; the three acts have been played, and the actors have departed. Let me try to follow them; I have had comedy enough for one night."

Chicot, who, since he had seen tombstones moving and confessionals occupied, had changed his mind about staying in the church till daylight, gently raised the latch, cautiously pushed open the door, and put his foot outside the box. He had noticed in a corner a ladder designed for use in cleaning windows. He lost no time. Extending his arms, moving his feet carefully, he reached the corner without noise, put his hand on the ladder, and placed it against a window. By the moonlight he saw that he had not been mistaken in his reckoning. The window opened on the convent cemetery, which bordered on the Rue Bordelle.

He opened the window, placed himself on the sill as on a saddle, and drawing the ladder to him with that force and address which fear or joy always gives, he drew it from the inside to the outside. When he had descended, he hid the ladder in a hedge which was planted at the bottom of the wall and jumped from tomb to tomb, until he reached the outside wall, over which he clambered. Once in the street he breathed more freely; he had escaped with a few scratches from the place where he had several times felt his life in danger. He went straight to the Corne d'Abondance, where he knocked at the door without hesitation or delay. It was opened by Claude Bonhomet himself, who knew him at once, although he went out dressed as a cavalier, and returned as a monk.

"Ah! is it you, my gentleman?" cried he. "Welcome!"

Chicot gave him a crown, and asked for Gorenflot.

The host smiled, and said, "Look!"

Brother Gorenflot lay snoring in the same place where Chicot had left him.

"*Ventre de biche!* my respectable friend," said Chicot; "you have had, without suspecting it, a terrible nightmare."

CHAPTER XXII

HOW MONSIEUR AND MADAME DE SAINT-LUC MET WITH A TRAVELLING-COMPANION

THE next morning, about the time when Gorenflot woke from his nap, warmly rolled in his frock, our reader, if he had been travelling on the road from Paris to Angers, might have seen a gentleman and his page, riding quietly side by side. These cavaliers had arrived at Chartres the evening before with foaming horses, one of which had fallen with fatigue as they stopped. They entered the inn, and half an hour after set out on fresh horses. Once in the country, still bare and cold, the taller of the two approached the other, and said, as he opened his arms, "Dear little wife, embrace me, for now we are safe."

Then Madame de Saint-Luc, leaning forward and opening her thick cloak, placed her arms round the young man's neck, and gave him the long and tender kiss which he had asked for. They stopped for the night in the little village of Courville, four leagues only from Chartres, which from its isolation seemed to them a secure retreat; and it was on the following morning that they were, as we said, pursuing their way. This day, as they were more easy in their minds, they travelled no longer like fugitives, but like school-children seeking for moss, for the first few early flowers, enjoying the sunshine, and amused at everything.

" *Morbleu!* " cried Saint-Luc, at last, " how delightful it is to be free! Have you ever been free, Jeanne? "

" I? " she replied in a joyous tone; " never. It is the first time I ever felt so. My father was suspicious, and my mother lazy. I never went out without a governess, two waiting-maids, and a tall lackey; so that I do not remember having run on the grass since, when a laughing child, I ran in the woods of Méridor with my dear Diane, challenging her to race, and rushing through the branches. But you, dear Saint-Luc,—you were free, at least? "

" I free? "

" Doubtless; a man! "

" Never. Brought up with the Duc d'Anjou, taken by him to Paris, condemned never to leave him by the perpetual rule of etiquette; pursued, if I tried to go away, by that doleful voice, crying, ' Saint-Luc, my friend, I am *ennuyé*, come and amuse me.' Free, with that stiff corset which choked my stomach, and that great ruff which scratched my neck! No, I have never been free till now, and I enjoy it."

" If they should catch us, and send us to the Bastille? "

" If they only put us there together we can bear it."

" I do not think they would. But there is no fear, and we shall be well concealed. If you only knew Méridor,—its great oaks, and its endless thickets, its rivers, its lakes, its flower-beds and lawns; and, then, in the midst of all, the queen of this kingdom, the beautiful, the good, the incomparable Diane, —a heart of diamond in a setting of gold. You will love her, Saint-Luc."

" I love her already; she has loved you."

" Oh, I am sure that she loves me still and will love me always; she is not capricious in her friendships. Think of the happy life we shall lead there."

" Let us push on; I am in haste to get there."

They quickened their pace, and completed the journey to Chartres au Mans, where they remained over night, and next morning set off with the intention of reaching Méridor that evening. They had already reached the woods and thought themselves in safety, when they saw behind them a cavalier advancing at a rapid pace. Saint-Luc grew pale.

" Let us fly," said Jeanne.

" Yes, let us fly, for there is a plume on that hat which disquiets me; it is of a colour much in vogue at the court, and he looks to me like an ambassador from our royal master." And taking Jeanne's horse by the bridle, he entered the forest.

But the trees were so numerous as to form before them a wall of branches, and the soil was so sandy that the horses sank into it at every step. Meantime, the cavalier rapidly approached, and they could hear the gallop of his horse.

" He is stopping," said the young woman.

" And in fact he dismounts," said Saint-Luc. " He enters the wood. Ah, my faith! were it the Devil himself I will go and meet him."

" Wait," said Jeanne, detaining her husband; " wait, I think he is calling."

The unknown, after tying his horse to a tree, entered the wood, calling out,—

" Eh, Monsieur, do not run away; I bring you something you have lost."

" What does he say? " asked Jeanne.

" He says we have lost something."

" Eh, Monsieur," cried the unknown, again, " you left a bracelet in the hotel at Courville. *Diable!* a lady's portrait,— that of Madame de Cossé. For the sake of that dear mamma, do not run away."

" I know that voice," said Saint-Luc.

" And then he speaks of my mother."

" Why, it is Bussy! " cried Saint-Luc.

" The Comte de Bussy, our friend? " said Jeanne.

" Yes, certainly, our friend," said Saint-Luc; and he hastened to meet him with as much eagerness as he had shown in avoiding him.

" Saint-Luc! I was not mistaken, then," said Bussy, with his sonorous voice; and he approached them with a bound. " Good-morning, Madame," said he, laughing, and giving her the bracelet.

" Have you come from the king to arrest us? " said Jeanne, smiling.

" No, indeed; I am not sufficiently his Majesty's friend for such a mission. No, I found your bracelet at the hotel, which showed me that you preceded me on my way."

"Then," said Saint-Luc, with a lingering suspicion, "it is chance which brings you on our path."

"Chance, or rather Providence."

Every remaining shadow of distrust vanished before the sincere smile and bright eyes of the handsome speaker.

"Then you are travelling?" asked Jeanne.

"I am," said Bussy, mounting his horse.

"But not like us?"

"Unhappily, no."

"I mean in disgrace. Where are you going?"

"Towards Angers, and you?"

"We also."

"Ah! I should envy your happiness if envy were not so vile."

"Eh, M. de Bussy! marry, and you will be as happy as we are," said Jeanne; "it is so easy to be happy when you are loved."

"Ah, Madame, every one is not so fortunate as you."

"But you, the man loved by every one."

"To be loved by every one is as though you were loved by no one, Madame."

"Well, let me find you a wife and you will know the happiness you deny."

"I do not deny the happiness, Madame; I deny only that it exists for me."

"Will you allow me to find you a wife?" repeated Madame de Saint-Luc.

"If you marry me according to your taste, no; if according to mine, yes."

"You say that like a man determined to remain single."

"Perhaps."

"Are you then in love with a woman whom you cannot marry?"

"Count," said Bussy, "beg your wife not to plunge daggers in my heart."

"Take care, Bussy; you will make me think it is with her that you are in love."

"If it were so, you will confess, at least, that I am a lover full of delicacy, and that husbands have no reason to be jealous of me."

"True," said Saint-Luc, remembering how Bussy had brought him his wife. "But confess that your heart is captured."

"I avow it."

"By a love or by a caprice?" asked Jeanne.

" By a passion, Madame."

" I will cure you."

" I do not believe it."

" I will see that you are married."

" I doubt it."

" And I will make you as happy as you ought to be."

" Alas, Madame, my only happiness now is to be unhappy."

" I am very determined, I warn you," said Jeanne.

" And I also."

" Well, will you accompany us? "

" Where are you going? "

" To the Château de Méridor."

The blood mounted to the cheeks of Bussy, and then he grew so pale that his secret would certainly have been betrayed, had not Jeanne been looking at her husband with a smile. Bussy therefore had time to recover himself, and said, " Where is that?"

" It is the property of one of my best friends."

" One of your best friends? And is she at home? "

" Doubtless," said Jeanne, who was completely ignorant of the events of the last two months; " but have you never heard of the Baron de Méridor, one of the richest noblemen in France, and—"

" And—" repeated Bussy, seeing that she hesitated.

" Of his daughter, Diane, the most beautiful girl ever seen? "

" No, Madame," replied Bussy, almost suffocated by emotion. And he asked himself by what singular good fortune he found on the road companions to talk to him of Diane de Méridor,— to echo the only thought which he had in his mind.

" Is this château far off, Madame? " asked he.

" About seven leagues; we shall sleep there to-night. You will come, will you not? "

" Yes, Madame."

" Good! that is already a step towards the happiness I promised you.'

" And the baron, what sort of a man is he? "

" A perfect gentleman, a chevalier who, had he lived in King Arthur's time, would have had a place at the Round Table."

" And," said Bussy, steadying his voice, " to whom is his daughter married? "

" Diane married? "

" Would that be extraordinary? "

" Of course not; only I should have been the first to hear of it."

Bussy could not repress a sigh. "Then," said he, "you expect to find Mademoiselle de Méridor at the château with her father?"

"We trust so."

There was a moment of silence while each followed his own thought.

"Ah!" cried Jeanne, suddenly, "there are the turrets of the château. Look, M. de Bussy, through that great leafless wood, which in a month will be so beautiful; do you not see the roof?"

"Yes," said Bussy, with an emotion which astonished himself; "and is that the Château de Méridor?"

And he thought of the poor prisoner shut up in the Rue St. Antoine.

CHAPTER XXIII

THE OLD MAN

Two hours later they reached the château. Bussy had been debating within himself whether or not to confide to his friends what he knew about Diane. But there was much that he could tell to no one, and he feared their questions; and, besides, he wished to enter Méridor as a stranger.

Madame de Saint-Luc was surprised, when the porter sounded his horn to announce a visit, that Diane did not run as usual to meet them. Instead of Diane appeared an old man bent and leaning on a stick, and his white hair flying in the wind. He crossed the drawbridge, followed by two great dogs, and when quite near, he said in a feeble voice, "Who is there? And who does a poor old man the honour to visit him?"

"It is I, Seigneur Augustin!" cried the laughing voice of the young woman.

But the baron, raising his head slowly, said, "You? I do not see. Who is it?"

"Oh, *mon Dieu!*" cried Jeanne, "do you not know me? It is true, my disguise——"

"Excuse me," said the old man, "but I can see little; the eyes of old men are not made for weeping, and if they weep too much, the tears burn them."

"Must I tell you my name? I am Madame de Saint-Luc."

"I do not know you."

"Ah; but my maiden name was Jeanne de Cossé-Brissac."

"Ah, *mon Dieu!*" cried the old man, trying to open the gate with his trembling hands. Jeanne, who did not understand this strange reception, still attributed it only to his declining faculties, but seeing that he remembered her, jumped off her horse and ran to throw herself into his arms; but in embracing the baron she felt his cheek wet with tears.

"It is with joy," she thought, "ah! the heart is always young."

"Come," said the old man, turning towards the house, without even noticing the others. The château had a strange, sad look; all the blinds were down, and the servants whom they saw were dressed in black.

"Is Diane unfortunately not at home?" asked Jeanne.

The old man stopped, and looked at her with an almost terrified expression. "Diane!" said he. At this name the two dogs uttered a mournful howl. "Diane!" repeated the old man; "do you not, then, know?" And his voice, trembling before, was extinguished in a sob.

"But what has happened?" cried Jeanne, clasping her hands.

"Diane is dead!" cried the old man, with a torrent of tears.

"Dead!" cried Jeanne, growing as pale as death.

"Dead!" thought Bussy; "then he has let him also think her dead. Poor old man! how he will bless me some day!"

"Dead!" cried the old man, again; "they killed her."

"Ah, my dear baron!" cried Jeanne, bursting into tears, and throwing her arms round the old man's neck.

"But," said he, at last, "though desolate and empty, the old house is none the less hospitable. Enter."

Jeanne took the old man's arm, and they went into the dining-hall, where he sank into his armchair. The valet opened a window to admit the air and withdrew to a corner of the chamber.

Jeanne did not dare to break the silence; she feared to reopen the old man's wounds by questioning him. Nevertheless she was like all who are young and happy; she could not regard as real the misery which he expressed. There is a period of life in which one cannot fathom the abyss of death, because one does not believe in it.

It was the baron who spoke first. "You have told me that you are married, my dear Jeanne. Is Monsieur"—indicating Bussy—"your husband?"

"No, Seigneur Augustin; this is M. de Saint-Luc."

M. de Saint-Luc advanced and bowed to the old man, who tried to smile as he saluted him, then, turning to Bussy, said, "And this gentleman?"

" He is our friend, M. Louis de Clermont, Comte de Bussy d'Amboise, gentleman of M. le Duc d'Anjou."

At these words the old man started up, threw a withering glance at Bussy, and then sank back with a groan.

" What is it? " said Jeanne.

" Does the baron know you, M. de Bussy? " asked Saint-Luc.

" It is the first time I ever had the honour of seeing M. de Méridor," said Bussy, who alone understood the effect which the name of the Duc d'Anjou had produced on the old man.

" Ah! you are a gentleman of the Duc d'Anjou! " cried the baron,—" of that monster, that demon, and you dare to avow it! You have the audacity to present yourself here! "

" Is he mad? " asked Saint-Luc of his wife.

" Grief must have turned his brain," replied she, in terror.

" Yes, that monster! " cried he, again; " the assassin who killed my child! Ah, you do not know," continued he, taking Jeanne's hands; " but the duke killed my Diane, my child,— he killed my child! "

He uttered these words with such an accent of grief that tears came to the eyes of Bussy himself.

" Seigneur," said the young woman, " were it so, which I do not understand, you cannot accuse M. de Bussy of this dreadful crime,—the most noble and generous gentleman living. See, my good father, he weeps with us. Would he have come had he known how you would receive him? Ah, dear baron, tell us how this catastrophe happened! "

" Then you did not know? " said the old man to Bussy.

Bussy bowed without answering.

" Eh, *mon Dieu!* no," cried Jeanne, " we none of us knew."

" My Diane is dead, and her best friend did not know it! Oh, it is true! I wrote to no one; it seemed to me that everything must die with her. Well, this prince, this disgrace to France, saw my Diane, and, finding her so beautiful, had her carried away to his Château de Beaugé to dishonour her. But Diane, my pure and noble Diane, chose death instead. She threw herself from the window into the lake, and they found nothing but her veil floating on the surface." And the old man finished with a burst of sobs which overwhelmed them all.

" Oh, Count," cried Saint-Luc, " you must abandon this infamous prince; a noble heart like yours cannot remain friendly to a ravisher and an assassin! "

The old man, a little comforted by these words, awaited

Bussy's response, which would determine his opinion of that gentleman.

But Bussy, instead of replying to Saint-Luc's apostrophe, advanced to M. de Méridor. "Monsieur the Baron," said he, "will you grant me the honour of a private interview?"

"Listen to M. de Bussy, dear seigneur," said Jeanne; "you will see that he is good and may help you."

"Speak, Monsieur," said the baron, trembling; for he perceived a strange significance in the young man's expression.

Bussy turned to Saint-Luc and his wife, and said, "Will you permit me?"

The young couple went out, and then Bussy said, "Monsieur the Baron, you have accused the prince whom I serve in terms which force me to ask for an explanation." The old man made a movement. "Oh, do not misconceive the entirely respectful meaning of my words; it is with the most profound sympathy and the most earnest desire to soften your griefs that I beg of you to recount to me the details of the sad catastrophe. Let us see whether everything took place as you believe, and whether all hope is lost."

"Monsieur, I had once a moment's hope. A noble and loyal gentleman, M. de Monsoreau, loved my poor daughter, and interested himself for her."

"M. de Monsoreau! Well, what was his conduct in all this?"

"Ah, generous; for Diane had refused his hand. He was the first to tell me of the infamous projects of the duke; he showed me how to baffle them, only asking, if he succeeded, for her hand. I gave my consent with joy; but alas! it was useless. He arrived too late,—my poor Diane had saved herself by death!"

"And since then have you received any intelligence from him?"

"It is only a month since these events occurred, and the poor man has doubtless been reluctant to appear before me, having failed in his generous design."

"Well, Monsieur," said Bussy, "I am charged by the Duc d'Anjou to bring you to Paris, where his Highness desires to speak to you."

"To speak to me! to me! Shall I go into the presence of that man after the death of my daughter?" cried the baron. "And what can the murderer have to say to me?"

"Who knows? To justify himself perhaps."

"No, M. de Bussy, no, I will not go to Paris; it would be too far away from where my child lies in her cold bed."

"Monsieur the Baron," said Bussy, firmly, "permit me to insist. It is my duty to conduct you to Paris, and I have come expressly for that purpose."

"Well, I will go," cried the old man, trembling with anger; "but woe to those who have ruined me! The king will hear me, or, if he will not, I will appeal to all the gentlemen of France. Yes, M. de Bussy, I will accompany you."

"And I, Monsieur the Baron," said Bussy, taking his hand, "recommend to you the patience and calm dignity of a Christian nobleman. God is merciful to noble hearts, and you know not what he reserves for you. I beg you also, while waiting for that day, not to count me among your enemies, for you do not know what I will do for you. Till to-morrow, then, Baron; and early in the morning we will set off."

"I consent," replied the old baron, moved by Bussy's tone and words; "but meanwhile, friend or enemy, you are my guest, and I will show you to your room."

CHAPTER XXIV

HOW RÉMY LE HAUDOUIN HAD, IN BUSSY'S ABSENCE, ESTABLISHED COMMUNICATION WITH THE RUE ST. ANTOINE

MONSIEUR AND MADAME DE SAINT-LUC could hardly recover from their surprise. Bussy holding secret interviews with M. de Méridor, and then setting off with him for Paris, appearing to take the lead in a matter which at first seemed strange and unknown to him, was to the young people an inexplicable phenomenon. In the morning the baron took leave of his guests, begging them to remain in the château. Before Bussy left, however, he whispered a few words to Madame de Saint-Luc which brought the colour to her cheeks, and smiles to her eyes.

It was a long way from Méridor to Paris, especially for the old baron, covered with wounds from all his battles, and for his old horse, whom he called Jarnac. Bussy studied earnestly during the journey to find his way to the heart of the old man by his care and attentions, and without doubt he succeeded, for on the sixth morning, as they arrived at Paris, M. de Méridor said, "It is singular, Count; I am nearer than ever to the source of my misfortune, and yet I feel less unquiet at the end than I did at the beginning of my journey."

"Two hours more, Monsieur the Baron, and you shall have judged me as I deserve."

"Where are we going,—to the Louvre?"

"Let me first take you to my hotel, that you may refresh yourself a little, and be fit to see the person to whom I am leading you."

The count's people had been very much alarmed at his long absence, for he had set off without telling any one but Rémy. Thus their delight on seeing him again was great, and they all crowded round him with joyous exclamations. He thanked them, and then said, "Now assist this gentleman to dismount, and remember that I look upon him with more respect than I should have for a prince."

When M. de Méridor had been shown to his room and had had some refreshment, he asked if they should set out.

"Soon, Baron; and be easy,—it will be a happiness not only for you, but for me also."

"What do you mean? And how does it happen that you so often say what I cannot understand?"

"I have spoken to you of a Providence compassionate for great souls; we approach the moment when in your name I shall make an appeal to that Providence."

The baron looked at Bussy with astonishment; but Bussy, making a respectful gesture which meant, "I will return immediately," went out with a smile on his lips. As he had supposed, Rémy awaited him near the door. He took the young man by the arm and led him into a cabin. "Well, dear Hippocrates!" said he, "is there anything new?"

"Nothing; all goes well."

"Then the husband has not returned?"

"Yes, he has, but without success. It seems there is a father who is expected to turn up to make the *dénouement*."

"Good!" said Bussy, "but how do you know all this?"

"Why, Monseigneur, as your absence made my position a sinecure, I thought I would try to make some little use of my time; so I took some books and a sword to a little room which I hired at the corner of the Rue St. Antoine, whence I could see the house that you know."

"Very good."

"But as I feared, if I were constantly watching, to pass for a spy, I thought it prudent to fall in love."

" In love ? "

" Oh, yes, desperately, with Gertrude; she is a fine girl, only two inches taller than myself, and an excellent narrator."

" Narrator ? "

" Yes; through her I know all that happens in the house. I thought you might not dislike to have communications with it."

" Rémy, you are a good genius, whom chance, or rather Providence, has placed in my way. Then you are received in the house ? "

" Last night I made my entrance on the points of my toes, by the door you know."

" And how did you manage it ? "

" Quite naturally. The day after my taking possession of the little chamber, I waited at my door till the lady of my thoughts came out to buy provisions, which she does every morning. She recognised me, uttered a cry, and ran away."

" Then ? "

" Then I ran after her, but could hardly catch her, for she runs fast; but still, petticoats are always a little in the way. '*Mon Dieu!*' she cried. 'Holy Virgin!' said I. That gave her a favourable idea of me. Another, less pious than I, would have cried, '*Morbleu!*' or '*Corbœuf!*' 'The doctor!' she said. 'The charming housekeeper!' I responded. She smiled, but said, 'You are mistaken, Monsieur, I do not know you.' 'But I know you,' I replied; 'and for the last three days I have lived but for you. And I adore you so much that I no longer live in the Rue Beautreillis, but at the corner of this street; and I changed my lodging only to see you pass in and out.'"

" So that now you are— "

" As happy as a lover can be—with Gertrude, you understand; all is relative. But I am not only happy, I am at the height of felicity in having accomplished what I designed in your interest."

" Does she suspect you come from me ? "

" Oh, no; how should the poor doctor know a great lord like M. de Bussy ? No; I said, 'And how is your young master ?' 'What young master ?' 'The one I cured.' 'He is not my master.' 'Oh! I thought as he was in your mistress's bed—' 'Oh, no, poor young man! we have seen him only once since.' 'Do you know his name ?' 'Oh, yes! he is the Seigneur de Bussy.' 'What! the brave Bussy ?' 'Yes, himself.' 'And your mistress ?' 'Oh, she is married!' 'Yes, but still she

may think sometimes of a handsome young man when she has
seen him lying wounded in her bed.' 'Oh, to be frank, I do
not say she does not think of him; we talk of him very often.'
'What do you say about him?' I asked. 'I recount all I hear
about his prowess, and I have even taught her a little song
about him, which she sings constantly.'"

Bussy pressed the young man's hand; he felt supremely
happy. "Is that all?" said he,—so insatiable is man in his
desires.

"All, Monseigneur. Oh! but I shall learn more later. What
the devil! one can't find out everything in a day, or rather, in
a night."

CHAPTER XXV

THE FATHER AND DAUGHTER

On descending into the court, M. de Méridor found a fresh
horse, which Bussy had had prepared for him; another waited
for Bussy, and attended by Rémy, they started. As they went
along, the baron could not but ask himself by what strange
confidence he had accompanied, almost blindly, the friend of
the prince to whom he owed all his misfortunes. Would it not
have been better to have braved the Duc d'Anjou, and instead
of following Bussy where it pleased him to lead, to have gone
at once to the Louvre, and thrown himself at the feet of the
king? What could the prince say to him? How could he
console him? Could soft words heal his wounds?

When they stopped, "What!" said the baron, "does the
Duc d'Anjou live in this humble house?"

"Not exactly, Monsieur, but if it is not his dwelling, it is
that of a lady whom he has loved."

A cloud passed over the face of the old gentleman. "Monsieur," said he, "we provincials are not used to the easy manners
of Paris; they annoy us. It seems to me that if the Duc
d'Anjou wishes to see the Baron de Méridor, it ought to be at
his palace, and not at the house of one of his mistresses."

"Come, come, Baron!" said Bussy, with his smile, which
always carried conviction with it, "do not hazard false conjectures. On my honour, the lady whom you are going to see is
perfectly virtuous and worthy in all respects."

"Who is she then?"

"She is—the wife of a friend of yours."

" Really! but then, Monsieur, why did you say the duke loved her? "

" Because I always speak the truth. But enter, and you shall see accomplished all I have promised you."

" Take care. I wept for my child, and you said, ' Console yourself, Monsieur, the mercy of God is great; ' to promise me a consolation to my grief was almost to promise me a miracle."

" Enter, Monsieur," said Bussy, with his bright smile.

Bussy went in first, and running up to Gertrude, said, " Go and tell Madame de Monsoreau that M. de Bussy is here, and desires to speak to her. But," continued he, in a low voice, " not a word of the person who accompanies me."

" Madame de Monsoreau! " said the old man, in astonishment. But as he feebly mounted the staircase, he heard the voice of Diane crying, " M. de Bussy, Gertrude? Oh, let him come in! "

" That voice! " cried the baron, stopping. " Oh, *mon Dieu! mon Dieu!* "

At that moment, as the baron tremblingly held on to the baluster, and looked around him, he saw at the top of the staircase, Diane, smiling, and more beautiful than ever. At this sight the old man uttered a cry and would have fallen, had he not caught hold of Bussy, who stood by him.

" Diane alive! Diane! my Diane, who they told me was dead! Oh, my God! "

" *Mon Dieu!* M. de Bussy! " cried Diane, running down, " what is the matter with my father? "

" He thought you dead, Madame, and he wept, as a father must weep for a daughter like you."

" How! " cried Diane; " and no one undeceived him? "

" No one."

" No," cried the old man, recovering a little, " no one, not even M. de Bussy."

" Ungrateful! " said Bussy, in a tone of gentle reproach.

" Oh, yes! you are right; for this moment repays me for all my griefs. Oh, my Diane! my beloved Diane! " cried he, drawing his daughter to him with one hand, and extending the other to Bussy. But all at once he cried, " But you said I was to see Madame de Monsoreau. Where is she? "

" Alas, my father! " murmured Diane.

Bussy summoned up all his strength. " M. de Monsoreau is your son-in-law," he said.

" What! my son-in-law? and every one—even you, Diane —left me in ignorance."

" I feared to write, my father; he said my letters would fall into the hands of the prince. Besides, I thought you knew all."

" But why all these strange mysteries? "

" Ah, yes, my father; why did M. de Monsoreau let you think me dead, and not let you know I was his wife? "

The baron, overwhelmed, looked from Bussy to Diane. " M. de Monsoreau my son-in-law! " stammered he.

" That cannot astonish you, Father; did not you order me to marry him? "

" Yes, if he saved you."

" Well! he did save me," said Diane, sinking down on a chair, " not from unhappiness, but at least from shame."

" Then why did he let me think you dead,—I, who wept for you so bitterly? Why did he let me die of despair, when a single word would have restored me? "

" Oh! there is some hidden mystery," cried Diane. " My father, you will not leave me again; M. de Bussy, you will protect us? "

" Alas, Madame! it belongs to me no more to enter into your family secrets. Seeing the strange manœuvres of your husband, I wished to bring you a defender. You have your father; I retire."

" He is right," said the old man, sadly. " M. de Monsoreau feared the Duc d'Anjou, and so does M. de Bussy."

Diane cast a glance at the young man, which meant, " You, whom they call ' the brave Bussy,' are you, like Monsoreau, afraid of the Duc d'Anjou? "

Bussy understood the look, and smiled. " Monsieur the Baron," he said, " excuse, I beg, the singular question I am about to ask; and you also, Madame, for I wish to serve you. Monsieur the Baron, ask Madame de Monsoreau if she be happy in the marriage which she has contracted in obedience to your orders."

Diane burst into tears for her only answer. The eyes of the baron filled also, for he began to fear that his friendship for M. de Monsoreau had tended to make his daughter unhappy.

" Now," said Bussy, " is it true that you voluntarily promised him your daughter's hand? "

" Yes, if he saved her."

" And he did save her. Then, Monsieur, I need not ask if you mean to keep your promise."

" It is a law for all, and, above all, for gentlemen; you know that, M. de Bussy. My daughter must be his."

" Ah! " murmured the young woman, " would I were dead! "

" Madame," said Bussy, " you see I was right, and that I can do no more here. Monsieur the Baron gives you to M. de Monsoreau, and you have promised yourself to him when you should see your father again safe and well."

" Ah! you tear my heart, M. de Bussy," cried Diane, approaching the young man; " my father does not know that I fear this man, that I hate him. My father persists in seeing him as my saviour, and I—I, whom my instincts enlighten—I persist in saying that he is my executioner."

" Diane! Diane! " cried the baron, " he saved you! "

" Yes," cried Bussy, carried beyond the bounds within which his prudence and delicacy had restrained him until then, " but if the danger were less than you thought,—if the danger were fictitious? What do we know? There is some mystery in all this, which I must clear up. But I protest to you that if I had had the happiness to be in the place of M. de Monsoreau, I would have saved your young and beautiful daughter without exacting a price for it."

" He loved her," said M. de Méridor, who, however, perceived how odious Monsoreau's conduct had been; " and to love we must forgive much."

" And I, then—" cried Bussy; and although he stopped, frightened at what he was about to say, Diane heard and understood.

" Well! " cried she, reddening, " my brother, my friend, can you do nothing for me? "

" But the Duc d'Anjou? " said the baron.

" I am not one of those who fear the anger of princes," said Bussy; " and besides, I am much mistaken if we have anything to fear from him. If you wish, M. de Méridor, I will put you on so good terms with the prince that he will protect you against M. de Monsoreau, from whom comes, believe me, the real danger, —a danger unknown, but certain; invisible, but perhaps inevitable."

" But if the duke learns that Diane is alive, all is lost."

" I see," said Bussy, " you believe M. de Monsoreau more than me. Say no more; you refuse my aid. Throw yourself, then, into the arms of the man who has already so well merited your confidence. I have accomplished my task; I retire. Adieu, Baron; adieu, Madame. You will see me no more."

" Oh! " cried Diane, taking his hand. " Have you seen me waver for an instant? Have you ever seen me soften towards him? No. I beg you on my knees, M. de Bussy, not to abandon me."

Bussy seized her hands, and all his anger melted away like snow before the sun. "Then so be it, Madame," said he; "I accept the mission, and in three days—for I must have time to go to Chartres to the prince—you shall see me again." Then, in a low tone to her, he said, "We are allied against this Monsoreau; remember that it was not he who brought you back your father, and be faithful to me."

CHAPTER XXVI

HOW BROTHER GORENFLOT AWOKE, AND THE RECEPTION HE MET WITH AT HIS CONVENT

CHICOT, after seeing with pleasure that Gorenflot still slept soundly, told Maître Bonhomet to retire and to take the light with him, charging him not to say anything of his absence. Now Maître Bonhomet, having remarked that the relations between the monk and Chicot were such that Chicot paid the bills, had a great deal of consideration for him, promised to observe silence in regard to what had occurred during the night, and departed, leaving the two friends in darkness.

Chicot immediately noticed with admiration that Brother Gorenflot could snore and talk at the same time. It indicated, not, as might be thought, a conscience harrowed by remorse, but a stomach overloaded with food. The words pronounced by Gorenflot in his sleep were a strange mixture of sacred eloquence and bacchanalian maxims. Meanwhile Chicot discovered that if he remained in complete darkness he should find it difficult to accomplish the restitution of the monk's frock, which still remained to be achieved, so that Gorenflot, on awaking, might mistrust nothing; in fact, he might in that complete darkness step on some one or more of the monk's four limbs, whose location he could not determine, and thus arouse him from his lethargy. He therefore blew upon the coals in the brazier to light up the room a little.

At the sound of that blowing Gorenflot stopped snoring and murmured, "My brethren, here is a mighty wind. It is the Lord; it is his breath inspiring me;" and he betook himself to snoring again.

Chicot waited a moment for sleep to resume its sway, and then began to unwrap the monk.

" Brrrou! " said Gorenflot. " How cold! That will hinder the ripening of the grapes."

Chicot stopped in the midst of his work, which he resumed a moment later.

" You know my zeal, Brethren," continued the monk, " for the Church and for Monseigneur le Duc de Guise."

" *Canaille !* " said Chicot.

" That is my opinion," said Gorenflot, " but it is certain—"

" What is certain? " asked Chicot, as he lifted the monk to put on his frock.

" It is certain that man is stronger than wine; Brother Gorenflot has wrestled with wine as Jacob wrestled with the angel, and Brother Gorenflot has overcome the wine."

Chicot shrugged his shoulders; and that untimely movement made the monk half open his eyes. He saw the smiling face of Chicot, which in that weird light seemed pale and sinister.

" Ah! " said the monk; " come now, no ghosts, no foolishness! " as if he were remonstrating with some familiar demon, unmindful of his agreement.

" He is dead drunk," said Chicot; and he finished putting on the robe, and then put the monk's hood on his head.

" All right! " muttered Gorenflot; " the sacristan has closed the door of the choir and the wind has stopped blowing in."

" Wake up now whenever you please," said Chicot; " it is all one to me."

" The Lord has heard my prayer," murmured the monk; " and the north wind which he had sent to freeze the vines is changed to a gentle zephyr."

" Amen! " said Chicot. And making a pillow of the napkins and table-cloth, after placing the empty bottles and dirty plates as they would naturally be scattered about, he lay down to sleep by the side of his companion. Daylight at last awakened Gorenflot, who sat up, and began to look about him at the remains of their last night's repast, and at Chicot, who, although also awake, lay snoring while he watched.

" Broad daylight! " said the monk. " *Corbleu,* I must have passed the night here! " Then, collecting his ideas, " And the abbey! " he said; " oh, oh! " His eyes rested on Chicot, who, observing it, snored with redoubled energy. " What a fine thing it is to be drunk! " said Gorenflot, looking at him with admiration. " How happy he is to sleep thus! " he continued.

" Ah! he is not in my position," and he sighed. " Shall I wake him to ask for advice? No, no, he will laugh at me; I can surely invent a falsehood without him. But whatever I invent, it will be hard to escape punishment. It is not so much the imprisonment, it is the bread and water I mind. Ah! if I had but some money to bribe the brother jailer."

Chicot, hearing this, adroitly slipped his purse from his pocket and put it under him. This precaution was not useless, for Gorenflot, who had been looking about him, now approached his friend softly, and murmuring, " Were he awake, he would not refuse me a crown, but his sleep is sacred, and I will take it," advanced and began feeling his pockets. " It is singular," said he, " nothing in his pockets. Ah! in his hat perhaps."

While he searched there, Chicot adroitly poured the money into his hand and stuffed the empty purse into his breeches' pocket.

" Nothing in the hat," said the monk. " Ah! I forgot," and thrusting in his hand, he drew from the pocket the empty purse. " *Mon Dieu!* " cried he, " empty! and who will pay the bill! "

This thought made a profound impression on the monk; for he immediately stood up, and with a step that was still somewhat irregular, though rapid, he started for the door, crossed the kitchen without responding to his host's overture to conversation, and fled.

Then Chicot put his money in his purse, and his purse in his pocket, and leaning against the window, already touched by rays of the sun, he forgot Gorenflot in a profound meditation.

Meantime Gorenflot pursued his way, searching for some magnificent lie by which to explain his absence the night before. As he approached the convent, his fears grew strong, and seeing a concourse of monks standing talking on the threshold, he felt inclined to fly. But some of them approached to meet him; he knew that flight was hopeless, and resigned himself. The monks seemed at first to hesitate to speak to him, but at last one said, " Poor dear brother! "

Gorenflot sighed, and raised his eyes to heaven.

" You know the prior waits for you? "

" Ah, *mon Dieu!* "

" Oh, yes, he ordered that you should be brought to him as soon as you came in."

" I feared it," said Gorenflot. And more dead than alive, he entered the convent, whose doors closed on him. They led him to the prior. Gorenflot did not dare to raise his eyes on finding himself alone with a superior who would doubtless be angry, and justly so.

" Ah! it is you at last," said the abbé.

" Reverend sir—"

" What anxiety you have given us! "

" You are too good, my father," said Gorenflot, astonished at this indulgent tone.

" You feared to come in after the scene of last night? "

" I confess it."

" Ah, dear brother, you have been very imprudent."

" Let me explain, Father."

" There is no need of explanations; your sally—"

" Oh! so much the better," thought Gorenflot.

" I understand it perfectly. A moment of enthusiasm carried you away; enthusiasm is a holy virtue, but virtues exaggerated become almost vices, and the most honourable sentiments when carried to excess are reprehensible."

" Pardon, my Father," said Gorenflot, timidly, " but I do not understand. Of what sally do you speak? "

" Of yours last night."

" Out of the convent? "

" No; in the convent."

" I made a sally in the convent,—I? "

" Yes, you."

Gorenflot rubbed the end of his nose; he began to see that they were playing at cross purposes.

" I am as good a Catholic as you, but your audacity frightened me."

" My audacity? I have been audacious, then? "

" More than audacious, my son; you have been rash."

" Alas! you must pardon me, my father. I will endeavour to correct myself."

" Yes; but meanwhile, I fear the consequences for you and for all of us. Had the affair happened among ourselves only, it would have been nothing."

" What! " said Gorenflot, " is the matter generally known? "

" Doubtless; you know well there were more than a hundred laymen listening to your discourse."

" My discourse! " said Gorenflot, more and more astonished.

" I admit that it was fine, that the applause may have intoxicated you, and that the unanimous approval probably turned your head; but to propose to make a procession through the streets of Paris, with a helmet on your head and a partisan on your shoulder, appealing to all good Catholics, was rather too strong, you will allow."

Gorenflot looked at the prior with eyes which passed through all the expressions of astonishment.

"Now," continued the prior, "this religious fervour, which burns so strongly in your heart, will injure you in Paris. I wish you therefore to go and expend it in the provinces."

"An exile!" cried Gorenflot.

"If you remain here, much worse may happen to you, my dear brother."

"What?"

"Perpetual imprisonment, or even death."

Gorenflot grew frightfully pale; he could not understand how he had incurred all this by getting tipsy in an inn, and passing the night out of the convent.

"By submitting to this temporary exile, my dear brother, not only will you escape this danger, but you will plant the banner of our faith in the provinces, where such words are less dangerous than here, under the eyes of the king. Set off at once, then, Brother; perhaps the archers are already out to arrest you."

"Oh, reverend father, what are you saying?" stammered Gorenflot, rolling his eyes in terror. "The archers, do you say? And what have I to do with the archers?"

"You have nothing to do with them; but it may easily happen that they will have something to do with you. Go, then, go!"

"It is easy to say 'go;' but how am I to live?"

"Oh, nothing more easy. You will find plenty of partisans who will let you want for nothing. But go, in Heaven's name, and do not come back till you are sent for!" And the prior, after embracing him, pushed him to the door. There he found all the community waiting for him, to touch his hands or his robe.

"Adieu!" said one, embracing him, "you are a holy man; do not forget me in your prayers."

"I, a holy man!" thought Gorenflot.

"Adieu, brave champion of the faith," said another.

"Adieu, martyr," said a third, "the light will soon come."

Thus was he conducted to the outside of the convent, and as he went away he exclaimed, "Devil take me, but either they are all mad, or I am!"

CHAPTER XXVII

HOW BROTHER GORENFLOT REMAINED CONVINCED THAT HE WAS A SOMNAMBULIST, AND BITTERLY DEPLORED THIS INFIRMITY

UP to this inauspicious day—the day when that unexpected persecution fell on the poor monk—Brother Gorenflot had led a contemplative life.   Trusting in God and in the abbey kitchen, his ambition had been limited to procuring for himself occasional luxuries, very mundane and not very frequent, at the Corne d'Abondance.   These luxuries were subject to the caprices of the faithful, and were dependent on the alms they gave in money. Such charities on their way to the convent were diminished somewhat by Brother Gorenflot's expenditure on his own private account.   He had, indeed, Chicot for a friend,—a man fond of good feasts and good fellows; but Chicot was very fanciful in his mode of life.   The monk would sometimes see him three or four days in succession, and then there would be a fortnight, a month, six weeks, in which he would not appear,—perhaps because he was shut up with the king, or attended him on some pilgrimage, or was off on some expedition in furtherance of his own affairs or fancies.

Gorenflot, then, was one of those monks for whom, as for certain soldiers, the world begins with the superior of the house, that is to say, the colonel of the convent,—and ends at the empty soup-kettle.   So this soldier of the Church, this child of the frock, so to speak, had never imagined that the day would come when he should be obliged to go out into the world in search of adventures.   Still if he had had some money—but the prior's answer to his demand had been simple and without apostolic embellishment, like that fragment from Saint Luke, "Seek, and ye shall find."   Gorenflot, while considering that he must seek far away, found that he was tired before beginning.

However, the principal thing was to avoid the danger then threatening,—a danger unknown, but according to the prior's words, imminent.   The poor monk was not one of those who could disguise their appearance and escape by some skilful metamorphosis.   He resolved, therefore, in the first place, to gain the open country; with that purpose he went out by the Porte Bordelle at a rather rapid pace, but making himself as small as possible, in the fear that those archers of whom the prior had spoken might prove to be too grasping realities.

But once in the open air, once in the level country, when he had gone five hundred steps from the gate of the city; when he saw the inviting armchairs offered by the early growth of spring, the joyous sun near the horizon, himself in solitude upon the right hand and upon the left, the city murmuring behind him,—he sat down on a slope by the wayside, rested his double chin on his large fat hand, rubbed his nose with his finger, and fell into a reverie attended by an accompaniment of groans.

Except that he had no harp, Brother Gorenflot resembled not a little one of those Hebrews who, hanging their harps on the willow, furnished at the time of the desolation of Jerusalem the text of the famous line, " Super flumina Babylonis," and the subject of a thousand melancholy pictures.

Gorenflot's groaning increased as nine o'clock drew near,— the convent hour for dinner,—for the monks, not up with civilisation, being separated from the world, still followed, in the year 1578, the custom of the good King Charles V., who dined at eight o'clock in the morning, after his Mass.

It would be as practicable to count the grains of sand raised by a tempest on the seashore as to enumerate the conflicting ideas which, one after the other, entered the head of hungry Gorenflot. The first idea, and that which he dismissed with the most difficulty, was to return to Paris, to go straight to the convent, and declare to the abbé that he would decidedly prefer the dungeon to exile, and would consent even to submit to any extreme of discipline, provided only that his meals should be properly attended to, which he would consent should be reduced to five daily.

To this idea, after a good quarter of an hour, succeeded another, slightly more reasonable. It was to go straight to the Corne d'Abondance, inquire for Chicot, whom he might find there still asleep, represent to him the deplorable condition to which he had been brought by Chicot's festive allurements,— allurements to which he, Gorenflot, had weakly yielded,—and obtain from that generous friend an alimentary provision. This plan occupied Gorenflot another quarter of an hour; for he had a judicial mind, and the idea was not without merit.

Gorenflot entertained also the audacious idea of taking a turn round the walls of Paris, entering by another gate and continuing his collections clandestinely in the city. This plan was especially attractive to him; that was the sort of life to which he seemed to be naturally adapted. But to carry out that plan and follow that mode of life, he must remain in Paris and at

every step risk meeting the archers, the sergeants, or the eccle-
siastical authorities,—a class of men who would be dangerous
to a vagabond monk.

And then another inconvenience suggested itself. The
treasurer of the convent was an administrator too prudent to
leave Paris without an alms-gatherer for the convent; so that
Gorenflot would run the risk of coming face to face with a
colleague who would have over him the incontestable advantage
of being in the legitimate exercise of his functions. This idea
made Gorenflot shudder,—and with good reason.

The monk had proceeded thus far in his meditations when he
saw a cavalier leaving the city at full gallop by way of the
Porte Bordelle. He saw him dismount near a house situated
about a hundred feet from where he was sitting. The man
knocked; the gate was opened, and horse and horseman disappeared. Gorenflot noted this incident with special attention
because he envied the good fortune of the cavalier in having a
horse, which he might sell. But in a few moments the cavalier
came out of the house and went to a place between a grove
of trees and a mass of rocks, where he took an attitude of
concealment.

"This is certainly an ambush," murmured Gorenflot. "If
I was on better terms with the archers, I would go and inform
them; or if I were brave I would interfere."

At this moment the man in ambush, who with a certain
appearance of uneasiness was casting rapid glances to the right
and left, saw Gorenflot sitting immovable, with his chin in his
hand. The sight annoyed him. He began to walk about with
an affected air of indifference. Suddenly he sank down, as if the
muscles of his legs had given way. He had heard the noise of
horses' feet coming from the city gate. He looked out and saw
three men, two of whom seemed to be lackeys, with three good
mules and three large portmanteaus, coming slowly from the
direction of the city. Immediately he shrank into as small a
space as possible, and crawling rather than walking, he gained
the group of trees, and selecting the largest, hid behind it in the
attitude of a hunter on the watch. The cavalcade passed
without noticing him, while he, on the contrary, seemed to
devour them with his eyes.

"It is I who have prevented the consummation of the crime,"
said Gorenflot to himself; "and my presence on the road at
just that moment was a manifestation of the divine will, since
I needed some one to provide me with a breakfast."

The cavalcade having passed, the man in hiding re-entered the house.

"Good!" said Gorenflot, "here is an incident which unless I am greatly mistaken will procure me the alms I seek. A man who watches dislikes to be observed. I have his secret, and were it worth only six deniers I will turn it into money;" and without delay Gorenflot moved on towards the house. But as he approached, he recalled the martial form of the cavalier, his long sword, and the terrible eye with which he had watched the passing cavalcade. He said to himself, "I really think that I have made a mistake; a man like that won't allow himself to be intimidated."

On arriving at the gate, Gorenflot had become altogether convinced, and began scratching his ear. Suddenly his face brightened up. "An idea!" said he.

Such was the process of the awaking of an idea in the monk's sleepy brain that he was himself astonished by the coming of this idea; but it was already a proverb that "necessity is the mother of invention."

"An idea!" he repeated, "and an idea quite ingenious. I will say to him, ' Monsieur, every man has his projects, his desires, his hopes. I will pray for your projects; give me something.' If his projects are evil, of which I have no doubt, he will have double need of my prayers, and will bestow on me a charity. And I will submit the matter to the first doctor of the Church whom I shall meet; I will ask of him whether one should pray for projects unknown, when one has conceived a doubt as to their character; whatever the doctor may tell me I will do, and he, not I, will be responsible. If perchance I should not meet any doctor, as is quite probable, I will abstain. Meantime I shall have breakfasted on the charity of that man of evil intentions."

In consequence of that determination, Gorenflot stood close to the wall and waited. Five minutes later the gate opened and the horse and man appeared, the one carrying the other. Gorenflot drew near. "Monsieur," said he, "if five *Paters* and five *Aves* for the success of your projects would be agreeable to you—"

"Gorenflot!" cried the cavalier.

"M. Chicot!"

"Where the devil are you going?"

"I do not know. And you?"

"Oh! I am going straight before me."

" Very far? "

" Till I stop.   But since you cannot tell me with what purpose you are here, I suspect something."

" What is it? "

" That you were playing the spy on me."

" God forbid! I saw you, that is all."

" Saw what? "

" Saw you watch the mules going by."

" You are crazy."

" But you were there, behind those stones, watching."

" Listen, Gorenflot! I wish to build a house outside the walls.   Those stones are mine, and I was assuring myself of their quality."

" Ah! that is another thing," said the monk, who did not believe a word of Chicot's reply; " I was mistaken."

" But what are you doing outside the barriers? "

" Alas, M. Chicot! I am exiled," said Gorenflot, with an enormous sigh.

" What? "

" Exiled, I tell you.   My brothers reject me from their bosom; I am anathematised, excommunicated."

" Bah! what for? "

" Listen, M. Chicot; you will not believe me perhaps, but I do not know."

" Perhaps you were met last night gadding about."

" Do not joke; you know quite well what I was doing last night."

" Yes, from eight till ten, but not from ten till three."

" How, from ten till three? "

" Yes, at ten you went out."

" I? "

" Yes, and I asked you where you were going."

" And what did I say? "

" That you were going to pronounce a discourse."

" There was some truth in that," murmured Gorenflot.

" Yes, and you even told me part of it; it was very long, and there were terrible things against the king in it."

" Bah! "

" So terrible that I should not wonder if you were arrested for them."

" M. Chicot, you open my eyes; did I seem quite awake when I spoke? "

" I must say you seemed very strange; you looked like a man who talks in his sleep."

"Yet I feel sure I awoke this morning at the Corne d'Abondance."

"Well, of course; you came in again at three o'clock. And to prove it, I will even tell you that you left the door open, and I was very cold."

"And I also,—I remember that."

"So you see!" said Chicot.

"If what you tell me is true—"

"What? if what I tell you is true? Ask Maître Bonhomet."

"Maître Bonhomet?"

"Yes; he opened to you on your return. And you were so full of pride when you came in that I said to you, ' Fie, comrade; pride does not become mortals, more especially monks.' "

"And of what was I proud?"

"Of the success your discourse had met with, and the compliments paid to you by the Duc de Guise and M. de Mayenne."

"Now I understand all."

"That is lucky. Then you confess you went to the assembly; what did you call it? Oh! the holy Union."

Gorenflot groaned. "I am a somnambulist," he said; "I have long suspected it."

"Somnambulist? what does that mean?"

"It means that with me mind is stronger than matter; so that while the body sleeps the spirit wakes, and sometimes is so powerful that it forces the body to obey."

"Ah, comrade; that sounds much like magic. If you are possessed, tell me so frankly; for really, a man who walks and gesticulates and makes discourses in his sleep in which he attacks the king,—that is not natural. Avaunt, Beelzebub! ' Vade retro, Satanas! ' "

"Then," cried Gorenflot, "you also abandon me. ' Tu quoque, Brute! ' Ah! I could not have believed that of you."

Chicot took pity on him. "What did you tell me just now?" said he.

"I do not know. I feel half mad; my head is full and my stomach is empty."

"You spoke of travelling?"

"Yes, the holy prior has invited me to travel."

"In what direction?"

"Wherever I like."

"And you are going?"

"I know nothing about it. For God's sake, M. Chicot, lend me two crowns to help me on my journey."

" I will do better than that," said Chicot.

" Ah! what will you do? "

" I also am travelling, and will take you with me."

Gorenflot looked bewildered.

" Well! do you accept? " continued Chicot.

" Accept! I should think so.   But have you money to travel with? "

" Look," said Chicot, drawing out his purse.

Gorenflot jumped for joy.

" How much? " said he.

" One hundred and fifty pistoles."

" And where are we going? "

" You shall see."

" When shall we breakfast? "

" Immediately."

" What shall I ride? "

" Not my horse, *corbœuf!* you would kill it."

" Then what must I do? " said Gorenflot, disappointed.

" Nothing more simple; I will buy you an ass."

" You are my benefactor, M. Chicot.   Let the ass be strong. Now, where do we breakfast? "

" Here; look over this door and read."

Gorenflot looked up, and saw, " Here eggs, ham, eel-pies, and white wine may be had."   At this sight Gorenflot's whole face expanded with joy.

" Now," said Chicot, " go and get your breakfast, while I go and look for an ass for you."

CHAPTER XXVIII

HOW BROTHER GORENFLOT TRAVELLED UPON AN ASS NAMED PANURGE, AND LEARNED MANY THINGS HE DID NOT KNOW BEFORE

WHAT made Chicot so indifferent to his own repast was that he had already breakfasted plentifully.   Therefore when Gorenflot sat down to eggs and bacon, he went among the peasants to look for an ass.   He found a pacific creature, four years old, gave twenty-two livres for it, and brought it to Gorenflot, who was enchanted at the sight of it, and christened it Panurge.   Chicot, seeing by the appearance of the table that there would be no cruelty in staying his companion's repast, said, " Come, now we must go on; at Melun we will lunch.

Gorenflot got up, merely saying, " At Melun; at Melun."

They went on for about four leagues; then Gorenflot lay down on the grass to sleep, while Chicot began to calculate. One hundred and twenty leagues, at ten leagues a day, would take twelve days.   Ten leagues was as much as he could reason- ably expect from the combined forces of a monk and an ass. But Chicot shook his head.   " It will not do," he said; " If he wants to follow me, he must make fifteen leagues daily."

He pushed the monk to wake him, who, opening his eyes, said, " Are we at Melun?   I am hungry."

" Not yet, comrade, and that is why I woke you; we must get on; we go too slowly, *ventre de biche !* "

" Eh! that troubles you, dear M. Chicot,—to go slowly?   The journey of life is an ascent, even to the sky, and it is fatiguing to ascend.   Besides, there is no hurry; the longer time we put into the journey, the longer we shall be together. Am I not travelling for the propagation of the faith, and you for pleasure? Well, the slower we go, the better the faith will be propagated, and the more you will amuse yourself. My advice is to stay some days at Melun, where they make excellent eel-pies.   What do you say, M. Chicot? "

" I say that my advice is to go as fast as possible, not to lunch at Melun, and to stop for supper only at Montereau,—to make up for lost time."

Gorenflot looked at his companion as if he did not under- stand.

" Come, let us get on," said Chicot.

The monk sat still and groaned.

" If you wish to stay behind and travel at your ease, you are welcome."

" No, no! " cried Gorenflot, in horror of that isolation from which he had just escaped, as by miracle,—" no, no, M. Chicot; I will follow you.   I love you too much to leave you! "

" Then to your saddle at once."

Gorenflot got on his ass this time sideways, as a lady sits,— pretending that it was more convenient for conversation; but the fact was that, fearing they were to go faster, he wished to be able to hold on both by mane and tail.

Chicot started off at a smart pace, and the ass followed.   The first moments were terrible for Gorenflot, but he managed to keep his seat.   From time to time Chicot stood up in his stirrups and looked forward, and then, not seeing what he looked for, redoubled his speed.

" What are you looking for, dear M. Chicot? "

" Nothing; but we are not getting on."

" Not getting on! we are trotting without break."

" Gallop! gallop!" said Chicot, urging his horse into that gait.

Panurge, following the example, also began to gallop, but with an ill-disguised rage which boded no good to his rider.

Gorenflot's troubles increased. " Say, then," said he, as soon as he could speak, " do you call this travelling for pleasure? It does not amuse me at all."

" On! on!"

" It is dreadful!"

" Stay behind, then!"

" *Ventrebleu !* no! for nothing in this world!"

" Well, then, as I said before, on! on!" and Chicot urged his horse to greater speed.

" Panurge can do no more; he is stopping."

" Then adieu, comrade!"

Gorenflot felt half inclined to reply in the same manner; but he remembered that the horse, whom he felt ready to curse, bore on his back a man with a hundred and fifty pistoles in his pocket, so he resigned himself and beat his ass to make him gallop once more.

" I shall kill my poor Panurge!" cried he, dolefully, thinking to move Chicot.

" Well, kill him," said Chicot, quietly, " and we will buy a mule."

All at once Chicot, on arriving at the top of a hill, reined in his horse suddenly. Gorenflot, a less skilful horseman, and who, besides, instead of a bridle had only a halter, continued on his way.

" Stop! *corbœuf*, stop!" cried Chicot.

But the ass had taken a notion to gallop, and the notions of an ass are persistent.

" Will you stop?" cried Chicot. " On my honour, I will send you a pistol-ball!"

" What devil of a man is that!" said Gorenflot to himself; " and by what animal has he been bitten?"

Then, Chicot's voice becoming more threatening, the monk, fancying that he already heard the whistling of the ball, executed a manœuvre for which his manner of riding gave him every

facility; he slipped off and sat on the ground. Still holding
fast to the halter, he was dragged forward in that position a few
feet by the beast, who finally came to a stop.

"Here I am!" said Gorenflot; and he looked for Chicot,
expecting to see his face lighted up with admiration of a
manœuvre so skilfully performed. Chicot was hidden behind
a rock, and continued there his signs and his threats. The
monk began to surmise that something important was taking
place, and looking on ahead he saw at a distance of about five
hundred feet three men quietly riding along on their mules.
At the first glance he recognised the travellers who had left Paris
in the morning, and whom Chicot from behind a tree had so
eagerly watched.

Chicot waited in concealment until the three travellers were
out of sight. Then he rejoined his companion, who had remained
sitting in the same place, still holding Panurge by the halter.

"Ah, there!" said Gorenflot, who was beginning to lose
patience, "explain to me a little, dear M. Chicot, the affair in
which we are engaged. In the first place we must gallop at all
speed, and then we must stop short here."

"My good friend," said Chicot, "I wished to ascertain
whether your ass was of good stock, and whether I had been
cheated in paying for it twenty-two livres. Now the trial has
been made, and I am entirely satisfied."

The monk was not duped, but was too lazy to enter on a
discussion. "No matter," he said; "I am very tired and very
hungry."

"And so am I," said Chicot, "and at the first hotel we come
to we will order a couple of fricasseed chickens, some ham, and
a jug of their best wine."

"Really, is it true this time?"

"I promise you, comrade."

"Well, then, let us go and seek it. Come, Panurge, you shall
have some dinner."

Chicot remounted his horse, and Gorenflot led his ass. The
much-desired inn soon appeared, but to the surprise of Gorenflot,
Chicot caused him to make a _détour_ and pass round the back.
At the front door were standing the mules of the three travellers.

CHAPTER XXIX

HOW BROTHER GORENFLOT CHANGED HIS ASS FOR A MULE, AND HIS MULE FOR A HORSE

HOWEVER, Gorenflot's troubles were near their end for that day, for after the *détour* they went on a mile, and then stopped at a rival hotel. Chicot took a room which looked upon the high-road, and ordered supper. But even while he was eating, he was constantly on the watch. However, at ten o'clock, as he had seen nothing, he went to bed, first, however, ordering that the horse and the ass should be ready at daybreak.

" At daybreak? " uttered Gorenflot, with a deep sigh.

" Yes, you should be used to getting up at that time."

" Why so? "

" For matins."

" I had an exemption from the superior."

Chicot ordered Gorenflot's bed to be placed in his room. At daylight he was up and at the window, and before very long he saw three mules coming along. He ran to Gorenflot and shook him.

" Can I not have a moment's rest? " cried the monk, who had been sleeping for ten hours.

" Be quick! get up and dress, for we are going."

" But the breakfast? "

" Is on the road to Montereau."

" Where is Montereau? "

" It is the city where we breakfast, that is enough for you. Now, I am going down to pay the bill, and if you are not ready in five minutes I go without you."

A monk's toilet does not require much time; however, Goren-flot took six minutes for his, and when he came down Chicot had set off. But Panurge, stimulated by double rations provided by Chicot, started at a gallop of his own accord, and soon overtook the Gascon. Chicot was standing in his stirrups; Gorenflot followed his example, and saw the three travellers descending beyond a small hill. The monk sighed as he thought of the effect upon his fortunes of that foreign influence.

This time Chicot kept his word, and they breakfasted at Mon-tereau. This day passed much like the former one, and the next presented almost the same succession of events. Gorenflot was beginning to get accustomed to this accidental mode of life, when towards the evening he noticed that Chicot was gradually losing all his gaiety. Since noon he had seen nothing of the three travellers; therefore he was in a very bad humour at supper, and slept badly. Gorenflot ate and drank for two, and sang his best songs; but Chicot was impassive. They were off at daybreak and galloped till noon, but all in vain; no mules were visible. Chicot stopped at a turnpike, and asked the man if he had seen three travellers pass on mules.

"Not to-day," was the reply; "yesterday evening about seven o'clock."

"What were they like?"

"They looked like a master and two servants."

"It was they," said Chicot; "*ventre de biche!* they have twelve hours' start of me. But courage!"

"Listen, M. Chicot!" said Gorenflot, "my ass can do no more; even your horse is almost exhausted." Chicot looked, and saw that the poor animals were indeed trembling from head to foot.

"Well, Brother," said he, "we must take a resolution. You must leave me."

"Leave you! why?"

"You go too slow."

"Slow! I go like the wind. Why, we have galloped for five hours this morning."

"That is not enough."

"Well, then, let us go on. The quicker we go, the sooner we shall arrive, for I suppose we shall stop at last."

"But our animals are exhausted."

"What shall we do, then?"

"Leave them here, and take them as we come back."

"Then how are we to proceed?"

"We will buy mules."

"Very well," said Gorenflot, with a sigh.

"Bravo! comrade; you are beginning to form yourself. Commend Bayard and Panurge to the care of the innkeeper, while I make the purchases."

Gorenflot faithfully discharged his commission. During the four days of his acquaintance with Panurge, he had appreciated, we do not say his merits, but his faults, and had noticed that they were the same as those to which he was himself inclined,— laziness, luxury, and gluttony. That observation had touched his heart, and it was not without regret that he separated from his ass. But Gorenflot was not only lazy, luxurious, and a glutton, he was still more an egotist; and he was willing to part with Panurge rather than with Chicot, who, as we have said, carried the purse.

Two mules were soon found, and they went so well that in the evening Chicot saw with joy those of the three travellers standing at the door of a farrier's. But they were without harness, and both master and lackeys had disappeared. Chicot trembled. "Go," said he to Gorenflot, "and ask if those mules are for sale, and where their owners are."

Gorenflot went, and soon returned, saying that a gentleman had sold them, and had afterwards taken the road to Avignon.

"Alone?"

"No, with a lackey."

"And where is the other lackey?"

"He went towards Lyon."

"Strange! And why does the gentleman go to Avignon? I thought he was going to Rome. But I speak of matters of which you know nothing."

"Yes, I know about them. Ah! that surprises you."

"What? You know about them?"

"Yes. He goes to Avignon because the pope has sent thither a legate with full power."

"Good!" said Chicot, "I understand. And how did they go on?"

"On horses which they bought."

"Of whom?"

"Of a captain of troopers who was here. They sold their mules to a dealer, who is trying to sell them again to those Franciscan monks whom you see there."

"Well, take our two mules and go and offer them to the monks instead; they ought to give you the preference."

"But then how shall we go on?"

"On horseback, *morbleu!*"

"The devil!"

"Oh! a good rider like you."

"Bah!" said Gorenflot. "But where shall I find you?"

"In the Grand Place."

"Go and await me there."

The monk advanced with a resolute step towards the Franciscans, while Chicot, by a cross street, went to the central square of the town. There he found the captain of the troopers drinking wine at an inn, and from him gained further information which confirmed at all points that which he had received from Gorenflot.

In a few moments Chicot had traded with him for two horses, and it remained only to fix a price on the saddles and bridles, when he saw the monk reappear, carrying the saddles and bridles of the mules.

" Oh! you have kept the harness? "

" Yes."

" And sold the mules? "

" For ten pistoles each."

" Which they paid you? "

" Here is the money."

" *Ventre de biche!* you are a great man; let us go on."

" But I am thirsty."

" Well, drink while I saddle the beasts, but not too much."

" A bottle? "

" Very well."

Gorenflot drank two, and came to give the rest of the money back to Chicot, who felt half inclined to give it to him; but reflecting that if Gorenflot had money he would no longer be obedient, he refrained. They rode on, and the next evening Chicot came up with Nicolas David, still disguised as a lackey, and kept him in sight all the way to Lyon, whose gates they all three entered on the eighth day after their departure from Paris.

CHAPTER XXX

HOW CHICOT AND HIS COMPANION INSTALLED THEMSELVES AT THE HOSTELRY OF LA CROIX, AND HOW THEY WERE RECEIVED BY THE HOST

CHICOT watched Nicolas David into the principal hotel of the place, and then said to Gorenflot, " Go in and bargain for a private room; say that you expect your brother, then come out and wait about for me. I will come in when it is dark, and you can guide me straight to my room. Do you understand? "

" Perfectly."

" Choose a good room, looking on the street, as near as possible to that of the traveller who has just arrived; and on no account pronounce my name."

Gorenflot acquitted himself marvellously of the commission. Their room was separated by only a partition from that of Nicolas David.

" You deserve a recompense," said Chicot to him, " and you shall have sherry wine for supper."

" I never got tipsy on that wine; it would be agreeable."

" *Ventre de biche!* you shall in two hours."

Chicot sent for the host, who replied that his new guest must have patience, since he was engaged with a traveller who, having arrived before him, had a right to prior service. Chicot divined that the traveller was his advocate. " What can they have to talk about? " he said.

" Do you think, then, that the host and your man are in collusion? "

" Well, you see; the host converses with a man dressed like a lackey."

" Ah! " said Gorenflot, " he has changed his clothes; he is now dressed all in black."

" A reason the more; the host is doubtless a man of intrigue."

" Shall I try to confess his wife? "

" No, it would suit me better if you would take a walk about the town."

" But the supper? "

" It shall be ready against your return; here is a crown meanwhile."

Gorenflot went off quite happy, and then Chicot made with a gimlet a hole in the partition at about the height of his eye. Through this he could hear what was said, and could see the host talking to Nicolas David; the latter was professing to have been sent on a mission by the king, to whom he professed great fidelity. The host did not reply, but Chicot fancied he could see an ironical smile on his lip whenever the king's name was mentioned.

" Is he a Leaguer? " thought Chicot; " I will find out."

When the host left David he came to visit Chicot, who said, " Pray sit down, Monsieur, and before we make a definitive arrangement, listen to my history. You saw me this morning with a monk? "

" Yes, Monsieur."

" Silence! that monk is proscribed."

" What! is he a disguised Huguenot? "

Chicot took an offended air. " Huguenot, indeed! he is my relative, and I have no Huguenot relatives. On the contrary, he is so fierce an enemy of the Huguenots that he has fallen into disgrace with his Majesty Henri III., who protects them, as you know."

The host began to look interested. " Be careful! " said he.

" Why, have you any of the king's people here? "

" I fear so; there is a traveller in there."

" Then we must fly immediately, for, proscribed and menaced—"

" Where will you go? "

" We have two or three addresses given to us by an inn-keeper we know, M. la Hurière."

" Do you know La Hurière? "

" Yes, we made his acquaintance on the night of Saint Bartholomew."

" Well, I see that you and your relative are holy people; I also know La Hurière. Then you say this monk—"

" Had the imprudence to preach against the Huguenots, and with so much success that the king wanted to put him in prison."

" And then? "

" Faith! I carried him off."

" And you did well."

" M. de Guise offered to protect him."

" What! the great Henri? "

" Himself; but I feared civil war."

" If you are friends of M. de Guise, you know this; " and he made a sort of masonic sign by which the Leaguers recognised one another.

Chicot, who had seen both this and the answer to it twenty times during that famous night, replied, " And you this? "

" Then," said the innkeeper, " you are at home here; my house is yours. I look on you as a brother, and if you have no money—"

Chicot drew out his purse. The sight of a well-filled purse is always agreeable, even to a generous host.

" Our expenses," continued Chicot, " are paid by the treasurer of the holy Union, for we travel to propagate the faith. Tell us of an inn where we may be safe."

" *Morbleu!* nowhere more so than here."

" But you spoke just now of a man lodging here."

" Yes; but let him be careful, for on the first sign that he is watching you, out he goes, on the honour of Bernouillet."

" Your name is Bernouillet? "

" That is my name, Monsieur,—known to the faithful in the province, if not in the capital. Say the word, and I will turn him out."

" Oh, no; it is better to have our enemies near, that you

may watch them. But what makes you think he is our enemy?
I say our enemy," continued the Gascon, with a tender smile,
" because I see clearly that we are brothers."

" Well! he came disguised as a lackey, then he put on an
advocate's dress; and I am sure he is no more an advocate
than he is a lackey, for I saw a long rapier under his cloak.
Then he avowed he had a mission from M. de Morvilliers, who
is, as you know, a minister of Nebuchadnezzar."

" Of Herod, as I call him."

" Sardanapalus."

" Bravo! "

" Ah! I see we understand each other."

" Then we are to remain here? "

" I should think so."

" Not a word about my relative."

" Of course not."

" Nor of me."

" Oh, no! But hush! here is some one."

" Oh, it is the worthy man himself! "

The host turned to Gorenflot, and made the sign of the
Leaguers. Gorenflot was struck with terror and astonishment.

" Reply, my brother," said Chicot; " he knows all,—he is a
member."

" Of what? "

" Of the holy Union," said Bernouillet, in a low tone.

" You see all is safe; reply," said Chicot.

Gorenflot replied, to the great joy of the innkeeper.

" But," said Gorenflot, who did not like the conversation,
" you promised me some sherry."

" Sherry, Malaga, Alicant,—every wine in my cellar is at
your disposal, my brother."

Gorenflot looked at Chicot in amazement.

Three days in succession Gorenflot got drunk, first on sherry,
next on Malaga, then on Alicant; afterwards he declared he
liked Burgundy best, and returned to that. Meanwhile, Chicot
had never stirred from his room, and had constantly watched
Nicolas David, who, having appointed to meet Pierre de Gondy
at this inn, would not leave the house. On the morning of the
sixth day he declared himself ill, and the next day worse.
Bernouillet came to tell Chicot.

" What! do you think him in danger? "

" High fever, my dear brother; he is delirious, and tried to strangle me and beat my servants. The doctors do not understand his complaint."

" Have you seen him? "

" Of course,—I tell you he tried to strangle me."

" How did he seem? "

" Pale and furious, and constantly crying out."

" What? "

" Take care of the king! they want to hurt the king! Then he is always saying that he expects a man from Avignon, and wishes to see him before he dies."

" Ah! he speaks of Avignon? "

" Every minute."

" *Ventre de biche !* " said Chicot.

" Say, then, it would be queer if he should die."

" Very queer; but I wouldn't have him die before the man from Avignon arrives."

" Why not? The sooner he dies, the sooner we are rid of him."

" Yes; but I don't carry hatred so far as to wish the ruin of both soul and body. And since this man is coming from Avignon to confess him—"

" Eh! that is only a feverish fancy, a notion that sickness has put into his head; he expects no one."

" Bah! who knows? " said Chicot.

" Ah! you are a good Christian," replied the host.

" Render good for evil,—it is the divine law."

The host withdrew, wondering.

As for Gorenflot, he grew visibly fatter every day, so much so that he announced to Chicot with terror one day that the staircase was narrowing. Neither David, the League, nor religion occupied him; he thought of nothing but how to vary his dinner and wine,—so that Bernouillet often exclaimed in astonishment, " To think that that man should be a torrent of eloquence! "

CHAPTER XXXI

HOW THE MONK CONFESSED THE ADVOCATE, AND THE ADVOCATE THE MONK

AT last M. Bernouillet came into Chicot's room, laughing immoderately.

"He is dying," said he; "and the man has arrived from Avignon."

"Have you seen him?"

"Of course."

"What is he like?"

"Little and thin."

"It is he," thought Chicot; and he said, "Tell me about his arrival."

"An hour ago I was in the kitchen, when I saw a great horse, ridden by a little man, stop before the door. 'Is Maître Nicolas here?' asked he. 'Yes, Monsieur,' said I. 'Tell him that the person he expects from Avignon is here.' 'Certainly, Monsieur; but I must warn you that he is very ill.' 'All the more reason for doing my bidding at once.' 'But he has a malignant fever.' 'Really! then I advise you to hurry!' 'What! you persist?' 'I persist.' 'In spite of the danger?' 'In spite of everything, I must see him.' So I took him to the room, and there he is now. Is it not odd?"

"Very odd."

"I wish I could hear them."

"Go in."

"He forbade me to go in, saying he was going to confess."

"Listen at the door."

Bernouillet went, and Chicot went also to his hole; but they spoke so low that he could hear nothing, and in a few minutes Gondy rose and took leave. Chicot ran to the window, and saw a lackey waiting with a horse, which M. de Gondy mounted and rode off.

"*Mordieu!*" said Chicot; "if only he has not carried off the genealogy. Never mind, I shall soon catch him if necessary; but I suspect it is left here. Where can Gorenflot be?"

M. Bernouillet returned, saying, "He is gone."

"The confessor?"

"He is no more a confessor than I am."

"Will you send me my brother as soon as he comes in."

" Even if he be drunk? "

" In whatever state he is."

Bernouillet went, and Chicot remained in a state of indecision as to what to do; for he thought, " If David is really so ill, he may have sent on the despatches by Gondy." Presently he heard Gorenflot's voice, singing a drinking-song as he came up the stairs.

Chicot ran to the door. " Silence, drunkard! " said he.

" Drunkard, indeed! "

" Yes; but come here and speak seriously, if you can."

" What is it now? "

" It is that you never think of the duties of your profession, that you wallow in greediness and drunkenness, and leave religion to take care of itself, *corbœuf ! *"

Gorenflot looked astonished. " I? " he gasped.

" Yes, you; you are disgraceful to see. Your robe is torn; your left eye is circled with black. You have been fighting."

" I? " said Gorenflot, more and more astonished at these unwonted reproaches.

" Certainly; you are covered with mud up to the knees,— and white mud, which proves that you have been drinking in the faubourgs."

" It is too true! "

" If you go on so, I will abandon you."

" Chicot, my friend, you will not do that? Am I very guilty? "

" There are archers at Lyon."

" Oh, pity! my dear protector, pity! " stammered the monk, who began, not to weep, but to bellow like a bull.

" Fie! the ugly beast! " continued Chicot. " And in what a moment, I ask you, do you abandon yourself to such misconduct? When our neighbour is dying! "

" It is true," said Gorenflot, with an air of deep contrition.

" Are you a Christian or not? "

" I not a Christian! "

" Then do not let a neighbour die without confession."

" I am ready, but I must drink first, for I am thirsty."

Chicot passed him a jug of water, which he nearly emptied.

" Now, who is it that I am to confess? "

" Our unlucky neighbour who is dying."

" Let them give him a pint of wine with honey in it."

" He needs spiritual aid as well as temporal. Go to him."

" Am I fit? " said Gorenflot, timidly.

" You! I have never seen you so full of unction as you are at this moment. You will bring him back to righteousness if he has wandered, and will direct him straight to Paradise if he is seeking the way."

" Then I will go."

" Stay; I must tell you what course to follow."

" Why so? I know my business after being twenty years a monk."

" Yes, but you do not know what I wish."

" What you wish? "

" If you execute it well, I will deposit one hundred pistoles at the Corne d'Abondance, for you to eat or drink as you may choose."

" What must I do? "

" Listen; your robe gives you authority. In the name of God and the king, summon him to give up the papers he has just received from Avignon."

" What for? "

" To gain one hundred pistoles, stupid."

" Ah! true; I go."

" Wait a minute. He will tell you he has confessed."

" But if he has? "

" Tell him he lies; that the man who has just left him is no confessor, but an intriguer like himself."

" But he will be angry."

" What does that matter, since he is dying? "

" That is true."

" Now, then, you understand. You will speak of God, you will speak of the Devil, you will speak of what you please; but in one way or another, you must get hold of those papers."

" If he refuses? "

" Refuse him absolution, curse him, anathematise him—"

" Or I will take them by force."

" Good; and when you have got them, knock on the wall."

" And if I cannot get them? "

" Knock also."

" Then in any case I am to knock? "

" Yes."

Gorenflot went, and Chicot placed his ear to the hole in the wall. When Gorenflot entered, the sick man raised himself in his bed, and looked at him with wonder.

" Good-day, Brother," said Gorenflot.

" What do you want, my father? " murmured the sick man, in a feeble voice.

" My son, I hear you are in danger, and I come to speak to
you of your soul."

" Thank you, but I think your care is needless; I feel
better."

" You think so? "

" I am sure of it."

" It is a ruse of Satan, who wishes you to die without confession."

" Then he will be deceived, for I have just confessed."

" To whom? "

" To a worthy priest from Avignon."

" He was not a priest."

" Not? "

" No."

" How do you know? "

" I knew him."

" You knew the man who has just gone? "

" Yes; and as you are not better, and this man was not a
priest, you must confess."

" Very well," replied the patient, in a stronger voice; " but
I will choose to whom I will confess."

" You will have no time to send for another priest; and I am
here."

" What! I shall have no time," cried the sick man, in a voice
which was becoming continually stronger, " when I tell you that
I feel better, when I say to you that I am sure of recovery? "

Gorenflot shook his head. " I tell you, my son, that you are
condemned by the doctors and by Providence. You may think
it cruel to tell you so; but it is what we must all come to sooner
or later. Confess, my son; confess."

" But I assure you, Father, that I feel much stronger; it is
probably an effect of your holy presence."

" A mistake, my son; the lamp flares up at the last, just
before it goes out. Come," continued the monk, taking a seat
near the bed, " confess to me your plots, your intrigues, and
machinations! "

" My intrigues, my plots, my machinations! " repeated
Nicolas David, recoiling from this singular monk, whom he did
not know, but who seemed to know him so well.

" Yes; and when you have told all that, give me up the
papers, and perhaps God will let me absolve you."

" What papers? " cried the sick man, in a voice as strong as
though he were quite well.

"The papers that the pretended priest brought you from Avignon."

"And who told you that he brought me papers?" cried the patient, putting one leg out of bed.

Gorenflot began to feel frightened, but he said firmly, "He who told me knew well what he was saying; give me the papers, or you shall have no absolution."

"I laugh at your absolution," cried David, jumping out of bed, and seizing Gorenflot by the throat; "and you shall see if I am too ill to strangle you."

Gorenflot was strong, and he pushed David back so violently that he fell in the middle of the room. But he rose furious, and seizing a long sword which hung on the wall behind his clothes, presented it to the throat of Gorenflot, who sank on a chair in terror.

"It is now your turn to confess," said he; "speak, or you die."

Gorenflot, completely sobered by that disagreeable pressure of cold steel against his throat, comprehended the gravity of the situation. "Oh!" said he, "then you were not ill; your pretended suffering was a comedy, then?"

"It is not for you to question, but to answer."

"To answer what?"

"Who are you?"

"You can see that?"

"That is not answering," said the advocate, pressing the sword a little.

"What the devil! Take care! If you kill me before I answer, you will learn nothing."

"You are right. Your name?"

"Brother Gorenflot."

"You are then a real monk?"

"I should think so."

"What brings you to Lyon?"

"I am exiled."

"What brought you to this inn?"

"Chance."

"How long have you been here?"

"A fortnight."

"Why did you watch me?"

"I did not."

"How did you know that I had the papers?"

"Because I was told so."

" Who told you? "

" He who sent me here."

" Who was that? "

" That is something I cannot tell you."

" And that is something you will tell me, nevertheless."

" Oh, oh! I will cry out."

" And I will kill."

Gorenflot cried out, and a spot of blood appeared on the point of the sword.

" His name? " cried David.

" Oh! I can hold out no more."

" Speak."

" It was Chicot."

" The king's jester? "

" Himself."

" And where is he? "

" Here! " cried a voice, and Chicot appeared at the door, pale, grave, and with a drawn sword in his hand.

CHAPTER XXXII

HOW CHICOT, HAVING MADE A HOLE WITH A GIMLET, MAKES ANOTHER WITH HIS SWORD

NICOLAS DAVID, on recognising him whom he knew to be his mortal enemy, could not repress a movement of terror, during which Gorenflot slipped a little to the side, crying out, " Help, friend! come to my aid! "

" Ah, M. David, it is you, then? " said Chicot.

" Yes," faltered David,—" yes, certainly, it is I."

" Delighted to meet you again," said Chicot. Then, turning to Gorenflot, he said, " My good Gorenflot, your presence as monk was very necessary just now, when we believed Monsieur dying; but now that he is so well, he no longer needs a confessor. He is going to have an affair with a gentleman."

David affected a derisive laugh.

" Yes, with a gentleman," said Chicot, " who will show you that he is of good family. My dear Gorenflot," he continued, addressing the monk, " do me the favour to stand sentinel on the threshold, and prevent any one from coming in to interrupt our little conversation."

Gorenflot, who asked nothing better than to go, was soon out of the room. Chicot, always with the same coolness, closed the door after him and bolted it. David, having now recovered from his surprise, and confident in his skill as a swordsman, stood waiting for Chicot, with his sword in his hand and a smile on his lips.

"Dress yourself, Monsieur," said Chicot; "I do not wish to take any advantage of you. Do you know what I have come to seek in this room?"

"The rest of the blows which I have owed you on account of the Duc de Mayenne, since that day when you jumped so quickly out of the window."

"No, Monsieur; I know the number, and will return them to him who had them given me, you may be assured. What I have come for is a certain genealogy which M. Pierre de Gondy took to Avignon, without knowing what he carried, and equally in ignorance, has just now intrusted to you."

David turned pale. "What genealogy?" he said.

"That of M. de Guise, who descends, as you know, in a direct line from Charlemagne."

"Ah, you are a spy! I thought you only a buffoon."

"Dear M. David, I will be both if you wish it; a spy to hang you, and a buffoon to laugh at it after."

"To hang me?"

"High and dry, Monsieur; I hope you do not lay claim to be beheaded like a gentleman."

"And how will you do it?"

"Oh, very easily; I will relate the truth, that is all. I must tell you, dear M. David, that I assisted last month at the meeting held in the convent of Ste. Geneviève."

"You!"

"Yes; I was in the confessional in front of yours. Very uncomfortable, are they not?—the more so in my case, at least, because I couldn't leave my box till all was finished, and the affair was tediously prolonged. Yes, I was a listener to the discourse of M. de Monsoreau, of La Hurière, and of a certain monk whose name I have forgotten, but who seemed to me very eloquent. I witnessed the coronation of M. d'Anjou, which was not very amusing; but the afterpiece was very funny. They played The Genealogy of MM. de Lorraine, revised, augmented, and corrected by Maître Nicolas David. It was a very droll farce, which wanted only the approbation of his Holiness."

"Ah! you know about the genealogy?" cried David, biting his lips with anger.

"Yes, and I found it very ingenious, especially that part about the Salic law; only it is a misfortune to have so much intellect,—one gets hanged for it. Therefore, feeling myself moved with tender pity for so ingenious a man, I said to myself, 'Shall I let this brave M. David be hanged?' and I took the resolution of travelling with, or rather behind, you. You came out by the Porte Bordelle, did you not? I was watching you. You didn't see me, and that is not surprising, for I was well concealed. From that moment I have followed you,—losing you, overtaking you again, taking a great deal of trouble, I assure you. At last we arrived at Lyon. I entered the hotel an hour after you, and have been in the adjoining room. Look, there is only a partition between; and, as you may imagine, I did not travel all the way from Paris to Lyon to lose sight of you here. I pierced a little hole, through which I had the pleasure of watching you when I liked, and I confess I gave myself this pleasure several times a day. At last you fell ill; the host wished to get rid of you, but you were determined to wait here for M. de Gondy. It was a stratagem that only half deceived me; but you might be really ill,—since we are all mortal, the truth of which I will show you presently,—so I sent you a brave monk, to excite you to repentance. But, hardened sinner that you are, you tried to kill him, forgetting the Scripture maxim, 'He who strikes with the sword shall perish with the sword.' Then I came to you, and said, 'We are old friends; let us arrange the matter.'"

"In what manner?"

"M. David, you are an accomplished man. Fencing, horsemanship, chicanery, the art of putting fat purses in large pockets, —you are skilful in all. It would be a pity that such a man as you should disappear from the world. Well, then, dear M. David, give up plots, trust to me, break with the Guises, give me your papers, and, on my honour, I will make your peace with the king."

"While, on the contrary, if I do not give them to you?"

"Ah! then, on my honour, I will kill you. Does the matter still seem laughable to you, dear M. David?"

"More and more," said the advocate, caressing his sword.

"But if you give them to me, dear M. David," continued Chicot, "all shall be forgotten. You do not believe me, perhaps, for your nature is bad, and you think my resentment crusts my heart like rust on iron. No, I hate you, it is true; but I hate M. de Mayenne more. Give me what will ruin him, and I will save you. And then,—perhaps you will not believe this either, for you love nothing,—I love the king, foolish and corrupted as he is, and I wish that he should reign tranquilly, which is impossible with the Mayennes and the genealogies of Nicolas David. Therefore, give me up the genealogy, and I promise to conceal your name and make your fortune."

David made no reply.

"Well," said Chicot, "I see all that I say to you is but wasted breath, and that you do not believe me. But I have a way to punish you for your ancient wrongs towards me, and to rid the earth of a man who no longer believes in probity or humanity. I am going to get you hanged. Adieu, M. David;" and he stepped backwards towards the door, with his eye on the advocate.

The advocate made a bound towards him. "And you think I shall let you go out?" he cried. "No, no, my fine spy; no, no, Chicot, my friend! When one knows secrets like that of the genealogy, he dies! When one threatens Nicolas David, he dies! When one enters here as you have entered, he dies!"

"You put me quite at my ease," said Chicot, still calm. "I hesitated only because I am sure to kill you. Crillon, the other day, taught me a particular thrust, only one; but that will suffice. Come, give me the papers," he added in a terrible voice, "or I kill you! And I will tell you how,—I will pierce your throat just where you wished to bleed my friend Gorenflot."

Chicot had hardly spoken these words when David rushed on him with a savage laugh. The two adversaries were nearly matched in height, but Chicot, who fenced almost every day with the king, had become one of the most skilful swordsmen in the kingdom. David soon began to perceive this, and he retreated a step.

"Ah, ah!" said Chicot, "now you begin to understand. Once more; the papers!"

David, for answer, threw himself again upon Chicot, and a new combat ensued, longer and fiercer than the first, although Chicot contented himself with parrying, and had not yet struck a blow. This second contest ended, like the first, in a backward step by the advocate.

"Ah, ah!" said Chicot, "it is now my turn;" and he made a step forward. Nicolas David met him. Chicot parried once more, beat down his adversary's guard, reached the place which he had indicated in advance, and plunged his sword half its length through M. David's throat. "That is the stroke," said he.

David did not reply, but fell at Chicot's feet, pouring out a mouthful of blood. But by a natural movement he tried to drag himself towards his bed so as to defend his secret to the last.

"Ah!" cried Chicot, "I thought you cunning; but I see you are a fool. I did not know where the papers were, and you have shown me." While David rolled in the agonies of death, he ran to the bed, raised the mattress, and found under it a roll of parchment. At the moment when he unrolled it to see if it was the document he sought, David raised himself in a rage and then fell back dead. Chicot saw with joy that he held what he wanted. The pope's legate had written at the bottom, "Fiat ut voluit Deus; Deus jura hominum fecit." After placing it in his breast, he took the body of the advocate, who had died without losing more blood, the nature of the wound making him bleed inwardly, put it back in the bed, turned the face to the wall, and opening the door, called Gorenflot.

"How pale you are!" said the monk, as he entered.

"Yes, the last moments of that man caused me some emotion."

"Then he is dead?"

"There is every reason to think so."

"He was so well just now."

"Too well; he swallowed something difficult of digestion, and died of it."

"Oh, oh! The wretch wanted to strangle me, a holy man, and it has brought misfortune to him."

"Pardon him; you are a Christian."

"I do, although he frightened me much."

"You must do more; you must light the lamps, and say some prayers by his bed."

"Why?"

"That you may not be taken prisoner as his murderer."

"I a murderer! it was he who tried to murder me!"

"*Mon Dieu !* yes, and as he could not succeed, his rage made him break a blood-vessel. But till your innocence is established they might annoy you much."

"I fear you are right."

"Then do what I tell you. Install yourself here, and recite all the prayers you know, or do not know; then, when evening comes, go out quietly and without haste, and call at the iron-monger's at the corner of the street. There you will find your horse; mount him, and take the road to Paris. At Villeneuve le Roi sell him, and take Panurge back."

" Ah! that good Panurge; I shall be delighted to see him again. But how am I to live? "

Chicot drew from his pocket a handful of crowns and put them into the large hand of the monk.

" Generous man! " cried Gorenflot. " Let me stay with you at Lyon; I love Lyon."

" But I do not stay here; I set off at once, and travel too rapidly for you to follow me."

" So be it, then."

Chicot installed the monk by the bed, and went downstairs to the host. " M. Bernouillet," said he, " a great event has taken place in your house."

" What do you mean? "

" The hateful Royalist, the enemy of our religion upstairs, received to-day a messenger from Rome."

" I know that; it was I who told you."

" Well, our holy Father the Pope had sent him to this conspirator, who, however, probably did not suspect for what purpose."

" And why did he come? "

" Go upstairs, lift up the bedclothes, look at his neck, and you will see."

" You frighten me."

" I say no more. The pope did you honour in choosing your house for the scene of his vengeance."

Then Chicot put ten crowns into the hand of the host, and went down to the stable to get out the horses. M. Bernouillet went up and found Gorenflot praying. He looked as directed, and found the wound. " May every enemy of our religion die thus! " said he to Gorenflot.

" Amen," replied the monk.

These events took place about the same time that Bussy brought the Baron de Méridor back to his daughter.

CHAPTER XXXIII

HOW THE DUC D'ANJOU LEARNED THAT DIANE WAS NOT DEAD

THE last days of the month of April had arrived. The great cathedral of Chartres was hung with white, and the king was standing barefooted in the nave. The religious ceremonies, which were for the purpose of praying for an heir to the throne of France, were coming to an end, when Henri, in the midst of the general silence, heard what seemed to him a stifled laugh. He turned round to see if Chicot were there, for he thought no one else would have dared to laugh at such a time. It was not, however, Chicot who had laughed at the sight of the two chemises of the holy Virgin which were said to have such a prolific power, and which were just drawn from their golden box; but it was a cavalier who had stopped at the door of the church, and who was making his way with his muddy boots through the crowd of courtiers in their penitents' robes and sacks. Seeing the king turn, he stopped for a moment, and Henri, irritated at seeing him arrive thus, threw an angry glance at him. The new-comer, however, continued to advance until he knelt by the velvet chair of M. le Duc d'Anjou, who, absorbed in his thoughts rather than in his prayers, was not giving the least attention to what took place near him. However, when he felt the touch of this new-comer, he turned suddenly, and in a low tone exclaimed, "Bussy!"

"Good-morning, Monseigneur," Bussy replied, as if he had left the duke the evening before, and nothing of importance had occurred since they were together.

"Are you mad?"

"Why so?"

"To come here to see this nonsense."

"Monseigneur, I wish to speak to you at once."

"Where have you been for the last three weeks?"

"That is just what I have to tell you."

"Well, you must wait until we leave the church."

"So much the worse."

"Patience, here is the end."

Indeed, the king was putting on one of these chemises, and the queen another. Then they all knelt down, and afterwards the king, taking off his holy tunic, left the church.

"Now, Monseigneur," said Bussy, "shall we go to your house?"

"Yes, at once, for you ought to have many things to tell me."

"I have, Monseigneur, and things which you do not expect."

When they were in the hotel the duke said, "Now sit down and tell me all; I feared you were dead."

"Very likely, Monseigneur."

"You left me to look after my beautiful unknown. Who is this woman, and what am I to expect?"

" You will reap what you have sown, Monseigneur,—plenty of shame."

" What do you mean? " cried the duke.

" What I said."

" Explain yourself, Monsieur; who is this woman? "

" I thought you had recognised her."

" Then it was she? "

" Yes, Monseigneur."

" You saw her? "

" Yes."

" And she spoke to you? "

" Certainly; it is only ghosts who do not speak. Doubtless you had reason to think her dead, and you perhaps hoped she was so."

The duke grew pale, surprised by the rudeness of his manner.

" Yes, Monseigneur," continued Bussy, " although you pushed to despair a young girl of noble race, she escaped from death; but do not breathe yet, do not think yourself absolved, for in preserving her life, she found a misfortune worse than death."

" What is it?   What has happened to her? " said the duke, trembling.

" Monseigneur, a man preserved her honour and saved her life; but he made her pay for this service so dearly that she regrets his having rendered it."

" Finish."

" Well, Monseigneur, Mademoiselle de Méridor, to escape becoming the mistress of the Duc d'Anjou, has thrown herself into the arms of a man whom she detests, and is now Madame de Monsoreau."

" What do you say? "

" I say that Diane de Méridor is to-day Madame de Monsoreau."

At these words the blood rushed furiously into the duke's face. " Blood of Christ! " he exclaimed furiously; " is that true? "

" *Pardieu!* I said it," said Bussy, haughtily.

" I did not mean that,—I did not doubt your word, Bussy; I wondered only if it were possible that one of my gentlemen had had the audacity to interfere between me and a woman whom I honoured with my love."

" And why not? "

" Then you would have done so? "

"I would have done better; I would have warned you that your honour was drifting away."

"Listen, Bussy," said the prince, becoming calmer; "I do not justify myself, but M. de Monsoreau has been a traitor towards me."

"Towards you?"

"Yes; he knew my intentions."

"And they were?"

"To try and make Diane love me."

"To make her love you?"

"Yes, but in no case to use violence."

"Those were your intentions?" said Bussy, with an ironical smile.

"Certainly, and these intentions I preserved to the last, although M. de Monsoreau constantly combated them."

"Monseigneur, what do you say? This man incited you to dishonour Diane?"

"Yes."

"By his counsels?"

"By his letters. Would you like to see them?"

"Oh, if I could believe that!"

"You shall see." And the duke, opening a little cabinet, and taking out a letter, said, "Since you doubt your prince's words, read."

Bussy took it and read,—

MONSEIGNEUR,—Be quite easy; the *coup de main* can be executed without risk, for the young person sets off this evening to pass a week with an aunt who lives at the Château de Lude. I charge myself with it, and you need take no trouble. As for the scruples of the young lady, be sure that they will vanish in the presence of your Highness. Meanwhile I act; and this evening she will be at the Château de Beaugé.
        Your Highness's respectful servant,
                BRYAN DE MONSOREAU.

"Well, what do you say, Bussy?"

"I say that you are well served, Monseigneur."

"You mean betrayed."

"Ah, true; I forgot the end."

"The wretch! he made me believe in the death of a woman—"

"Whom he stole from you; it is black enough."

"How did he manage?"

"He made the father believe you the ravisher, and offered himself to rescue the lady, presented himself at the Château de Beaugé with a letter from the Baron de Méridor, brought a boat to the windows, and carried away the prisoner, then shut her up in the house you know of, and by constantly working upon her fears, forced her to become his wife."

" Is not that an infamous disloyalty? "

" Placed under shelter of your own, Monseigneur," replied Bussy, with his usual boldness.

" Ah, Bussy, you shall see how I will revenge myself! "

" Princes do not revenge themselves, they punish," said Bussy. " You will charge this Monsoreau with his infamous conduct, and punish him."

" How can I punish him? "

" By restoring happiness to Madame de Monsoreau."

" But can I? "

" Certainly."

" How? "

" By restoring her to liberty. The marriage was forced, therefore it is null."

" You are right."

" Get it set aside, then, and you will have acted like a gentleman and a prince."

" Ah, ah! " said the prince, " what warmth! you are interested in it, Bussy."

" I! not at all, except that I do not wish people to say that Louis de Clermont serves a perfidious prince and a man without honour."

" Well, you shall see. But how to break the marriage? "

" Nothing more easy; make her father act."

" But he is buried in Anjou."

" Monseigneur, he is here in Paris."

" At your house? "

" No, with his daughter. Speak to him, Monseigneur, that he may see in you, not what he does now, an enemy, but a protector,—that he who now curses your name may bless you."

" He is a powerful nobleman in his country," said the duke; " and it is said has great influence through all the province."

" Yes, Monseigneur; but what you ought to consider before everything else is that he is a father, that his daughter is unhappy, and he with her."

" And when can I see him? "

" As soon as you return to Paris."

" Very well."

" It is agreed, then? "

" Yes."

" On your word as a gentleman? "

" On my faith as a prince."

" And when do you return? "

" This evening; will you accompany me? "

" No, I go first; where shall I meet your Highness? "

" To-morrow at the king's levee."

" I will be there, Monseigneur."

Bussy did not lose a moment, and the distance that the duke required fifteen hours to accomplish, sleeping in his litter, the young man who returned to Paris in an exaltation of joy and love, did in five, to console the baron and Diane the sooner.

CHAPTER XXXIV

HOW CHICOT RETURNED TO THE LOUVRE, AND WAS RECEIVED BY THE KING HENRI III.

ALL was quiet at the Louvre, for the king, fatigued with his pilgrimage, had not yet risen, when two men presented themselves together at the gates.

" M. de Chicot," cried the younger, " how are you this morning? "

" Ah, it is Seigneur de Bussy. Wonderfully well, Monsieur," replied Chicot, with easy politeness.

" You come for the king's levee, Monsieur? "

" And you also, I presume? "

" No; I come to see M. le Duc d'Anjou. You know I have not the honour of being among the favourites of his Majesty."

" The reproach is for the king, and not for you."

Bussy bowed. " Do you come from far? " he asked; " I heard you were travelling."

" Yes, I was hunting; but have not you also made a journey? "

" Yes, I have been in the provinces; and now will you be good enough to render me a service? "

" I shall be delighted."

" Well, you can penetrate into the Louvre, while I remain in the antechamber; will you tell the duke I am waiting for him? "

" Why not come in with me? "

" The king would not be pleased."

" Bah! "

" *Diable!* he has not accustomed me to his most gracious smiles."

" Henceforth, for some time, all that will change."

" Ah, ah! are you a necromancer, M. Chicot? "

" Sometimes; come, take courage, and come in with me."

They entered together; one went towards the apartments of the Duc d'Anjou, and the other towards those of the king.

Henri was awake, and had rung. A crowd of valets and friends had rushed in; already the chicken broth and the spiced wine were served, when Chicot entered briskly, and without saying a word, sat down to eat and drink.

" *Par la mordieu!* " cried the king, delighted, although he affected anger; " it is that knave of a Chicot, that fugitive, that vagabond! "

" What is the matter, my son? " said Chicot, placing himself on the immense seat, embroidered with *fleur de lis,* on which the king was seated.

" Here is my misfortune returned, and I shall hear only disagreeable things," said Henri; " for three weeks I have been so tranquil."

" Bah! you always grumble. One would think you were one of your own subjects. Let me hear, Henriquet, how you have governed this kingdom in my absence."

" Chicot! "

" Have you hanged any of your curled gentlemen? Ah, pardon, M. Quélus, I did not see you."

" Chicot, we shall quarrel."

" Is there a little money left in our coffers or in those of the Jews? That wouldn't be bad; we must amuse ourselves. *Ventre de biche!* life is very wearisome."

The king laughed at him as usual. " Come," he said, " where have you been? Do you know that I have had you sought for in all the bad places in Paris? "

" Did you search the Louvre? "

Just then M. de Monsoreau entered.

" Ah! it is you, Monsieur," said the king; " when shall we hunt again? "

" When it shall please your Majesty; I hear there are plenty of wild boars at St. Germain en Laye."

" The wild boar is dangerous," said Chicot; " King Charles IX., I remember, was nearly killed by one. And then the spears are hard, and they make blisters on our little hands, do they not, my son? "

M. de Monsoreau looked sidewise at Chicot.

" Stay," said the Gascon to Henri, " your chief huntsman must have met a wolf not long ago."

" Why so? "

" Because he has caught the likeness,—in the eye, especially; it is striking."

M. de Monsoreau grew pale, and turning to Chicot, said, " M. Chicot, I am not used to jesters, having lived little at court, and I warn you that before my king I do not like to be humiliated,—above all, when I speak of my duties."

" Well, Monsieur," said Chicot, " we are not like you; we court people laughed heartily at the last joke."

" And what was that? "

" Making you chief huntsman. You see that the dear Henriquet, if less a buffoon than I am, is far more crazy."

Monsoreau looked daggers at Chicot.

" Come, come," said Henri; " let us speak of something else."

" Yes, let us speak of the merits of Notre-Dame de Chartres."

" Chicot, no impiety," said the king, in a severe tone.

" I impious? it is you, on the contrary; there were two chemises accustomed to be together, and you separated them. Join them together and a miracle may happen."

This allusion to the estrangement of the king and queen made every one laugh.

Monsoreau then whispered to Chicot, " Pray withdraw with me into that window, I wish to speak to you." When they were alone, he went on, " Now, M. Chicot, buffoon as you are, a gentleman forbids you,—do you understand?—forbids you to laugh at him, and reminds you that others may finish what M. de Mayenne began."

" Ah! you wish me to become your creditor, as I am his, and to give you the same place in my gratitude."

" It seems to me that among your creditors you forget the principal."

" Indeed, I have generally a good memory. Who may it be? "

" M. Nicolas David."

" Oh! you are wrong; he is paid."

At this moment Bussy entered. " Monsieur," said he to the count, " M. le Duc d'Anjou desires to speak with you."

" With me? "

" With you, Monsieur."

" Do you accompany me? "

" No, I go first, to tell the duke that you are coming; " and he returned as he had come, gliding, with his customary address, through the throng of courtiers.

The Duc d'Anjou was waiting in his cabinet, and reading again the letter with which we are already acquainted. Hearing some one enter, he thought it was Monsoreau, and hid the letter. Bussy appeared.

" Well? " said the duke.

" He is coming."

" And he suspects nothing? "

" Nothing; but if he did, what matter. Is he not your creature? Does he seem to you less guilty than he did yesterday? "

" No, a hundred times more so."

" He has carried off, by treason, a young girl of noble rank, and married her equally treasonably; either he must ask for the dissolution of the marriage himself, or you must do it for him."

" That is decided upon."

" And in the name of the father, in the name of the young girl, in the name of the Château de Méridor, in the name of Diane, I have your word? "

" You have."

" Remember that they know and are anxiously waiting."

" She shall be free, Bussy; I pledge my honour."

Bussy kissed the hand which had signed so many false promises. As he did so, M. de Monsoreau entered, and Bussy went to the corridor, where were several other gentlemen. Here he had to wait as patiently as might be for the result of this interview, on which all his future happiness was at stake. He waited for some time, when suddenly the door of the duke's room opened, and the sound of M. de Monsoreau's voice made Bussy tremble, for it sounded almost joyful. Soon the voices approached, and Bussy could see M. de Monsoreau bowing and retiring, and he heard the duke say, " Adieu, my friend, the thing is settled."

" ' My friend! ' " murmured Bussy. " *Sang Dieu!* what is the meaning of that? "

Then Monsoreau said, " Your Highness agrees with me that publicity is best? "

" Yes, yes; an end to all mysteries."

" Then this evening I will present her to the king."

" Do so; I will prepare him."

" Gentlemen," then said Monsoreau, turning towards those in the corridor, " allow me to announce to you a piece of news. Monseigneur permits me to make public my marriage with

Mademoiselle Diane de Méridor, who has been my wife for more than a month, and whom under his auspices I shall this evening present at the court."

Bussy, who had been hidden behind a *portière*, staggered and almost fell at this unexpected blow. He came forward, and he and the duke, both pale, exchanged glances,—of contempt on Bussy's part, of terror on the part of the duke. Bussy made a movement as if to approach the duke, who saw it, and shut his door; and Bussy heard the key turn in the lock. Feeling that if he stayed a moment longer he should betray before every one the violence of his grief, he ran downstairs, got on his horse, and galloped to the Rue St. Antoine. The baron and Diane were eagerly waiting for him, and they saw him enter, pale and trembling.

"Madame," cried he, "hate me, despise me; I believed I could do something, and I can do nothing. Madame, you are now the recognised wife of M. de Monsoreau, and are to be presented this evening. I am a fool, a miserable dupe,—or rather, as you said, Monsieur the Baron, the duke is a coward and a villain."

And leaving the father and daughter overcome with grief, he rushed wildly away.

CHAPTER XXXV

WHAT TOOK PLACE BETWEEN M. DE MONSOREAU AND THE DUKE

It is time to explain the duke's sudden change of intention with regard to M. de Monsoreau. When he first received him, he was in a state of mind entirely favourable to Bussy's wishes. His anger was fed from two sources,—his wounded self-love, and his fear of an exposure, threatened by Bussy, in the name of M. de Méridor.

"Your Highness sent for me?" said Monsoreau, very calm, and examining the tapestries as if demanding of them an explanation of the duke's purposes.

"Fear nothing, Monsieur," said the duke; "there is no one behind those curtains. We can talk freely and frankly."

Monsoreau bowed.

"For you are a good servant, Monsieur the Grand Huntsman of France, and you have an attachment to my person?"

" I think so, Monsieur."

" I am sure of it. Often you have told me of the plots against me, have aided my enterprises, forgetting your own interests, and exposing your life."

" Your Highness—"

" Even lately, in this last unlucky adventure—"

" What adventure, Monseigneur? "

" This carrying off of Mademoiselle de Méridor,—poor young creature! "

" Alas! " murmured Monsoreau.

" You pity her, do you not? " said the duke.

" Does not your Highness? "

" I! you know how I have regretted this fatal caprice. And indeed it required all my friendship for you, and the remembrance of all your good services, to make me forget that without you I should not have carried off this young girl."

Monsoreau felt the blow. " Monseigneur," said he, " your natural goodness leads you to exaggerate; you no more caused the death of this young girl than I did."

" How so? "

" You did not intend to use violence to Mademoiselle de Méridor."

" Certainly not."

" Then the intention absolves you; it is a misfortune, nothing more."

" And besides," said the duke, looking at him, " death has buried all in eternal silence."

The tone of his voice and his look struck Monsoreau. " Monseigneur," said he, after a moment's pause, " shall I speak frankly to you? "

" Why should you hesitate? " said the prince, with astonishment mingled with hauteur.

" Indeed, I do not know why I should hesitate."

" That is to say? "

" Oh, Monseigneur, I wish to say that with a prince so eminent by his intelligence and his nobleness of heart, frankness should enter henceforth as a principal element in this conversation."

" Henceforth!—which means? "

" That at the beginning your Highness has not thought proper to use that frankness towards me."

" Really! " cried the duke, with an explosive laugh that betrayed a furious anger.

" Monseigneur, I know what your Highness meant to say to me."

" Speak, then."

" Your Highness wished to make me understand that perhaps Mademoiselle de Méridor was not dead, and that therefore those who believed themselves her murderers might be free from remorse."

" Oh, Monsieur, you have taken your time before making this consoling reflection to me. You are a faithful servant, on my word; you saw me sad and afflicted, you heard me speak of the wretched dreams I had since the death of this woman, and you let me live thus, when even a doubt might have spared me so much suffering. How must I consider this conduct, Monsieur? "

" Monseigneur, is your Highness accusing me? "

" Traitor! " cried the duke, " you have deceived me; you have taken from me this woman whom I loved—"

Monsoreau turned pale, but did not lose his proud, calm look.
" It is true," said he.

" Ah! it is true? The impudent knave! "

" Please to speak lower, Monseigneur; your Highness forgets that you speak to a gentleman and a good servant."

The duke laughed convulsively.

" A good servant to the king," continued Monsoreau, still unmoved.

That word checked the duke. " What do you mean? " he murmured.

" I mean," replied Monsoreau, with obsequious gentleness, " that I might wish to have that woman, since you yourself have wished to have her."

The duke could make no reply, stupefied by such audacity.

" My excuse is," the chief huntsman humbly continued, " that I loved Mademoiselle de Méridor ardently."

" I also," replied François, with dignity.

" It is true, Monseigneur; but she did not love you."

" And she loved you,—you? "

" Perhaps," murmured Monsoreau.

" You lie! you lie! You used force as I did; only I, the master, failed, while you, the servant, succeeded, because I had only power, while you could use treason."

" Monseigneur, I loved her."

" What is that to me? "

" Monseigneur—"

" Threats, serpent? "

" Monseigneur, take care! " said Monsoreau, lowering his head like a tiger about to spring. " I loved her, I tell you; and I am not one of your servants, as you said just now. My wife is mine, like my land, and no one can take her from me, not even the king. I wished to have her, and I took her."

" Really! " said François, springing towards a silver bell on the table, " you took her! Well, you shall give her up."

" You are wrong, Monseigneur," cried Monsoreau, darting towards the table to stop the duke. " Dismiss your evil intention to do me a wrong; for if you call once, if you do me a public injury—"

" You shall give up this woman, I tell you! "

" Give her up! she is my wife before God—"

" If she is your wife before God, you shall give her up before men. I know all, and I will break this marriage, I tell you. To-morrow, Mademoiselle de Méridor shall be restored to her father; you shall set off into the exile I impose on you; you shall have sold your place. These are my conditions, and take care, or I will break you as I break this glass." And he threw down violently a crystal cup.

" I will not give up my wife; I will not give up my place; and I will remain in France! " replied Monsoreau.

" You will not! "

" No, I will ask my pardon of the King of France,—of the king anointed at the Abbey Ste. Geneviève; and this new sovereign, so good, so noble, so blessed with divine favour, so recently crowned, too, will not, I am sure, refuse the first request proffered to him."

François grew deadly pale, and nearly fell. " Well, well," stammered he; " this request, speak lower—I listen."

" I will speak humbly, as becomes the servant of your Highness. A fatal love was the cause of all. Love is the most imperious of the passions. To make me forget that your Highness had cast your eyes on Diane, I must have been no longer master of myself."

" It was treasonable, Count, as I told you."

" Do not overwhelm me, Monseigneur," said Monsoreau, in a low tone; " I saw you rich, young, and happy, the first Christian prince in the world,—for you are so, and between you and supreme rank there is now only a shadow easy to dispel. I saw all the splendour of your future, and, comparing your proud position with my humble one, I said, ' Leave to the prince his brilliant prospects and splendid projects; scarcely will he miss the pearl that I steal from his royal crown.' "

"Count! Count!" said the duke, intoxicated in spite of himself by the charms of that future.

"You pardon me, Monseigneur, do you not?"

At this moment the duke raised his eyes, and saw Bussy's portrait on the wall. It seemed to exhort him to courage, and he said, "No, I cannot pardon you. It is not for myself that I hold out; it is because a father in mourning—a father unworthily deceived—cries out for his daughter; because a woman, forced to marry you, cries for vengeance against you; because, in a word, the first duty of a prince is justice."

"Monseigneur, if justice be a duty, gratitude is not less so; and a king should never forget those to whom he owes his crown. Now, Monseigneur, you owe your crown to me."

"Monsoreau!" cried the duke, in terror. "Are you, then, a traitor to the king as well as to the prince?"

"I attach myself to those who sustain me, Sire," said Monsoreau, in a louder tone.

"Unhappy man!" The duke looked again at Bussy's portrait. "I cannot do it," he said. "You are a gentleman, —you know I cannot approve of what you have done."

"Why not?"

"Because it is a deed unworthy of you, and of me. Renounce that woman. Eh! my dear count, this one more sacrifice. I will recompense you for it; I will give you all you ask."

"Then your Highness loves her still!" cried Monsoreau, pale with jealousy.

"No, I swear I do not."

"Then why should I? I am a gentleman; who can enter into the secrets of my private life?"

"But she does not love you."

"What matter?"

"Do this for me, Monsoreau."

"I cannot."

"Then—" began the duke, who was terribly perplexed.

"Reflect, Sire."

"You will denounce me?"

"To the king dethroned for you,—yes, your Majesty; for if my new king destroyed my honour and happiness, I would return to the old."

"It is infamous!"

"True, Sire; but I love enough to be infamous."

" It is cowardly ! "

" Yes, your Majesty; but I love enough to be cowardly."

The duke made a movement towards Monsoreau; but the latter stopped him with a smile.

" You would gain nothing by killing me, Monseigneur," he said; " there are secrets which float with the corpse. Let us be as we are,—you a king full of clemency, I the most humble of your subjects."

The duke clasped his hands, and tore them with his finger-nails.

" Come, Monseigneur, do something for the man who has served you so well in everything."

" What do you want? "

" That you should pardon me."

" I will."

" That you should reconcile me with M. de Méridor."

" I will try."

" That you will sign my marriage contract with Mademoiselle de Méridor."

" Yes," said the prince, in a hoarse voice.

" And that you shall honour my wife with a smile on the day when she will appear formally in the queen's circle, to whom I wish the honour of presenting her."

" Yes; is that all? "

" All, Monseigneur."

" You have my word."

" And you shall keep the throne to which I have raised you. Adieu, Sire. There remains now only," thought Monsoreau, " to find out who told the duke."

CHAPTER XXXVI

CHICOT AND THE KING

THAT same evening M. de Monsoreau presented his wife in the queen's circle. Henri, tired, had gone to bed, but after sleeping three or four hours, he woke, and feeling no longer sleepy, proceeded to the room where Chicot slept, which was the one formerly occupied by Saint-Luc. Chicot slept soundly, and the king called him three times before he woke. At last he opened his eyes and cried out, " What is it? "

" Chicot, my friend, it is I."

" You; who? "

" I, Henri."

" Decidedly, my son, the pheasants must have disagreed with you; I warned you at supper, but you would eat so much of them, as well as of those crabs."

" No; I scarcely tasted them."

" Then you are poisoned, perhaps. *Ventre de biche!* how pale you are! "

" It is my mask," said the king.

" Then you are not ill? "

" No."

" Then why wake me? "

" Because I am annoyed."

" Annoyed! if you wake a man at two o'clock in the morning, at least you should bring him a present. Have you anything for me? "

" No; I come to talk to you."

" That is not enough."

" Chicot, M. de Morvilliers came here last evening."

" You receive very bad company, Henri. What did he come for? "

" To ask for an audience."

" Ah! there is a man who knows something,—that is not like you, who come to one's chamber without notice at two o'clock in the morning."

" What can he want to say to me, Chicot? "

" What! is it only to ask that that you wake me? "

" Chicot, you know he occupies himself with the police.".

" No; I did not know it."

" Do you doubt his watchfulness? "

" Yes, I do, and I have my reasons."

" What are they? "

" Will one suffice you? "

" Yes, if it be good."

" And you will leave me in peace afterwards? "

" Certainly."

" Well, one day—no, it was one evening—I beat you in the Rue Froidmentel; you had with you Quélus and Schomberg."

" You beat me? "

" Yes, all three of you."

" What was it for? "

" You had insulted my page. You received the blows, and M. de Morvilliers has not discovered who gave them."

" What! it was you, wretch? "

" I myself," said Chicot, rubbing his hands; " do I not hit hard? "

" Wretch! "

" You confess it was true? "

" I will have you whipped, Chicot."

" That is not the question. Is it true or not? that is all I ask you."

" You know well that it is true, you scoundrel."

" Did you send for M. de Morvilliers the next day? "

" You know I did, for you were there when he came."

" And you told him the accident that had happened to one of your friends? "

" Yes."

" And you ordered him to find out the criminal? "

" Yes."

" Did he find him? "

" No."

" Well, then, go to bed, Henri; you see your police is bad." And, turning round, Chicot refused to say another word, and was soon snoring again.

The next day the council assembled. It consisted of Quélus, Maugiron, D'Epernon, and Schomberg. Chicot, seated at the head of the table, was making paper boats and arranging them in a fleet. M. de Morvilliers was announced, and came in, looking grave. After a profound salutation, responded to by Chicot, he approached the king. " Am I," said he, " before your Majesty's council? "

" Yes, before my best friends; speak freely."

" Well, Sire, I have a terrible plot to denounce to your Majesty."

" A plot! " cried all.

Chicot abandoned his fleet and began to listen.

" Yes, your Majesty," said M. de Morvilliers, in the half-suppressed tone that presages terrible confidences.

" Oh, is it a Spanish plot? "

At this moment the Duc d'Anjou, who had been summoned to attend the council, entered.

" My brother," said Henri, " M. de Morvilliers comes to announce a plot to us."

The duke threw a suspicious glance round him. " Is it possible? " he said.

" Alas, yes, Monseigneur," said M. de Morvilliers.

" Tell us all about it," said Chicot.

" Yes," stammered the duke; " tell us all about it, Monsieur."

" I listen," said Henri.

" Sire, for some time I have been watching some malcontents; but they were shopkeepers, or junior clerks, a few monks and students."

" That is not much," said Chicot.

" I know that malcontents always make use either of war or of religion."

" Very sensible!" said the king.

" In the army I had officers devoted to your Majesty, who informed me of everything; in religion the affair was more difficult. I put men on the watch."

" Still very sensible," said Chicot.

" In short, through my agents, I persuaded a man connected with the provostship of Paris to watch the preachers, who go about exciting the people against your Majesty."

" Oh, oh!" thought Chicot. " Has he an eye on my friend?"

" They are prompted by a party hostile to your Majesty, and this party I have studied."

" Very well," said the king.

" Quite sensible," said Chicot.

" And I am acquainted with their purposes," added Morvilliers, triumphantly.

" It is superb!" cried Chicot.

The king made a sign to him to keep still. The Duc d'Anjou kept his eyes on the speaker.

" For more than two months," said the chancellor, " I have had in your Majesty's pay men of much skill, of tried courage, of an insatiable cupidity, it is true; but I have taken care to turn that to the profit of the king, since, though paying much, I gain more. For a good round sum of money I shall learn the chief rendezvous of the conspirators."

" That is good," said Chicot. " Pay it, my king; pay it!"

" Eh! let not that stop you," cried Henri; " but let us have it, Chancellor,—what is the aim of this plot? What do the conspirators expect?"

" Sire, they think of nothing less than a second Saint Bartholomew."

" Against whom?"

" Against the Huguenots."

" About how much has that cost you?" said Chicot.

" One hundred and seventy-five thousand livres."

Chicot turned to the king, saying, " If you like, for one thousand crowns, I will tell you all the secrets of M. de Morvilliers."

" Speak."

" It is simply the League, instituted ten years ago; M. de Morvilliers has discovered what every Parisian knows as well as his *Ave*."

" Monsieur," interrupted the chancellor.

" I speak the truth, and I will prove it," cried Chicot.

" Tell me, then, their place of meeting."

" Firstly, the public streets; secondly, the public streets."

" M. Chicot is joking," said the chancellor; " tell me their rallying sign."

" They are dressed like Parisians, and shake their legs when they walk."

A burst of laughter followed this speech; then M. de Morvilliers said, " They have had one meeting-place which M. Chicot does not know of."

The Duc d'Anjou turned pale.

" Where? " asked the king.

" The Abbey Ste. Geneviève."

" Impossible! " murmured the duke.

" It is true," said M. de Morvilliers, triumphantly.

" And what did they do? What did they decide? " asked the king.

" That the Leaguers should choose chiefs; that every one enrolled should arm; that every province should receive a deputy from the conspirators; and that all the Huguenots cherished by his Majesty,—that was their expression—"

The king smiled.

" Should be massacred on a given day."

" Is that all? " said the duke.

" No, Monseigneur."

" I should hope not," said Chicot; " if the king got only that for one hundred and seventy-five thousand livres, it would be a shame."

" There are chiefs—"

Chicot observed that the duke's doublet was agitated by the beating of his heart. " What! " he cried; " a conspiracy that has chiefs! how wonderful! But we ought to have more than that for one hundred and seventy-five thousand livres."

" Their names? " asked the king.

" Firstly, a fanatic preacher; I gave ten thousand livres for his name."

" Very well."

" A monk called Gorenflot."

" Poor devil! " said Chicot, with true commiseration.

" Gorenflot? " said the king, writing down the name; " well? "

" Oh! " said the chancellor, with hesitation, " that is all."
And he looked round as if to say, " If your Majesty were alone,
you should hear more."

" Speak, Chancellor," said the king; " I have none but
friends here."

" Oh, Sire, I hesitate to pronounce such powerful names."

" Are they more powerful than I am? " cried the king.

" No, Sire; but one does not tell secrets in public."

" Monsieur," said the Duc d'Anjou, " we will retire."

The king signed to the chancellor to approach him, and to
the duke to remain. M. de Morvilliers had just bent over the
king to whisper his communication, when a great clamour was
heard in the court of the Louvre. The king jumped up, but
Chicot, running to the window, called out, " It is M. de Guise
entering the Louvre."

" The Duc de Guise? " stammered the Duc d'Anjou.

" How strange that he should be in Paris! " said the king,
reading in M. de Morvilliers's face the name which the latter
had intended to give him. " Was it of him you were about to
speak? " he asked in a low tone.

" Yes, Sire; he presided over the meeting."

" And the others? "

" I know no more."

Henri consulted Chicot with a glance.

" *Ventre de biche !* " cried the Gascon, taking a royal attitude;
" admit my cousin of Guise! " And leaning towards Henri, he
said, " You need not write that name on your tablets! you
will not forget it."

The ushers noisily opened the door.

" Only one door, gentlemen," said Henri; " only one,—the
two are for the king."

The Duc de Guise was near enough to hear these words; but
they made no change in the smile with which he had determined
to meet the king.

CHAPTER XXXVII

WHAT M. DE GUISE CAME TO DO AT THE LOUVRE

BEHIND M. de Guise there entered a great number of officers, courtiers, and gentlemen, and behind was a concourse of the people,—an escort less brilliant, but more formidable; and it was their cries that had resounded as the duke entered the Louvre.

" Ah! it is you, my cousin," said the king; " what a noise you bring with you! Did I not hear the trumpets sound? "

" Sire, the trumpets sound in Paris only for the king, and in campaigns for the general. Here the trumpets would make too much noise for a subject; there they do not make enough for a prince."

Henri bit his lips. " *Par la mordieu !* " he said, after a silence devoted to a scrutiny of the Lorraine prince, " you are very brilliant, my cousin. Is it possible that you have arrived from the siege of La Charité only to-day? "

" Only to-day, Sire," replied the duke, with a heightened colour.

" Faith! your visit is a great honour to us."

" Your Majesty jests, no doubt. How can my visit honour him from whom all honour comes? "

" I mean, M. de Guise," replied Henri, " that every good Catholic is in the habit, on returning from a campaign, to visit God first in one of his temples; the king comes only second. ' Honour God, serve the king,' you know, my cousin."

The heightened colour of the duke became now still more distinct; and the king, happening to turn towards his brother, saw with astonishment that he was as pale as the duke was red. He was struck by this emotion in each, but he said, " At all events, Duke, nothing equals my joy to see that you have escaped all the dangers of war, although you sought them, I was told, in the rashest manner; but danger knows you and avoids you."

The duke bowed.

" But I must beg you, my cousin, not to be so ambitious of mortal perils, for you put to shame sluggards like us, who sleep, eat, and invent new fashions and new prayers."

" Yes, Sire," replied the duke, " we know you to be a pious prince, and that no pleasure can make you forget the glory of

God and the interests of the Church. That is why we have come with so much confidence to your Majesty."

"With confidence! Do you not always come to me with confidence, my cousin?"

"Sire, the confidence of which I speak refers to the proposition I am about to make to you."

"You have a proposition to make to me! Well, speak, as you say, with confidence. What have you to propose?"

"The execution of one of the most beautiful ideas which has been originated since the Crusades."

"Continue, Duke."

"Sire," said the duke, now raising his voice so as to be heard in the antechamber, "the title of most Christian king is not a vain one; it makes an ardent zeal for religion incumbent on its possessor. The eldest son of the Church—that is your title, Sire—should be ever ready to defend his mother."

"Behold," said Chicot, "my cousin who preaches with a long sword at his side, and a helmet on his head; it is comical! I am no longer surprised that the monks want to fight. Henri, I demand a regiment for Gorenflot."

The duke pretended not to hear. Henri crossed his legs and rested his elbow on his knee and his chin on his hand. "Is the Church menaced by the Saracens once more," he said, "or do you aspire perchance to be king—of Jerusalem?"

"Sire, the great concourse of people who followed me, blessing my name, honoured me with this reception only because of my zeal to defend the Church. I have already had the honour of speaking to your Majesty of the project of an alliance among all true Catholics."

"Yes, yes," said Chicot, "the League; *ventre de biche!* Henri, the League. By Saint Bartholomew! how can you forget so splendid an idea, my son?"

The duke cast a disdainful glance on Chicot, while D'Anjou, who stood by, as pale as death, tried by signs to make the duke stop.

"Look at your brother, Henri," whispered Chicot. Henri quickly glanced at the Duc d'Anjou, caught the signal, and understood its meaning.

"Sire," continued the Duc de Guise, "the Catholics have indeed called this association the holy League, and its aim is to fortify the throne against the Huguenots, its mortal enemies; but to form an association is not enough, and in a kingdom like France, several millions of men cannot assemble without the consent of the king."

"Several millions!" cried Henri, almost with terror.

"Several millions!" repeated Chicot,—"a small number of malcontents, which under skilful management (of which there can be no doubt) may bring forth pretty results."

"Sire," cried the duke, "I am astonished that your Majesty allows me to be interrupted so often when I am speaking on serious matters."

"Quite right," said Chicot; "silence there!"

"Several millions!" repeated the king; "and against these millions, how many Huguenots are there in my kingdom?"

"Four," said Chicot.

This new sally made the king and his friends laugh; but the duke frowned, and his gentlemen murmured loudly.

The king turned slowly, and with that dignified expression which he could sometimes assume, towards the door of the antechamber whence these murmurs proceeded, and they immediately ceased. Then, turning towards the duke with the same dignity, "Let us see, Monsieur," he said, "what you wish; to the point, to the point!"

"I wish, Sire,—for the popularity of my king is dearer to me than my own,—I wish your Majesty to show clearly that you are as superior to us in your zeal for the Catholic religion as in all other things; you will thus take from the discontented every pretext of beginning war again."

"Ah! if it is a question of war, my cousin," said Henri, "I have troops; even under your command, in the camp from which you have come to give me this excellent counsel, you have, I believe, about twenty-five thousand men."

"Sire, when I speak of war, I ought perhaps to explain myself."

"Explain yourself, my cousin. You are a great captain, and you may be sure that I shall take pleasure in hearing you discourse on such subjects."

"Sire, I meant to say that at the present time kings are called to maintain two wars,—moral war, if I may so express myself, and political war; war against ideas, and war against men."

"*Mordieu!*" said Chicot, "how powerfully expounded!"

"Silence, fool!" said the king.

"Men," continued the duke, "are visible, palpable, mortal. You can meet, attack, subdue them; and when they are subdued you can subject them to trial and hang them. But ideas you cannot oppose in that way, Sire. They glide unseen; they penetrate; they hide themselves especially from the sight of those who would destroy them. Hidden in the depth of the soul, they there throw out deep roots. The more you cut off the branches which imprudently appear, the more powerful and inextirpable become the roots below. An idea, Sire, is a young giant, which must be watched night and day; for the idea which yesterday crawled at your feet, to-morrow will dispose of your head. An idea, Sire, is a spark falling upon straw. There is need of good eyes to discover the beginning of the conflagration; and this is why, Sire, millions of watchers are necessary. It is in order to provide for and direct that watchfulness that I propose to your Majesty that you appoint a chief for the holy Union."

"Have you spoken, my cousin?" asked Henri.

"Yes, Sire, and without circumlocution, as your Majesty has perceived."

Chicot heaved a tremendous sigh, while the Duc d'Anjou, recovered from his first fright, smiled on the Lorraine prince.

"Well!" said the king to those who surrounded him, "what do you think of it, my friends?"

Chicot, without saying a word, drew out a lion's skin from a corner, and threw himself on it.

"What are you doing, Chicot?" asked the king.

"Sire, they say that night brings good counsel,—that must be because of sleep; therefore I am going to sleep, and to-morrow I will reply to my cousin Guise."

The duke cast a furious glance on Chicot, who replied by a loud snore.

"Well, Sire!" said the duke, "what does your Majesty say?"

"I think that, as usual, you are in the right, my cousin. Convoke, then, your principal Leaguers; come at their head; and I will choose the chief."

"When, Sire?"

"To-morrow."

The Duc de Guise then took leave, and the Duc d'Anjou was about to do the same, when the king said,—

"Stay, my brother, I wish to speak to you."

CHAPTER XXXVIII

CASTOR AND POLLUX

THE king dismissed all his favourites, and remained with his brother. The duke, who had managed to preserve a tolerably composed countenance throughout, believed himself unsuspected, and accepted Henri's invitation without distrust. He had no suspicion of the glance sent him by the king at Chicot's instigation, and which had surprised his indiscreet finger too near his lips.

" My brother," said Henri, after assuring himself that with the exception of Chicot no one remained in the room, " do you know that I am a very happy prince? "

" Sire, if your Majesty be really happy, it is a recompense from Heaven for your merits."

" Yes, happy," continued the king, " for if great ideas do not come to me, they do to my subjects. It is a great idea which has occurred to my cousin Guise."

The duke made a sign of assent, and Chicot opened his eyes to watch the king's face.

" Indeed," continued Henri, " to unite under one banner all the Catholics, to arm all France on this pretext from Calais to Languedoc, from Bretagne to Burgundy, so that I shall always have an army ready to march against England, Holland, or Spain, without alarming any of them,—do you know, François, it is a magnificent idea."

" Is it not, Sire? " said the duke, delighted.

" Yes, I confess I feel tempted to reward largely the author of this fine project."

Chicot opened his eyes, but he shut them again, for he had seen on the face of the king one of those almost imperceptible smiles, visible to him alone, who knew the king better than any one else; and that smile reassured him.

" Yes," continued Henri, " I repeat, such a project merits recompense, and I will do what I can for him who has conceived it. Is it really the Duc de Guise who is the originator of that fine idea, or rather of that good work,—for the work is begun, is it not, my brother? "

The duke indicated by a sign of assent that the execution of the project had already begun.

"Better and better; my subjects not only conceive these good ideas, but in their anxiety to be of use to me, hasten to put them in execution. But I ask you, my dear François, if it be really to the Duc de Guise that I am indebted for this royal thought?"

"No, Sire, it occurred to the Cardinal de Lorraine twenty years ago, and the Saint Bartholomew only prevented its execution, or rather, made its execution needless."

"Ah! what a pity he is dead; but," continued Henri, with that air of frankness which made him the first comedian of the day, "his nephew has inherited it, and brought it to bear. What can I do for him?"

"Sire," said François, completely duped by his brother, "you exaggerate his merits. He has, as I say, but inherited the idea, and another man has given him great help in developing it."

"His brother the cardinal?"

"Doubtless he has been occupied with it, but I do not mean him."

"Mayenne, then?"

"Oh, Sire, you do him too much honour."

"True, how could any good ideas come to such a butcher? But to whom, then, am I to be grateful for his aid to my cousin Guise?"

"To me, Sire."

"To you!" cried Henri, as if in astonishment. "How! when I saw all the world unchained against me,—the preachers against my vices, the poets against my weaknesses,—while my friends laughed at my powerlessness, and my situation was so harassing that it gave me grey hairs every day, such an idea came to you, François,—to you, whom I confess (for man is feeble and kings are blind) I did not always believe to be my friend! Ah, François, how guilty I have been!" And Henri, moved even to tears, held out his hand to his brother.

Chicot opened his eyes again.

"Oh!" continued Henri, "the idea is triumphant. Not being able to raise troops without raising an outcry, scarcely to walk, sleep, or love without exciting ridicule, this idea of M. de Guise—or rather, yours, my brother—gives me at once an army, money, friends, and repose. But my cousin spoke of a chief?"

"Yes, doubtless."

"This chief, you understand, François, cannot be one of my favourites; none of them has at once the head and the heart necessary for so important a post. Quélus is brave, but is occupied only by his amours. Maugiron is also brave, but he thinks only of his toilet; Schomberg also, but he is not clever. D'Epernon is a valiant man; but he is a hypocrite, whom I could not trust, although I am friendly to him. But, you know, François," said the king, with increasing effusiveness, " that one of the heaviest taxes on a king is the necessity of dissimulation; therefore, when I can speak freely from my heart, as I do now, —ah! I breathe."

Chicot closed both eyes.

" Well, then, if my cousin Guise originated this idea, in the development of which you have assisted, the execution of it belongs to him."

" What do you say, Sire? " said François, uneasily.

" I say that to direct such a movement we must have a prince of high rank."

" Sire, take care."

" A good captain and a skilful negotiator."

" The last, particularly."

" Well, is not M. de Guise all this? "

" My brother, he is very powerful already."

" Yes, doubtless; but his power makes my strength."

" He holds already the army and the *bourgeois ;* the cardinal holds the Church; and Mayenne is their instrument. It is a great deal of power to be concentrated in one family."

" It is true, François; I had thought of that."

" If the Guises were French princes, their interest would be to aggrandise France."

" Yes, but they are Lorraines."

" Of a house always rival to ours."

" Yes, François; you have touched the sore. I did not think you so good a politician. Yes, there does not pass a day but one or other of these Guises, either by address or by force, carries away from me some particle of my power. Ah, François, if we had but had this explanation sooner, if I had been able to read your heart as I do now, certain of support in you, I might have resisted better, but now it is too late."

" Why so? "

" Because all combats fatigue me; therefore I must make him chief of the League."

" You will be wrong, Brother."

" But whom could I name, François? Who would accept this perilous post? Yes, perilous; for do you not see that he intended me to appoint him chief, and that should I name any one else to the post, he would treat him as an enemy?"

"Name some one so powerful that, supported by you, he need not fear all the three Lorraine princes together."

"Ah, my good brother, I know no such person."

"Look around you, Brother."

"Around me I see only you and Chicot, my brother, who are truly my friends."

"Well, Brother?"

Henri looked at the duke as if a veil had fallen from his eyes. "Surely you would never consent, Brother! It is not you who could teach all these *bourgeois* their exercises, who could look over the discourses of the preachers, who, in case of battle, would play the butcher in the streets of Paris; for all this, one must be triple, like the duke, and have a right arm called Charles and a left called Louis. What! you would like all this? You, the first gentleman of our court! *Mort de ma vie!* how people change with the age!"

"Perhaps I would not do it for myself, Brother, but I would do it for you."

"Excellent brother!" said Henri, wiping away a tear which never existed.

"Then," said the duke, "it would not displease you for me to assume this post?"

"Displease me!" cried Henri. "*Corne du diable!* no, it does not displease me, it delights me, on the contrary. So you too, you had thought of the League. So much the better! *Mordieu!* so much the better! You too, you had a little end of the idea,—what do I say, a little end? The big end! After what you have told me, upon my word, I am filled with astonishment. In fact, I have around me only superior intelligences and am myself the great ass of my kingdom."

"Oh! your Majesty jests."

"I? God forbid! the situation is too grave. I say what I think, François. You will deliver me from a great embarrassment, the greater because for some time past I have been ill; my faculties are depressed. Miron often explains that to me. But what need have I of intelligence while I can light my way by the brilliancy of yours? It is agreed, then, that I shall appoint you chief of the League?"

François trembled with joy. "Oh! if your Majesty thinks me worthy of this confidence."

"Confidence! When you are the chief what have I to

fear? The League itself? That cannot be dangerous, can it, François?"

"Oh, Sire!"

"No, for then you would not be chief,—or at least, when you are chief there will be no danger. But, François, the duke is doubtless certain of this appointment, and he will not lightly give way."

"Sire, you grant me the command?"

"Certainly."

"And you wish me to have it?"

"Particularly; but I dare not too much displease M. de Guise."

"Oh, make yourself easy, Sire; if that be the only obstacle, I pledge myself to arrange it."

"When?"

"At once."

"Are you going to him? That will be doing him too much honour."

"No, Sire; he is waiting for me."

"Where?"

"In my room."

"Your room! I heard the cries of the people as he left the Louvre."

"Yes; but after going out at the great door he came back by the postern. The king had the right to the first visit, but I to the second."

"Ah, Brother, I thank you for keeping up our prerogative, which I have the weakness so often to abandon. Go, then, François, and do your best."

François bent down to kiss the king's hand; but he, opening his arms, gave him a warm embrace, and then the duke left the room to go to his interview with the Duc de Guise. The king, seeing his brother gone, gave an angry growl, and rapidly made his way through the secret corridor, until he reached a hiding-place whence he could distinctly hear the conversation between the two dukes.

"*Ventre de biche!*" cried Chicot, starting up, "how touching these family scenes are! For an instant I believed myself in Olympus, assisting at the reunion of Castor and Pollux after six months' separation."

CHAPTER XXXIX

IN WHICH IT IS PROVED THAT LISTENING IS THE BEST WAY TO HEAR

THE Duc d'Anjou was well aware that there were few rooms in the Louvre which were not built so that what was said in them could be heard from the outside; but completely beguiled by his brother's manner, he forgot to take any precautions. Henri III. entered his place of observation at the moment when his brother entered his chamber, so that not a word of the two interlocutors escaped his hearing.

"Why, Monseigneur," said the Duc de Guise, "how pale you are!"

"Visibly?"

"Yes, to me."

"The king saw nothing?"

"I think not; but he retained you?"

"Yes."

"Doubtless to speak of the proposition which I had made to him."

"Yes, Monsieur."

There was then a moment of embarrassing silence, the meaning of which Henri in his hiding-place completely understood.

"And what says his Majesty, Monseigneur?" asked the Duc de Guise.

"He approves the idea; but the greater it appears, the more he hesitates to place a man like you at the head."

"Then we are likely to fail?"

"I fear so, my dear duke; the League seems to be suppressed."

"The devil!" said the duke; "that would be to die before birth, to end before beginning."

At this moment Henri, hearing a noise, turned and saw Chicot by his side, listening also. "You followed me, knave!" said he.

"Hush, my son!" said Chicot; "you prevent me from hearing."

The king shrugged his shoulders; but as Chicot was the only human being in whom he had entire confidence, he resumed his listening.

"Monseigneur," said the Duc de Guise, "it seems to me that

in that case the king would have refused at once.   Does he wish to oust me?"

"I believe so," said the prince, with hesitation.

"Then he would ruin the enterprise?"

"Yes; but I aided you with all my power."

"How, Monseigneur?"

"In this,—the king has left me almost master, to kill or reanimate the League."

"How so?" cried the duke, with sparkling eyes.

"Why, if instead of dissolving the League, he named me chief—"

"Ah!" cried the duke, while the blood mounted to his face.

"Good! the dogs are going to fight over their bones," said Chicot; but to his surprise and the king's, the Duc de Guise suddenly became calm, and exclaimed in an almost joyful tone, "You are an adroit politician, Monseigneur, if you did this."

"Yes, I did; but I would not conclude anything without speaking to you."

"Why so, Monseigneur?"

"Because I did not know what it would lead us to."

"Well, I will tell you, Monseigneur, not to what it will lead us,—God alone knows that,—but how it will serve us.   The League is a second army; and as I hold the first, and my brother the Church, nothing can resist us as long as we are united."

"Without counting," said the Duc d'Anjou, " that I am heir presumptive to the throne."

"Ah, ah!" said Henri.

"He is right," said Chicot; " and it is your fault, my son,— you still keep separate the two chemises of Notre-Dame de Chartres."

"But, Monseigneur," said the Duc de Guise, " heir presumptive though you are, calculate your bad chances."

"I have done so a hundred times."

"There is, first, the King of Navarre."

"Oh! I do not mind him; he is entirely occupied by his amours with La Fosseuse."

"He, Monseigneur, will dispute every inch with you.   He watches you and your brother; he hungers for the throne.   If any accident should happen to your brother, see if he will not be here with a bound from Pau to Paris."

"An accident to my brother?" repeated François, slowly, fixing his eyes inquiringly on the Duc de Guise.

"Listen, Henri," said Chicot.

"Yes, Monseigneur," said the Duc de Guise; "an accident. Accidents are not rare in your family; you know that as well as I do. One prince is in good health, and all at once he falls ill; another is counting on long years, when perhaps he has but a few hours to live."

"Do you hear, Henri?" said Chicot, taking the hand of the king, who shuddered at what he heard.

"Yes, it is true," said the Duc d'Anjou, "the princes of my house are born under fatal influences; but my brother Henri is, thank God, strong and well. He supported formerly the fatigues of war, and now that his life is nothing but recreation—"

"Yes; but, Monseigneur, remember one thing,—these recreations are not always without danger. How did your father, Henri II., die, for example?—he, who also had happily escaped the dangers of war. The wound by M. de Montgomery's lance was an accident. Then your brother François also died unfortunately, that worthy prince. You will say, Monseigneur, that it was of a malady of the ears; and who the devil would take that for an accident? But it was one, nevertheless, of the gravest kind; for I have more than once heard it said in the camp, in the city, even in the court, that that mortal malady was poured into the ear of King François II. by some one whom it would be a great mistake to call Chance, since he bore another name well known."

"Duke!" murmured François, reddening.

"Yes, Monseigneur; the name of king has long brought misfortune with it. Look at Antoine de Bourbon, who died from an arquebuse-wound in the shoulder, which to any one but a king would have been by no means fatal. Then there was Jeanne d'Albret, the mother of the Béarnais, who died from smelling a pair of perfumed gloves,—an accident very unexpected, although there were people who had great interest in this death. Then Charles IX., who died neither by the eye, the ear, nor the shoulder, but by the mouth—"

"What do you say?" cried François, starting back.

"Yes, Monseigneur, by the mouth. Those hunting-books are very dangerous, of which the pages stick together, and can be opened only by wetting the finger constantly."

"Duke! Duke! I believe you invent crimes."

"Crimes! who speaks of crimes? I speak of accidents. Was it not also an accident that happened to Charles IX. at the chase? You know what chase I mean,—that of the boar, where, intending to kill the wild boar which had turned on your brother, you, who never before had missed your aim, did so then; and the king would have been killed, as he had fallen from his horse, had not Henri de Navarre slain the animal which you had missed."

"But," said the Duc d'Anjou, trying to recover himself, "what interest could I have had in the death of Charles IX., when the next king would be Henri III.?"

"Oh, Monseigneur, there was already one throne vacant,—that of Poland. The death of Charles IX. would have left another, that of France; and even the kingdom of Poland might not have been despised. Besides, the death of Charles would have brought you a degree nearer the throne, and the next accident would have benefited you."

"What do you conclude from all this, Duke?" said the Duc d'Anjou.

"Monseigneur, I conclude that each king has his accident, and that you are the inevitable accident of Henri III., particularly if you are chief of the League."

"Then I am to accept?"

"Oh! I beg you to do so."

"And you?"

"Oh, be easy! my men are ready, and to-night Paris will be curious."

"What are they going to do in Paris to-night?" asked Henri of Chicot.

"Why, don't you understand?" replied Chicot, "to-night they sign the League publicly. For a long time they have been signing it in secret, awaiting your assent. You gave it this morning; and this evening, *ventre de biche!* they sign. You see, Henri, your 'accidents'—for you have two of them—lose no time."

"It is well," said the Duc d'Anjou, "till this evening, then."

"Yes," repeated the listening Henri, "till this evening."

"What!" said Chicot, "you will not risk going into the streets to-night?"

"Yes, I shall."

"You are wrong, Henri; remember the 'accidents.'"

"Oh! I shall be well accompanied. Will you come with me?"

"What! do you take me for a Huguenot? No, I am a good Catholic, and I mean to sign the League; I will do it ten times rather than once, and a hundred times rather than ten."

"Still one word," said the king, stopping Chicot as he moved away; "what do you think of all this?"

"I think that every one of the kings, your predecessors, was not forewarned of his 'accident;' so Henri II. did not guard his eye, François II. did not guard his ear, Antoine de Bourbon did not guard his shoulder, Jeanne d'Albret did not guard her nose, Charles IX. did not guard his mouth. You have, therefore, a great advantage over them, Maître Henri, for, *ventre de biche!* you know your brother, do you not?"

"Yes, and, *mordieu!* before long he shall find it out."

CHAPTER XL

THE EVENING OF THE LEAGUE

PARIS presented a fine sight, as through its then narrow streets thousands of people pressed towards the same point; for at eight o'clock in the evening M. le Duc de Guise was to receive the signatures of the *bourgeois* to the League. A crowd of citizens, dressed in their best clothes, as for a fête, but fully armed, directed their steps towards the churches. What added to the noise and confusion was that large numbers of women, disdaining to stay at home on such a great day, had followed their husbands, and many had brought with them a batch of children. It was in the Rue de l'Arbre Sec that the crowd was the thickest. The streets were literally choked, and the crowd pressed tumultuously towards a bright light suspended below the sign of the Belle Etoile. On the threshold a man, with a cotton cap on his head and a naked sword in one hand and a register in the other, was crying out, "Come, come, brave Catholics, enter the hostelry of the Belle Etoile, where you will find good wine! come, to-night the good will be separated from the bad and to-morrow morning the wheat will be known from the tares! Come, gentlemen, you who can write, come and sign! you who cannot write, come and tell your names to me, Maître la Hurière, or to my assistant, M. Croquentin! Gentlemen, it is for the Mass! Gentlemen, it is for the holy religion!" A tall man elbowed his way through the crowd, and in letters half an inch long wrote his name, "Chicot," in the register of M. Croquentin. He then approached the register of Maître la Hurière, who, having seen his magnificent signature, received him, not only with open arms, but with open register. Chicot took the pen and wrote his name a second time, with a flourish a hundred times more magnificent than the first. Then he asked

La Hurière if he had not a third register. La Hurière did not understand raillery, and answered angrily. Chicot retorted, and a quarrel seemed imminent, when Chicot, feeling some one touch his arm, turned, and saw the king, disguised as a simple *bourgeois*, and accompanied by Quélus and Maugiron, also disguised, and carrying arquebuses on their shoulders.

"What!" cried the king, "good Catholics disputing among themselves; *par la mordieu!* it is a bad example."

"Do not mix yourself with what does not concern you," replied Chicot, without seeming to recognise him. But a new influx of the crowd distracted the attention of La Hurière, and separated the king and his companions from the hotel.

"Look to your left, Sire," said Chicot; "there,—what do you see?"

"Ah, ah! M. de Mayenne's broad face, and the cardinal's sharp nose."

"Hush, Sire; one plays a sure game when one knows where his enemies are, while they do not know where he is."

"Do you think, then, I have anything to fear?"

"Eh, *mon Dieu!* in a crowd like this it is so easy for one man to put a knife into his neighbour, who utters an oath and gives up the ghost."

"Have I been seen?"

"I think not; but you will be if you stay longer."

"Vive la messe! vive la messe!" cried a mob which came from the market-places and surged like a tide into the Rue de l'Arbre Sec.

"Hurrah for M. de Guise!" "Hurrah for the cardinal!" "Hurrah for M. de Mayenne!" replied the crowd standing about La Hurière's door, who had recognised the two Lorraine princes.

"Oh, oh! what are those cries?" said Henri, frowning.

"They are cries which show that every one has his own place, and should stay in it,—M. de Guise in the streets, and you in the Louvre. Go to the Louvre, Sire; go to the Louvre."

"Are you coming with us?"

"I? oh, no. You do not need me, my son,—you have your guards. Forward, Quélus! Forward, Maugiron! I propose to see the spectacle to the end; I find it interesting, if not amusing."

"Where are you going?"

"I am going to write my name on the other registers. I want a thousand of my autographs to be found to-morrow in the streets of Paris. Here we are upon the quay. Good-night,

my son. Turn to the right; I turn to the left, and hurry off
to St. Méry to hear a famous preacher."

"Oh, oh! what is this new outcry, and what are the people
running for?"

Chicot stood on tiptoe, but could at first see nothing but a
mass of people crying, howling, and pushing, appearing to carry
some one or something in triumph. At last the mass opened;
and like the monster borne by the waves to the feet of Hippo-
lytus, a man who seemed to be the principal personage in that
burlesque scene was driven by those human waves to the feet
of the king. The man was a monk mounted on an ass. The
monk spoke and gesticulated, and the ass brayed.

"*Ventre de biche!*" cried Chicot, "I spoke of a famous
preacher at St. Méry; it isn't necessary to go so far. Listen
to this one."

"A preacher on a donkey!" cried Quélus.

"Why not?"

"Why, it is Silenus," said Maugiron.

"Which is the preacher?" said the king, "for they speak
both at once."

"The one underneath is the most eloquent," said Chicot,
"but the one at the top speaks the best French; listen, Henri."

"My brethren," said the monk, "Paris is a superb city;
Paris is the pride of France, and the Parisians are a fine people."
Then he began to sing, but the ass joined in with an accompaniment so loud and so spirited that he shut off the speech of
his rider. The crowd burst out laughing.

"Hold your tongue, Panurge! hold your tongue!" cried the
monk. "You shall speak in your turn, but let me speak first."

The ass was quiet.

"My brothers," continued the preacher, "the earth is a valley of
grief, where man often can quench his thirst only with his tears."

"Why, he is drunk," said the king.

"I should think so," said Chicot.

"I, who speak to you," continued the monk, "I am returning from exile like the Hebrews of old, and for a week Panurge
and I have been living on alms and privations."

"Who is Panurge?" asked the king.

"The superior of his convent, probably; but let me listen."

"Who made me endure this? It was Herod; you know
what Herod I speak of. I and Panurge have come from Villeneuve le Roi in three days, to assist at this great solemnity;
now we see, but we do not understand. What is taking place,

my brothers? Is it to-day that they depose Herod? Is it to-day that they put Brother Henri in a convent? Gentlemen," continued he, "I left Paris with two friends,—Panurge, who is my ass, and Chicot, who is his Majesty's jester. Can you tell me what has become of my friend Chicot?"

Chicot made a grimace.

"Oh," said the king, "he is your friend." Quélus and Maugiron burst out laughing. "He is handsome and respectable," continued the king. "What is his name?"

"It is Gorenflot, of whom M. de Morvilliers spoke to you."

"The incendiary of Ste. Geneviève?"

"Himself!"

"Then I will have him hanged!"

"Impossible!"

"Why?"

"He has no neck."

"My brothers," continued Gorenflot, "I am a true martyr; and it is my cause that they defend at this moment, or rather, that of all good Catholics. You do not know what is taking place in the provinces; we have been obliged at Lyon to kill a Huguenot who preached revolt. While one of them remains in France, there will be no tranquillity for us. Let us exterminate them. To arms! to arms!"

Several voices repeated, "To arms!"

"*Par la mordieu!*" said the king, "make this fellow hold his tongue, or he will make a second Saint Bartholomew!"

"Wait," said Chicot, and with his stick he struck Gorenflot with all his force on the shoulders.

"Murder!" cried the monk.

"It is you!" cried Chicot.

"Help me, M. Chicot, help me! The enemies of the faith wish to assassinate me; but I will not die without making my voice heard. Death to the Huguenots! Death to the Béarnais!"

"Will you hold your tongue, animal?" cried Chicot.

"To the devil with the Gascons!" continued the monk.

But at this moment a second blow fell on the shoulders of the monk with such force that he cried out with real pain. Chicot, astonished, looked round him, but saw nothing but the stick. The blow had been given by a man who had immediately disappeared in the crowd after administering this punishment.

"Who the devil could it have been?" thought Chicot, and he began to run after the man, who was gliding away, escorted by a single companion.

CHAPTER XLI

THE RUE DE LA FERRONNERIE

Chicot had good legs, and he would have made good use of them to join the man who had beaten Gorenflot if something strange in the appearance of the man, and especially in that of his companion, had not suggested that there might be danger in seeking an acquaintance which they seemed to avoid. They evidently sought to escape from observation in the crowd, and turned at the corners of the streets to assure themselves that they were not followed.

Chicot thought the best way not to seem to watch them was to pass them; so he ran on, and passed them at the corner of the Rue Tirechappe, and then hid himself at the end of the Rue des Bourdonnais. The two men went on, their hats slouched over their eyes, and their cloaks drawn up over their faces, with a quick and military step, until they reached the Rue de la Ferronnerie. There they stopped and looked round them. Chicot, who was still ahead, saw in the middle of the street, before a house so old that it appeared as if falling to pieces, a litter, attached to which were two horses. The driver had fallen asleep, while a woman, apparently anxious, was looking through the blind. Chicot hid himself behind a large stone wall, which served as stalls for the vegetable sellers on the days when the market was held in this street, and watched. Scarcely was he hidden, when he saw the two men approach the litter, one of whom, on seeing the driver asleep, let fall a "*Cap de diou !*" strongly accented; while the other, still more impatient, pricked the driver with his poniard.

"Oh, oh!" said Chicot, "I was not mistaken, then. They are compatriots; and that is why they leathered Gorenflot when he spoke contemptuously of the Gascons."

The lady now leaned out of the window, and Chicot saw that she was young, very pale, but very beautiful. The two men approached the litter, and the taller of the two took in both of his the little white hand which was stretched out to him.

"Well, my dear, my little heart, my pet," he said, "how are you?"

The lady shook her head with a sad smile, and showed her flask of salts.

"Still those faintings, *ventre-saint-gris !*"

" Why the devil did you bring Madame to Paris? " said the other man, rudely. " It is a curse to you, upon my word, that you must always have a petticoat tacked to your doublet! "

" Ah, dear Agrippa," replied the man who had spoken first, " it is so great a grief to part from one you love."

" *Cordioux!* on my soul, you drive me mad with your talk. Did you come to Paris to make love? It seems to me that Béarn is large enough for your sentimental promenades, without continuing them in this Babylon, where you have nearly got us killed twenty times to-day. Go home, if you wish to make love, but here, *mordioux!* keep to your political intrigues, my master."

" Let him scold, my dear, and don't be disturbed by what he says. I think he would be ill, like you, if he couldn't growl."

" But, at least, get into the litter and say your sweet things to Madame; you will run less risk of being recognised there than in the open street."

" You are right, Agrippa. You see, my love, that he is not so bad an adviser as he appears. There, make room for me, my darling,—if you will permit me to sit by you."

" Permit, Sire; I desire it ardently," replied the lady.

" Sire! " murmured Chicot, who, carried away by an impulse, tried to raise his head, and knocked it against the stone wall. " Sire! what is she saying there? "

Meanwhile, the happy lover profited by the permission given, and the creaking of the litter announced an increase of its burden. To the creaking succeeded the sound of kissing.

" Oh, how happy I am! " cried the man in the litter, without attending in the least to the impatience of his friend. " *Ventre-saint-gris!* this is a good day. Here are my good Parisians, who execrate me with all their souls, and would kill me if they could, working to smooth my way to the throne, and I have in my arms the woman I love. Where are we, D'Aubigné? when I am king I will erect here a statue to the genius of the Béarnais."

" The Béarn— " began Chicot, but he stopped, for he had given his head a second bump.

" We are in the Rue de la Ferronnerie, Sire," said D'Aubigné; " and it does not smell nice."

" It seems to me," continued Henri,—for our readers have doubtless already recognised the King of Navarre,—" it seems to me that I am looking forward into the course of my life; that I see myself king; that I am on the throne, strong and powerful, but perhaps not so much loved as I am at this moment; and that my view embraces all the future, to the hour of my death. Oh, tell me again that you love me, for my heart melts at the sound of your voice!" And the Béarnais, yielding to a feeling of sadness that sometimes overwhelmed him, sighed profoundly and let his head fall on his mistress's shoulder.

"Oh, *mon Dieu!*" said the young woman, frightened, "are you ill, Sire?"

"Good! that alone was wanting," said D'Aubigné,—"fine soldier, fine general, fine king, fainting away!"

"No, my love, be easy," said Henri; "if I were to faint near you it would be with happiness."

"Really, Sire, I don't see why you sign yourself 'Henri de Navarre;' you should sign 'Ronsard' or 'Clement Marot.' *Cordioux!* how is it that you get on so badly with Madame Margot when you are both so inclined to poetry?"

"Ah, D'Aubigné! for pity's sake don't speak of my wife! *Ventre-saint-gris!* you know the proverb,—suppose we should meet her!"

"Although she is in Navarre?"

"*Ventre-saint-gris!* am I not also in Navarre? Am I not supposed to be there, at least? Come, Agrippa, you have made me shiver; get in and let us be moving."

"Faith, no! I will follow behind; I should annoy you, and what is worse, you would annoy me."

"Shut the door, then, bear of Béarn, and do as you like." Then to the coachman he said, "Lavarenne, you know where."

The litter went slowly away, followed by D'Aubigné.

"Let me see," said Chicot, "must I tell Henri what I have seen? Why should I? Two men and a woman, who hide themselves; it would be cowardly. No, I will not tell; that I know it myself is the important point, for is it not I who reign? His love was very pretty, but he loves too often, this dear Henri of Navarre. A year ago it was Madame de Sauve, and I suppose this was La Fosseuse. However, I love the Béarnais, for I believe some day he will do an ill turn to those dear Guises. Well, I have seen every one to-day but the Duc d'Anjou; he alone is wanting to my list of princes. Where can my François III. be? *Ventre de biche!* I must look for the worthy monarch."

Chicot was not the only person who was seeking for the Duc d'Anjou, and was concerned by his absence. The Guises had also sought for him on all sides, but they were not more successful than Chicot. M. d'Anjou was not the man to risk himself imprudently, and we shall see what precautions had kept him from his friends. Once Chicot thought he had found him in the Rue Béthisy. A numerous group was standing at the door of a wine-merchant; and in this group Chicot recognised M. de Monsoreau and M. de Guise, and fanced that the Duc d'Anjou could not be far off. But he was wrong. MM. de Monsoreau and Guise were occupied in exciting still more an orator in his stammering eloquence. This orator was Gorenflot, recounting his journey to Lyon, and his duel in an inn with a dreadful Huguenot. M. de Guise was listening intently, for he began to fancy it had something to do with the silence of Nicolas David. Chicot was terrified; he felt sure that in another moment Gorenflot would pronounce his name, which would throw a fatal light on the mystery. He lost no time. In an instant he cut the bridles of some of the horses that were fastened there, and giving them each a violent blow, sent them galloping among the crowd, which opened, and began to disperse in different directions. Chicot passed quickly through the groups, and approaching Gorenflot, took Panurge by the bridle and turned him round. The Duc de Guise was already separated from them by the rush of the people, and Chicot led off Gorenflot to a kind of *cul de sac* by the church of St. Germain l'Auxerrois.

" Ah, drunkard! " said he to him, " ah, traitor! you will, then, always prefer a bottle of wine to your friend."

" Ah, M. Chicot! " stammered the monk.

" What! I feed you, wretch, I give you drink, I fill your pockets and you stomach, and you betray me! "

" Ah, M. Chicot! "

" You tell my secrets, wretch! "

" Dear friend."

" Hold your tongue! you are but a sycophant, and deserve punishment."

And the monk, vigorous and strong, powerful as a bull, but overcome by wine and repentance, remained without defending himself in the hands of Chicot, who shook him like a balloon full of air.

" A punishment to me, to your friend, dear M. Chicot! "

" Yes, to you," said Chicot, striking him over the shoulders with his stick.

" Ah! if I were but fasting."

" You would beat me, I suppose,—me, your friend."

" My friend! and you treat me thus! "

" He who loves well chastises well," said Chicot, redoubling his proofs of friendship. " Now," said he, " go and sleep at the Corne d'Abondance."

" I can no longer see my way," cried the monk, from whose eyes tears were falling.

" Ah!" said Chicot, " if you could weep the wine you have drunk, that might sober you a little. But no, I shall have to guide you."

And taking the ass by the bridle, he led him to the hotel, where two assistants of Maître Bonhomet assisted Gorenflot to dismount, and led him up to the room which our readers already know.

" It is done," said the host, returning.

" He is in bed? "

" Yes, and snoring."

" Very well. But as he will awake some day or other, remember that I do not wish that he should know how he came here; indeed, it will be better that he should not know that he has been out since the famous night when he made such a scandal in the convent, and that he should believe that all that has happened since is a dream."

" Very well, M. Chicot; but what has happened to the poor monk? "

" A great misfortune. It appears that at Lyon he quarrelled with an agent of M. de Mayenne's and killed him."

" Oh, *mon Dieu !* "

" So that M. de Mayenne has sworn that he will have him broken on the wheel."

" Make yourself easy, Monseiur; he shall not go out from here on any pretext."

" Good! And now," said Chicot, as he went away, " I must find the Duc d'Anjou."

PART SECOND

CHAPTER I

THE PRINCE AND THE FRIEND

WE may remember that the Duc de Guise had invited the Duc d'Anjou to meet him in the streets of Paris on the evening of the League. That invitation had disturbed the prince. He had reflected, and after reflection he surpassed the serpent in prudence. However, as his interest seemed to require that he should see with his own eyes whatever might take place that evening, he decided to accept the invitation; but he determined not to go out of his palace unless he was well accompanied. Therefore the duke went to seek his sword, which was Bussy d'Amboise. The duke must have been seized by strong apprehensions before making up his mind to that step. Since his deception of Bussy in regard to M. de Monsoreau, Bussy had kept himself away from him; and François admitted to himself that were he in Bussy's place, and supposing that in taking his place he took his courage, he should feel more than contempt for a prince who should have betrayed him so cruelly. Bussy, like all fine natures, felt sorrow more vividly than pleasure; for it is rare that a man intrepid in danger, cold and calm in the face of fire and sword, does not give way to grief more easily than a coward. Those from whom a woman can draw tears most easily are those most to be feared by men. Bussy had seen Diane received at court as Comtesse de Monsoreau, and as such admitted by the queen into the circle of her maids of honour, he had seen a thousand curious eyes fixed on her unrivalled beauty, which he had, so to speak, discovered and rescued from the tomb in which it was buried. During the whole evening he had fastened his ardent gaze on her. She did not once look at him; and he, unjust, like every man in love, failed to consider that perhaps she was suffering because she did not dare to meet his sympathising glance.

"Oh," said he to himself, seeing that he waited uselessly for a look, "women have skill and audacity only when they want to deceive a guardian, a husband, or a mother; they are awkward and cowardly when they have simply a debt of gratitude to

pay. They fear so much to seem to love, they attach so exaggerated a value to their least favour, that they do not mind
breaking their lover's heart if such be their humour. Diane
might have said to me frankly, ' I thank you for what you have
done for me, but I do not love you.' The blow would have
killed or cured me. But no, she prefers letting me love her
hopelessly; but she has gained nothing by it, for I no longer
love her, I despise her."

And he went away with rage in his heart.

" I am mad," thought he, " to torment myself about a person
who disdains me. But why does she disdain me, or for whom?
Not, surely, for that long livid skeleton, who, always by her
side, covers her incessantly with his jealous glances. If I wished
it, in a quarter of an hour I could hold him mute and cold
under my knee with ten inches of steel in his heart; and
if I cannot be loved, I could at least be terrible and hated.
Oh, her hatred, rather than her indifference! Yes, but to act
thus would be to do what a Quélus or a Maugiron would do
if they knew how to love. Better to resemble that hero of
Plutarch whom I have so much admired,—the young Antiochus,
dying of love and never avowing it, nor uttering a complaint.
Yes, I will be silent,—I, who have contended in close conflict
with all the strong fighting men of the time, who have seen
Crillon (the brave Crillon himself) disarmed before me, holding
his life at my mercy,—yes, I will stifle my grief in my soul.
Nothing is impossible to me, Bussy, who, like Crillon, am
surnamed the ' brave; ' and all that those heroes have done I
will do."

On saying to himself these words, Bussy relaxed his clinched
hands, wiped the sweat from his forehead, and went slowly to
the door. He summoned all his endurance and gentleness, and
went out with a smile on his lips, calmness on his brow, and a
volcano in his heart. It is true that, meeting the Duc d'Anjou
on his way, he turned away his head; for he knew that with
all the firmness of his soul, he could not smile upon, or even
greet, the prince who called him his friend, and had so odiously
betrayed him. In passing, the prince called him by name, but
Bussy appeared not to hear him.

Bussy returned home. He placed his sword on a table, took
his poniard from its sheath, unfastened his cloak and doublet,
and sat down in a large armchair, leaning his head against a
coat-of-arms designed on its back. His attendants saw that he
was preoccupied; they thought he wished to rest, and withdrew

Bussy did not sleep; he dreamed. He spent several hours in that way without noticing that at the other end of the chamber a man, sitting, like himself, was watching him attentively, without movement or speech. At length an icy shiver shook Bussy's shoulders, and his eyes wandered; the observer did not stir. Then the count's teeth chattered; his arms stiffened; his head slipped along the back of his chair and fell on his shoulder. Then the man watching him rose from his chair, uttered a sigh, and approached him. "Monsieur the Count," said he, "you are in a fever."

The count raised his face, empurpled by the fever's heat. "Ah, it is you, Rémy," said he.

"Yes, Count, I was waiting here for you."

"Here! and why?"

"Because one does not long remain in the place where he is suffering."

"Thanks, my friend," said Bussy, pressing the young man's hand.

Rémy held in his own that terrible hand, now more feeble than that of a child, and pressed it to his heart with affection and respect. "Now," said he, "the question is whether you wish to continue in this condition. Do you wish the fever to increase until it overcomes you? Then remain as you are. Do you wish to conquer it? Then go to bed and have some one read to you from a good book from which you may draw example and strength."

The count had nothing in the world to do but to obey; he obeyed. So, then, all his friends who came to visit him found him in bed.

All the next day Rémy remained with the count. He exercised a double function, as physician for the body and physician for the soul. He had refreshing drinks for the one, and pleasant words for the other. But on the following day—the day on which M. de Guise came to the Louvre—Bussy looked for him in vain.

"Poor lad!" thought he, "he is tired and wants to enjoy the air, the sun, and the springtime. And then doubtless Gertrude expected him. She is but a *femme de chambre*, but she loves him; and a *femme de chambre* who loves is better than a queen who does not."

The day passed, and Rémy did not return. Bussy became angry and impatient. "Oh!" cried he, "I, who still believed in gratitude and friendship, will henceforth believe in nothing."

Towards evening he heard voices in his antechamber, and a servant entered, saying, " It is Monseigneur le Duc d'Anjou."

" Let him enter," said Bussy, frowning.

The duke, on entering the room, which was without lights, said, " It is too dark here, Bussy."

Bussy did not answer; disgust closed his mouth.

" Are you really ill," said the duke, " that you do not answer?"

" I am really ill."

" Then that is why I have not seen you for two days? "

" Yes, Monseigneur."

The prince, piqued at these short answers, took two or three turns round the room, looking at the sculptures that stood out in the dim light, and feeling of the upholstery.

" You seem to me well lodged, Bussy," said he.

Bussy did not reply.

" Bussy must be very ill," said the duke to an attendant who stood by; " why was not Miron called? The king's doctor is not too good for Bussy."

The servant shook his head in a mannner that arrested the duke's attention.

" Come, Bussy, are you in grief? " asked the duke, almost obsequiously.

" I do not know."

The duke approached, becoming more and more gracious as he was rebuffed. " Come, speak to me frankly, Bussy," said he.

" What am I to say, Monseigneur? "

" You are angry with me? "

" I! for what? Besides, it is of no use to be angry with princes; what good could that do? "

The duke was silent.

" But," said Bussy, " we are losing time in preambles; to the point, Monseigneur! You have need of me, I suppose? "

" Ah, M. de Bussy! "

" Yes, doubtless; do you think I believe that you come here through friendship,—you, who love no one? "

" Oh, Bussy, to say such things to me! "

" Well, be quick, Monseigneur, what do you want? When one serves a prince, and he dissimulates to the extent of calling you his friend, one must pay for the dissimulation by being ready to sacrifice everything, even life. Speak! "

The duke coloured; but it was too dark for Bussy to observe that fact. " I wanted nothing of you, Bussy, and you deceive yourself in thinking my visit interested. I desire only, seeing the fine evening, and that all Paris is out to sign the League, that you should accompany me a little about the streets."

Bussy looked at him. "Have you not Aurilly to go with you?"

"A lute-player!"

"Ah, Monseigneur, you do not mention all his qualities; I believed that he fulfilled other functions for you. Besides, you have a dozen other gentlemen; I hear them in the antechamber."

The *portière* was gently raised.

"Who is there?" said the duke, haughtily. "Who enters unannounced where I am?"

"I, Rémy," replied the young man, without any embarrassment.

"Who is Rémy?"

"Rémy, Monseigneur, is the doctor," said the young man.

"Rémy," said Bussy, "is more than the doctor, Monseigneur, —he is the friend."

"Ah!" said the duke, feeling the blow.

"You heard what Monseigneur asks?" said Bussy, preparing to get out of bed.

"Yes, that you should accompany him; but—"

"But what?" said the duke.

"But you will not accompany him, Monsieur."

"And why so?" cried the duke.

"Because it is too cold out of doors."

"Too cold!" cried the duke, surprised that any one should dare to oppose him.

"Yes, too cold. Therefore I, who answer for M. Bussy's life to his friends, and especially to myself, must forbid him to go out." Bussy none the less continued his movement to get out of bed, but Rémy's hand found his and pressed it significantly.

"Very well," said the duke, "if the risk be so great, he must stay." And he turned angrily to the door.

Bussy did not move. The duke came back to the bed. "So," he said, "it is decided; you will not risk yourself?"

"Monseigneur, you hear that the doctor forbids me."

"You ought to see Miron; he is a great doctor."

"I prefer my friend."

"Then adieu."

"Adieu, Monseigneur."

The duke went out with a great noise. He had hardly departed when Rémy, who had followed him with his eyes till

he had gone from the hotel, hastened to his patient, saying,
" Now, Monsieur, get up at once, if you please."

" What for? "

" To come out with me. This room is too warm."

" You said just now to the duke that it was too cold outside."

" The temperature has changed since."

" So that—" said Bussy, with curiosity.

" So that now I am convinced that the air will do you good."

" I do not understand."

" Do you understand the medicines I give you? Yet you
take them. Come, get up; a walk with M. d'Anjou would be
dangerous, with the doctor it will be beneficial. Have you lost
confidence in me? If so, send me away."

" Well, as you wish it." And he rose, pale and trembling.

" An interesting paleness," said Rémy; " the handsome
invalid."

" But where are we going? "

" To a place where I have analysed the air to-day."

" And this air? "

" Is a sovereign remedy for your complaint, Monseigneur."

Bussy dressed, and they went out.

CHAPTER II

ETYMOLOGY OF THE RUE DE LA JUSSIENNE

REMY took his patient by the arm, and led him by the Rue
Coquillière down to the rampart.

" It is strange," said Bussy; " you take me near the marsh
of the Grange Batelière, and call it wholesome."

" Oh, Monsieur, a little patience; we are going to turn round
by the Rue Pagavin, and get into the Rue Montmartre,—you will
see what a fine street that is."

" As if I did not know it."

" Well, so much the better; I need not lose time in showing
you its beauties, and I will lead you at once into a pretty little
street."

Indeed, after going a few steps down the Rue Montmartre,
they turned to the right.

" This," said Rémy, " is the Rue de la Gypecienne, or
Egyptienne, as you prefer,—a street which the people are
already beginning to call ' Rue de la Gyssienne,' and which before

long they will call 'Rue de la Jussienne,' because it is softer, and the tendency in language is, as you go towards the south, to multiply the vowels. You ought to know that, Monseigneur, —you, who have been in Poland."

"Very likely; but as I can't suppose that we have come here to take a course in philology, come, tell me, where are we going?"

"Do you see that little church?" said Rémy. "How nicely it is situated! I dare say you never remarked it before."

"No, I did not know it."

"Well, now that you have seen the exterior, let us enter and look at the windows; they are very curious."

There was such a pleased smile on the young man's face that Bussy felt sure that he must have some other reason for wishing him to enter than to look at windows which it was too dark to see. There was, however, something else to see,—for the interior of the church was lighted up for service; there were some of those naïve paintings of the sixteenth century, such as Italy, thanks to its fine climate, still preserves, while with us, moisture and vandalism have effaced those traditions of a past age, those evidences of a faith which no longer exists. The artist had painted in fresco for François I., and by order of that king, the life of Saint Mary the Egyptian. Now, among the most interesting scenes of that life, the artist, simple-minded, and a great lover of truth,—historical, if not anatomical,—had selected and placed conspicuously in the chapel that critical moment when Saint Mary, having no money to pay the boatman, offers herself in payment for her passage.

It is, however, but just to say that notwithstanding the veneration of the faithful for Mary the Egyptian, converted, many honest women of the quarter thought that the artist might have put that work in some other place, or at least might have treated his subject in a different manner; and the reason which they give—or rather, which they did not give—was that certain details in that fresco attracted too often the eyes of the shop-clerks whom their employers brought to the church on Sundays and fête-days.

Bussy looked at Rémy, who, becoming for the moment a shop-clerk, gave close attention to that painting.

"Are you expecting," said Bussy, "to awaken in me Anacreontic ideas with your chapel of Ste. Marie l'Egyptienne? If so, you have mistaken your subject; you should bring hither monks and students."

"God forbid!" said Rémy. "Omnis cogitatio libidinosa cerebrum inficit."

"Come, you had some other object in bringing me here than to make me look at the knees of Saint Mary the Egyptian."

"*Ma foi!* no."

"Then let us go."

"Wait a moment; the service is closing. If we go out now we shall disturb the faithful."

"Now let us go," said Bussy; "they are moving;" and he moved towards the door, visibly indifferent and absent-minded.

"Well," said Rémy, "here you are going away without taking the holy water. Where the devil is your head?"

Bussy, obedient as a child, directed his course towards the holy-water font.

Rémy took advantage of the opportunity to make a sign to a woman, who, upon that signal, went in the same direction that Bussy had taken. So at the moment when the count extended his hand towards the font, another hand, somewhat large and red, but the hand of a woman, was extended towards his own, and its fingers were dipped in the holy water. Bussy's eyes naturally wandered from the hand, large and red, to the face of the woman. Then he recoiled and turned pale, for he recognised Gertrude, half-concealed as she was by a veil. She saluted him and passed on; but behind her came a figure which, although closely veiled, made his heart beat fast. Rémy looked at him, and Bussy knew now why he had brought him to this church. Bussy followed the lady, and Rémy followed him. Gertrude had walked on before until she came to an alley closed by a door. She opened it and let her mistress pass. Bussy followed, and the two others disappeared.

It was half-past seven in the evening, and near the beginning of May; the air began to have the feeling of spring, and the leaves were beginning to unfold themselves. Bussy looked round him, and found himself in a little garden fifty feet square, surrounded by high walls covered with vines and moss. The first lilacs which had begun to open in the morning sun sent out their sweet emanations; and the young man felt tempted to think that so much perfume and warmth and life came to him only from the presence of the woman he loved so tenderly.

On a little wooden bench sat Diane, twisting in her fingers a sprig of wall-flower, which she had picked without knowing what she did. As Bussy approached her she raised her head and said timidly, "Monsieur the Count, all deception would be unworthy of us; if you found me at the church of Ste. Marie l'Egyptienne, it was not chance that brought you there."

"No, Madame; Rémy took me out without my knowing where I was going, and I swear to you that I was ignorant—"

"You do not understand me, Monsieur. I know well that M. Rémy brought you there, by force, perhaps."

"No, Madame, not by force; I did not know that he was going to take me to see any one."

"That is a harsh speech," said Diane, sadly, and with tears in her eyes. "Do you mean that had you known, you would not have come?"

"Oh, Madame!"

"It would have been but just, Monsieur; you did me a great service, and I have not thanked you. Pardon me, and receive all my thanks."

"Madame—" Bussy stopped; he felt so overcome that he had neither words nor ideas.

"But I wished to prove to you," continued Diane, "that I am not ungrateful nor forgetful. It was I who begged M. Rémy to procure for me the honour of this interview; it was I who sought for it. Forgive me if I have displeased you."

"Oh, Madame! you cannot think that."

"I know," continued Diane, who was the strongest, because she had prepared herself for this interview, "how much trouble you had in fulfilling my commission; I know all your delicacy. I know it and appreciate it, believe me. Judge, then, what I must have suffered from the idea that you would misunderstand the sentiments of my heart."

"Madame, I have been ill for three days."

"Oh, I know," cried Diane, with a rising colour; "and I suffered more than you, for M. Rémy—he deceived me, no doubt—made me believe—"

"That your forgetfulness caused it. Oh, it is true!"

"Then I have been right to do as I have done,—to see you, to thank you for your kindness, and to swear to you an eternal gratitude. Do you believe that I speak from the bottom of my heart?"

Bussy shook his head sadly and did not reply.

"Do you doubt my words?" said Diane.

"Madame, those who feel a kindness for any one show it when they have the opportunity. You knew I was at the palace the night of your presentation, you knew I was close to you, you must have felt my looks fixed on you; yet you never raised your eyes to me, you never let me know by a word, a sign, or a gesture, that you were aware of my presence. But perhaps you did not recognise me, Madame; you have seen me only twice." Diane replied with so sad a glance of reproach that Bussy was moved by it.

"Pardon, Madame," said he; "you are not an ordinary woman, and yet you act like them. This marriage——"

"You know I was forced to it."

"Yes, but it was easy to break."

"Impossible, on the contrary."

"Did you not know that near you watched a devoted friend?"

"It was that especially that made me fear."

"And you did not think of what my life would be when you belonged to another. But perhaps you kept the name of Monsoreau from choice?"

"Do you think so?." murmured Diane; "so much the better." And her eyes filled with tears.

Bussy walked up and down in great agitation. "In short," he said, "I am to become what I was before; that is to say, a stranger to you."

"Alas!"

"Your silence says so."

"I can only speak by my silence."

"At the Louvre you would not see me, and now you will not speak to me."

"At the Louvre I was watched by M. de Monsoreau; and he is jealous."

"Jealous! What does he want then? *Mon Dieu!* whose happiness can he envy, when all the world is envying his?"

"I tell you he is jealous; for the last two or three days he has seen some one wandering round our new abode."

"Then you have left the Rue St. Antoine?"

"What!" cried Diane, thoughtlessly, "then it was not you?"

"Madame, since your marriage was publicly announced,—since that evening at the Louvre, where you did not deign to look at me,—I have been in bed, devoured by fever; so you see that your husband could not be jealous of me, at least."

"Well, Monsieur the Count, if it be true that you had any desire to see me, you must thank this unknown man; for knowing M. de Monsoreau as I know him, this man made me tremble for you, and I wished to see you and say to you, ' Do not expose yourself so, Monsieur the Count; do not make me more unhappy than I am.'"

" Reassure yourself, Madame; it was not I."

" Now let me finish what I have to say. In the fear of this man—whom I do not know, but whom M. de Monsoreau does, perhaps—he exacts that I should leave Paris; so that," said Diane, holding out her hand to Bussy, " you may look upon this as our last meeting, Monsieur the Count. To-morrow we start for Méridor."

" You are going, Madame? "

" There is no other way to reassure M. de Monsoreau,—no other way for me to be at peace. Besides, I myself detest Paris, the world, the court, and the Louvre. I wish to be alone with my souvenirs of my happy past; perhaps a little of my former happiness will return to me there. My father will accompany me, and I shall find there Monsieur and Madame de Saint-Luc, who expect me. Adieu, M. de Bussy."

Bussy hid his face in his hands. " All is over for me," he murmured.

" What do you say? " said Diane.

" I say, Madame, that this man exiles you; that he takes from me the only hope left to me,—that of breathing the same air as yourself, of seeing you sometimes, of touching your dress as you pass. Oh, this man is my mortal enemy, and if I perish for it, I will destroy him with my own hands! "

" Oh, Monsieur the Count! "

" The wretch! it is not enough for him that you are his wife, —you, the most beautiful and most charming of creatures; but he is still jealous. Jealous! The devouring monster would absorb the whole world! "

" Oh! calm yourself, Count; *mon Dieu!* he is excusable, perhaps."

" He is excusable! you defend him, Madame? "

" Oh, if you knew! " cried Diane, covering her face with her hands, as if she feared that notwithstanding the darkness Bussy might see her blushes.

" If I knew! Oh, Madame, I know one thing,—he who is your husband is wrong to think of the rest of the world."

" But! " cried Diane, in a broken voice, " if you were wrong, Monsieur the Count,—if he were not? "

And the young woman, touching with her cold hand the burning ones of Bussy, rose and fled among the sombre alleys of the garden, seized Gertrude's arm and dragged her away, before Bussy, astonished and overwhelmed with delight, had time to stretch out his arms to retain her. He uttered a cry and tottered; Rémy arrived in time to catch him in his arms and make him sit down on the bench that Diane had just left.

CHAPTER III

HOW D'EPERNON HAD HIS DOUBLET TORN, AND HOW SCHOMBERG WAS STAINED BLUE

WHILE M. la Hurière accumulated signatures; while Chicot consigned Gorenflot to the Corne d'Abondance; while Bussy returned to life in the happy little garden full of perfume and love,—Henri, annoyed at all he had seen in the city, and furious against his brother, whom he had seen pass in the Rue St. Honoré, accompanied by MM. de Guise and Mayenne, and a train of gentlemen whom M. de Monsoreau appeared to direct,— Henri, we say, re-entered the Louvre, accompanied by Maugiron and Quélus. He had gone out with all four of his friends; but at a short distance from the Louvre, Schomberg and D'Epernon had profited by the first crush to disappear, counting on some adventures in such a turbulent night. Before they had gone one hundred yards D'Epernon had passed his sword-sheath between the legs of a citizen who was running, and who tumbled down in consequence; and Schomberg had pulled the cap off the head of a young and pretty woman. But both had badly chosen their day for attacking these good Parisians, generally so patient; for a spirit of revolt was prevalent in the streets. The *bourgeois* rose, crying, "Down with the heretic!" and sprang upon D'Epernon. The young woman cried out, "Down with the favourite!" which was still worse; and her husband, who was a dyer, launched his apprentices on Schomberg. Schomberg was brave; therefore he stopped, put his hand on his sword, and spoke in a high tone. D'Epernon was prudent; he fled.

Henri had entered his room at the Louvre, and seated in his great armchair, was trembling with impatience, and seeking a good pretext for getting into a passion. Maugiron was playing with Narcissus, the large greyhound, and Quélus was sitting near.

"They go on," cried Henri; "their plot advances. Sometimes tigers, sometimes serpents, when they do not spring, they crawl."

"Oh, Sire!" said Quélus, "are there not always plots in a kingdom? What the devil could all the sons, brothers, and cousins of kings do if they did not plot?" And Quélus irreverently turned his back to the king.

"Come, Maugiron," said Henri, "am I right or wrong, *mordieu?* Should one try to lull me with twaddle and commonplaces, as if I were a common king, or a shopkeeper afraid of losing his favourite cat?"

"Well, Sire," said Maugiron, who was always of the same opinion with Quélus, "if you are not a common king, prove it by acting the great king. What the devil! here is Narcissus. He is a good dog; but when you pull his ears he growls, and when you tread on his toes he bites."

"Good!" said Henri; "and now the other compares me to my dog!"

"Not so, Sire; I place Narcissus far above you, for he knows how to defend himself, and you do not." And he also turned his back.

"That is right," cried the king; "my good friends, for whom they accuse me of despoiling the kingdom, abandon me, insult me! Ah, Chicot! if you were here."

At this moment, however, the door opened, and D'Epernon appeared without hat or cloak, and with his doublet all torn.

"*Bon Dieu!*" cried Henri, "what is the matter?"

"Sire," said D'Epernon, "look at me; see how they treat the friends of your Majesty!"

"Who has treated you thus?"

"*Mordieu!* your people; or rather the people of M. le Duc d'Anjou, who cried, 'Vive la messe!' 'Vive Guise!' 'Vive François!'—*vive* every one, in fact, except the king."

"And what did you do to be treated thus?"

"I? nothing. What can a man do to a people? They recognised me for your Majesty's friend, and that was enough."

"But Schomberg?"

"Well?"

"Did he not come to your aid? Did he not defend you?"

"*Corbœuf!* he had enough to do on his own account."

"How so?"

"I left him in the hands of a dyer whose wife's cap he had pulled off, and who, with his five or six apprentices, seemed likely to make him pass an unpleasant quarter of an hour."

"*Par la mordieu!* and where did you leave my poor Schomberg? I will go myself to his aid. They may say," continued he, looking at Maugiron and Quélus, "that my friends abandon me; but they shall never say that I abandon them."

"Thanks, Sire," said a voice behind Henri; "thanks, but here I am. I extricated myself without assistance; but, *mein Gott!* it was not without trouble."

"It is Schomberg's voice," cried all; "but where the devil is he?"

"Here I am," cried the voice; and indeed, in the dim light they saw coming towards them, not a man, but a shadow.

"Schomberg!" cried the king, "where do you come from, and why are you of that colour?"

Indeed, Schomberg from head to foot was of a most beautiful blue. "*Der Teufel!*" cried he, "the wretches! It is not wonderful that the people ran after me."

"But what is the matter?" asked Henri. "If you were yellow, that might be explained by fear; but blue!"

"The matter is that they dipped me in a vat, the knaves! I believed that it was only water; but it was indigo."

"Oh, *mordieu!*" cried Quélus, bursting out laughing, "indigo is very dear; you must have carried away at least twenty crowns' worth of it."

"I wish you had been in my place."

"And you did not kill any one?" asked Maugiron.

"I left my poniard somewhere, that is all I know, up to the hilt in a sheath of flesh; but in a second I was taken, carried off, dipped in a vat, and almost drowned."

"And how did you get out of their hands?"

"I had the courage to do an act of cowardice, Sire."

"What was that?"

"I cried, 'Vive la Ligue!'"

"That was like me; only they made me add, 'Vive le Duc d'Anjou!'" said D'Epernon.

"And me also," cried Schomberg; "but that is not all."

"What, my poor Schomberg, did they make you cry something else?"

"No, that was enough, God knows; but just as I cried, 'Vive le Duc d'Anjou,' guess who passed."

"How can I guess?"

"Bussy,—his cursed Bussy, who heard me."

"He could not understand," said Quélus.

"*Parbleu!* it was not difficult to understand. I had a poniard at my throat, and I was in a vat."

"And he did not come to your rescue?"

"He seemed to be occupied with something else. With

wings he would have flown away; he hardly touched the ground as he walked."

"And then," said Maugiron, "perhaps he didn't recognise you."

"As if that were likely!"

"Had you already become blue?"

"Ah! that is true," said Schomberg.

"He would be excusable," said the king; "for indeed, my poor Schomberg, I should hardly have known you myself."

"Never mind; we shall meet some other time when I am not in a vat."

"Oh, as for me," said D'Epernon, "it is not the valet I should like to punish, but the master; it is not with Bussy I should deal, but with Monseigneur le Duc d'Anjou."

"Yes, yes!" cried Schomberg, "with Monseigneur le Duc d'Anjou, who wishes to kill us with ridicule while waiting to kill us with a poniard."

"The Duc d'Anjou, whose praises they are singing all over Paris," said Quélus and Maugiron together.

"The fact is that it is he, and not the king, who is master of Paris to-night," said D'Epernon. "Go out a little way, and you will see whether they respect you more than us."

"Ah, my brother! my brother!" murmured the king, in a threatening tone.

"Ah, yes, Sire; you cry, 'My brother!' but you do nothing against him. And yet it is clear to me that he is at the head of some plot," said Schomberg.

"Eh, *mordieu!* that is what I was saying, just before you came in, to these gentlemen; and they replied by shrugging their shoulders and turning their backs."

"Not because you said there was a plot, Sire, but because you do nothing to suppress it."

"And now," said Quélus, "we say: Save us, Sire,—or rather save yourself, for when we have fallen you will perish. To-morrow M. de Guise will come to the Louvre and ask you to name a chief for the League; to-morrow you will name the Duc d'Anjou, as you have promised. And then, once chief of the League,—that is to say, at the head of one hundred thousand Parisians, warmed up by this night's orgies,—the Duc d'Anjou will do with you whatever he wishes."

"Then," said Henri, "if I take a decisive step, you will support me?"

"Yes, Sire."

" If, Sire, you will only give me time to change my dress," said D'Epernon.

" Go to my room, D'Epernon; my *valet de chambre* will give you what you want."

" And I, Sire, must have a bath," said Schomberg.

" Go to my bath, Schomberg, and my bather will attend to you."

" Then I may hope, Sire, that my insult will not remain unavenged? "

Henri remained silent a moment, and then said, " Quélus, ask if M. d'Anjou has returned to the Louvre."

Quélus went out. D'Epernon and Schomberg awaited with the others Quélus's return,—so much was their zeal revived by the imminence of danger. It is not in the storm, but in the calm, that sailors are mutinous.

" Sire," asked Maugiron, " your Majesty will act, then? "

" You will see," replied the king.

Quélus came back. " Monsieur the Duke has not yet returned," he said.

" Very well," replied the king. " D'Epernon, go and change your clothes; Schomberg, go and change your colour; you, Quélus and Maugiron, go down and watch for my brother's entrance."

" And when he has entered? "

" Have all the doors shut."

" Bravo, Sire! " said Quélus.

" I will be back in ten minutes, Sire," said D'Epernon.

" I cannot say when I shall return; that will depend on the quality of the dye," said Schomberg.

" Come as soon as possible," said the king.

The young men went out, and the king, left alone, kneeled down on his *prie-Dieu*.

CHAPTER IV

CHICOT MORE THAN EVER KING OF FRANCE

THE gates of the Louvre were generally closed at twelve, but Henri had wisely reasoned that the Duc d'Anjou would certainly sleep that night at the Louvre, so as to afford less ground for the suspicions which the tumults of the evening might awaken in the king's mind. He had therefore ordered that the gates should remain open till one o'clock.

At quarter past twelve Quélus came up; " Sire," said he, " the duke has come in."

" What is Maugiron doing? "

" Watching that he does not go out again."

" There is no danger."

" Then—"

" We will let him go to bed quietly.   Whom has he with him? "

" M. de Monsoreau and his ordinary gentlemen."

" And M. de Bussy? "

" No; he is not there."

" So much the better."

" What are your orders, Sire? "

" Tell Schomberg and D'Epernon to be quick, and let M. de Monsoreau know that I wish to speak to him."

Five minutes after, Schomberg and D'Epernon entered,— the former with only a slight blue tint left, which it would take several baths to eradicate, and the latter newly clothed.   After them, M. de Monsoreau appeared.

" The captain of the guards has just announced to me that your Majesty did me the honour to send for me," said he.

" Yes, Monsieur.   When I was out this evening, I saw the stars so brilliant, and the moon so clear that I thought it would be splendid weather for a chase to-morrow; so, Monsieur the Count, set off at once for Vincennes, and get a stag roused ready for me."

" But, Sire, I thought that to-morrow your Majesty had given a rendezvous to M. le Duc d'Anjou and M. de Guise, in order to name a chief for the League."

" Well, Monsieur? " said the king, haughtily.

" Sire, there might not be time."

" There is always time, Monsieur, for those who know how to employ it; that is why I tell you to set off at once, so that you may have all ready for to-morrow morning at ten.   Quélus, Schomberg, have the door of the Louvre opened for M. de Monsoreau, and have it closed behind him."

The chief huntsman retired in astonishment.   " It is, then, a whim of the king's? " he asked the young men.

" Yes," they laconically answered.

M. de Monsoreau saw that he could get nothing from them, and asked no more questions.   " Oh, oh! " he murmured, casting a glance towards the apartments of the Duc d'Anjou, " it seems to me that this promises no good to his royal Highness." But he had no way of giving warning to the prince.   Quélus and Schomberg had him between them. For a moment he imagined that they held him as a prisoner, under private orders; and it was not until the gate had closed behind him that he dismissed the suspicion.

At the end of ten minutes Schomberg and Quélus were again with the king.

"Now," said Henri, "silence, and all four of you follow me!"

"Where are we going, Sire?" said D'Epernon.

"Those who follow will see."

The king took a lantern in his hand, and led the young men along the secret corridor which led to his brother's rooms. A *valet de chambre* watched here; but before he had time to warn his master, Henri ordered him to be silent, and the young men pushed him into a room and locked the door.

Henri opened his brother's door. François had gone to bed full of dreams of ambition, which the events of the evening had nourished; he had heard his name exalted, and the king's abused. Conducted by the Duc de Guise, he had seen the Parisians open their heart to him and his gentlemen, while the gentlemen of the king were insulted and hooted. Never since the beginning of his career had he been so popular, and consequently so hopeful. He had placed on the table a letter from M. de Guise, which had been brought to him by M. de Monsoreau, who at the same time urged him not to fail to be present in the morning at the king's levee. The duke had no need of that counsel; he had already promised himself not to be absent at the hour of triumph. His surprise and terror were great when he saw the secret door open, and still more when he recognised the king. Henri signed to his companions to remain on the threshold, and advanced to the bed, frowning, but silent.

"Sire," stammered the duke, "the honour that your Majesty does me is so unlooked for—"

"That it frightens you, does it not? But stay where you are, my brother; do not rise."

"But, Sire, only—permit me—" and he drew towards him the letter of M. de Guise.

"You were reading?" asked the king.

"Yes, Sire."

"Something interesting, to keep you awake at this time of night?"

"Oh, Sire, nothing very important; the evening courier—"

"Oh, yes, I understand,—courier of Venus; but no, I see I

am wrong,—they do not fasten with seals of such dimensions
the notes brought by Iris or by Mercury."

The duke hid the letter altogether.

"How discreet this dear François is!" said the king, with a
smile which frightened his brother.

However, making an effort to recover himself, "Did your
Majesty wish to say anything to me in private?" asked the
duke, who noticed that the four gentlemen at the door were
listening to and enjoying the opening of the interview.

"What I have to say to you, Monsieur, I wish to say before
witnesses. Here, gentlemen," continued he, turning to the four
young men, "listen to us; the king permits it."

"Sire," said the duke, with a glance full of rage and hatred,
"before insulting a man of my rank, you should have refused
me the hospitality of the Louvre; in the Hôtel d'Anjou at least
I should have been free to reply to you."

"Really, you forget, then, that wherever you are, you are
my subject; that I am the king, and that every house is mine."

"Sire, I am at the Louvre, at my mother's."

"And your mother is in my house. But to the point; give
me that paper."

"Which?"

"That which you were reading, which was on your table,
and which you hid when I came in."

"Sire, reflect."

"On what?"

"On this,—that you are making a request unworthy of a
gentleman, and fit only for a police-officer."

The king grew livid. "That letter, Monsieur!"

"A woman's letter, Sire."

"There are some women's letters very good to see, and
dangerous not to see,—such as those our mother writes."

"Brother!"

"This letter, Monsieur!" cried the king, stamping his foot,
"or I will have it torn from you by my Swiss!"

The duke jumped out of bed, with the letter crumpled in his
hand, evidently with the intention of approaching the fireplace
so as to burn the letter. "You would do that," he said, "to
your brother?"

Henri, divining his intention, placed himself between him
and the fire. "Not to my brother," said he, "but to my most
mortal enemy. Not to my brother, but to the Duc d'Anjou,
who went all through Paris this evening with M. de Guise, who

tries to hide from me a letter from one of his accomplices, the Lorraine princes."

"This time," said the duke, "your police are wrong."

"I tell you I saw on the seal the three merlets of Lorraine. Give it to me, *mordieu!* or—"

Henri advanced towards his brother and laid his hand on his shoulder. François had no sooner felt the touch of his hand than, falling on his knees, he cried out, "Help! help! my brother is going to kill me!"

These words, uttered in an accent of profound terror, startled the king and mitigated his rage. The idea passed quickly through his mind that in their family, as by a curse, brother had always assassinated brother.

"No, my brother," said he, "you are wrong; I do not wish to hurt you, but you cannot contend with me. I am the master; and if you did not know it before you know it now."

"Yes, my brother, I acknowledge it."

"Very well, then, give me that letter; the king orders it."

The duke let it fall, and the king picked it up, but without reading it, put it in his pocket-book.

"Is that all," said the duke, with his sinister glance.

"No, Monsieur, you must keep your room until my suspicions with respect to you are completely dissipated. The room is commodious, and not much like a prison; stay here. You will have good company,—at least, outside the door,—for this night these four gentlemen will guard you; to-morrow they will be relieved by a guard of Swiss."

"But my friends, cannot I see them?"

"Whom do you call your friends?"

"M. de Monsoreau, M. de Ribeirac, M. d'Antragues, and M. de Bussy."

"Oh, yes; he, of course."

"Has he had the misfortune to displease your Majesty?"

"Yes."

"When, Sire?"

"Always, but particularly to-night."

"To-night! what did he do?"

"Insulted me in the streets of Paris."

"You?"

"My followers, which is the same thing."

"Bussy has insulted some one to-night in the streets of Paris? You have been deceived, Sire."

"I know what I say, Monsieur."

"Sire, M. de Bussy has not been out of his hotel for two days. He is at home, ill in bed, burning with fever."

The king turned to Schomberg, who said, "If he had fever, at all events he had it in the Rue Coquillière."

"Who told you he was there?" said the duke.

"I saw him."

"You saw Bussy out of doors!"

"Yes, looking well and happy, and accompanied by his ordinary follower, that Rémy."

"Then I do not understand it. I saw him in bed myself; he must have deceived me."

"It is well; he will be punished with the rest," said the king.

The duke, who thought he might divert from himself to Bussy the anger of the king, no longer defended his gentleman. "If M. de Bussy has done that," he said,—"if after refusing to go out with me he went out alone,—it was doubtless because he had intentions which he could not confess to me, whose devotion to your Majesty he knew so well."

"You hear, gentlemen, what my brother says. But we will talk of Bussy another time; now I recommend my brother to your care. You will have the honour of serving as guard to a prince of the blood."

"Oh, Sire!" said Quélus, with a look that made the duke shudder, "be satisfied; we know what we owe to his Highness."

"It is well; adieu, gentlemen."

"Sire," cried the duke, more terrified by the absence of the king than he had been by his presence, "am I really a prisoner? Are my friends not to visit me; and am I not to go out?" And he thought of what was to take place in the morning, when his presence would be so necessary to M. de Guise. "Sire," cried he again, "let me at least remain near your Majesty; it is my place, and I can be as well guarded there as elsewhere. Sire, grant me this favour."

The king was about to yield to this request and say, "Yes," when his attention was attracted to the door, where a long body, with its arms, its head, and everything that it could move, was making the most violent negative gestures that any one could invent and execute without dislocating his bones. It was Chicot.

"No," said Henri to his brother; "you are very well here, and here you must stay."

"Sire—"

"Since that is the good pleasure of the King of France, it

seems to me you should be satisfied, Monsieur," added Henri, with an air of pride which completed the duke's defeat.

"And I said that I was the real King of France!" murmured Chicot.

CHAPTER V

HOW CHICOT PAID A VISIT TO BUSSY, AND WHAT FOLLOWED

THE next morning, about nine, Bussy was eating his breakfast and talking with Rémy over the events of the previous day.

"Rémy," said he, "did you not think you had seen somewhere that gentleman whom they were dipping in a vat in the Rue Coquillière?"

"Yes, Monsieur the Count; but I cannot think of his name."

"Then you didn't recognise him, either?"

"No; he was already quite blue."

"I ought to have helped him," said Bussy, "it is a duty one gentleman owes to another; but really, Rémy, I was too much occupied with my own affairs."

"But he must have recognised us, for we were of our natural colour; and it seemed to me that he rolled his eyes frightfully and shook his fist at us."

"Are you sure of that, Rémy? We must find out who it was; I cannot let such an insult pass."

"Oh!" cried Rémy, "I know now who he was."

"How so?"

"I heard him swear."

"I should think so; any one would have sworn in such a situation."

"Yes; but he swore in German."

"Bah!"

"Yes, he said, 'Gott verdamme!'"

"Then it was Schomberg?"

"Himself, Monsieur the Count."

"Then, my dear Rémy, get your salves ready."

"Why so, Monsieur?"

"Because, before long, you will have to apply them either to his skin or to mine."

"You would not be so foolish as to get killed, now that you are so well and so happy. Saint Mary the Egyptian has resuscitated you once; but she will get tired of working a miracle which Christ himself performed on only two occasions."

"On the contrary, Rémy, you cannot tell how pleasant it feels to risk your life when you are happy. I assure you I never fought with a good heart when I had lost large sums at play, when I had surprised my mistress in a fault, or when I had anything to reproach myself with; but when my purse is full, my heart light, and my conscience clear, I go boldly to the field, —for I am sure of my hand. It is then I am brilliant. I should fight well to-day, Rémy; for, thanks to you," said he, extending his hand to the young man, "I am very happy."

"Stay a moment, however; you will, I hope, deprive yourself of this pleasure. A beautiful lady of my acquaintance made me swear to keep you safe and sound, under pretext that your life belongs to her."

"Good Rémy!"

"You call me good Rémy because I brought you to see Madame de Monsoreau; but shall you call me so when you are separated from her?—and unluckily the day approaches, if it be not come."

"What do you mean?"

"Do you not know that she is going to Anjou, and that I myself have the grief of being separated from Gertrude? Ah—"

Bussy could not help smiling at the pretended grief of the young man.

"You love her, then?" he said.

"I should think so; you should see how she beats me."

"And you let her do it?"

"Yes; for the love of science. She has driven me to the invention of a pomade which is a sovereign remedy for blue spots."

"In that case you should send a few pots of it to Schomberg."

"Let us speak no more of Schomberg; it is agreed that we leave him to get himself clean in his own way."

"Yes, and let us return to Madame de Monsoreau,—or rather, to Diane de Méridor, for you know—"

"Oh, *mon Dieu!* yes, I know."

"Rémy, when shall we start?"

"Ah! I expected that. On the latest possible day, I should say."

"Why so?"

"Firstly, because it seems to me that M. le Duc d'Anjou will want you here."

" And then? "

" And then, because M. de Monsoreau, by a special blessing, does not suspect you in the least, and would suspect something immediately if he saw you disappear from Paris at the same time as his wife, who is not his wife."

" Well, is it of any consequence to me what he suspects? "

" It is of much consequence to me. I charge myself with curing the sword-strokes received in duels,—for, as you manage your sword well, you never receive very serious ones,—but I refuse to take charge of the blows given secretly by jealous husbands; they are animals who in such cases strike hard."

" Well, my dear friend, if it is my destiny to be killed by M. de Monsoreau—"

" Well? "

" Well, he will kill me."

" And then, a week, a month, a year after, Madame de Monsoreau will be reconciled to her husband, which will dreadfully enrage your poor soul, which will see it from above—or below —without being able to prevent it."

" You are right, Rémy; I will live."

" Very good; but to live is not all,—you must be charmingly polite to the Monsoreau. He is at present frightfully jealous of the Duc d'Anjou, who, while you were ill in bed, promenaded before the house with his Aurilly. Make advances, then, to this charming husband who is not a husband. Do not even ask him what has become of his wife; that would be useless, since you know already. He will report everywhere that you are the only gentleman possessing the virtues of Scipio,—sobriety and chastity."

" You are right, Rémy, I believe. Now that I am no longer jealous of the bear, I will try to tame him; that will be comical to the last degree. Ah, now, Rémy, demand of me what you will; everything is easy to me. I am happy."

At this moment some one knocked at the door.

" Who is there? " cried Bussy.

" Monsieur," replied a page, " there is a gentleman below who wishes to speak to you."

" To speak to me so early; who is it? "

" A tall gentleman dressed in green velvet, with rose-coloured stockings, a face somewhat amusing, but the appearance of an honest man."

" Can it be Schomberg? "

" He said a tall man."

" True; then Monsoreau, perhaps."

" He said ' the appearance of an honest man.' "

" You are right, Rémy; it is probably neither of them. Let him come in."

After a minute the visitor entered.

" Ah, *mon Dieu!* " cried Bussy, rising precipitately at the sight of his visitor, while Rémy, like a discreet friend, withdrew.

" M. Chicot! " cried Bussy.

" Himself, Monsieur the Count."

Bussy's gaze was fixed on him with an astonishment which plainly said, " Monsieur, what are you doing here? " And so, without waiting for other questioning, Chicot replied in a serious tone, " Monsieur, I come to propose to you a little bargain."

" Speak, Monsieur," said Bussy, in great surprise.

" What will you promise me if I render you a great service? "

" That depends on the service, Monsieur," replied Bussy, disdainfully.

Chicot feigned not to remark this air of disdain. " Monsieur," said he, sitting down and crossing his long legs, " I remark that you do not ask me to sit down."

The colour mounted to Bussy's face.

" Monsieur," continued Chicot, " have you heard of the League? "

" I have heard much of it," said Bussy.

" Well, Monsieur, you ought to know that it is an association of honest Christians, united for the purpose of religiously massacring their neighbours, the Huguenots. Are you of the League, Monsieur? I am."

" But—Monsieur—"

" Say only yes or no."

" Allow me to express my astonishment—"

" I did myself the honour of asking you if you belonged to the League? "

" M. Chicot, as I do not like questions whose import I do not understand, I beg you to change the conversation; and I will wait a few minutes, for courtesy's sake, before repeating to you that not liking questions, I naturally do not like questioners."

" Very well; courtesy is courteous, as that dear M. de Monsoreau remarks when he is in good humour."

At that name, which the Gascon pronounced without apparent intention, Bussy began to listen with interest. " Eh! " he said to himself, " has he suspected something and sent this Chicot as a spy?" Then aloud, "Come, M. Chicot, to the point! You know we have but a few minutes left."

"Well, in a few minutes one can say a great deal; however, I might have dispensed with asking you the question, since if you do not belong to the League now, you soon will, as M. d'Anjou does."

"M. d'Anjou! Who told you that?"

"Himself, speaking to me in person, as the gentlemen of the law say, or rather write,—for example, that dear M. Nicolas David, that light of the *Forum Parisiense*,—a light extinguished without its being known who blew it out. Now you understand that as M. d'Anjou belongs to the League, you cannot help belonging to it also,—you, who are his right arm. The League knows better than to accept a maimed chief."

"Well, M. Chicot, what then?"

"Why, if you do belong to it, or they think you are likely to do so, what has happened to his royal Highness will certainly happen to you."

"And what has happened to him?"

"Monsieur," said Chicot, rising and imitating the attitude which Bussy had taken a moment before, "I do not like questions nor questioners, therefore I have a great mind to let them do to you what they have done to-night to the duke."

"M. Chicot," said Bussy, with a smile containing all the excuses that a gentleman could make, "speak, I beg of you; where is the duke?"

"He is in prison."

"Where?"

"In his own room. Four of my good friends guard him: M. de Schomberg, who was dyed blue yesterday, as you know, since you passed during the operation; M. d'Epernon, who is yellow from the fright he had; M. de Quélus, who is red with anger; and M. de Maugiron, who is white with ennui. It is beautiful to see,—not to speak of the duke, who is turning green with terror, so that we shall have a perfect rainbow to delight our eyes."

"Then, Monsieur, you think my liberty in danger?"

"Danger, Monsieur! I suppose that they are, they may be, or they should be, already on the way to arrest you."

Bussy shuddered.

"Do you like the Bastille, M. de Bussy? It is a good place for meditation; and M. Laurent Testu, the governor, keeps a good cook."

"They would send me to the Bastille?"

"Now I think of it, I ought to have in my pocket something like an order to conduct you there. Would you like to see it?" and Chicot drew from his pocket an order from the king in due form, to apprehend, wherever he might be, M. Louis de Clermont, Seigneur de Bussy. "Written very nicely by M. de Quélus," continued Chicot.

"Then, Monsieur," cried Bussy, "you are really rendering me a service?"

"I think so; do you agree with me?"

"Monsieur, I beg you to tell me why you do it; for you love the king, and he hates me."

"Monsieur the Count, I save you; think what you please of my action. But do you forget that I asked for a recompense?"

"Ah, true."

"Well?"

"Most willingly, Monsieur."

"Then some day you will do what I ask you?"

"On my honour, if it is anything that is possible."

"That is enough. Now mount your horse and disappear; I go to carry this order to those who are to use it."

"Then you were not to arrest me yourself?"

"I! for what do you take me? I am a gentleman, Monsieur."

"But I should abandon my master."

"Have no scruples; he has already abandoned you."

"You are a gallant gentleman, M. Chicot."

"*Parbleu!* I am aware of it."

Bussy called Rémy. To do him justice, he was listening at the door. He entered immediately.

"Rémy, our horses!"

"They are saddled, Monsieur."

"Ah!" said Chicot, "this young man knows what he is about."

"*Parbleu!*" said Rémy, "I am aware of it." And they saluted each other in the style of Guillaume Gorin and Gauthier Gargouille, fifty years later.

Bussy got together a few heaps of crowns, which he crammed into his pockets and those of Rémy; after which, having thanked Chicot again, he prepared to descend.

"Where are we going?" said Rémy.

"Well—" said Bussy, hesitating.

"What do you say to Normandy?" said Chicot.

"It is too near."

"Flanders, then?"

"Too far."

"Anjou is at a reasonable distance, Monsieur," said Rémy.

"Well, then, Anjou," said Bussy, colouring.

"Adieu, Monsieur!" said Chicot.

"It is destiny," said Rémy, when he had gone.

"Let us be quick, and perhaps we may overtake her," said Bussy.

CHAPTER VI

THE CHESS OF M. CHICOT, AND THE CUP AND BALL OF M. QUÉLUS

CHICOT returned joyfully to the Louvre. He enjoyed the threefold satisfaction of having rendered a service to a brave man like Bussy, of having been engaged in an intrigue, and of having rendered possible to the king a political stroke which the circumstances demanded. Indeed, what with Bussy's head, and especially his heart, and the organising force of MM. de Guise, a stormy day was likely to rise on the good city of paris.

All that the king had feared, and all that Chicot had anticipated, came to pass, as might have been expected.

M. de Guise, after having received in the morning the principal Leaguers, who came to bring him the registers filled with signatures, and after having made them all swear to recognise the chief that the king should appoint, went out to visit M. d'Anjou, whom he had lost sight of at about ten o'clock the evening before. Chicot had anticipated this visit; and therefore, on leaving Bussy he had lounged in the neighbourhood of the Hôtel d'Alençon. As M. de Guise approached, Chicot hid himself at a corner of the street, and the duke entered without seeing him.

The duke found the prince's valet somewhat concerned about his master's absence, but he imagined that he had slept at the Louvre. The duke asked to speak to Aurilly, who was most likely to know where his master was. Aurilly came, but stated that he had been separated from the prince the evening before by a pressure of the crowd, and had come to the Hôtel d'Alençon to wait for him, not knowing that his Highness had intended to sleep at the Louvre. He added that he had sent to the Louvre three times to inquire, and repeated to him the reply brought by the three messengers that the duke was still asleep.

" Asleep at eleven o'clock! not likely. You ought to go to the Louvre, Aurilly."

" I did think of it, Monseigneur; but I feared that this was only a tale invented to satisfy my messenger, and that the prince was seeking pleasure elsewhere, and might be annoyed at my seeking him."

" Oh, no; the duke has too much sense to be pleasure-seeking on a day like this. Go to the Louvre; you will be sure to find him there."

" I will if you wish it; but what shall I say to him? "

" Say that the convocation at the Louvre is fixed for two o'clock, and that it is necessary that we should have a conference first. It is not at a time when the king is about to choose a chief for the League that he should be sleeping."

" Very well, Monseigneur, I will beg his Highness to come here."

" And say that I am waiting impatiently for him. Meanwhile I will go and seek M. de Bussy."

" But if I do not find his Highness, what am I to do? "

" Then make no further search for him. In any event I shall be at the Louvre at a quarter before two."

Aurilly saluted the duke and started out. Chicot observed his departure, and divined its purpose. If the Duc de Guise should learn of M. d'Anjou's arrest, all would be lost, or at least all would fall into confusion. Chicot therefore hastened with all the speed of his long legs and arrived quickly at the Louvre.

Aurilly passed through the courtiers who crowded the Louvre, and made his way to the duke's apartments. At the door Chicot was playing chess, alone, and seemed to be absorbed in a profound combination. Aurilly tried to pass, but Chicot, with his long legs, blocked up the doorway. He was forced to touch him on the shoulder.

" Ah, it is you, M. Aurilly? "

" What are you doing, M. Chicot? "

" Playing chess, as you see."

" All alone? "

" Yes, I am studying; do you play? "

" Very little."

" Yes, I know you are a musician; and music is so difficult an art that those who give themselves to it must sacrifice all their time."

" You seem very serious over your game."

" Yes; it is my king who disquiets me. You must know, M. Aurilly, that at chess the king is a very insignificant person, who has no will, who can go only one step forward or back, or one to the right or left, while he is surrounded by active enemies, —by knights who jump three squares at a time, by a crowd of pawns who surround him,—so that if he be badly counselled he is a ruined king in no time."

" But, M. Chicot, how does it happen that you are studying this at the door of his royal Highness's room? "

" Because I am waiting for M. Quélus, who is in there."

" Where? "

" With his Highness."

" With his Highness! What is he doing there? I did not think they were such friends."

" Hush! " Then he whispered in Aurilly's ear, " he is come to ask pardon of the duke for a little quarrel they had yesterday."

" Really? "

" It was the king who insisted on it; you know on what excellent terms the brothers are just now. The king would not suffer an impertinence of Quélus's to pass, and ordered him to apologise."

" Really? "

" Ah, M. Aurilly, I think that we are entering the golden age; the Louvre is about to become Arcadia, and the two brothers *Arcades ambo*."

Aurilly smiled and passed into the antechamber, where he was courteously saluted by Quélus, between whose hands a superb cup and ball of ebony inlaid with ivory were making rapid evolutions.

" Bravo, M. Quélus! " said Aurilly, on seeing the young man accomplish a difficult feat.

" Ah, my dear M. Aurilly, when shall I play cup and ball as well as you play the lute? "

" When you have studied your plaything as long as I have my instrument. But where is Monseigneur? I thought you were with him."

" I have an audience with him; but Schomberg is before me."

" What! M. de Schomberg, also? "

" Oh, *mon Dieu!* yes. The king settled all that. He is in the next room. Enter, M. Aurilly, and remind the prince that we are waiting for him."

Aurilly opened the second door and saw Schomberg reclining on a kind of couch, where he was amusing himself by sending from a tube little balls of earth through a gold ring, suspended from the ceiling by a silk thread, while a favourite dog brought him back the balls as they fell.

"Ah, *guten morgen*, M. Aurilly! you see I am amusing myself while I wait for my audience."

"But where is Monseigneur?"

"Oh, he is occupied in pardoning D'Epernon and Maugiron. But will you not enter,—you who are so privileged?"

"Perhaps it would be indiscreet."

"Not at all; enter, M. Aurilly, enter." And he pushed him into the next room, where the astonished musician perceived D'Epernon before a mirror, occupied in stiffening his mustaches, while Maugiron, seated near the window, was cutting out engravings by the side of which the bas-reliefs on the temple of Venus Aphrodite would have looked holy.

The duke, without his sword, was in his armchair between these two men, who looked at him only to watch his movements, and spoke to him only to say something disagreeable. Seeing Aurilly, he got up to meet him.

"Take care, Monseigneur," said Maugiron; "you are stepping on my figures."

"*Mon Dieu!*" cried the musician, "he insults my master!"

"Dear M. Aurilly," said D'Epernon, still arranging his mustaches, "how are you?"

"Be so kind as to bring me here your little dagger," said Maugiron.

"Gentlemen, gentlemen," said Aurilly, "do you not remember where you are?"

"Yes, yes, my dear Orpheus, that is why I ask for your dagger; you see Monsieur the Duke has none."

"Aurilly!" cried the duke, in a tone full of grief and rage, "do you not see that I am a prisoner?"

"A prisoner! to whom?"

"To my brother; you might know that by my jailers."

Aurilly uttered a cry of surprise. "Oh, if I had but guessed it!" said he.

"You would have brought your lute to amuse his Highness," said a mocking voice behind them; "but I thought of it, and sent for it. Here it is."

"How does your chess go on, Chicot?" inquired D'Epernon.

"I believe I shall save the king; but it is not without trouble. Come, M. Aurilly, give me your poniard in return for the lute, —a fair exchange."

The astonished musician obeyed, and went and sat on a cushion at the feet of his master.

"There is one rat in the trap," said Quélus, who returned to his post in the antechamber, only exchanging his cup and ball for Schomberg's shooting-tube.

"It is amusing to vary one's pleasures," said Chicot; "so for a change I will go and sign the League."

CHAPTER VII

THE RECEPTION OF THE CHIEFS OF THE LEAGUE

THE time for the great reception drew near. Paris, nearly as tumultuous as the evening before, had sent towards the Louvre its deputation of Leaguers, its bodies of workmen, its sheriffs, its militia, and its constantly increasing masses of spectators.

The king, on his throne in the great hall, was surrounded by his officers, his friends, his courtiers, and his family, waiting for all the corporations to defile before him, when M. de Monsoreau entered abruptly.

"Look, Henriquet!" said Chicot, who was standing near the king.

"At what?"

"At your chief huntsman; *pardieu!* he is well worth it. See how pale and dirty he is!"

Henri made a sign to M. de Monsoreau, who approached. "How is it that you are at the Louvre, Monsieur? I thought you were at Vincennes."

"Sire, the stag was roused at seven o'clock this morning; but when noon came, and I had no news, I feared that some misfortune had happened to your Majesty, and I hurried back."

"Really!"

"Sire, if I have done wrong attribute it to an excess of devotion."

"Yes, Monsieur; and I appreciate it."

"Now," said the count, hesitatingly, "if your Majesty wishes me to return to Vincennes, as I am reassured—"

"No, no, stay; this chase was a fancy which came into my head, and which went as it came. Do not go away; I want near me devoted subjects, and you have just classed yourself among those on whose devotion I can rely."

Monsoreau bowed, and said, " Where does your Majesty wish me to remain? "

" Will you give him to me for half an hour? " said Chicot to the king, in a low voice.

" What for? "

" To torment him a little. You owe me some compensation for obliging me to be present at this tiresome ceremony."

" Well, take him."

" Where does your Majesty wish me to stand? " again asked M. de Monsoreau.

" Where you like; go behind my armchair, that is where I put my friends."

" Come here," said Chicot, making room for M. de Monsoreau; " come and get the scent of these fellows. Here is game which can be tracked without a hound. Here are the shoemakers who pass, or rather who have passed; then here are the tanners. *Mort de ma vie!* if you lose their scent I will take away your place."

M. de Monsoreau listened mechanically; he seemed preoccupied, and looked round him anxiously.

" Do you know what your chief huntsman is hunting for now? " said Chicot, in an undertone, to the king.

" No."

" Your brother."

" The game is not in sight, at any rate," said Henri, smiling.

" Just ask him where his countess is."

" What for? "

" Just ask and you will see."

" Monsieur the Count," said Henri, " what have you done with Madame de Monsoreau? I do not see her here."

The count started, but replied, " Sire, she is ill. The air of Paris did not agree with her; so having obtained leave from the queen, she set out last night with her father for Méridor."

" Paris is not good for women in her situation," said Chicot. " ' Gravidis uxoribus Lutetia inclemens.' I advise you, Henri, to imitate the example of the count, and send the queen away somewhere when she is—"

Monsoreau grew pale and looked furiously at him. " Who has told you, impertinent, that Madame the Countess was *enceinte?* "

" And is she not? " said Chicot. " It would be more impertinent to suppose that, it seems to me."

" She is not, Monsieur."

I

"Ah, do you hear that, Henri? It seems that your grand huntsman has made your mistake,—he has forgotten to bring together the chemises of Notre-Dame. That poor countess!" continued Chicot, "she will die of ennui by the way."

"I said that she travelled with her father."

"A father is very respectable, I allow, but not very amusing; and if she had only that worthy baron to amuse her, it would be sad. But luckily—"

"What?" cried the count.

"What?"

"What do you mean by 'luckily'?"

"Ah, you made an ellipsis just then."

The count shrugged his shoulders.

"Oh, but it was. Ask Henri, who is a man of letters."

"Yes," said the king; "but what did your adverb mean?"

"What adverb?"

"'Luckily.'"

"'Luckily' means luckily. Luckily, then, there exist some of our friends, and very amusing ones, who, if they meet the countess, will amuse her; and as they are going the same way, it is probable they will. Oh, I see them from here; do you not, Henri,—you, who are a man of imagination? There they go, on a good road, well mounted, and saying sweet things to Madame the Countess, which she likes very much, dear lady."

This was a second dagger, sharper than the first, planted in the grand huntsman's breast. M. de Monsoreau was furious, but he could not show it before the king; so he said as mildly as he could, "What! have you friends travelling to Anjou?"

"You might even say we have, Monsieur the Count; for those friends are even more yours than mine."

"You surprise me, M. Chicot; I know no one who—"

"Good! pretend to be mysterious."

"I swear to you—"

"Oh! you know they are there, although I saw you just now seeking for them mechanically among the crowd by force of habit."

"You saw me?"

"Yes, you,—the palest of all chief huntsmen, past, present, and future, from Nimrod to M. d'Aulefort, your predecessor."

"M. Chicot!"

"The palest, I repeat."

"Monsieur, will you return to the subject of which you spoke, and be so good as to name those friends if your superabundant imagination will let you."

"Seek, Monsieur. *Morbleu!* it is your occupation to hunt out animals,—witness the unlucky stag whom you disturbed this morning, and who thought it very unkind of you. Seek!"

The eyes of M. de Monsoreau wandered anxiously again. "What!" cried he, seeing a vacant place by the king, "not the Duc d'Anjou?"

"*Taïaut! taïaut!* the beast is found."

"He has set out to-day?" exclaimed the count.

"He is gone to-day; but it is possible that he set out last night. When did your brother disappear, Henri?"

"Last night."

"The duke gone!" murmured Monsoreau, pale and trembling. "Ah, *mon Dieu! mon Dieu!* what are you telling me, Sire?"

"I do not say that he has gone; I say only that he disappeared last night, and that his best friends do not know where he is," said the king.

"Oh!" cried the count, "if I thought so——"

"Well; what would you do? Besides, what harm if he does talk nonsense to Madame de Monsoreau? He is the gallant of the family, you know."

"I am lost!" murmured the count, trying to go away. But Chicot detained him.

"Keep still; *mordieu!* you shake the king's chair. *Mort de ma vie*, I should like to be in your wife's place, were it only to see every day a prince with a double nose, and to hear M. Aurilly, who plays the lute like the late Orpheus. What a chance your wife has,—what a chance!"

Monsoreau trembled with anger.

"Quietly, Monsieur," continued Chicot; "hide your joy. Here is the business beginning. You should not show your feelings so openly; listen to the discourse of the king."

M. de Monsoreau was forced to keep quiet. M. de Guise entered and knelt before the king, not without throwing an uneasy glance of surprise on the vacant seat of M. d'Anjou. The king rose, and the heralds commanded silence.

CHAPTER VIII

HOW THE KING APPOINTED A CHIEF FOR THE LEAGUE, WHO WAS NEITHER THE DUC DE GUISE NOR M. D'ANJOU

"Gentlemen," said the king, after assuring himself that his four friends, now replaced by ten Swiss, were behind him, "a king hears equally the voices which come to him from above and those which come from below; that is to say, what God commands, and what the people command. I understand perfectly that there is a guarrantee for my people in the association of all classes which has been formed to defend the Catholic faith; and therefore I approve of the counsels of my cousin Guise. I declare, then, the holy League duly constituted; and as so great a body must have a powerful head, and as it is necessary that the chief called to sustain the Church should be one of its most zealous sons, I choose a Christian prince for the chief, and declare that this chief shall be"—he made a slight pause—"Henri de Valois, King of France and Poland."

Henri, in pronouncing these words, had raised his voice, to mark his triumph and to gratify the enthusiasm of his friends, ready to break out, and also to complete the prostration of the Leaguers, whose half-suppressed murmurs betrayed their dissatisfaction, surprise, and fear.

The Duc de Guise was thunderstruck. Large drops stood on his forehead, and he looked from one to the other of his brothers. The cardinal stole up to his brother Mayenne, and whispered, "François, I fear we are no longer in safety here. Let us haste to take leave, for the populace is uncertain; and the king, whom they execrated yesterday, will be their idol for two or three days."

"So be it," said Mayenne; "let us go. Wait here for our brother; I will arrange for the retreat."

During this time the king had signed the act prepared beforehand by M. de Morvilliers,—the only person, with the exception of the queen-mother, who was in the secret; then he passed the pen to the Duc de Guise, saying, "Sign, my cousin,—there, below me; now pass it to Monsieur the Cardinal and M. de Mayenne."

But these two had already disappeared. The king remarked their absence, and added, "Then pass the pen to M. de Monsoreau."

The duke did so, and was about to retire; but the king said,

" Wait." And while the others signed, he added, " My cousin, it was your advice, I believe, to guard Paris with a good army, composed of all the forces of the League. The army is made, and properly made, since the natural general of the Parisians is the king."

" Assuredly, Sire," said the duke, without well knowing what he said.

" But I do not forget that there is another army to command, and that this belongs of right to the bravest soldier in my kingdom; therefore go and command the army."

" And when am I to set out, Sire? "

" Immediately."

" Henri, Henri! " whispered Chicot; but in spite of his signs and grimaces, the king gave the duke his brevet ready signed. He took it and went out. The cardinal awaited him at the door of the hall, and the Duc de Mayenne awaited them both at the gate of the Louvre. They mounted instantly; and ten minutes later all three were outside of Paris. The rest of the assembly dispersed gradually, crying, " Vive le roi! " and " Vive la Ligue! "

" Oh, Sire! " cried the favourites, approaching the king, " what a sublime idea you have had! "

" They think that gold is going to rain on them like manna," said Chicot, who followed his master about everywhere with lamentations.

As soon as they were left alone, " Ah, M. Chicot! " said Henri, " you are never content. The devil! I do not ask for complaisance, but for good sense."

" You are right, Henri; it is what you want most."

" Confess I have done well."

" That is just what I do not think."

" Ah! you are jealous, M. Roi de France."

" I! Heaven forbid! I shall choose better subjects for jealousy."

" Corbleu! "

" Oh, what ferocious self-love! "

" Am I or am I not king of the League? "

" Certainly you are; but—"

" But what? "

" You are no longer King of France."

" And who is king, then? "

" Everybody, except you; firstly, your brother—"

" My brother? "

" Yes, M. d'Anjou."

" Whom I hold prisoner."

" Yes, but prisoner as he is, he was consecrated."

" By whom was he consecrated? "

" By the Cardinal de Guise. Really, Henri, you have a fine police. They consecrate a king at Paris before thirty-three people, in the church of Ste. Geneviève, and you do not know of it! "

" Oh! and you do? "

" Certainly I do."

" How can you know what I do not? "

" Ah! because M. de Morvilliers manages your police, and I am my own police."

The king frowned.

" Well, then, without counting Henri de Valois, we have François d'Anjou for king," continued Chicot; " and then there is the Duc de Guise."

" The Duc de Guise! "

" Yes, Henri de Guise, Henri de Balafré."

" A fine king! whom I exile, whom I send to the army."

" Good! as if you were not exiled to Poland; and La Charité is nearer to the Louvre than Cracow is. Ah, yes, you send him to the army,—that is so clever; that is to say, you put thirty thousand men under his orders, *ventre de biche!* and a real army, not like your army of the League. No, no, an army of *bourgeois* is good for Henri de Valois, king of the favourites; but Henri de Guise must have an army of soldiers. And what soldiers!—hardened warriors, capable of destroying twenty armies of the League; so that if, being king in fact, Henri de Guise had the folly one day to wish to be so in name, he would only have to turn towards the capital, and say, ' Let us swallow Paris and Henri de Valois and the Louvre at a mouthful,' and the rogues would do it. I know them."

" You forget one thing in your argument, illustrious politician."

" Ah, the devil! it is possible! If you mean a fourth king—"

" No; you forget that before thinking of reigning in France, when a Valois is on the throne, it would be necessary to look back and count your ancestors. That such an idea might come to M. d'Anjou is possible; his ancestors are mine, and it is only a question of primogeniture. But M. de Guise,—come now, Maître Chicot, study heraldry, my friend, and tell me if the *fleur de lis* of France are not of higher rank than the merlets of Lorraine."

" Ah! that is just where you are in error."

" How so? "

" M. de Guise is of a better race than you think."

" Better than I, perhaps," said Henri, smiling.

" There is no perhaps in it, my little Henriquet."

" You are mad.   Learn to read, my friend."

" Well, Henri, you who can read, read this; " and he drew from his pocket the genealogy which we know already.   Henri turned pale as he recognised, near to the signature of the legate, the seal of Saint Peter.

" What do you say, Henri?   Are not your *fleur de lis* thrown a little into the background?   *Ventre de biche!* the merlets seem to me to fly as high as the eagle of Cæsar.   Take care, my son."

" But how did you get this genealogy? "

" I!   Do I seek these things?   It came to seek me."

" Where? "

" Under the bolster of an advocate."

" And what was his name? "

" Maître Nicolas David."

" Where was he? "

" At Lyon."

" And who took it from under the bolster? "

" One of my good friends."

" Who is he? "

" A monk."

" His name? "

" Gorenflot."

" What! that abominable Leaguer, who uttered those incendiary discourses at Ste. Geneviève, and again yesterday in the streets of Paris? "

" You remember the history of Brutus, who pretended to be a fool? "

" He is, then, a profound politician?   Did he take it from the advocate? "

" Yes, by force."

" Then he is brave? "

" Brave as Bayard."

" And having done this he has not asked for any recompense? "

" He returned humbly to his convent, and asks only that it may be forgotten that he ever came out."

" Then he is modest? "

" As Saint Crépin."

"Chicot, your friend shall be made a prior on the first vacancy."

"Thanks for him, Henri.—*Ma foi!*" said Chicot to himself, "if he escapes being hanged by Mayenne, he will have an abbey."

CHAPTER IX

ETEOCLES AND POLYNICES

THIS day of the League terminated brilliantly and tumultuously, as it began. The friends of the king rejoiced; the preachers proposed to canonise Brother Henri, and spoke everywhere of the great deeds of the Valois. The favourites said, "The lion is roused." The Leaguers said, "The fox has discovered the snare."

The three Lorraine princes, as we have seen, had left Paris; and their principal agent, M. de Monsoreau, was leaving the Louvre to make his preparations for departure, in the hope of overtaking the Duc d'Anjou. But as he was going out, Chicot accosted him. The Leaguers had gone, and the Gascon had no further fears for his king. "Where are you going in such a hurry?" said he.

"To his Highness."

"His Highness?"

"Yes, I am concerned about him. We do not live in times when a prince ought to travel without a good escort."

"Oh! he is so brave," said Chicot, "even to rashness."

The grand huntsman looked at the Gascon. "Well," said the latter, "if you are anxious, I am still more so."

"About whom?"

"About his Highness also."

"Why?"

"Do you not know what they say?"

"That he has gone to Anjou?"

"No; that he is dead," whispered the Gascon in the ear of his interlocutor.

"Bah!" said Monsoreau, with a tone of surprise not unmixed with joy, "you told me he was travelling."

"The devil! they persuaded me to believe so; I am so credulous that I am taken in by every lie that is told me. But now I have good reason to think that if the poor prince be travelling it is to another world."

"What gives you these mournful ideas?"

"He entered the Louvre yesterday, did he not?"

"Certainly, I came in with him."

"Well, he has never been seen to come out."

"From the Louvre?"

"No."

"Where is Aurilly?"

"Disappeared."

"But his people?"

"Disappeared."

"You are joking, are you not, M. Chicot?"

"Ask."

"Whom?"

"The king."

"I cannot question his Majesty."

"Oh, yes! if you go about it in the right way."

"Well," said the count, "I cannot remain in this uncertainty." And leaving Chicot, or rather preceding him, he went to the king's apartments.

"Where is the king?" he asked. "I have to render an account to him of the execution of some orders he gave me."

"With M. le Duc d'Anjou," replied the man whom he addressed.

"With the Duc d'Anjou?" said the count to Chicot; "the prince is not dead, then?"

"I am not so sure of that."

M. de Monsoreau was thoroughly bewildered; it was becoming clear to him that M. d'Anjou had not left the Louvre. But as he did not know the true cause of the prince's absence at a time so critical, that absence astonished him beyond measure.

The king had, in fact, gone to visit the Duc d'Anjou; but the grand huntsman, notwithstanding his strong desire to know what was going on, was obliged to wait for news in the corridor.

Immediately after the sitting, Quélus, Maugiron, Schomberg, and D'Epernon, in spite of the ennui they experienced there, were so anxious to be disagreeable to the duke that they returned to their posts, — Schomberg and D'Epernon in the salon, Maugiron and Quélus in the chamber of his Highness. He, on his part, was weary of his confinement as well as anxious; and, it must be confessed, the conversation of these gentlemen was not calculated to comfort him.

"Do you know, Quélus," said Maugiron, calling from one end of the chamber to the other as if the prince were not there,

" that it is only now that I begin to appreciate our friend Valois? really, he is a great politician."

" Explain yourself," said Quélus, who was lounging on a chair.

" While he was afraid of the conspiracy, he kept it quiet. Now he speaks of it openly; therefore he is no longer afraid of it."

" Well? "

" If he no longer fears it, he will punish it. You know Valois; he has certainly many good qualities, but clemency is not one of them."

" Granted."

" Then if he punishes these conspirators there will be a trial, and we shall have a fine spectacle."

" Unless, which is possible, on account of the rank of the accused, they arrange it all quietly."

" That would be my advice, certainly. It is better in family affairs; and this last conspiracy was really a family affair."

Aurilly glanced anxiously at the prince.

" Faith," said Maugiron, " I know one thing,—that in the king's place I would not spare the high heads, which are always the most guilty. I would make an example of one or two,— one, at all events."

" I think it would be well to revive the famous invention of sacks."

" What was that? "

" A royal fancy which dates from about 1350: they shut up a man in a sack, in company with three or four cats, and threw them into the water. The minute the cats felt the water they attacked the man, and there occurred in the sack things which unluckily could never be seen."

" Really, Quélus, you are a well of science, and your conversation is most interesting."

" They could not apply this invention to the chiefs. They have the right to be beheaded; but to the small fry, I mean the favourites, squires, stewards, and lute-players—"

" Gentlemen—" stammered Aurilly, pale with terror.

" Do not reply to them, Aurilly," said François; " it cannot be addressed to me, nor, consequently, to my household. Princes of the blood are not a subject for jesting in France."

" No, they are treated more seriously," said Quélus; " they are beheaded."

At this point in the conversation the door opened, and the

king appeared on the threshold. The duke rose. " Sire," cried
he, " I appeal to your justice against the unworthy treatment I
meet with from your followers."

Henri did not seem either to see or to hear his brother.
" Good-morning, Quélus," said he, kissing his favourite on both
cheeks,—" good-morning, my child; the sight of you rejoices
my soul. And you, my poor Maugiron, how are you? "

" I am dying of ennui, Sire. When I undertook to guard your
brother, I thought he was more amusing. Oh, the tiresome
prince! are you sure he is the son of your father and mother? "

" Sire, you hear! " cried the prince; " is it your wish that
your brother should be insulted? "

" Silence, Monsieur! " said Henri; " I do not like my prisoners
to complain."

" Prisoner or not, I am your—"

" The title which you are about to invoke," interrupted the
king, " is fatal to you. My brother, guilty, is doubly guilty."

" But if he is not? "

" He is."

" Of what crime? "

" Of having displeased me."

" Sire, have our family quarrels need of witnesses? "

" You are right, Monsieur. My friends, let me speak a little
to my brother."

" Sire," said Quélus, in a low tone, " it is not prudent for your
Majesty to remain with two enemies."

" I will take away Aurilly," said Maugiron, in the other ear
of the king.

The two gentlemen took Aurilly away, who was at once burning with curiosity and dying of anxiety.

" Now we are alone, Monsieur," said the king, when they had
gone.

" I have waited for this moment impatiently."

" And I also. Ah, you want my crown, my worthy Eteocles:
you made of the League a means, and of the throne an aim, and
were consecrated in a corner of Paris in a retired church, so that
you might show yourself to the Parisians shining with holy
oil."

" Alas! your Majesty will not let me speak."

" What for,—to lie, or to tell me things which I know already?
But no, you would lie; for to confess what you have done would
be to confess that you merit death. You would lie; and I
would spare you that shame."

"My brother, is it your intention to overwhelm me with outrages?"

"If what I say is an outrage, it is I who lie; and I ask nothing better than that what I say should be proved untrue. Speak, then; I listen. Show me that you are not a traitor, and what is worse, a blunderer."

"I do not know what your Majesty means; you speak in enigmas."

"Then I will explain my words," cried the king, in a voice full of threatening. "You have conspired against me, as formerly you conspired against my brother Charles; only then it was by the aid of Henri de Navarre, and now it is with the assistance of the Duc de Guise. It is true that formerly you crawled like a serpent; now you wish to spring like the lion. After perfidy, open force; after poison, the sword."

"Poison! what do you mean?" cried François, with flashing eyes.

"The poison with which you assassinated our brother Charles, which you destined for Henri de Navarre, your associate. That fatal poison is known; our mother has used it so often. That, doubtless, is the reason why you renounced it on this occasion. That is why you wished to assume the style of a captain, commanding the forces of the League. But look me in the face, François," continued Henri, making a threatening step towards his brother, "and be assured that a man like you will never kill a man like me."

François shivered under that fierce attack; but without pity for his prisoner the king continued, "A sword! Ah! I should like to see you here in this room alone with me, holding a sword. I have conquered you in cunning; and in a combat you would be killed. Dream no longer of struggling against me in any manner, for from this moment I act as king, as master, as despot; I shall watch you everywhere, follow you everywhere, and at the least suspicion, I will throw you to the axe of my executioner. This is what I had to say to you about our family affairs, my brother; this is why I wished to speak privately with you, François. And I will order you to be left alone to-night to ponder over my words."

"Then, Sire, for a suspicion, I have fallen into disgrace with you."

"Say, under my justice."

"But at least, Sire, fix a term to my captivity, that I may know what to expect."

" You will know when you hear your sentence read."

" Can I not see my mother? "

" What for? There were but three copies in the world of the famous hunting-book which killed my poor brother; and of the two others, one is in London and the other at Florence. Besides, I am not a Nimrod, like my poor brother; adieu, François.

" Gentlemen," said the king, opening the door, " the Duc d'Anjou has requested to be alone to-night to reflect on an answer he has to make to me to-morrow morning. Leave him then alone, except for occasional visits of precaution. You will perhaps find your prisoner a little excited by the conversation just now closed; but remember that in conspiring against me M. le Duc d'Anjou has renounced the title of my brother. He consequently is here only as a captive under guard. No ceremony then; if the captive troubles you, call me. I have the Bastille ready; and the governor, M. Laurent Testu, is the best man in the world to conquer ill-tempers."

" Sire," cried François, trying a last effort, " remember I am your—"

" You were also the brother of Charles IX., I think."

" At least restore to me my friends."

" I deprive myself of mine to give them to you." And Henri shut the door, while the duke fell in despair into his armchair.

CHAPTER X

HOW PEOPLE DO NOT ALWAYS LOSE THEIR TIME BY SEARCHING EMPTY DRAWERS

THE scene which the duke had just had with the king made him regard his position as desperate. The favourites had not allowed him to be ignorant of what had taken place at the Louvre. They had exhibited in exaggerated outlines the defeat of MM. de Guise and the triumph of Henri. He had heard what was to him incomprehensible,—the people crying, " Vive le roi! " and " Vive la Ligue! " He perceived that he was abandoned by the other chiefs, who had themselves to save. In his quarrels with his brother Charles he had always had for confidants, or rather dupes, those two devoted men, Coconnas and La Mole; and for the first time in his life, feeling himself alone and isolated, he felt a kind of remorse at having sacrificed them. During that time his sister Marguerite had loved and consoled him. How had he recompensed her?

He had recently had near him a brave and valiant heart and sword,—Bussy, the brave Bussy; and he had offended him to please Monsoreau, who had his secret, with which he always threatened him, and which was now known to the king. He had therefore quarrelled with Bussy gratuitously, which, as a great politician once said, "was more than a crime, it was a mistake!" How he would have rejoiced in his present situation to know that Bussy was watching over him,—Bussy the invincible, Bussy the loyal, Bussy the universal favourite. It would have been probable liberty and certain vengeance.

But, as we have said, Bussy, wounded to the heart, kept away from the prince; so that the prisoner remained fifty feet above the ground, with the four favourites in the corridor, without counting the courtyard full of Swiss. Besides this, one or another of his guards entered from time to time, and without seeming even to notice the prince, went round the room, examined the doors and windows, looked under the beds and tables, and glanced at the curtains and sheets.

"Faith!" said Maugiron, after one of these visits, "I have done; I am not going to look after him any more to-night."

"Yes," said D'Epernon, "as long as we guard him, there is no need of going to look at him."

"And he is not handsome to look at," said Quélus.

"Still," said Schomberg, "I think we had better not relax our vigilance, for the devil is cunning."

"Yes; but it is not enough to be cunning to pass over the bodies of four men like us."

"That is true," said Quélus.

"Oh!" said Schomberg, "do you think, if he wants to escape, he will choose to come through our corridor? If he really means to escape, he will make a hole in the wall."

"With what?"

"Then he has the windows."

"Ah, the windows! bravo, Schomberg! Would you jump forty-five feet?"

"I confess that forty-five feet—"

"Yes; and he who is lame and heavy, and timid as—"

"You," said Schomberg.

"My dear fellow," said D'Epernon, "you know I fear nothing but ghosts,—that is an affair of the nerves."

"The fact is," said Quélus, "that all those whom he had killed in duels appeared to him one night."

"However," said Maugiron, "I have read of wonderful escapes,—with sheets, for instance."

"Ah! that is more sensible," said D'Epernon; "I saw myself, at Bordeaux, a prisoner who escaped by the aid of his sheets."

"You saw?" said Schomberg.

"Yes; but he had his leg broken and his neck too. His sheets were thirty feet too short, and he had to jump; so that while his body escaped from prison, his soul escaped from his body."

"Besides," said Quélus, "if he escapes, we shall have a chase for a prince of the blood; we will follow him, and in the pursuit some mischief may happen to him."

So they dismissed the subject. They were correct in the supposition that the duke was not likely to attempt a perilous escape. From time to time his pale face was at the window which overlooked the fosses of the Louvre, beyond which was an open space about fifteen feet broad, and then the Seine rolled calm as a mirror. On the other side rose, like a giant, the tower of Nesle.

He had watched the sunset and the gradual extinction of all the lights. He had contemplated the beautiful spectacle of old Paris, with its roofs gilded by the last rays of the sun, and silvered by the first beams of the moon; then little by little he was seized with a great terror at seeing immense clouds roll over the sky, announcing a storm. Among his other weaknesses, the Duc d'Anjou was afraid of thunder, and he would have given anything to have had his guardians with him again, even if they insulted him. He threw himself on his bed, but found it impossible to sleep. He tried to read; but the letters danced before his eyes like black devils. He resorted to drinking; but the wine tasted bitter. He touched with his finger-ends Aurilly's lute, hanging on the wall; but the vibration of the chords affected his nerves and made him want to cry. Then he set himself to swearing like a pagan and breaking everything within reach. It was a family failing, and they were accustomed to it at the Louvre. The young men had opened the door to see what the noise meant; and seeing that it was the duke amusing himself, they had shut it again, which redoubled his anger. He had just broken a chair, when a crashing of glass was heard at the window, and he felt a sharp blow on his thigh. His first idea was that he was wounded by the discharge of an arquebuse, fired by some emissary of the king.

" Ah, I am dead! " he cried, and fell on the carpet. But as he fell, his hand came in contact with a larger and rougher substance than an arquebuse-bullet.

" Oh! a stone," thought he; and feeling his leg, he found it uninjured. He picked up the stone and looked at it, and saw that it was wrapped in a piece of paper. Then the duke's ideas began to change. Might not this stone come from a friend as well as an enemy? He approached the light, cut the silk which tied the paper round the stone, and read:—

Are you tired of keeping your room? Do you love open air and liberty? Enter the little room where the Queen of Navarre hid your poor friend, M. de la Mole; open the cabinet, and by displacing the lowest bracket you will find a double bottom. In this there is a silk ladder; attach it yourself to the balcony. Two vigorous arms will hold it at the bottom. A horse, swift as thought, will lead you to a safe place.　　　　A Friend.

" A friend! " cried the prince; " oh, I did not know I had a friend! Who is this friend who thinks of me? " And the duke ran to the window, but could see no one.

" Can it be a snare? " thought he; " but first let me see if there is a double bottom and a ladder."

The duke then, leaving the light where it was, for precaution, groped his way to the cabinet, which he knew so well. He opened the closet, felt for the bottom shelf, and to his great joy found what he looked for. As a thief escapes with his booty, the duke rushed into the next room with his prey. Ten o'clock struck; the duke thought of his hourly visitors, and hid his ladder under a cushion, on which he sat down. Indeed, five minutes had not passed before Maugiron appeared in a dressing-gown, with a sword in one hand and a light in the other. As he came in, one of his friends said to him, " The bear is furious, —he was breaking everything just now; take care he does not devour you, Maugiron."

Maugiron made his usual examination; he saw that a window was broken, but thought the duke had done it in his rage.

" Maugiron! " cried Schomberg, from outside, " are you already eaten that you do not speak? In that case, sigh, at least, that we may know what has happened, and may avenge you."

The duke trembled with impatience.

" No, no," said Maugiron; " on the contrary, my bear is quite conquered."

And so saying, he went out and locked the door. When the key had ceased to turn in the lock, the duke murmured, " Take care, gentlemen; the bear is a very cunning beast."

CHAPTER XI

VENTRE-SAINT-GRIS

LEFT alone, the duke, knowing that he had at least an hour before him, drew out his ladder, and carefully examined it. " The ladder is good," said he, at length, " and is not offered me as a contrivance for getting my ribs broken." Then he unrolled it all, and counted thirty-eight rounds fifteen inches apart. " The length is sufficient," said he; " there is nothing to fear on that point. Ah! but if it were some of those cursed favourites who sent me to the ladder? They will allow me to attach it to the balcony; and while I am descending they will cut the cords. But no; they could not be foolish enough to think I would fly without barricading the door, and they would remember that I should have time to fly before they could force it. Moreover, how could any one suppose that I would trust to the innocence of that ladder, found in a closet of the Queen of Navarre? For, in short, who is there in the world who could know about that ladder except my sister Marguerite? Let us see; who is the friend? The note is signed, ' a friend.' Who is the friend so well acquainted with the closets in my apartments, or those of my sister Marguerite? "

The duke had hardly finished that statement of the problem, when, reading the note again, to recognise the signature if possible, he was seized by a sudden idea. " Bussy! " he cried. Bussy, whom so many women loved; who seemed a hero to the Queen of Navarre; Bussy, discreet, versed in the knowledge of closets; was it not, in all probability, Bussy, the only one among all his friends on whom the duke could rely,—was it not Bussy who had sent the note? Everything made him think so. The duke, of course, did not know all Bussy's reasons for being angry with him, for he did not know his love for Diane, and believed him to be too noble to think of resentment when his master was a prisoner. He approached the window again, and fancied he could see in the fog the indistinct forms of three horses and two men by the river. Two men,—these must be Bussy and Rémy. He then looked through the keyhole, and saw his four guardians; two were asleep, and two had inherited Chicot's chessboard and were playing. He extinguished his light.

Then he opened his window, and looked over the balcony; the gulf below him looked fearful in the darkness, and he drew back. But air and liberty have an attraction so irresistible to a prisoner that François, on withdrawing from the window, felt as if he were being stifled; and for an instant something like disgust of life and indifference to death passed through his mind. He fancied he was growing courageous; and profiting by this moment of excitement, he seized the ladder, fixed it to the balcony, then barricaded the door as well as he could, and returned to the window. The darkness was now great, and the first growlings of the storm began to make themselves heard; a great cloud with silver fringes extended itself like a recumbent elephant from one side to the other of the river. A flash of lightning broke the immense cloud for a moment; and the prince thought he saw below him in the fosse the horses and the men. A horse neighed; there was no more doubt,—he was waited for.

The duke shook the ladder to see if it was firm, then he put his leg over the balustrade and placed his foot on the first step. Nothing can describe the anguish of the prisoner at this moment, placed between a frail silk cord for his sole support, on the one hand, and his brother's cruel menaces on the other. But as he stood there he felt the ladder stiffened; some one held it. Was it a friend or an enemy? Were they open arms, or arms bearing weapons which waited for him? An irresistible terror seized him; he still held the balcony with his left hand and made a movement to remount, when a very slight pull at the ladder came to him like a solicitation. He took courage and tried the second step. The ladder was held as firm as a rock; and he found a steady support for his foot. He descended rapidly, almost gliding down, when all at once, instead of touching the earth, which he knew to be near, he felt himself seized in the arms of a man who whispered, " You are saved." Then he was carried along the fosse till they came to the end, when another man seized him by the collar and drew him up; and after his companion had ascended in the same way, they ran to the river, where stood the horses. The prince knew he was at the mercy of his saviours, so he jumped at once on a horse, and his companions did the same. The same voice now said, " Quick! " and they set off at a gallop.

" All goes well at present," thought the prince; " let us hope it will end so. Thanks, my brave Bussy," said he to his companion on the right, who was entirely covered with a large cloak.

"Quick!" replied the other.

They arrived thus at the great ditch of the Bastille, which they crossed on a bridge improvised by the Leaguers the night before. The three cavaliers rode towards Charenton, when all at once the man on the right entered the forest of Vincennes, saying only, "Come." The prince's horse neighed, and several others answered from the depths of the forest. François would have stopped if he could, for he feared they were taking him to an ambush; but it was too late, and in a few minutes he found himself in a small open space, where eight or ten men on horseback were drawn up.

"Oh! oh!" said the prince, "what does this mean, Monsieur?"

"*Ventre-saint-gris!* it means that we are saved."

"You, Henri?" cried the duke, stupefied, "you my liberator?"

"Does that astonish you? Are we not related?" Then looking around for his other companion, "Agrippa," he said, "where the devil are you?"

"Here I am," said D'Aubigné.

"Are there two fresh horses with which we can go a dozen leagues without stopping?"

"But where are you taking me, my cousin?" asked François.

"Where you like, only be quick,—for the King of France has more horses than I have, and is rich enough to kill a score of horses if he takes it into his head to pursue us."

"Really, then, I am free to go where I like?"

"Certainly, I await your orders."

"Well, then, to Angers."

"To Angers; so be it, there you are at home."

"But you?"

"I! when we are in sight of Angers I shall leave you and ride on to Navarre, where my good Margot expects me, and must be very weary of my absence."

"But no one knew you were here?"

"I came to sell three diamonds of my wife's."

"Ah, very well!"

"And also to know if this League was really going to ruin me."

"You see there is nothing in it."

"Thanks to you, yes."

"How, thanks to me?"

"Certainly. If, instead of refusing to be chief of the League
when you knew it was directed against me, you had accepted
and made common cause with my enemies, I should have been
ruined. Therefore, when I heard that the king had punished
your refusal with imprisonment, I swore to release you, and I
have done so."

"Always so simple-minded," thought François; "really, it is
easy to deceive him."

"Go, my cousin," said the Béarnais,—"go to Anjou. Ah,
M. de Guise! I send you a companion you do not want."

When the fresh horses ordered by Henri were brought, he
and the Duc d'Anjou leaped into the saddles and set off at a
gallop, accompanied by Agrippa d'Aubigné, who followed them,
growling.

CHAPTER XII

THE FRIENDS

WHILE Paris was in this ferment, Madame de Monsoreau,
escorted by her father and two servants, pursued their way to
Méridor, by stages of ten leagues a day. She began to enjoy her
liberty, precious to those who have suffered. The azure of the
sky compared to the sky extended, always menacing, over the
black towers of the Bastille, the trees already green, the beautiful
paths winding through the heart of the forest,—all appeared to
her fresh and young, beautiful and new, as if she had really come
out of the watery grave where her father had believed her to be
buried. He, the old baron, had become twenty years younger.
We will not attempt to describe their long journey, free from
incidents. Sometimes, on coming to rising ground, Diane would
allow the others to pass her, and remaining behind would search
the depths of the valley for signs of any one following. Then her
father, watching her from the corner of his eye, would say, "Do
not fear, Diane."

"Fear what?"

"Were you not looking to see if M. de Monsoreau was following
us?"

"Ah, it is true; yes, I was thinking of that," said the young
woman, with another look behind.

At last, on the eighth day, they reached the Château de
Méridor, and were received by Madame de Saint-Luc and her
husband. Then began for these four people one of those

existences of which every man has dreamed in reading Virgil or Theocritus. The baron and Saint-Luc hunted from morning till evening; you might have seen troops of dogs rushing from the hills in pursuit of some hare or fox, and startling Diane and Jeanne, as they sat side by side on the moss, under the shade of the trees.

"Tell me," said Jeanne, "all that happened to you in the tomb,—for you were dead to us. See, the hawthorn is shedding on us its last flowers, and the elders send out their perfume. Not a breath in the air, not a human being near us; tell me all about it, little sister."

"What can I say?"

"Tell me, are you happy? Those beautiful eyes encircled by bluish shadows, that paleness of your cheeks, that mouth which tries a smile which it never finishes,—Diane, you must have many things to tell me."

"No, nothing."

"You are, then, happy with M. de Monsoreau?"

Diane shuddered.

"You see!" said Jeanne, with tender reproach.

"With M. de Monsoreau! Why did you pronounce that name? Why do you evoke that phantom in the midst of our woods, our flowers, our happiness?"

"Well, I know now why your beautiful eyes are encircled with blue, and why they are so often raised towards heaven; but I have not yet discovered why your lips begin those smiles."

Diane sadly shook her head.

"You told me, I think," said Jeanne, embracing Diane's shoulders with her white round arm, "that M. de Bussy showed much interest in you."

Diane reddened even to her delicate round ears.

"M de Bussy is a charming cavalier," said Jeanne; and she sang,—

> "Un beau chercheur de noise,
> C'est le Seigneur d'Amboise."

Diane rested her head on her friend's bosom and murmured in a voice softer than the warbling of birds,—

> "Tendre, fidèle aussi,
> C'est le brave—"

"Bussy? say it, then," said Jeanne, joyously kissing the eyes of her friend.

"Enough of foolishness," said Diane, suddenly; "M. de Bussy thinks no longer of Diane de Méridor."

"That is possible; but I believe he pleases Diane de Monsoreau a little."

"Do not say that."

"Does it displease you?"

"I tell you he thinks no more of me; and he does well—oh, I was cowardly."

"What do you say?"

"Nothing, nothing!"

"Now, Diane, you are going to cry, and to accuse yourself. You cowardly! you, my heroine! you were under constraint."

"I believed it; I saw dangers, gulfs under my feet. Now, Jeanne, those dangers seem to me chimerical; those gulfs, a child could cross them. I was cowardly, I tell you; oh, if only I had had time to reflect!"

"You speak in enigmas."

"No," cried Diane, rising in great excitement, "it was not my fault,—he did not wish it. I recall the situation, which seemed terrible to me. I hesitated; I doubted. My father offered me his support; and I was frightened. *He, he* offered me his protection; but he did not offer it in a way to convince me. The Duc d'Anjou was against him; the Duc d'Anjou was in league with M. de Monsoreau, you will say. Well, of what account are the Duc d'Anjou and the Comte de Monsoreau? When one really wishes a thing; when one really loves,—oh! it would be neither prince nor master that should keep me back. I tell you, Jeanne, if once I should love—" And Diane, overcome by her excitement, leaned back against a tree, as if, the soul having broken the body, the latter could no longer sustain itself."

"Be calm, dear friend."

"I tell you, we were cowardly."

"'We!' of whom do you speak? That 'we' is eloquent, my dearest Diane."

"I mean my father and I; you did not think anything else, did you? My father is a nobleman; he might have spoken to the king. I am proud, and do not fear a man when I hate him. But, you see, the secret of that cowardice was this: I understood that *he* did not love me."

"You lie to yourself! you know the contrary, little hypocrite!"

"You may believe in love, Jeanne,—you, whom M. de Saint-Luc married in spite of the king; you, whom he carried away from Paris; you, who pay him by your caresses for proscription and exile."

" And he thinks himself richly repaid."

" But I (reflect a little, do not be egotistical),—I, whom that fiery young man pretended to love; I, who fixed the regards of that invincible Bussy, of that man who fears no obstacles,—I trusted myself to him in the cloister of La Gypecienne. We were alone; he had Gertrude and Rémy, his two accomplices, and myself,—another accomplice. He could have carried me off under his cloak! At that moment I saw him suffering because of me; I saw his eyes languishing, his lips pale and parched with fever. If he had asked me to die to restore the brightness to his eyes, and the freshness to his lips, I would have died. Well, I went away; and he did not think of holding me back by a corner of my veil. Wait; still more—oh, you don't know what I suffer! He knew that I was leaving Paris, that I was returning to Méridor; he knew that M. de Monsoreau—I blush as I tell it—is my husband only in name; he knew that I travelled alone. And along the road, dear Jeanne, I kept turning, thinking every moment that I heard the gallop of his horse behind us; but no, it was only the echo of my own. I tell you he does not think of me. I am not worth a journey to Anjou while there are so many beautiful women at the court of France, whose smiles are worth a hundred avowals from the provincial buried at Méridor. Do you understand now? Am I forgotten, despised—"

She had not finished when the foliage of the oak rustled, a quantity of mortar and moss fell from the old wall, and a man threw himself at the feet of Diane, who uttered an affrighted cry.

Jeanne ran away; she recognised him.

" Here I am! " cried Bussy, kneeling and kissing the edge of Diane's robe, which he held in his trembling hand.

She too recognised him; and overcome by this unexpected happiness, she opened her arms and fell unconscious upon the breast of him whom she had just accused of indifference.

CHAPTER XIII

BUSSY AND DIANE

Swoons of joy are not of long duration, nor are they very dangerous. Diane soon opened her eyes, and found herself in Bussy's arms, for he would not yield to Madame de Saint-Luc the privilege of receiving Diane's first look.

" Oh! " she murmured, " it was shocking, Count, to surprise us thus."

Bussy waited for her to say something further; possibly (men are so exacting) he expected something more than words. But Diane said nothing more, and disengaging herself gently from his arms, went to rejoin her friend, who, with a woman's interest is that charming spectacle of a reunion of lovers, had very quietly returned, not to take part in the conversation, but near enough not to lose any of it.

" Is it thus that you receive me, Madame? "

" No, M. de Bussy; but—"

" Oh! no ' but,' Madame," sighed Bussy, drawing near again.

" No, no! not so, not on your knees, M. de Bussy! "

" Oh, let me pray to you an instant thus! " cried the count. " I have so longed for this place."

" Yes; but to come to it you jumped over the wall. Not only is it not suitable for a man of your rank, but it is very imprudent."

" How so? "

" If you had been seen! "

" Who could have seen me? "

" Our hunters, who a quarter of an hour ago passed by this wall."

" Do not be uneasy, Madame; I hide myself too carefully to be seen."

" Hidden! oh, really," said Jeanne, " that is very romantic; tell us about it, M. de Bussy."

" Let me say first that if I did not join you on the road it was not my fault; I took one route and you another. You came by Rambouillet, and I by Chartres. And then,—listen, and judge if your poor Bussy be not in love,—I did not dare to join you. It was not in the presence of your father and your servants that I wished to meet you again, for I did not desire to compromise you; so I made the journey stage by stage, devoured by impatience. At last you arrived. I had taken a lodging in the village, and, concealed behind the window, I saw you pass."

" Oh, *mon Dieu!* are you, then, at Angers under your own name? "

" For what do you take me? No; I am a travelling merchant. Look at my costume; it is of a colour much worn among drapers and goldsmiths. I have not been noticed."

" Bussy, the handsome Bussy, two days in a provincial town

and not noticed! Who would believe that at court?" said Jeanne.

"Continue, Count," said Diane, blushing; "how do you come here from the town?"

"I have two horses of a choice stock. I leave the village on one, stopping to look at all the signs and writings; but when out of sight my horse takes to a gallop, which brings him the four miles in twenty minutes. Once in the wood of Méridor I ride to the park wall; but it is very long, for the park is large. Yesterday I explored this wall for more than four hours, climbing up here and there, hoping to see you. At last, when I was almost in despair, I saw you in the evening returning to the house; the two great dogs of the baron were jumping round you. When you had disappeared, I jumped over, and saw the marks on the grass where you had been sitting. I fancied you might have adopted this place, which is charming, during the heat of the sun; so I broke away some branches that I might know it again, and, sighing, which hurts me dreadfully—"

"From want of habit," said Jeanne.

"I do not say no, Madame; well, then, sighing, I retook my way to the town. I was very tired, I had torn my dress in climbing trees; but I had seen you, and I was happy."

"It is an admirable recital," said Jeanne; "and you have surmounted frightful obstacles. It is quite heroic; but in your place I would have preserved my doublet, and, above all, have taken care of my white hands. Look at yours, all scratched by the briers."

"Yes; but then I should not have seen her whom I came to see."

"On the contrary, I should have seen her better than you did."

"What would you have done, then?"

"I would have gone straight to the Château de Méridor. Monsieur the Baron would have pressed me in his arms; Madame de Monsoreau would have placed me by her at table; M. de Saint-Luc would have been delighted to see me, and his wife also. It was the simplest thing in the world; but lovers never think of what is straight before them."

Bussy shook his head, with a smile and a glance addressed to Diane. "Oh, no!" he said, "no, what you say you would have done might have answered for any one else, but not for me."

Diane blushed like a child; and the same smile and glance were reflected in her eyes and on her lips.

" Then I no longer understand what good manners are."

" No," said Bussy; " I could not go to the château. Monsieur the Baron owes to the husband of his daughter, whoever he may be, a strict vigilance."

" Good! " said Jeanne, " here is a lesson for me; " and kissing Diane on the forehead, she ran away. Diane tried to stop her; but Bussy seized her hands, and she let her friend go. They remained alone. Diane looked at Madame de Saint-Luc, who was picking flowers as she went along, and then sat down, blushing.

Bussy lay at her feet. " Have I not done well, Madame," said he, " and do you not approve? "

" I do not desire to feign," said Diane,—" besides, it would be useless; you know I approve. But here must stop my indulgence; in wishing for you, in calling for you as I did just now, I was mad, I was guilty."

" *Mon Dieu!* What do you say? "

" Alas, Count, the truth; I have a right to make M. de Monsoreau unhappy, who has driven me to this extremity,—but only while I refrain from giving happiness to another. I can refuse him my presence, my smile, my·love; but if I give those favours to another, I rob him who is, in spite of me, my master."

Bussy listened patiently to all that moralising, softened, it is true, by Diane's grace and gentleness. " It is my turn to speak," he said, " is it not? "

" Speak! "

" Well! of all that you have just said, you do not find one word in your heart."

" What do you mean? "

" Listen patiently; you have overwhelmed me with sophisms. The commonplaces of morality do not apply here. This man is your master, you say; but did you choose him? No; a fatality imposed him on you, and you submitted. Now, do you mean to suffer all your life the consequences of this odious constraint? I will deliver you from it."

Diane tried to speak, but Bussy stopped her.

" Oh, I know what you are going to say,—that if I provoke M. de Monsoreau and kill him, you will see me no more. So be it. I may die of grief, but you will live free and happy; and you may render happy some gallant man, who in his joy will sometimes bless my name, and cry, ' Thanks, Bussy, thanks, for having delivered us from that horrible Monsoreau! ' and you yourself, Diane, who will not dare to thank me while living, will thank me when I am dead."

Diane seized his hand, and pressed it tenderly.

"You have not yet implored me, Bussy," she said; "you begin with menaces."

"Menace you! oh, could I have such an intention, — I, who love you so ardently, Diane? I know you love me. Do not deny it, and class yourself with those vulgar souls whose words are contradicted by their actions. I know it, for you have avowed it. Now, a love like mine shines like the sun and animates all hearts that it touches; and so I will not supplicate you, I will not pine in despair. No, I place myself at your knees, which I kiss; and I say to you, my hand on my heart, which has never lied either from interest or from fear, ' Diane, I love you for my whole life; Diane, I swear to you in the face of Heaven that I will die for you, I will die adoring you.' If you still say to me, ' Go; do not steal the happiness of another,' I will go without a sigh or complaint from this place where I am so happy, and I will say, ' This woman does not love me, and never will love me.' Then I will go away, and you will see me no more. But as my devotion for you is even greater than my love; as my desire to make you happy will survive the certainty that I shall not be happy myself; as I shall not have stolen the good fortune of another,—I shall have the right to take from that other his life, while sacrificing my own. That is what I shall do, Madame; and I shall do it that you may not be forever a slave, and that you may not have a pretext for rendering miserable any brave man who may love you."

Bussy uttered these words with strong emotion. Diane read in his eyes, so brilliant and so loyal, all the force of his resolution; she understood that he would do what he said he would do,— that his words would certainly be translated into action. And as the snow of April melts under the rays of the sun, her resistance melted under the fire of his eyes. "Well," she said, "I thank you for the violence you do me; it is still a delicacy on your part, to take from me thus even remorse for having yielded to you. Now, will you love me, as you have said, even to death? Shall I not be the toy of your caprice, and will you not sometimes leave me to the odious regret of not having listened to the love of M. de Monsoreau? But, no, I have no conditions to make. I am vanquished; I surrender; I am yours, Bussy, in love at least. Remain then, friend; and now that my life is yours, protect us."

On saying these words, Diane placed one of her white and delicate hands upon Bussy's shoulder, and offered him the other, which he pressed warmly to his lips; Diane trembled under that kiss. Then they heard the light steps of Jeanne, accompanied by a warning cough. Instinctively the clasped hands parted. Jeanne saw the movement.

"Pardon, my good friends, for disturbing you," said she; "but we must go in if we do not wish to be sent for. Monsieur the Count, regain, if you please, your excellent horse, and let us go to the house. See what you lose by your obstinacy, M. de Bussy,—a dinner at the château, which is not to be despised by a man who has had a long ride and has been climbing trees, without counting all the amusement we could have had, or the heart-warming glances that might have been exchanged. Come, Diane, come away."

Bussy looked at the two friends with a smile. Diane held out her hand to him.

"Is that all?" said he. "Have you nothing to say?"

"Till to-morrow," replied she.

"Only to-morrow?"

"To-morrow, and always."

Bussy uttered a joyful exclamation, pressed his lips to her hand, and ran off. Diane watched him till he was out of sight.

"Now," said Jeanne, when he had disappeared, "will you talk to me a little?"

"Oh, yes," said the young woman, with a start, as if the voice of her friend awoke her from a dream, "I hear you."

"Well, to-morrow I shall go to the chase with Saint-Luc and your father."

"What! you will leave me alone at the château?"

"Listen, dear friend; I also have my principles, and there are certain things that I cannot consent to do."

"Oh, Jeanne!" cried Diane, growing pale, "can you say such things to me?"

"Yes, I cannot continue thus."

"I thought you loved me, Jeanne. What cannot you continue?"

"Continue to prevent two poor lovers from talking to each other at their ease."

Diane seized in her arms the laughing young woman and covered her face with kisses.

"Listen!" said Jeanne, "there are the hunters calling us; and poor Saint-Luc is impatient."

CHAPTER XIV

HOW BUSSY WAS OFFERED THREE HUNDRED PISTOLES FOR HIS HORSE, AND PARTED WITH HIM FOR NOTHING

THE next day Bussy left Angers before the earliest waking *bourgeois* had had their breakfast. He flew along the road; and Diane, mounted on a terrace in front of the château, saw him coming, and went to meet him. The sun had scarcely risen over the great oaks, and the grass was still wet with dew, when she heard from afar, as she went along, the horn of Saint-Luc, which Jeanne incited him to sound, to remind her friend of the service she was rendering her in leaving her alone. Diane arrived at the meeting-place just as Bussy appeared on the wall. He saw her running to the place of meeting, and uttered a cry of joy, hastening to her with open arms. With both hands upon her heart she approached him quickly, and their morning salutation was a long and warm embrace.

The day passed like an hour. What had they to say? That they loved each other. What had they to wish for? They were together.

" Diane," said Bussy at length, " it seems to me as though my life had begun only to-day. You have shown me what it is to live."

" And I," replied she, " who not long ago would have willingly thrown myself into the arms of death, shudder now at the thought of dying and losing your love. But why do you not come to the château, Louis? My father would be glad to see you; and M. de Saint-Luc is your friend, and is discreet."

" Alas, Diane, if I came once, I should be always there. All the province would know it; and if it came to the ears of that ogre, your husband, he would hasten hither. You forbid me to deliver you from him—"

" Oh, yes ! "

" Well, then, for our safety—that is to say, for the security of our happiness—we must guard our secret. Madame de Saint-Luc knows it, and her husband soon will. I have written him a line this morning, asking him for an interview at Angers; and when he comes I will make him promise never to breathe a word of this. It is the more important, dear Diane, as doubtless they are seeking me everywhere. Things looked grave when I left Paris."

" You are right; and then my father is so scrupulous that in spite of his love for me, he is capable of denouncing me to M. de Monsoreau."

" Let us hide ourselves well, then; and if God delivers us to our enemies, at least we can say that we did all that was possible."

" God is good, Louis. Do not distrust him at a time like this."

" I do not distrust God; I fear some evil spirit, jealous of our happiness."

" Say adieu to me, then; do not ride so fast,—your horse frightens me."

" Fear nothing; he knows the way already, and is the gentlest and safest horse I ever rode. When I return to the city, buried in sweet thoughts, he takes the way without my touching the bridle."

At last the sound of the returning chase was heard, the horns playing an air agreed upon with Jeanne; and Bussy left. As he approached the city, he remarked that the time was approaching when the gates of the city would be closed. He was preparing to ride on quickly, when he heard behind him the gallop of horses. For a lover who wishes to remain concealed, as for a robber, everything seems threatening. Bussy asked himself whether he should ride on or draw up and let the cavaliers pass; but their course was so rapid that they were up to him in a moment. There were two.

" Here is the city," said one, with a Gascon accent. " Three hundred more blows with the whip, and one hundred with the spur; courage and vigour!"

" The beast has no more breath; he shivers and totters. He will not go on; and yet I would give a hundred horses to be in my city before nightfall."

" It is some Angers man out late," thought Bussy. " But look! the horse is falling. Take care, Monsieur!" cried he; " leave your horse,—he is about to fall."

Indeed, as he spoke, the animal fell heavily on his side, shook his legs convulsively, then suddenly his breath stopped, his eyes grew dim, and he was dead.

" Monsieur!" cried the cavalier to Bussy, " three hundred pistoles for your horse!"

" Ah, *mon Dieu!*" cried Bussy, drawing near.

" Do you hear me, Monsieur? I am in haste."

" Ah, my prince; take it for nothing," cried Bussy, who had recognised the Duc d'Anjou.

At the same moment they heard the click of a pistol, which was cocked by the duke's companion.

"Stop, M. d'Aubigné," cried the duke. "Devil take me, it is Bussy!"

"Oh, yes, my prince, it is I. But what the devil are you doing, killing horses on the road at this hour?"

"Ah! is it M. de Bussy?" said D'Aubigné; "then you do not want me any more. Permit me to return to him who sent me."

"Not without receiving my sincere thanks and the promise of a lasting friendship."

"I accept all, Monseigneur, and will recall your words to you some day."

"M. d'Aubigné! I am in the clouds," murmured Bussy.

"Did you not know? As you are here, did you not expect me?" said the prince, with an air of suspicion which did not escape Bussy, who began to reflect that his secret residence in Anjou might seem very strange to the prince.

"I did better than expect you," said Bussy; "and as you wish to enter the town before the gates are closed, jump into the saddle, Monseigneur."

The prince accepted, and Bussy mounted behind him, asking himself if this prince dressed in black were not the evil spirit sent already to disturb his happiness.

"Where do we go now, Monseigneur?" said he, as they entered the city.

"To the château. Let them hoist my banner and convoke the nobility of the province."

"Nothing more easy," said Bussy, resolving to acquiesce in everything so as to gain time,—and besides, too much surprised to be otherwise than passive.

The news was immediately spread through the city that the duke had arrived, and a crowd soon collected.

"Gentlemen," cried the duke, "I have come to throw myself into my good city of Angers. At Paris the most terrible dangers have menaced my life; I had lost even my liberty. I succeeded in escaping, thanks to some good friends, and now that I am here, my tranquillity and my life are assured."

The magistrates, stupefied, feebly cried, "Long live our lord!"

The people, hoping for the usual gratuities, shouted lustily, "Hail!"

"Now let me sup," said the prince; "I have had nothing since the morning."

The city was illuminated; guns were fired; the bells of the cathedral were rung; and the wind carried to Méridor the noisy joy of the good Angevins.

CHAPTER XV

THE DIPLOMACY OF THE DUC D'ANJOU

WHEN the duke and Bussy were left alone, the duke said, "Let us talk."

François, who was very quick, had perceived that Bussy had made more advances to him than usual; therefore he judged that he was in some embarrassing situation, and that he might, by a little address, get an advantage over him. But Bussy had had time to prepare himself, and he was quite ready.

"Yes, let us talk, Monseigneur," replied he.

"The last day I saw you, my poor Bussy, you were very ill."

"It is true, Monseigneur, I was very ill; and it was almost a miracle that saved me."

"There was near you a doctor very devoted to you, for he growled at every one who approached you."

"True, Prince, Rémy loves me."

"He kept you rigorously to your bed, did he not?"

"At which I was in a great rage, as your Highness might have seen."

"But if that were the case, why did you not send the doctor to the devil, and come out with me as I begged you to do? But as it was a grave affair, you were afraid to compromise yourself."

"Did you say I was afraid?"

"I did say so."

"Well, then, it was a lie!" said Bussy, jumping up from his chair; "you lied to yourself, Monseigneur, for you do not believe a single word of what you say. There are twenty scars on my body which prove the contrary. I never knew fear; and on my soul, I know many who cannot say as much,—at any rate, cannot prove it."

"You have always unanswerable arguments, M. de Bussy," cried the duke, turning very pale; "when you are accused, you cry louder than your accuser, and then you think you are right."

"Oh! I am not always right, I know well; but I know on what occasions I am wrong."

"And what are they?"

"When I serve ungrateful people."

"Really, Monsieur, I think you forget yourself," said the duke, suddenly rising with that dignity which he could assume upon occasions.

"Very well! I forget myself, Monseigneur," said Bussy. "For once in your life do as much; forget yourself or forget me."

Bussy moved towards the door; but the prince stopped him. "Do you deny, Monsieur," said he, "that after refusing to go out with me, you went out directly?"

"I deny nothing, Monseigneur; but I will not be forced to confession."

"Tell me then why you remained so persistently in your hotel."

"Because I had business."

"At home?"

"At home or elsewhere."

"I thought that when a gentleman was in the service of a prince his principal business was that of the prince."

"And who does your business generally, Monseigneur, if not I?"

"I do not say no; generally I find you faithful and devoted, and, I will say more, I excuse your bad humour."

"Ah! you are very good."

"Yes, for you had some reason to be angry."

"You admit it, Monseigneur?"

"Yes, I promised you the disgrace of M. de Monsoreau. It seems you hate him very much."

"I? not at all. I find him very ugly, and should be pleased if he were away from the court, so that I might not have to look at him. It seems, however, that you admire him. There is no use in disputing about tastes."

"Well, then, as that was your sole excuse for sulking towards me, like a spoiled child, you were doubly wrong to refuse to accompany me, and then to go out afterwards and commit follies."

"Follies! what did I do?"

"Doubtless you do not like M. d'Epernon and M. de Schomberg; neither do I, but one must have some prudence. Kill them, and I shall be grateful to you; but do not exasperate them."

"What did I do to them?"

"Why, you had D'Epernon stoned."

"I?"

" Yes, so that his clothes were torn to pieces."

" Good! and what about M. de Schomberg? "

" You will not deny that you had him dyed in indigo? When
I saw him, three hours after, he was still bright blue. Do you
call that a joke? " and the prince laughed in spite of himself;
and Bussy, recalling Schomberg's appearance in his vat, broke
into peals of laughter.

" Then," said Bussy, " they think it is I who played them
these tricks? "

" *Pardieu!* it is I, perhaps."

" And you have the conscience to reproach a man who has
such fine ideas? Come, I just now told you that you are ungrateful."

" Agreed. Well, if you really went out for that I forgive
you."

" Do you mean it? "

" Yes, word of honour; but you are not at the end of my
complaints."

" Go on."

" Let us speak of myself a little."

" Well? "

" What did you do to deliver me from my unlucky situation? "

" You see,—I came to Anjou."

" It seems to me that you would have been more useful
nearer."

" Ah! there we differ; I preferred coming to Anjou."

" Your caprice is a bad reason."

" But if I came to gather your partisans? "

" Ah, that is different. What have you done? "

" I will explain that to you to-morrow; at present I must
leave you."

" Why? "

" I have an appointment with a person of the highest importance."

" Oh, very well; go, Bussy, but be prudent."

" Prudent! are we not the strongest here? "

" Never mind; risk nothing. Have you done much? "

" I have been here only two days."

" But you keep yourself concealed, I hope."

" I should think so. Look at my dress; am I in the habit of
wearing cinnamon-coloured clothes? "

" And where are you lodging? "

" Ah! I hope you will appreciate my devotion,—in a tumbledown old house near the ramparts. But you, my prince, how did you get out of the Louvre? How was it that I found you on the road, with M. d'Aubigné for a companion? "

" Because I have friends."

" You, friends! come, now! "

" Yes, friends that you do not know."

" Well, and who are they? "

" The King of Navarre and D'Aubigné, whom you saw."

" The King of Navarre! Ah, true! did you not conspire together? "

" I never conspired, M. de Bussy."

" No? Ask poor La Mole and Coconnas."

" La Mole," said the prince, gloomily, " died for another crime than the one alleged against him."

" Well, let us leave La Mole,—with the more reason, Monseigneur, because we should hardly agree on that subject. Let us return to yourself. How the devil did you get out of the Louvre? "

" Through the window."

" Which window? "

" That of my bedroom."

" Then you knew of the rope-ladder? "

" What rope-ladder? "

" In the cabinet."

" Ah, it seems you knew it! " cried the prince, turning pale.

" Oh, your Highness knows I have sometimes had the happiness of entering that room."

" In the time of my sister Margot? Then you came in by the window."

" As you came out. What astonishes me is that you knew of the ladder."

" It was not I who found it."

" Who then? "

" I was told of it."

" By whom? "

" By the King of Navarre."

" Ah, the King of Navarre knew of it! I should not have thought so. However, now you are here safe and sound, we will put Anjou in flames, and Béarn and Angoumois will catch the light; so we shall have a fine blaze."

" But did you not speak of a rendezvous? "

" It is true; the interest of the conversation was making me forget. Adieu, Monseigneur."

" Do you take your horse? "

" If it will be useful to you, Monseigneur, you may keep it; I have another."

" Well, I accept! we will settle that later."

The duke gave Bussy his hand, and they separated.

CHAPTER XVI

THE IDEAS OF THE DUC D'ANJOU

BUSSY returned home, but instead of Saint-Luc, whom he expected, he found only a letter from him saying that he would arrive the next day.

Accordingly, at about six o'clock the next morning, Saint-Luc left Méridor with one attendant and took his way towards Angers. He arrived on foot at the walls at about the time when the gates were opened, and without noticing the excitement among the people, went to Bussy's lodgings. The two friends cordially embraced.

" Accept the hospitality of my poor hut, Saint-Luc," said Bussy; " I am encamped here."

" Yes, like a conqueror on the field of battle."

" What do you mean? "

" I mean, dear Bussy, that my wife has no secrets from me, and has told me all. Receive my compliments; but since you have sent for me, permit me to give you a piece of advice."

" Well? "

" Get rid as soon as possible of that abominable Monsoreau. No one at court knows of your love for his wife; so when you marry the widow no one will say you killed him on purpose."

" There is but one obstacle to this project, which presented itself to my mind, as to yours."

" What is it? "

" That I have sworn to Diane to respect the life of her husband —so long, at least, as he does not attack me."

" You were very wrong."

" Why so? "

" Because if you do not take the initiative, he will discover you and will kill you."

" That will be as shall please God," said Bussy, smiling. " But not only I can't break my promise to Diane not to kill her husband—"

" Her husband!—you know well that he is not."

" Yes; but he has the title, at any rate. Not only must I keep my promise to her, but should I kill him every one would assail me; and he who to-day is in all eyes a monster would, in his coffin, seem an angel put to death by me."

" Therefore I do not advise you to kill him yourself."

" Oh, Saint-Luc, no assassins! "

" Who spoke of assassins? "

" What did you mean, then? "

" Nothing; an idea passed through my mind. I will tell you what it was at another time. I do not love this Monsoreau much more than you, although I have not the same reason to detest him; so let us speak of the wife instead of the husband."

Bussy smiled. " You are a capital companion, Saint-Luc," said he; " and you may count on my friendship. As you know, my friendship consists of three things,—my purse, my sword, and my life. Now, what about Diane? "

" I wished to ask if you were not coming to Méridor."

" My dear friend, I thank you; but you know my scruples."

" I know all. At Méridor you fear to meet Monsoreau, although he is eighty leagues off,—fear to have to shake his hand, and it is hard to shake the hand of the man you wish to strangle; you fear to see him embrace Diane, and it is hard to see the woman you love embraced by another."

" Ah, how well you understand! " cried Bussy, with rage; " but, my dear friend, did you not hear last night the noise of bells and guns? "

" Yes; and we wondered what it meant."

" It meant that the Duc d'Anjou arrived last night."

Saint-Luc jumped up. " The duke here? We heard he was imprisoned at the Louvre."

" That is just why he is now at Angers. He managed to escape through a window, and came here."

" Well? "

" Well, here is an excellent opportunity to revenge yourself for the king's persecutions. The prince has already a party; he will soon have troops; and we shall have something like a little civil war."

" Oh, oh! "

" And I reckoned on you to help us."

" Against the king? " said Saint-Luc, with sudden coldness.

" Not precisely against the king, but against those who fight against us."

"My dear Bussy, I came here for country air, not to fight against his Majesty."

"But let me present you to Monseigneur."

"Useless, my dear Bussy; I do not like Angers, and intend to go away soon. It is a tiresome place and gloomy; its rocks are as soft as cheese, and its cheese as hard as rocks."

"My dear Saint-Luc, you will do me a great service by consenting; the duke asked me what I came here for, and, not being able to tell, because of his own passion for Diane, I said that I had come to draw to his cause all the gentlemen in the canton. I even told him I had a rendezvous with one this morning."

"Well, tell him you have seen the gentleman, and that he asks six months to consider. Listen: I am bound to nothing in the world but my wife; you are bound only to your mistress. I will always help you to defend Diane; you shall help me to defend my wife. We will make a treaty for love, but not for politics. Thus only shall we be able to agree."

"I see that I must yield to you, Saint-Luc, for you have the advantage over me. I want you, and you have no need of me."

"On the contrary, it is I who claim your protection."

"How so?"

"Suppose the rebels besiege and sack Méridor."

The two friends laughed; then, as the duke had sent to inquire for Bussy, they pledged themselves anew to a comradeship outside of politics, and parted much pleased with each other.

Bussy went to the ducal palace, where already all the nobility of the provinces were arriving. He hastened to arrange an official reception, a repast, and speeches, and having thus cut out some hours' occupation for the prince, mounted his other horse, and galloped to Méridor. The duke made some good speeches, and produced a great effect, giving himself out for a prince persecuted by the king on account of the love of the Parisians for him. When Bussy returned, it was four in the afternoon; he dismounted, and presented himself to the duke all covered with dust.

"Ah, my brave Bussy! you have been at work?"

"You see, Monseigneur."

"You are very hot."

"I have ridden fast."

"Take care not to get ill again."

"There is no danger."

" Whence do you come? "

" From the environs. Is your Highness content? Have you had a numerous assemblage? "

" Yes, I am pretty well satisfied; but I missed some one."

" Who is it? "

" Your *protégé*, the Baron de Méridor."

" Ah! " said Bussy, changing colour.

" And yet we must not neglect him," continued the duke; " he is influential here."

" You think so? "

" I am sure of it. He was the correspondent of the League at Angers, chosen by M. de Guise; and the Guises choose their men well. He must come, Bussy."

" But if he does not come? "

" I will go to him."

" To Méridor? "

" Why not? "

" Oh, why not, certainly! " cried Bussy, with flashing eyes; " a prince may do anything."

" Then you think he is still angry with me? "

" How should I know? "

" You have not seen him? "

" No."

" As one of the great men of the province, I thought—"

" I was not sufficiently fortunate in the former promises I made him to be in a hurry to present myself to him."

" Has he not attained his object? "

" How so? "

" He wanted his daughter to marry the count; and she has done so."

Bussy turned his back on the duke, who at the same moment moved towards another gentleman who entered the room. Bussy began to reflect on what the duke's projects might be with regard to the baron,—whether they were purely political, or whether he was still seeking to approach Diane; but he imagined that, embroiled with his brother, banished from the Louvre, and the chief of a provincial insurrection, he had sufficiently grave interests at stake to outweigh his love fancies. He passed the night banqueting with the duke and the Angevin gentlemen, and in dancing with the Angevin ladies. It is needless to say that he excited the admiration of the latter and the hatred of the husbands, several of whom looked at him in a way which did not please him; so that, curling his mustaches, he invited three or four of them to take a walk with him by moonlight. But his reputation had preceded him, and they all declined.

At the door Bussy found a laughing face waiting for him, which he believed to be eighty leagues away.

" Ah! " cried he, joyfully, " it is you, Rémy."

" Yes, Monsieur."

" I was going to write to you to join me."

" Really? "

" On my word."

" That is capital; I was afraid you would scold me."

" For what? "

" For coming without leave. But I heard that M. le Duc d'Anjou had escaped, and had fled hither. I knew you were here also, and I thought there might be civil war, and many holes made in skins, so I came."

" You did well, Rémy; I wanted you."

" How is Gertrude, Monsieur? "

" I will ask Diane the first time I see her."

" And in return, every time I see Gertrude I will ask for news of Madame de Monsoreau."

" You are charming."

Meanwhile they had reached Bussy's lodging.

" Here is my palace; you must lodge as you can."

" It will not be difficult; I could sleep standing, I am so tired."

Bussy rose early the next morning and went to the ducal palace, leaving word for Rémy to follow him. The duke had prepared a list of important things to be done,—a walk round the walls to examine the fortifications; a review of the inhabitants and their arms; a visit to the arsenal; correspondence.

" Ah! " cried the duke, " you already? "

" Faith, yes, Monseigneur! I could not sleep, your Highness's interests were so much on my mind. What shall we do this morning? Shall we hunt? "

" What! " said the duke, " you pretend to have been thinking all night of my interests, and the result of so much meditation is to propose to me a hunt? "

" True," said Bussy; " besides, we have no hounds."

" And no chief huntsman."

" Upon my word, the chase would be, to me, more agreeable without him."

" Ah, I am not like you; I want him. He would have been very useful to us here."

" How so? "

" He has property here."

" He? "

" He or his wife."

Bussy bit his lips.

" Méridor is only three leagues off, you know that," continued the duke,—" you, who brought the old baron to me."

" I brought him because he hung on to my cloak. However, my protection did not do him much good."

" Listen," said the duke; " I have an idea."

" The devil! " said Bussy, who was always suspicious of the duke's ideas.

" Yes; it is that if Monsoreau had the advantage over you at first, you shall have it now."

" What do you mean? "

" It is very simple; you know me, Bussy? "

" I have that misfortune."

" Think you I am the man to submit to an affront with impunity? "

" Explain yourself, Monseigneur."

" Well, he stole a young girl I loved and made her his wife; now I, in my turn, will steal his wife and make her my mistress."

Bussy tried to smile, but notwithstanding his best efforts could succeed only in making a grimace. " Steal his wife! " he stammered.

" Nothing more easy. She is here, and you told me she hated her husband; therefore, without too much vanity, I may flatter myself she will give me the preference, especially if I promise her—what I will promise."

" And what will you promise her, Monseigneur? "

" To get rid of her husband for her."

" You will do that? "

" You shall see. Meanwhile I will pay a visit to Méridor."

" You will dare? "

" Why not? "

" You will present yourself before the old baron, whom you abandoned after promising me—"

" I have an excellent excuse to give him."

" Where the devil, then, do you find it? "

" Oh! I will say to him, ' I did not break this marriage, because Monsoreau, who knew that you were one of the principal agents of the League, and that I was its chief, threatened to sell us both to the king.' "

" Has your Highness invented that? "

" Not entirely."

" Then I understand."

" Yes, I shall make him believe that by getting his daughter married I saved his life."

" It is superb."

" Well, order the horses, and we will go to Méridor."

" Immediately, Monseigneur." Bussy then went to the door, but turned back, and said, " How many horses will your Highness have? "

" Oh, four or five,—what you like."

" If you leave it to me, I shall take a hundred."

" What for? " cried the prince, surprised.

" To have at least twenty-five I can rely on in case of attack." The duke was startled. " In case of attack? " said he.

" Yes; I have heard that there are thick woods in that neighbourhood, and it would not surprise me if we fell into some ambush."

" Ah, do you think so? "

" Monseigneur knows that true courage does not exclude prudence; I will order one hundred and fifty." And he moved towards the door.

" A moment," said the prince. " Do you think I am in safety at Angers? "

" Why, the town is not very strong, but if it is well defended—"

" Yes, but it may be badly defended; however brave you are, you can be but in one place at a time."

" True."

" Then if I am not in safety here—and I am not if Bussy doubts—"

" I did not say I doubted."

" If I am not safe, I had better make myself so. I will go to the château and intrench myself."

" You are right, Monseigneur."

" And then another idea."

" The morning is fruitful."

" I will make the Méridors come here."

" Monseigneur, you are grand to-day. Now let us visit the château."

Bussy went out while the prince was getting ready, and found Rémy waiting. He wrote hastily a little note, picked a bunch of roses from the conservatory, rolled the note round the stems, went to the stable, saddled Roland, invited Rémy to mount, and giving him the bouquet, led him out of the city into a sort of path.

"Now," said he, "let Roland go; at the end of this path you will find the forest, in the forest a park, round the park a wall, and at that part of the wall where Roland stops, throw over this bouquet."

"He whom you expect does not come," said the note, "because he who was not expected has come, and is more menacing than ever, for he loves still. Take with the lips and the heart all that is invisible to the eyes in this paper."

In half an hour Rémy reached his destination, carried by his horse, and threw over the bouquet; a little cry from the other side told him it had been received. Then Rémy returned, much to Roland's dissatisfaction, who evinced a lively discontent at being deprived of his accustomed repast on the acorns. Rémy joined Bussy as he was exploring a cave with the prince.

"Well," said he to his messenger, "what have you seen? What have you heard? What have you done?"

"A wall, a cry, seven leagues," replied Rémy, briefly.

CHAPTER XVII

A FLIGHT OF ANGEVINS

BUSSY contrived to occupy the duke so well with his preparations for war during the next two days that he found no time to think of Méridor; and from time to time, under pretext of examining the outer fortifications, Bussy jumped on Roland, and arrived at a certain wall, which he got over all the more quickly because each time he made some stone fall, and was in fact gradually making a breach.

Towards the end of the third day, as an enormous convoy of provisions was entering the city, the produce of a requisition levied by the duke on his good Angevins; as M. d'Anjou, to make himself popular, was tasting the black bread and salt fish of the soldiers,—a great noise was heard at one of the gates of the city, where a man, mounted on a white horse, had presented himself. Now Bussy had had himself named captain-general of Anjou, and had established the most severe discipline in Angers; no one could go out of or enter the town without a password,—all which had no other aim than to prevent the duke from sending a messenger to Méridor without his knowledge.

The man on the white horse had arrived at a furious gallop, and had attempted to enter, but had been stopped.

"I am D'Antragues," said he, "and desire to speak to the Duc d'Anjou."

"We do not know D'Antragues," replied the commander of the post, "but as for seeing the duke, you shall be satisfied, for we shall arrest you, and conduct you to him."

"You are a nice fellow, truly, to talk of arresting Charles Balzac d'Antragues, Baron de Cuneo, and Comte de Graville."

"We will do so, however," replied the *bourgeois*, who had twenty men behind him and only one before him.

"Wait a little, my good friends. You do not know the Parisians, do you? Well, I will show you a specimen of what they can do."

"Let us arrest him! let us lead him to Monseigneur!" cried the furious militia.

"Softly, my little lambs of Anjou; it is I who will have that pleasure."

"What does he say?" asked the *bourgeois*.

"He says," said D'Antragues, "that his horse has travelled only ten leagues, and will ride over you all if you don't give room. Stand aside, then, or *ventre-bœuf*—" And as the *bourgeois* of Angers appeared not to comprehend the Parisian oath, D'Antragues drew his sword, and swinging it furiously round, he cut off the blades of the nearest halberds, and in less than ten minutes fifteen or twenty of them were changed into broom-handles.

"Ah! this is very amusing!" cried he, laughing, and as he spoke, stunning one of the *bourgeois* with a blow on the head with the flat of his sword. However, as more and more *bourgeois* crowded to the attack, and D'Antragues began to feel tired, he said, "Well, you are as brave as lions; I will bear witness to it. But you see you have nothing left but the handles of your halberds, and you do not know how to load your muskets. I had resolved to enter the city; but I did not know it was guarded by an army of Cæsars. I abandon the attempt to conquer you. Good-evening, I am going away; only tell the prince that I came here from Paris expressly to see him."

Meantime, the captain had managed to communicate the fire to the match of his musket, but just as he was raising it to his shoulder, D'Antragues gave him such a furious blow upon the fingers that he dropped it.

"Kill him! kill him!" cried several voices. "Do not let him escape!"

" Ah! " said D'Antragues, " a moment ago you would not let me come in; now you will not let me go out. Take care! that will change my tactics, and instead of the flat of my sword I will use the point; instead of cutting the halberds, I will cut the wrists. Come, now, my lambs of Anjou, will you let me go? "

" No, no! he is tired, kill him! "

" Very well! it is to be played in earnest, then? "

" Yes, yes! "

" Well, then, take care of your hands! "

Scarcely had he spoken and made ready to put his threat into execution, when another cavalier appeared, riding furiously also, who cried out as he approached, " D'Antragues! eh! what the devil are you doing among all these *bourgeois* ? "

" Livarot! " cried D'Antragues. " *Mon Dieu!* you are welcome! Montjoie and Saint-Denis, to the rescue! "

" I heard four hours ago that you were before me, and I have been trying to catch you. But what is the matter; do they want to massacre you? "

" Yes; they are our friends of Anjou, who will neither let me in nor out."

" Gentlemen," said Livarot, holding his hat in his hand, " will you please to step either to the right or left, and let us pass."

" They insult us! kill them! " cried the people.

" Oh, this is Angers manners! " said Livarot, putting on his hat with one hand and drawing his sword with the other.

" Yes; you see, unluckily, there are so many of them."

" Bah! if there were three of us we would made an end of them."

" And here is Ribeirac coming."

" Do you hear him? "

" I see him. Here, Ribeirac! "

" Are you fighting? " cried Ribeirac. " Good-morning, Livarot; good-morning, D'Antragues."

" Let us charge them," said D'Antragues.

The *bourgeois* looked in stupefaction at this reinforcement which had joined the two friends, who were now about to pass from the condition of the assailed to that of assailants.

" They are a regiment," said the captain of the militia to his men. " Gentlemen, our order of battle seems to me defective; I propose that we make a half-turn to the left."

The *bourgeois*, with characteristic skill in the execution of military movements, immediately began a half-turn to the right.

" It is only an advance guard," cried some, who wished to give themselves a pretext for flight.

" We are fathers of families, and our lives belong to our wives and children. Save yourselves!" roared the captain.

A frightful tumult then arose in the street, and blows fell like hail among the spectators who, crowding too near, hindered the flight of the terrified militia.

At this stage of the affair Bussy and the prince arrived, followed by twenty cavaliers, to ascertain the cause of the tumult. They were told that it was three incarnate devils from Paris who were making all the disturbance.

" Three men, Bussy; see who they are."

Bussy raised himself in his stirrups, and his quick eye soon recognised Livarot.

" *Mort de ma vie*, Monseigneur!" cried he; " they are our friends from Paris who are besieging us."

" No!" cried Livarot, " on the contrary, it is the friends of Anjou who are killing us."

" Down with your arms, knaves!" cried the duke; " these are friends."

" Friends!" cried the *bourgeois*, " then they should have had the password; for we have been treating them like Pagans, and they us like Turks."

Livarot, D'Antragues, and Ribeirac advanced in triumph to kiss the duke's hand.

" Monseigneur," said Bussy, " how many militia do you think there were here?"

" At least one hundred and fifty."

" You have not very famous soldiers, since three men beat them."

" True, but I shall have the three men who beat them."

CHAPTER XVIII

ROLAND

THANKS to the reinforcement which had arrived, M. le Duc d'Anjou could go where he pleased; he explored the ramparts and the surrounding country and châteaux. The Angevin gentlemen found liberty and amusement at the court of the duke; and the three friends were soon intimate with many of these nobles, especially those who had pretty wives. The general joy was at its height when twenty-two riding-horses, thirty carriage-horses, and forty mules, together with litters, carriages, and waggons, arrived at Angers, all the property of the duke. We must allow that the saddles were not paid for, and that the coffers were empty; but still the entrance of that *cortège* produced a magnificent effect. The duke's reputation for wealth was henceforward solidly established, and all the province remained convinced that he was rich enough to war against all Europe if need were; therefore they did not grudge the new tax which the prince imposed upon them. One never regrets the money he lends or gives to the rich. The worthy prince lived like a patriarch on the fat of the land. Numerous cavaliers arrived to offer to him their adhesion, or their services.

The Duc d'Anjou meanwhile carried on his reconnoitring expeditions, still in search of a certain treasure. Bussy had managed so that none of those expeditions reached the château inhabited by Diane; for he reserved that treasure to himself, plundering on his own account that little corner of the province, which, after a proper defence, had finally surrendered at discretion.

Now, while M. d'Anjou reconnoitred and Bussy plundered, M. de Monsoreau, mounted on a hunting-horse, arrived at the gates of Angers. It was about four o'clock in the afternoon. In order to arrive at that time he had ridden eighteen leagues that day; therefore his spurs were red, and his horse covered with foam, and half-dead. They no longer made difficulties about letting strangers enter, therefore M. de Monsoreau went straight through the city to the palace, and asked for the duke.

" He is out reconnoitring," replied the sentinel.

" Where? "

" There," said the sentinel, pointing in the direction of one of the four cardinal points.

" The devil! " said Monsoreau; " what I have to say to him is very pressing. What am I to do? "

" First put your horse in the stable, for if you don't lean him against a wall, he will fall."

" The advice is good; where are the stables? "

As he spoke, a man approached and asked for his name. M. de Monsoreau gave it. The major-domo (for it was he) bowed respectfully, for the chief huntsman's name was well known in Anjou.

" Monsieur," said he, " please to enter and take some repose. Monseigneur has not been out more than ten minutes, and will not be back till eight o'clock."

" Eight o'clock! I cannot wait so long; I am the bearer of news which cannot be too soon known to his Highness. Can I not have a horse and a guide? "

" There are plenty of horses; but a guide is a different thing, for his Highness did not say where he was going."

" Well, I will take a fresh horse, and try to find him."

" Probably you will hear where he has passed, Monsieur."

" Did they set off at a rapid pace? "

" At a walk, Monsieur; at a walk."

" Very well, that settles it; show me the horse I am to take."

" Will Monsieur come into the stables and choose one? They all belong to the duke."

Monsoreau entered. Ten or twelve fine horses, quite fresh, were feeding from the manger, which was filled with grain. Monsoreau looked over them, and then said, " I will take this bay."

" Roland? "

" Is that his name? "

" Yes, and he is his Highness's favourite horse. M. de Bussy gave him to the duke, and it is quite a chance that he is here to-day."

Roland was soon saddled, and Monsoreau rode out of the stable.

" In which direction did they start? " asked he.

The man pointed it out.

" Upon my word," said Monsoreau, on seeing that the horse took that direction of his own accord, " the horse seems to know the way."

Indeed, the animal set off without being urged, and went deliberately out of the city; he even went out of the main road to take a shorter course to the gate. As he approached the gate, he accelerated his pace.

" In truth," Monsoreau murmured, " they didn't say too much of him. Since you know the way so well, go, Roland, go; " and he dropped the reins on the horse's neck. He went along the boulevard, then turned into a shady lane, which cut across the country, passing gradually from a trot to a gallop.

" Oh! " thought Monsoreau, as they entered the woods, " one would say we were going to Méridor. Can his Highness be there? " and his face grew black at the thought. " Oh! " he murmured, " I who was going to see the prince, and putting off till to-morrow to see my wife, shall I see them both at the same time? "

The horse went on, turning always to the right.

" We cannot be far from the park," said he.

At that moment his horse neighed, and another answered him. In a minute Monsoreau saw a wall, and a horse tied to a neighbouring tree. " There is some one here! " said he, turning pale.

CHAPTER XIX

WHAT M. DE MONSOREAU CAME TO ANNOUNCE

As M. de Monsoreau approached, he remarked the dilapidation of the wall; it was almost in steps, and the brambles had been torn away, and were lying about. He looked at the horse standing there. The animal had a saddle-cloth embroidered in silver, and in one corner an F and an A. There was no doubt, then, that it came from the prince's stables; the letters stood for François d'Anjou. The count's suspicions at this sight became real alarm. The duke had come here, and had come often; for besides the horse waiting there, there was a second that knew the way. He tied up his horse near to the other, and began to scale the wall. It was an easy task; there were places for both feet and hands, and the branches of an oak-tree, which hung over, had been carefully cut away. Once up, he saw at the foot of a tree a blue mantilla and a black cloak, and not far off a man and woman, walking with arms interlaced, their backs turned to the wall, and nearly hidden by the trees. Unluckily for M. de Monsoreau, a stone fell from the wall and struck the ground with a great noise.

At this noise the lovers must have turned and seen him, for the cry of a woman was heard, and a rustling of the branches as they ran away like startled deer. At this cry Monsoreau felt cold drops on his forehead, for he recognised Diane's voice. Full of fury, he jumped over the wall, and with his drawn sword in his hand, tried to follow the fugitives; but they had disappeared, and there was not a trace or a sound to guide him. What should he do in that solitude? In what direction should he run? The park was extensive; he might, in pursuing those whom he sought, encounter those whom he did not seek. He concluded that the discovery he had made was enough for the time; and besides, he considered that he was too much under the influence of violent passion to act with the prudence necessary against a rival so powerful as François,—for he had no doubt that his rival was the prince. And then, if by chance it were not he, he had a mission to the Duc d'Anjou which must be discharged at once; and when he should be in the duke's presence, he would easily come to a conclusion in regard to his guilt or innocence. Then a sublime idea occurred to him; it was to climb back again over the wall, and carry off with his own the horse he had seen there. He retraced his steps to the wall and climbed up again; but on the other side no horse was to be seen. His idea was so good that before it came to him it had come to his adversary. He uttered a howl of rage, clinching his fists, but started off at once on foot. In two hours and a half he arrived at the gates of the city, dying with thirst, heat, and fatigue, but determined to interrogate every sentinel, and find out by what gate a man had entered with two horses. The first sentinel he applied to said that about two hours before a horse without a rider had passed through the gate, and had taken the road to the palace; he feared some accident must have happened to his rider. Monsoreau ground his teeth with passion, and went on to the ducal palace. In the palace was much animation, a great noise, great hilarity. The windows shone like suns; the kitchens sent forth enticing odours. But the wickets were closed, and it was necessary to have them opened. There a difficulty presented itself. Monsoreau called the *concierge* and gave his name; but the *concierge* would not recognise him. "You were erect," he said; "and now you are bent."

"It is fatigue."

"You were pale, and now you are red."

"It is the heat."

"You were mounted, and you return on foot."

"Because my horse took fright and threw me, and returned without a rider. Have you not seen my horse?"

"Ah, yes!" said the *concierge*.

"At least, call the major-domo."

The *concierge*, delighted at that opening to a release from all responsibility, sent for M. Rémy, who came and immediately recognised Monsoreau. "*Mon Dieu!* whence do you come, and in such a state?" he asked.

Monsoreau repeated the same story he had told the *concierge*.

"In fact," said the major-domo, approaching, "we were very anxious when we saw the horse return without a rider,—Monseigneur, especially, to whom I had the honour of announcing your arrival."

" Ah! Monseigneur appeared anxious? " said M. de Monsoreau.

" Very anxious."

" And what did he say? "

" That you must be sent to him immediately on your return."

" Very well; I will take time only to visit the stable to see that nothing has happened to his Highness's horse."

He went to the stable and found his horse in the stall he had taken him from; then, without changing his dress, he went to the dining-room. The prince and all his gentlemen were sitting round a table magnificently served and lighted. The duke, who had been told of his arrival, received him without surprise, and told him to sit down and sup with him.

" Monseigneur," replied he, " I am hungry, tired, and thirsty; but I will neither eat, drink, nor sit down till I have delivered to your Highness a message of the highest importance."

" You come from Paris? "

" Yes, in great haste."

" Well, speak."

Monsoreau advanced with a smile on his lips and hatred in his heart, and said, " Monseigneur, your mother is advancing hastily to visit you."

The duke looked delighted. " It is well," said he. " M. de Monsoreau, I find you to-day, as ever, a faithful servant; let us continue our supper, gentlemen."

Monsoreau sat down with them, but gloomy and preoccupied. He still seemed to see the two figures among the trees, and to hear the cry of Diane.

" You are overcome with weariness," said the prince to him; " really, you had better go to bed."

" Yes," said Livarot, " or he will go to sleep in his chair."

" Pardon, Monseigneur; I am tired out."

" Get tipsy," said D'Antragues; " there is nothing so refreshing as that. To your health, Count! "

" You must give us some good hunts," said Ribeirac; " you know the country."

" You have horses and woods here," said D'Antragues.

" And a wife," added Livarot.

" We will hunt a boar, Count," said the prince.

" Oh, yes, to-morrow! " cried the gentlemen.

" What do you say, Monsoreau? "

" I am always at your Highness's orders, but I am too much

fatigued to conduct a chase to-morrow; besides which, I must examine the woods."

"And we must leave him time to see his wife," cried the duke.

"Granted," cried the young men; "we give him twenty-four hours to do all he has to do."

"Yes, gentlemen, I promise to employ them well."

"Now go to bed," said the duke; and M. de Monsoreau bowed, and went out, very happy to escape.

CHAPTER XX

HOW THE KING LEARNED OF HIS BELOVED BROTHER'S FLIGHT, AND WHAT FOLLOWED

WHEN Monsoreau had retired, the repast continued, and was more gay and joyous than ever.

"Now, Livarot," said the duke, "go on with the story of your flight from Paris, which Monsoreau interrupted."

Livarot continued; but as our title of historian gives us the privilege of knowing better than Livarot himself what had occurred, we will substitute our recital for that of the young man. The story may suffer loss in point of vivacity, but it will gain in intelligibility, since we know as Livarot could not what took place at the Louvre.

Towards the middle of the night Henri III. was awakened by an unaccustomed noise in the palace. There were oaths, blows on the wall, rapid steps in the galleries, and, amid all, these words, repeated by a thousand echoes, "What will the king say?"

Henri sat up and called Chicot, who was asleep on the couch. Chicot opened one eye.

"Ah, you were wrong to call me, Henri," said he; "I was dreaming that you had a son."

"But listen."

"To what? You say enough follies to me by day, without breaking in on my nights."

"But do you not hear?"

"Oh, oh! I do hear cries."

"'What will the king say? What will the king say?' Do you hear?"

" It is one of two things,—either your dog Narcissus is ill, or the Huguenots are taking their revenge for Saint Bartholomew."

" Help me to dress."

" If you will first help me to get up."

" What a misfortune! what a misfortune!" they heard repeated in the antechambers.

" The devil! this looks serious," said Chicot.

" Shall we arm ourselves?" said the king.

" We had better go first and see what is the matter."

Almost immediately they went out by the secret door into the gallery which led to the Duc d'Anjou's apartments. There they saw arms uplifted towards the heavens, and heard exclamations of despair.

" Oh, oh!" cried Chicot, " I understand. Your unhappy prisoner has hanged himself in his prison. I congratulate you, Henri; you are a better politician than I thought."

" Oh, no; it cannot be that."

" So much the worse."

" Come on;" and they entered the duke's chamber. The window was open, and the ladder still hung from it. Henri grew as pale as death.

" Oh, my son, you are not so *blasé* as I thought!" said Chicot.

" Fled! escaped!" cried Henri, in such a thundering voice that all the gentlemen who were crowded round the window turned in terror. Schomberg tore his hair, Quélus and Maugiron struck themselves like madmen; as for D'Epernon, he had vanished, upon the plausible pretence of pursuing the Duc d'Anjou.

Upon seeing the punishment which in their despair his favourites inflicted on themselves the king suddenly became calm. " Gently, my son," said he, laying hold of Maugiron.

" No! *mordieu!* " cried he, " I will kill myself!" and he knocked his head against the wall.

" Holloa! help me to hold him!" cried Henri.

" Ho, comrade!" said Chicot; " there is a pleasanter death than that,—run your sword through your body."

" Will you hold your tongue, brute?" said Henri, with tears in his eyes.

Meantime Quélus was pounding his cheeks with his fist.

" Quélus, my child," said the king, " you will be as blue as Schomberg when he came out of the indigo."

Quélus stopped; but Schomberg still continued to tear at his hair.

" Schomberg, Schomberg! a little reason, I beg!"

" It is enough to drive one mad."

" Indeed, it is a terrible misfortune, and so you must preserve your reason, Schomberg. Yes, it is a frightful calamity; I am ruined! Here is civil war begun in my kingdom. Who did it? Who furnished the ladder? *Mordieu!* I will hang all the city! Who was it? Ten thousand crowns to whomsoever will tell me his name, and one hundred thousand to whomsoever will bring him to me, dead or alive!"

" It must have been some Angevin," said Maugiron.

" *Pardieu!* you are right," cried Henri.

" Ah, the Angevins; they shall pay for it!"

As if that word had been a spark lighting a train of powder, a terrible explosion of cries and threats broke out against the Angevins.

" Oh, yes, the Angevins!" cried Quélus.

" Where are they?" roared Schomberg.

" Let them be ripped open!" shouted Maugiron.

" A hundred gibbets for a hundred Angevins!" said Henri.

Chicot could not remain silent in the midst of that general madness. He drew his sword; and striking right and left with its flat side, he attacked the favourites and beat the walls, rolling his eyes and crying out, " Oh, *ventre de biche!* Oh, noble rage! Ah, damnation! The Angevins, *mordieu!* Death to the Angevins!"

That cry, " Death to the Angevins!" was heard throughout the city, as the cry of the Hebrew mothers was heard throughout all Rama.

Meantime, the king had disappeared; he had thought of his mother, and without saying a word, had gone to her. When he entered, she was half lying in a great armchair. She heard the news without answering.

" You say nothing, Mother. Does not this flight seem to you criminal, and worthy of punishment?"

" My dear son, liberty is worth as much as a crown; and remember, I advised you to fly in order to gain a crown."

" My mother, he braves me; he outrages me!"

" No; he only saves himself."

" Ah! this is how you take my part."

" What do you mean, my son?"

" I mean that with age the feelings grow calm,—that you do not love me as much as you used to do."

" You are wrong, my son," said Catherine, coldly; " you are

my beloved son, but he of whom you complain is also my son."

" Well, then, Madame, I will go to find other counsellors capable of feeling for me and of aiding me."

" Go, my son; and may God guide your counsellors, for they will have need of it to aid you in this strait! "

" Adieu, then, Madame! "

" Adieu, Henri! I do not pretend to counsel you,—you do not need me, I know,—but beg your counsellors to reflect well before they advise, and still more before they execute."

" Yes, for the position is difficult; is it not, Madame? "

" Very grave," she replied, raising her eyes to heaven.

" Have you any idea who it was that carried him off? "

Catherine did not reply.

" I think it was the Angevins," continued the king.

Catherine smiled scornfully. " The Angevins? " she repeated.

" You do not think so? "

" Do you, really? "

" Tell me what you think, Madame."

" Why should I? "

" To enlighten me."

" Enlighten you! I am but a doting old woman, whose only influence lies in her prayers and repentance."

" No, Mother; speak,—you are the cleverest of us all."

" Useless; I have only the ideas of another age. Can Catherine—an old woman—still give counsel worth hearing?— that, my son, is impossible."

" Well, then, Mother, refuse me your counsel; deprive me of your aid. In an hour I will hang all the Angevins in Paris."

" Hang all the Angevins! " exclaimed Catherine, in amazement.

" Yes, hang, slay, massacre, burn; already my friends are running through the city to break the bones of those cursed rebels."

" Let them beware, unhappy man! " said Catherine, aroused by the seriousness of the situation. " They will ruin themselves,—which would be nothing; but they will ruin you also."

" How so? "

" Blind! Will kings eternally have eyes, and not see? "

" Kings must avenge their injuries,—it is but justice; and in this case all my subjects will rise to defend me."

" You are mad."

" Why so? "

"You will make oceans of blood flow. The standard of revolt will soon be raised; and you will arm against you a host who never would rise for François."

"But if I do not revenge myself they will think I am afraid."

"Did any one ever think I was afraid? Besides, it was not the Angevins."

"Who was it, then? It must have been my brother's friends."

"Your brother has no friends."

"But who was it then?"

"Your enemy."

"What enemy?"

"Eh! my son, you know you have never had but one,— yours, mine, your brother Charles's; always the same."

"Henri de Navarre, you mean?"

"Yes, Henri de Navarre."

"He is not at Paris."

"Do you know who is at Paris and who is not? Do you know anything? Have you eyes and ears? Have you around you those who see and hear? No, you are all deaf; you are all blind."

"Henri de Navarre?" repeated Henri.

"My son, in every disappointment you meet with, in every misfortune that happens to you of which the author is unknown, do not seek or conjecture; it is useless. Cry out, 'It is Henri de Navarre;' and you will be sure to be right. Strike on the side where he is, and you will be sure to strike right. Oh, that man, that man!—he is the sword suspended over the head of the Valois."

"Then you think I should countermand my orders about the Angevins?"

"At once, without losing an instant. Hasten! perhaps you are already too late."

Henri flew out of the Louvre to find his friends, but found only Chicot sitting on a stone, and drawing geographical outlines in the sand.

CHAPTER XXI

HOW, AS CHICOT AND THE QUEEN-MOTHER WERE AGREED, THE KING BEGAN TO AGREE WITH THEM

" Is this how you defend your king? " cried Henri.

" I defend him in my own way, and I think it is a good one."

" Good, indeed! "

" I maintain it, and I will prove it."

" I am curious to hear this proof."

" It is easy; but first, we have committed a great folly."

" How so? " cried Henri, struck by the agreement between Chicot and his mother.

" Yes," replied Chicot, " your friends are crying through the city, ' Death to the Angevins! ' and now that I reflect, it was never proved that they had anything to do with the affair. And your friends, crying thus through the city, will raise that nice little civil war of which MM. de Guise have so much need, and which they did not succeed in raising for themselves. Besides which, your friends may get killed,—which would not displease me, I confess, but which would afflict you,—or else they will chase all the Angevins from the city, which will please M. d'Anjou enormously."

" *Mordieu!* " cried the king, " do you think, then, that things are already so bad as that? "

" Yes, if not worse."

" But all this does not explain what you do here, sitting on a stone."

" I am tracing a plan of all the provinces that your brother will raise against us, and am computing the number of men each will furnish to the revolt."

" Chicot, Chicot, I have, then, around me only birds of ill omen."

" The owl sings at night, my son; it is his hour. Now it is dark, Henri, so dark that one might take the day for the night, and I sing what you ought to hear. Look! "

" At what? "

" My geographical plan. Here is Anjou, something like a tartlet, you see; there your brother will take refuge. Anjou, well managed, as Monsoreau and Bussy will manage it, will alone furnish to your brother ten thousand combatants."

" Do you think so? "

" That is the minimum. Let us pass to Guyenne; here it is, —this figure like a calf walking on one leg. Of course, you will not be astonished to find discontent in Guyenne; it is an old focus for revolt, and the English are hardly out of it. Guyenne, then, will be quick to rise, not against you, but against France. They can furnish eight thousand soldiers; that is not much, but they are well trained. Then we have Béarn and Navarre; you see these two divisions, which look like an ape on the back of an elephant,—they may furnish about sixteen thousand. Let us count now: ten thousand for Anjou, eight thousand for Guyenne, sixteen thousand for Béarn and Navarre,—making a total of thirty-four thousand."

" You think, then, that the King of Navarre will join my brother? "

" I should think so."

" Do you believe that he had anything to do with my brother's escape? "

Chicot looked at him. " That is not your own idea, Henriquet."

" Why not? "

" It is too clever, my son."

" Never mind whose idea it was; answer my question."

" Well! I heard a *ventre-saint-gris* in the Rue de la Ferronerie."

" You heard a *ventre-saint-gris?* " cried the king.

" Faith, yes," replied Chicot; " I was recalling it only to-day."

" He was in Paris? "

" I think so."

" And what makes you think so? "

" I saw him."

" You saw Henri de Navarre in Paris? "

" Yes."

" You saw my mortal enemy here, and did not tell me? "

" A man is a gentleman or he is not," said Chicot.

" Well? "

" Well, if one is a gentleman he is not a spy,—that's all."

Henri became thoughtful. " So," said he, " Anjou and Béarn!—my brother François and my cousin Henri! "

" Without counting the three Guises, you understand."

" What! do you think they will join the alliance? "

" Thirty-four thousand men to begin with," said Chicot, counting on his fingers,—" ten for Anjou, eight for Guyenne, sixteen for Béarn; twenty or twenty-five thousand more under command of M. de Guise, as lieutenant-general of your armies; total, fifty-nine thousand men. If we call it fifty thousand, on account of gout, rheumatism, sciatica, and other infirmities, it is still, as you see, my son, a very pretty total."

" But Henri de Navarre and the Duc de Guise are enemies."

" Which will not prevent their uniting against you; they will be free to fight with each other when they have conquered you."

" You are right, Chicot, and my mother is right; we must prevent an outbreak. Help me get together the Swiss."

" Oh, yes! Quélus has them."

" My guards, then."

Schomberg has them."

" My household, at least."

" They have gone with Maugiron."

" Without my orders? "

" And when do you ever give orders, Henri? Ah! when it is a question of processions or flagellations, perhaps you do; but when there is a question of war, when there is a question of government,—why that concerns M. de Schomberg, M. de Quélus, and M. de Maugiron. As to D'Epernon I say nothing, since he hides himself."

" *Mordieu !* " cried Henri, " is that the way things are going on? "

" Allow me to say, my son," said Chicot, " that you discover rather late in the day that you are the seventh or eighth king in your kingdom."

Henri bit his lips and stamped with his foot.

" Eh! " said Chicot, peering into the darkness.

" What is it? " asked the king.

" *Ventre de biche !* there they are! See, Henri, there are your men." And he pointed out to the king three or four cavaliers who were running, followed at a distance by men on horseback, and a crowd of men on foot. The cavaliers were about to re-enter the Louvre, not seeing those two men standing near the ditch, and half concealed in the dim light.

" Schomberg! " cried the king, " this way! "

" Holloa! " said Schomberg; " who calls? "

" Come, my child, come! "

Schomberg thought he recognised the voice and approached. " Eh! " said he, " God damn me, it is the king! "

" Yes, impatiently awaiting you; what have you done? "

" What have we done? " said a second cavalier, approaching.

"Ah! come here, Quélus," said the king; "and do not go away again without my permission."

"There is no need," said a third, in whom the king recognised Maugiron, "since all is finished."

"All is finished?" repeated the King.

"God be praised!" said D'Epernon, suddenly appearing.

"Hosanna!" cried Chicot, lifting his hands towards the heavens.

"You have killed them, then?" said the king, and added in a low voice, "At any rate the dead never return."

"You have killed them?" said Chicot. "Ah! if you have killed them there is nothing to say."

"Oh! we had not that trouble; the cowards ran away,— we had scarcely time to cross our swords with them."

Henri grew pale. "With whom?" said he.

"With D'Antragues."

"You killed him, at any rate?"

"On the contrary, he killed a lackey of Quélus's."

"They were, then, on their guard?" asked the king.

"*Parbleu!* I should think so!" cried Chicot. "You shout 'Death to the Angevins!' you fire the cannon, you ring the bells, you set all the old iron in Paris trembling; and you expect those honest men to be as deaf as you are stupid."

"Oh!" murmured the king, "here is a civil war lighted up." Quélus started. "The devil!" he said, "it is true."

"Ah!" said Chicot, "you begin to perceive it, do you? That is fortunate. Here are MM. de Schomberg and de Maugiron, who have as yet no suspicion of it."

"We reserve ourselves," replied Schomberg, "to defend the person and the crown of his Majesty."

"Eh, *pardieu!*" said Chicot, "for that we have M. de Crillon, who doesn't cry as loud as you do, but is worth quite as much."

"But, M. Chicot, you cried with us, 'Death to the Angevins!'"

"Oh, that is a different thing! I am a fool, and you are clever men."

"Come, peace, gentlemen; we shall have enough of war soon."

"What are your Majesty's orders?"

"That you employ the same ardour in calming the people as you have done in exciting them, and that you bring back all the Swiss, my guards, and my household, and have the doors of the Louvre closed; so that perhaps to-morrow the *bourgeois* may take the whole thing for a drunken frolic."

The young men went off, and Henri returned to his mother.

" Well," said she, " what has happened? "

" All that you foresaw, Mother."

" They have escaped? "

" Alas, yes! "

" What else? "

" Is not that enough? "

" The city? "

" Is in tumult. But that is not what disquiets me; I hold it under my hand."

" No, it is the provinces."

" Which will revolt," said Henri.

" What shall you do? "

" I see but one thing."

" What is that? "

" To withdraw the army from La Charité and march on Anjou."

" And M. de Guise? "

" Oh, I will arrest him if necessary."

" And you think violent measures will succeed? "

" What can I do, then? "

" All that you propose is impossible, my son."

" Ah! " cried Henri, in deep disgust, " I am, then, badly inspired to-day? "

" No; but you are troubled. Recover yourself first, and then we will see."

" Then, Mother, have ideas for me. Let us do something; we must act."

" Send an ambassador."

" To whom? "

" To your brother."

" An ambassador to that traitor! You humiliate me, Mother."

" This is not a moment to be proud," said Catherine, sternly.

" An ambassador who will ask for peace? "

" Who will buy it if necessary."

" And, *mon Dieu !* for what advantage? "

" If it were only to secure quietly, afterwards, those who have gone to make war on you."

" Oh! I would give four provinces of my kingdom for that? "

" Well, then, the end is worth the means."

" I believe you are right, Mother; but whom shall I send? "

" Seek among your friends."

"My mother, I do not know a single man to whom I could confide such a mission."

"Confide it to a woman, then."

"To a woman! My mother, would you consent?"

"My son, I am very old and very weak, and death will perhaps await me on my return; but I will make this journey so rapidly that your brother and his friends will not have had time to learn their own power."

"Oh, my good mother!" cried Henri, kissing her hands, "you are my support, my benefactress, my providence!"

"That means that I am still Queen of France," murmured Catherine, regarding her son with an expression in which there was as much pity as tenderness.

CHAPTER XXII

IN WHICH IT IS PROVED THAT GRATITUDE WAS ONE OF SAINT-LUC'S VIRTUES

THE next morning M. de Monsoreau rose early, and descended into the courtyard of the palace. He entered the stable, where Roland was in his place.

"Are the horses of Monseigneur taught to return to their stable alone?" he asked of the man who stood there.

"No, Monsieur the Count."

"But Roland did so yesterday."

"Oh, he is remarkably intelligent."

"Has he ever done it before?"

"No, Monsieur; he is generally ridden by the Duc d'Anjou, who is a good rider, and never gets thrown."

"I was not thrown," replied the count, "for I also am a good rider. No, I tied him to a tree while I entered a house, and when I returned he had disappeared. I thought he had been stolen, or that some passer-by had played a bad joke by carrying him away; that was why I asked how he returned to the stable."

"He returned alone, as the major-domo had the honour to inform Monsieur the Count yesterday."

"It is strange. Monseigneur often rides this horse, you say?"

"Nearly every day."

"His Highness returned late last night?"

"About an hour before you."

" And what horse did he ride? Was it a bay with a white star on his forehead? "

" No, Monsieur; he rode Isolin, which you see here."

" And in the prince's escort is there any one who rides such a horse as I describe? "

" I know of no one."

" Well," said Monsoreau, impatiently, " saddle me Roland."

" Roland? "

" Yes; are there any orders against it? "

" No; on the contrary, I was told to let you have any horse you pleased."

When Roland was saddled, Monsoreau said to the man, " What are your wages per year? "

" Twenty crowns, Monsieur."

" Will you earn ten times that sum at once? "

" *Pardieu!* But how? "

" Find out who rode yesterday the horse I described."

" Ah, Monsieur, what you ask is very difficult; so many gentlemen come here."

" Yes, but two hundred crowns are worth some trouble."

" Certainly, Monsieur the Count, and I will do my best to discover."

" That is right, and here are ten crowns to encourage you."

" Thanks, Monsieur the Count."

" Well, tell the prince I have gone to reconnoitre the wood for the chase."

As he spoke, he heard steps behind him, and turned. " Ah, M. de Bussy! " he cried.

" Why, Monsieur the Count, who would have thought of seeing you here! "

" And you, Monsieur,—you are said to be ill."

" So I am; my doctor orders absolute rest, and for a week I have not left the city. Ah, you are going to ride Roland; I sold him to the duke, who is so well pleased with him that he rides him almost every day."

Monsoreau turned pale. " Yes," said he, " I understand that. He is an excellent animal; I rode him yesterday."

" Which makes you wish for him again to-day? "

" Yes."

" Pardon! " continued Bussy; " you spoke of preparing for a chase? "

" Yes, the prince wishes for one."

" And where is it to be? "

" Near Méridor. Will you come with me? "

" No, thank you, I shall go to bed; the fever is gaining on me."

" Oh!" cried a voice from behind, " there is M. de Bussy out without permission."

" The Haudouin," said Bussy; " good! now I am on sure ground. Adieu, Count; I commend Roland to you."

Bussy went away, and Monsoreau jumped into the saddle.

" What is the matter? " said Rémy; " you look so pale that I almost believe you are really ill."

" Do you know where he is going? "

" No."

" To Méridor."

" Well, did you hope he would not? "

" Mon Dieu! what will happen, after what he saw yesterday? "

" Madame de Monsoreau will deny everything."

" But he saw her."

" She will say he did not."

" She will never have the courage."

" Oh, M. de Bussy, is it possible you do not know women better than that? "

" Rémy, I feel very ill."

" So I see. Go home, and I will prescribe for you."

" What? "

" A slice of fowl and ham, and some lobster."

" Oh, I am not hungry."

" The more reason I should order you to eat."

" Rémy, I fear that that wretch will make a great scene at Méridor. I ought to have gone with him when he asked me."

" What for? "

" To sustain Diane."

" Oh, she will sustain herself. Besides, you ought not to be out; we agreed you were too ill."

" I could not help it, Rémy, I was so uneasy."

Rémy carried him off, and made him sit down to a good breakfast.

M. de Monsoreau wished to see if it were chance or habit that had led Roland to the park wall; therefore he left the bridle on his neck. Roland took precisely the same road as on the previous day; and before very long M. de Monsoreau found himself in the same spot as before, only now the place was solitary, and no horse was there. The count climbed the wall again, but no one was to be seen; judging that it was useless to watch for people on their guard, he went on to the park gates. The baron, seeing his son-in-law coming over the draw-bridge, advanced ceremoniously to meet him. Diane, seated under a magnificent sycamore, was reading poetry, while Ger-trude was embroidering at her side. The count, after greeting the baron, perceived them. He got off his horse and approached them.

Diane rose, took three steps towards the count, and made to him a grave reverence.

"What calmness, or rather, what perfidy!" murmured the count; "what a tempest I shall raise on the bosom of those quiet waters!"

A lackey approached; Monsoreau threw him the bridle, and then, turning towards Diane, "Madame," said he, "will you grant me the favour of an interview?"

"Willingly, Monsieur."

"Do you do us the honour of remaining at the château?" asked the baron.

"Yes, Monsieur, until to-morrow at least."

The baron went away to give orders; and Diane reseated herself, while Monsoreau took Gertrude's chair, and with a look which would have intimidated the most resolute man, said, "Madame, who was in the park with you yesterday?"

Diane looked at her husband with eyes that were clear and undisturbed. "At what time?" she asked with a voice from which she succeeded in banishing all emotion.

"At six."

"Where?"

"Near the copse."

"It must have been some one else; it was not I."

"It was you, Madame."

"What do you know about it?"

"Tell me the man's name!" cried Monsoreau, furiously.

"What man?"

"The man who was walking with you."

"I cannot tell, if it was some other woman."

"It was you, I tell you," said Monsoreau, striking the earth with his foot.

"You are wrong, Monsieur," replied Diane, coldly.

"How dare you deny it? I saw you."

"You, Monsieur?"

"Yes, Madame, myself. And there is no other lady here."

" You are wrong again; there is Jeanne de Brissac."

" Madame de Saint-Luc? "

" Yes; my friend."

" And M. de Saint-Luc? "

" Never leaves her; theirs was a love-match. It was Monsieur and Madame de Saint-Luc whom you saw."

" It was not M. de Saint-Luc; it was not Madame de Saint-Luc. It was you, whom I clearly recognised, with a man whom I do not know, but whom I will know, I swear to you."

" You persist, then, in saying that it was I, Monsieur? "

" But I tell you that I recognised you; I tell you that I heard the cry you uttered."

" When you are more reasonable, Monsieur, I shall be ready to hear you; at present I will retire."

" No, Madame," said Monsoreau, holding Diane by the arm; " you shall stay."

" Monsieur, here are Monsieur and Madame de Saint-Luc; I trust you will contain yourself in their presence."

Indeed, Monsieur and Madame de Saint-Luc approached. Jeanne bowed to Monsoreau; and Saint-Luc gave him his hand, then leaving his wife to Monsoreau, took Diane, and they moved on towards the house, warned by the bell for dinner, which was early at Méridor, as the baron preserved the old customs. The conversation at dinner was general, and turned naturally on the Duc d'Anjou and the movement his arrival had caused. Diane sat far from her husband, between Saint-Luc and the baron.

CHAPTER XXIII

THE PROJECT OF M. DE SAINT-LUC

WHEN the repast was over, Monsoreau took Saint-Luc's arm and went out. " Do you know," said he, " that I am very happy to have found you here? The solitude of Méridor frightened me."

" What! " said Saint-Luc, " with your wife? As for me, with such a companion I should find a desert too populous."

" I do not say no," replied Monsoreau, biting his lips; " but still—"

" Still, what? "

" I am very glad to have met you here."

" Really, Monsieur, you are very polite; for I cannot believe that you could possibly fear ennui with such a companion, and in such a country."

" Bah! I pass half my life in the woods."

" The more reason for being fond of them, it seems to me. See this admirable park; I know I shall be very sorry to leave it. Unfortunately I fear I shall be forced to do so before long."

" Why so? "

" Oh, Monsieur, when is man the arbiter of his own destiny? He is like the leaf of the tree, which the wind blows about. You are very fortunate."

" Fortunate; how? "

" To live among these splendid trees."

" Oh, I do not think I shall stay here long. I am not so fond of nature, and I fear these woods; I think they are not safe."

" Why,—on account of their loneliness, do you mean? "

" No, not that, for I suppose you see friends here."

" Faith, no," said Saint-Luc, with a perfect naïveté, " not a soul."

" Ah, really! You do not sometimes receive a visitor? "

" Not since I have been here, at least."

" Not one gentleman from the court at Angers? "

" Not one."

" Impossible."

" It is true."

" Then I am mistaken on that point."

" Entirely; but why is not the park safe? Are there bears here? "

" Oh, no."

" Wolves? "

" No."

" Robbers? "

" Perhaps. Tell me, Monsieur, is not Madame de Saint-Luc very pretty? She appeared so to me."

" Why, yes."

" Does she often walk in the park? "

" Often; she adores the woods, like myself. But why that question? "

" For nothing. And do you accompany her? "

" Always."

" Almost always," continued the count.

" What the devil are you driving at? "

" Oh, *mon Dieu!* nothing,—or at least a trifle."

" I listen."

" They told me—"

" Well? "

" You will not be angry? "

" I never am so."

" Besides, between husbands, these confidences are right; they told me a man had been seen wandering in the park."

" A man? "

" Yes."

" Who came for my wife? "

" Oh! I do not say that."

" You would be wrong not to tell me, my dear Monsoreau. Who saw him? Pray tell me."

" Oh, to tell you the truth, I do not think it was for Madame de Saint-Luc that he came."

" For whom, then? "

" Ah! I fear it was for Diane."

" Ah! bah! " said Saint-Luc, " I should prefer that."

" What! you would prefer that? "

" Certainly; you know we husbands are an egotistical set. Every one for himself, and God for us all."

" The devil, rather."

" Then you think a man entered here? "

" I more than think," said Monsoreau, " for I saw him."

" You saw a man in the park? "

" Yes."

" When? "

" Yesterday."

" Alone? "

" With Madame de Monsoreau."

" Where? "

" Just here to the left." And as they had walked down to the old copse, Monsoreau, from where he was, could point out the place to his companion.

" Ah! " said Saint-Luc, " here is a wall in a bad state; I must warn the baron."

" Whom do you suspect? " asked Monsoreau.

" Of what? "

" Of climbing over here to talk to my wife."

Saint-Luc seemed to plunge himself into a profound meditation, the result of which M. de Monsoreau awaited with anxiety.

" Well? " said he.

" Why," said Saint-Luc, " it must have been—"

" Who ? " asked the count, eagerly.

" Why, yourself ! "

" You are joking, M. de Saint-Luc," said the count, petrified.

" Upon my word, no; when I was first married I did such things. Why shouldn't you ? "

" Come ! you are trying to put me off; but do not fear, I have courage. Help me in my search; you will do me an immense favour."

Saint-Luc shook his head. " It must have been you," said he.

" Do not jest, I beg of you; the thing is serious."

" Do you think so ? "

" I am sure of it."

" That is another thing, then; and how does this man come ? "

" He comes secretly, *parbleu !* "

" Often ? "

" I should think so! Look at the marks in the wall."

" They are there, it is true."

" Have you never seen anything of what I now tell you ? "

" Oh ! " said Saint-Luc, " I did indeed suspect something of the kind."

" Ah! you see," said the count, agitated; " and then? "

" And then? I was not uneasy; I supposed it was you."

" But since I tell you that it was not ? "

" I believe you, my dear sir."

" Well, then—"

" It must have been some one else."

Monsoreau began to look black; but Saint-Luc preserved his easy nonchalance. " I have an idea," said he.

" Tell me."

" If it were—"

" Well ! "

" But, no."

" Pray speak."

" The Duc d'Anjou."

" I thought so at first; but I have made inquiries, and it could not have been he."

" Oh ! he is very cunning."

" Yes, but it was not he."

" Wait, then."

" Well ? "

" I have another idea; if it was neither you nor the duke, it must have been I."

" You? "

" Why not? "

" You to come on horseback to the outside of the park, when you live inside! "

" Oh, *mon Dieu !* I am such a capricious being."

" You, who fled away when you saw me! "

" Oh! any one would do that."

" Then you were doing wrong? " cried the count, no longer able to keep in his anger.

" I do not say I was not."

" You are mocking me," cried the count, growing very pale, " and have been doing so for a quarter of an hour."

" You are wrong, Monsieur," said Saint-Luc, drawing out his watch, and looking at Monsoreau with an expression which made him shudder, in spite of his fierce courage; " it has been twenty minutes."

" But you insult me, Monsieur."

" And do you imagine that you are not insulting me, Monsieur, with your police questions? "

" Ah! now I see clearly."

" How wonderful, at ten o'clock in the morning! But what do you see? "

" I see that you act in concert with the traitor, the coward, whom I saw yesterday."

" I should think so! he is my friend."

" Then I will kill you instead of him."

" Bah! in your own house, suddenly, without warning! Ah! M. de Monsoreau, how badly you have been brought up, and how living among beasts spoils the manners! Fie! "

" Do you not see that I am furious? " roared the count, standing before Saint-Luc with his arms crossed, and his features contracted by a frightful expression of the despair in his soul.

" Yes, *mordieu !* I see it; and really, fury is not at all becoming to you. You are horrible to look at when you are like that, my dear M. de Monsoreau."

The count, beside himself, put his hand to his sword.

" Ah! " said Saint-Luc, " you try to provoke me; you see I am perfectly calm."

" Yes, I do provoke you."

" Take the trouble to get over the wall; on the other side we shall be on neutral ground."

" What do I care? "

" I do; I do not want to kill you in your own house."

" Very well," said Monsoreau, climbing over.

" Take care! Pray do not hurt yourself, my dear count; those stones are loose," said Saint-Luc. Then he also got over.

CHAPTER XXIV

HOW M. DE SAINT-LUC SHOWED M. DE MONSOREAU THE THRUST THAT THE KING HAD TAUGHT HIM

" Are you ready? " cried Monsoreau.

" No; I have the sun in my eyes."

" Move then; I warn you I shall kill you."

" Shall you really? Well, man proposes, and God disposes. Look at that bed of poppies and dandelions."

" Well! "

" Well, I mean to lay you there." And Saint-Luc drew his sword, smiling. Monsoreau began the combat furiously, but Saint-Luc parried his thrusts skilfully. " *Pardieu!* M. de Monsoreau," said he, " you use your sword very well; you might kill any one but Bussy or me."

Monsoreau grew pale on discovering the skill of his adversary.

" You are perhaps surprised," continued Saint-Luc, " to find me handling my sword so properly. It is because the king, who loves me, as you know, has taken the trouble to give me a great many lessons; he has taught me among other things a thrust, which you shall see presently. I tell you so that if I should happen to kill you with that thrust, you may have the pleasure of knowing you are killed by the king's method,—it will be very flattering to you." And then suddenly he rushed furiously on Monsoreau, who, half wild with rage as he was, parried five thrusts, but received the sixth full in his chest.

" Ah! " said Saint-Luc, " you will fall just where I said you would," as Monsoreau sank down on the poppies. Then, wiping his sword, Saint-Luc stood quietly by, watching the changes which came over the face of the dying man.

" Ah, you have killed me! " cried Monsoreau.

" I intended to do so; but now I see you dying, devil take me if I am not sorry for what I have done! You are horribly jealous, it is true; but you were brave." And quite satisfied with that funeral oration, Saint-Luc knelt by Monsoreau, and said to him, " Have you any last wish? If so, tell it to me; and on the faith of a gentleman, it shall be executed. Are you thirsty? Shall I get you water?"

Monsoreau did not reply. He turned over with his face to the earth, biting the ground, and struggling in his blood.

"Poor devil!" said Saint-Luc, rising. "Oh, Friendship, Friendship, thou art an exacting divinity!"

Monsoreau opened his fading eyes, tried to raise his head, and fell back with a groan.

"Come, he is dead; let me think no more about him. Ah! but that is not so easy, when you have killed a man." And jumping back over the wall, he went to the château. The first person he saw was Diane talking to his wife. "How well she will look in black!" he thought. Then, approaching them, "Pardon me," said he, "but may I say a few words to Jeanne?"

"Do so; I will go to my father."

"What is it?" said Jeanne, when Diane was gone; "you look rather gloomy."

"Why, yes."

"What has happened?"

"Oh, *mon Dieu!* an accident."

"To you?"

"Not precisely to me, but to a person who was near me."

"Who was it?"

"The person I was walking with."

"M. de Monsoreau?"

"Alas, yes! poor dear man!"

"What has happened to him?"

"I believe he is dead."

"Dead!" cried Jeanne, starting back in horror.

"Yes."

"He who was here just now talking—"

"Yes, that is just the cause of his death; he talked too much."

"Saint-Luc, you are hiding something from me!" cried Jeanne, seizing his hands.

"I? Nothing; not even the place where he lies."

"Where is it?"

"Down there behind the wall,—just where Bussy used to tie his horse."

"It is you who killed him!"

"*Parbleu!* who else could it be? There were only two of us; I come back alive, and I tell you he is dead. It is not very difficult to determine which of us two killed the other."

"How unfortunate for you!"

" Ah, dear friend! he provoked me, insulted me, drew the sword first."

" It is dreadful! the poor man! "

" Good! I was sure of it; before a week is over he will be called Saint Monsoreau."

" But you cannot stay here in the house of the man you have killed."

" So I thought at once, and that is why I came to ask you to get ready."

" He has not wounded you? "

" At last! although it comes a trifle late, it is a question which reconciles me to you. No, I am entirely unhurt."

" Then we will go."

" As quickly as possible, for you know the accident may be discovered at any moment."

" Then Diane is a widow."

" That is just what I thought of."

" After you killed him? "

" No, before."

" Well, I will go and tell her."

" Spare her feelings."

" Do not laugh. Meanwhile get the horses saddled. But where shall we go? "

" To Paris."

" But the king? "

" Oh, he will have forgotten everything by this time; besides, if there is to be war, as seems probable, my place is at his side. But I must have pen and ink."

" For what? "

" To write to Bussy; I cannot leave Anjou without telling him why."

" No, of course not; you will find all you require in my room."

Saint-Luc went in, and wrote,—

DEAR FRIEND,—You will learn ere long, by report, of the accident which has happened to M. de Monsoreau; we had together, by the old copse, a discussion on broken-down walls and horses that go home alone. In the heat of the argument he fell on a bed of poppies and dandelions so hard that he died there.—Your friend for life,   SAINT-LUC.

P.S.—As you may think this rather improbable, I must add that we had our swords in our hands. I set off at once for Paris to make peace with the king, Anjou not seeming to me very safe after what has occurred.

Ten minutes after, a servant set off for Angers with this letter, while Monsieur and Madame de Saint-Luc went out by another door, leaving Diane much grieved at their departure, and much embarrassed how to tell the baron what had occurred. She had turned away her eyes from Saint-Luc as he passed.

"That is the reward for serving your friends," said he to his wife; "decidedly, every one is ungrateful except myself."

CHAPTER XXV

IN WHICH WE SEE THE QUEEN-MOTHER ENTER THE TOWN OF ANGERS, BUT NOT TRIUMPHANTLY

AT the same time that M. de Monsoreau fell under the sword of Saint-Luc, a flourish of trumpets sounded at the closed gates of Angers. It was Catherine de Médicis, who had come to enter Angers at the head of a considerable troop of attendants. The arrival was announced to Bussy, who rose from his bed and went to the prince, who immediately got into his. Certainly the airs played by the trumpets were fine, but they had not the virtue of those which made the walls of Jericho fall, for the gates did not open. Catherine leaned out of her litter to show herself to the guards, hoping that the majesty of a royal countenance would have more effect than the sound of the trumpets. They saw her, and saluted her courteously, but did not open the gates. Then she sent a gentleman to demand admittance; but they replied that Angers being in a state of war, the gates could not be opened without certain indispensable formalities. Catherine was furious. At last Bussy appeared, with five other gentlemen.

"Who is there?" cried he.

"It is her Majesty the Queen-mother, who has come to visit Angers."

"Very well; go to the left, and about eighty feet from here you will find the postern."

"A postern for her Majesty!" cried the gentleman.

But Bussy was no longer there to hear; he and his friends, who were laughing quietly, had ridden off towards the place indicated.

"Did your Majesty hear?" asked the gentleman,—"the postern!"

"Oh, yes, Monsieur, I heard; let us go there, if that be the only way to get in." And the flash from her eyes frightened the blunderer, who had thus emphasised her humiliation.

The *cortége* turned to the left, and the postern opened.

Bussy, on foot, with his unsheathed sword in his hand, advanced and bowed respectfully to Catherine. "Your Majesty is welcome to Angers," said he.

"Thank you, M. de Bussy," said the queen, descending from her litter, and advancing towards the little door.

Bussy stopped her. "Take care, Madame!" said he, "the door is low, and you will hurt yourself."

"Must I then stoop?" replied she. "It is the first time I ever entered a city so."

Her Majesty's litter was hoisted over the wall, so that she could resume her place in it to go to the palace. Bussy and his friends rode on either side.

"Where is my son?" cried she. "Why do I not see M. d'Anjou?" These words, which she would have preferred to repress, were forced from her by a resistless wrath. The absence of François at such a moment capped the insult.

"Monseigneur is ill, Madame, or else your Majesty cannot doubt that he would have come himself to do the honours of *his* city."

Catherine was sublime in hypocrisy. "Ill! my poor child ill!" she cried. "Ah! let us hasten to him! He is well cared for, I trust?"

"We do our best," said Bussy, looking at her with surprise, as if asking whether in that woman there was a remnant of maternal feeling.

"Does he know that I am here?" asked Catherine, after a pause.

"Yes, Madame; to be sure."

"He must suffer much, then," she added in a tone of compassion.

"Horribly; he is subject to these sudden indispositions."

"It was sudden, then?"

"*Mon Dieu!* yes, Madame."

When they arrived at the palace, Bussy ran up first to the duke.

"Here she is!" cried he; "beware!"

"Is she furious?"

"Exasperated."

"Does she complain?"

"No, she does worse, she smiles."

"What do the people say?"

"They looked at her in mute terror; now, Monseigneur, be careful."

"We stick to war?"

" *Pardieu,* ask one hundred to get ten, and with her you will only get five."

" Bah! you think me very weak.   Are you all here?   Where is Monsoreau? "

" I believe he is at Méridor."

" Her Majesty the Queen-mother! " cried the usher at the door.

Catherine entered, looking pale, and dressed in black, according to her custom. The duke made a movement to rise; but she threw herself into his arms and half stifled him with kisses. She did more,—she wept.

" We must take care," said D'Antragues to Ribeirac, " each tear will be paid for by blood."

Catherine now sat down on the foot of the bed. At a sign from Bussy every one went away but himself.

" Will you not go and look after my poor attendants, M. de Bussy?—you who are at home here," said the queen.

It was impossible not to go, so he replied, " I am happy to please your Majesty; " and he retired, without having been able to make any sign to the duke. Catherine suspected him, and did not lose sight of him for a moment.

Catherine wished to discover whether her son was really ill or was only feigning. But he, worthy son of such a mother, played his part to perfection. She had wept; he had a fever. Catherine, deceived, thought him really ill, and hoped to have more influence over a mind weakened by suffering. She overwhelmed him with tenderness, embraced him, and wept so much that at last he asked her the reason.

" You have run so great a risk, my child," she replied.

" In escaping from the Louvre, Mother? "

" No, afterwards."

" How so? "

" Those who aided you in this unlucky escape—"

" Well? "

" Were your most cruel enemies."

" She wishes to find out who it was," thought he.

" The King of Navarre," continued she, " the eternal scourge of our race—"

" Ah! she knows," thought François.

" Can you believe," she said, " that he boasts of it, and thinks he has gained everything? "

" That is impossible, for he had nothing to do with it; and if he had, I am quite safe, as you see. I have not seen the King of Navarre for two years."

" It is not of that danger alone that I speak to you, my son,"
said Catherine, perceiving that the stroke had failed.

" Of what, then? " replied the duke, smiling, as he saw the
tapestry shake behind the queen.

" The king's anger," said she, in a solemn voice,—" the
furious anger which menaces you—"

" This danger is something like the other, Madame.   He may
be furious; but I am safe here."

" You believe so? " she said in a tone that might have
intimidated the most audacious.

The tapestry moved.

" I am sure of it," replied the duke; " and it is so true, my
good mother, that you have come yourself to tell me so."

" How so? " said Catherine, disturbed by the duke's tranquillity.

" Because if you had been charged only with menaces, you
would not have come; and the king in that case would have
hesitated to place such a hostage in my hands."

" A hostage!   I! " she cried in terror.

" A most sacred and venerable one," replied the duke, with
a triumphant glance at the wall.

Catherine let fall her arms in despair; she did not know that
Bussy was encouraging the duke by signs.

" My son," said she at length, " you are quite right; they
are words of peace I bring to you."

" I listen, Mother; and I think we shall now begin to understand each other."

CHAPTER XXVI

LITTLE CAUSES AND GREAT EFFECTS

CATHERINE had, as we have seen, had the worst of the argument.   She was surprised, and began to wonder if her son were
really as decided as he appeared to be, when a slight event
changed the aspect of affairs.   Bussy had been, as we said, encouraging the prince secretly at every word that he thought
dangerous to his cause.   Now his cause was war at any price,
for he wished to stay in Anjou, watch M. de Monsoreau, and
visit his wife.   That policy, extremely simple, complicated in
the highest degree the politics of France.   Great effects have
small causes.   For the reason given, Bussy, with many winks
of the eyes, with furious grimaces, with trenchant gestures, with

frightful play of the eyebrows, urged his master to an obdurate course. The duke, who was afraid of Bussy, allowed himself to be urged; and we have seen how obstinate he was.

Catherine was beaten at all points, and was thinking only of effecting an honourable retreat, when a little event, as unlooked for as the obstinacy of the Duc d'Anjou, came to her support.

Suddenly, when the conversation between mother and son was most lively, and the duke's resistance full of force, Bussy felt his cloak pulled. Wishing to lose nothing of the conversation, he reached out his hand, without turning, and touched a wrist and then an arm and then the shoulder of a man. Thinking then that the matter might be important, he turned. The man was Rémy. Bussy wished to speak; but Rémy put a finger on his lips and drew his master gently into an adjoining chamber.

" What is it, then, Rémy? " asked the count, very impatiently; " and why do you disturb me at such a moment? "

" A letter," said Rémy, in a low tone.

" The devil take you! For a letter you take me away from an interview of so great importance? "

Rémy seemed not to be disturbed by that attack. " There are letters and letters," said he.

" Doubtless," thought Bussy. " Whence does it come? " he asked.

" It is from Méridor."

" Oh! " said Bussy, with eagerness, " from Méridor! Thank you, my good Rémy."

" Then I was not wrong? "

" Can you ever be wrong? Where is that letter? "

" Ah! that is what made me think it of importance,—the messenger would give it only to yourself."

" Is he here? "

" Yes."

" Bring him in."

Rémy opened the door, and a groom entered.

" Here is M. de Bussy," said Rémy.

" Give it to me; I am he whom you seek," said Bussy, putting a half-pistole in his hand.

" Oh, I know you well," said the man, giving him the letter.

" Did she give it to you? "

" No, he."

" What he? " asked Bussy, quickly, as he looked at the writing.

" M. de Saint-Luc."

" Ah, ah! "

Bussy had turned pale slightly, for at that word " he " he imagined for a moment that he had to do with the husband instead of the wife. He turned away to read the letter, and to conceal, while reading it, the emotion which every one must fear to exhibit in reading an important letter, unless he is a Cæsar Borgia, Machiavel, Catherine de Médicis, or the Devil. As he read the letter—with which we are already acquainted— the blood mounted to his head, and filled his eyes; he became purple instead of pale, stood for a moment stupefied, and then, seeing that he was about to fall, threw himself into an armchair near the window.

" Go! " said Rémy to the groom, who was astounded at the effect produced by the letter he had brought. He went away at once, thinking that the letter contained bad news, and fearing that his half-pistole would be taken from him.

Rémy went to the count and shook him by the arm. " *Mordieu!* " he cried; " speak to me this instant, or by the holy Æsculapius, I will bleed you in four places! "

Bussy rose; he was no longer red, no longer stupefied,—he was gloomy. " See, " he said, " what Saint-Luc has done for me; " and he handed the letter to Rémy.

Rémy read it eagerly. " Well, " said he, " this seems to me very fortunate; and Saint-Luc is a gallant man. "

" It is incredible! " stammered Bussy.

" Certainly; but that is not to the point. Here is our position quite changed; I shall have a Comtesse de Bussy for a patient. "

" Yes; she shall be my wife. "

" It seems to me, " said Rémy, " that it will be no great affair to bring that about; she is your wife already more than she was the wife of her husband. "

" Monsoreau dead! "

" Dead! " Rémy repeated; " it is written. "

" Oh, it seems like a dream, Rémy. What! shall I see no more that spectre always coming between me and happiness? Rémy, we are deceiving ourselves. "

" Not the least in the world. *Mordieu!* read it again: ' He fell on a bed of poppies and dandelions so hard that he died there.' "

" But Diane cannot stay at Méridor,—I do not wish it; she must go where she will forget him. "

" Paris will be best; people soon forget at Paris."

" You are right; we will return to the little house in the Rue des Tournelles, and she shall pass there her months of widowhood in obscurity."

" But to go to Paris you must have——"

" What? "

" Peace in Anjou."

" True; oh, *mon Dieu!* what time lost! "

" That means that you are going at once to Méridor."

" No, not I, but you; I must stay here. Besides, she might not like my presence just now."

" How shall I see her? Shall I go to the château? "

" No, go first to the old copse and see if she is there; if she is not, then go to the château."

" What shall I say to her? "

" Say that I am half mad." And pressing the young man's hand, he returned to his place behind the tapestry.

Catherine had been trying to regain her ground. " My son," she had said, " it seemed to me that a mother and son could not fail to understand each other."

" Yet you see that happens sometimes."

" Never when she wishes it."

" When they wish it, you mean," said the duke, seeking a sign of approbation from Bussy for his boldness.

" But I wish it! " cried Catherine. " Do you understand, François? I wish it! " And the expression of her voice was in contrast with her words, for her words were imperative, while her voice was almost supplicating.

" You wish it? " replied the Duc d'Anjou, smiling.

" Yes," said Catherine; " I wish it, and every sacrifice to that end will be readily made."

" Ah! ah! " said François; " the devil! "

" Yes, dear child. What do you ask? What do you demand? Speak."

" Oh, my mother! " said François, almost embarrassed at a victory so complete that it left him no opportunity to act as a stern conqueror.

" Listen, my son. You do not wish to drown the kingdom in blood,—it is not possible; you are neither a bad Frenchman nor a bad brother."

" My brother insulted me, Madame, and I owe him nothing either as brother or king."

" But I, François,—you cannot complain of me? "

" Yes, Madame, you abandoned me," replied the duke, thinking that Bussy was still there and could hear him as before.

" Ah, you wish to kill me! Well, a mother does not care to live to see her children murder each other," cried Catherine, who wished very much to live.

" Oh, do not say that, Madame, you tear my heart!" cried François, whose heart was not torn at all.

Catherine burst into tears. The duke took her hands and tried to reassure her, not without uneasy glances towards the tapestry.

" What do you want?" said Catherine. " At least declare your desires, that we may know where we are."

" What do you want yourself? Come, Mother," said François, " speak! I listen."

" I wish you to return to Paris, dear child,—to return to your brother's court, who will receive you with open arms."

" No, Madame, it is not he whose arms are open to receive me; it is the Bastille."

" No; return, and on my honour, on my love as a mother, I solemnly swear that you shall be received by the king as though you were king and he the Duc d'Anjou."

The duke looked at the tapestry.

" Accept, my son; you shall have honours, guards."

" Oh, Madame, your son gave me guards,—guards of honour, even, since he chose his four favourites."

" Do not reply so; you shall choose your own guards, and M. de Bussy shall be their captain, if you like."

Again the duke glanced at the wall, and to his surprise saw Bussy smiling and applauding by every possible method.

" What is the meaning of this change?" thought the duke. " Is it that he may be captain of my guards?—Then must I accept?" said he aloud, as though talking to himself.

" Yes, yes!" signed Bussy, with head and hands.

" Leave Anjou, and return to Paris?"

" Yes!" signed Bussy, more decidedly than ever.

" Doubtless, dear child," said Catherine; " is it, then, so disagreeable to return to Paris?"

" Faith!" said the duke to himself, " I am all at sea. It was agreed between us that I should refuse her everything, and now he urges me to peace and friendship!"

" Well," asked Catherine, anxiously, " what do you say?"

" Mother," said the duke, who wished to consult with Bussy

in regard to that change of front, " I will reflect, and to-
morrow—"

" I have won," thought Catherine.

They embraced once more, and separated.

CHAPTER XXVII

HOW M. DE MONSOREAU OPENED AND SHUT HIS EYES,
WHICH PROVED THAT HE WAS NOT DEAD

RÉMY rode along, wondering in what humour he should find
Diane, and what he should say to her. He had just arrived at
the park wall, when his horse, which had been trotting, stopped
so suddenly that had he not been a good rider, he would have
been thrown headlong. Rémy, astonished, looked around for
the cause, and saw before him a pool of blood, and a little farther
on, a body lying against the wall. " It is Monsoreau! " he exclaimed, and dismounting, he went forward towards the body.
" It is strange," he said; " he lies dead here, and the blood is
down there. Ah! there is the track; he must have crawled
hither from down there, or rather, that good M. de Saint-Luc
leaned him up against the wall that the blood might not fly to
his head. He died with his eyes open too."

All at once Rémy started back in horror; the two eyes, that
he had seen open, shut again, and a paleness more livid than
ever spread itself over the face of the defunct. Rémy became
almost as pale as M. de Monsoreau, but as he was a doctor, he
quickly recovered his presence of mind, and said to himself, " If
he has shut his eyes he is not dead." And as notwithstanding
his self-possession, the situation was trying, and as the joints of
his knees betrayed a greater weakness than was agreeable, he
sat down, or rather he slid down, to the foot of the tree which
supported him, and so was face to face with the corpse. " And
yet I have read," thought he, " of strange movements after
death, which indicate the beginning of decay. This devil of a
fellow frightens one even when he is dead. Yes, his eyes are quite
closed. There is one method of ascertaining whether he is dead
or not, and that is to shove my sword into him; if he does not
move then, he is certainly dead." And Rémy was preparing
for this charitable action, when suddenly the eyes opened again.
This second incident produced on Rémy an effect contrary to
that of the first. He jumped up as if moved by a spring, and a

cold sweat bathed his forehead. This time the eyes of the dead man remained open. " He is not dead! " murmured Rémy; " he is not dead! Here we are in a nice position! Yes, but if I kill him he will be dead." And he looked at Monsoreau, who seemed also to be looking at him earnestly, as if he divined his thoughts.

" Oh! " cried Rémy, " I cannot do it. God knows that if he were upright before me I would kill him with all my heart; but as he is now, helpless and three parts dead, it would be worse than a crime, it would be an infamy."

" Help! " murmured Monsoreau, " I am dying."

" *Mordieu!* " thought Rémy, " my position is embarrassing. I am a doctor, and as such, bound to succour my fellow-creatures when they suffer. It is true that Monsoreau is so ugly that he can scarcely be called a fellow-creature; still, he is of the same species,—*genus homo*. Come, I must forget that I am the friend of M. de Bussy, and do my duty as a doctor."

" Help! " repeated the wounded man.

" Here I am," said Rémy.

" Bring me a priest and a doctor."

" The doctor is here, and perhaps he will enable you to dispense with the priest."

" Rémy," said Monsoreau, " by what chance—"

As may be seen, Monsoreau was faithful to his character. In his agony he was still suspicious and asked questions.

Rémy understood all that the question might mean. This was no beaten road, and no one was likely to be there except upon particular business; the question was therefore quite natural.

" How is it that you are here? " repeated Monsoreau, to whom his suspicions restored a portion of his strength.

" *Pardieu!* " Rémy replied, " because a mile or two from here I met M. de Saint-Luc—"

" Ah! my murderer."

" And he said, ' Rémy, go to the old copse; there you will find a man dead.' "

" Dead? "

" Yes; he thought so. You mustn't think badly of him for that; then I came, I saw, you were conquered."

" And now tell me frankly, am I mortally wounded? "

" Ah, the devil! " said Rémy, " that is a great question. However, I will find out; let us see."

Rémy approached Monsoreau carefully, took off his cloak, his doublet, and shirt. The sword had penetrated between the sixth and seventh ribs.

" Hum! " said Rémy, " do you suffer much? "

" In my back, not in my chest."

" Ah, let me see; where? "

" Below the shoulder-bone."

" The steel must have come against a bone." And he began to examine. " No, I am wrong," said he; " the sword came against nothing, but passed right through."

Monsoreau fainted after this examination.

" Ah, that is all right! " said Rémy,—" syncope, low pulse, cold in the hands and legs. The devil! the widowhood of Madame de Monsoreau will not last long, I fear."

At this moment a slight bloody foam rose to the lips of the wounded man. Rémy drew from his pocket his lancet-case, then, tearing off a strip from the patient's shirt, bound it round his arm. " We shall see," said he. " If the blood flows, Madame Diane is perhaps not a widow; but if it does not flow— Ah, ah! it flows! Pardon, my dear M. de Bussy, pardon! but, faith, one is a doctor before everything."

Presently the patient breathed, and opened his eyes. " Oh! " stammered he, " I thought all was over."

" Not yet, my dear monsieur; it is even possible—"

" That I shall live? "

" Oh, *mon Dieu!* yes; but let me close the wound. Stop; do not move. Nature at this moment is aiding my work. I make the blood flow, and she stops it. Ah! nature is a great doctor, my dear monsieur. Let me wipe your lips. See, the bleeding has stopped already. Good; all goes well,—or rather, badly."

" Badly? "

" No, not for you; but I know what I mean. My dear M. de Monsoreau, I am afraid I shall have the happiness to cure you."

" You think I shall get well? "

" Alas, yes! "

" You are a singular doctor, M. Rémy."

" Never mind, as long as I cure you," said he, rising.

" Do not abandon me," said the count.

" Ah! you talk too much. Too much talking is injurious. That wouldn't be bad,—I ought to tell him to cry out."

" I don't understand you."

" Fortunately. Now your wound is dressed. I will go to the château and fetch assistance."

" And what must I do meanwhile? "

" Keep quite still; do not stir; breathe lightly, and try not to cough.   Which is the nearest house? "

" The Château de Méridor."

" How shall I reach it? " said Rémy, affecting ignorance.

" Get over the wall, and you will find yourself in the park; or follow the park wall and you will come to the gate."

" Very well; I go."

" Thanks, generous man."

" Generous, indeed, if you only knew all."

He soon arrived at the château, where all the inhabitants were busy looking for the body of the count; for Saint-Luc, to gain time, had given them a wrong direction.   Rémy came among them like a thunderbolt, and was so eager to bring them to the rescue that Diane looked at him with surprise.

" I thought he was Bussy's friend," she murmured, as Rémy disappeared, taking with him a wheelbarrow, lint, and water.

CHAPTER XXVIII

HOW M. LE DUC D'ANJOU WENT TO MÉRIDOR TO CONGRATULATE MADAME DE MONSOREAU ON THE DEATH OF HER HUSBAND, AND FOUND HIM THERE BEFORE HIM

As soon as the duke left his mother, he hastened to Bussy, to know the meaning of all his signs.   Bussy, who was reading Saint-Luc's letter for the fifth time, received the prince with a gracious smile.

" What!   Monseigneur takes the trouble to come to my house to seek me? "

" Yes, *mordieu!*   I want an explanation."

" From me? "

" Yes, from you."

" I listen, Monseigneur."

" You tell me to steel myself against the suggestions of my mother, and to sustain the attack valiantly.   I do so; and in the hottest of the fight you tell me to surrender."

" I gave you all those charges, Monseigneur, because I was ignorant of the object for which your mother came; but now that I see that she has come to promote your Highness's honour and glory—"

" What do you mean? "

" To be sure. What does your Highness want? To triumph over your enemies, do you not? For I do not believe, as some people say, that you dream of becoming King of France."

The duke looked sullen.

" Some might counsel you to it, but, believe me, they are your most cruel enemies. Consider for yourself, Monseigneur. Have you one hundred thousand men, ten millions of livres, alliances with foreigners; and, above all, would you turn against your king? "

" My king did not hesitate to turn against me."

" Ah! there you are right. Well! declare yourself; get crowned; take the title of King of France. And if you succeed, I ask nothing better; I should grow great with you."

" Who speaks of being king? " cried the duke, angrily, " you discuss a question which I have never proposed, even to myself."

" Well, then, that is settled. Let them give you a guard and five hundred thousand livres. Obtain, before peace is signed, a subsidy from Anjou, to carry on the war. Once you have it, you can keep it. So we shall have men, money, power; and we can go to—God knows what! "

" But once they have me at Paris, they will laugh at me."

" Oh! impossible, Monseigneur; did you not hear what the queen-mother offered you? "

" She offered me many things."

" That disquiets you? "

" Yes."

" But, among other things, she offered you a company of guards, even if I commanded it."

" Yes, she offered that."

" Well, accept; I will be captain, D'Antragues and Livarot lieutenants, and Ribeirac ensign. Let us get up your company for you, and see if they dare to laugh at you then."

" Faith! I believe you are right, Bussy; I will think of it."

" Do so, Monseigneur."

" What were you reading so attentively when I came in? "

" Oh! a letter, which interests you still more than me. Where the devil were my brains, that I did not show it to you? "

" What is it? "

" Sad news, Monseigneur; Monsoreau is dead."

" What! " cried the duke, with a surprise which Bussy thought was a joyful one.

" Dead, Monseigneur."

" Dead? M. de Monsoreau? "

" *Mon Dieu!* yes; are we not all mortal? "

" Yes; but one doesn't die suddenly like that."

" It depends on circumstances; suppose you are killed? "

" Then he was killed? "

" So it seems; and by Saint-Luc, with whom he quarrelled."

" Oh, that dear Saint-Luc! "

" I did not think he was one of your Highness's friends."

" Oh, he is my brother's, and, since we are to be reconciled, his friends are mine. But are you sure? "

" As sure as I can be. Here is a letter from Saint-Luc, announcing it; and I have sent Rémy, my doctor, to present my condolences to the old baron."

" Dead! Monsoreau dead! " repeated the Duc d'Anjou; " dead *by himself!* "

These words, " by himself," like " that dear Saint-Luc," were a naïve betrayal of his thought.

" He is not dead by himself," said Bussy, " since Saint-Luc killed him."

" Oh, I understand! " said the duke.

" Had Monseigneur perchance given orders to have him killed by some one else? "

" Faith, no! and you? "

" Oh! I, Monseigneur,—I am not a great prince, to do that sort of work by others; I am obliged to do such things myself."

" Oh, Monsoreau! Monsoreau! " cried the prince, with his malignant smile.

" Why, Monseigneur, one would say you hated the poor count."

" No, it was you who hated him."

" And with good reason," said Bussy, blushing in spite of himself; " did he not subject me to a terrible humiliation on the part of your Highness? "

" You remember it still? "

" Oh, *mon Dieu!* no,—as you see; but you, Monseigneur, whose friend and tool he was—"

" Well, well; get my horse saddled, Bussy."

" What for? "

" To go to Méridor; I wish to pay a visit of condolence to Madame de Monsoreau. I have been intending a visit for some time, and I do not know why it has not taken place sooner."

" Now that Monsoreau is dead," thought Bussy; " now that I am no longer afraid of his selling his wife to the duke,—it is no matter if he does see her. If he should attack her, I can defend her. Come, since I have the chance to see her again, let me profit by it."

A quarter of an hour after, the prince, Bussy, and ten gentlemen, rode to Méridor, with that pleasure which fine weather, turf, and youth inspire in men and in horses.

Upon seeing that magnificent cavalcade approach, the porter at the château came to ask the names of the visitors.

"The Duc d'Anjou," replied the prince.

The porter blew his horn; and soon windows were opened, and they heard the noise of bolts and bars as the door was unfastened, and the old baron appeared on the threshold, holding in his hand a bunch of keys.

"It is wonderful how little Monsoreau is regretted!" said the duke; "see, Bussy, every one looks as if nothing had happened."

A woman appeared on the steps.

"Ah! there is the beautiful Diane!" cried the duke. "Do you see, Bussy; do you see?"

"Yes, to be sure, I see her," said the young man; "but," he added in a low voice, "I don't see Rémy."

Diane, indeed, came out of the house, and behind her came a litter, on which lay Monsoreau. His eyes were bright with fever, or with jealousy, and he resembled a sultan of the Indies on his palanquin, rather than a dead man on his funeral couch.

"What does this mean?" cried the duke to his companion, who had turned whiter than the handkerchief with which he was trying to hide his emotion.

"Long live the Duc d'Anjou!" cried Monsoreau, raising his hand in the air by a violent effort.

"Take care; you will hurt yourself," said a voice behind him. It was Rémy.

Astonishment does not last long at court,—on the face, at least; so with a smile the duke said, "Oh, my dear count, what a happy surprise! Do you know we heard you were dead?"

"Come near, Monseigneur, and let me kiss your hand. Thank God, not only I am not dead, but I shall live, I hope, to serve you with more ardour than ever."

As for Bussy, who was neither prince nor husband,—those two social positions in which dissimulation is of the first necessity,—he felt stunned, and scarcely dared to look at Diane. This treasure, twice lost to him, it made him ill to see so near her possessor.

"And you, M. de Bussy," said Monsoreau, "receive my thanks, for it is almost to you that I owe my life."

" To me? " stammered the young man, who thought the count was mocking him.

" Yes; indirectly, it is true, for here is my saviour," said he, turning to Rémy, who would willingly have sunk into the earth. " My friends owe it to him that they have me still with them." Then, in spite of the signs made by the poor doctor for him to remain silent, which he understood to be made with reference to his feeble condition, he spoke emphatically of the care, the skill, and the zeal which Rémy had manifested in his behalf.

The duke frowned; Bussy looked at Rémy with a terrible expression. The poor follow, standing behind Monsoreau, could reply only with a gesture which said, " Alas! it is not my fault."

" I hear," continued the count, " that Rémy one day found you dying, as he found me. It is a tie of friendship between us, M. de Bussy; and when Monsoreau loves, he loves well. It is true that when he hates, it is also with all his heart."

" Come, then," said the duke, getting off his horse, and offering his hand to Diane, " deign, beautiful Diane, to do us the honours of the house, which we thought to find in grief, but which we find still the abode of joy. As for you, Monsoreau, rest; you require it."

" Monseigneur," said the count, " it shall never be said that Monsoreau, while he lived, allowed another to do the honours of his house to you; my servants will carry me, and wherever you go, I shall follow."

It seemed as if the duke recognised the real thought of the count, for he dropped the hand of Diane. Then Monsoreau breathed freely. Bussy approached Diane, and Monsoreau smiled; he took her hand, and he still smiled.

" Here is a great change, Monsieur the Count," said Diane, in a low tone.

" Alas! why is it not greater? "

CHAPTER XXIX

THE INCONVENIENCE OF LARGE LITTERS AND NARROW DOORS

BUSSY did not leave Diane; the smiles of Monsoreau gave him a liberty which he was only too glad to make use of.

" Madame," said he to Diane, " I am in truth the most miserable of men. On the news of Monsoreau's death, I advised the prince to return to Paris, and to come to terms with his mother. He consented; and now you remain in Anjou."

"Oh, Louis," she replied, pressing Bussy's hand, "do you dare to say that we are unhappy? So many happy days, so many unspeakable delights the remembrance of which makes my heart quiver,—do you forget them all?"

"I forget nothing, Madame; on the contrary, I remember but too much, and that is why I suffer as I do at losing this happiness. What shall I do if I return to Paris, a hundred leagues from you? My heart sinks at the thought, Diane."

Diane looked at him, and saw so much grief in his eyes that she lowered her head, and reflected. The young man clasped his hands and looked at her imploringly.

"Very well!" said Diane, suddenly; "you will go to Paris, Louis, and I will go also."

"What!" cried the young man, "you will leave M. de Monsoreau?"

"No, he would not allow me to do so; he must come with us."

"Wounded, ill as he is? Impossible!"

"He will come, I tell you." And leaving Bussy, she went to the prince, who, in a bad humour, was speaking to Monsoreau. At sight of Diane the count's face brightened; but she approached the duke, and he frowned.

"Monseigneur," said she, "they say your Highness is fond of flowers; if you will come with me, I will show you the most beautiful in Anjou."

The duke offered her his hand.

"Where are you about to take Monseigneur?" asked Monsoreau, uneasily.

"Into the greenhouse."

"Ah, well! carry me there."

"Faith!" thought Rémy, "I believe now that I did well in not killing him; thank God, he will kill himself."

Diane smiled on Bussy, and said to him in a low voice, "Do not let M. de Monsoreau suspect that you are about to leave Anjou, and I will manage all."

"Good!" said Bussy; and approaching the prince, he whispered, "Monseigneur, be prudent; do not let Monsoreau know that we intend to make peace."

"Why not?"

"Because he might tell the queen-mother, to make a friend of her; and she would be less inclined to bestow bounties on us."

"You are right; you suspect him, then?"

"Yes, I do."

"Well, so do I; I believe he only counterfeited death to deceive us."

"No, he really received a sword-thrust through his body; and but for that fool of a Rémy, he would have died. His soul must be glued to his body."

They arrived at the conservatory, and Diane continued to smile charmingly on the prince. He passed first, then Diane, and Monsoreau wished to follow, but it was impossible. His litter was too large to go through the door. At sight of the narrow door he uttered a groan. Diane went on quietly, without looking at him; but Bussy, who understood her, said to him, " It is useless to try, Monsieur the Count; your litter will not pass."

"Monseigneur!" cried Monsoreau, "do not go into that conservatory; some of the flowers exhale dangerous perfumes." Then he fainted.

Rémy resumed his authority; he directed that the wounded man should be conveyed to his chamber. "Now," said he to the young man, "what must I do?"

"Eh, *pardieu!*" said Bussy; "finish what you have so well begun. Remain with him and cure him." Then he informed Diane of what had happened.

Diane immediately left the duke and returned to the château.

"Have we succeeded?" said Bussy to her as she passed.

"I hope so; do not go away without having seen Gertrude."

When Monsoreau opened his eyes again, he saw Diane standing at his bedside. "Ah, it is you, Madame," said he; "to-night we leave for Paris."

Rémy cried out in horror; but Monsoreau paid no attention to him.

"Can you think of such a thing, with your wound?" said Diane, quietly.

"Madame, I would rather die than suffer; and though I may die on the road, we start to-night."

"As you please, Monsieur."

"Then make your preparations."

"My preparations are soon made; but may I ask the reason of this sudden determination?"

"I will tell you, Madame, when you have no more flowers to show to the prince, and when my doors are large enough to admit litters."

Diane bowed.

"But, Madame—" said Rémy.

" Monsieur the Count wishes it," replied she, " and my duty is to obey." And she left the room.

As the duke was making his adieux to the Baron de Méridor, Gertrude appeared, and said aloud to the duke that her mistress regretted that, being detained near the count, she could not have the honour of saying farewell to his Highness; then she said softly to Bussy that Diane would set off for Paris that evening.

The party of visitors set out on their return. On the way, the duke, unaware of Monsoreau's purpose, meditated on the danger there would be in yielding too easily to the queen-mother's wishes; for the smiles of Diane made Anjou attractive to him. Bussy had foreseen this, and was very sure he would wish to remain.

" Do you know, Bussy," said the duke, " I have been reflecting."

" Good, Monseigneur, and about what? "

" That it is not wise to give in at once to my mother."

" You are right; she thinks herself clever enough without that."

" Whereas, you see, if we keep the matter open for a week, and give fêtes, and call together the nobility around us, she will see how strong we are."

" Well reasoned, but still—"

" I will stay here a week; depend upon it, I shall draw new concessions from the queen."

Bussy appeared to reflect. " Well, Monseigneur," said he, " perhaps you are right; but the king, not knowing your intentions, may become annoyed. He is very irascible."

" You are right; I must send some one to greet my brother in my name, and announce to him my return,—that will give me the week I need."

" Yes; but that some one will run great risks."

" If I change my mind, you mean? "

" Yes, and in spite of your promise, you would do so if you thought it for your interest."

" Perhaps."

" Then they will send your messenger to the Bastille."

" I will give him a letter, and not let him know what he is carrying."

" On the contrary, give him no letter, and let him know."

" Then no one will go."

" Oh, I know some one."

" Who? "

" I, Monseigneur."

" You? "

" Yes, I like difficult negotiations."

" Bussy, my dear Bussy, if you will do that, I shall be eternally grateful."

Bussy smiled; he knew the measure of that eternal gratitude. The duke thought he hesitated.

" And I will give you ten thousand crowns for your journey," added he.

" Thanks, Monseigneur; but these things cannnot be paid for."

" Then you will go? "

" Yes."

" When? "

" Whenever you like."

" The sooner the better."

" This evening if you wish it."

" Brave Bussy! dear Bussy! you really consent, then? "

" Do I consent? " said Bussy. " You know well, Monseigneur, that in the service of your Highness I would pass through fire. It is agreed, then; I go to-night. You will stay here and enjoy yourself, and get me something good from the queen-mother."

" I will not forget."

Bussy then prepared to depart as soon as the signal should come from Méridor. It did not come till the next morning, for the count had felt himself so feeble that he had been forced to take a night's rest. But early in the morning a messenger came to announce to Bussy that the count had set off for Paris in a litter, attended by Rémy, Diane, and Gertrude, on horseback. Bussy jumped on his horse, and took the same road.

CHAPTER XXX

WHAT TEMPER THE KING WAS IN WHEN SAINT-LUC REAPPEARED AT THE LOUVRE

SINCE the departure of Catherine, Henri, although relying on his ambassador, had thought only of arming himself against the attacks of his brother. He occupied himself in drawing up long lists of proscriptions, in which were inscribed in alphabetical order all who had not shown themselves zealous for his cause. The lists became longer every day; and under S and L—that is to say, twice over—was inscribed the name of M. de Saint-Luc. And besides, the anger of the king was stimulated by the comments of the court, by the treacherous insinuations of the courtiers, and by bitter accusations based on Saint-Luc's flight to Anjou,—a flight which became treasonable on the day when the duke, himself a fugitive, directed his course to that province. In fact, should not Saint-Luc be regarded as the duke's quartermaster going to Angers to prepare quarters for the prince?

In the midst of all this movement and agitation, Chicot, encouraging the favourites to sharpen their daggers and rapiers to cut and stab the enemies of his most Christian Majesty, was magnificent to behold; and the more so because, while appearing to play the part of a fly on a coach, he was in fact engaged in serious occupations. Little by little, and, so to speak, man by man, he got ready an army for the service of the king.

Suddenly one afternoon when the king was taking supper with the queen, Chicot entered and stood with legs and arms stretched apart like those of a manikin, which are pulled apart by a string.

" *Ouf !* " he said.

" What is it? " asked the king.

" M. de Saint-Luc," replied Chicot.

" M. de Saint-Luc! " exclaimed his Majesty.

" Yes."

" At Paris? "

" Yes."

" At the Louvre? "

" Yes."

On that triple affirmation the king rose from the table, red and trembling. It would have been difficult to say by what sentiments he was agitated. He went hastily out of the chamber, Chicot following. Once outside, he exclaimed in excited tones, " What has he come for,—the traitor? "

" Who knows? "

" He comes, I am sure, as deputy from the States of Anjou,— as an envoy from my rebellious brother. He makes use of the rebellion as an opportunity to come here and insult me."

" Who knows? "

" Or perhaps," said Henri, walking up and down the gallery with an irregular step which betrayed his agitation, " he comes to ask me for his property, of which I have kept back the revenues,—which may have been rather an abuse of power, as, after all, he has committed no crime."

" Who knows? "

" Ah, you repeat always the same thing! *Mort de ma vie!* you irritate me with your eternal ' Who knows? ' "

" Eh, *mordieu!* do you think you are very amusing with your everlasting questions? "

" At least you might reply something."

" And what should I reply? Do you take me for an ancient oracle? Do you take me for Jupiter, for Apollo, or for Manto? It is you who are tiresome with your foolish suppositions."

" M. Chicot! "

" Well, what is it, M. Henri? "

" Chicot, my friend, you see my grief and laugh at me."

" Do not have any grief, *mordieu!* "

" But every one betrays me."

" Who knows? *Ventre de biche!* who knows? "

Henri went down to his cabinet, where, at the news of Saint-Luc's return, a number of gentlemen had assembled, who were looking at him with evident distrust and animosity. He, however, seemed quite unmoved by this. He had brought his wife with him also, and she was seated, wrapped in her travelling-cloak, when the king entered in an excited state.

" Ah, Monsieur, you here? " he cried.

" Yes, Sire," replied Saint-Luc.

" Really, your presence at the Louvre surprises me."

" Sire, I am only surprised that under the circumstances your Majesty did not expect me."

" What do you mean, Monsieur? "

" Sire, your Majesty is in danger."

" Danger! " cried the courtiers.

" Yes, gentlemen; a real, a serious danger, in which the king has need of the smallest as well as the greatest of those devoted to him. Therefore I come to lay at his feet my humble services."

" Ah! " said Chicot, " you see, my son, that I was right to say, ' Who knows? ' "

Henri did not reply at once; he would not yield immediately. After a pause, he said, " Monsieur, you have only done your duty; your services are due to us."

" The services of all the king's subjects are due to him, I know, Sire; but in these times many people forget to pay their debts. I, Sire, come to pay mine, happy if your Majesty will deign to number me always among your debtors."

Henri, placated by that gentleness and humility, took a step towards Saint-Luc. "Then," said he, "you return without any other motive than that which you state,—without any mission, or safe-conduct?"

"Sire, I return simply and purely for that reason. Now, your Majesty may throw me into the Bastille, or have me shot; but I shall have done my duty. Sire, Anjou is on fire; Touraine is about to revolt; Guyenne is rising. M. le Duc d'Anjou is hard at work in the west and south of France."

"He is well supported, is he not?"

"Sire," said Saint-Luc, who understood the meaning of the question, "neither counsel nor argument can stay the duke; but M. de Bussy, firm as he is, cannot reassure your brother under the terror with which your Majesty inspires him."

"Ah! he trembles then, the rebel?" said the king; and he smiled under his mustache.

"*Tudieu!*" said Chicot, caressing his chin, "that is a man of genius." And pushing the king with his elbow, "Stand aside, Henri," said he, "so that I may go and shake hands with M. de Saint-Luc."

The king followed him, and going up to his old favourite, and laying his hand on his shoulder, said, "You are welcome, Saint-Luc!"

"Ah, Sire," cried Saint-Luc, kissing the king's hand, "I find again my beloved master!"

"Yes; but you, my poor Saint-Luc,—you have grown thin."

"It is with grief at having displeased your Majesty," said a feminine voice.

Now, although the voice was soft and respectful, Henri frowned, for it was as distasteful to him as the noise of thunder was to Augustus. "Madame de Saint-Luc!" said he. "Ah! I forgot."

Jeanne threw herself at his feet.

"Rise, Madame," said he; "I love all that bear the name of Saint-Luc." Jeanne took his hand and kissed it; but he withdrew it quickly.

"You must convert the king," said Chicot to the young woman; "you are pretty enough for it."

But Henri turned his back to her, and passing his arm round Saint-Luc's neck, said, "Then we have made peace, Saint-Luc?"

"Say rather, Sire, that the pardon is granted."

"Madame," said Chicot, "a good wife should not leave her husband;" and he pushed her after the king and Saint-Luc.

CHAPTER XXXI

IN WHICH WE MEET TWO IMPORTANT PERSONAGES WHOM WE HAVE LOST SIGHT OF FOR SOME TIME

THERE are two of the personages mentioned in this story, about whom the reader has the right to ask for information. We mean an enormous monk, with thick eyebrows and large lips, whose neck was diminishing every day; and a large donkey whose sides were gradually swelling out like a balloon. The monk resembled a hogshead; and the ass was like a child's crib, supported by four posts. The one inhabited a cell at Ste. Geneviève, and the other the stable at the same convent. The one was called Gorenflot, and the other Panurge. Both were enjoying the most properous lot that ever fell to a monk and an ass.

The monks surrounded their illustrious brother with cares and attentions; and Panurge fared well for his master's sake. If a missionary arrived from foreign countries, or a secret legate from the pope, they pointed out to him Brother Gorenflot, that double model of the church preaching and militant; they showed Gorenflot in all his glory,—that is to say, in the midst of a feast, seated at a table in which a hollow had been cut for his sacred stomach,—and their hearts dilated with noble pride as they showed the holy traveller that Gorenflot consumed the rations of eight ordinary monks. And when the new-comer had piously contemplated this spectacle, " An admirably gifted nature! " the prior would say, clasping his hands with an upward look. " Brother Gorenflot is a gastronome; and he also cultivates the arts. You see what an eater he is; ah! if you had but heard his sermon one famous night, in which he offered to devote himself for the triumph of the faith. It is a mouth which speaks like that of Saint Chrysostom, and swallows like that of Gargantua."

Sometimes, however, it happens that in the midst of all these splendours a cloud settles on Gorenflot's brow. He loses his appetite for the allurements of the table, and his desire for wine; he is sad; he dreams. Then the report goes around that the worthy monk is in an ecstasy like Saint Francis, or in a swoon like Saint Theresa, and the admiration increases. He is no longer a monk, he is a saint; he is even a demigod. " Hush! " they would say; " let us not disturb Brother Gorenflot's meditations." The prior awaits the moment when he gives some

M

signs of life; he then approaches the monk, takes his hand, and respectfully addresses him. Gorenflot raises his head and looks at the prior with lustreless eyes; he comes forth from another world.

" What are you doing, my worthy brother? " asks the prior.

" I? " Gorenflot says.

" Yes, you; you are doing something? "

" Yes, my father; I am composing a sermon."

" Like that you gave us on the night of the holy League? "

Every time that any one spoke of that sermon, Gorenflot sighed and said, " What a pity I did not write it! "

" A man like you has no need to write," the prior would reply. " No, you speak from inspiration; you open your mouth, and the words of God flow from your lips."

" Do you think so? " sighed Gorenflot.

However, Gorenflot was not entirely happy. He, who at first thought his banishment from the convent an immense misfortune, discovered in his exile infinite joys before unknown to him. He sighed for liberty,—liberty with Chicot, the joyous companion; with Chicot, whom he loved without knowing why. Since his return to the convent, he had never been allowed to go out. He made no attempt to combat this decision, but he grew sadder from day to day. The prior saw this, and at last said to him, " My dear brother, no one can fight against his vocation; yours is to fight for the faith. Go, then; fulfil your mission. Only watch well over your precious life, and return for the great day."

" What great day? "

" That of the Fête Dieu."

" Ita," replied Gorenflot, with an air of profound wisdom. " But give me some money to bestow in alms in a Christian manner."

The prior went at once for a large purse, which he offered, open, to Gorenflot. Gorenflot plunged in his great hand. " You will see what I shall bring back to the convent," he said, transferring to a pocket in his frock the money he borrowed from the prior.

" You have your text, have you not, dear brother? "

" Yes, certainly."

" Confide it to me."

" Willingly, but to you alone; it is this, ' The flail which beats the corn, beats itself.' "

" Oh, magnificent! sublime! " cried the prior.

" Now, my father, am I free? "

" Yes, my son, go and walk in the way of the Lord."

Gorenflot saddled Panurge, mounted him with the aid of two vigorous monks, and left the convent about seven in the evening. It was the same day on which Saint-Luc arrived at Paris from Méridor.

Gorenflot, having passed through the Rue St. Etienne, was on the point of turning to the right, when suddenly Panurge stopped; a strong hand was laid on his croup.

" Who is there? " cried Gorenflot, in terror.

" A friend."

Gorenflot tried to turn, but he could not. " What do you want? " said he.

" Will my venerable brother show me the way to the Corne d'Abondance? "

" *Morbleu!* it is M. Chicot! " cried Gorenflot, joyfully.

" Precisely; I was going to seek you at the convent, when I saw you come out, and followed you until we should be alone. *Ventre de biche!* how thin you are! "

" But what are you carrying, M. Chicot? " said the monk; " you appear laden."

" It is some venison which I have stolen from the king."

" Dear M. Chicot! and under the other arm? "

" A bottle of Cyprus wine sent by a king to my king."

" Let me see! "

" It is my wine, and I love it much; do not you, Brother? "

" Oh, oh! " cried Gorenflot, raising his eyes and hands to heaven, and beginning to sing in a voice which shook the neighbouring windows. It was the first time he had sung for a month.

CHAPTER XXXII

DIANE'S SECOND JOURNEY TO PARIS

LET us leave the two friends entering the Corne d'Abondance (whither Chicot, the reader will have noticed, never conducted Gorenflot without a purpose in so doing, the importance of which the monk was far from suspecting), and return to the litter of M. de Monsoreau and to Bussy, who set out with the intention of following them. It is not difficult for a cavalier well mounted to overtake foot travellers, but still he incurs a risk,—that of going by them; and this happened to Bussy.

It was towards the end of May. The heat was great, and about noon M. de Monsoreau wished to make a halt in a little wood, which was near the road; and as they had a horse laden with provisions, they remained there until the great heat of the day had gone by. During this time Bussy passed them. But he had not travelled, as we may readily believe, without inquiring if a party on horseback, and a litter carried by peasants, had been seen. Until he had passed the village of Durtal, he had obtained the most satisfactory information, and, convinced that they were before him, had ridden on slowly, standing in his stirrups whenever he came to an elevation, to look for the party whom he followed. But suddenly all traces of them vanished, and on arriving at La Flèche he felt certain he must have passed them on the road. Then he remembered the little wood, and doubted not that they had been resting there when he passed. He installed himself at a little inn which had the advantage of being opposite the principal hotel, where he was sure that Monsoreau would stop; and he remained at the window watching. About four o'clock he saw a courier arrive, and half an hour afterwards the whole party. He waited till nine o'clock, and then he saw the courier set out again, and after him the litter, then Diane, Rémy, and Gertrude on horseback. He mounted his horse and followed them, keeping them in sight. Monsoreau scarcely allowed Diane to move from his side. He talked to her, or rather he scolded her. That visit to the conservatory served as a text for inexhaustible comments, and a multitude of malicious questions.

Rémy and Gertrude were sulky towards each other, or to speak more correctly Rémy meditated, and Gertrude sulked towards him. The explanation of that coolness is very simple: Rémy saw no further necessity for being in love with Gertrude, since Diane was in love with Bussy.

The *cortège* advanced, some disputing, others sulking. At length Bussy, who followed the cavalcade at a considerable distance, gave a long shrill whistle, with which he had been in the habit of calling his servants at his hotel. Rémy recognised it at once. Diane started and looked at the young man, who made an affirmative sign; then he came up to her and whispered, "It is he!"

"Who is speaking to you, Madame?" said Monsoreau.

"To me, Monsieur?"

"Yes, I saw a shadow pass close to you, and heard a voice."

"It is M. Rémy; are you also jealous of him?"

"No, but I prefer that those around me speak aloud; it interests me."

"There are some things which cannot be said aloud before Monsieur the Count, however," said Gertrude, coming to the rescue.

"Why not?"

"For two reasons,—because some would not interest you, and because some would interest you too much."

"And of which kind is what M. Rémy has just whispered?"

"Of the latter."

"What did Rémy say to you, Madame?"

"I said, Monsieur the Count, that if you excite yourself so much, you will be dead before we have gone a third of the way."

Monsoreau grew deadly pale.

"He is expecting you behind," whispered Rémy, again; "ride slowly, and he will overtake you."

Monsoreau, who heard a murmur, tried to rise and look back after Diane.

"Another movement like that, Monsieur the Count, and you will bring on the bleeding again," said Rémy.

Diane turned and rode back a little way, while Rémy walked by the litter to occupy the count's attention. A few seconds after, Bussy was by her side. They had no need of speech to understand each other; they remained for some moments in a tender embrace.

"You see that when you go away I follow you," said Bussy, breaking the silence.

"Oh, I shall be happy if I know you are always so near to me!"

"But by day he will see us."

"No; by day you can ride afar off. It is only I who will see you, my Louis. From the summit of some hill, at the turn of some road, your plume waving, your handkerchief fluttering in the breeze, will speak to me in your name, and tell me that you love me."

"Speak on, my beloved Diane; you do not know what music I find in your voice."

"And when we travel by night, which we shall often do, for Rémy has told him that the freshness of the evening is good for his wounds, then, as this evening, from time to time I will stay behind; from time to time I shall be able to press you in my arms, and to tell you, with a rapid pressure of the hand, all that I shall have thought of you during the day!"

" Oh, I love you! I love you! " murmured Bussy.

" Do you know," said Diane, " I think that our souls are so closely united that even when we are apart from each other, without speaking to or even seeing each other, we can be happy in our thoughts."

" Oh, yes! but to see you, to hold you in my arms,—oh, Diane, Diane! "

The horses came together, and the two lovers embraced each other, and forgot the world.

Suddenly they heard a voice which made them both tremble, Diane with fear, and Bussy with anger.

" Diane! " it cried, " where are you? Answer me."

" Oh, it is he! I had forgotten him," said Diane. " Sweet dream, frightful awaking! "

" Listen, Diane; we are together. Say one word, and nothing can separate us more; Diane, let us fly! What prevents us? Before us is happiness and liberty. One word, and we go; one word, and, lost to him, you belong to me forever."

" And my father? "

" When he shall know how I love you? "

" Oh! a father! "

That single word recalled Bussy to himself. " I will do nothing by violence, dear Diane," said he; " order, and I obey."

" Listen," said Diane, offering her hand; " our destiny is there. Let us be stronger than the demon who persecutes us. Fear nothing, and you shall see if I know how to love."

" Must we then separate? "

" Countess! " cried the voice, " reply, or if I kill myself in doing it, I will jump from this infernal litter."

" Adieu, Bussy; he will do as he says."

" You pity him? "

" Jealous! " said Diane, with an adorable smile.

Bussy let her go.

In a moment she was by the litter, and found the count half fainting.

" Ah! " cried he, " where were you, Madame? "

" Where should I have been, if not behind you? "

" At my side, Madame; do not leave me again."

From time to time this scene was renewed. Rémy said to himself, " if he is strangled by rage, the physician's honour is safe." But he did not die; on the contrary, at the end of ten days, when they arrived at Paris, he was decidedly better. During these ten days Diane had conquered all Bussy's pride, and had persuaded him to come and visit Monsoreau, who always showed him much friendship. Rémy tended the husband and gave notes to the wife.

"Æsculapius and Mercury," said he; "my functions accumulate."

CHAPTER XXXIII

HOW THE AMBASSADOR OF THE DUC D'ANJOU ARRIVED AT THE LOUVRE, AND THE RECEPTION HE MET WITH

MEANTIME neither Catherine nor the Duc d'Anjou reappeared at the Louvre, and the report of a dissension between the brothers became every day more widely extended and more important.

The king had received no message from his mother, and instead of concluding, according to the proverb, "No news, good news," he shook his head and said, "No news, bad news." The favourites added, "François, badly counselled, has detained your mother."

"Badly counselled." In fact, all the policy of this singular reign and of the three preceding reigns was comprised in those words. Badly counselled was Charles IX. when he authorised the massacre of Saint Bartholomew. Badly counselled was François II. when he ordered the massacre at Amboise. Badly counselled had been Henri II. when he burned so many heretics and conspirators. And now they dared not say, "Your brother has the family blood in his veins. He wishes, like the rest, to dethrone or poison; he would do to you what you did to your elder brother,—what your elder brother did to his, what your mother has taught you to do to one another." No, a king at that period, a king of the sixteenth century, would have taken such remarks as insulting,—for a king was then a man; and civilisation alone has availed to make of him a facsimile of God, like Louis XIV., or an irresponsible myth, like a constitutional king. The favourites said, therefore, to Henri III., "Sire, your brother is badly counselled."

Now, as only one person was able to counsel François, it was against Bussy that the cry was raised, which became every day more and more furious. At last the news arrived that the duke had sent an ambassador.

How did that news come? Who brought it? Who published it? It would be as easy to say whence come the whirlwinds that rise in the air, or the whirlwinds of dust in the country, or the whirlwinds of noise in the cities. There is a demon who puts wings to certain kinds of news and lets them loose like eagles into space.

When this news of which we now speak arrived at the Louvre there was a general excitement. The king became pale with anger, and the favourites, outdoing, according to their custom, the passion of their master, became livid. They swore. It would be difficult to repeat all that they swore; but they swore among other things that if that ambassador was an old man he should be scoffed at, derided, and imprisoned; if he was a young man he should be cut into small pieces, which should be sent to all the provinces as an example of royal wrath. And the favourites, according to their custom, took to sharpening their swords, exercising themselves in fencing, and practising with their daggers. Chicot left his sword in its scabbard, and his dagger in its sheath, and gave himself up to profound reflection.

The king, seeing Chicot reflect, and remembering that on one occasion he had been of the same mind with the queen-mother, whose opinion had been justified by the event, understood that in Chicot was embodied the wisdom of his kingdom, and he questioned him.

" Sire," Chicot replied, " either the Duc d'Anjou sends an ambassador or he does not."

" *Pardieu !* " said the king, " it was hardly worth while to make a hole in your cheek with your fist to discover that fine dilemma."

" If he sends an ambassador, it is because he feels himself strong,—he who is prudence itself. Now, if he is strong, we must temporise with him. Let us respect his ambassador, and receive him with civility. That engages you to nothing. Do you remember how your brother embraced Admiral Coligny, who came as ambassador from the Huguenots? "

" Then you approve of the policy of my brother Charles? "

" Not so, but I cite a fact; and I say to you, do not hurt a poor devil of a herald or ambassador. Perhaps we may find the way to seize the master, the mover, the chief,—the great Duc d'Anjou,—with the three Guises; and if you can shut them up in a place safer than the Louvre, do it."

" That is not so bad."

" Then why do you let your friends bellow so? "

" Bellow ! "

" Yes; I would say ' roar ' if they could be taken for lions. I say ' bellow ' because— See, Henri, it really makes me sick to look at those fellows,—playing ghost, like little boys, and trying to frighten men by crying, ' Hoo! hoo! ' If the Duc d'Anjou sends no ambassador, they will imagine that they have prevented it, and will think they are of some importance."

" Chicot, you forget that the men of whom you speak are my friends, my only friends."

" Do you want me to win a thousand crowns from you, O my king ? "

" Speak."

" Bet with me that those fellows will remain faithful against every temptation, and I will bet that before to-morrow night I shall have gained over three of the four, body and soul."

Chicot's assurance in saying this made Henri reflect, in his turn. He made no reply.

" Ah ! " said Chicot, " so you also meditate; you also bury your pretty hand in your charming jaw. You are stronger than I thought, my son; for now you are getting a smell of the truth."

" Well, what do you advise ? "

" To wait, my son. Half the wisdom of Solomon lies in that word. If an ambassador arrive, receive him courteously. And as to your brother, kill him if you can and like, but do not degrade him. He is a great knave, but he is a Valois; besides, he can do that well enough for himself."

" It is true, Chicot."

" One more lesson that you owe me. Now let me sleep, Henri; for the last week I have been engaged in fuddling a monk."

" A monk ! the one of whom you have already spoken to me ? "

" Yes. You promised him an abbey."

" I ? "

" *Pardieu !* it is the least you can do for him, after all he has done for you."

" He is then still devoted to me ? "

" He adores you. By the way, my son—"

" What ? "

" In three weeks it will be the Fête Dieu."

" Well ? "

" Are we to have some pretty little procession ? "

" I am the most Christian king, and it is my duty to set an example to my subjects."

" And you will, as usual, stop at the four great convents of Paris ? "

" Yes."

" At Ste. Geneviève? "

" Yes, that is the second at which I shall stop."

" Good."

" Why do you ask? "

" Oh, nothing; I was curious. Now I know all I want. Good-night, Henri! "

But just as Chicot prepared to leave, a great noise was heard.

" What is that noise? " said the king.

" It is ordained that I am not to sleep. Henri, you must get me a room in the town, or I must leave your service; upon my word, the Louvre is becoming uninhabitable."

At this moment the captain of the guards entered, saying, " Sire, it is an envoy from M. le Duc d'Anjou."

" With a suite? "

" No, Sire, alone."

" Then you must receive him doubly well, Henri; for he is a brave fellow."

" Well," said the king, very pale, but trying to look calm, " let all my court assemble in the great hall."

CHAPTER XXXIV

WHICH IS ONLY THE END OF THE PRECEDING ONE

HENRI sat on his throne in the great hall, and around him was grouped an eager crowd. He looked pale and frowning. All eyes were turned towards the door by which the captain of the guards would introduce the envoy.

" Sire," whispered Quélus to the king, " do you know the name of the ambassador? "

" No; but what does it matter? "

" Sire, it is M. de Bussy; the insult is doubled."

" I see no insult," said the king, with affected coolness.

" Perhaps your Majesty does not see it," said Schomberg; " but we see it clearly."

Henri did not reply. He perceived that wrath and hatred were at work around his throne, and congratulated himself that between him and his enemies there were two ramparts of so much strength. Quélus, pale and red by turns, rested both hands on the hilt of his sword. Schomberg took off his gloves and half drew his dagger from its sheath. Maugiron took his sword from the hands of a page and attached it to his belt. D'Epernon turned up his mustaches to his eyes, and placed himself behind his companions. As for Henri, like a hunter who hears his dogs barking at a boar, he let his favourites do as they would, and smiled. "Let the ambassador enter," he said.

At these words a deathlike silence pervaded the hall; and in the depth of that silence one might fancy that he heard the dull murmur of the king's wrath. Then a step and the jingling of spurs were heard in the corridor. Bussy entered, holding his hat in his hand, with his head erect, and a calm countenance. No one of those around the king attracted the young man's haughty glance. He advanced directly to Henri, saluted profoundly, and waited to be addressed,—standing proudly before the throne, but with a pride wholly personal, the pride of a gentleman, which comprised nothing offensive to the royal majesty.

"You here, M. de Bussy!" said the king; "I thought you were in Anjou."

"Sire, I was; but, as you see, I have left that place."

"And what brings you to our capital?"

"The desire of presenting my humble respects to your Majesty."

The king and courtiers looked at one another; it was evident that they had expected quite other language from the impetuous young man.

"And nothing else?" said the king.

"I will add, Sire, the orders I received from the Duc d'Anjou to join his respects to mine."

"And the duke said nothing else?"

"Only that he was on the point of returning with the queen-mother, and wished me to apprise your Majesty of the return of one of your most faithful subjects."

The king, almost suffocated with surprise, was unable to continue. Chicot took advantage of the interruption to approach the ambassador. "Good-morning, M. de Bussy," said he.

Bussy turned, astonished to find a friend in that assembly. "Ah, M. Chicot!" said he; "I greet you with all my heart. How is M. de Saint-Luc?"

"Why, very well; he is at this moment out walking with his wife."

"Is that all you have to say, M. de Bussy?" asked the king.

"Yes, Sire; anything that remains to be said will be said by the duke himself."

" Very well," said the king; and silently rising, he descended the two steps of the throne. The audience was at an end; the group broke up. Bussy noticed, from the corner of his eye, that he was surrounded by the four favourites, and enclosed as it were in a living circle full of excitement and threatening. At the end of the hall the king conversed in a low tone with his chancellor. Bussy affected to notice nothing and continued his conversation with Chicot. Then the king, as if he were in the plot to isolate Bussy, called Chicot away. Bussy remained alone in the circle; then he changed the expression of his countenance. He had been calm before the king; he had been polite with Chicot. He now became condescending. Seeing Quélus approach, he said, " Eh! good-morning, M. de Quélus; may I have the honour of asking how you are? "

" Not very well, Monsieur."

" Oh, *mon Dieu !* what is the matter? "

" Something annoys me infinitely."

" Something! And are you not powerful enough to get rid of it? "

" It is not something, but some one, that M. de Quélus means," said Maugiron, advancing.

" And whom I advise him to get rid of," said Schomberg, coming forward on the other side.

" Ah, M. de Schomberg! I did not recognise you."

" Perhaps not; is my face still blue? "

" Not so; you are very pale. Are you in poor health, Monsieur? "

" Monsieur," said Schomberg, " if I am pale, it is with anger."

" Oh! then you are like M. de Quélus; you also have some one who annoys you? "

" Yes, Monsieur."

" Like me," said Maugiron; " I also have some one who annoys me."

" Still lively, my dear M. de Maugiron! " said Bussy. " But really, gentlemen, the more I look at you, the more your discomposed features interest me."

" You forget me, Monsieur," said D'Epernon, planting himself fiercely before Bussy.

" Pardon me, M. d'Epernon; you were behind the others, as usual, and I have the pleasure of knowing you so slightly that it was not for me to address you first."

It was strange to see Bussy smiling and calm among those four furious men, whose eyes spoke with so terrible an eloquence that he must have been blind or stupid not to have understood their language; but Bussy was able to appear as if he did not understand. He maintained his self-control, and the same smile remained on his lips. Quélus, whose patience was first to give way, stamped on the floor, exclaiming, " Let us finish! "

Bussy raised his eyes to the ceiling, and looked around. "Monsieur," said he, " do you notice what an echo there is in this hall? Nothing gives back sound like marble walls, and the voice sounds doubly loud under plastered ceilings. On the contrary, in the open country sounds are disseminated, and, on my honour, I believe the clouds take up some part of them. I advance that proposition after Aristophanes. Have you read Aristophanes, gentlemen? "

Maugiron approached the young man to speak to him privately. Bussy stopped him. " No confidences here, Monsieur, I beg of you," said he. " You know how jealous his Majesty is; he might think that we were talking against him."

Maugiron withdrew, more furious than ever. Schomberg took his place, and with a tone of importance said,—

" I am a German, very dull, very obtuse, but very frank. I speak loud, to give those who listen every chance to hear me. But when my words, which I try to make as clear as possible, are not heard because he to whom they are addressed is deaf, or are not understood because he to whom I speak does not wish to understand, then I—"

" You? " said Bussy, fixing on the young man a look like those which tigers send forth from their fathomless eye-balls,— looks that seem to spring up from an abyss and to emit torrents of flame; " you? "

Schomberg paused. Bussy shrugged his shoulders and turned on his heel. He found himself face to face with D'Epernon. D'Epernon could not withdraw. " See, gentlemen," he said. " how provincial M. de Bussy has become: he has a beard, and no knot to his sword; he has black boots and a grey hat."

" It is an observation that I was just making to myself, my dear M. d'Epernon. Seeing you so well dressed, I said to myself, ' How much harm a few weeks' absence does to a man! Here am I, Louis de Clermont, forced to take a little Gascon gentle-man as a model of taste.' But let me pass. You are so near to me that you tread on my feet, and M. de Quélus also; and I feel it in spite of my boots," he added with a charming smile.

At that moment Bussy, passing between D'Epernon and Quélus, extended his hand to Saint-Luc, who had just come in.

Saint-Luc found his hand dripping with perspiration. He comprehended that something extraordinary was taking place, and drew Bussy out of the group and then out of the hall.

A strange murmur arose among the favourites and spread to the other groups of courtiers.

" It is incredible," said Quélus; " I insulted him, and he did not reply."

" I," said Maugiron, " provoked him, and he did not reply."

" I stepped on his foot," cried D'Epernon,—" stepped on his foot, and he did not reply."

" It is clear that he did not wish to understand," said Quélus; " there is something underneath."

" And I know what it is," said Schomberg.

" What is it? "

" He knows that we four will kill him, and he doesn't want to be killed."

At that moment the king approached them, Chicot whispering in his ear.

" Well," said the king, " what, then, does M. de Bussy have to say? I thought I heard loud talking in this direction."

" Do you wish to know what M. de Bussy said, Sire? " asked D'Epernon.

" Yes; you know that I am curious," said Henri, smiling.

" Faith! nothing good, Sire," said Quélus; " he is no longer a Parisian."

" And what is he, then? "

" He is a countryman. He stands aside."

" Oh, oh! " said the king; " what does that mean? "

" It means," said Quélus, " that I am going to train a dog to bite his calves; and yet, who knows if he will feel it through his boots? "

" And I," said Schomberg,—" I have a quintain in my house; I shall name it Bussy."

" For my part," said D'Epernon. " I will act more directly, and will go farther. To-day I have stepped on his foot; to-morrow I will box his ears. He is a sham hero, a hero of vanity; he says to himself, ' I have fought enough for honour; now I will save my life.' "

" Eh, what! gentlemen," said Henri, with pretended anger, " have you dared insult, in my house, in the Louvre, a gentleman of my brother's suite? "

" Alas, yes! " said Maugiron, replying with affected humility to the king's pretended wrath; "and although we insulted him vigorously, Sire, I swear to you that he made no response."

The king turned, smiling, towards Chicot, and in a low tone said, "Do you still think that they bellow? It seems to me that they have roared, eh?"

"Perhaps," said Chicot, "they have mewed. The cry of a cat has a horrible effect on the nerves of some persons; perhaps M. de Bussy is one of them, and for that reason went out without replying."

"Do you think so?"

"Those who live will see," responded Chicot, very sententiously.

"Let him go, then," said Henri; "like master, like valet."

"Do you mean, Sire, by those words, that Bussy is your brother's valet? You are mistaken."

"Gentlemen," said Henri, "I am going to visit the queen, with whom I shall dine."

The assembly bowed, and the king went out by the great door. Precisely at that moment Saint-Luc entered by another. "Pardon, M. de Quélus," he said, bowing, "Do you still live in the Rue St. Honoré?"

"Yes, my dear friend; why do you ask?"

"I have two words to say to you."

"Ah!"

"And you, M. de Schomberg, may I venture to ask your address?"

"Rue Béthisy," said Schomberg, astonished.

"D'Epernon's address I know."

"Rue de Grenelle."

"You are my neighbour. And you, Maugiron?"

"Near the Louvre. But I begin to understand; you come from M. de Bussy."

"Never mind from whom I come; I have to speak to you, that is all."

"To all four of us?"

"Yes."

"Then if you cannot speak here, let us all go to Schomberg's; it is close by."

"So be it."

And the five gentlemen went out of the Louvre arm in arm.

CHAPTER XXXV

HOW M. DE SAINT-LUC ACQUITTED HIMSELF OF THE COMMISSION GIVEN TO HIM BY BUSSY

LET us leave Saint-Luc a little while in Schomberg's ante-chamber, and see what had taken place between him and Bussy.

Once out of the hall, Saint-Luc had stopped, and looked anxiously at his friend.

"Are you ill?" said he. "You are so pale you look as though you were about to faint."

"No, I am only choking with anger."

"You do not surely mind those fellows?"

"You shall see."

"Come, Bussy, be calm."

"You are charming, really. Be calm, indeed! if you had had half said to you that I have had, some one would have been dead before this."

"Well, what do you want?"

"You are my friend; you have already given me a terrible proof of it."

"Ah! my dear friend," said Saint-Luc, who believed Monsoreau dead and buried, "do not thank me; it is not worth while. Certainly the thrust was a good one, and succeeded admirably; but it was the king who showed it me, when he kept me here a prisoner at the Louvre."

"Dear friend—"

"Never mind Monsoreau; tell me about Diane. Was she pleased at last? Does she pardon me? When will the wedding take place?"

"Oh, my dear friend, we must wait till Monsoreau is dead."

"What!" cried Saint-Luc, starting back as though he had put his foot on a pointed nail.

"Yes; poppies are not such dangerous plants as you thought. He did not die from his fall on them, but is alive and more furious than ever."

"Really?"

"Yes, and he talks of nothing but vengeance, and of killing you on the first occasion."

"He lives?"

"Alas! yes."

"And who, then, is the ass of a doctor who cured him?"

"My own, dear friend."

"What! I did not succeed?" cried Saint-Luc, overwhelmed by that revelation. "Ah! I am dishonoured! I have announced his death to every one; he will find his heirs in mourning. But he shall not give me the lie. I will find him; and at our next meeting, instead of one thrust of the sword, I will give him four if necessary."

"In your turn, calm yourself, my dear Saint-Luc. Really, I am better off than you would think; it is the duke whom he suspects, and of whom he is jealous. I am his dear Bussy,—his precious friend. That is only natural, for it was that fool of a Rémy who cured him."

"What an idiot he must have been!"

"He has an idea that as a doctor it is his duty to cure people."

"The fellow is visionary!"

"In short, Monsoreau says he owes his life to me, and confides his wife to my care."

"Ah! I understand that this makes you wait more patiently for his death. However, I am quite thunderstruck at the news."

"But now, my friend, let us leave Monsoreau."

"Yes, let us enjoy life while he is still ill; but once he is well, I shall order myself a suit of mail, have new locks put on my doors, and you must ask the Duc d'Anjou if his mother has not given him some antidote against poison. Meanwhile, let us amuse ourselves."

"Well, my dear friend, you see you have rendered me only half a service."

"Do you wish me to complete it?"

"Yes, in another way."

"Speak."

"Are you on good terms with those four gentlemen?"

"Faith! we are something like cats and dogs in the sun; as long as we all get the heat, we agree, but if one of us took the warmth from another, then I would not answer for the consequences."

"Well! will you go for me to M. de Quélus?"

"Ah!"

"And ask him what day it will please him that I should cut his throat, or he mine?"

"I will."

"You do not mind it?"

"Not the least in the world. I will go at once if you wish it."

"One moment; as you go, just call on M. de Schomberg and make him the same proposal."

"Schomberg too? The devil! how you go on! Well, as you wish."

"Then, my dear Saint-Luc, as you are so amiable, go also to M. de Maugiron, and ask him to join the party."

"What! three? Bussy, you cannot mean it. I hope that is all."

"No; from him go to D'Epernon."

"Four?"

"Even so, my dear friend; I need not recommend to a man like you to proceed with courtesy and politeness towards these gentlemen. Let the thing be done in gallant fashion."

"You shall be content, my friend. What are your conditions?"

"I make none; I accept theirs."

"Your arms?"

"What they like."

"The day, place, and hour?"

"Whatever suits them."

"But—"

"Oh, never mind such trifles, but do it quickly. I will walk in the little garden of the Louvre; you will find me there when you have executed your commission."

"Expect me, then; but it may be somewhat tedious waiting."

"I have time."

We know how Saint-Luc found the four young men and accompanied them to Schomberg's house. Saint-Luc remained in the antechamber, waiting until, according to the etiquette of the day, the four young men should be installed in the salon ready to receive him. Then an usher came and saluted Saint-Luc, who followed him to the threshold of the salon, where he announced M. d'Epinay de Saint-Luc.

Schomberg then rose and saluted his visitor, who, to mark the character of the visit, instead of returning it, put on his hat. That formality gave to his visit colour and intention. Schomberg then, turning towards Quélus, said, "I have the honour to present to you M. Jacques de Levis, Comte de Quélus."

The two gentlemen bowed, and then the same ceremony was performed with the others. This done, the four friends sat down, but Saint-Luc remained standing, and said to Quélus, "Monsieur the Count, you have insulted M. le Comte Louis de Clermont d'Amboise, Seigneur de Bussy, who presents to you his compliments, and calls you to single combat on any day and hour, and with such arms as may please you. Do you accept?"

" Certainly; M. de Bussy does me much honour."

" Your day, Monsieur the Count? "

" I have no choice,—only, I should prefer to-morrow to the day after, and the day after to any later date."

" Your hour? "

" In the morning."

" Your arms? "

" Rapier and dagger, if that suits M. de Bussy."

Saint-Luc bowed. Then he addressed the same questions to the others, and received the same answers.

" If we all should happen to choose the same day and hour, —chance sometimes works so strangely,—M. de Bussy would be rather embarrassed," said Schomberg.

" Certainly," replied Saint-Luc, " M. de Bussy might be embarrassed, as would any other gentleman in combat with four brave men like you; but he says the circumstance would not be new to him, as it has already happened at the Tournelles."

" And he would fight us all four? " asked D'Epernon.

" All four."

" Separately? " Schomberg inquired.

" Separately, or at once."

The four young men looked at one another; then Quélus, red with anger, said, " It is very fine of M. de Bussy; but however little we may be worth, we can each do our own work. We will accept, therefore, the count's proposal, and will fight him separately, or rather,—which will be still better, as we do not seek to assassinate a gallant man,—chance shall decide which of us shall fight M. de Bussy."

" And the three others? " asked D'Epernon.

" Oh, M. de Bussy has too many friends, and we too many enemies, for them to remain with folded arms. Do you agree to this, gentlemen? "

" Yes! " cried all.

" If MM. de Ribeirac, d'Antragues, and de Livarot would join the party, it would be complete."

" Gentlemen," said Saint-Luc, " I will transmit your desires to M. de Bussy; and I believe I may promise that he is too courteous not to agree to your wishes. It therefore only remains for me to thank you in his name."

Then he took his leave, after throwing his purse to the four lackeys, whom he found outside, that they might drink to their masters' health.

CHAPTER XXXVI

IN WHAT RESPECT M. DE SAINT-LUC WAS MORE CIVILISED THAN
M. DE BUSSY, THE LESSONS WHICH HE GAVE HIM, AND THE
USE WHICH M. DE BUSSY MADE OF THEM

SAINT-LUC returned, proud of having executed his commission
so well. Bussy thanked him, but looked sad, which was not
natural to him.

" Have I done badly? " said Saint-Luc.

" Upon my word, my dear friend, I only regret you did not
say, ' at once.' "

" Ah, patience! The Angevins have not yet returned. And
then where is the necessity for you to make so suddenly a heap
of the dead and dying? "

" It is because I wish to die as soon as possible."

Saint-Luc looked at him in astonishment.

" Die! at your age, with your name, and Diane? "

" Yes; I shall kill them, I know, but I shall receive some
good blow which will tranquillise me for ever."

" What black ideas, Bussy! "

" A husband whom I thought dead, and who has returned to
life; a wife who can no longer leave the bedside of the pretended dying man! Not to see her, smile on her, touch her
hand!—*mordieu!* I want to cut some one in pieces! "

Saint-Luc interrupted him with a burst of laughter. " Oh,"
cried he, " the innocent man! To think that women love this
Bussy,—a tyro! Why, my dear fellow, you have lost your
senses. There is no other lover on earth so fortunate as you."

" Ah, very good! prove that to me, married man."

" *Nihil facilius,* as the Jesuit Triquet, my teacher, would say.
You are the friend of M. de Monsoreau? "

" Yes, for the honour of human intelligence I am ashamed to
confess it; that booby calls me his friend."

" Well, be his friend."

" Oh! and abuse this title! "

" *Prorsus absurdum,* Triquet would again remark. Is he
really your friend? "

" He says so."

" No, for he makes you unhappy. Now the end of friendship
is to make men happy in their relations to one another. At
least, so his Majesty says, and he is learned in friendship. So,

if he makes you unhappy he is not your friend; therefore you
may treat him either as a stranger, and take his wife from him,
or as an enemy, and kill him if he murmurs."

"In fact, I hate him."

"And he fears you."

"Do you think he does not love me?"

"The devil! Take away his wife, and you will see."

"Is that still the logic of Father Triquet?"

"No, it is my own."

"I congratulate you."

"It satisfies you?"

"No, I prefer to be a man of honour."

"And let Madame de Monsoreau cure her husband both
physically and morally; for it is certain that if you get yourself
killed, she will attach herself to the only man who remains
to her."

Bussy frowned.

"But," added Saint-Luc, "here is my wife; she always gives
good advice. She has been picking herself a bouquet in the
gardens of the queen-mother, and will be in a good humour.
Listen to her; she speaks gold."

Jeanne arrived radiant, full of happiness and fun. Bussy
saluted her in a friendly manner, and she held out her hand to
him, saying with a smile, "How go on the love-affairs?"

"They are dying."

"They are wounded and fainting," said Saint-Luc; "perhaps
you can restore them, Jeanne."

"Let me see; show me the wound."

"In two words this is it: M. de Bussy does not like smiling
on M. de Monsoreau, and he thinks of retiring."

"And leaving Diane to him?" cried Jeanne, with fright.

"Oh, Madame, Saint-Luc does not tell you that I wish to die."

"Poor Diane!" murmured Jeanne; "decidedly men are
ungrateful."

"Good! this is the conclusion my wife draws."

"I ungrateful," cried Bussy, "because I fear to render my
love vile by practising a disgraceful hypocrisy?"

"Oh, Monsieur, that is only a pretext! If you were really
in love you would fear but one thing,—not to be loved in
return."

"But, Madame, there are sacrifices—"

"Not another word. Confess that you love Diane no longer;
it will be more worthy of a gallant man."

Bussy grew pale.

" You do not dare to tell her; well, I will."

" Madame! Madame!"

" You are rich, you men, with your sacrifices. And does she make none? What! she exposes herself to be murdered by that tiger of a Monsoreau; she preserves her position only by employing a strength of will of which Samson or Hannibal would have been incapable! Oh, I swear, Diane is sublime; I could not do a quarter of what she does every day."

" Thank you!" said Saint-Luc.

" And he hesitates!" continued she. " He does not fall on his knees and say his *mea culpa!*"

" You are right," said Bussy; " I am but a man,—that is to say, an imperfect creature, inferior to the most commonplace woman."

" It is well that you are convinced of it."

" What do you order me to do?"

" To go at once and pay a visit—"

" To M. de Monsoreau?"

" Who speaks of him? To Diane."

" But he never leaves her."

" When you went so often to see Madame de Barbezieux, had she not always near her that great ape, who bit you because he was jealous?"

Bussy began to laugh, and Saint-Luc and Jeanne followed his example.

" Madame," then said Bussy, " I am going to M. de Monsoreau's house; adieu." He went to Monsoreau's house, and found him in bed. The count uttered exclamations of joy on seeing him. Rémy had just promised that his wound should be cured in less than three weeks. Bussy related to him the history of the commission with which he had been charged by the Duc d'Anjou, the visit to the court, the king's embarrassment, and the cold demeanour of the favourites.

" Cold demeanour," was Bussy's expression; Diane smiled on hearing it.

Monsoreau, becoming thoughtful, asked Bussy to lean towards him, and whispered in his ear, " The duke has still projects on foot, has he not?"

" I believe so."

" Do not compromise yourself for that bad man. I know him; he is perfidious, and will not hesitate to betray you."

" I know it."

" You are my friend; and I wish to put you on your guard."

" You must sleep after the dressing of your wound," said Rémy.

" Yes, my dear doctor. My friend, take a turn in the garden with Madame de Monsoreau."

" I am at your orders," replied Bussy.

CHAPTER XXXVII

THE PRECAUTIONS OF M. DE MONSOREAU

SAINT-LUC was right, and Jeanne was right; and at the end of a week Bussy perceived it and rendered them justice. As for Diane, she gave herself up to the two instincts that Figaro recognises as inborn in mankind,—to love and to deceive. M. de Monsoreau grew better and better. He had escaped from fever,—thanks to the application of cold water, that new remedy which Providence had discovered to Ambrose Paré,— when all at once he received a great shock: he learned that the Duc d'Anjou had arrived in Paris with the queen-mother and the Angevins.

The count had good reason for anxiety, for on the day after his arrival, the duke, under the pretext of inquiring about his health, presented himself at his hotel. It was impossible to close his door against a prince who showed so much interest in him; M. de Monsoreau therefore was obliged to receive the prince, who was most amiable to him and to his wife. As soon as he was gone, M. de Monsoreau took Diane's arm, and in spite of Rémy's remonstrances, walked three times round his arm-chair; and from his satisfied air, Diane was sure he was meditating on some project.

But this concerns the private history of the house of Monsoreau. Let us return, then, to the arrival of the Duc d'Anjou, which belongs to the epic part of this book.

It may easily be imagined that the day when Monseigneur François de Valois returned to the Louvre was an interesting day to the observers at court. And this is what they saw,— angry contempt on the part of the king; an ostentatious in-difference on the part of the queen-mother; and on the part of the Duc d'Anjou, a vulgar insolence which seemed to say, " Why the devil did you call me back, if you make faces at me when I arrive? "

On that day Chicot moved about more actively than Cæsar on the eve of the battle of Pharsalia. Then the sensation died out, and things went on as before.

The next day the duke came again to visit the wounded man. This time, since Monsoreau was daily becoming stronger, as soon as the duke had gone, he took Diane's arm again, and instead of going three times around his armchair, he took one turn around his room; after which he resumed his seat still more satisfied than before. That evening Diane warned Bussy that her husband had certainly some project in his head. A few minutes after, when Bussy and Monsoreau were alone, "When I think," said Monsoreau, " that this prince who smiles on me is my mortal enemy, and tried to have me assassinated by M. de Saint-Luc—"

" Oh, assassinated! take care, Monsieur the Count! Saint-Luc is a gentleman; and you confess yourself that you provoked him, drew the sword first, and received your wound in fair fight."

" Certainly; but it is not the less true that he obeyed the wishes of M. d'Anjou."

" Listen! I know M. de Saint-Luc, and I can assure you he is devoted to the king, and hates the duke. If your wound had come from D'Antragues, Livarot, or Ribeirac, it might be so; but from Saint-Luc—"

" You do not know," replied Monsoreau, obstinate in his opinion. At last he was able to go down into the garden. " That will do," said he; " now we will move."

" Why move? " said Rémy.   " Is not the air good here, or do you want amusement? "

" On the contrary," said Monsoreau, " there is too much. M. d'Anjou fatigues me with his visits, and he always brings with him a crowd of gentlemen; the noise of their spurs destroys my nerves."

" But where are you going? "

" I have ordered them to get ready my little house at the Tournelles."

Bussy and Diane exchanged a look of loving remembrance.

" What! that little place? " cried Rémy, imprudently.

" What! do you know it? "

" Who does not know the houses of the chief huntsman, particularly I, who lived in the Rue Beautreillis? "

" Yes, yes, I will go there. One can receive there only four persons at most. It is a fortress; and you can see from the window a hundred yards off who is coming to visit you."

"What good does that do?" asked Rémy.

"You can avoid them if you wish, particularly when you are well!"

Bussy bit his lips; he feared a time might come when Monsoreau would avoid him. Diane sighed; she thought of the time when she had seen Bussy in that house lying fainting on the bed.

"You cannot do it," said Rémy.

"Why not, if you please, Monsieur?"

"Because the chief huntsman of France must hold receptions, must keep valets and equipages. Let him have a palace for his dogs, if he likes, but not a dog-kennel for himself."

"It is true; but—"

"But I am the doctor of the mind as of the body; it is not your residence here that displeases you."

"What then?"

"That of Madame; therefore send her away."

"Separate myself from her?" cried Monsoreau, fixing on Diane a look which certainly expressed more of anger than of love.

"Then give up your place; send in your resignation. I believe it would be wise. If you do not do your duty, you will displease the king; and if you do—"

"I will do anything but leave the countess," said Monsoreau, with closely shut teeth. As he spoke, they heard in the courtyard a noise of voices and horses' feet.

Monsoreau shuddered. "The duke again!" he cried.

"Yes," said Rémy, going to the window.

The prince entered immediately, and Monsoreau saw his first glance given to Diane. He brought to her as a present one of those masterpieces of which the artists of that day produced two or three in the course of a lifetime. It was a poniard, with a handle of chased gold. This handle was a smelling-bottle; and on the blade a chase was carved with admirable skill,—horses, dogs, trees, game, and hunters, mingled together in harmonious confusion on this blade of azure and gold.

"Let me see," cried Monsoreau, who feared there was a note hidden in the handle.

The prince separated the two parts. "To you, who are a hunter," said he, "I give the blade; to the countess, the handle. Good-morning, Bussy; you are, then, a friend of the count's now?"

Diane reddened; but Bussy said, "Your Highness forgets that you asked me to inquire after M. de Monsoreau."

"It is true."

The prince sat down, and began to talk to Diane. In a few minutes he said, "Count, it is very warm in your rooms; I see the countess is stifling. I will give her my arm for a turn in the garden."

The husband and the lover exchanged wrathful looks. Diane, being invited to descend, arose and placed her arm on that of the prince.

"Give me an arm," said Monsoreau to Bussy; and he got up and followed his wife.

"Ah!" said the duke, "it seems you are better."

"Yes, Monseigneur; and I hope soon to be able to accompany Madame de Monsoreau wherever she goes."

"Good; but meanwhile do not fatigue yourself."

Monsoreau was compelled by his feebleness to sit down; but he sat where he could keep them in view.

"Count," said he to Bussy, "will you be amiable enough to escort Madame de Monsoreau this evening to my house at the Tournelles?"

"No," said Rémy to his master, "you cannot do that, Monsieur."

"Why not?"

"Because M. d'Anjou would never forgive you if you helped to play him such a trick."

Bussy was about to cry, "What do I care?" but a glance from Rémy stopped him.

"Rémy is right," said Monsoreau,—"it would injure you; to-morrow I will go myself."

"You will lose your place."

"It is possible; but I shall keep my wife."

The next day they went to the old house; Diane took her old room, with the bed of white-and-gold damask. A corridor only separated it from that of the count. Bussy tore his hair with rage. Saint-Luc maintained that rope-ladders had reached a high degree of perfection and were an excellent substitute for stairways. Monsoreau rubbed his hands, and smiled as he thought of the Duc d'Anjou's annoyance.

CHAPTER XXXVIII

A VISIT TO THE HOUSE AT LES TOURNELLES

THE duke became more and more in love with Diane as she seemed always to escape him; and with his love for her his hatred of Monsoreau increased. On the other hand, he had not renounced his political hopes, but had resumed his underhand machinations. The moment was favourable, for many wavering conspirators, encouraged by the triumph which the weakness of the king and the cunning of Catherine had afforded to the Angevins, gathered around the Duc d'Anjou, uniting by imperceptible but strong threads the cause of the prince to that of the Guises, who remained prudently in the background, and preserved a silence which filled Chicot with alarm.

However, the duke no longer confided his projects to Bussy; he showed him only a hypocritical friendship. He was vaguely uneasy at seeing him at Monsoreau's house, and envious of the confidence that Monsoreau, so suspicious of himself, placed in him. He was frightened also at the joy and happiness which shone in Diane's face. He knew that flowers bloom only in the light of the sun, and women in that of love. She was visibly happy, and this annoyed him. Determined to use his power, both for love and vengeance, he thought it would be absurd to be stayed in this purpose by such ridiculous obstacles as the jealousy of a husband and the repugnance of a wife. One day he ordered his equipages, intending to visit Monsoreau. He was told that he had moved to his house in the Rue St. Antoine. "Let us go there," said he to Bussy.

Soon the place was in commotion at the arrival of the twenty-four handsome cavaliers, each with two lackeys, who formed the prince's suite. Both Bussy and the prince knew the house well. They both went in; but while the prince entered the room, Bussy remained on the staircase. It resulted from this arrangement that the duke was received by Monsoreau alone; while Bussy was received in the arms of Diane, who embraced him tenderly, while Gertrude kept watch.

Monsoreau, always pale, grew livid at sight of the prince. "Monseigneur! here! really, it is too much honour for my poor house!" cried he, with open irony.

The prince smiled. "Wherever a suffering friend goes, I follow him," replied he. "How are you?"

" Oh, much better; I can already walk about, and in a week I shall be quite well."

" Was it your doctor who prescribed for you the air of the Bastille?" asked the prince, with an innocent air.

" Yes, Monseigneur."

" Did you not like the Rue des Petits Pères?"

" No, Monseigneur. I had too much company there; they made too much noise."

" But you have no garden here."

" I did not like the garden."

The prince bit his lips. " Do you know, Count," said he, after a moment of silence, " that many people are asking the king for your place?"

" On what pretext, Monseigneur?"

" They say you are dead."

" Monseigneur, you can answer for it that I am not."

" I answer for nothing; you bury yourself as though you were dead."

It was Monsoreau's turn to bite his lips. " Well, then, I must lose my place," said he.

" Really?"

" Yes; there are things I prefer to it."

" You are very disinterested."

" It is my character, Monseigneur."

" Then of course you will not mind the king's knowing your character?"

" Who will tell him?"

" Why, if he asks me about you, I must repeat our conversation."

" Faith, Monseigneur! if all they say in Paris were reported to the king, his two ears would not be enough to listen with."

" What do they say at Paris, Monsieur?" asked the prince, sharply.

Monsoreau saw that the conversation had taken a turn too serious for a convalescent not yet at liberty to act; he suppressed the wrath which raged in his soul, and assuming an appearance of indifference, " How should a poor invalid, such as I am, know?" said he. " If the king is angry at seeing his work badly done, he is wrong."

" How so?"

" Because doubtless my accident proceeds, to some extent, from him."

" Explain yourself."

"M. de Saint-Luc, who wounded me, is a dear friend of the king's. It was the king who taught him the thrust by which he wounded me; and it might have been the king who prompted him."

"You are right; but still the king is the king."

"Until he is so no longer."

The duke trembled. "By the way, is not Madame de Monsoreau here?" said he.

"Monseigneur, she is ill, or she would have come to present her respects to you."

"Ill! poor woman! it must be grief at seeing you suffer."

"Yes, and the fatigue of moving."

"Let us hope it will be a brief indisposition. You have so skilful a doctor."

"Yes, that dear Rémy—"

"Why, he is Bussy's doctor."

"He has lent him to me."

"You are, then, great friends?"

"He is my best, I might say my only friend," replied Monsoreau, coldly.

"Adieu, Count!"

As the duke raised the tapestry he fancied he saw the skirt of a dress disappear into the next room, and immediately Bussy appeared at his post in the middle of the corridor. Suspicion grew stronger with the duke.

"We are going," said he to Bussy, who ran downstairs without replying; while the duke, left alone, tried to penetrate the corridor where he had seen the silk dress vanish. But, turning, he saw that Monsoreau had followed, and was standing at the door.

"Your Highness mistakes your way," said he.

"True," said the duke; "thank you." And he went down with rage in his heart. On the way home, which was long, he and Bussy did not interchange a word. Bussy left the duke at the door of his hotel. When the duke had entered and was alone in his cabinet, Aurilly mysteriously glided in.

"Well," said the duke, on perceiving him, "I am baffled by the husband!"

"And perhaps also by the lover, Monseigneur."

"What do you say?"

"The truth, your Highness."

"Speak, then."

"I hope your Highness will pardon me; it was in your service."

"I pardon you in advance. Go on."

"After your Highness had gone upstairs, I watched under a shed in the courtyard."

"Ah! What did you see?"

"I saw a woman's dress; I saw this woman lean forward; I saw two arms twined around her neck; and then I heard the sound of a long and tender kiss."

"But who was the man?"

"I cannot recognise a man by his arms, Monseigneur."

"No, but you might recognise the gloves."

"Indeed, it seemed to me——"

"That you recognised them?"

"It was only a guess."

"Never mind; speak out."

"Well, Monseigneur, they looked like the gloves of M. de Bussy."

"Buff, embroidered with gold, were they not?"

"Yes, Monseigneur."

"Ah, Bussy! yes, it was Bussy. Oh, I was blind—or rather, no, I was not blind; but I could not believe in so much audacity."

"Be careful!" said Aurilly; "I think your Highness is speaking rather loud."

"Bussy!" repeated the duke, calling to mind a thousand circumstances unnoticed before, but now taking on a new significance.

"But your Highness must not believe too lightly; might there not have been a man hidden in her room?"

"Yes, doubtless; but Bussy, who was in the corridor, would have seen him."

"That is true."

"And then the gloves——"

"Yes; and besides the kiss, I heard——"

"What?"

"Three words, ' Till to-morrow evening.' "

"Oh, *mon Dieu!*"

"So that if you like, we can make sure."

"Aurilly, to-morrow evening we will be there."

"Your Highness knows I am at your orders."

"Very well. Ah, Bussy!" repeated the duke between his teeth; "Bussy, traitor to his chief! Bussy, that bugbear to every one! Bussy, the honest man! Bussy, who does not wish me to be King of France;" and the duke, smiling with an infernal joy, dismissed Aurilly, that he might reflect at his ease.

CHAPTER XXXIX

THE WATCHERS

The duke kept Bussy near him all day, so as not to lose sight of his movements. Bussy asked nothing better than to attend the prince during the day, for in that way he might have freedom for the evening. At ten o'clock he wrapped himself in his cloak, and with a rope-ladder under his arm went towards the Bastille. The duke, who did not know that he had a ladder, and could not believe that any one would walk alone in that way through the streets of Paris, thought Bussy would certainly call at his hotel for a horse and a servant, and lost ten minutes in preparations. During those ten minutes, Bussy, active and in love, had already gone three-fourths of the distance. He was lucky, as brave people generally are; he met with no accident by the way, and on arriving saw a light in the windows. It was the signal agreed on between him and Diane. He threw his ladder up to the balcony; it had six hooks, and was sure to fasten itself somewhere. At the noise, Diane put out her light and opened the window to fasten the ladder. The thing was done in a moment. Diane looked all around; the street seemed deserted. Then she signed to Bussy to mount, and he was up in five seconds. The moment was happily chosen, for while he got in at the window, M. de Monsoreau, after having listened patiently for a quarter of an hour at his wife's door, descended the stairs painfully, leaning on the arm of a confidential valet, and it so happened that he opened the street-door just as the ladder was drawn up and the window closed. He looked around; but the streets were deserted.

"You have been badly informed," said he to the servant.

"No, Monsieur, I have just left the Hôtel d'Anjou, and they told me that the duke had ordered two horses for this evening. But perhaps it was not to come here."

"Where else should he go?" asked Monsoreau, with a sombre air. He, like all jealous persons, thought the whole world had nothing to do but to torment him.

"Perhaps I should have done better to stay in her room," he murmured. "But they probably have signals for corresponding; she would have warned him of my presence, and I should have learned nothing. It is better to watch outside. Come, conduct me to the hiding-place, whence you say one can see everything."

" Come, Monsieur."

About twenty-five steps from the door was an enormous heap of stones that had come from the ruins of demolished houses, and served as fortifications to the children of the neighbourhood when they played at battles. In the midst was a space which could contain two people. The valet spread a cloak, on which Monsoreau sat down, while his servant sat at his feet with a loaded musket placed beside him. Diane had prudently drawn her thick curtains, so that scarcely a ray of light showed through, to betray that there was life in this gloomy house. They had been watching about ten minutes, when two horses appeared at the end of the street. The valet pointed to them.

" I see," said Monsoreau.

The two men got off their horses, and tied them up at the corner of the Hôtel des Tournelles.

" Monseigneur," said Aurilly, " I believe that we have arrived too late; he must have gone straight from your hotel, and must have entered."

" Perhaps so; but if we did not see him go in, we can see him come out."

" Yes, but when? "

" When we please."

" Would it be too curious to ask how you mean to manage? "

" Nothing is more easy; we have but to knock at the door, and ask after M. de Monsoreau. Our lover will be frightened at the noise; and as you enter the house he will come out at the window, and I, who am hidden outside, shall see him."

" And Monsoreau? "

" What can he say? I am his friend, and was uneasy about him, as he looked so ill yesterday; nothing can be more simple."

" It is very ingenious, Monseigneur."

" Do you hear what they say? " asked Monsoreau of his valet.

" No, Monsieur; but we soon shall, for they are coming nearer."

" Monseigneur," said Aurilly, " here is a heap of stones, which seems made on purpose for us."

" Yes, but wait a moment; perhaps we can see through the opening of the curtain."

Diane had relighted her lamp, and a faint ray appeared at the edges of the curtain. The duke and Aurilly went from place to place for more than ten minutes, trying to find a place to peep through. Meanwhile, Monsoreau was boiling with impatience, and his hand approached the musket.

"Oh! shall I suffer this?" murmured he. "Shall I swallow this affront also? No, my patience is worn out. *Mordieu!* that I can neither sleep nor wake nor even suffer quietly, because a shameful caprice has lodged in the idle brain of this miserable prince. No, I am not a complaisant valet. I am the Comte de Monsoreau, and if he comes near, on my word, I will blow his brains out. Light the match, René."

At this moment, just as the prince, finding that he could not look into the chamber, returned to his first project, and prepared to hide himself among the stones while Aurilly should go and knock at the door, suddenly Aurilly, forgetting the distance between him and the prince, placed his hand eagerly on the prince's arm.

"Well, Monsieur," said the prince, in astonishment, "what is the matter?"

"Come away, Monseigneur; come."

"Why so?"

"Do you not see something shining there to the left? Come, Monseigneur; come."

"I see a spark in that heap of stones."

"It is the match of a musket or arquebuse."

"Ah! who the devil can be in ambush there?"

"Some friend or servant of Bussy's. Let us go and make a *détour*, and return another way. The servant will give the alarm, and we shall see Bussy come out of the window."

"You are right; come;" and they went to their horses.

"They are going," said the valet to Monsoreau.

"Yes. Did you recognise them?"

"They seemed to me to be the prince and Aurilly."

"Precisely. But I shall soon be more sure still."

"What does Monseigneur propose to do?"

"Come."

Meanwhile the duke and Aurilly turned into the Rue Ste. Catherine, intending to return by the boulevard of the Bastille. Monsoreau went in and ordered his litter.

What the duke had foreseen happened. At the noise that Monsoreau made, Bussy took the alarm, the light was extinguished, the ladder fixed; and Bussy, to his great regret, was obliged to fly, like Romeo, but without having, like him, seen the sun rise and heard the lark sing. Just as he touched the ground, and Diane had thrown him the ladder, the Duke and

Aurilly arrived at the corner of the Bastille. They saw a shadow suspended from Diane's window; but this shadow disappeared almost instantaneously at the corner of the Rue St. Paul.

"Monsieur," said the valet to Monsoreau, "we shall wake up the household."

"What do I care?" cried Monsoreau, furiously. "I am master here, I believe; and I have at least the right to do what M. d'Anjou wished to do."

The litter was got ready, and, drawn by two stout horses, it was soon at the Hôtel d'Anjou. The duke and Aurilly had so recently come in that their horses were not unsaddled. Monsoreau, who had the privilege of ready admission to the duke's presence, appeared on the threshold just as the duke, after having thrown his hat on a chair, was holding out his boots to a valet to pull off. A servant, preceding him by some steps, announced M. de Monsoreau. A thunderbolt breaking his windows could not have astonished the prince more.

"M. de Monsoreau!" cried he, with an uneasiness he could not hide.

"Myself, Monseigneur," replied he, trying to repress his emotion; but the effort he made over himself was so violent that his legs failed him, and he fell on a chair which stood near.

"But you will kill yourself, my dear friend," said the duke; "you are so pale you look as though you were going to faint."

"Oh, no; what I have to say to your Highness is of too much importance. I may faint afterwards."

"Speak, then, my dear count," said François, quite overcome.

"Not before your people, I suppose."

The duke dismissed every one, even Aurilly.

"Your Highness has just come in?" said Monsoreau.

"As you see, Count."

"It is very imprudent of your Highness to go by night in the streets."

"Who told you I had been in the streets?"

"The dust on your clothes, Monseigneur."

"M. de Monsoreau," said the prince, in a tone that could not be misunderstood, "have you another employment besides that of chief huntsman?"

"Yes, that of spy, Monseigneur; all the world follows that calling now more or less, and I also like the rest."

"And what does this profession bring you, Monsieur?"

"Knowledge of what is taking place."

" It is curious," said the prince, getting nearer to his bell, so that he might sound it if the occasion should arise.

" Very curious," said Monsoreau.

" Well, tell me what you have to say."

" I came for that."

" You permit me to sit down? " said the duke.

" No irony, Monseigneur, towards an old and faithful servant like me, who comes at this hour and in this state to do you a service.   If I sat down, on my honour, it was because I could not stand."

" A service? to do me a service? "

" Yes."

" Speak, then."

" Monseigneur, I come on the part of a great prince."

" From the king? "

" No; from M. le Duc de Guise."

" Ah! that is quite a different thing.   Approach, and speak low."

CHAPTER XL

HOW M. LE DUC D'ANJOU SIGNED, AND AFTER HAVING SIGNED, SPOKE

THERE was a moment's silence.   Then the duke said, " Well, Monsieur the Count, what have you to say to me from the Duc de Guise? "

" Much, Monseigneur."

" They have written to you? "

" No; the duke writes no more since that strange disappearance of Nicolas David.   They have come to Paris."

" MM. de Guise are at Paris? "

" Yes, Monseigneur."

" I have not seen them."

" They are too prudent to expose themselves or your Highness to any risk."

" And I was not told! "

" I tell you now."

" What have they come for? "

" They come, Monseigneur, to the rendezvous you gave them."

" That I gave them? "

" Doubtless; on the day when your Highness was arrested

you received a letter from M. de Guise and replied to it verbally, through me, that they were to come to Paris from the 31st of May to the 2nd of June. It is now the 31st of May; and if your Highness has forgotten them, they have not forgotten you."

François grew pale. So many events had occurred since, that he had forgotten the appointment. "It is true," said he, at length; "but the relations which then existed between us exist no longer."

"If that be so, Monseigneur, you would do well to tell them, for I believe they think differently."

"How so?"

"You, perhaps, think yourself free as regards them; but they feel bound to you."

"A snare, my dear count, in which a man does not let himself be taken twice."

"And where was Monseigneur taken in a snare?"

"Where? At the Louvre, *mordieu!*"

"Was it the fault of MM. de Guise?"

"I do not say so; but they did not assist me to escape."

"It would have been difficult; they were flying themselves."

"It is true."

"But when you were in Anjou, did they not charge me to tell you that you could always count on them, as they on you, and that the day you marched on Paris, they would do the same?"

"It is true, but I did not march on Paris."

"You are here."

"Yes; but as my brother's ally."

"Monseigneur will permit me to observe that he is more than the ally of the Guises."

"What then?"

"Their accomplice."

The duke bit his lips.

"And you say they charged you to announce their arrival to me?"

"They did me that honour."

"But they did not tell you the motive of their return?"

"They told me all, knowing me to be the confidant of your Highness,—their motives and their projects."

"Then they have projects? What are they?"

"The same always."

"And they think them practicable?"

"They look upon them as certain."

" And these projects have for an aim—"

The duke stopped, not daring to finish.

" To make you King of France; yes, Monseigneur."

The duke felt the flush of joy mount to his face.

" But," said he, " is the moment favourable? "

" Your wisdom must decide."

" My wisdom? "

" Yes; the facts cannot be contradicted. The nomination of the king as head of the League was only a comedy, quickly seen through and appreciated. Now the reaction has commenced; and the entire state is rising against the tyranny of the king and his creatures. Sermons are a call to arms; and churches are places where they curse the king instead of praying to God. The army trembles with impatience; the *bourgeois* league together; our emissaries bring in nothing but signatures and new adherents to the League. In a word, the king's reign touches on its close. Now do you renounce your former projects? "

The duke did not reply.

" Monseigneur knows that he may speak frankly to me."

" I think," said the duke, " that considering my brother has no children, that his health is uncertain, and that after him the crown will come naturally to me, there is no reason why I should compromise my name and my dignity in a useless struggle, and try to take, with danger, what will come to me in due course without danger."

" Your Highness is in error; your brother's throne will only come to you if you take it. MM. de Guise cannot be kings themselves; but they will only allow a king of their own making to reign, whom they will substitute for the present king. They count on your Highness; but if you refuse, they will seek another."

" And who will dare to seat himself on the throne of Charlemagne? "

" A Bourbon instead of a Valois, Monseigneur; a son of Saint Louis instead of another son of Saint Louis."

" The King of Navarre? "

" Why not? He is young and brave."

" He is a Huguenot."

" Was he not converted at the Saint Bartholomew? "

" Yes; and he abjured afterwards."

" Oh, Monseigneur, what he did for his life he will do again for the crown."

" They think, then, that I will yield my rights without a struggle."

" The case is provided for."

" I will fight."

" They are men of war."

" I will put myself at the head of the League."

" They are the soul of it."

" I will join my brother."

" Your brother will be dead."

" I will call the kings of Europe to my aid."

" The kings of Europe will readily enough make war on kings, but they will think twice before making war on a people."

" My party will stand by me."

" Your party, I believe, consists of M. de Bussy and myself."

" Then I am tied."

" Nearly so. You can do nothing without the Guises; with them, everything. Say the word, and you are king."

The duke walked about for a few minutes in great agitation, then stopped, and said, " Go on, Count."

" This, then, is the plan. In a week the Fête Dieu will take place; and the king meditates on that day a great procession to the convents of Paris. There the guards will remain at the door; the king will stop before each altar, kneel down, and say five *Paters* and five *Aves*."

" I know all that."

" He will go to Ste. Geneviève—"

" Yes."

" He will enter with a suite of five or six persons, and behind them the doors will be closed."

" And then—"

" Your Highness knows the monks who will do the honours of the abbey to his Majesty."

" They will be the same—"

" Who were there when your Highness was crowned."

" They will dare to lay hands on the Lord's anointed? "

" Oh! to shave him, only."

" They will never dare to do that to a king."

" He will not be a king then."

" How so? "

" Have you never heard of a holy man who preaches sermons, and is going to perform miracles? "

" Brother Gorenflot? "

" Precisely."

" The one who wished to preach the League with his arquebuse on his shoulder? "

" The same."

" Well, they will conduct the king into his cell. Once there, he will be asked to sign his abdication; then, when he has signed, Madame de Montpensier will enter, scissors in hand. She wears them now, hanging to her side; they are charming scissors, made of gold, and admirably chased, to do him honour. You understand the rest. We announce to the people that the king, experiencing a holy repentance for his sins, has announced his intention of never more leaving the convent. If there are any who doubt, M. de Guise holds the army, Monsieur the Cardinal the Church, and M. de Mayenne the *bourgeois ;* and with these three powers thus disposed you can make the people believe what you like."

" But they will accuse me of violence," said the duke.

" You need not be there."

" They will look on me as a usurper."

" Monseigneur forgets the abdication."

" The king will refuse."

" It seems that Brother Gorenflot is not only clever, but strong."

" The plan is then settled? "

" Quite."

" And they do not fear that I shall denounce it? "

" No, Monseigneur; for in that case, they have another, not less sure."

" Ah ! "

" Yes."

" And this one? "

" I do not know; they thought me too much your friend to trust me with it."

" Well, I yield, Count. What must I do? "

" Approve."

" Very well, I approve."

" Yes; but words are not enough."

" How, then, is it necessary to approve? "

" In writing."

" It is a folly to suppose I will ever consent to that."

" And why not? "

" If the conspiracy fail—"

" It is just in case it should that they ask for your signature."

" Then they wish to shelter themselves behind my name? "

" Nothing else."

" Then I refuse a thousand times."

" You cannot."

" I cannot refuse? "

" No."

" Are you mad? "

" To refuse is to betray."

" Let them think as they like; at all events I will choose my own danger."

" Monseigneur, you choose badly."

" I will risk it," cried François, endeavouring to keep firm.

" For your own interest I advise you not to do so."

" But I shall compromise myself by signing."

" In refusing, you assassinate yourself."

François shuddered.

" They would dare? " said he.

" They would dare anything, Monseigneur. The conspirators have gone so far that they must succeed at any cost."

The duke fell into a state of indecision easy to understand.

" I will sign," said he, at last.

" When? "

" To-morrow."

" No, Monseigneur; if you sign, it must be at once."

" But M. de Guise must draw up the agreement."

" It is already drawn; here it is; " and Monsoreau drew a paper from his pocket. It was a full adhesion to the scheme. The duke read it through, growing more and more pale as he did so.

" Here is the pen, Monseigneur."

" Then I must sign? "

" If you wish to do so; no one forces you."

" Yes, they do, since they menace me with assassination."

" I do not menace you, Monseigneur; I only warn you."

" Give me the pen."

And snatching it eagerly, he signed the paper. Monsoreau watched him with an eye full of hatred and hope; and no sooner had the duke finished than, exclaiming " Ah! " he seized the paper, buttoned it into his doublet, and wrapped his cloak over it. François looked at him with astonishment, for a flash of ferocious joy played over his face.

" And now, Monseigneur, be prudent," said he.

" How so? "

" Do not run about the streets with Aurilly, as you did just now."

" What do you mean? "

" I mean that this evening you pursued with your love a woman whom her husband adores, and of whom he is jealous enough to kill any one who approaches her without permission."

" Is it of yourself and your wife that you are speaking? "

" Yes, Monseigneur. I have married Diane de Méridor; she is mine, and no one shall have her while I live,—not even a prince! I swear it by my name and on this poniard! " and he almost touched with his poniard the breast of the prince, who started back.

" Monsieur, you menace me! " cried François, pale with rage.

" No, Monseigneur; once more I say, I only warn you."

" Of what? "

" That no one shall make love to my wife."

" And I warn you that you are too late, and that some one has her already."

Monsoreau uttered a terrible cry and buried both hands in his hair. " It is not you," he stammered; " it is not you, Monseigneur? "

" You are mad, Count," said the duke, making a movement to ring the bell.

" No; I see clearly, I talk intelligibly, I understand correctly. You have just said that some one possesses my wife; you have said it."

" I repeat it."

" Name that person, and prove the statement."

" Who was hidden this evening, twenty steps from your door, with a musket? "

" I."

" Well, Count, during that time there was a man with your wife."

" You saw him go in? "

" I saw him come out."

" By the door? "

" No, by the window."

" Did you recognise him? "

" Yes."

" Name him, Monseigneur, or I do not answer for myself."

The duke half smiled. " Monsieur the Count," said he, " on my faith as a prince, on my soul, within a week I will tell you his name."

" You swear it? "

" I swear it."

" Well, Monseigneur, you have a week," said he, touching the paper in his breast; " in a week or—you understand? "

" Come back in a week."

" Good! in a week I shall have regained all my strength, and shall be ready for vengeance."

CHAPTER XLI

A PROMENADE AT LES TOURNELLES

IN course of time the Angevin gentlemen had returned to Paris, although not with much confidence. They knew too well the king, his brother, and mother, to hope that all would terminate in a family embrace. They returned therefore timidly and glided into the town armed to the teeth, ready to fire on the least suspicion, and fifty times before reaching the Hôtel d'Anjou drew their swords on harmless *bourgeois*, who were guilty of no crime but that of looking at them. The duke gave them a cordial welcome. He said to them, " My friends, they are thinking here of killing you. Receptions of that sort are in the air; take care of yourselves."

" Should we not offer our very humble respects to his Majesty? " asked D'Antragues; " for if we hide ourselves, that will do little honour to Anjou. What do you think? "

" You are right," said the duke; " and if you wish I will go with you."

The three young men looked at one another in consultation. At this moment Bussy entered the hall and went to embrace his friends. " Eh! " said he, " you are late in returning. But what is this I hear,—his Highness proposing to get himself killed in the Louvre, like Cæsar in the Roman senate? Consider, then, that each one of the favourites would gladly carry away under his cloak a small piece of Monseigneur."

" But, dear friend, we propose to rub down those gentlemen a little."

Bussy kept his secret. " Eh, eh! " he said, " we shall see; we shall see."

The duke looked at him attentively.

" Let us go to the Louvre," said Bussy, " but alone; Monseigneur can remain in his garden, knocking off poppy-heads."

François was glad to escape the disagreeable visit.

The Angevins presented themselves at the Louvre, magnificently dressed in silk, velvet, and embroidery. Henri III. would not receive them; they waited vainly in the gallery. It was MM. de Quélus, de Maugiron, de Schomberg, and d'Epernon who came to announce this news to them with great politeness, and expressing many regrets.

" Ah, gentlemen," said D'Antragues, " the news is sad; but coming from your mouths, it loses half its bitterness."

" Gentlemen," said Schomberg, " you are the flower of grace and courtesy. Would it please you to change the reception which you have missed into a little promenade? "

" Ah, gentlemen, we were about to propose it."

" Where shall we go? " said Quélus.

" I know a charming place near the Bastille," said Schomberg.

" We follow you; go on."

Then the eight gentlemen went out arm in arm, talking gaily on different subjects. On arriving, Quélus said, " Here is a solitary place, with a good footing."

" Faith! yes," said D'Antragues, trying it in different places.

" Well," Quélus continued, " we thought that you would one day accompany us here to meet M. de Bussy, who has invited us all here."

" It is true," said Bussy to his astounded friends.

" Do you accept, gentlemen of Anjou? " said Maugiron.

" Certainly; we rejoice at such an honour."

" That is well," said Schomberg. " Shall we each choose an opponent? "

" No," said Bussy, " that is not fair; let us trust to chance, and the first one that is free can join the others."

" Let us draw lots, then," said Quélus.

" One moment," said Bussy; " first let us settle the rules of the game."

" They are simple; we will fight till death ensues."

" Yes, but how? "

" With sword and dagger."

" On foot? "

" Oh, yes! on horseback one's movements are not so free."

" Then, on foot."

" What day? "

" The soonest possible."

" No," said D'Epernon, " I have a thousand things to settle and a will to make; I would rather wait five or six days."

" That is speaking like a brave man," said Bussy, ironically.
" Is it agreed? "

" Yes; we understand one another marvellously well."

" Let us draw lots, then," said Bussy.

" One moment! divide the ground into four compartments,
each for a pair."

" Well said."

" I propose for number one the long square between the
chestnuts; it is a fine place."

" Agreed."

" But the sun? One would be turned to the east."

" No," said Bussy, " that is not fair; " and he proposed a
new position, which was agreed to.

Schomberg and Ribeirac came first, Quélus and D'Antragues,
second, Livarot and Maugiron, third; D'Epernon, who saw
himself left to Bussy, grew very pale.

" Now, gentlemen," said Bussy, " until the day of the combat,
we belong to one another; we are friends for life to death.
Will you accept a dinner at the Hôtel Bussy? "

All agreed, and returned with Bussy to his hotel, where a
sumptuous banquet kept them together till morning.

CHAPTER XLII

IN WHICH CHICOT SLEEPS

THE movements of the young men had been remarked by the
king and by Chicot. The king walked up and down, waiting
impatiently for his friends to return; but Chicot followed them
at a distance, and saw enough to be satisfied of their intentions.
When he returned to the house, he found the king walking up
and down, muttering.

" Ah, my dear friend! do you know what has become of
them? " cried Henri.

" Whom,—your favourites? "

" Alas! yes, my poor friends."

" They must lie very low by this time."

" Have they been killed? " cried Henri. " Are they dead? "

" Dead, I fear— "

" And you laugh, wretch? "

" Oh, my son! dead drunk."

"Oh, Chicot! how you terrified me. But why do you calumniate these gentlemen?"

"On the contrary, I praise them."

"Be serious, I beg; do you know that they went out with the Angevins?"

"Of course I know it."

"What was the result?"

"What I tell you,—that they are dead drunk or pretty near it."

"But Bussy?"

"He is intoxicating them; he is a dangerous man."

"Chicot, for pity's sake—"

"Yes; Bussy has given a dinner to your friends. How do you like that?"

"Impossible! They are sworn enemies."

"Exactly; if they were friends they wouldn't need to get drunk together. Listen; have you good legs?"

"What do you mean?"

"Would you go even to the river?"

"I would go to the end of the world to see such a thing."

"Well, go only to the Hôtel Bussy."

"Will you accompany me?"

"Thank you, I have just come from there."

"But—"

"Oh, no; I who have seen do not need to be convinced. Go, my son; go."

The king looked at him angrily.

"You are very good," said Chicot, "to get angry on account of those fellows. They laugh; they feast; they make opposition to your government. Let us respond to all those things philosophically. They laugh; let us laugh. They feast; let us be served with something good and hot. They make opposition; let us go to bed after supper."

The king could not help smiling.

"You can flatter yourself that you are a true sage," said Chicot. "There have been in France long-haired kings, a bold king, a grand king, lazy kings; I am sure that you will be called 'Henri the Patient.' Ah, my son! it is so excellent a virtue—when one has no other."

"Betrayed!" said the king to himself. "Those fellows haven't even the manners of gentlemen!"

"Ah, there!" cried Chicot, urging the king towards the hall in which supper awaited them, "you are uneasy about your friends. You first lament them as if they were dead; and when you hear they are not dead, you are uneasy still—"

" You are intolerable, M. Chicot."

" Would you have preferred that they should each have had seven or eight wounds by a rapier? "

" I should like to be able to depend on my friends."

" Oh, *ventre de biche!* depend upon me. I am here, my son; only feed me. I want pheasant and truffles."

Henri and his only friend went to bed early, the king still sighing because his court was so empty, Chicot short of breath because his stomach was so full.

The next day, at the *petite* levee of the king, MM. de Quélus, de Schomberg, de Maugiron, and d'Epernon presented themselves. Chicot still slept. The king jumped from his bed in a fury, and tearing off the perfumed mask from his face, cried, " Go out from here! "

The young men looked at one another in wonder.

" But, Sire, we wished to say to your Majesty—"

" That you are no longer drunk, I suppose."

Chicot opened his eyes.

" Your Majesty is in error," said Quélus, gravely.

" And yet I have not drunk the wine of Anjou."

" Oh, I understand," said Quélus, smiling.

" What? "

" If your Majesty will remain alone with us, we will tell you."

" I hate drunkards and traitors."

" Sire! " cried three of the gentlemen.

" Patience, gentlemen," said Quélus, " his Majesty has slept badly, and had unpleasant dreams. A few words will set all right."

" Speak, then, but be brief."

" It is possible, Sire, but difficult."

" Yes; one turns long round certain accusations."

" No, Sire, we go straight to it," replied Quélus, looking again at Chicot and the usher, as though to reiterate his request that they might be left alone.

The king signed to the usher to leave the room; but Chicot said, " Never mind me, I sleep like a top," and closing his eyes again, he began to snore with all his strength.

CHAPTER XLIII

WHERE CHICOT WAKES

"YOUR Majesty," said Quélus, " knows only half the business, and that the least interesting half. We have, it is true, all dined with M. de Bussy, and, to the honour of his cook be it said, dined well."

"There was especially," said Schomberg, " a certain wine from Austria or Hungary which really appeared to me marvellous."

"Oh, that low-minded German!" said the king; "he loves wine, I always suspected that."

"I was sure of it," said Chicot; "I have seen him drunk twenty times." Schomberg turned towards him. "Pay no attention to me," said the Gascon, "Henri will tell you that I dream aloud."

Schomberg returned to Henri. "Faith, Sire," he said, "I conceal neither my likes nor my dislikes, — good wine is good."

"Let us not call a thing good which leads us to forget our sovereign," said the king, in a tone of reserve.

Schomberg was about to reply, doubtless unwilling to abandon so good a cause, when Quélus made a sign to him.

"You are right," said Schomberg; "go on."

"I was about to say, Sire," Quélus resumed, "that during the repast, or rather after it, we had a most serious and interesting conversation concerning your Majesty's affairs."

"You make the exordium very long," said Henri; "it is a bad sign."

"*Ventre de biche!* how talkative that Valois is!" cried Chicot.

"Oh, oh! Maître Gascon," said Henri, "if you do not sleep, you must leave the room."

"*Pardieu!* it is you who keep me from sleeping, your tongue clacks so fast."

Quélus, seeing it was impossible to speak seriously, shrugged his shoulders, and rose in anger.

"Sire," said D'Epernon, "we were speaking of grave matters."

"Grave matters?" repeated Henri.

"Yes, if the lives of eight brave gentlemen seem to your Majesty worthy of attention."

"What does that mean?" exclaimed the king.

"It means," said Quélus, "that I am waiting until the king will deign to listen."

"I listen, my son; I listen," said Henri, placing his hand on Quélus's shoulder.

"Well, then, as I was saying, Sire, we have had a serious conversation, and this is the conclusion to which it led,—the royal cause is imperilled and enfeebled."

"That is to say, every one seems to conspire against it," cried Henri.

"It resembles," continued Quélus, "those strange gods who, like the gods of Tiberius and Caligula, arrived at old age and could not die, but in their immortality followed the course of human infirmity; they could be arrested in that course only by some noble sacrifice on the part of a devotee, by which they were rejuvenated. Then, regenerated by transfusion of young blood, generous and glowing, they began again to live, and became vigorous and powerful. Well, Sire, your royalty resembles those gods,—it can live only by sacrifices."

"He speaks gold," said Chicot. "Quélus, my son, go and preach in the streets of Paris, and I will wager an ox against an egg that you will surpass Lincestre, Cahier, Cotton, and even that thunder of eloquence called Gorenflot."

Henri made no reply. It was evident that his mood had changed. He had at first assailed the favourites with disdainful looks, but gradually, an idea of the truth having taken possession of him, he became thoughtful, gloomy, and anxious. "Go on," he said; "you see that I am listening to you, Quélus."

"Sire, you are a great king; but you have no horizon before you. The nobility have raised so many barriers before your eyes that you can see nothing, if it be not the still higher barriers that the people have raised. When, Sire, in battle one battalion places itself like a menacing wall before another, what happens? Cowards look behind them, and seeing an open space, they fly; the brave lower their heads and rush on."

"Well, then, forward!" cried the king. "Mordieu! am I not the first gentleman in my kingdom? Were they not great battles that I fought in my youth? Has the now closing century many names more resounding than Jarnac and Moncontour? Forward, then, gentlemen! and I, according to my custom, will march before you to the centre of conflict."

"Oh, yes, Sire! forward!" exclaimed the young men, electrified by that warlike demonstration of the king.

Chicot sat up. "Silence, there, you others!" he said, "let

my orator speak. Go on, Quélus; go on, my son. You have already said beautiful and excellent things, and it is for you to say more of them. Continue, my friend; continue."

"Yes, Chicot, you are right, as you often are. Yes, I will continue, and will say to his Majesty that the time has come for royalty to consent to one of those sacrifices of which I have spoken. Against these ramparts which are closing round your Majesty, four men will march, sure to be applauded by you, and glorified by posterity."

"What do you mean, Quélus?" cried the king, with eyes in which joy was tempered by solicitude. "Who are these four men?"

"I and these other gentlemen," replied Quélus, with the sentiment of pride which exalts every man who stakes his life for a principle or for a passion. "I and these gentlemen devote ourselves, Sire."

"To what?"

"To your safety."

"Against whom?"

"Against your enemies."

"Private enmities of young men?"

"Oh, Sire, that is the expression of vulgar prejudice; speak like a king, Sire, not like a *bourgeois*. Do not profess to believe that Maugiron detests D'Antragues, that Schomberg dislikes Livarot, that D'Epernon is jealous of Bussy, and that I hate Ribeirac. Oh, no! they are all young and agreeable, and we might love one another like brothers. It is not therefore a rivalry between man and man which places the swords in our hands; it is the quarrel of France with Anjou, the dispute as to the rights of the populace against the prerogatives of the king. We present ourselves as champions of royalty in those lists where we shall be met by the champions of the League; and we came to say, 'Bless us, Sire; smile on those who are going to die for you.' Your blessing will perhaps give us the victory; your smile will make us die happy."

Henri, overcome with emotion, opened his arms to Quélus and the others. He united them in his heart; and it was not a spectacle without interest, a picture without expression, but a scene in which manly courage was allied to softer emotions, sanctified by devotion. Chicot looked on, and his face, ordinarily indifferent or sarcastic, was not the least noble and eloquent of the six.

"Ah, my heroes," cried the king at length, "it is a splendid sacrifice, a noble undertaking; and I am proud to-day, not of being King of France, but of being your friend. At the same time, as I know my own interests best, I will not accept a sacrifice of which the result will deliver me up, if you fall, into the hands of my enemies. You may be sure that France is strong enough to contend with Anjou. I know my brother, the Guises, and the League; often during my life have I subdued horses more fiery and contumacious."

"But, Sire," cried Maugiron, "soldiers do not reason thus; they cannot admit the consideration of possible bad luck into the examination of questions of this kind,—questions of honour, questions of conscience, in which a man acts by conviction rather than by reason."

"Pardon me, Maugiron; a soldier may act blindly, but the captain reflects."

"Reflect, then, Sire, and let us act, who are only soldiers," said Schomberg. "Besides, I know no ill luck; I am always successful."

"Friend, friend," said the king, sadly, "I could not say as much. It is true you are but twenty years old."

"Sire," said Quélus, "on what day shall we meet MM. de Bussy, de Livarot, d'Antragues, and de Ribeirac?"

"Never; I forbid it absolutely."

"Sire, pardon, the rendezvous was arranged yesterday before the dinner; our word is given, and cannot be withdrawn."

"Excuse me, Monsieur," said Henri; "the king absolves from oaths and promises by saying, 'I will, or I will not,' for the king is all-powerful. Tell these gentlemen, therefore, that I have menaced you with all my anger if you come to blows; and that you may not doubt it yourselves, I swear to exile you if—"

"Stop, Sire!" said Quélus; "for if you can release us from our promises, God alone can release you from yours. Do not swear, then, because, if for such a cause we have merited your anger, and this anger shows itself by exiling us, we will go into exile with joy; for then, being no longer on your Majesty's territories, we can keep our promises, and meet our adversaries."

"If these gentlemen approach you within range of an arquebuse, I will throw them all into the Bastille."

"Sire, if you do so we will all go barefooted, and with cords round our necks, to M. Testu, the governor, and pray to be incarcerated with them."

"I will have them beheaded, *mordieu!* I am king, I hope."

" We will cut our throats at the foot of their scaffold."

Henri kept silent for a long time, then, raising his eyes, said, " Indeed, here is a good and brave nobility. If God does not bless a cause defended by such men as these—"

" Do not be impious; do not blaspheme," Chicot said solemnly, arising from his couch and approaching the king. " Yes, they are noble hearts; do what they wish, and fix a day for their meeting. That is your proper business, and not to dictate his duty to the Almighty."

" Oh, *mon Dieu! mon Dieu!* " murmured Henri.

" Sire, we pray you! " cried all the four gentlemen, bending their knees.

" Well, so be it! Indeed, God is just; he will give us the victory. But let us prepare for the conflict in a Christian manner. Dear friends, do you remember that Jarnac performed his devotions with exactness before fighting La Chateigneraie? The latter was a rough swordsman; but he abandoned himself to feasts and gaieties; he visited women,—an abominable sin! In short, he tempted God, who perhaps would have smiled on his youth, his beauty, and his strength, and would have saved his life. Jarnac killed him, however. Listen: we will enter upon a devotion. If I had time, I would send all your swords to Rome, that the pope might bless them. But we have the shrine of Ste. Geneviève, which contains most precious relics; let us fast and do penance, and keep holy the great day of the Fête Dieu, and then the next day—"

" Ah, Sire, thanks! that is in a week! " cried the young men.

And they seized the hands of the king, who embraced them all once more, and going into his oratory, melted into tears.

" Our cartel is ready," said Quélus; " we have but to add the day and hour. Write, Maugiron, the day after the Fête Dieu. Here is a table."

" It is done," said Maugiron; " now who will carry the letter? "

" I will, if you please," said Chicot, approaching; " but I wish to give you a piece of advice. His Majesty speaks of fasts and macerations. That is all very well after the combat; but before, I prefer good nourishment, generous wine, and eight hours' sleep every night."

" Bravo, Chicot! "

" Adieu, my little lions," replied the Gascon, " I go to the Hôtel Bussy." He went three steps and returned and said,

" Apropos, do not leave the king during the Fête Dieu; do not go to the country, any of you, but stay by the Louvre. Now I will do your commission."

CHAPTER XLIV

THE FÊTE DIEU

DURING this week events were preparing themselves, as a tempest gathers in the heavens during the calm days of summer. Monsoreau had an attack of fever for twenty-four hours, then he rallied, and betook himself to watching for the thief of his honour; but as he discovered no one, he became more than ever convinced of the hypocrisy of the Duc d'Anjou and of his bad intentions with regard to Diane.

Bussy did not discontinue his visits by day, but, warned by Rémy of this constant watchfulness, came no more at night to the window.

Chicot divided his time between the king—whom he watched as a mother watches her child—and his friend Gorenflot, whom he had persuaded to return to his convent, whither he had himself conducted him, and where he had received from the abbé a charming hospitality. At that first interview they talked of the piety of the king, and the prior seemed exceedingly grateful to his Majesty for the honour he would do the abbey by his proposed visit. That honour was to be even more marked than had been at first intended; Henri, being urged by the venerable abbé, had consented to spend the day and night in retirement at the convent. Chicot confirmed the abbé in that expectation; and as it was known that he had the ear of the king, he was invited to repeat his visit,—which he promised to do. As for Gorenflot, he became six cubits taller in the estimation of the monks. It was indeed a masterly stroke to secure thus Chicot's entire confidence. Machiavel would not have done better.

Being invited to return, Chicot returned; and as he carried with him in his pockets, under his cloak, and in his large boots, flasks of wine of rarest and most excellent vintage, Brother Gorenflot received him even more cordially than the abbé. Then he would remain for hours at a time shut up in the cell of the monk, sharing with him, according to the general report, his studies and his ecstasies. He spent in the convent the entire night preceding the Fête Dieu, and in the morning a rumour ran through the abbey that Gorenflot had persuaded Chicot to take the robe.

As for the king, he gave constant lessons in fencing to his friends, teaching them new thrusts, and, above all, exercising D'Epernon, to whom fate had appointed so skilful an adversary, and who was so visibly preoccupied by expectations of the decisive day.

Any one walking in the streets of Paris at certain hours of the night might have met the strange monks of whom we have already furnished some description, and who resembled troopers more than monks. Then, to complete the picture, we must add that the Hôtel de Guise had become at once mysterious and turbulent, peopled within and deserted without; that meetings were held every night in the great hall, and with all the blinds and windows hermetically closed; and that these meetings were preceded by dinners to which none but men were invited, and which were presided over by Madame de Montpensier. Of all these meetings, however, important though they were, the police suspected nothing. On the morning of the great day the weather was superb, and the flowers which filled the streets sent their perfumes through the air. Chicot, who for the last fortnight had slept in the king's room, waked him early; no one had yet entered the royal chamber.

" Oh, Chicot," cried the king, " plague on you! I never saw a man so unreasonable. You have waked me from one of the sweetest dreams I ever had in my life."

" What was it, my son? "

" I dreamed that Quélus had run D'Antragues through the body, and was swimming in the blood of his adversary. Let us go and pray that my dream may be realised. Call, Chicot; call! "

" What do you want? "

" My hair-cloth and my scourge."

" Would you not prefer a good breakfast? "

" Pagan, would you go to hear Mass on the Fête Dieu with a full stomach? "

" Even so."

" Call, Chicot! "

" Patience; it is scarcely eight o'clock, and you will have plenty of time to scourge yourself. Let us talk first. Converse with your friend; you will not repent it, Valois, on the faith of a Chicot."

" Well, talk; but be quick."

" How shall we divide our day, my son? "

" Into three parts."

" In honour of the Trinity; very well, let me hear these three parts."

" First, Mass at St. Germain l'Auxerrois."

" Well? "

" Return to the Louvre for a collation."

" Very good."

" Then, a procession of penitents through the streets, stopping at the principal convents of Paris, beginning at the Jacobins and finishing at Ste. Geneviève, where I have promised the prior to stay till to-morrow in the cell of a saint, who will spend the night in prayer to assure the success of our arms."

" I know him."

" The saint? "

" Yes, perfectly."

" So much the better; you shall accompany me, and we will pray together."

" Yes; make yourself easy."

" Then dress yourself, and come."

" Wait a little."

" What for? "

" I have more to ask."

" Be quick, then, for time passes."

" What is the court to do? "

" Follow me."

" And your brother? "

" Will accompany me."

" Your guard? "

" The French guard will wait for me at the Louvre, and the Swiss at the door of the abbey."

" That will do; now I know all."

" Then I may call? "

" Yes."

Henri struck on his gong.

" The ceremony will be magnificent," said Chicot.

" God will accept our homage, I hope."

" We shall see about that to-morrow. But tell me, Henri, before any one comes in, have you nothing else to say to me? "

" No. Have I forgotten some detail of the ceremonial? "

" I am not speaking of that."

" Of what, then? "

" Of nothing."

" But you ask me—"

" If it is settled that you go to the abbey of Ste. Geneviève."

" Certainly."

" And that you spend the night there? "

" I have promised."

" Well, my son, I tell you I do not like that part of the programme."

" How so? "

" When we have dined I will tell you another plan that has occurred to me."

" Well, I consent to it."

" Whether you consent or not it will be all the same thing."

" What do you mean? "

" Hush! here are your attendants."

As he spoke, the ushers opened the door; and the barber, perfumer, and valet of the king entered, and began to perform upon his Majesty one of those toilets which we have described elsewhere. When the king was dressing, the Duc d'Anjou was announced. He was accompanied by M. de Monsoreau, d'Epernon, and Aurilly. Henri, at the sight of Monsoreau, still pale and looking more frightful than ever, could not repress a movement of surprise. The duke perceived that movement, which the count also noticed.

" Sire," said the duke, " it is M. de Monsoreau, who comes to pay homage to your Majesty."

" Thank you, Monsieur," said Henri; " and I am the more affected by your visit because you have been wounded, have you not? "

" Yes, Sire."

" At the chase, they told me."

" Yes, Sire."

" But you are better now? "

" I am well."

" Sire," said the duke, " would it please you that after our devotions M. de Monsoreau should go and prepare a chase for us in the woods of Compiègne? "

" But do you not know that to-morrow—"

He was going to say, " four of your friends are to fight four of mine; " but he stopped, for he remembered that it was a secret.

" I know nothing," said the duke; " but if your Majesty will inform me—"

" I meant that as I am to pass the night at the abbey of Ste.

Geneviève, I should perhaps not be ready for to-morrow; but
let the count go. If it be not to-morrow it shall be the day
after."

" You hear? " said the duke to Monsoreau.

" Yes, Monseigneur."

At this moment Quélus and Schomberg entered. The king
received them with open arms.

Monsoreau said softly to the duke, " You exile me, Monseigneur."

" Is it not your duty to prepare the chase for the king? "
said the duke, smiling.

" I understand; this is the last day of the week which your
Highness asked me to wait, and you prefer sending me to
Compiègne to keeping your promise. But be careful; before
night I can with a single word—"

François seized the count by the wrist. " Be quiet! " said
he; " I hold to my promise."

" Explain yourself."

" Your departure will be publicly known, since the order is
official."

" Well? "

" Well, you will not go, but you will hide near your house;
then, believing you gone, the man you wish to know will come.
The rest concerns yourself; I believe I promised nothing more."

" Ah! if that be so—"

" You have my word."

" I have better than that, I have your signature."

" Oh, yes, *mordieu !* I know that."

Aurilly touched D'Epernon's arm and said, " It is done;
Bussy will not fight to-morrow."

" Not fight? "

" I answer for it."

" Who will prevent it? "

" What matter, so long as he doesn't fight? "

" If it be so, my dear sorcerer, there are one thousand crowns
for you."

" Gentlemen," said the king, who had finished his toilet, " to
St. Germain l'Auxerrois! "

" And from there to Ste. Geneviève? " asked the duke.

" Certainly," replied Henri, passing into the gallery, where
all his court were waiting for him.

CHAPTER XLV

WHICH WILL EXPLAIN THE PREVIOUS CHAPTER

THE evening before, after everything had been agreed upon and arranged between the Guises and the Angevins, M. de Monsoreau had returned to his home, and had found Bussy there. Then, in his friendship for this brave gentleman, he had taken him aside and said, " Will you permit me to give you a piece of advice? "

" Pray do."

" If I were you, I should leave Paris to-morrow."

" I! and why so? "

" All that I can tell you is that your absence may save you from great embarrassment."

" From great embarrassment? " Bussy replied, looking at the count with a searching gaze.

" Are you ignorant of what is to take place to-morrow? "

" Completely."

" On your honour? "

" On my word as a gentleman."

" M. d'Anjou has confided nothing to you? "

" Nothing; M. d'Anjou confides nothing to me beyond what all the world knows."

" Well! I, who am not the Duc d'Anjou, who love my friends for their own sakes, and not for mine, I will tell you, my dear count, that he is preparing for grave events to-morrow, and that the parties of Guise and Anjou meditate a stroke which may end in the fall of the king."

Bussy looked at M. de Monsoreau with suspicion; but his whole manner expressed so much sincerity that it was impossible to doubt him.

" Count," replied he, " my sword belongs to the Duc d'Anjou. The king, against whom I have done nothing, hates me, and has never let slip an occasion of doing or saying something wounding to me; and to-morrow even," continued Bussy, lowering his voice,—" I tell this to you, but to you alone, remember,—to-morrow I am about to risk my life to humiliate Henri de Valois in the person of his favourites."

" Then you are resolved to risk all the consequences of your adherence to the duke? "

" Yes."

" You know to what it may lead you? "

" I know where I intend to stop. Whatever complaints I have against the king, I will never lift a hand against him; but I will let others do what they like, and I will follow M. d'Anjou to protect him in case of need."

" My dear count," said Monsoreau, " the Duc d'Anjou is perfidious and a traitor; a coward, capable, from jealousy or fear, of sacrificing his most faithful servant, his most devoted friend. Abandon him. Take a friend's counsel; pass the day in your little house at Vincennes; go where you like, except to the procession of the Fête Dieu."

" But why do you follow the duke yourself? "

" For reasons which concern my honour. I have need of him for a little while longer."

" Well, that is like me; for things which concern my honour I must follow the duke."

The Comte de Monsoreau pressed his hand, and they parted.

The next morning Monsoreau, on returning home from his interview with the king, announced to his wife his approaching departure for Compiègne, and gave all the necessary orders. Diane heard the news with joy. She knew from her husband of the duel which was arranged between Bussy and D'Epernon, but had no fear for the result, and looked forward to it with pride.

Bussy had presented himself in the morning to the Duc d'Anjou, who, seeing him so frank, loyal, and devoted, felt some remorse; but two things combated this return of good feeling, —the great influence Bussy had over him, as every powerful mind has over a weak one, and which made him fear that if he should attain to the throne Bussy would be the real king; and then, besides that, Bussy's love for Diane, which awoke all the tortures of jealousy in his heart. However, he said to himself, —for Monsoreau also inspired him with anxiety,—" Either Bussy will accompany me, and supporting me by his courage will secure the triumph of my cause,—and then if I triumph, I shall not care what Monsoreau may say or do,—or Bussy will abandon me, and then I shall owe him nothing, and will abandon him in return."

When they were in the church, the duke saw Rémy enter, and going up to his master, slip a note into his hand.

" It is from her," thought he; " she sends him word that her husband is leaving Paris."

Bussy put the note into his hat, opened and read it; and the duke saw his face radiant with joy and love. "Ah! it will be bad for you," he said, "if you abandon me." The duke looked round; if Monsoreau had been there, perhaps the duke would not have had patience to wait till the evening to denounce Bussy to him.

The Mass over, they returned to the Louvre, where a collation waited for the king in his room, and for the gentlemen in the gallery. On entering the Louvre, Bussy approached the duke.

"Pardon, Monseigneur," said he; "but can I say two words to you?"

"Are you in a hurry?"

"Very much so."

"Will it not do during the procession? We shall walk side by side."

"Monseigneur must excuse me, but what I wished to ask is that I need not accompany you."

"Why so?"

"Monseigneur, to-morrow is to be a great day, as your Highness is aware, since it is to determine the quarrel between Anjou and France; I desire therefore to spend this day in retirement at my little house in Vincennes."

"Then you do not join the procession with the king and court?"

"No, Monseigneur, if you will excuse me."

"Will you not rejoin me at Ste. Geneviève?"

"Monseigneur, I wish to have the whole day to myself."

"But if anything should occur during the day to make me need my friends?"

"As Monseigneur would need me then only that I might draw sword against the king, it is a double reason for excusing myself," replied Bussy; "my sword is engaged against M. d'Epernon."

Monsoreau had told the duke the night before that he might reckon on Bussy; this change, therefore, must have been occasioned by Diane's note.

"Then," said the duke, with closed teeth, "you abandon your chief and master?"

"Monseigneur, he who is about to risk his life in a bloody duel, as ours will be, has but one master; and it is to him my last devotions will be paid."

"You know that I am playing for a throne, and you leave me."

"Monseigneur, I have worked pretty well for you; I will

work for you again to-morrow. Do not ask me for more than my life."

"It is well!" said the duke, in a hollow voice, "you are free; go, M. de Bussy."

Bussy, without caring for the prince's evident anger, ran down the staircase of the Louvre, and went rapidly to his own house.

The duke called Aurilly. "Well, he has condemned himself," said he.

"Does he not follow you?"

"No."

"He goes to the rendezvous to which the note invited him?"

"Yes."

"Then it is for this evening?"

"It is."

"Is M. de Monsoreau warned?"

"Of the rendezvous—yes; but not yet of the man."

"Then you have decided to sacrifice the count?"

"I have determined to revenge myself; I fear now but one thing."

"What is that?"

"That Monsoreau will trust to his strength, and that Bussy will escape him."

"Reassure yourself, Monseigneur."

"Why?"

"Is M. de Bussy irrevocably condemned?"

"Yes, *mordieu!*—a man who dictates to me, who takes from me my will and substitutes his own, who takes from me my mistress and makes her his own; a sort of lion, of whom I am less the master than the keeper,—yes, Aurilly, he is condemned without mercy."

"Well, then, be easy, for if he escapes Monsoreau, he will not escape from another."

"And who is that?"

"Does your Highness order me to name him?"

"Yes, I do."

"It is M. de Epernon."

"D'Epernon! who was to fight him to-morrow?"

"Yes, Monseigneur."

"How is that?"

Aurilly was about to reply, when the duke was summoned, for the king was at table, and had sent for his brother.

"You shall tell me during the procession," said the duke.

Since we shall not have leisure to follow the duke and Aurilly in the streets of Paris, we will at once tell our readers what had taken place between D'Epernon and the lute-player. In the morning, at about daybreak, D'Epernon had gone to the Hôtel d'Anjou, and called for Aurilly. They had long known each other, for Aurilly had taught D'Epernon to play on the lute, and as he was fond of music, they were often together. He called upon Aurilly to talk with him of his approaching duel, which disquieted him not a little. Bravery was never one of D'Epernon's prominent qualities; and he looked on a duel with Bussy as certain death.

At the first word that D'Epernon spoke to the musician on the subject he had at heart, Aurilly, who knew what hatred his master cherished against Bussy, entered into sympathy with his pupil, and told him that for the last week M. de Bussy had practised fencing two hours every morning with a member of the guards,—the most cunning swordsman that then could be found in Paris; a sort of artist in sword-thrusts, who, a traveller and philosopher, had borrowed from the Italians their cautious play, from the Spaniards their subtle and brilliant feints, from the Germans firmness of the wrist and the method of parry and thrust, and from the savage Poles—then called Sarmatians— their springs and bounds, their sudden prostrations, and their close embrace, body to body.

During this recital D'Epernon appeared greatly terrified. " Ah! why, I'm a dead man," said he, half laughing, and turning pale.

" *Pardieu !* " answered Aurilly.

" But it is absurd to go out with a man who is sure to kill me. It is as if one should play at dice with a man who is sure to throw double sixes every time."

" You should have thought of that before making the engagement."

" *Peste !* I will break the engagement. He is a fool who gives up his life willingly at twenty-five. But, now I think of it— *mordieu !* yes, it is good logic, listen."

" Well? "

" M. de Bussy is sure to kill me, you say? "

" I do not doubt it."

" Then it will not be a duel, but an assassination."

" That is true."

" And if it be, it is lawful to prevent an assassination by—"

" By? "

" By—a murder."

" Doubtless."

" What prevents me, since he wishes to kill me, from killing him first? "

" Oh, *mon Dieu!* nothing; I thought of that myself."

" Is not my reasoning clear? "

" Clear as day."

" Natural? "

" Very natural."

" Only, instead of killing him cruelly with my own hands, as he wishes to do to me, I, who have an abhorrence of blood, will leave that task to some other person."

" That is to say, you will hire assassins? "

" Faith! yes, as M. de Guise did for Saint-Mégrin."

" It will cost you dear."

" I will give three thousand crowns."

" You will only get six men for that, when they know with whom they have to deal."

" Are not six enough? "

" M. de Bussy would kill four before they touched him. Do you remember the fight in the Rue St. Antoine? "

" I will give six thousand if necessary. *Mordieu!* if I do the thing at all, I want to do it well, and so thoroughly that he cannot escape."

" Have you your men? "

" Oh, there are plenty of unoccupied men,—soldiers of fortune."

" Very well; but take care."

" Of what? "

" If they fail they will denounce you."

" I have the king to protect me."

" That will not hinder M. de Bussy from killing you."

" That is true."

" Should you like an auxiliary? "

" I should like anything which would aid me to get rid of that mad dog."

" Well, a certain enemy of your enemy is jealous."

" Ah, ah! "

" And he is now laying a snare for him."

" Well? "

" But he wants money; with your six thousand crowns he will take care of your affairs as well as his own. You do not wish the honour of the thing to be yours, I suppose? "

" *Mon Dieu !* no; I ask only to remain in obscurity."

" Send your men, and he will use them."

" But I must know who it is."

" I will show you this morning."

" Where? "

" At the Louvre."

" Then he is noble? "

" Yes."

" Aurilly, you shall have the six thousand crowns."

" Then it is settled? "

" Irrevocably."

" To the Louvre, then! "

" To the Louvre."

We have seen in the preceding chapter how Aurilly said to D'Epernon, " Be easy, Bussy will not fight to-morrow."

CHAPTER XLVI

THE PROCESSION

As soon as the collation was over, the king had entered his chamber with Chicot, to put on his penitent's robe, and had come out an instant after, with bare feet, a cord round his waist, and his hood over his face; the courtiers had made the same toilet. The weather was magnificent, and the pavements were strewn with flowers; an immense crowd lined the roads to the four places where the king was to stop. The clergy of St. Germain l'Auxerrois led the procession, and the Archbishop of Paris followed, carrying the holy sacrament; between them walked young men shaking censers, and young girls scattering roses. Then came the king, followed by his four friends, bare-footed and frocked like himself.

The Duc d'Anjou followed in his ordinary dress, accompanied by his Angevins. Next came the principal courtiers, and then the *bourgeois*. It was one o'clock when they left the Louvre. Crillon and the French guards were about to follow; but the king signed to them to remain. It was near six in the evening when the head of the *cortége* arrived before the old abbey, where they saw the prior and the monks drawn up on the threshold to wait for his Majesty. The Duc d'Anjou, a little before, had pleaded great fatigue, and had asked leave to retire to his hotel, which had been granted to him. His gentlemen had retired with him, as if to proclaim that they followed the duke and not the king; and besides, three of them were to fight on the following day, and were reluctant to fatigue themselves unduly. At the door of the abbey the king dismissed his four favourites, that they also might take some repose. The archbishop also, who had officiated all day without eating, was so exhausted that he was on the point of falling; the king took pity on him and on the other priests, and dismissed them all. Then, turning to the prior, Joseph Foulon, " Here I am, my father," said he, in nasal tones; " I come, sinner as I am, to seek repose in your solitude."

The prior bowed, and the royal penitent mounted the steps of the abbey, striking his breast at each step; and the door was immediately closed behind him. The king was so deeply absorbed in his meditations that he appeared not to notice that circumstance; and besides, there was nothing extraordinary in it, since he had dismissed his suite.

" We will first," said the prior, " conduct your Majesty into the crypt, which we have ornamented in our best manner to do honour to the King of heaven and earth."

The king merely made a gesture of assent and followed the prior.

No sooner had the king passed through the sombre arcade, lined with monks, and turned the corner which led to the chapel, than twenty hoods were thrown into the air, and eyes were seen brilliant with joy and triumph. Certainly those were not the faces of idle and cowardly monks; bristling mustaches and embrowned skins indicated among them force and activity. A considerable number showed faces furrowed by scars; and by the side of the proudest of all, who displayed the scar which was the most celebrated, stood a woman covered with a frock, and looking triumphant and happy. This woman, shaking a pair of golden scissors which hung by her side, cried, " Ah, my brothers, at last we have the Valois!"

" Upon my word, Sister, I believe so."

" Not yet," murmured the cardinal.

" How so?"

" Shall we have enough *bourgeois* troops to make head against Crillon and his guards?"

" We have better than *bourgeois* troops," replied the Duc de Mayenne; " and, believe me, there will not be a musket-shot exchanged."

" How so?" said the duchess; " I should have liked a little disturbance."

" Well, Sister, you will be deprived of it. When the king is taken he will cry out, but no one will answer; then, by persuasion, or by violence, but without showing ourselves, we shall make him sign his abdication. The news will soon spread through the city, and dispose in our favour both the *bourgeois* and the troops."

" The plan is good, and cannot fail," said the duchess.

" It is rather rough," said the Duc de Guise; " and besides, the king will refuse to sign the abdication. He is brave, and will rather die."

" Let him die, then," cried Mayenne and the duchess.

" Not so," replied the duke, firmly. " I will mount the throne of a prince who abdicates and is despised, but not of an assassinated man who is pitied. Besides, in your plans you forget M. le Duc d'Anjou, who if the king is killed will claim the crown."

" Let him claim, *mordieu!*" said Mayenne; " he shall be included in his brother's act of abdication. He is in relation with the Huguenots, and is unworthy to reign."

" With the Huguenots? Are you sure of that?"

" *Pardieu!* did he not escape from the Louvre by the aid of the King of Navarre?"

" Well?"

" Then another clause in favour of our house shall follow; this clause shall make you lieutenant-general of the kingdom, from which to the throne is only a step."

" Yes, yes," said the cardinal, " all that is settled; but it is probable that the French guards, to make sure that the abdication is a genuine one, and above all, a voluntary one, will insist upon seeing the king, and will force the gates of the abbey if they are not admitted. Crillon does not understand joking, and he is just the man to say to the king, ' Sire, your life is in danger; but, before everything, let us save our honour.' "

" The general has taken his precautions. If it be necessary to sustain a siege, we have here eighty gentlemen, and I have distributed arms to a hundred monks. We could hold out for a month against an army; besides, in case of danger, we have the cave to fly to with our prey."

" What is the Duc d'Anjou doing?"

" In the hour of danger he has failed, as usual. He has gone home, no doubt, waiting for news of us through Bussy or Monsoreau."

" *Mon Dieu!* he should have been here, not at home."

" You are wrong, Brother," said the cardinal; " the people and the nobles would have seen in that union of the two brothers a snare to entrap the family. As you said just now, we must, above all things, avoid playing the part of usurper. We inherit, that is all. By leaving the Duc d'Anjou free, and the queen-mother independent, we shall win approbation and admiration, and no one will have anything to say against us. If we act otherwise, we shall have against us Bussy and a hundred other dangerous swords."

" Bah! Bussy is going to fight against the king's favourites."

" *Pardieu!* he will kill them, and then he will join us," said the Duc de Guise; " he is a superior man, and one whom I much esteem. I will make him general of the army in Italy, where war is sure to break out."

" And I," said the Duchesse de Montpensier, " to show that I esteem him no less than you do, if I become a widow, will marry him."

" Who is with the king? " asked the duke.

" The prior and Brother Gorenflot."

" Is he in the cell? "

" Oh, no! he will look first at the crypt and the relics."

" And then? "

" Then the prior will address to him a few sonorous words on the vanity of the good things of the world; after which, Brother Gorenflot—you know him, he who delivered that magnificent discourse on the evening of the League—"

" Yes, go on."

" Brother Gorenflot will try to obtain from his conviction that which we are reluctant to wrest from his feebleness."

" Indeed, it will be infinitely better so," said the duke, reflecting.

" Bah! Henri is superstitious and weak," said Mayenne. " I will guarantee that he will yield to the fear of hell."

" And I am not less convinced than you," said the duke; " but our ships are burned, and there is no longer any possibility of going back. After the attempt by the prior and the discourse of Gorenflot, if both fail we will try the last resort,— intimidation."

" And then I shall shear my Valois," cried the duchess, reverting still to her favourite idea.

At this moment a bell sounded.

" The king is returning," said the Duc de Guise; " let us

become monks again." And immediately the hoods covered ardent eyes and speaking scars, and twenty or thirty monks, conducted by the three brothers, went towards the crypt.

CHAPTER XLVII

CHICOT I

THE king was absorbed in a meditativeness which promised an easy success to the projects of MM. de Guise. He visited the crypt, kissed the relics, often striking his breast, and murmuring the most doleful psalms. The prior began his exhortations, to which the king listened with the same signs of fervent contrition. Presently, upon a signal of the Duc de Guise, the prior said, " Sire, will it please you now to come and lay your earthly crown at the feet of the Eternal King? "

" Let us go," said the king, simply; and they all proceeded towards the cells. Henri continued to beat his breast, and appeared to be very much affected.

They arrived at the cell, on the threshold of which stood Gorenflot, his eyes brilliant as carbuncles.

" Here? " said the king.

" Right here," replied the fat monk.

Henri entered. " Hic portus salutis? " murmured he.

" Yes," replied the prior; " here is the door."

" Leave us! " said Gorenflot, with a majestic gesture; and immediately the door shut, and they were left alone.

" Here you are, then, Herod, Pagan, Nebuchadnezzar! " cried Gorenflot, suddenly.

" Is it to me you speak, my brother? " cried the king, appearing to be surprised.

" Yes, to you. Can one accuse you of anything so bad that it is not true? "

" My brother! " murmured the king.

" Bah! you have no brother here. I have long been meditating a discourse, and now you shall have it. I divide it into three heads: first, you are a tyrant; second, you are a satyr; third, you are dethroned."

" Dethroned, my brother? " exclaimed the king.

" Neither more nor less. This abbey is not like Poland, and you cannot fly."

" Ah, a snare! "

"Oh, Valois, learn that a king is but a man."

"You are violent, my brother."

"*Pardieu!* do you think we imprison you to flatter you?"

"You abuse your religious calling."

"Is there any religion?" cried Gorenflot.

"Oh, you are a saint, and say such things!"

"I have said it."

"You will expose yourself to damnation."

"Is there any damnation?"

"You speak like an infidel, my brother."

"Come, no preaching; are you ready, Valois?"

"To do what?"

"To resign your crown; I am charged to demand it of you."

"You are committing a mortal sin."

"Oh, I have right of absolution, and I absolve myself in advance. Come, renounce, Brother Valois."

"Renounce what?"

"The throne of France."

"Rather death!"

"Oh, then you shall die! Here is the prior returning. Decide!"

"I have my guards, my friends; they will defend me."

"Yes, but you will be killed first."

"Leave me at least a little time for reflection."

"Not an instant, not a second!"

"Your zeal carries you away, Brother," said the prior, opening the door; and saying to the king, "Your request is granted," he shut it again.

Henri fell into a profound reverie. "I accept the sacrifice," he said, after the lapse of ten minutes. Some one was heard knocking on the door of the cell.

"It is done! he accepts!" cried Gorenflot.

The king heard a murmur of joy and surprise in the corridor.

"Read him the act," said a voice which startled the king to such a degree that he looked out through the grating of the door. A monk handed a roll of parchment into the cell. Gorenflot read the act to the king, who was in great grief, and listened with his head buried in his hands.

"If I refuse to sign?" cried he, shedding tears.

"It will be doubly your ruin," said the Duc de Guise, from under his hood. "Look on yourself as dead to the world, and do not force your subjects to shed the blood of a man who has been their king."

" I will not be forced."

" I feared so," said the duke to his sister. Then, turning to Mayenne, " Go, my brother; let every one arm and prepare," said he.

" For what? " cried the king, in a plaintive tone.

" For everything," said the prior.

The king's despair redoubled.

" *Corbleu !* " cried Gorenflot, " I hated you before, Valois, but now I despise you! Sign, or you shall perish by my hand! "

" Have patience," said the king; " let me pray to my Divine Master for resignation."

" He wishes to reflect again! " said Gorenflot.

" Give him till midnight," said the cardinal.

" Thanks, charitable Christian! " cried the king, in a paroxysm of despair. " May God reward you! "

" His brain has really become enfeebled," said the duke; " we serve France by dethroning him."

" I shall have great pleasure in clipping him! " said the duchess.

Suddenly a dull noise was heard outside of the convent.

" Silence! " said the Duc de Guise.

The most profound silence ensued. Presently they could distinguish blows, struck forcibly and at regular intervals on the resounding door of the abbey. Mayenne ran thither as quickly as his rotundity would permit. " My brothers," said he, " there is a troop of armed men outside."

" They have come to seek him," said the duchess.

" The more reason that he should sign quickly," said the cardinal.

" Sign, Valois, sign! " roared Gorenflot.

" You gave me till midnight," said the king, piteously.

" Ah! you hoped to be rescued."

" He shall die if he does not sign! " cried the duchess.

Gorenflot seized the wrist of the king and offered him the pen. The noise outside increased.

" A new troop! " cried a monk; " they are surrounding the abbey."

" Come! " cried Mayenne and the duchess, impatiently. The king dipped the pen in the ink.

" The Swiss," cried the prior, " are advancing on the right! "

" Well, we will defend ourselves; with such a hostage in our hands, we need not surrender."

" He has signed!" cried Gorenflot, tearing the paper from Henri, who buried his face in his hands.

" Then you are king!" cried the cardinal to the duke; " take the precious paper."

The king overturned the little lamp which alone lighted the scene; but the duke already held the parchment.

" What shall we do?" said a monk, under whose frock was a gentleman, completely armed. " Here is Crillon, with his guards, threatening to break in the doors. Listen!"

" In the king's name!" cried the powerful voice of Crillon.

" There is no king!" cried Gorenflot through the window.

" Who says that, scoundrel?" cried Crillon.

" I! I!" said Gorenflot, proudly.

" Let some one show me that rascal and plant a few bullets in his carcase."

Gorenflot, seeing the guards level their weapons, fell on his back in the middle of the cell.

" Break in the doors, M. Crillon!" said, from outside, a voice which made the hair of all the monks, real and pretended, stand on end.

" Yes, Sire," replied Crillon, giving a tremendous blow on the door with an axe.

" What do you want?" said the prior, appearing at the window in great agitation.

" Ah! it is you, M. Foulon," replied the same voice, " I want my jester, who came to spend the night in one of your cells. I want Chicot; I am lonely at the Louvre."

" And I have been much amused, my son," said Chicot, throwing off his hood, and pushing his way through the crowd of monks, who recoiled with a cry of terror.

At this moment the Duc de Guise, advancing to a lamp, read the signature obtained with so much labour. It was " Chicot I."

" Chicot!" cried he; " thousand devils!"

" Let us fly!" said the cardinal, " we are lost!"

" Ah!" cried Chicot, turning to Gorenflot, who was nearly fainting; and he began to strike him with the cord he had round his waist.

CHAPTER XLVIII

PRINCIPAL AND INTEREST

As the king spoke and the conspirators recognised him, they passed from astonishment to terror. The abdication signed " Chicot I." changed their terror to rage. Chicot threw back his frock upon his shoulders, crossed his arms, and while Gorenflot fled at his utmost speed, sustained, firm and smiling, the first shock. It was a terrible moment, for the gentlemen, furious at the cruel hoax of which they had been the dupes, advanced menacingly on the Gascon. But this man without weapons, his breast covered only by his arms, this laughing face, arrested their steps even more than did the remonstrance of the cardinal, who said to them that Chicot's death could serve no end, but, on the contrary, would be terribly avenged by the king, who was the jester's accomplice in this scene of terrible buffoonery. The result was that daggers and rapiers were lowered before Chicot, who continued to laugh in their faces.

Meanwhile, the king's menaces and Crillon's blows became more vehement. It was evident that the door could not long resist such an attack, which no attempt was made to repel; and therefore, after a moment's deliberation, the Duc de Guise gave the order for retreat. This order made Chicot smile, for during his nights with Gorenflot he had examined the cellar. He had discovered the door and informed the king of its location, who had placed there Toquenot, lieutenant of the Swiss guards. It was evident, then, that the Leaguers, one after another, were about to throw themselves into the trap. The cardinal made off first, followed by about twenty gentlemen. Then Chicot saw the duke pass with about the same number, and afterwards Mayenne. When Chicot saw him go he laughed outright. Ten minutes passed, during which he listened earnestly, expecting to hear the noise of the Leaguers sent back into the cellar; but to his astonishment, the sound continued to go farther and farther off. His laugh began to change into oaths. Time passed, and the Leaguers did not return; had they seen that the door was guarded, and found another way out? Chicot was about to rush from the cell, when all at once the door was obstructed by a mass which fell at his feet, and began to tear its hair.

" Ah! wretch that I am!" cried the monk. " Oh, my good M. Chicot, pardon me, pardon me!"

How did Gorenflot, who went first, return now alone? was the question that presented itself to Chicot's mind.

"Oh, my good M. Chicot," he continued to cry, "pardon your unworthy friend, who repents at your knees!"

"But how is it you have not fled with the others?"

"Because the Lord in his anger has struck me with obesity, and I could not pass where the others did. Oh, unlucky stomach! Oh, miserable paunch!" cried the monk, striking with his two hands the part he apostrophised. "Ah, why am not I thin like you, M. Chicot?"

Chicot understood nothing of the lamentations of the monk.

"But the others are escaping somewhere, then?" cried he, in a voice of thunder.

"Pardieu! what should they do,—wait to be hanged? Oh, unlucky paunch!"

"Silence, and answer me."

Gorenflot raised himself on his knees. "Question me, M. Chicot," he said; "you certainly have the right."

"How are the others escaping?"

"As fast as they can."

"So I imagine; but where?"

"By the hole."

"Mordieu! what hole?"

"The hole in the cavern of the cemetery."

"Is that what you call the cellar? Answer quickly."

"Oh, no; the door of that was guarded outside. The great cardinal, just as he was about to open it, heard a Swiss say, 'Mich durstet,' which means, 'I am thirsty.'"

"Ventre de biche! I know what that means. So then they took another way?"

"Yes, dear M. Chicot, they are getting out into the cavern of the cemetery."

"What does that open into?"

"On one side into the crypt, on the other into the Porte St. Jacques."

"You lie! I should have seen them repass before this cell."

"No, dear M. Chicot; they thought they had not time for that, so they are creeping out through the air-hole."

"What hole?"

"One which looks into the garden, and serves to light the passage."

"So that you—"

" I was too big, and could not pass, and they drew me back by my legs, because I intercepted the way for the others."

" But," cried Chicot, his face suddenly illumined by a strange joy, " if you couldn't pass—"

" No; and yet I made the greatest efforts. See my shoulders; see my breast."

" Then he who is bigger than you?"

" He! who?"

" Oh, Holy Virgin! I promise you a dozen wax candles if he also cannot pass."

" M. Chicot."

" Get up."

The monk raised himself from the ground as quickly as he could.

" Now lead me to the hole."

" Where you wish."

" Go on, then, wretch."

Gorenflot went on as fast as he was able, while Chicot stimulated his pace, striking him with the cord. They traversed the corridor, and descended into the garden.

" Here! this way," said Gorenflot.

" Hold your tongue, and go on!"

" There it is," said the monk; and exhausted by his efforts, he sank on the grass, while Chicot, hearing groans, advanced, and saw something protruding through the hole. By the side of this something lay a frock and a sword. It was evident that the individual in the hole had taken off successively all the loose clothing which increased his size; and now, as Gorenflot had done, he was making useless efforts to get through.

" *Mordieu! ventrebleu! sang Dieu!*" cried a stifled voice. " I would rather pass through the midst of the guards. Do not pull so hard, my friends; I shall come through gradually. I feel that I advance,—not quickly, it is true, but I do advance."

" *Ventre de biche!*" murmured Chicot, " it is M. de Mayenne. Holy Virgin! you have gained your candles;" and he made a noise with his feet like some one running fast.

" They are coming," cried several voices from inside.

" Ah!" cried Chicot, as if out of breath, " it is you, miserable monk!"

" Say nothing, Monseigneur!" murmured the voices; " he takes you for Gorenflot."

" Ah, it is you, heavy mass,—*pondus immobile ;* it is you, *indigesta moles!*"

And at each apostrophe, Chicot, arrived at last at his desired vengeance, let fall the cord with all the weight of his arm on the body before him.

"Silence!" whispered the voices again; "he takes you for Gorenflot."

Mayenne only uttered groans, and made immense efforts to get through.

"Ah, conspirator!" cried Chicot again; "ah, unworthy monk, this is for your drunkenness, this for idleness, this for anger, this for gluttony, and this, and this, and this, for all the vices you have."

"M. Chicot, have pity!" whispered Gorenflot, covered with perspiration.

"And here, traitor, this is for your treason!" continued Chicot, still striking.

"Mercy!" murmured Gorenflot, feeling on his own person all the blows that fell on Mayenne,—"mercy, dear M. Chicot!"

But Chicot, instead of stopping, became intoxicated with his vengeance, and redoubled his blows. All Mayenne's control over himself was insufficient to repress his groans.

"Ah!" said Chicot, "why did it not please God to substitute for your vulgar carcase the high and mighty shoulders of the Duc de Mayenne, to whom I owe a volley of blows, the interest of which has been accumulating for seven years!"

"Chicot!" cried the duke.

"Yes, Chicot, unworthy servant of the king, who wishes he had the hundred arms of Briareus for this occasion." And more and more excited, he repeated his blows with such violence that the sufferer, making a tremendous effort, pushed himself through, and fell torn and bleeding into the arms of his friends. Chicot's last blow fell into empty space. He turned, and saw that the true Gorenflot had fainted with terror.

CHAPTER XLIX

WHAT WAS TAKING PLACE NEAR THE BASTILLE WHILE CHICOT WAS PAYING HIS DEBT TO M. DE MAYENNE

IT was eleven at night, and the Duc d'Anjou was waiting impatiently at home for a messenger from the Duc de Guise announcing the abdication of the king. He walked restlessly up and down, looking every minute at the clock. All at once

he heard a horse in the courtyard, and thinking it was that of
the messenger, he ran to the window; but he saw only a groom
leading up and down a horse which was waiting for its master,
who almost immediately came out. It was Bussy, who, as captain of the duke's guards, came to give the password for the
night. The duke, seeing this handsome and brave young man,
of whom he had never had reason to complain, experienced an
instant's remorse; but in the light of a torch, carried by Bussy's
valet, his face was revealed, and in that face the duke saw so
much joy, hope, and happiness that all his jealousy returned.
Meanwhile, Bussy, ignorant that the duke was watching him,
jumped into his saddle and rode off to his own hotel, where he
gave his horse to the groom. There he saw Rémy.

"Ah! you, Rémy?"

"Myself, Monsieur."

"Not yet in bed?"

"I have just come in. Indeed, since I have no longer a
patient, it seems to me that the days have forty-eight hours."

"Are you out of spirits?"

"I am afraid I am."

"Then Gertrude is abandoned?"

"Entirely."

"You grew tired?"

"Of being beaten. That was how her love showed itself."

"And does your heart not speak for her to-night?"

"Why to-night?"

"Because I would have taken you with me."

"To the Bastille?"

"Yes."

"You are going there?"

"Yes."

"And Monsoreau?"

"Is at Compiègne, preparing a chase for the king."

"Are you sure, Monsieur?"

"The order was given publicly this morning."

"Ah!"

Rémy remained thoughtful a moment. "Then?" he asked,
after a pause.

"Then I spent the day thanking God for the happiness he
has sent me for this night; and I am going to spend the night
in the enjoyment of that happiness."

"Very well; Jourdain, my sword," said Rémy.

"You have changed your mind?"

" I will accompany you to the door for two reasons."

" What are they? "

" First, lest you should meet any enemies."

Bussy smiled.

" Oh, *mon Dieu!* yes, I know you fear no one, and that Rémy the doctor is but a poor companion; still, two men are not so likely to be attacked as one. Secondly, because I have a great deal of good advice to give you."

" Come, my dear Rémy, come. We will speak of her; next to the pleasure of seeing the woman you love, I know none greater than talking of her."

Bussy then took the arm of the young doctor, and they set off. Rémy had said that he had a great deal of good advice to give the count; and as soon as they were well started he began to adduce a thousand imposing Latin quotations to prove to Bussy that he did wrong in visiting Diane that night instead of remaining quietly in his bed, since ordinarily a man fights badly when he has slept badly. Bussy smiled. Rémy insisted.

" You see, Rémy," said the count, " when my arm holds a sword, it becomes so identified with it that the fibres of flesh take the hardness and spring of steel, and the steel seems to become animated and warm like living flesh. From that moment my sword is an arm and my arm is a sword. So that, do you see, there is no longer any question of strength and energy. A sword does not become fatigued."

" No, but it becomes dull."

" Fear nothing."

" Ah, my dear master, to-morrow you are to enter a combat like that of Hercules against Antæus, like that of Theseus against the Minotaur, like that of Bayard, like something Homeric, gigantic, impossible. I wish people to speak of it in future times as the combat *par excellence*, and that in it you shall not receive a scratch."

" Be easy, my dear Rémy, you shall see wonders. This morning I put swords in the hands of four fencers, who during eight minutes could not touch me once, while I tore their doublets to pieces."

So conversing, they arrived in the Rue St. Antoine.

" Adieu! here we are," said Bussy.

" Shall I wait for you? "

" Why? "

" To make sure that you will return before two o'clock, and have at least five or six hours' sleep before your duel."

" If I give you my word? "

" Oh, that will be enough; Bussy's word is never doubted."

" You have it, then. In two hours, Rémy, I will be at the hotel."

" Then, adieu, Monsieur."

" Adieu, Rémy."

Rémy watched and saw Bussy enter, not this time by the window, but boldly through the door, which Gertrude opened for him. Then Rémy turned to go home; but he had gone only a few steps, when he saw coming towards him five armed men, wrapped in cloaks. Five men at that hour,—it was an event. Rémy hid behind the corner of a house. When they arrived about ten feet from him, they said good-night to each other, and four went off in different directions, while the fifth remained stationary.

" M. de Saint-Luc! " said Rémy.

" Rémy! "

" Rémy, in person. Is it an indiscretion to ask what your Lordship is doing at this hour so far from the Louvre? "

" I am examining, by the king's order, the physiognomy of the city. He said to me, ' Saint-Luc, walk about the streets of Paris, and if you hear any one say I have abdicated, contradict him.' "

" And have you heard it? "

" Nowhere; and as it is just midnight, and I have met no one but M. de Monsoreau, I have dismissed my friends, and am about to return."

" M. de Monsoreau! "

" Yes."

" You have met M. de Monsoreau? "

" With a troop of armed men; ten or twelve at least."

" M. de Monsoreau! Impossible! "

" Why so? "

" He ought to be at Compiègne."

" He ought to be, but he is not."

" But the king's order? "

" Bah! who obeys the king? "

" You have met M. de Monsoreau with ten or twelve men? "

" Certainly."

" Did he know you? "

" I believe so."

" You were but five? "

" My four friends and I."

" And he did not attack you? "

" On the contrary, he avoided me, which astonished me, as on seeing him I expected a terrible battle."

" In what direction was he going? "

" Towards the Rue de la Tixeranderie."

" Ah, *mon Dieu !* "

" What? " asked Saint-Luc, frightened by the young man's tone.

" M. de Saint-Luc, a great misfortune is about to happen."

" To whom? "

" To M. de Bussy."

" Bussy! *Mordieu !* speak, Rémy; I am his friend, you know."

" Oh! M. de Bussy thought him at Compiègne."

" Well? "

" And, profiting by his absence, is with Madame de Monsoreau."

" Ah! " said Saint-Luc, " that means trouble."

" Do you not see. He has had suspicions, and has feigned to depart, that he might appear unexpectedly."

" Wait a moment," said Saint-Luc, striking his forehead.

" Have you an idea? "

" The Duc d'Anjou is at the bottom of it."

" Why, it is the Duc d'Anjou who this morning instigated Monsoreau's departure."

" Another reason. Have you good lungs, Rémy? "

" *Corbleu !* like a blacksmith's bellows."

" Well! let us run, without losing an instant. You know the house? "

" Yes."

" Go on, then." And the young men set off like hunted deer.

" Is he much in advance of us? " said Rémy.

" Who? Monsoreau? "

" Yes."

" About a quarter of an hour."

" If we do but arrive in time! "

CHAPTER L

THE ASSASSINATION

BUSSY, himself without disquietude or hesitation, had been received by Diane without fear, for she believed herself sure of the absence of M. de Monsoreau. Never had this beautiful woman been more beautiful; never had Bussy been so happy. In certain moments, whose importance is perceived by the soul, or rather by the instinct of self-preservation, a man combines his moral faculties with all the physical resources afforded by his senses. With all his energies he enjoys the life which at any moment he may lose, without divining by what disaster he loses it.

Diane was agitated,—and the more because she sought to hide her emotion. Moved by her fears of the threatening to-morrow, she appeared more tender, because sadness, pervading all love, gave to hers the perfume of poesy which it lacked. True passion is not sportive; and the eyes of a woman sincerely in love will be moist oftener than joyous. So she began by checking the amorous young man. What she had to say to him in that interview was that his life was her life; what she had to discuss with him was the surest way to escape,—for not only was it necessary to conquer in the approaching conflict, it would be necessary afterwards to avoid the wrath of the king. Henri would never forgive the conqueror for the defeat or the death of his favourites. " And then," said she, putting her arm around Bussy's neck, and devouring with her eyes her lover's face, " are you not already acknowledged to be the bravest man in France? Why make it a point of honour to augment your glory? You are already superior to other men, and you do not wish to please any other woman but me, Louis. Therefore, guard your life, or rather—for I think there is not a man in France capable of killing you, Louis, except by treason—I should say, take care of wounds, for you may be wounded. Indeed, it was through a wound received in fighting with these same men that I first made your acquaintance."

" Make yourself easy," said Bussy, smiling; " I will take care of my face. I shall not be disfigured."

" Oh, take care of yourself altogether! Think of the grief you would experience if you saw me brought home wounded and bleeding! Well, I should feel the same grief on seeing your

blood. Be prudent, my too courageous hero,—that is all I ask.
Act like the Roman of whom you read to me the other day.
Let your friends fight; aid the one who needs it most; but if
three men, if two men attack you, fly. You can turn, like
Horatius, and kill them one after another."

" Yes, my dear Diane."

" Oh, you reply without hearing me, Louis; you look at me,
and do not listen."

" But I see you; and you are very beautiful."

" Do not think of my beauty just now! *Mon Dieu !* it is your
life I am speaking of,—our life. Stay, I will tell you something
that will make you more prudent,—I shall have the courage to
witness this duel."

" You ? "

" I shall see it."

" Impossible, Diane ! "

" No; listen. There is, in the room next to this, a window
looking into a little court, but with a side-view of the Tournelles."

" Yes, I remember; the window from which I threw crumbs to
the birds the other day."

" From there I can have a view of the ground; therefore,
above all things, take care to stand so that I can see you. You
will know that I am there; but do not look at me, lest your
enemy should profit by it."

" And kill me, while I had my eyes fixed upon you. If I had
to choose my death, Diane, that is the one I should prefer."

" Yes; but now you are not to die, but live."

" And I will live; therefore tranquillise yourself, Diane.
Besides, I am well seconded; you do not know my friends.
D'Antragues uses his sword as well as I do; Ribeirac is so steady
on the ground that his eyes and his arms alone seem to be alive;
and Livarot is as active as a tiger. Believe me, Diane, I wish
there were more danger, for there would be more honour."

" Well, I believe you, and I smile and hope; but listen, and
promise to obey me."

" Yes, if you do not tell me to leave you."

" It is just what I am about to do. I appeal to your reason."

" Then you should not have made me mad."

" No nonsense, but obedience,—that is the way to prove your
love."

" Order, then."

" Dear friend, your eyes are weary; you need a good sleep.
Leave me."

" Oh! already? "

" I am going to say my prayer, and you may kiss me."

" But one ought to pray to you, as to the angels."

" And do you think, then, that the angels do not pray to God? " said Diane, kneeling. " Lord," she prayed, " if thou art willing that thy servant should live happily and not die in despair, protect him whom thou hast placed in my path, for I love him and him only! "

As she finished these words, Bussy stooped to take her in his arms and raise her face to his lips. Suddenly a pane of the window flew into pieces, then the window itself, and three armed men appeared on the balcony while a fourth was climbing over. This one had his face covered with a mask, and held in his right hand a sword, and in his left a pistol.

Bussy remained paralysed for a moment by the frightful cry uttered by Diane at this sight. The masked man made a sign, and the three others advanced. One of these three was armed with an arquebuse.

Bussy put Diane aside with his left hand, and drew his sword with his right.

" Come, my brave fellows! " said a sepulchral voice from under the mask; " he is already half dead with fear."

" You are wrong," said Bussy; " I never feel fear."

Diane drew near him.

" Go back, Diane," said he. But she threw herself on his neck. " You will get me killed," said he; and she drew back.

" Ah! " said the masked man, " it is M. de Bussy, and I would not believe it, fool that I was! Really, what a good and excellent friend! "

Bussy said nothing; but biting his lips, he looked around for means of defence.

" He learns," continued the voice, in a mocking tone which made it seem more terrible,—" he learns that the husband is absent and has left his wife alone and fears she may be afraid; so he comes to keep her company, although on the eve of a duel. I repeat, he is a good and excellent friend! "

" Ah! it is you, M. de Monsoreau! " said Bussy. " Good! throw off your mask. Now I know with whom I have to do."

" I will do it," he replied, and threw away the mask of black velvet.

Diane uttered a feeble cry; the count was as pale as a corpse, but he smiled like a demon.

"Let us finish, Monsieur," said Bussy. "It was very well for Homer's heroes, who were demigods, to talk before they fought; but I am a man. Attack me or let me pass."

Monsoreau replied by a laugh which made Diane shudder, but raised Bussy's anger.

"Let me pass!" cried he.

"Oh, oh!" said Monsoreau, "'let me pass!' how you say that, M. de Bussy!"

"Then, draw and have done; I wish to go home, and I live far from here."

"You have come to lie here, Monsieur," said Monsoreau, "and here you will lie."

During this time two other men mounted into the balcony.

"Two and four make six," said Bussy; "where are the others?"

"Waiting at the door."

Diane fell on her knees, and in spite of her efforts Bussy heard her sobs. He gave her a rapid glance; then, turning towards the count, "My dear monsieur," he said, after reflecting, "you know I am a man of honour."

"Yes, you are; and Madame is a faithful wife."

"Good, Monsieur. It is severe, but it is deserved; and all that will be settled for at one time. Only, as I have an appointment for to-morrow with four gentlemen whom you know, and as they have a claim on me prior to yours, I beg to be allowed to retire to-night, and I pledge my word that you shall find me again, when and where you will."

Monsoreau shrugged his shoulders.

"I swear to you, Monsieur," said Bussy, "that when I have satisfied MM. Quélus, Schomberg, d'Epernon, and Maugiron, I shall be at your service. If they kill me, your vengeance will be satisfied; and if not—"

Monsoreau turned to his men. "On, my brave fellows!" said he.

"Oh!" said Bussy, "I was wrong; it is not a duel, but an assassination."

"*Parbleu!*" said Monsoreau.

"Yes, I see it; we have misunderstood each other. But consider, Monsieur,—the Duc d'Anjou will not like this."

"It is he who sent me."

Bussy shuddered. Diane raised her hands towards heaven with a groan.

"In that case," said the young man, "I must rely on Bussy.

Come on, my ruffians!" and he upset the *prie-Dieu*, drew a table towards him, and on it placed a chair, so that in a second he had formed a kind of rampart between himself and his enemies. This movement had been so rapid that the ball fired at him from the arquebuse struck only the *prie-Dieu*. Bussy threw down a magnificent credence-table, and added it to his defences. Behind this Diane concealed herself. She understood that she could aid Bussy only by her prayers; and she prayed. Bussy glanced at her, and then at his assailants, crying, "Come on, but take care, for my sword is sharp."

The men advanced, and one tried to seize the *prie-Dieu*, but before he reached it, Bussy's sword pierced his arm. The man uttered a cry, and fell back. Bussy then heard rapid steps in the corridor, and thought he was caught between two fires. He flew to the door to lock it! but before he could reach it, it was opened, and two men rushed in.

"Ah, dear master!" cried a well-known voice, "are we in time?"

"Rémy!"

"And I?" cried a second voice; "it seems they are attempting assassination here."

"Saint-Luc!" cried Bussy, joyfully. "Ah! M. de Monsoreau, I think now you will do well to let us pass, for if you do not, we will pass over you."

"Three more men!" cried Monsoreau. And they saw three new assailants appear on the balcony.

"Ah! is it, then, an army?" cried Saint-Luc.

"Oh, God protect him!" cried Diane.

"Wretch!" cried Monsoreau, and he advanced to strike her. Bussy saw the movement. Agile as a tiger, he bounded on him, and touched him in the throat; but the distance was too great; the wound was only a scratch. Five or six men rushed on Bussy; but one fell beneath the sword of Saint-Luc.

"Rémy!" cried Bussy, "carry away Diane."

Monsoreau uttered a yell and snatched a pistol from one of the men.

Rémy hesitated. "But you?" said he.

"Away! away! I confide her to you."

"Come, Madame," said Rémy.

"Never! I will never leave him."

Rémy seized her in his arms.

"Bussy, help me! Bussy!" cried Diane. The poor woman was wild, and could no longer distinguish between her friends and her enemies; whatever separated her from Bussy was death to her.

"Go," cried Bussy, "I will rejoin you."

At this moment Monsoreau fired, and Bussy saw Rémy totter, and then fall, dragging Diane with him. Bussy uttered a cry, and turned.

"It is nothing, Master," said Rémy. "It is I who have received the ball. She is safe."

As Bussy turned, three men threw themselves on him; Saint-Luc rushed forward, and one of them fell. The two others drew back.

"Saint-Luc," cried Bussy, "by her you love, save Diane!"

"But you?"

"I am a man."

Saint-Luc rushed to Diane, seized her in his arms, and disappeared through the door.

"Here, my men, from the staircase!" shouted Monsoreau.

"Ah, coward!" cried Bussy.

Monsoreau retreated behind his men. Bussy gave a back stroke and a thrust; with the first he cleft open a head, and with the second pierced a breast.

"That clears!" cried he; then he returned to his rampart.

"Fly, Master!" cried Rémy.

"I, fly!—fly from assassins!" then, bending over the young man, he added, "Diane must first escape; but you, are you much hurt?"

"Take care!" said Rémy, "take care!"

In fact, four men rushed in through the door from the staircase. Bussy saw himself between two troops, but his only cry was, "Ah, Diane!" Then, without losing a second, he rushed on the four men; and taken by surprise, two fell, one dead, one wounded. Monsoreau advanced; and he retreated again behind his rampart.

"Push the bolts, and turn the key," cried Monsoreau; "we have him now."

During this time, by a great effort, Rémy had dragged himself before Bussy, and added his body to the rampart. There was an instant's pause. Bussy looked around him. Seven men lay stretched on the ground, but nine remained. And seeing these nine swords, and hearing Monsoreau encouraging them, this brave man, who had never known fear, saw the image of death arise in the depths of the chamber, summoning him with its gloomy smile.

" I may kill five more," thought he; " but the other four will kill me. I have strength for ten minutes' more combat; in that ten minutes let me do what man never did before."

And rushing forward, he gave three thrusts; and three times he pierced the leather of a shoulder-belt, or the buff of a jacket, and three times a stream of blood followed.

During this time he had parried twenty blows with his left arm, and his cloak, which he had wrapped round it, was hacked to pieces.

The men changed their tactics; seeing two of their number fall and one retire, they renounced the sword, and some tried to strike with the butt-ends of their muskets, while others fired at him with pistols. He avoided the balls by jumping from side to side, or by stooping; for he seemed not only to see, hear, and act, but to divine every movement of his enemies. It was to him one of those moments in which a created being reaches the height of perfection; he was less than a god because he was mortal, but certainly he was more than man. Then he thought that by killing Monsoreau he might end the combat, and sought him among his assailants; but Monsoreau was behind his men, loading their pistols, or himself firing from his place of shelter. But it was a simple thing for Bussy to make an opening. He threw himself into the midst of the assassins, who separated, and he found himself face to face with Monsoreau. Monsoreau, who held a loaded pistol, fired, and the ball, striking Bussy's sword, broke it off six inches from the handle.

" Disarmed! " cried Monsoreau.

Bussy drew back, picking up his broken blade, and in an instant it was fastened to his wrist with a handkerchief; and the battle was resumed, presenting the extraordinary spectacle of a man almost without arms, but also almost without wounds, keeping six enemies at bay, and with ten corpses at his feet for a rampart. Monsoreau, while his men renewed the attack on Bussy, divining that the young man was seeking for a weapon, drew to himself all those that were within his reach. Bussy was surrounded; the blade of his sword bent and shook in his hand, and fatigue began to deaden his arm. He looked around, and suddenly one of the bodies rose to its knees, and placed in his hand a long and strong sword. It was Rémy's last act of devotion. Bussy uttered a cry of joy, and threw away his broken sword; at the same moment Monsoreau fired at Rémy, and the ball entered his brain. This time he fell to rise no more.

Bussy roared. His strength returned to him; and he whirled

round his sword in a circle, cutting through a wrist at his right hand and laying open a cheek at his left. By that double stroke he had cleared the way to the door. He sprang towards it, and with an effort that shook the wall he tried to force it open; but the bolts prevented. Exhausted by the effort, he let his right arm fall for a moment, while with his left he tried to undraw the bolts behind him, turning his face to his adversaries. During this second, he received a ball in his thigh, and two swords pierced his sides; but he had drawn the bolts and turned the key. Sublime with rage, he rushed on Monsoreau, and wounded him in the breast.

" Ah ! " cried Bussy, " I begin to think I shall escape."

The four men rushed on him; but they could not touch him, and were repulsed with blows. Monsoreau approached him twice more, and twice more was wounded. But three men grasped the handle of his sword, and tore it from him. Bussy seized a stool of carved wood, struck three blows with it, and knocked down two men; but it broke on the shoulder of the third, who sent his dagger into Bussy's breast.

Bussy took hold of his wrist, drew out the dagger, and turning it against his adversary, forced him to stab himself. The last man jumped out of the window. Bussy made two steps to follow him; but Monsoreau, raising himself from the floor where he was lying, wounded him in the leg with his dagger. The young man seized a sword which lay near, and plunged it so vigorously into his breast that he pinned him to the floor. " Ah ! " he cried, " I do not know if I shall live, but at least I shall have seen you die ! "

Bussy dragged himself to the corridor, while blood poured from his wounds. He threw a last glance behind him. The moon was shining brilliantly, and its light penetrated this room inundated with blood, illuminated the walls pierced by balls and hacked by blows, and lighted up the pale faces of the dead, which for the most part preserved in death the fierce look of assassins. Bussy, at the sight of this field of battle, peopled by him with slain, experienced a feeling of pride, though himself almost dying. As he had intended, he had done what no man had done before him. There now remained to him only to fly.

But all was not over for the unfortunate young man. On arriving at the staircase, he saw arms glittering in the court; some one fired, and the ball pierced his shoulder. The court was guarded. He then thought of the little window where Diane had said she would sit to see the combat; and as quickly as he could he dragged himself thither, and locked the door behind him. Then he mounted the window with great difficulty, and measured with his eyes the distance to the iron trellis, wondering if he could jump to the other side of it.

"Oh, I shall never have the strength!" cried he.

But at that moment he heard steps coming up the staircase; it was the second troop mounting. He collected all his strength, and made a spring; but his foot slipped, and he fell on the iron spikes, of which some entered his body and others caught his clothes, and he hung suspended. He thought of his only friend. "Saint-Luc!" cried he, "help! Saint-Luc!"

"Ah, it is you, M. de Bussy," answered a voice from behind some trees.

Bussy shuddered, for it was not the voice of Saint-Luc.

"Saint-Luc!" cried he again, "come to me! Diane is safe! I have killed Monsoreau!"

"Ah! Monsoreau is killed?" said another voice.

"Yes."

"Good!"

Then Bussy saw two men come out from behind the trees; both were masked. "Gentlemen," cried he, "in Heaven's name, help an unfortunate man, who may still escape if you aid him."

"What do you say, Monseigneur?" said one.

"Imprudent!" said the other.

"Monseigneur," cried Bussy, who heard the conversation, "deliver me, and I will pardon you for betraying me."

"Do you hear?" said the duke.

"What do you order?"

"That you deliver him—" Then he added with a laugh which his mask partly concealed, "—from his sufferings."

Bussy turned his head to look at the man who laughed at such a time. "Oh, I am lost!" he murmured.

At that moment the muzzle of an arquebuse was placed against his breast; and the weapon was discharged. Bussy's head fell on his shoulder, and his hands stiffened. "Assassin!" he said, "be accursed!" And he died uttering the name "Diane." Drops of his blood fell upon him who had been addressed as Monseigneur.

"Is he dead?" cried several men, who, after forcing the door, appeared at the windows.

"Yes," said Aurilly. "But fly; remember that his Highness the Duc d'Anjou was the friend and protector of M. de Bussy."

The men instantly made off; and when the sound of their steps was lost, the duke said, " Now, Aurilly, go up into the room and throw out of the window the body of Monsoreau."

Aurilly obeyed, and the blood fell over the clothes of the duke, who, however, raised the coat of the dead man, and drew out the paper which he had signed.

" This is all I wanted," said he; " so now let us go."

" And Diane? "

" *Ma foi !* I care no more for her; and as she has not recognised us, untie her, and Saint-Luc also, and let them go whither they will."

Aurilly disappeared.

" I shall not be King of France by this stroke," murmured the duke, tearing up the paper; " but at all events, I shall not be beheaded for high treason."

CHAPTER LI

HOW BROTHER GORENFLOT FOUND HIMSELF MORE THAN EVER BETWEEN A GALLOWS AND AN ABBEY

THE conspiracy had ended in a comedy. Neither the Swiss nor the French guards had been able to lay hands on one of the conspirators; all had gone out by the subterranean passage. As soon as the door was broken down, Crillon put himself at the head of thirty men and, with the king, invaded Ste. Geneviève. The silence of death reigned throughout the vast and gloomy structure. Crillon, a man of experience, would have preferred a great noise; he feared an ambush. But in vain they sent out scouts; in vain they opened doors and windows; in vain they searched the crypt,—the place was deserted.

The king went at the head, sword in hand, crying at the top of his voice, " Chicot! Chicot! " No one answered. " Can they have killed him? " said he. " *Mordieu !* if they have they shall pay for my fool the price of a gentleman."

" And with good reason, Sire," replied Crillon, " for he is one of the bravest."

Chicot did not reply, because he was occupied in beating M. de Mayenne, which gave him so much pleasure that he neither heard nor saw what was taking place in his vicinity. However, when the duke had disappeared and Gorenflot had fainted, and nothing remained to occupy his mind, he heard and recognised the royal voice.

" Here, my son, here! " he cried, trying at the same time to raise Gorenflot, who, beginning to recover himself, cried, " M. Chicot! "

" Ah! you are not dead, then? "

" My good M. Chicot," continued the monk, trying to join his hands in front of his enormous stomach, " is it possible, then, that you will deliver me to my persecutors,—me, Gorenflot? "

" Wretch! " said Chicot, with an accent of tenderness poorly disguised.

Gorenflot began to howl, and having succeeded in joining his hands, he tried to wring them. " I, who have had so many good dinners with you," he continued; " I, who drank so well that you always called me the king of the sponges; I, who loved so much the capons you used to order at the Corne d'Abondance that I never left anything but the bones! "

This climax appeared sublime to Chicot, and determined him to clemency.

" Here they are! *Mon Dieu!* " cried Gorenflot, vainly trying to rise, " here they come! I am lost! Oh, good M. Chicot, help me! " and finding he could not rise, he threw himself with his face to the ground.

" Get up," said Chicot.

" Do you pardon me? "

" We shall see."

" You have beaten me so much that it can go towards payment."

Chicot laughed; the poor monk was so beside himself that he fancied he had received the blows given to Mayenne.

" You laugh, M. Chicot."

" Yes, to be sure I laugh, animal."

" Then I shall live? "

" Perhaps."

" You would not laugh if your Gorenflot was about to die."

" It does not depend upon me, but on the king; he alone has the power of life and death."

Gorenflot made an effort and succeeded in rising to his knees.

At this moment lights appeared, and a crowd of embroidered dresses and swords shining in the light of the torches.

" Ah! Chicot! my dear Chicot, how glad I am to see you! " cried the king.

" You hear, good M. Chicot," whispered Gorenflot, " this great prince is glad to see you."

" Well? "

" Well! in his happiness he would not refuse you a favour; ask for my pardon."

" What! from Herod? "

" Oh! silence, dear M. Chicot."

" Well, Sire, how many have you caught? " said Chicot, advancing.

" *Confiteor*," said Gorenflot.

" Not one," said Crillon, " the traitors must have found some opening unknown to us."

" It is probable."

" But you saw them? " said the king.

" Certainly I saw them."

" All? "

" From the first to the last."

" *Confiteor*," said Gorenflot.

" You recognised them, no doubt? "

" No, Sire."

" Not recognise them? "

" That is to say, I recognised only one."

" Who was that? "

" M. de Mayenne."

" M. de Mayenne, to whom you owed—"

" Yes, Sire; we are quits."

" Ah! tell me about that, Chicot."

" Afterwards, my son; now let us think of the present."

" *Confiteor*," repeated Gorenflot.

" Ah! you have made a prisoner," said Crillon, laying his large hand on the monk's shoulder.

Chicot was silent for a minute, leaving Gorenflot a prey to all the anguish of profound terror. Gorenflot almost fainted again on seeing around him so much wrath unappeased.

At last, after a silence in which Gorenflot thought he heard sounding in his ears the trumpet of the last judgment, Chicot said, " Sire, look well at this monk."

One of the assistants brought a torch near Gorenflot's face. He closed his eyes that he might have less to do in passing from this world to another.

" The preacher Gorenflot! " cried Henri.

" *Confiteor, confiteor !* " repeated the monk, eagerly.

" Himself," said Chicot.

" He who—"

" Precisely," interrupted Chicot.

" Ah, ah ! " said the king, with an air of satisfaction.

Gorenflot shook with terror, for he heard the sounds of swords clashing.

" Wait," said Chicot, " the king must know all." And taking him aside, " My son," said he, " thank God for having permitted this holy man to be born thirty-five years ago, for it is he who has saved us all."

" How so ? "

" It was he who recounted to me the whole plot, from the Alpha to the Omega."

" When ? "

" About a week ago ; so that if ever your Majesty's enemies catch him he will be a dead man."

Gorenflot heard only the last words, " a dead man ; " and he covered his face with his hands.

" Worthy man," said the king, casting a benevolent look on the mass of flesh before him, " we will cover him with our protection."

Gorenflot caught in its flight that look of pity, and like an ancient mask, smiled on one side while he wept on the other.

" You will do well, my king," said Chicot, " for he is a servant of wonderful merit."

" What must we do with him ? "

" I think that as long as he remains in Paris he will be in danger."

" If I gave him guards ? "

Gorenflot heard this proposition of Henri's. " Well ! " thought he, " I shall get off with imprisonment ; I prefer that to beating, if they only feed me well."

" Oh, no, that is needless," said Chicot, " if you will allow me to take him with me."

" Where ? "

" Home."

" Well ! take him, and return to the Louvre, whither I am going, to find our friends and prepare them for to-morrow."

" Get up, reverend father," said Chicot.

" He mocks me," murmured Gorenflot.

" Get up, brute," whispered Chicot, giving him a nudge in the back with his knee.

" Ah ! I have deserved it," cried Gorenflot.

" What does he say ? " asked the king.

"Sire, he is thinking over all his fatigues and his tortures; and when I promised him your protection, he said, 'Oh! I have well merited that.'"

"Poor devil!" said the king, "take good care of him."

"Oh, be easy, Sire, he will want for nothing with me."

"Oh, M. Chicot, dear M. Chicot," cried Gorenflot, "what will they do with me?"

"You will know soon. Meanwhile, monster of iniquity, thank his Majesty."

"What for?"

"Thank him, I tell you."

"Sire," stammered Gorenflot, "since your gracious Majesty—"

"Yes," interrupted Henri, "I know all you did for me in your journey from Lyon, on the evening of the League, and again to-day. Be easy, you shall be recompensed according to your merits."

Gorenflot sighed.

"Where is Panurge?" said Chicot.

"In the stable, poor beast."

"Well! go and fetch him, and return to me."

"Yes, M. Chicot."

And the monk went away as fast as he could, much astonished not to be followed by guards.

"Now, my son," said Chicot, "keep twenty men for your own escort, and send ten with M. Crillon to the Hotel d'Anjou, and let them bring your brother here."

"Why?"

"That he may not escape a second time."

"Did my brother—"

"Have you repented following my advice to-day?"

"No, *par la mordieu!*"

"Then do what I tell you."

Henri gave the order to Crillon, who set off at once.

"And you?" said Henri.

"Oh! I am waiting for my saint."

"And you will rejoin me at the Louvre?"

"In an hour; go, my son."

Henri went; and Chicot, proceeding to the stables, met Gorenflot coming out on his ass. The poor devil had not an idea of endeavouring to escape from the fate that he thought awaited him.

"Come, come," said Chicot; "we are waited for."

Gorenflot made no resistance; but he shed many tears.

CHAPTER LII

WHERE CHICOT GUESSES WHY D'EPERNON HAD BLOOD ON HIS FEET AND NONE IN HIS CHEEKS

THE king, returning to the Louvre, found his friends peacefully asleep, except D'Epernon, whose bed was empty.

" Not come in yet; how imprudent! " murmured the king to Chicot, who had also returned, and was standing with him by their beds.   " The fool! having to fight to-morrow with a man like Bussy,—the bravest man in France, the most dangerous man in the world,—and to take no more care than this.   Let them seek M. d'Epernon," said he, going out of the room, and speaking to an usher.

" M. d'Epernon is just coming in, Sire," replied the man.

Indeed, D'Epernon came softly along, hoping to glide unperceived to his room.   On seeing the king, he looked confused.

" Ah! here you are at last," said Henri, " come here and look at your friends.   They are wise.   They understand the importance of the duel to-morrow; but you, instead of praying and sleeping like them, have been running about the streets.   *Corbleu !* how pale you are!   What will you look like to-morrow? "

D'Epernon was indeed pale; but at the king's remark he coloured.

" Now go to bed," continued Henri, " and sleep if you can."

" Why not? "

" Much time you will have.   You are to fight at daybreak; and at this time of year the sun rises at four.   It is now two; you have but two hours to sleep."

" Two hours well employed go a long way."

" You will sleep, then? "

" Soundly, Sire! "

" I do not believe it."

" Why not? "

" Because you are agitated; you think of to-morrow."

" I will sleep, Sire, if your Majesty will only let me."

" That is just," said Chicot.

Indeed D'Epernon undressed and get into bed with a calm and satisfied look that seemed both to the king and Chicot to augur well.

" He is as brave as a Cæsar," said the king.

" So brave," said Chicot, scratching his ear," that on my word of honour I can't understand it."

" See, he sleeps already."

Chicot approached the bed, for he could not believe that D'Epernon's tranquillity was so well assured as that would indicate.

" Oh! " said he.

" What is it? "

" Look; " and he pointed to D'Epernon's boots.

" Blood! "

" He has been walking in blood, my son. Brave fellow! "

" Can it be that he is wounded! " said the king, anxiously.

" Bah! he would have told us; and besides, unless he had been wounded, like Achilles, in the heel——"

" See, the sleeve of his doublet is also spotted. What can have happened to him? "

" Perhaps he has killed some one to keep his hand in."

" It is singular," said the king.

Chicot scratched his ear more seriously. " Hum! hum! " said he.

" You do not answer me."

" Yes, I say ' hum! hum! '—that means a great deal, it seems to me."

" Mon Dieu ! " said Henri, " what is going on around me, and what is the future that awaits me? Fortunately to-morrow—"

" To-day, my son. You are always confounding."

" Yes, it is true."

" Well, to-day? "

" To-day I shall be tranquil."

" Why so? "

" Because those cursed Angevins will be killed."

" You think so, Henri? "

" I am sure of it; my friends are brave."

" I never heard that the Angevins were cowards."

" No, doubtless; but my friends are so strong. Look at Schomberg's arm; what muscle! "

" Ah! if you saw D'Antragues's! Is that all that reassures you? "

" No; come, and I will show you something."

" Where? "

" In my room."

" And this something makes you confident of victory? "

" Yes."

" Come, then."

" Wait, and let me take leave of them. Adieu, my good friends," murmured the king, as he stooped and imprinted a light kiss on each of their foreheads.

Chicot was not superstitious, but as he looked on, his imagination pictured a living man making his adieux to the dead.

" It is singular," thought he; " I never felt so before. Poor fellows! "

As soon as the king left the room, D'Epernon opened his eyes, and, jumping out of bed, began to efface, as well as he could, the spots of blood on his clothes. Then he went to bed again.

As for Henri, he conducted Chicot to his room, and opened a long ebony coffer lined with white satin.

" Look! " said he.

" Swords! "

" Yes! but blessed swords, my dear friend."

" Blessed! by whom? "

" By our Holy Father the Pope, who granted me this favour. To send this box to Rome and get it back cost me twenty horses and four men; but I have the swords."

" Are they sharp? "

" Doubtless; but their great merit is that they are blessed."

" Yes, I know that; but still I should like to be sure they are sharp."

" Pagan! "

" Let us talk of something else."

" Well, be quick."

" You want to sleep? "

" No, to pray."

" In that case we will talk. Have you sent for M. d'Anjou? "

" Yes, he is waiting below."

" What are you going to do with him? "

" Throw him into the Bastille."

" That is very wise; only choose a dungeon that is deep and safe,—such, for example, as those which were occupied by the Constable de Saint-Pol, or Jacques d'Armagnac."

" Oh! be easy."

" I know where they sell good black velvet, my son."

" Chicot! he is my brother."

" Ah! true; the family mourning is violet. Shall you speak to him? "

" Yes, certainly; if only to show him that his plots are discovered."

" Hum ! "

" Do you disapprove ? "

" In your place I should cut short the conversation, and double the imprisonment."

" Let them bring here the Duc d'Anjou," said the king.

A minute after the duke entered, very pale, and disarmed. Crillon followed him.

" Where did you find him ? " asked the king.

" Sire, his Highness was not at home, but I took possession of his hotel in the king's name; and soon after he returned, when we arrested him without resistance."

" That is fortunate." Then, turning to the prince, he said, " Where were you, Monsieur ? "

" Wherever I was, Sire, be sure it was on your business."

" I doubt it."

François bowed.

" Come, tell me where you were while your accomplices were being arrested."

" My accomplices ! "

" Yes; your accomplices."

" Sire, your Majesty is making some mistake."

" Oh, this time you shall not escape me; your measure of crime is full."

" Sire, be moderate; there is certainly some one who slanders me to you."

" Wretch ! you shall die of hunger in a cell of the Bastille ! "

" I bow to your orders, whatever they may be."

" Hypocrite ! But where were you ? "

" Sire, I was serving your Majesty, and working for the glory and tranquillity of your reign."

" Really ! your audacity is great."

" Bah ! " said Chicot, " tell us about it, my prince; it must be curious."

" Sire, I would tell your Majesty, had you treated me as a brother; but as you have treated me as a criminal, I will let the event speak for me."

Then, bowing profoundly to the king, he turned to Crillon and the other officers, and said, " Now, which of you gentlemen will conduct the first prince of the blood to the Bastille ? "

Chicot had been reflecting, and a thought struck him. " Ah ! " murmured he, " I believe I guess now why M. d'Epernon had so much blood on his feet and so little in his cheeks."

CHAPTER LIII

THE MORNING OF THE COMBAT

A BEAUTIFUL day rose over Paris. None of the citizens knew what was appointed for that day; but the Royalist gentlemen and those of the Guise party—the latter still stupefied—awaited the event, and took cautious measures to congratulate the conqueror. The king, as we have seen, did not sleep at all that night; he prayed and wept. About three o'clock in the morning he set off, accompanied by Chicot, to examine the ground where the combat was to take place. Dressed in clothes of a sombre hue, enveloped in a large cloak, his sword by his side, and his hair and eyes concealed under the rim of his hat, he followed the Rue St. Antoine to within a hundred yards of the Bastille. Having reached that point, he saw a crowd gathered at a place a little above the Rue St. Paul; and not wishing to encounter it, he took the Rue Ste. Catherine, and reached the enclosure of the Tournelles by a back way.

It may easily be conjectured what that crowd was doing there; they were counting the dead. The king avoided them and consequently knew nothing of what had taken place.

Chicot explained to the king the conditions of the combat and the partition of the ground among the combatants. Henri, being thus informed, immediately began to measure the space, looked among the trees, estimated the position of the sun, and said, " Quélus will be exposed to the sun; he will have it at his right, just in his only eye,[1] whereas Maugiron, who has good eyes, will be in the shade. That is badly managed. As for Schomberg, his place is good; but Quélus, my poor Quélus ! "

" Do not torment yourself so, my king; it is useless."

" And D'Epernon; I am really unjust not to think of him— he, who is to fight Bussy; how he will be exposed ! Look, my brave Chicot,—to the left a barrier; to the right, a tree; behind, a ditch. And he will have to give way constantly, for Bussy is like a tiger, a lion, a serpent; he is a living sword."

" Bah ! " said Chicot; " I am not concerned about D'Epernon."

" You are wrong; he will be killed."

" Not he; be sure he has taken precautions."

" What do you mean ? "

" I mean that he will not fight."

[1] Quélus had previously lost his left eye in a duel.

P

" Did you not hear what he said before going to bed? "

" That is just why I think he will not fight."

" Incredulous and distrustful! "

" I know my Gascon, Henri. But if you will take my advice, you will return to the Louvre; it is full daylight."

" Do you think I can stay there during the combat? "

" *Ventre de biche!* you will stay there; for if you should be seen here every one would say, in case your friends were victorious, that you had forced the victory by some sort of magic; and in case they were conquered, that you had brought misfortune to them."

" And what to me are rumours and interpretations? I shall love them to the end."

" I want you to be of a strong mind, Henri; I even congratulate you on your love for your friends,—it is a rare virtue among princes,—but I wish you not to leave M. d'Anjou alone at the Louvre."

" Is not Crillon there? "

" Crillon is only a buffalo, a rhinoceros, a wild boar; while your brother is a serpent, whose strength lies in his cunning."

" You are right; I should have sent him to the Bastille."

" I told you that you did wrong in seeing him."

" Yes, I have been conquered by his assurance, by his coolness, by the service which he pretends he has rendered me."

" Reason the more for distrusting him. Believe me, Henri, it is best that we return."

Henri followed Chicot's advice and started with him on the way to the Louvre, after giving one last look at the field of combat.

When Chicot and the king entered, the young men were being dressed by their valets.

" Good-morning, gentlemen," said the king; " I find you all in good spirits, I hope? "

" Yes, Sire," said Quélus.

" You look gloomy, Maugiron."

" Sire, I am superstitious, and I had bad dreams last night; so I am drinking a little wine to keep up my spirits."

" My friend, remember that dreams are the impressions of the previous day, and have no influence on the morrow."

" Yes, Sire," said D'Epernon; " I also had bad dreams last night, but in spite of that, my hand is steady and fit for action."

" Yes," said Chicot, " you dreamed you had blood on your boots; that is not a bad dream, for it signifies that you will be a conqueror, like Alexander or Cæsar."

" My friends," said Henri, " remember you fight only for honour. The past night has seated me firmly on my throne, therefore do not think of me; and, above all things, no false bravery. You wish to kill your enemies, not to die yourselves."

" Oh! as for myself," said D'Epernon, " I shall give no quarter."

" I," said Quélus, " will promise nothing; I will do what I can."

" And I," said Maugiron, " I assure your Majesty that if I die I shall kill my man, blow for blow."

The gentlemen were now ready, and it only remained to take leave of their master.

" Do you go on horseback? " he asked.

" No, Sire, on foot."

They each kissed his hand; and D'Epernon said, " Sire, bless my sword."

" Not so, D'Epernon; give up your sword. I have a better one for each of you. Chicot, bring them here."

" No, Sire, send your captain of the guards. I am but a Pagan; and the celestial benedictions might be changed to fatal enchantments if it should occur to my friend the Devil to look at my hands and observe what I was carrying."

" What are these swords, Sire? " said Schomberg, glancing at the box which an officer had just brought in.

" Italian swords, my son, forged at Milan."

" Thanks, Sire," said the four young men, with one voice.

" Now go; it is time," said the king, who could hardly control his emotion.

" Sire," said Quélus, " shall we not have your Majesty's presence to encourage us? "

" No, that would not be right; you will be supposed to fight without any one being cognisant of it, and without my sanction. Let it appear to be the result of a private quarrel."

When they were gone, the king threw himself down in tears.

" Now," said Chicot, " I will go to see this duel, for I have an idea that something curious will happen with regard to D'Epernon." And he went off.

Henri shut himself up in his own room, first saying to Crillon, who knew what was to take place, " If we are conquerors, Crillon, come and tell me; if not, strike three blows on the door."

CHAPTER LIV

THE FRIENDS OF BUSSY

THE friends of the Duc d'Anjou had passed as good and tranquil a night as those of the king, although their master had not taken the same care of them. After a good supper, they had all retired to sleep at D'Antragues's house, which was nearest to the field of battle. D'Antragues, before supper, had gone to take leave of a little milliner whom he adored, Ribeirac had written to his mother, and Livarot had made his will. They were up early in the morning, and dressed themselves in red breeches and socks, that their enemies might not see their blood, and they had doublets of grey silk. They wore shoes without heels, and their pages carried their swords, that their arms might not be fatigued.

The weather was splendid for love, war, or walking; and the sun gilded the roofs, on which the night dew was sparkling. The streets were dry, and the air delightful.

Before leaving the house the young men had sent to the Hôtel d'Anjou to inquire for Bussy, and had received a reply that he had gone out the evening before and had not yet returned.

" Oh ! " said D'Antragues, " I know where he is; the king ordered a grand chase at Compiègne, and M. de Monsoreau was to set off yesterday. It is all right, gentlemen. He is nearer the ground than we are, and may be there before us; we will call for him in passing."

The streets through which they passed were deserted. No one was to be seen except peasants coming from Montreuil or Vincennes, with milk or vegetables. The young men went on in silence until they reached the Rue St. Antoine. Then, with a smile, which indicated that they all had the same thought, they glanced at Monsoreau's house.

" One could see well from there; and I am sure poor Diane will be more than once at the window," said D'Antragues.

" I think she must be there already," said Ribeirac, " for the window is open."

" True, but what can be the meaning of that ladder before it ? "

" In fact, it is very strange," said D'Antragues.

All three approached the house with an inward presentiment that they were drawing near to some important revelation.

"We are not the only ones to wonder," said Livarot; "see those peasants who are stopping their carts to look."

The young men arrived under the balcony. "M. de Monsoreau," they cried, "do you intend to be present at our combat? If so, be quick, for we wish to arrive first."

They waited, but no one answered.

"Did you put up that ladder?" asked D'Antragues of a man who was examining the ground.

"God forbid!" replied he.

"Why so?"

"Look up."

"Blood!" cried Ribeirac.

"The door has been forced," said D'Antragues; and seizing the ladder, he was on the balcony in a moment. He looked into the chamber.

"What is it?" cried the others, seeing him turn pale.

A terrible cry was his only answer. Livarot mounted behind him. "Corpses! death everywhere!" cried he. And they both entered the room. Ribeirac remained below in fear of a surprise. The chamber bore horrible traces of the terrible combat of the previous night. A river of blood flowed over the room, and the curtains were hanging in strips from sword-cuts.

"Oh, poor Rémy!" cried D'Antragues, suddenly.

"Dead?"

"Yes."

"But a regiment of troopers must have passed through the room," cried Livarot. Then, seeing the door of the corridor open, and traces of blood indicating that one or more of the combatants had also passed through there, he followed it. Meanwhile, D'Antragues went into the adjoining room. There, also, blood was everywhere, and this blood led to the window. He leaned out and looked into the little garden. The iron spikes still held the livid corpse of the unhappy Bussy. At this sight it was not a cry, but a roar, that D'Antragues uttered. Livarot ran in.

"Look!" said D'Antragues, "Bussy dead!"

"Bussy assassinated! thrown out of the window! Come in, Ribeirac, come in!"

Livarot started for the court, and at the foot of the staircase met Ribeirac, whom he took with him. A little door opened from the court into the garden, and they passed through.

"It is indeed he!" cried Livarot.

"His wrist is cut."

" He has two balls in his breast."

" He is full of dagger-wounds."

" Ah, poor Bussy!" roared D'Antragues; " vengeance! vengeance!"

Livarot, turning round, stumbled against a second corpse. " Monsoreau!" cried he.

" What! Monsoreau also."

" Yes, pierced through and through, and his head is broken on the pavement."

" Ah, then, they have assassinated all our friends."

" And his wife,—Madame de Monsoreau?" cried D'Antragues.

No one answered. The populace began to swarm about the house. It was at that moment that the king and Chicot arrived opposite the Rue Ste. Catherine, and turned away to avoid the crowd.

" Bussy, poor Bussy!" cried Ribeirac, in despair.

" Yes, they wished to get rid of the most formidable of us all."

" It is cowardly! it is infamous!"

" Let us go and tell the duke."

" No," said D'Antragues; " let us not charge any one with the care of our vengeance. Look, my friends, at the noble face of the bravest of men. See his blood; it gives us an example, —he never charged another with the work of his vengeance. Bussy, we will act like you, and we will avenge you."

On saying these words, he took off his hat, pressed his lips to Bussy's, and drawing his sword, bathed it in Bussy's blood. " Bussy," said he, " I swear on your corpse that this blood shall be washed off by the blood of your enemies."

" Bussy," cried the others, " we swear to kill them or die!"

" Gentlemen," said D'Antragues, sheathing his sword, " we are agreed that there shall be no mercy, no pity!"

" No mercy, no pity!" they repeated, extending their hands over the corpse.

" But," said Livarot, " we shall now be only three against four."

" True; but we have assassinated no one, and God will strengthen the innocent. Adieu, Bussy!"

" Adieu, Bussy!" repeated the others; and they went out, horror-stricken and pale, from that cursed house. They had there found, with the image of death, that profound despair which multiplies one's forces; they had there been inspired by that generous indignation which makes one superior to his mortal state. They penetrated the crowd with difficulty, it had already become so large. Arriving on the ground, they found their opponents waiting for them.

" Gentlemen," said Quélus, rising and bowing, " we have had the honour of waiting for you."

" Excuse us," said D'Antragues; " but we should have been here before you, had we not been delayed by one of our company."

" M. de Bussy," said D'Epernon, " I do not see him. Where is he? "

" We have waited till now; we can wait longer for him," said Schomberg.

" He will not come," said D'Antragues.

All looked thunderstruck, except D'Epernon, who exclaimed, " Ah! the brave man *par excellence,*—is he, then, afraid? "

" That cannot be," said Quélus.

" You are right, Monsieur," said Livarot.

" And why will he not come? "

" Because he is dead."

" Dead! " cried the favourites. D'Epernon said nothing, and even turned slightly pale.

" And dead because he has been assassinated! " said D'Antragues. " Did you not know it, gentlemen? "

" No," said Quélus; " how should we? "

" Besides, is it certain? " asked D'Epernon.

D'Antragues drew his sword. " So certain that here is his blood," said he.

" Assassinated! " cried three of the king's friends; " M. de Bussy assassinated! "

D'Epernon continued to shake his head with an air of doubt.

" His blood cries for vengeance! " said Ribeirac; " do you not hear it, gentlemen? "

" What do you mean? "

" ' Seek whom the crime profits,' the law says," murmured Livarot.

" Ah, gentlemen, will you explain yourselves? " cried Maugiron.

" That is just what we have come for."

" Quick! our swords are in our hands! " said D'Epernon.

" Oh! you are in a great hurry, Monsieur the Gascon," said Livarot; " you did not crow so loud when we were four against four? "

" Is it our fault if you are only three? "

" Yes, it is your fault," cried D'Antragues. " He is dead

because you preferred that he should be lying in his blood instead of standing here; he is dead, with his wrist cut, that that wrist might no longer hold a sword; he is dead that you might not see the lightning of those eyes which dazzled you all. Do you understand me? Am I clear?"

"Enough, gentlemen!" said Quélus. "Retire, M. d'Epernon; we will fight three against three. These gentlemen shall see if we are men to profit by a misfortune which we deplore as much as themselves. Come, gentlemen," added the young man, throwing his hat behind him, and raising his left hand, while he whirled his sword with the right, "God is our judge if we are assassins!"

"Ah, I hated you before," cried Schomberg, "and now I execrate you!"

"On your guard, gentlemen!" cried D'Antragues.

"With doublets, or without?" said Schomberg.

"Without doublets, without shirts; our breasts bare, our hearts uncovered!"

The young men threw off their doublets and shirts.

"I have lost my dagger," said Quélus; "it must have fallen on the road."

"Or else you left it at M. de Monsoreau's, in the Place de la Bastille," said D'Antragues.

Quélus gave a cry of rage, and drew his sword.

"But he has no dagger, M. d'Antragues," cried Chicot, who had just arrived.

"So much the worse for him; it is not my fault," said D'Antragues.

CHAPTER LV

THE COMBAT

THE place where this terrible combat was to take place was sequestered, and shaded by trees. It was generally frequented only by children, who came to play there during the day, or by drunkards or robbers, who made a sleeping-place of it by night.

Chicot, his heart palpitating, although he was not of a very tender nature, seated himself before the lackeys and pages on a wooden balustrade.

He did not love the Angevins, and detested the minions; but they were all brave young men, and in their veins flowed a generous blood, which he was probably destined to see flow before long.

D'Epernon made a last bravado, "What! you are all afraid of me!" he cried.

"Hold your tongue!" said D'Antragues.

"Come away, bravest of the brave," said Chicot, "or else you will lose another pair of shoes."

"What do you mean?"

"I mean that there will soon be blood on the ground, and that you will walk in it, as you did last night."

D'Epernon became deadly pale, and moving away, he seated himself at some distance from Chicot.

The combat began as five o'clock struck, and for a few minutes nothing was heard but the clashing of swords; not a blow had taken effect. At last Schomberg touched Ribeirac in the shoulder, and the blood gushed out; Schomberg tried to repeat the blow, but Ribeirac struck up his sword, and wounded him in the side.

"Now let us rest a few seconds, if you like," said Ribeirac.

Quélus, having no dagger, was at a great disadvantage; for he was obliged to parry with his left arm, and as it was bare, every parry cost him a wound. His hand was soon bleeding in several places, and D'Antragues had also wounded him three times in the breast; but at each wound he repeated, "It is nothing."

Livarot and Maugiron were still unwounded.

Ribeirac and Schomberg recommenced; the former was pierced through the breast, and Schomberg was wounded in the neck. Ribeirac, mortally hurt, applied his left hand to his wound; Schomberg profited by the opportunity to give him a second thrust which penetrated his side. Ribeirac with his right hand seized the hand of his adversary, and with his left plunged his dagger into his heart. Schomberg fell back, dragging Ribeirac with him, still pierced by the sword.

Livarot, seeing his friend fall, ran rapidly to him, pursued by Maugiron. He gained several feet on the way, and aiding Ribeirac in his efforts to rid himself of Schomberg's sword, he drew that sword from his breast. But then, rejoined by Maugiron, he was obliged to defend himself with the disadvantage of slippery ground, an imperfect guard, and the sun shining into his eyes. At the end of a second a blow of the sword opened Livarot's head, who dropped his sword and fell upon his knees; then Maugiron hastened to give him another wound, and he fell altogether.

Quélus and Maugiron remained against D'Antragues. Quélus was bleeding, but from slight wounds. D'Antragues comprehended his danger; he had not the least wound, but he began to feel tired, so he pushed aside Quélus's sword and jumped over a barrier. But at the same moment Maugiron attacked him behind; D'Antragues turned, and Quélus profited by this movement to get under the barrier.

"He is lost!" thought Chicot.

"Vive le roi!" cried D'Epernon. "At him, my lions! at him!"

"Silence, if you please, Monsieur!" said D'Antragues. "Do not insult a man who fights even to his last breath."

At this instant Livarot, of whom no one was thinking, rose on his knees, hideous from the blood with which he was covered, and plunged his dagger between the shoulders of Maugiron, who fell, crying out, "*Mon Dieu!* I am killed!"

Livarot fell back again, fainting.

"M. de Quélus," said D'Antragues, "you are a brave man; yield. I offer you your life."

"And why yield?"

"You are wounded, and I am not."

"Vive le roi!" cried Quélus; "I have still my sword!" And he rushed on D'Antragues, who parried the thrust, and seizing his arm, wrested his sword from him, saying, "Now you have it no longer."

"Oh, a sword!" said Quélus; and bounding like a tiger on D'Antragues, he threw his arms round him.

D'Antragues struck him with his dagger again and again; but Quélus managed to seize his hands, and twisted round him like a serpent, with arms and legs. D'Antragues, nearly suffocated, reeled and fell, but on the unfortunate Quélus. He managed to disengage himself, for Quélus's powers were failing him, and leaning on one arm, gave him a last blow, which entered his breast. " There," said he, " are you satisfied? "

" Vive le r—" said Quélus, his eyes fast closing. It was all over; the silence and terror of death reigned on the field of battle.

D'Antragues rose, covered with blood, but it was that of his enemy. D'Epernon made the sign of the cross, and fled as if he were pursued by demons. Chicot ran and raised Quélus, whose blood was pouring out from nineteen wounds. The movement roused him, and he opened his eyes. " D'Antragues," said he, " on my honour, I am innocent of the death of Bussy."

" Oh, I believe you, Monsieur," cried D'Antragues, much moved.

" Fly! " murmured Quélus; " the king will never forgive you."

" I cannot abandon you thus, even to escape the scaffold."

" Save yourself, young man," said Chicot; " do not tempt Providence twice in one day."

D'Antragues approached Ribeirac, who still breathed. " Well? " asked he.

" We are victors," said D'Antragues, in a low tone, not to offend Quélus.

" Thanks," said Ribeirac; " now go." And he fainted again.

D'Antragues picked up his own sword, which he had dropped, then that of Quélus, which he presented to him. A tear shone in the eyes of the dying man. " We might have been friends," he murmured.

" Now fly," said Chicot; " you are worthy of being saved."

" And my companions? "

" I will take care of them, as of the king's friends."

D'Antragues wrapped himself in a cloak which his squire handed to him, so that no one might see the blood with which he was covered; and leaving the dead and wounded, he disappeared through the Porte St. Antoine.

CHAPTER LVI

THE END

THE king, pale with anxiety, and shuddering at the slightest noise, employed himself in conjecturing, with the experience of a practised man, the time that his friends would require for the combat, and also estimating the good or bad possibilities afforded by their character, their force, and their skill.

" Now," he had said at first, " they are crossing the Rue St. Antoine; now they are entering the field; now they have begun." And at these words the poor king, trembling, began to pray. Rising again almost immediately, he cried, " If Quélus only remembers the thrust I taught him! As for Schomberg, he is so cool that he ought to kill Ribeirac; Maugiron, also, should be more than a match for Livarot. But D'Epernon, he is lost; fortunately he is the one of the four whom I love least. But if Bussy, the terrible Bussy, after killing him, falls on the others! Ah, my poor friends! "

" Sire! " said Crillon, at the door.

" What! already? "

" Sire, I have no news but that the Duc d'Anjou begs to speak to your Majesty."

" What for? " said the king, still talking through the door.

" He says that the moment has come for him to tell you what service he rendered your Majesty, and that what he has to tell you will calm a part of your fears."

" Well, let him come."

At this moment they heard a voice crying, " I must speak to the king at once! "

The king recognised the voice, and opened the door.

" Here, Saint-Luc! " cried he. " What is it? But, *mon Dieu!* what is the matter? Are they dead? "

Indeed, Saint-Luc, pale, without hat or sword, and spotted with blood, rushed into the king's room.

" Sire! " cried he, " vengeance! I ask for vengeance! "

" My poor Saint-Luc, what is it? What can have caused you such despair? "

" Sire, one of your subjects, the bravest, noblest, was murdered last night,—traitorously murdered! "

The king, preoccupied by one idea, was reassured. It was

not any one of his four friends, since he had seen them all in the morning. "Of whom do you speak?" he said.

"Sire, you do not love him, I know; but he was faithful, and if need were, would have shed all his blood for your Majesty, else he would not have been my friend."

"Ah!" said the king, who began to understand; and something like a gleam of joy passed over his face.

"Vengeance, Sire, for M. de Bussy!"

"M. de Bussy?"

"Yes, M. de Bussy, whom twenty assassins poniarded last night. He killed fourteen of them."

"M. de Bussy dead?"

"Yes, Sire."

"Then he does not fight this morning?"

Saint-Luc cast a reproachful glance on the king, who turned away his head, and in doing so, saw Crillon still standing at the door. He signed to him to bring in the duke.

"No, Sire, he will not fight," said Saint-Luc; "and that is why I ask, not for vengeance,—I was wrong to call it so,—but for justice. I love my king, and am, above all things, jealous of his honour; and I think that it is a deplorable service which they have rendered to your Majesty by killing M. de Bussy."

The Duc d'Anjou had just arrived at the door; he stood there immovable as a bronze statue. Saint-Luc's words had enlightened the king as to the service his brother had boasted of having rendered him.

"Do you know what they will say?" continued Saint-Luc. "They will say, if your friends conquer, that it is because they first murdered Bussy."

"And who will dare to say that?"

"*Pardieu!* every one," said Crillon.

"No, Monsieur, they shall not say that," replied the king, "for you shall name the assassin."

"I will name him, Sire, to clear your Majesty from so heinous an accusation," said Saint-Luc.

"Well! do it."

The Duc d'Anjou stood quietly waiting.

"Sire," continued Saint-Luc, "last night they laid a snare for Bussy, while he visited a woman who loved him. The husband, warned by a traitor, came to his house with a troop of assassins; they were everywhere,—in the street, in the courtyard, even in the garden."

In spite of his power over himself, the duke grew pale at these last words.

"Bussy fought like a lion, Sire; but numbers overwhelmed him, and—"

"And he was killed," interrupted the king, "and justly; I will certainly not avenge an adulterer."

"Sire, I have not finished my tale. The unhappy man, after having defended himself for more than half an hour in the room, after having triumphed over his enemies, escaped, bleeding, wounded, and mutilated; he only wanted some one to lend him a saving hand, which I would have done had I not been seized by his assassins and bound and gagged. Unfortunately they forgot to take away my sight as well as my speech, for I saw two men approach the unfortunate Bussy, who was hanging on the iron railings. I heard him entreat them for help, for in these two men he had the right to reckon on two friends. Well, Sire, it is horrible to relate,—it was still more horrible to see and hear,—one ordered him to be shot, and the other obeyed."

"And you know the assassins?" cried the king, moved in spite of himself.

"Yes," said Saint-Luc; and turning towards the prince, he said, charging his words and his gestures with all the hate so long repressed, "It is Monseigneur! The assassin is the prince! The assassin is the friend!"

The king was expecting that blow, and the duke received it without emotion. "Yes," he said calmly, "M. de Saint-Luc is right. It was I, and your Majesty will appreciate my action, for M. de Bussy was my servant, it is true; but this morning he was to fight against your Majesty."

"You lie, assassin!" cried Saint-Luc. "Bussy, full of wounds, his hands cut to pieces, a ball through his shoulder, and hanging suspended on the iron trellis-work, might have inspired pity in his most cruel enemies; they would have succoured him. But you, the assassin of La Mole and of Coconnas,—you killed Bussy, as you have killed, one after another, all your friends. You killed Bussy, not because he was the king's enemy, but because he was the confidant of your secrets. Ah! Monsoreau knew well your reason for this crime."

"Cordieu!" cried Crillon, "why am I not king?"

"They insult me before you, Brother," said the duke, pale with terror.

"Leave us, Crillon," said the king.

The officer obeyed.

"Justice, Sire, justice!" cried Saint-Luc again.

"Sire," said the duke, "will you punish me for having saved your Majesty's friends this morning?"

"And I," cried Saint-Luc, "I say that the cause which you espouse is accursed and will be pursued by the anger of God. Sire, when your brother protects our friends, woe to them!"

The king shuddered. Then they heard hasty steps and voices, followed by a deep silence, and then, as if a voice from heaven came to confirm Saint-Luc's words, three blows were struck slowly and solemnly on the door by the vigorous arm of Crillon.

Henri turned deadly pale. "Conquered," cried he; "my poor friends!"

"What did I tell you, Sire?" cried Saint-Luc.

The duke clasped his hands in terror.

"Do you see, coward?" cried the young man, with a superb emphasis; "it is thus that assassins save the honour of princes! Come, then, assassinate me also; I have no sword;" and he flung his silk glove into the duke's face. François uttered a cry of rage and turned livid.

But the king saw nothing, heard nothing; he buried his face in his hands, and murmured, "Oh! my poor friends; they are conquered, wounded. Who will give me certain news of them?"

"I, Sire," said Chicot.

"Well!" cried Henri.

"Two are dead, and the third is dying."

"Which is the third who is not yet dead?"

"Quélus."

"Where is he?"

"At the Hôtel Boissy."

The king said no more, but rushed from the room with cries of lamentation.

Saint-Luc had taken Diane home to his wife; and this had kept him from appearing sooner at the Louvre. Jeanne passed three days and nights watching her through the most frightful delirium. On the fourth day, Jeanne, overcome by fatigue, went to take a little rest; two hours after, when she returned, Diane had disappeared.

Quélus died at the Hôtel Boissy, in the king's arms, after lingering for thirty days.

Henri was inconsolable. He raised three magnificent tombs for his friends, on which their effigies were sculptured in marble,

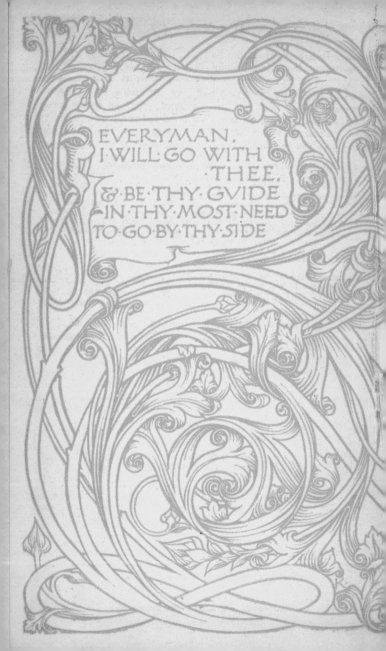

EVERYMAN,
I WILL GO WITH
THEE,
& BE THY GVIDE
IN THY MOST NEED
TO GO BY THY SIDE